*   *   *   *

Unlike so many of his gay buddies who fantasized about finding a dream lover, Chase Hyde had no interest in settling down. Still in top shape in his late forties, he was happy to cruise West Hollywood for exhilarating muscle sex with one hot bodybuilder after the next. A devout, self-acknowledged "roamosexual," his foremost objection to settling down was that having a partner would take him off the market. So even if love was never in the air, lust was always just around the corner.

Chase expected to continue his carefree lifestyle until, through a correspondence in cyber-space, he met Hunter Rowe, a younger, up-and-coming Madison Avenue advertising executive and fellow bodybuilder who pined for a long-term relationship with a mature muscleman.

Neither Chase nor Hunter can imagine the twists of fate that await in Muscle Bound, *a passionate tale about the turbulent pursuit of sexual conquest set against the world of muscle obsession, gym addiction and steroid abuse.*

*   *   *   *

MUSCLE BOUND

MUSCLE BOUND

A Novel

David Marlow

NOVEMBER, '08

FOR RAY —
I LOOK FORWARD TO THE
DAY YOU FINALLY RECOGNIZE
HOW SEXY YOU TRULY ARE;
WITH LOVE,
D. Marlow

iUniverse, Inc.
New York Bloomington Shanghai

Muscle Bound

iUniverse books may be ordered through booksellers or by contacting:

iUniverse
1663 Liberty Drive
Bloomington, IN 47403
www.iuniverse.com
1-800-Authors (1-800-288-4677)

Because of the dynamic nature of the Internet, any Web addresses or links contained in this book may have changed since publication and may no longer be valid.

This is a work of fiction. All of the characters, names, incidents, organizations, and dialogue in this novel are either the products of the author's imagination or are used fictitiously.

ISBN: 978-0-595-44739-8 (pbk)
ISBN: 978-0-595-68984-2 (cloth)
ISBN: 978-0-595-89060-6 (ebk)

Printed in the United States of America

For

David Shipley

and

David McGarity

BOOK ONE:

THE ROAMOSEXUAL AGENDA

"He felt an odd sense of ennui when too late
he discovered true love looks best from far away"

— Marcel Proust, Swann's Way
Remembrance of Things Past

YOU'VE GOT MALE

Chase Hyde always had a passion for muscle. As far back as he could remember, the sight of a well-built man flexing big biceps or bouncing powerful pecs got him so aroused, he embraced their appeal as the trumpet blare of his sexual calling. And once he recognized the potency of muscle's persistent lure, he also discovered that the best way to become a magnet for a man with muscles was to develop them himself.

His fascination with muscle fueled his unwavering motivation and made passionate his determination to stay in training. Fast approaching forty-nine, the six-footer never stopped striving to improve his exceptional physique, insuring he was fully loaded to fool around whenever the next hunk showed up on the muscular landscape. Ounce by ounce, pound after pound, inch by inch, year after year, he trained as hard as he could until he actuated himself into the bona fide, mature muscle hunk who smiled with satisfaction every morning at his reflection in his bathroom's full-length mirror.

Chase treasured the fact that he was still so fit at a time in life when most other guys, particularly straight men, had long since given up the painstaking pursuit of building muscle. An old bodybuilding myth suggested that once you developed muscles, they simply stayed put. No one back then mentioned either atrophy or the life-long obligation it took to hold on to your gains. Most hetero men stopped exercising after high school, and soon after went soft and then plump as they expanded into couch potatoes.

By contrast, Chase was still buff from hitting the weights. And seeing how his allegiance to staying fit and his quest for muscle were so deeply intertwined with his prolific libido, he knew that so long as he kept getting it up, he'd keep pumping it up. He could never afford to grow complacent, never let up on his commitment to constantly improve his powerful body. He vowed to keep working out until that bittersweet day when the loss of his sexual appetite stopped feeding his craving for muscle. Until then, his focus would remain firmly fixed on the gym. Only diligence and dedication yielded the blessed dividends of visible results.

Chase was long set in his well-ordered ways, and on the day our story begins, his inner clock woke him lazily, around eight. He slapped together ingredients for his protein-packed, egg-white frittata, zapped it in the microwave and, at the same time, brewed a pot of Kona coffee which jolted him awake, jump-starting his day.

After retrieving that morning's *Los Angeles Times* from his front doorstep, he settled in on his couch and spent a leisurely hour or so poring over the paper. A voracious reader, the walls of his living room were lined with shelves crammed with books collected over many years. By mid-morning and his third cup of coffee, Chase turned on the computer at his desk and devoted what he acknowledged was far too huge a chunk of his day to feeding his online fixation. He logged on, answered his e-mail, and then clicked on to a few of the muscle sites to which he subscribed. At the same time, he chatted and flirted with other bodybuilders from across the city, the country, and all over the globe.

Before he knew it, the morning was gone and Chase finally logged off the Internet and pulled himself away from the computer. He quickly stuffed his workout gear into his backpack and then blended and gulped down his pre-workout whey protein drink. After mounting his Serotta titanium ten-speed mountain bike, he sped from Hyde Park, the four-unit complex he owned and managed in Laurel Canyon, just off Lookout Mountain. In his highest gear, he pedaled pell-mell on his steep, seventeen-minute down-hill ride to Gold's gym in Hollywood, to meet up with Stack Robinson, his equally dedicated workout partner of the past seven years, with whom he trained consistently, three days on, one day off.

*   *   *   *

Chase locked his mountain bike outside the gym's main entrance, and after cooling down from his aerobic journey, he passed through the turnstile and headed upstairs to the men's locker area. The Gold's gym in Hollywood was one of the best facilities within their worldwide franchise. Cavernous workout areas offered a wide array of workout equipment accompanied by a communal sense of hard-driving energy, generated in no small part by the pulsating beat from the dozen or so television monitors airing nonstop music videos.

After stuffing his backpack into an empty metal compartment, Chase looked around at a dozen or so men in various states of undress and was reminded how, even in the most gay-oriented gyms, male behavior in their changing chambers often reeked of a prevailing atmosphere that was predominantly heterosexual. Locker rooms, in fact, seemed to be the one place where even the most nellie of queens felt some innate pressure to switch personas and project a reasonable facsimile of a butch manliness.

Chase was often bemused to see an inherently swishy gay man instantly raise his personal butch quotient, his own BQ, a solid ten to fifteen points just from the manly way in which he conducted himself while in the locker area, compared, for example, to how he might otherwise flail about on a dance floor late on a Saturday night after, say, three apple martinis or a tab of Ecstasy.

As men went about their business, undressing inside the locker area, an unwritten social dictum suggested that everyone all but ignore any inviting display of muscle. No staring at sweaty men pulling off their workout shirts. No gawking at guys with voluminous quads as they stepped in and out of their socks. Everyone pretended to be oblivious to any presentation of the superb flesh to which they found themselves fleetingly exposed.

A lean, athletic-looking young man in his early twenties, sitting next to Chase on a locker bench, lacing up a sneaker, looked over and spotted Chase pulling off his tee shirt. The young man tried not to appear too intrusive as he drank in Chase's movie-star good looks. He hoped to remain undetected as, furtively, he appraised Chase's chiseled pecs and saw they were … impeccable. When Chase reached for his navy-blue workout tank top, the young man silently observed the way Chase's back was lumpy in all the right places, his traps thick and well-defined. Boldly, he snuck in a quick glance at Chase's signature, seventeen-inch, perfectly peaked, vascular biceps. When Chase turned around to step into his SafeGard jock strap and then his gym shorts, the young man's eyes bulged involuntarily at the fleeting glimpse he caught of Chase's genitalia.

A popular misconception about bodybuilders suggested that many of them were overcompensating for their undersized dicks. Not Chase. The enormity and hefty girth of his manhood often proved a challenge to the most practiced of cocksuckers. Long ago, back in his high school locker room, his buddies had dubbed his mammoth member the Fifty-First State. At the time, Chase was simultaneously embarrassed and privately elated by the ribald attention his impressive endowment could arouse.

Compelled to initiate a conversation, to say *something*, the young man in the locker room looked up at Chase and observed, "You know, I have so much trouble putting on size. What would it take to get arms with peaks as big as yours?"

Chase relished the validation and welcomed the opportunity to serve as supportive influence to younger guys, especially those just getting into bodybuilding. He leaned over, placed an open hand atop the kid's bare shoulder, and stepped steadfastly into his alter ego as Coach Chase. "Patience and consistency are the keys to successful bodybuilding, Kiddo," he then counseled the young man. "Our bodies are *always* a work in progress."

The young man looked up at his would-be muscle mentor, beaming like he'd just witnessed the Sermon on the Mount. No doubt about it. Chase Hyde's fans were everywhere.

Gratified he helped motivate another well-intentioned novice, Chase winked at his freshly infatuated friend and then bounded out of the locker room. He trotted downstairs to the main floor just as Stack strutted through the gym's front door, psyched up as always for a heavy workout.

"Stack!" Chase greeted his training partner with their ritual sophomoric greeting as simultaneously, they bumped shoulders.

"Yo, Coach!" Stack barked at Chase. "Stack is jacked. Ready to pump some iron?"

"Lead the way!" Chase barked back, and nodded toward the crowded gym floor. "We're not packing on any muscle standing here."

∗   ∗   ∗   ∗

There were so many appealing muscular men working out on the gym floor, it was sometimes hard to concentrate on the weights. Among the attractive, predominantly gay clientele, were traffic-stopping actors, models and hustlers. Cliques of muscle buddies stood around in exclusive little circles, bonding through short stop-and-chat sessions of daily dish. All that hunkdom clumped together meant that along with the aroma of fresh perspiration, there was often a detectable sexual tension hovering in the air as members furtively checked one another out in a fashion more overt than the locker room subterfuge. These casual cruises and mini-flirtations were mostly short-lived, however, and one could only marvel at how easily infatuation could blossom and then wilt with the slam of a weight, in the blink of a set. Glances at first willingly exchanged often turned into glimpses ignored as instant enticement often waned into speedy disenchantment.

Cumbersome chromium equipment sat crammed together across the gym's gargantuan main floor. At any given hour, the enormous space was filled with a multitude of dedicated bodybuilders, some of whom were more than a little over-steroided.

Stack Robinson was just such a beyond-juiced bodybuilder — a six-foot-two, forty-three-year-old, sexily balding, mountain of a muscle monster. The massive muscleman was your basic butch-macho-jock muscle fantasy, and he arrived sporting a scruffy three-day's worth of five o'clock shadow as well as two Maori-inspired tattoos — one fanning across his upper back, the other slashed across the front of his left shoulder blade.

Stack's real name was Stan, but his nickname alluded to his penchant for lifting heavier and still heavier weights on any given machine; striving, sweating, and pounding away until he could ultimately lift up or pull down its entire stack. His nickname suited him aptly as it also observed how at any given time he was also usually stacking some potent combination of steroids in his enduring effort to pack on ever more muscle size.

Stack was a failed actor who now made his living working both as a certified personal trainer and also as a surreptitious seller of contraband steroids. He worked several days a week at an upscale women's gym/spa in Beverly Hills called Slim Chance. The women he trained there, all on a one-on-one basis, were mostly bored housewives. Fearful of aging, many of them paid dearly for Botox injections and cosmetic procedures, whatever it took to hold on to their once youthful faces, their once girlish figures, for as long as surgically possible. The one-hundred-and-twenty-five dollars the ladies doled out for their private, hourly training sessions with Stack may have been exorbitant, but the artificial confidence he inspired in them, despite their sagging bottoms, and the one-on-one attention they received from a bona-fide Adonis, were priceless.

When he wasn't busy tightening drooping buns in Beverly Hills, Stack preferred to work out with Chase at Gold's. It allowed him to get away from his needy clients, while establishing connections for selling his steroid cycles.

Stack prided himself on being well-read and up-to-speed on muscle medicines available on the black market — illicit anabolic drugs from all over the world, whether Mexico, Germany, Russia, Peru, or Thailand. He had a knack for concocting fast-acting, muscle-building cocktails, and often sold his clients a combination of several different types of steroids in the space of one cycle, hence *stacking* the juice.

A dozen years ago, the big fellow moved from Minnesota to Hollywood to become an actor and take up bodybuilding. He quickly discovered that stealthily black-marketing a contraband commodity in high demand was a whole lot easier and far more remunerative than spending hours at crowded cattle call auditions.

Once he began dealing the juice, one of the perquisites Stack enjoyed was that he no longer had to pay for any more steroids. Unburdened, he was carefree to careen from one cycle to the next, and lived for those joyful hours he spent working out and making contacts at the gym.

Best buddies Chase and Stack first met several years earlier, appropriately enough, at the gym. Sex between them was never an issue, mainly because Stack's taste in men was somewhat unusual. Most gay bodybuilders sweated to get as big as possible so they could attract other big bodybuilders. By contrast, the perfect sexual encounter for Stack was any lanky, twenty-three-year-old who tipped the scales at no more than a hundred thirty pounds, dripping wet. "My walking broomsticks," was how he affectionately referred to those underfed lads who stoked Stack's erotic imagination and became his never-ending prey.

Chase and Stack programmed their workouts to last seventy to ninety minutes. On that late September morning, they pumped triceps and biceps. Chase looked forward to all his workouts with Stack, but took the greatest pleasure when they pumped their biceps, his widely heralded Guns of Navarone. Guys at the gym often lauded Chase's great pythons, saying he probably possessed the best-damned arms in the gym — no small compliment given the incredible competition among the rest of the buffed membership.

They finished off their triceps routine at one of the cable stations, prosecuting a punishing drop set, pushing down the heavy metal bar until muscle failure kicked in and neither of them could pump out another repetition. As he did with every workout, every set, every rep, Chase took pains to incorporate perfect form. He knew full well his venerated muscularity could come crashing down if ever he got hurt while exercising. His bodybuilding program along with his considerable sex appeal could all collapse at the clumsy drop of a dumbbell. Bodybuilders got hurt all the time at his gym, some of them on a regular basis: the separated rotator cuff, the torn biceps tendon, the strained connective tissue, the wrenched neck, the pulled hamstring, the herniated spinal column, the perennially pained lower back. Sadly, the worst part about getting hurt was how damn long it took for injuries to heal. So if you got hammered and couldn't hit the gym for several weeks, the toll on your muscularity could be significant. Every bodybuilder knew it took forever to get into shape, and barely three days of inactivity before atrophy set in. After that, it was a rapid slide downhill into terminal schlubbyhood.

As the workout partners next approached one of the standing barbell racks to initiate their biceps workout, Chase took a good look at the sturdy Colossus. "By the way, Large One," he told him, "you are looking especially huge today!"

"Don't I know?" Stack boasted in agreement and bounced his pecs with pride. "Two sixty-two first thing this morning. Before breakfast. After pooping. That's five pounds in three weeks. I knew finishing my cycle with this Deca would kick butt!"

Chase sized up the powerfully built man. "Guess you can never be too rich or too big, huh?"

"Or too aggressive!" Stack added with a growl, at least half in jest. "My testosterone is so high by now, if I snap at you, or push my hand through the wall, you'll know it's not me — just my 'roids doing the raging."

"At least when I snap at you," Chase countered, "you know it's the real me doing the barking."

Stack pretended not to hear and then suggested innocently, as if they hadn't been over it a hundred times, "And when are you going to give up all your goody-two-shoes bullshit and finally let me design a dynamic cycle for you?"

"Call me crazy," Chase told his workout partner. "But I'm comfortable just the way things are. Here I am: six feet, two hundred five pounds of pure Coach Chase, every ounce fully earned and all natural, thank you. I have no complaints about all the muscle boys I attract to my bed."

"Maybe what you need, instead of reading all those books, is a steady boyfriend," Stack suggested.

"Right," Chase facetiously agreed. "I'll stop reading and take on another boyfriend just a soon as you stop using steroids and start dating men your own age."

"Real funny," said Stack, faking a laugh. "Still, I'd like to see you packing on another ten, fifteen pounds of hefty muscle. Bring you over the top, into the next level of hunkdom."

Stack was a terrific workout partner and a loyal friend. He was always trying to talk Chase into joining him in doing a cycle of steroids. Even offered to sell it to him at cost. But Chase resisted. He had no problem with all the rapid muscle growth steroids provided. He just wasn't ready to run the risk of sacrificing any of his organs or encountering any of the side effects that might develop from an adverse reaction to the shots.

Beyond the health threat, the least appealing element of steroids, and the bottom line for Chase, was that most of the muscle gains men earned while juicing came from water retention. So, even though you looked great while cycling, the lion's share of all your blissful improvements switched into reverse all too quickly and came to a fast end not long after the cycle ended. Once that unhappy event kicked in, your water weight evaporated as most of your muscle gains withered back down to where they'd been before you first began the whole process.

Stack often pointed out to Chase those bodybuilders on the gym floor doing steroids — who of them was on cycle, who was off, who was getting bigger and who looked smaller. He could tell, not just from the super-speedy gains a guy in question might be making, but also because he was usually the dealer who sold the illegal drugs to the bodybuilder in the first place.

As Chase and Stack began executing four sets of heavy barbell curls, taking turns spotting one another, Stack also stealthily launched his other requisite gym preoccupation: lining up a recruit for what he anticipated would turn into his afternoon blow job. The success Stack enjoyed as a bodybuilder infused him with a strong sense of entitlement. With his imposing physique, he was convinced any underfed pup he signaled out for seduction should feel humbled and honored to service him whenever chosen to do so.

When he wasn't straining in full contraction, Stack vigilantly scanned the room, looking for likely candidates to see who among them might be the lucky cadet who, post-pump, got invited out to the parking lot and into the spacious cab of the enormous man's Ford truck. While Stack eyeballed likely aspirants, Chase remained focused on the biceps exercise in play.

Chase knew Stack was an unrepentant sexaholic. But the huge bodybuilder was also an excellent workout partner. He'd always been there for Chase, and maybe that was why Chase put up with his buddy's often distracting cruising. As soon as they finished pounding out their curls, Stack studied himself in one of the wall-length mirrors, admiring the veins popping up across his pumped biceps. As they grew more prominent, he flexed and said to Chase, "I'm so hot, I swear, I'd give myself a blow job if I could!"

"Sounds like the perfect pairing," Chase agreed. "You ever meet a mirror that didn't smile back?"

"Hey, Buddy!" Stack cockily thumped a fist against his own massive pecs and issued a caveman grunt. "You want modesty — move to Modesto!"

By the time they got to their final biceps exercise, Stack had yet to single out any kid he wanted to approach about actually performing that afternoon's erotic service. Chase suggested they finish off their arms routine by tweaking their peaks with dumbbell hammer curls over the preacher's bench.

Four strict sets later, Stack felt his biceps muscles popping as he strutted off in search of his post-pump release. The moment Stack's chemically elevated testosterone levels and boundless sexual energy connected with his freshly oxygenated blood, they all cried out for instantaneous libidinous release. That's why he made it his business, at the conclusion of every workout with Chase, to zero in on some young man who might willingly fulfill that lustful need.

Stack scored surprisingly often in his oddball pursuit. Incongruously, for him the hunt was most often more satisfying than the capture. He had little patience when things didn't follow his chartered erotic path, and became indignant whenever an afternoon's skinny boy didn't care to swallow his eruption.

Following any workout, that day's lucky winner of Stack's prized pecker had to be willing, not only to put up with one of his impersonal slam-bam-thank-you-sir quickies inside his truck, but to also gulp down the muscle monster's entire ejaculation. If the kid wouldn't agree to that stipulation in advance, it was a deal-breaker.

Stack's aggressive, no-nonsense manner often made his dick a magnet for scrawny boys hoping to satisfy some long-held fantasy of servicing a huge, superhero muscle man. Since most of his lads resembled the proverbial ninety-eight-pound weakling, classically getting sand kicked in his face, there could be nothing sexier than getting hit on and picked up by a massive bodybuilder who looked like Stack.

While circumnavigating the gym floor, Stack relished a mini-high as fresh blood streamed into his freshly pumped biceps and triceps. He reviewed the hot crowd, feverishly lifting barbells, pressing dumbbells, pushing weights, pulling cables. Wherever he looked, grown men were grunting and groaning to the clanging of metal plates.

Over the years, Stack had gotten so accustomed to being gazed at, he took in stride most of the appreciation that never stopped flowing his way. At the end of his fast-clipped, nearly three-sixty walkabout, he turned the corner and, standing there like a dream come true, practically staring him in the face, was his afternoon blow-job.

A gangly, twenty-three-year-old skinny boy was returning a pair of fifteen- pound dumbbells to the rack. When he looked up and saw Stack smiling at him and heading his way, the underfed fledgling was sure he'd died and gone to muscle nirvana.

Walking a fine line between confidence and conceit, Stack approached his prey. After perfunctory introductions, a rapid negotiation was agreed upon, and Stack led his lamb to slaughter, directly to his truck in the parking lot.

Chase, meanwhile, hooked his feet into one of the gym's slant boards and stretched himself out to pump out several sets of tight crunches, further cementing his washboard abs. Then he retrieved his backpack from his upstairs locker, left the gym, and biked in his lowest gear back up Laurel Canyon, all the way home to Hyde Park.

*   *   *   *

Hunter Rowe always had a passion for danger. At the same time, all he ever really wished, since moving to Manhattan eleven years earlier, was to someday not just fall in love, but to fall in love forever. Apart from this outward longing to find a true and lasting romance, he simultaneously kept tucked deep within himself a dark side he had yet to act upon, even though it was something he had dwelled on and dreamt about for years.

As a kid, he loved nothing so much as getting all tingly with dread anticipation whenever he found himself cowering behind a door while playing hide and seek. Hair-raising roller coasters that scared him senseless and sent him into a screaming frenzy were his favorite rides. His early fixation with the sheer exhilaration that accompanied feeling frightened was only somewhat satisfied when horror slasher movies became his favorite form of cinematic escapism.

Hunter's primary subconscious sexual fantasy since his teens was to one day experience being romanced, made glorious love to and, at the same time, placed in harrowing jeopardy by a strong, mature man who would frighten him out of his wits.

Growing up, Hunter made it his business to ignore the obvious callings of his most basic nature, and instead sought out the acceptance of his heterosexual peers, even when that meant ignoring any worthy erotic exploration of his true inner self. Rather than face up to the appeal of men, especially the exhilaration he felt about in-shape, older men, he opted to follow the righteous path of sexual celibacy. His was a virtuous calling, one dictated by denial, by his need to sublimate the destiny of his incipient homosexuality.

Since Hunter had such a difficult time accepting his undeniable attraction to other men, it was much easier and far less stressful throughout the first quarter century of his life to simply remain in the closet. A comforting refuge, it was the easiest path available that might allow him to deny his true feelings. He refused to acknowledge his same-sex attraction, in part, because he so resented the gay lifestyle. He disapproved of what he saw as its rampant promiscuity, and pledged to wait until he knew he was truly in love before committing himself to what, for him, could only be a lifelong, monogamous relationship.

Rather than exploring the gay life running rampant throughout Manhattan, whether down in Chelsea and Greenwich Village, or on the Upper West Side, he instead willingly embraced his steadfast dedication to his promising career in advertising. Carefully, he choreographed his agenda by allowing his prominent standing and budding reputation as one of the up-and-coming Boy Wonders of Madison Avenue to serve as the most forceful presence in his life. His one-hundred-and-eighty-five-thou-a-year salary, plus benefits, enabled him to sit pretty.

Hunter long ago convinced himself that by not giving in to his secret longing and not acting out any of his wicked fantasies, he could remain both guilt-free and above reproach. While growing up, he sometimes got to wrestle around and roughhouse with other guys. Sometimes he and his opponent even finished off their erotic grappling with a round of mutual masturbation. But that was where he drew the line. As for actually committing himself to something as personal as kissing deeply, or participating in an activity as unseemly and hard to swallow as sucking dick — or diving into a practice as graphically off-putting as anal sex — Hunter vowed to steer clear of them all. He simply refused to engage in any such confounding behavior. By choice, he would wait for his true romance. He trusted that if he remained patient and unsullied until he was blessed with genuine feelings of strong, loving emotions, even if felt for another man, so true an adulation would likely mitigate any unpleasant aspects of a sexual congress undertaken in the name of love.

Still, there were times in his long-lived commitment to chastity, especially toward the end of his teen years, when his subconscious managed to escape from its imprisonment within his psyche and wreak havoc on his libido. It played tauntingly naughty eroticisms which video-streamed across his adolescent mind, broadcasting disturbing yet exciting scenes, each of which exposed his deep-seated attraction to fear and danger, his ever-expanding fascination with the hidden, darker sides of sensuality.

A decade later, by the time he turned twenty-eight, he was set in his ways. Ever resistant to change, he clung to the security that accompanied his pledge to chastity, and felt a comforting sense of accomplishment knowing how well his productive days and quiet nights conformed to the pattern of his organized routine. Driven by sheer force of habit, his work ethic was interrupted only by intermittent episodes of punishing migraines which sliced through his brain and rendered him pretty much useless.

He got up early every morning, often before dawn, with no alarm to rouse him. While sipping his coffee, he downed a banana along with a protein bar. As soon as the caffeine kicked in, he carefully made his bed, hospital corners and all, thoroughly scrubbed his coffee mug, and then scoured the kitchen sink. From the way his pristine apartment sparkled and gleamed, it was obvious he was a compulsive cleaner. Hunter found a soothing satisfaction in keeping everything in its proper place, all of it well-polished. He paid little attention to the barbs and quips made over the years by friends who often teased his zealous compulsion to keep things forever tidy. If you're going to be compelled by something, he reasoned, let it be keeping yourself and your home spotless.

Hunter next dressed quickly, tossed some work-related papers along with his workout gear into his thick attaché case, hurried from his one-bedroom, seventeenth-floor apartment, and rode the elevator down to the lobby of Hemisphere Arms, the fashionable, Upper East Side high-rise he called home. By then, it was six-forty-five in the morning.

Walking rapidly, like most of the other energetic New Yorkers scurrying up and down Third Avenue at that early hour, he crossed over to the subway station at Seventy-Seventh Street and hopped aboard the train to Grand Central Station. Once inside the cavernous terminal, he made his way through throngs of people, took a crowded escalator up to the lobby of the Met Life building, and squeezed himself into a sardine-packed elevator which carried him skyward to the nineteenth floor. When the elevator doors opened, Hunter stepped out into the lobby entrance of his lavish midtown Manhattan gym.

*   *   *   *

The Executive Sporting Club was one of those highly over-priced, super-luxurious gyms that provided every pampering for its well-to-do clientele short of blowing their noses for them. A self-service coffee bar offered urns of stimulating espresso and soothing chamomile tea. Water coolers filled with Gatorade provided instant energy. Guests were given their choice of five protein powders for their complimentary recovery drinks.

Hunter bounded through the enormous double glass doors of his fitness club a little before seven, signed in at the reception desk and then headed straight for the men's locker area. He quickly changed into his gym attire and walked out to the main floor. There, mounted high in various niches around the room, television monitors were tuned into half a dozen closed-circuit financial data stations, all with celluloid strips flashing across the bottom of their screens, each displaying the latest stock, bond, and commodity prices from a variety of global markets. If you had a vested interest in learning how well rubber futures opened in Malaysia that morning, this was the place to be.

After greeting several familiar club chums, the same amiable gaggle of Fortune 500 business executives who were there at the same time, morning after morning, year after year, Hunter climbed atop one of the elliptical machines encircling the perimeter of the gym. He began pressing his legs up and down, pushing hard to get his blood circulating, his heart pounding; his energy, his muscles, and his enthusiasm warmed up.

His twenty minutes of intense aerobics passed quickly, and by the time he got out on the gym floor and started lifting weights, Hunter was stoked. He worked out vigorously, using several of the club's gleaming, high-tech machines, pumping to failure on every set, breaking down two major muscle groups every time he worked out. On that early morning, he pumped back and delts.

Hunter enjoyed the company of these older men, and actually preferred his club's prevailing heterosexual atmosphere. He liked not having to deal with the intermittent flirtations that might otherwise be directed his way whenever he took a shower or removed his clothes in the locker room. While he might entertain the occasional coy flirtation from a safe distance, he still maintained his celebrated celibacy.

Most members of the Executive Sporting Club were prosperous capitalists: successful stockbrokers, CEOs of major corporations, powerful attorneys and, like him, high-ranking ad men. Unlike him, however, most of his more mature cronies were actually in pretty sorry shape.

Both far older and much softer than Hunter's well-developed self, the bulk of ESC members worked out with personal trainers who over-charged by the hour, and who still somehow managed to make their clients look, even after all their investment of time, energy, and especially money, as if they'd never once exercised in the first place. Sadly, most of the other members were saddled with voluminous love handles, flabby guts, and, all too often, overly large butts layered in fat.

Additionally, almost all the members were married men who lived in surrounding suburbia. Conforming to convention, most of them had two or three houses, two or three cars, two or three children, two or three ex-wives. Weekdays, they traveled by train into Manhattan, disembarked at Grand Central and then, before heading over to their midtown offices, first stopped off at their health club, nineteen floors overhead, to engage in their daily exercise, such as it was.

Tuition for a year at the ESC was a jolting two thousand, eight hundred dollars, a fee so exorbitant, the exclusive club was far too expensive for most bodybuilders' budgets, which was precisely how the successful proprietors of the swanky workout palace wanted it.

After polishing off his morning's training by dropping to a slant board and banging out three sets of twenty crunches each, Hunter walked around the gym floor, stopping here and there for a fast and friendly chat with other gym members. No one ever flirted, cruised, or came on to Hunter in this decidedly straight atmosphere and that was fine with him, especially since he could sense the respect and admiration these straight men afforded him for being in such terrific shape, for projecting so well his all-American good looks and accomplished athlete's physique. Hunter enjoyed the company of these older, successful straight men, especially since none of their harmless pleasantries ever threatened his ongoing commitment to celibacy.

Few of his gym pals ever inquired about his private life. Some may have quietly suspected that since he was still single at twenty-eight, he might be harboring undisclosed, unspoken secrets about his sexuality. However, since most stop-and-chats at the Club centered on matters of worldwide financial dealings, he was able to keep the trappings of his still closeted social life to himself.

With broad shoulders held high, Hunter strolled back into the men's dressing room, stepped out of his gym clothes, picked up one of the large, thick-piled white towels, flipped it over his shoulder and headed for the showers.

Hunter was hardly shy about showing off his body. He even felt comfortable walking around the locker area stark naked. The appealing hirsute configuration of his well-developed chest made his pecs appear powerful, like he was wearing a transparent warrior's breastplate. The full authority of his sturdy muscular build was on prominent display as he showered, shampooed his thick, blond hair, and then shaved in front of the mirror at the sink. He felt respected simply by standing out, not as the richest or most prominent, but at least as the best-built, most muscular member among the club's other mostly chubby schlubs.

Showered, shaved, and refreshed, Hunter returned to his locker, quickly stepped into his tan cotton slacks, pulled on his navy blue Izod shirt, grabbed his attaché case, and hurried out through the Club's double glass doors into the elevator. At fifteen minutes before nine, he stepped outside, onto a hectic, crowded Park Avenue. All set to attack the day ahead, an invigorated Hunter briskly walked the six blocks to his office building on Madison Avenue at Forty-Seventh Street.

While hurrying through its ornate, marble-laden lobby, Hunter took his customary glance at the building's detailed directory, and zoomed in on the name Broad & Harris Advertising before his eyes next panned down the roster and came to rest upon: *Hunter Rowe — Accounts Manager — 32nd Floor.*

Smiling with self-assurance, but hoping not to be perceived as smug, Hunter stepped into an elevator and was swept up thirty-two stories where he stepped out, directly into the Broad & Harris reception area.

The first thing Hunter did, after greeting his secretary Margo and getting settled into his spacious office overlooking Madison Avenue was turn on his computer and log on to the Internet to quickly click into that day's e-mail.

After glancing through his business-related correspondence, he clicked on a message from Phil, his septuagenarian cyber-buddy from Tampa.

From: PhloridaPhil@Hotmail.com

To: HunterRowe@Yahoo.com

Hunter,

Knowing how much you like roughhousing around with mature musclemen who somehow defy gravity and are still in tip-top shape, I'm attaching this picture I came across on a site called BigMuscle.com. Something tells me that if this hot stud isn't right up your alley, I just may have to give up trying to find you a husband!

Your Pal, Phil.

Hunter couldn't help but smile. Good old Phil — always trying to fix him up. His elderly cyber pal's life as a gay man about town had long since come and gone, and so he now lived vicariously through the muscle fantasies of his younger Internet pals. As such, he forwarded photos of hot-looking men to Hunter at least once a week. Hunter was always amused by the thoughtful gesture, even if, right after he glanced at their pictures, he usually deleted the dependably unappealing photos anyway.

So it was unusual when he didn't use his mouse to hit the delete button once the forwarded photo of Chase appeared on his computer monitor. In point of fact, the moment Hunter looked at the amazing muscleman's picture plastered across his monitor that late September morning, something deep inside him reacted so strongly, he was instantly aroused.

As if by instinct, Hunter knew he needed to hold on to the sexy photograph, and so he clicked "Save".

Hunter actually remained hard the whole of the next several minutes he spent just gazing at the picture of Chase's beautifully mature body. He pored over the incredibly hot double-biceps pose that had been forwarded to him. He quickly looked up Chase's AOL profile, MuscleCoach, and read that "Coach" Chase was not just a dedicated bodybuilder, but also the author of two books. As for his proclivities, his profile claimed he was a man who enjoyed erotic flexing and having hot muscle sex with well-muscled lads.

What in God's name was it about the lure of in-shape, well-seasoned, older men, so-called *mature* muscle, Hunter wondered, that always got him so heavily aroused, so dependably boned? Was it perhaps the sheer strength and power, mixed with the wisdom from the accumulated life experiences so many in-shape, older men exuded and brought to any equation?

WOOF! thought Hunter, still savoring the photo. *Right up my alley is right!*

Hunter knew he needed to ignore any nagging inhibitions, and take what was for him a major risk by initiating a correspondence. He felt a strong sexual attraction to Chase's photo, and sensed at once by some divine providence that this so-called Muscle Coach just might be the man for whom he'd been waiting.

As he continued admiring the enticing photo, Hunter impulsively composed a flirtatious note to Chase. Once written, he attached a photo of himself executing his own not so shabby double-biceps pose, and sent the e-mail straightaway to the new paradigm of his still mostly closeted muscle obsession, Coach Chase.

*   *   *   *

Chase used the lowest gear on his state-of-the-art bike, and by the time he finished pedaling back up Laurel Canyon, his body was thoroughly oxygenated. While catching his breath and retrieving the snail mail from his postal box, he spotted Gloria Bishop, one of his three tenants, en route to her small, one-bedroom bungalow at the rear of his property. In her mid-fifties, she was still a reasonably attractive character actress, one whose claim to fame, more than a quarter of a century ago, was when she had a recurring role over five seasons on "Knots Landing." Chase smiled and waved to her.

"Good afternoon, Chase!" Gloria called out to him. "Bicycling up that ridiculous hill would kill most everyone else. How do you manage it?"

"I take deep breaths!" Chase answered with a smile.

Gloria smiled back, and then gently closed her front door. The perfect tenant, quiet and never late with her rent, she'd been living in one of Chase's three comfortable rental units for the past nine years. She moved into Hyde Park right after her lady lover of twelve years ran off with a younger woman. Since that breakup long ago, Gloria had not dated again. Instead, she closed down, vowing to never again be so foolish as to romantically trust another living soul, male or female.

Chase entered his own eye-catching, two-bedroom, mid-century home, kicked off his sneakers, and then went into the kitchen to concoct his recovery protein drink.

A few minutes later, while luxuriating beneath the soothing pulsations of his long, hot shower, he allowed the pounding water to relax his freshly worked-out triceps and biceps. After drying off, he threw on a pair of blue shorts, a fresh tank-top, and then sat down at the desk in his study.

For the past decade, the Internet served as the ideal arena for the exploration of Chase's sexual needs. He found it the perfect venue for hooking up with other men into muscle. Any flirtation you initiated got directly to the point when you didn't have to wait to see what a prospective trick looked like shirtless. All you needed was the rapid exchange of photos provided by the click of a mouse.

Corresponding with and occasionally meeting other finely tuned bodybuilders became Chase's crusade. Muscle buddies who lived out of town turned out to be the most ideal sexual companions. You saw them only now and again, maybe two, three times a year. After several uncomplicated hours spent enjoying each other's bodies, you each went back to your own lives. No complications, no demands. None of them ever weighed you down, and your casual relationship never had time to grow stale.

Unlike so many of his gay buddies who dreamed of finding a dream lover, Chase had no plans to settle down. A practicing roamosexual, his foremost objection to setting up house was that having a partner would take him off the market. The notion of abandoning successive partners to the monotony of monogamy troubled him. Fidelity, throughout the long history of man, he reminded himself repeatedly, had never been truly successful in any known culture. *Love is for losers* was not only his eleventh commandment, but also his mantra. *Only wimps settle down* was his credo, and *get out before it gets ugly* his favored defense mechanism.

Chase stayed alert, knowing his next passing sexual interlude lay forever in wait. And even if love was never in the air, lust was always just around the corner as he looked forward to savoring the next well-muscled lad to cross his path or catch his eye. For Chase, beauty was its own reward, and every time he was seduced by a flirtation from another hot bodybuilder, the big question one might ask was: how long can so satisfying and intense a hookup last? The short answer for Chase, as with so many like-minded men, was always the same: at least until orgasm.

Before the Internet captured his imagination, the Coach had no idea there were so many other men out there as obsessed about or as excited over muscle as was he. By the time guys got their video cams hooked onto their computers, they could engage in long-distance muscle sex without even having to leave home. You could enjoy all the benefits of a micro-mini-romance right there on your screen. As for sexually transmitted diseases, there was nothing risky about having a pair of muscular images flexing for one another online via video cam, beating their boners in unison in virtual, two-dimensional, fluid animation, often thousands of miles apart. Surely, sex didn't get any safer than that.

Best of all for a guy like Chase was that, post-orgasm, the only thing required of you and your partner was to bid farewell and sign off. No waiting around impatiently, feigning tenderness until your sex partner finally got up, dressed, and left the house. No worries about allowing your fleeting, soon to be former lover to spend the night, both of you sleeping fitfully in the same bed.

Even with all the pleasure it afforded him, Chase acknowledged how his infatuation with muscle was not just ultimately shallow and superficial, but also unworthy of all the time and effort he so slavishly invested in its preoccupation. Still, like a poet drawn to his rhyme scheme, an addict to his needle, his fixation never stopped calling to him, an intoxicating siren.

On that sunny autumn afternoon, Chase logged on to his primary AOL handle, MuscleCoach, and then clicked into the BigMuscle site, where his profile, featured among tens of thousands of other bodybuilders, displayed the most recent photos of him flexing for the camera.

Chase clicked into his New Mail and read what he referred to as his *fan male*. These were often glowing missives from men who'd visited his Web page, or had seen his picture on one of the musclemen sites that sported his visage. After viewing him, many felt compelled to write to let him know how impressed they were with his physique. Most often, they praised his obvious dedication to his training, and reliably asked if he would like to hook up with them. No doubt about it. His fans were everywhere.

Chase went out of his way to be especially thoughtful whenever fan male arrived from a particularly unattractive or out-of-shape cyber buddy who wanted to meet. Coach was always polite and made an extra effort to let them down easy, often mentioning how much physical potential they had. He answered all letters of admiration with respect and consideration because they helped so much in fueling his motivation to stay in shape, even while satiating his daily craving for a hit of validation. Chase was the first to confess he was a confirmed roamosexual and likely to remain so. He relished spending time online prowling for muscle, chat room to chat room, often visiting myriad sites dedicated to the manly sport-pastime-preoccupation-obsession that made up bodybuilding: BigMuscle, MuscleMan4Man, BodybuildersM4M, Adam4Adam, DaddyHunt, older muscle, younger muscle, muscle worship, you name it, it was all there — the whole world of muscledom, all waiting to be explored on your monitor screen.

As a novelist, Chase was comfortable with the relative if limited success of his writing career, and felt grateful for his small inner circle of close friends.

He also kept a close kinship with his bodybuilding lifestyle, and that included his unwavering pursuit of the next muscular man. Whether they were younger or older didn't matter much to Chase. Being white, black, yellow, even orange was also of little consequence. All his muscle buddies needed to be were passably intelligent and in great shape.

Chase reveled in his chosen lifestyle, and felt satisfied and satiated in his role as satyr-like roamosexual. Nothing was likely to change any of that. At least up until the moment he opened his last New Mail that early afternoon and his interest was quickly captured by Hunter's note.

From: HunterRowe@Yahoo.com

To: MuscleCoach@AOL.com

Yo, Coach Chase —

I'm a twenty-eight year old bodybuilder who has always been attracted to older, muscular men. And WOW, Coach, are you ever in great shape! Ever since I was a kid, the sight of mature, sexy jocks working out, flexing their muscles, or sweating it out while roughhousing, has always been highly erotic for me.

When I saw your hot pics on BigMuscle, I felt such a strong sexual buzz, I just had to write to say hello. As it happens, I'm planning a business trip west in a couple of weeks, and am hoping you might want to meet.

I haven't been at this gay stuff very long, have so far pretty much only just fooled around, more or less roughhousing with other guys. I was on the wrestling team back in high school, and often got boned during practice.

You see, it's long been my as yet unrealized fantasy to be subdued, dominated, maybe even overwhelmed by an older, in-shape muscle man such as yourself. While admiring your hot photos, I wondered if you just might be that take-charge kinda guy to do the job.

I also read in your profile that you've had two novels published. Brains and Brawn, Coach. Your boy is mightily impressed.

Not to get too mystical here, but since your name is Chase and mine's Hunter, something tells me that with such thematically analogous monikers and our mutual interests in muscular bodies, we're clearly destined to hook up. Hell, maybe you'd even like to rough me up some. As an eager novice, I'm open to most anything and have attached my pic. Let me know what you think, okay, Boss? Until then, I remain,

Your New York Muscle Buddy,

Hunter

Coach enjoyed passionate interplay as much as the next guy, but had never gotten particularly excited over either roughhousing or erotic wrestling. He was all set to write back, to politely decline and say thanks, but no thanks, when he next downloaded the photo attached to Hunter's e-mail and suddenly everything changed.

Hunter's double biceps photo was dazzling. Smiling while flexing in a dark blue Speedo, the handsome younger man stood about six feet and looked like he weighed around two hundred pounds of solid muscle, the same as Chase. Carefully scrutinizing the photo still further, Chase took in the impressive mass that made up Hunter's well-developed pecs, the well-rounded peaks on his biceps, and especially that most difficult to achieve of all muscle missions: the young man's sexily sculpted six pack abs. Additionally, Chase figured this all-American looking kid must have swum through the lucky gene pool, since his handsome face and lean muscle mass were accompanied by impressive vascularity, and what looked in the photo, at least, like ideal proportions. In point of fact, the younger bodybuilder seemed to have it all, even great legs.

Chase hit the reply button, answered Hunter's e-mail and embedded a recent pic of himself, again showing off his signature Guns of Navarone. He sent his response and logged off.

*   *   *   *

After tossing promotional ideas back and forth from one coast to another, Hunter's three-hour video-teleconference finally ended. As he clicked off the conference room's closed-circuit TV monitor, the two executives working with him on their all-important account agreed their meeting with the people from the San Diego Bureau of Tourism had gone extremely well.

As they filed out of the conference room, one of Hunter's co-executives half-joked, "It's no big deal. All we have to do is turn a dreary San Diego into America's number one dream destination."

Back in his office, Hunter logged on to the Internet and perked up the moment he saw there was a reply waiting for him from MuscleCoach. He quickly opened and read the brief note:

From: MuscleCoach@aol.com

To: HunterRowe@Yahoo.com

Not sure how much I'd want to rough up a guy as good-looking as you, Hunter, mainly because I'm more a lover than a slugger. Still, after seeing that pic of your incredibly hot body, I do know I'd sure like to be all over each and every one of your major muscle groups. And you don't have to worry about any lack of experience if you and I meet, Kiddo. You'd be in good hands with Coach Chase. As it turns out, virgins are my specialty!

Your Muscle Buddy,

Chase

Titillated and excited while reading Chase's e-mail, Hunter got completely stiff as he viewed the intoxicating, fresh photo sent from Chase, and instructed his secretary, Margo, to hold his calls so he could respond to his muscle buddy's encouraging note.

From: HunterRowe@Yahoo.Com

To: MuscleCoach@aol.com

Yo, Coach Chase —

Your note was muscular music to my ears and your latest pic a sight for green eyes. I am more than ready to become your willing student. So, Coach Chase, if you think you want to take me down and make me your Star Varsity Wrestler, I'm ready to submit to your power, your will. You up to the job, Sir?

Your Muscle Boy,

Hunter

*   *   *   *

As soon as Chase opened the second muscle pic Hunter imbedded with his latest reply, an erection sprang up instantly inside his sweat pants. What was it about biceps and pecs, Chase wondered, that could always be counted upon to get him so fired up?

There were few things Coach Chase enjoyed more than a stimulating new challenge, and the sudden and unexpected sexual response triggered into full bloom by this younger hunk signaled he could turn out to be one very sexy prospect. Coach was impressed by this fellow's bravado in thinking they might share a sensual attraction to erotic wrestling. And, while not really a wrestler himself, the Coach still felt an aesthetic appreciation every now and again for wrestlers with hot bodies, whether amateur, collegiate, or pro. Beyond admiring their muscular developments, however, and outside of roughhousing around with his father and his bulldogs when he was a kid, the world of grappling held little interest or excitement for Chase. Sure, the sight of a pair of well-built jocks struggling, hot and sweaty, grunting and straining while being highly competitive, was gratifyingly homoerotic, but for Chase it was more the sensual, glistening movements of their musculature than their actual aggression that got him stimulated.

Ever since he was a kid, Chase got aroused by the sight of strapping jocks like football players, pole-vaulters, gymnasts, shot putters, wrestlers, and bodybuilders. He guessed that guys turned on by wrestling represented but a fraction of the general gay sexicon.

Wrestling, not unlike flexing and muscle sex, was more a sub-cult, a small slice of the huge pie that made up the cultural canon of the homosexual experience. If flexing was the *leit motif* of muscle sex, then erotic wrestling remained for most gay men a closeted sub-diversion. Rolling around in hot, sweaty contortions with another man was not something you heard much talk about in everyday gay circles.

Still, Coach had heard through the gayvine about a wrestling club in the Valley, and here and there had come across guys online in male chat rooms who boasted that they were turned on by gut punching or pec pounding, or by wrestling an opponent into submission. Some guys were more interested in pursuing pro-fantasy wrestling, where you *pretended* to beat each other up, while still others sought out violent, no-holds-barred matches, often with the winner earning the right to top the loser.

Without hesitation, Chase fired back a fast reply:

Yo, Muscle Boy —

Although wrestling has always appealed to me, at least in an abstract sense, it has never really been my gig. I usually stick to hot and heavy muscle sex. You know, celebrating another man's strong body by flexing together, massaging resilient, well-formed muscles, essentially exploring the sensual glories of mutual muscle appreciation. Okay, I admit it. I'm a Flexibitionist. Besides, it's safe and it's fun.

Still, make no mistake, Kiddo — I sure do like the idea of taking charge and dominating the situation. Especially since you seem so willing a team player.

How soon do you get to LA and how do we set up our meeting of the muscles?
Your Muscle Coach,
Chase.

Returning the visual favor, Chase embedded yet another photo of himself, one which captured the Coach lying atop a futon on his patio, clad in a blue Speedo, smiling proudly while flexing his prize-worthy, peaked biceps.

Since so few of the infinite flirtations initiated over the Internet ever panned out, Chase had no idea how, when or even if this particular sexual muscle fantasy might evolve into a reality. He instructed himself not to get excited, but to wait and see what, if anything, developed.

Sure enough, right there amidst his e-mail the following morning was Hunter's reply:

Yo, Coach —

Your boy, Kid Hunter here, reporting for duty, SIR!

I sure do like your style, Big Guy. And that hot pic of those amazing guns gave me another big instant lift-off right here within my Calvin briefs. I'm just afraid the sexual fulfillment of our possible forthcoming hookup might be rather short lived, as I'll probably pop the moment you flex those perfect orbs in my face.

I used the link you provided in your profile and ordered your first novel, "True Jock." I'm a bit embarrassed to admit it, but just reading the title got me hard.

Part of me is so turned on, I want to learn everything I can about you even before we hookup, while another slice of me is almost afraid to get to know you any better, fearing it just might spoil or burst the superhero image I've already created in my mind. So far, however, you're dazzling me.

I'll be heading out to San Diego in three weeks on business. My ad firm's been contracted to somehow make that unlikely destination tantalizingly appealing to tourists — no easy feat — so I'll be going there for strategy meetings with honchos from their Bureau of Tourism.

After that, I'm thinking of taking the train up to LA, probably staying at the Four Seasons. (Don't want to get in your way. But did I mention I have a huge, uhm, expense account?)

In point of fact, Coach, I'm planning to make the side trip up to LA primarily so I can meet you and feel the force of your powerful muscles up close and personal.

For now, however, I send a big flex, and an even bigger muscle hug.

Your Boy,

Hunter

*　　　*　　　*　　　*

Over the course of the next two weeks, Chase and Hunter built an intense cyber correspondence. Their daily e-mails and eventual phone conversations quickly evolved into lust-filled scenarios. Playfully, they detailed teasing taunts highlighting their individual sexual fantasies, including all they planned to do to one another once they finally realized the forthcoming meeting of their muscles.

In one of his detailed missives, Chase also made a firm point of making sure the Kid understood right from the opening bell, he was *not* searching for any lasting commitment, most certainly *not* looking to get involved in any LTR, online lingo for long term relationship.

"You mean you really wouldn't want to fall in love with someone?" Hunter asked, almost in disbelief, when next he called Chase.

"I didn't say that," Chase answered in all candor. "It's nothing personal. Just letting you know I'm not looking to set up house. That's not what I want."

"I thought that's what everyone wanted," Hunter responded, in earnest.

"Maybe not quite *everyone*," Chase smiled into his cell phone and eased himself further into the chaise on his patio, adding, "The simple truth is I'm having far too much fun playing the field."

"You never know," replied Hunter. "People change their minds all the time. Maybe settling down into an LTR could be just what you really need. Besides, Coach, I have a good feeling about you and me. About us."

"So do I," Chase allowed. "Let's just be clear on this particular point, okay? Don't want it to be a deal breaker down the road. One of the reasons we've gotten this far this fast is because you're over there on the other side of the country. Even with all your sterling qualities, Kiddo, that's the one I find most appealing. All I'm looking for, all I need in my life right now is another good muscle buddy. If we're real lucky, maybe we'll even become friends. So don't go daydreaming on me about any Hawaiian honeymoon, okay?"

"Got it, Sir!" said Hunter. "I promise not to bring this subject up again; at least not until I e-mail you later this evening."

As promised, their phone conversation segued over to the Internet hours later, when Hunter sent Chase an e-mail declaring only:

Took me a while to catch on, Coach, but now I understand: you're a roamosexual!

Chase replied quickly to the note, e-mailing back:

Took you long enough to figure it out, Kiddo. What was your first clue?

Hunter instantly answered their online-volley:

You can't kid this Kiddo, Chase. By now, I can spot a roamosexual, even from three thousand miles away. You guys are like bulls. You sleep with a cow but once before moving on to what you're convinced will be greener pastures. One conquest after the next. Don't fence me in. Give me those wide-open spaces. I gotta be me. Clearly, Boss, I have my work cut out for me.

The moment he finished reading Hunter's note, Chase hit the reply icon and quickly typed back:

I'm impressed, Kiddo. Most often, Coach's boys aren't around long enough to figure out what makes me tick. You nailed it even before we've met. Bravo. And here I thought you weren't paying attention."

"What we've got right now is ideal," Chase maintained when next they spoke by phone. "I live here and you live there. So, best case scenario? We meet, we click, we dick, maybe even like each other so much we'll want to fool around again every few months or so. Now, what's wrong with that?"

"Nothing," Hunter contended. "Except I want to play a bigger part in my man's life. When I was a little boy, my mother promised that when I grew up, I'd find the most wonderful person in the world, and we'd both live happily ever after."

"That's a fairytale, Kid," said Chase. "Doesn't always work out that way."

"You think my mother lied to me?"

"All mothers lie," said Chase. "It's part of their job description. Mine swore I'd grow up to become President of the United States."

"Hey …" suggested Hunter. "A guy can dream, can't he?"

"Be my guest, Lover Boy!" Chase allowed, and then warned pointedly, "But you should also know you're fast approaching the point where your overboard attention might not be so welcome. Truth is, if you weren't such a sexy muscle boy, I'd have kicked you to the curb a dozen e-mails ago."

"Kick me hard as you like, Coach!" Hunter beamed.

"Okay, Kiddo," Chase suggested. "Don't say you weren't warned."

Later that evening, Hunter responded to Chase's hesitancy when he sent still another e-mail, cavalierly dismissing his Coach's protestations:

Can I help it if I get stiff just looking at your pictures? Once we meet face to face, I'm confident you'll start feeling a whole lot better about our transcontinental connection.

I can be very persuasive, especially when it comes to going after something I want. But since I don't want to scare you off, I won't type something stupid like: "You can't escape — I am your destiny," ha-ha, and instead send a more humble but heartfelt muscle hug from,

Your Star Varsity Wrestler,
Hunter

* * * *

In an admittedly calculated effort to curry favor and insinuate himself into his new cyber pal's life, upon finishing *True Jock*, Hunter lavished exuberant praise on Chase's initial literary effort. He recalled his favorite passages, as well as choice bits of dialogue, and spoke extensively about how craftily Chase had developed his characters. Hunter so enjoyed Chase's writing, in fact, he went online and ordered a copy of Chase's second novel, *Pumping Irony*.

As their long-distance camaraderie strengthened, their cyber correspondence grew ever more enthusiastic concerning their forthcoming sexual tryst. They were each tantalized by how well most of their role-playing sexual fantasies seemed to mesh: father/son home alone in the den; marine sergeant/grunt recruit alone in the barracks; and of course, Hunter's most favored muscle role-playing illusion: coach/star varsity wrestler alone, down in the locker room, immediately following a grueling practice.

Hunter opened up further about his long-held fantasy to be totally dominated. He detailed his deeply suppressed and as yet unrealized yearning to be erotically roughed up and brought to orgasm while frightened to death. Over time, he grew so comfortable and trusting in his correspondence with Chase, he eventually "fessed up" and wrote forthrightly of the long-suppressed and mostly unexpressed muscle fantasy he'd harbored ever since he was a teenager.

What I've dreamt about in my darkest wishes, Hunter wrote in an e-mail, *is to be restrained by a powerful bodybuilder, forcibly taken down by him, and then raped. I have no idea why this excites me so much, especially since I never heard of a single rape victim proclaiming: Wow, that sure was fun! Can we do it again?*

Hunter hastened to explain he, of course, wanted his sexually violent mayhem executed in make-believe. All of it would be in the guise of homo-erotic roughhouse, enacted to satisfy his admittedly perverse curiosity to feel scared witless. Most importantly, his so-called rape fantasy would only work if accompanied by little or no pain.

As Hunter's visit to Southern California neared, Chase and Hunter began exchanging daily reflections that were not necessarily sexually related. They corresponded about other aspects of their lives, their careers, their politics, the movies they saw, the television they watched, the newspapers and books they read, the music they heard, their friends, their enemies, the best of their lives and the worst.

Hunter wrote about his abusive father, his late blooming sexuality, and also his love for books, horror movies, and anything to do with muscles. Chase wrote of his loving father and the generations of bulldogs they'd raised, the early and uncomplicated acceptance of his same sex attraction, and also his love for books, Hawaii, and anything to do with muscles.

As they got to know each other, they each looked forward to their lively cyber chats. It was almost as if they were becoming, of all unusual and unexpected developments … *friends.*

Uncharacteristically comfortable with the affirmation and attention Hunter was showering on him, Chase was more amused than threatened by Hunter's whimsical flights of fancy regarding their apparent future together as a couple. He was giving Hunter extra leeway over this matter not just because he lived so many miles away, but also because the Kid was so naïve, inexperienced and, truth to tell, mostly because he was so damn hot. Most other guys would have already been handed their walking papers. Not Hunter. In fact, a fresh ripple of excitement pulsated across Chase's gonads whenever he logged on and found a fresh e-mail from his sexy muscle boy.

Hunter was similarly elated whenever he went online and discovered correspondence from Chase. Whenever Chase embedded another photo of his muscular self, Hunter got instantly hard, sometimes even expelling a sloppy sprout of pre-orgasmic fluid into his shorts.

As a twenty-eight-year-old gay man who had yet to experience anal sex, Hunter was not only an anomaly, but also a hopeless romantic. His correspondence with Chase may have been filled with an aggressive bravado about his lofty muscle fantasies, but they were still all in his head. His lovemaking had yet to move past the confines of his imagination. He often reminded himself how, even with all his frankness and open willingness to put it out there and be vulnerable, his drawn out chastity was still by choice. And now that he'd finally singled Chase out as the intended popper of his cherished cherry, he was certainly not about to let so insignificant an obstacle as his heartthrob's stubborn resistance to any emotional commitment stand in their way.

Coach felt a relaxed ease over the winning way he and Hunter were hitting it off both in their cyber correspondence as well as in their coast-to-coast phoner-boners. Still, he was neither confident nor certain as to just how well they might actually react to one another once they finally hooked up in the harsh light of reality. Once face to face, would they still share so strong a mutual connection and so deeply intense a sexual attraction? What if he didn't like Hunter at all? Worse yet, what if the Coach didn't live up to the superhero image the Kid had already painted of him in his mind?

No matter how eagerly he anticipated hooking up with Hunter, Chase held fast to his conviction that the last thing he wanted was to end up getting hurt as he had twice before. After those painful episodes, he stuck to his rule never to allow any of his muscle boys to spend the entire night. Beyond that, even the notion of having a second date with any one of them was a rare occurrence.

*   *   *   *

On the afternoon of Hunter's arrival in Los Angeles, Chase biked uphill all the way home after his gym workout. He gulped down his recovery drink, stripped off his gym gear and jumped into the shower. As the steaming water cascaded across his rear delts, soothing his freshly pumped muscles, he made a note to himself to remain calm, even as he tried ignoring the gnawing anxiety deep in his gut. Why the hell was he getting so worked up about this? They hadn't even met yet.

Wasn't it common knowledge that all too many of the people who played online and engaged in cyber sex often turned out to be phonies or flakes? Ugly stories abounded about guys who, when they finally showed up in person, arrived on the scene ten years older and twenty pounds heavier than in photos they'd sent. Somehow the sheer anonymity inherent in the initiation of cyber flirtations gave men license to forgo reality and fashion themselves into something more idealized than they were: better looking, more muscular, taller, thinner, younger, whatever they chose to embellish. Often, the images they sent bore only feint resemblance to their present-day appearance.

Some guys in cyberspace went so far as to send out pictures of hot, well-built men who were not even themselves. Guys at the gym often spoke of cyber hookups that ended up as major disasters once the two parties finally met. Would his meeting with Hunter also turn into one of those unfortunate, hideous encounters?

Even if Hunter turned out to be exactly whom he claimed, Coach had always been a loner. Well, at least ever since that disastrous affair he'd lived through ten years earlier with Christian, a very married, very religious muscle monster. But that's another story. Ever since he had to get over the pain from that clumsy heartbreaker, and the depression he suffered after burying a best friend lost to AIDS, Chase vowed to be extra careful before ever allowing anyone to again penetrate his safely guarded emotional shield.

Driving south on the Hollywood Freeway, on his way downtown to pick up Hunter, Chase tried quieting his unexpected, unwelcome apprehension by forcing himself to lower his own far too elevated expectations.

It probably won't work out, so no big deal, he reasoned. *Count on nothing. Depend on no one. Never forget the pain that follows infatuation. Never forget the Eleventh Commandment: Love is for losers.*

         *   *   *   *

Chase pulled into Union Station, parked his car, and then walked quickly into the bustling terminal. On his way to the train platform, he ducked into the men's room. While washing his hands, he glanced up at his appearance in the mirror. A couple of weeks shy of forty-nine, fast approaching the big five-O, and never in better shape. The hint of salt and pepper in his thick hair placed a cap of dignity atop the mature muscle already embodied in his Coach persona.

What's your main objective? Chase silently asked his image. *Catch and release. Now go nail him!*

While descending the escalator toward the passenger arrival area, Chase passed a trio of sailors on the adjacent ascending escalator. One of the petty officers not only turned and glanced his way with an over-the-shoulder, cruisey look of appraisal, he also checked out how empowering Coach's big guns looked popping out from the short sleeves of his tight Izod shirt. Nothing like the rush of a mini-flirtation to fire up Chase's libido. No doubt about it. His fans were everywhere.

Chase found a sturdy column at the front of the platform and leaned against it as the train from San Diego slowly chugged to the end of its run. As commuters stepped out from rail cars, he kept a watchful eye on the dense crowd.

Scores of enthusiastic loved ones greeted riders as they stepped onto the platform, while other travelers were met by chartered chauffeurs holding up small signs displaying illegibly scribbled names.

Then, in the blink of an eye, Chase saw Hunter walking slowly toward him. A black camera bag was tossed over his right shoulder, he wore a backpack, and towed behind him a small suitcase on rollers.

From across the platform, at the same exact moment, they each caught an initial glimpse of one another.

It only took that inaugural passing glance for Hunter to know for certain his prayers had been answered. He could tell from the thumping of his heart and the sudden, throbbing jolts to his groin that this was the real thing, exactly what he'd been waiting for his entire life.

No doubt about it. He was in love.

Chase was relieved when Hunter not only turned out to be just who he claimed he was, but even sexier, more handsome in the flesh. The Coach took a few steps forward, opened his huge arms wide, and warmly embraced his muscle boy. While forcefully hugging Hunter, capturing him in a strong embrace, his big dick sprang to life inside his shorts, and Chase could recall nothing that ever felt quite so gratifying.

No doubt about it. He was in lust.

Locked together in their exuberant, immobilizing hug, the Coach and his Star Varsity Wrestler stood motionless on the platform, squeezing tightly as each of them savored the extended moment of their first physical contact.

"Welcome to L.A., Kiddo," Chase whispered into Hunter's ear.

"Can't believe I'm finally here, Coach," Hunter whispered back. "Right here in your strong arms, exactly as I imagined them."

Chase smiled and squeezed still tighter.

Hunter returned the forceful embrace with equal intensity and implored in a hesitant, low voice, "Hey, do me a favor, will ya, Coach? Don't let go of me, okay? Not just yet. I need to hold on to this moment, not just for posterity, but also because I just popped major wood. The beast within needs to settle down before this caravan can move on."

Chase pressed his fingers into Hunter's taut back muscles. "Take all the time you need, muscle boy. You feel so good in my arms, I could stand here for a month."

They stood in place, hugging solidly, four big, strong arms wrapped around two big, strong men. They held on to one another as if for dear life, absorbing the sparks of sexual tension fairly exploding about them, even as oblivious pedestrians involved in their own personal traveling sagas scurried by. These other busy commuters barely took notice of two men openly hugging with such apparent affection.

Airports and bus and railroad stations were among the select few places where men could actually get away with flaunting the taboo of displaying same sex affection in public. There seemed to be something intangibly inoffensive about warm hellos or fond farewells that tolerated private tactile moments enacted before the public eye.

*   *   *   *

Chase scooted in behind the wheel of his Jeep Cherokee, turned to face Hunter in the passenger seat and, after a quick glance around to ensure the open parking area was deserted, forcefully took Hunter into his arms and kissed him smack on the lips.

Neither of them could tell how long their initial kiss may have lasted because, along with reality, their collective sense of the fourth dimension dissolved as lips collided, tongues wrestled, and tonsils jostled. Breathing in unison, their conjoined oxygen intakes floated rhythmically back and forth, invigorating each of them with skyrocketing sexual arousal.

Coach sure knows how to kiss, Hunter thought to himself, and his inner core went numb with a weird tingling sensation as Chase forcefully grabbed a fistful of blond hair from the back of his head and pulled it tight.

Never imagined it would feel this sweet, this soon, thought Chase. *So far so good.*

While Coach kept one hand tightly clenched on Hunter's hair at the back of the Kid's head, he allowed his free hand to roam. As his fingers charted a path down Hunter's shirt, he gently squeezed his muscle boy's resilient pecs, then moved further down and caressed the protruding outer ripples along the Kid's hard abs. Chase's fingers then wandered down still further and his open hand softly caressed his muscle buddy's pronounced stiffness.

Hunter, too, gave his left hand license to travel down to Chase's crotch so he could gently rub his fingers against the solid bulge that greeted its arrival.

When at last the Coach finally pulled his lips apart from Hunter's sensual mouth, the Kid leaned back against the passenger door and casually commented, "Well, Coach, I sure hope this is the first of many long weekends together."

Whoa! That did it all right. Chase drew himself away from Hunter and vehemently wrapped his hands around the steering wheel, even as his rigid cock took a major swan dive, went fleetingly flaccid, and then decidedly limp. "Let's not get ahead of ourselves here," he advised, sagely. "After all our intense correspondence about this, you must know that getting stuck on me is a real fast road to nowhere."

"I'll take my chances," Hunter smiled with unwarranted confidence.

Chase was amused by the Kid's moxie. "And here I was sure you had more smarts than that."

Hunter kissed Chase again softly on the lips, licked the bottom of his nose, and whispered, "Have it your way, Coach."

They kissed again, strongly, passionately, gluing their interlocking lips. As the Fifty-First State put in an impressive return engagement, the blare of a horn on the other side of the parking area snapped Chase and Hunter back to reality.

After reluctantly breaking their protracted embrace, Coach started the engine, pulled out from the train station's parking spot, and headed to Hunter's hotel.

*   *   *   *

Hunter checked in at the Four Seasons and Chase began kissing him all over again the moment they stepped in and closed the door to his room.

"Where'd you learn to kiss like that?" Hunter finally asked as, between extended kisses, he flipped the lock on the door.

"You kidding, Kiddo?" Coach smiled a brutish grin. "I *majored* in kissing."

"Doesn't surprise me," said Hunter, planting soft kisses along the length of his Coach's athletic neck.

Chase again clutched a tightly drawn clump of hair at the back of Hunter's head, even as he slowly steered the two of them over to the foot of the huge bed, all the while still kissing him deeply. Never freeing Hunter's lips from his own, Chase carefully eased his muscle buddy down onto the bed, positioned himself on top so they were chest to chest, and then wrapped his arms around Hunter's shoulders, and squeezed tightly. Time again froze for the two of them, and they kissed blissfully for another interval that toyed with infinity.

"I swear, Coach, I don't think I've ever been kissed like this!" Hunter admitted.

Chase broke himself away, stood up and clapped his hands together. "This is it, Soldier!" he commanded, raising his voice. "On your feet! Front and center! The time has come for a balls-to-the-wall muscle inspection."

"Sir, yes Sir!" Hunter shouted out as willingly, he sprang to his feet and snapped to rigid attention.

Chase stepped forward, took a hold of both sides of the lapels on Hunter's shirt and then, with no warning, willfully ripped the Kid's stylish plaid shirt wide apart. As buttons popped to the floor like beads from a broken necklace, Coach then grabbed the bottom front tails of Hunter's now torn shirt and rapidly shredded the rest of the garment, pulling it up and then apart by its seams, before ripping it completely off him.

"Holy shit, Coach!" Hunter cried out. "That was a brand new shirt! Wore it today just for you!"

"I'll buy you another!" Chase grinned with a dismissive shrug.

"Don't bother!" Hunter grinned emphatically. "That was worth the whole trip here. I nearly shot when you did that. Honest. You can take me to the airport now, Coach. I'll return home a happy puppy."

"Not just yet, Soldier," Chase smiled. "First let's have a good look at you."

As Hunter stood before Chase, shirtless and vulnerable, the Coach sized his sexy buddy up and down, eyeing the young man's beautifully muscled body. "Even better in person, Kiddo!" he pronounced approvingly, then ordered, "Okay, Hunter, let's see you flex those big cannons for your Coach."

"Sir, yes Sir!" Hunter beamed and, raising his arms high into the air, struck a powerful double biceps stance.

"Sheer perfection!" Chase muttered softly and welcomed his stiff cock back to the party. Still standing eye to eye, directly in front of Hunter, he asked, "You of course have heard about the Guns of Navarone, haven't you, Kiddo?"

"Who hasn't?" Hunter asked playfully. "Famous in song and story."

"Well, now say hello to them in person," Chase offered as he lifted his arms to flex his own signature double biceps pose.

At first, Hunter said nothing. "Just incredible," he finally uttered favorably, even as he placed a grateful hand around each of the peaks of Coach's incredible guns, and held on, grasping each of them tightly. "I am so thrilled to finally be here, face to face with them. And of course with you, Coach. Can't believe how great you look, how incredible you feel to hold, to touch. Will you take off your shirt so I can see more, or should I just rip it off you?"

"I'll save you the trouble," Coach said with a smile as he yanked his tight blue short sleeve shirt up over his head and dropped it to the floor. The near perfection of his entire sculptured torso exposed at last, Chase again flexed his double biceps for his entranced muscle boy.

Hunter looked at Chase in near veneration. "Coach, you're driving me nuts," he confessed as he stared at Chase's crotch. "And I can't wait any longer to see the rest of you."

Reaching forward, Hunter slowly unzipped Chase's khaki shorts and lowered them to the floor. It was apparent from the bulge in Coach's Jocko briefs that lift-off had already been achieved and was shooting skyward.

Hunter quickly dropped to his knees, untied the laces on each of Coach's sneakers and helped him kick them off. He then assisted as Chase stepped out of his shorts. Hunter kicked off his own shoes, unzipped his navy Armani slacks, stepped out of them and left them on the floor in a clump. Clad only in their briefs, they stood before one another, kissing voraciously.

Slowly, Coach again lowered Hunter onto the bed, carefully eased him down on his back before he again dropped his full weight on top of the Kid and planted another powerful kiss across his boy's thick lips. And all the while they kissed, their hands wandered and probed, exploring the landscape, feeling out the topography of each other's solid muscle groups. Rolling around intensely, kissing intimately, hugging tightly, being this affectionate, this connected and energized, Hunter hoped their foreplay would never end. He looked up into Chase's dark blue eyes and told him, "Feels great having you on top of me, Coach."

After embracing a lot more while locked in deeply powerful, wet kisses, Coach again eased Hunter over onto his back, then sat up and straddled the Kid's abs. Flexing his huge, exhilarating guns while hovering over his boy, he asked, "Is it too early to declare victory in our wrestling match?"

"You're too tough for me, Coach," said Hunter, slapping the comforter. "I'm tapping out." Reaching up and squeezing the peaks of Chase's baseball biceps, he further acknowledged, "I wanted you soon as I saw your picture online and then again the moment I stepped off the train, Boss. I'm all yours. Do with me as you wish!"

"Well, for openers," Chase tugged at Hunter's Calvin's. "Let's get you out of these damn dopey drawers."

"Gladly," said Hunter. "And how 'bout we lose your sexy boxers, as well?"

Playfully, they yanked off each other's underwear before they flopped down again on their backs, shoulder to shoulder, both their impressive erections standing straight up in the air, saluting like good soldiers. The Fifty-First State swelled a couple of inches higher into the air than Hunter's phallus. If their dicks were a metaphoric New York skyline, Chase was The Empire State Building, Hunter the Chrysler Building.

Hunter gazed over at Chase's stiff manhood, and with glowing satisfaction regarded the size and thickness of his Coach's prized member. He eased himself down the bed, squeezed himself in snugly between Chase's thighs, and positioned his face directly before Coach's crotch. The Kid then wrapped each of his arms around the girth of Chase's thickly muscled thighs and brought his nose face-to-face with Chase's big hard dick. Intimidated and at the same time challenged by the enormity of the task at hand, Hunter looked up at Chase and told him, "You know, Coach, I've never been a size queen. But in your case, I'm prepared to make an exception."

"Give me your best shot, Kiddo. Let's see what you got."

Hunter smiled and quietly announced, "Had I known it was this big, I would have practiced on something like a loaf of French bread. But I'm a tough soldier, so

I'll try to devour the whole thing. As you know, I'm just getting my feet wet with all this gay stuff. Blowjobs are still a foreign country to me, and I didn't bring my passport. So I hope you'll be patient."

"Sure thing, Kiddo," Chase smiled as he clasped his hands smugly behind his head and looked up at the ceiling. "Take your time. Not sure how often I mentioned this, but as it happens, virgins are Coach Chase's specialty."

"I recall," Hunter smiled. "And I hope you'll train me. Don't be afraid to tell me how I might improve my technique in serving you better, Boss. Twenty years from now, I don't want to hear after all our time together that your boy has been giving a lousy blow job."

"Won't be a problem, Hunter," Coach responded. "I promise to teach you everything I know."

Sizing up the monumental erection bobbing back and forth before his dazed gaze, Hunter observed, "Gosh, Coach, it's so darn ... *big!*"

"Nonsense," Chase was dismissive. "It's about the same size as my Dad's. And I never once heard my mother complain."

"Oh, believe me, Boss, I'm not complaining. Still, it may take some practice before I get the whole thing down."

"Relax," said Chase, as he eased his head back down against the pillow and closed his eyes. He flexed his great guns hard, exhaled deeply and then added, "The Guns of Navarone and the Fifty-First State aren't going anywhere ... we're right here for you."

His mission clear, his purpose set, Hunter squeezed each of Chase's heavily muscled thighs still tighter, and rubbed them against the cheeks of his face. Then, exhilarated and relieved about how incredibly well the two of them were hitting it off, just as he'd hoped and prayed, the Kid brought his open mouth down to the fat mushroom head of Chase's thick hard member, and finally went down on his lifelong muscle fantasy.

*   *   *   *

Their marathon sexcapade lasted more than three hours. Hunter and Chase kissed and caressed and fondled and massaged one another with abandon. They stood up before the hotel room's floor-to-ceiling mirror, flexing for one another while acting out an erotic pose-down. They slathered each other's torsos up and down, draining an entire bottle of baby oil in the process. Their bodies shined, their muscles glistened.

Entwined like muscular pretzels, they flopped back down atop the bed and rolled around in circles, all over the hotel linens. They went down on one another, feverishly sixty-nine-ing, getting Chase so aroused and excited that he actually broke his long-held safety rule of never engaging in oral sex on a first date.

When, at last, they could no longer hold back, the Coach and the Kid each continued masturbating their own erections as Chase again eased Hunter over on to his back and again straddled his boy's abs. Then, while he flexed his big left gun, Hunter returned the favor, copying the gesture as he fiercely flexed one of his own beautifully sculptured biceps.

Vehemently, they whacked away in tandem until Chase slammed his full lips against Hunter's, kissing him so forcefully, they both exploded at the same time, their tongues locked, their spurts of sperm spewing their mutual orgasms all over the Kid's ravishing abs.

*   *   *   *

They lay still together for the longest time, each of them drifting in and out of a semi-slumber, basking in the private, primal intimacy of their shared, post-orgasmic euphoria. In time, Hunter retrieved a warm wet washcloth from the bathroom, and then carefully wiped clean both their torsos. He then jumped back into bed and snuggled up right next to his muscle mentor. Flat on their backs, quiet and reflective, they remained for the longest time both immobile and mute. Hunter's head rested against his coach's shoulder. Finally astride his chosen mate, Hunter never felt safer or more secure. He eventually broke the serenity of their reverie, commenting, "Feels like I died and went straight to muscle heaven. So when do we get to wrestle?"

"Isn't that what we were doing?" asked Chase, feigning naiveté.

"Not quite," Hunter smiled. "What we just finished was a lot closer to making love than making war. So when are you going to toss me around the room, Boss?"

"Who knows?" Chase laughed. "You're the wrestler, remember? So far, I'm having far too much fun just kissing you and being all over you. But don't worry. I'll try working up enough steam to take you down more forcefully next time."

"Oh, yeah?" Hunter asked with a mock bravado, as he clenched pseudo-threatening fists. "You and what army, old man?"

"What'd you just call me?" Chase pretended to be offended.

"Whoops ..." Hunter quickly slammed his hand across his open mouth.

"Take it back!" Chase shouted out as he jumped on top of Hunter and twisted the Kid's arm into a tight contortion behind his back. "Apologize! Now!"

"Fat chance!" Hunter retorted in defiant protest.

Chase twisted Hunter's arm harder.

"Ouch! Stop!" Hunter shouted, both laughing and complaining at the same time. "You're breaking my arm! Hey — that hurts!"

"Say it!" Chase demanded as he wrapped Hunter's neck in a headlock with his free hand and used his other to twist the Kid's arm still further up behind his back.

"Ow-OW!" Hunter cried out. "Stop — you're killing me. Stop!"

"Let me hear you say it!"

"Okay, okay," Hunter howled at the same time he spontaneously sported major wood. "I give! I'm sorry ... Okay? I GIVE! I'M SORRY!"

Chase released Hunter and again flexed his big left gun in Hunter's face as he quietly asked, "You don't really want to mess with your coach, now do you, Muscle Boy!" Then he started kissing Hunter deeply, passionately, all over again.

Two more muscle-motivated orgasms later, Chase and Hunter were thoroughly spent as they lay entwined together in bed. When Chase looked out the hotel room window, he saw it was dark outside. "Will you look at the time? Coach and his boy need to down some protein, feed these hungry machines, and I mean pronto."

"How 'bout if I take you to dinner?" asked Hunter, sitting up with a semi-smart salute. "Any damn place you like."

"Works for me," Chase happily accepted. "Let's go to Paris."

"I meant some place within driving distance," Hunter smiled. "I'm here in Southern California on business, you know, and I don't just mean our muscular monkey business. You must know some fun spot with inflated prices where your boy can pad his substantial expense account."

Chase and Hunter shared a steamy shower, taken up by heated kisses and soaped-up, scrubbed-down body rubs.

Hunter stood beneath the cascading hot water and placed his hands on each side of his waist. He tensed his wet abdominal muscles as he taunted Chase, challenging, "Go ahead, big man. Hit me. Go on. Just lemme have it, okay? Test out these rock hard abs. Go on, Coach. Take your best shot."

Chase made a fist and, as requested, smacked it flush against Hunter's rigid six-pack. The splashing water intensified the sound of his punch. Hunter easily absorbed the blow.

"That's it? That's the best you got?" Hunter asked, dismissively, and gritted his teeth. "Come on. Don't be afraid. Hit me again. You can't hurt me."

Chase smiled and again erotically struck his fist smack up against Chase's still resilient gut. Oomph.

Hunter moaned with glee and, in true pro wrestling spirit, made believe it hurt far more than it did. "Now that's more like it!" He said once he caught his breath. "You see, you *can* be a wild animal!"

"AAAARRGGGHHHH!!! Chase responded with affectionate ire, in his best bull-dog growl, as he twirled shut the shower faucets.

They dried one another off and dressed for dinner. Rather than drive all the way up to Hyde Park so he could change, Hunter loaned Chase his newest pair of tan Abercrombie & Fitch slacks, as well as a fresh, deep green, Tommy Hilfiger short sleeve shirt. Hunter wore his navy Armani slacks and one of his green Calvin Klein long-sleeved shirts. By no coincidence, the shirt was the same color as his eyes.

Chase looked sharp clad in the Kid's clothes. Since he and Hunter were both about the same size, with similar builds, Coach realized he'd be acquiring a whole new, hot-looking wardrobe should they, down the path, wind up together as a couple.

Whoa! Chase quickly slammed on the brakes of his own confusion as a voice inside his head articulated its outrage. *You've had one incredible session of muscle sex, and so far you and this guy are having a lot of fun together. But it's a little soon to start picking out china patterns. So take a deep breath and a short step back — and fast.*

At the open door, ready to leave the hotel room a few minutes later, Hunter turned, leaned in toward Chase, opened his arms wide for a hearty embrace and forthrightly requested, "How 'bout a big muscle hug for the road?"

Chase seized the moment to telegraph a subtle withdrawal. He lifted his left arm straight out and froze it in place as his fist came flush up against the middle of Hunter's advancing pecs, stopping his boy in his tracks. "Hold on, Hunter," Chase said with forced laughter. "If I get my arms around you again, I'll have to hug you so hard, not only won't I be able to stop, I'll also wrinkle your perfectly starched shirt so badly, you'd look like a major slob at dinner."

"You make a good point, Coach," Hunter said as he leaned back on his heels, and took Chase's minor rebuff in stride. "How 'bout if I grab you later?"

"As they say out here in Hollywood: you got a deal!"

*   *   *   *

They dined a few blocks from the hotel, on the candlelit patio at Orso, the Northern Italian perennial hot spot on Third Street. After a few sips of the pricey California Coppola pinot noir ordered by Hunter, the Kid lowered his voice to take Chase into his confidence as he timidly revealed, "Coach, I have a confession to make."

"Don't tell me you're really a lesbian!"

"Not quite," Hunter edged his chair closer to Chase. "Well ... you already know I haven't been especially active since more or less coming out to myself not so long ago, right?"

"Yes, I knew that, Kiddo," Chase answered. "And I keep telling you it's not a problem."

"I know," said Hunter. "But here's the funny part. And don't laugh! Truth is, I've never been topped by a guy — for that matter, never even topped one. I *really* am a virgin"

Chase looked surprised. "You mean you were telling the truth?"

"'Fraid so," Hunter shrugged and blushed.

"This could be a cyberspace first," suggested Chase. "I was sure when you wrote you were inexperienced, well, that you meant it as a metaphor for still not having had much emotional interplay with other men. I never dreamed you meant it quite so literally. You been living in a cave?"

"May as well have been," Hunter shrugged. "Took me years to start fooling around with guys, even on the most innocuous level. I was convinced my attraction to musclemen was a transitory phase, something I'd eventually outgrow. Hell, even after I came to grips with my fixation for muscle, and partially accepted being gay, I still avoided getting down and dirty. I sublimated my same-sex urges by turning to wrestling. It's physical, it's muscular, fun, safe, satisfying. But most of all ... it doesn't have to be all out gay sex."

"Hunter ... you are dazzling me with your footwork," Chase told him. "But let me get this straight. In all your twenty-eight years, you've never once experienced anal sex?"

"Never."

"How 'bout the other side of the coin?" Chase wanted to know. "Ever had sex with a woman?"

"Once," Hunter answered softly. "On my fifteenth birthday. It's a long story. I hate to admit this, Coach, but after that initial encounter, I didn't have sex again till four years ago."

Feigning astonishment, Chase placed a supportive hand on Hunter's shoulder. "Still pure as the driven snow, huh? It's like having dinner with Saint Francis of Assisi."

"But it's the truth," Hunter admitted, reluctantly. "I could count on three fingers the number of times I've even gone down on a guy, and that includes this afternoon. I'm what you might call a late boner bloomer."

"I'll say!" Chase agreed, and then wanted to know, "And may I ask just why you waited until now to bring this up?"

"I didn't want to scare you off," Hunter answered, honestly. "Some guys would have run away from that kind of inexperience, right off the bat."

"Not me," said Chase. "You already knew that."

Hunter placed his hand under the table and affectionately squeezed Chase's inner thigh. "I decided as soon as I saw you today that the time had finally come. You're the one I want to do the deed. I even purchased my first tube of lube and brought some condoms just in case we really clicked and, man oh man, have we ever clicked."

"Now don't start getting mushy on me again, Kiddo," Said Chase, forcing an evil grin. "We've got three thousand miles and almost twenty years between us. Past that, we both want different things out of life. You know I ain't the marryin' kind!"

"Details!" proclaimed Hunter, casually dismissing Chase's protestations. "If it's good, we can make it work. If it works, we can make it good."

"I think you've been reading too many fortune cookies."

"You bet your boots I have, Boss. With me, the cup is always half full. At the office, I'm known not just for my superb organizational skills, but also my unflagging optimism."

A waiter arrived at the table to take their order. Hunter looked straight at Chase and asked, practically in a whisper, "So? After all I've told you, are you, pardon the expression, still up for it?"

"That depends," Chase answered quietly with a sexy wink. "How soon can we get back to your hotel room?"

*　　　*　　　*　　　*

At the end of their dinner, after downing miniature cups of decaf espresso, Hunter whipped out his credit card and signed for the check.

They both remained quiet while driving the few blocks back over to the Four Seasons. Hunter leaned himself against his coach's shoulder, and placed his left hand firmly on Chase's huge strong right thigh, caressing it with care.

While Hunter ruminated over how their forthcoming sexual drama might unfold with the relinquishing of his hallowed virginity, Chase worked at pumping up his own confidence so he could rise to the occasion, particularly after polishing off that bottle of red wine. While the pinot noir relaxed him, he hoped its alcohol would not come between him and his treasured virility. Feeling the need to say *something* just in case things didn't go according to plan, Chase patted Hunter's pecs and came clean. "And now I have something to admit to you, Kiddo."

"I'm all ears, Coach," said Hunter, squeezing himself closer to Chase.

"Just want you to know that when it comes to … insertion, I'm a bit, how shall we say … rusty?"

"You mean out of practice?" asked Hunter.

"Exactly," Chase answered. "It's been quite a while, maybe ten years since I last … made love to a man."

"Seems a real long stretch, Coach," said Hunter. "Especially for such a studly guy. Don't you like doing it?"

Chase speedily maneuvered his Jeep around a sharp corner, and told Hunter, "Truth is, I've always been more interested in muscle. So back when AIDS first reared its ugly head, I just figured it might be a lot easier, safer, to give up rear entry for a while, just not do it, and concentrate on staying HIV-negative, limiting myself to nothing more intense than muscle sex."

"I can relate," Hunter smiled.

"Figured you might," Chase smiled back. "And after losing a best friend to the plague, I decided to wise up and only play safe — to stay alive, if only for his sake."

"Understandably."

"And I've been comfortable with that, simply beating off with another body-builder while getting off on our mutual muscle appreciation — fast, easy, fun, uncomplicated, clean, only temporarily emotional, and best of all, safe."

"Sounds like we've been living somewhat parallel sex lives, Coach."

"Fact is, even knowing how effective condoms can be, I've resisted all that back-door business. Fine about it, that is, Hunter, until you came into the picture."

"I'm flattered, Boss. Truly."

"I decided to stop fucking around with guys until I met someone that meant more than just another passing orgasm. I needed to have more than just my genitals stimulated, so I promised myself I just wouldn't do it again until there was someone with whom I really *wanted* to do it, someone who meant more to me — not just physically, but emotionally, intellectually, maybe even spiritually."

"Now I'm more than just flattered," Hunter smiled and pressed himself even closer against his coach. "Daddy, I'm honored."

"For good reason, Son," said Chase, almost in jest. "This is not going to be your everyday pop, Pal. Tonight I hope to give you something you're going to hold on to … forever."

"Great!" Hunter expressed his excitement. "Because in taking me down for the first time, I'd like you to also rip me a new asshole!"

"Sounds anatomically challenging," suggested Chase.

"Naw — you can do it," Hunter insisted, brashly. "And I know for sure I can take it."

Chase made a sharp left turn into the hotel's semi-circular driveway and pulled up to the valet station outside the entrance. He killed the engine, stroked the back of Hunter's head and pointedly offered, "You mean you think you can take it!"

*　　*　　*　　*

After setting the Do Not Disturb sign in place, Hunter locked the door to his hotel room. As he turned around, Coach placed his hands around the Kid, forcefully pulled him into his huge arms, and kissed him deeply. Lips locked, their hunger for one another found them fumbling about, unbuttoning, unbuckling, unzipping, stripping off each other's clothes.

Minutes later, naked again and working up another sweat, they flexed for one another's excitement. Coach flipped the Kid over on to his stomach and started massaging the enticing rounded mounds of his sumptuous bubble butt, before gently easing his fingers back and forth between the fleshy divide within Hunter's firm cheeks. He reached for the tube of lube on the night stand, and tenderly slid a lubricated finger into the softness of his boy's virgin butt.

After several more minutes of this intimate, erotic butt play, Chase withdrew his lubricated fingers, then leaned forward and softly yet firmly whispered into Hunter's ear, "Okay, Kiddo. Time for Coach Chase to put an end to his boy's long-suffering chastity. Does the condemned prisoner have any last wishes?"

"My only goal, Coach …" Hunter admitted, "is to see that you're happy. So make me your boy, and don't you dare be gentle with me."

"Gentle?" Chase sneered sardonically. "Not likely. You must know by now Coach Chase is so take-charge — I may just pound you into the next room."

"Promises, promises," Hunter smiled into his pillow. "Okay, Boss, it's just you and me. Coach and his Star Varsity Wrestler together, down in the locker room after practice, finally getting plowed good and hard by my muscle coach."

Chase planted a kiss on the back of Hunter's neck, and whispered into his ear, "I'm going to unite us now, Hunter."

"I like the sound of that, Big Daddy!" Hunter said, tensing up.

Confident, in control, and by then rigid as a rocket on the launch pad, Chase was ready for take-off. With no need for Viagra, he flipped Hunter over onto his back and looked straight into his green eyes. Their gazes remained locked as Chase positioned one of the Kid's legs over each of his big shoulders. He shoved a nearby pillow beneath the small of Hunter's back and reached for one of the condoms Hunter had placed next to the pillow. He tore open the small foiled packet, rolled the prophylactic onto his enormous erection, quickly greased it with a glob of lube, and commanded Hunter's attention with knowing assurance. "Now relax," he said quietly.

"Relax and breathe. Let it all go. I'm in charge now, and I'm going to take real good care of you."

"I know you will, Coach."

"It's just you and me — Coach and his boy. Now give me the opposite of a solid flex and loosen up. Just exhale, relax, and most importantly, trust me."

"With all my heart," Hunter muttered and then, following his Coach's instructions, he tried to relax, no easy feat given his elevated level of sexual anxiety.

Chase held firmly onto Hunter's elevated thighs and then, while still bending all the way forward so he could feverishly kiss his beautiful sex partner, he also positioned himself as he brought the fat head of his stiff cock flush up against the sensitive wall of Hunter's lubricated inner flesh.

Willingly, Hunter placed all his faith in his new best friend, his most extraordinary muscle coach, and closed his eyes as he tried to relax and accept the inevitable.

Authoritative yet patient, measured yet forceful, Chase triumphantly forged his way into their shared bliss.

*   *   *   *

By the time their initial lovemaking finally climaxed, it culminated in a pair of simultaneous, ecstatic orgasms. Chase collapsed on top of Hunter and fought to catch his breath. Sweaty and musky, they remained motionless, silently enjoying their quasi-conscious euphoria. Entangled together in comfort, they breathed in unison as time slipped away.

"Gosh, Pop," Hunter finally interrupted their reverie. "I'm sure glad Mom and Sis went shopping at the mall so we could finally fool around."

"You and me both, Son," Chase went along good-naturedly with Hunter's cute role-play.

Hunter changed the subject, calmly suggesting out of nowhere, "I bet guys are always falling in love with you."

Chase stretched to the end of the bed for a towel, and responded, at least semi-facetiously, "One after the other. All part of their training program."

"And what happens when they do?" Hunter wanted to know.

"Well," Chase smiled mischievously. "If they play their cards right, they sometimes get invited to have another private session down in the locker room with their Coach, right after practice."

"Then that's what I aspire to!" Hunter decreed, as he accepted the towel from Chase and began wiping them both off. "And how do you react when one of your boys say he's fallen in love with you?"

"It's no biggie, Kiddo," Chase conveniently sidestepped the issue by pretending to yawn. "I hear it all the time."

"And then what?" Hunter wanted to know. "Tell the truth. Do you walk away? Do you … disengage?"

"More often than not, sure," Coach answered, candidly. "I've been burned twice. Three strikes and I'm out. That's why I usually like to leave while it's still hot. Why wait around until the relationship loses its spark? Shouldn't romance be more than some pathetic, flickering candle?"

Hunter sat up, too, and kissed Chase directly on his full lips. He held his Coach's face in both his hands and firmly told him, "Well, here's the big difference, Boss. In case I haven't mentioned this at least a dozen times — Boy Wonders of Madison Avenue get spoiled rotten. We get things done our way, often just the way we want. And right now, you and I are having too much damn fun to call it quits. So hear me well, Chase Hyde, because I plan to do whatever it takes to make sure we never lose steam or flicker out."

Chase removed Hunter's hands from his face and held them tightly in his own. "Fine with me, Kiddo," he decreed. "Just know you've been warned."

"I understand, Coach," Hunter beamed. "Your boy accepts the danger inherent in this challenging assignment. And may the best man win ... you!"

Minutes later, they were showering together again in the hotel's plush bathroom. As Hunter soaped up and vigorously massaged the solid muscles of Chase's back, Coach sighed contentedly, quietly observing, "I don't know about you, but I'm wiped out. You'd think I was the one who'd just taken the pounding. Gonna sleep real well tonight, guaranteed!"

"Don't you mean *we're* going to sleep real well tonight?" asked Hunter.

Uh-oh. Another early sign of trouble? Chase wondered as his protection meter pricked up and raised its red flag alarm. Was it time to slam on the brakes?

Chase turned to face Hunter. As water rained down upon them both, he asked with calm resolve, "You don't really mind if I go home now, do you, sleep in my own bed — like always?"

"Mind?" asked Hunter, facetiously. "Why would I mind? Just because I assumed we'd spend the night together after I traveled a hundred twenty miles from San Diego just to see you?"

"Sleeping with another guy is never easy," Chase answered, guardedly. "All that snoring and clearing of throats, the coughing and constantly getting up to pee, monopolizing the covers, farting, waking up hysterical from a nightmare. Hell, I consider it a major accomplishment just getting me to sleep in the same bed with *me*."

Hunter looked Chase squarely in the eye and asked slyly, "Could my coach be wrestling not just with me, but also with issues involving ... *intimacy?*"

"Has nothing to do with intimacy!" Chase was defensive. "I just don't like sleeping with another man. Period."

"How would you know?" asked Hunter. "When did you last try it?"

"Long time ago," Chase shot back. "At least ten years." Forcefully, he twirled the hot and cold shower knobs, terminating the water's cascade.

"Well, then, we're practically even," Hunter told him. "Because I've never done it at all. Never even wanted to sleep an entire night next to someone else. Not until now."

Hunter slid open the glass shower door, reached for an enormous white bath towel and started drying off Chase's muscular chest. "How 'bout if we just give it a shot," he suggested while firmly rubbing his Coach. "What have you got to lose?"

"I'm not sure," Chase answered honestly. "For one thing, I'd never be able to fall asleep with the air conditioner on so high."

"I can't tolerate much heat," Hunter acknowledged. "Guess I'm something of a penguin."

"I like feeling comfortable," said Chase. "But you've got the A/C up so high, you could store cadavers in here."

"Okay, then, how's this, Coach? If you'll stay, I'll lower the air conditioning. And then, if you're not comfortable sleeping next to me, you can just get up any time during the night and head home. No hard feelings. Fair enough?"

Chase leaned back against the tiles of the bathroom wall while Hunter finished drying him off. He then went against his better judgment as well as his usually well-guarded protective instincts as he forced a smile and acquiesced. "Fair enough, Kiddo," he told Hunter. "We'll try it your way."

*   *   *   *

They fell asleep abutting each other, tush to tush. Chase was surprised when he slept as soundly as a bulldog puppy. He awoke around three in the morning to pee. When he returned to the bed and snuggled up next to Hunter, the Kid, still deep in slumber, instinctively placed an affectionate arm around Chase's broad shoulders. He eased himself closer until they were again both cozily snoozing into the cool night, a pair of strapping, snoozing soup spoons.

Early the next morning, Chase was slowly stirred into semi-consciousness when he felt a warm, wet, highly pleasurable sensation coming from the vicinity of his loins. It took him a moment to focus before he remembered that he wasn't waking up at home alone in his own bed. When he opened his eyes, he glanced down to find Hunter straddled between his legs, giving him impassioned head.

"Mmmm," Chase moaned with satisfaction. "This hotel sure has good room service."

"Gotta practice on my hot man," Hunter gasped, between slurps. "Gotta get more proficient at this."

Chase reached down, placed a calming hand on each side of Hunter's face, gently pulled him up and with great affection, kissed him forcefully on the lips. As their lips locked, the stiffness of their members attested to their exhilaration.

When they weren't kissing deeply in their morning passion, they went down on each other. While Chase was more accustomed to being the recipient of any proffered fellatio, there was something so exhilarating about the intensity of this new alliance, something so remarkable about its heat that made him want to give back as good as he was getting. He found himself not only happy to accept the great oral sex Hunter was offering, but eager to reciprocate in the erotic gesture as well.

In an impulsive moment fomented by primal lust, Chase flipped Hunter onto his back and straddled the Kid's solid abs. Growling like a caveman, he leaned forward, took hold of each of Hunter's open hands and pinned them to the bed sheet.

Hunter loved being restrained by the force of Chase's arms. The powerful older man's total domination filled him with a nervous excitement. As he lay beneath his new boyfriend, defenseless and exposed, he privately hoped his sex partner might also take the time to frighten him silly. "I'm ready for anything you want, Coach," he allowed, submissively. "I want to be your number-one boy."

Chase was by then ready to explode. "In that case," he asked Hunter, "are you prepared for another first?"

"You know I am, Boss!"

"I bet you've never swallowed another man's cum."

"That is correct, Sir!" Hunter answered.

"Well, the time has come to change that."

Suddenly petrified, Hunter pointed to Chase's robust erection. "Not with *that*!" he protested, half in awe, half in fear. And not just your everyday, cold fear, but the very kind he favored most — a fright that came with no guarantee of safety. "You'll drown me!"

"Too late to back out now," Chase breathed heavily, his exhilaration escalating, set to erupt. "I'm about to shoot. Can you take it?"

"TAKE IT?!" Hunter repeated in astonishment as his eyes went wide with amazement. "Sure," he then uttered with resolution. "If that's what you want, Coach. Let me have it!"

"But you gotta take all of me!"

"I'll do my best, Sir!" Hunter declared, his fear fueling his trepidation, heightening his excitement. "Gimme your best shot!"

Chase grabbed the back of Hunter's neck and vigorously forced the whole of his huge cock all the way down Hunter's mouth, fucking his boy's face.

"That's it — you've got it now!" Chase shouted while holding onto the back of Hunter's head. Refusal was no longer an option, and as the gathering sperm surged en masse from deep within Chase's testicles, all three hundred fifty million swirling spermatozoa swam upstream into the urethral opening atop his rigid hose, erupting in a glorious, gushing geyser which sent an astonishing load of creamy gism deep into Hunter's throat. As Chase surrendered his incredible orgasm, he demanded sexily, "Take the whole thing, muscle boy. Take it now!"

Feeling overwhelmed and momentarily disoriented by the force of Coach's thick liquid assault, Hunter tensed in place as he gagged and nearly choked. Still, his mission was clear. He had to excite Chase and was committed to becoming not just his Star Varsity Wrestler, not just his best muscle buddy ever, but also his future lover and life partner.

Refusing to disappoint, Hunter gave in to the turmoil and allowed himself to absorb the whole of his man's huge payload. Straining to take it all in, he gulped down the entire gooey package, every last drop of his coach's prolific orgasm.

As Chase completed his rapturous release, Hunter realized this was the most exciting sexual moment of his thus far sheltered and repressed gay life and, without even touching himself, discharged an explosive ejaculation all his own.

At last, spent and depleted, Chase collapsed on top of his muscle boy and squeezed him tightly as they both caught their breath and slowly drifted back into a trouble-free slumber.

*   *   *   *

When they awoke again a short while later, Hunter called room service and ordered a huge protein-packed breakfast. Egg white omelets arrived atop an enormous cart, accompanied by turkey sausage links, sides of steamed spinach, bowls of fresh raspberries, honeydew melon, and a huge pot of steaming coffee.

They ate in their underpants, Hunter in his navy blue Calvin briefs, Coach in his Jocko shorts.

"I sure enjoyed bottoming for you last night," Hunter said while spooning raspberries into a bowl. "So for my money, and if it's okay with you, I'd love it if you stay in charge. When I'm with you, I prefer catching to pitching."

"Not a problem, Kiddo," Chase assured him. "Coach is only too happy to captain our ship of state."

"Oh, and one more thing," Hunter added, matter-of-factly, "I also think it might be even more fun if you got a lot rougher with me."

"Yeah, yeah," Chase humored him. "We all know what a tough guy you are."

After spending the rest of the morning and the whole of the afternoon in bed, alternately snoozing and necking, Hunter took Chase out that evening for an early birthday dinner at Patina in the Disney Hall.

"You must have one impressive expense account," Chase observed while scanning the menu. "These prices are pretty steep."

"It's only money, Coach," said Hunter. "Besides, I plan to spoil you silly. About time someone did. Especially since it's almost your forty-ninth birthday."

"Not for another nine days," Chase protested affably. "Don't rush me."

"What's it matter, anyway?" asked Hunter. "Fifty's the new forty. And when you look as good as you, Coach, believe me, if anything, your age is an asset."

Back in Hunter's hotel room, Chase and he kissed with abandon as they quickly undressed. From the combustible spontaneity Chase exhibited as he once again proceeded to make love to Hunter, you'd think they'd just met. The Coach couldn't understand why sex with Hunter just kept getting better. Not that he was complaining.

All the while they kissed, Hunter fantasized ahead to a time when he and Chase might be living together in harmony while sharing a mortgage, joint bank accounts, dual gym memberships, maybe even a second home in Hawaii. He didn't dare share his lofty visions with Chase since he sensed such finely conceived plans were the last thing an orthodox roamosexual needed to hear.

Spent after so much lovemaking, they remained wrapped cozily in each other's arms until they both drifted into a sound sleep. Chase was amazed when once again he had no trouble getting a good night's rest.

On Sunday, after polishing off another hearty room-service breakfast, the two new best buddies drove up Laurel Canyon, to Chase's comfortable compound in the hills. The towering trio of eighty-year-old avocado trees that canopied the units lent an air of bucolic enchantment to the property. When Hunter saw the inviting hot tub that sat in the middle of Chase's sun-dappled patio, he said he hoped he might one day get to dip more than just his big toe.

Hunter felt right at home in Chase's house. As he took notice of the many framed photos on prominent display of the Hyde dynasty of bulldogs, Athena to Zeus, along with all the medals they won at dog shows, he realized how bonded Chase must have been with his former canine companions. So he made a point of letting him know how special they seemed; that is, in a beautiful/ugly sort of way.

"My father and I raised them," Chase told Hunter. "One generation after the next until they finally all died out. They get sick a lot, which is why they're known as the heartbreak breed."

Hunter pointed to a picture of a brindle-and-white bulldog. "I like the mug on this guy," he told Chase.

"That was Mars," Chase told him.

"The God of war?" asked Hunter. "Wasn't he ferocious?"

"Only in his puppy dreams," said Chase. "Looks can be deceptive. In reality, bulldogs have the world's sweetest dispositions."

"Then why don't you get another one?" Hunter asked while admiring still another wrinkled canine's photo.

"Believe me, I plan to," Chase answered with assurance. "Soon as I'm flush again. For now, they're a little out of my league. These days, pedigree bully pups go for two, three thou a pop."

"Do they drool?" Hunter wanted to know.

"Only most of the time."

"Then what's the attraction?"

"Beats me," Chase answered with an honest shrug. "Maybe bulldogs are a lot like guys with muscles. You're either excited by them or you're not."

Hunter looked at another picture on the wall, a father-son shot of Chase as a twelve-year-old boy, standing alongside an athletic-looking, well-built man in his early thirties. In the photo, each of them held up a huge surfboard.

"That you and your dad?" Hunter wanted to know.

"That's us, surfing in Hawaii," Chase told him, as he led Hunter through the kitchen and into the garage.

"Quite the hunk!" Hunter observed, impressed with the handsome man's physicality.

"Yeah," Chase agreed. "He was a true jock. Ever since that trip, it's been my dream to go back there someday. Maybe visit one of the other islands."

Chase heaved his mountain bike, as well as the one he'd borrowed from his work-out partner, Stack, into the back of his Jeep; and he and Hunter drove out to Santa Monica. After parking near the beach, they donned their backpacks and pedaled over to the paved bike path that ran parallel with the ocean for twelve miles, all the way down to Manhattan Beach.

It was another sublimely autumnal Southern California day, warm, breezy, cloud-less. Chase and Hunter smeared their torsos in sunblock and then biked the entire distance shirtless. Their torsos gleamed against the scattered luminescence dancing off a shimmering Pacific Ocean. They stopped at a bench along the Manhattan Beach pier, unpacked their backpacks and then ate their picnic lunch of cold roast chicken along with the pair of salads they'd picked up earlier at Whole Foods. Hunter whipped out his Nikon digital and snapped some pics of his new favorite subject.

"Flex 'em for me, Big Daddy!" Hunter requested with a big grin.

Never too shy when invited to show off, Chase proudly flexed his formidable double biceps pose and smiled ebulliently for his muscle buddy. *Click!*

"Give me another playful smile, will ya, Coach?" *Click!* "Perfect. Now show me you can also be serious." *Click!* "Good job. How 'bout a nice profile shot, Handsome?" *Click!*

After biking all the way back up the ocean path, they piled the bikes into the rear of Chase's Jeep and drove back into town. Along the way, Chase surprised no one more than himself when he turned to Hunter and asked, "Since this is your last night here, Kiddo, why don't you check out of your hotel and spend the night over at my place? That way I can drive you to the airport first thing tomorrow morning."

Hunter was so flabbergasted and flattered by Chase's generosity, he was almost moved to tears. But he quickly put a lid on any display of sappy emotion, even as he acknowledged to himself how meaningful this significant gesture was. "You sure I won't be too much in your face, Big Daddy?" asked Hunter.

"This may sound nuts, especially coming from me," Chase said as he affection-ately rubbed the back of Hunter's head. "But right now, right here in my face is exactly where I want you."

*   *   *   *

That night, their last together for this initial meeting of the muscles, Hunter orchestrated an elaborate pornographic scenario the two of them could enact. The basic setup was that Chase would play a prison warden who catches inmate Hunter trying to escape, and needs to punish him in the prison dungeon with a mean and nasty rape.

After wrestling around the bed a bit, rolling over repeatedly while roughhousing together, Chase quickly tired of growling like one of his bulldogs, and felt detached by so much physical effort exerted for the sake of faux-violent hostility. He wanted to satisfy Hunter's odd request to get placed in peril and be scared silly. But at his core, all Chase really wanted to drum up with Hunter was grand and glorious lovemaking. Which is exactly what he did.

Slowly, Chase directed their every move as they kissed and fondled one another, segueing in and out from one erotic orifice to the next. For their passion-filled finale, Coach lifted the kid's butt off the mattress and, while Hunter pretended he was both restrained and completely powerless, Chase skillfully entered him with as much brutish energy as he could summon, intermingled with his own sincere affection.

Their heated sexual foray culminated with a bang, after which Chase collapsed alongside Hunter, and they both remained entangled, gripped by each other's solid embrace.

"So what's the deal with this rape fantasy?" Chase asked, once his heart rate returned to normal and he caught his breath.

"Started back when I was on the wrestling team in high school," Hunter lifted his head to explain. "I fantasized about being taken down to the showers and raped by the hottest guys on the squad."

"Ouch!" Chase squinted at the notion. "Sounds kind of painful."

"Pain-Shmain!" Hunter shrugged. "That's not what excited me. I was attracted to the high drama, the sheer intensity of the experience."

"I bet it'd be a lot less fun in real life than in your imagination."

"Maybe so," Hunter allowed.

"You're probably better off," Chase teased him. "I doubt you were tough enough to take on the entire squad."

"Oh, yeah?" Hunter protested as he broke away from Chase. "I'll show you who's tough! Let's arm wrestle!"

Hunter slammed his right upper arm atop the sheet, raised his forearm straight up, and assumed the classic arm wrestling stance.

"Right now?" Chase asked, quizzically. "Here on the bed?"

"Right here, right now!" Hunter declared. "That is, if you're man enough to take on an opponent as tough as me."

Amused, Chase accepted Hunter's challenge, flipped over onto his stomach and leveled his left arm on the bedding, directly before Hunter's. They clasped hands and tensed their bodies.

"Okay, now …" Hunter said quietly. "At the count of three. Ready?"

"Ready!"

"Okay: One, two, three!"

The contest commenced. Chase and Hunter strained with all their might against the other man's strong resistance. After a few moments of intense muscle contraction, Chase got the upper hand in their test of wills, and slowly forced Hunter's strong arm down until he slammed it against the mattress.

"You won!" Hunter decreed with a smile.

"Nothing to it," Chase smiled back. "Hell, I didn't even have to cheat."

"What most men don't know is how much more fun it is to lose," Hunter confessed. "To be able to submit to someone you respect. For me, the excitement of defeat has always been more appealing than the so-called thrill of victory."

"In that case," Chase responded. "I'll try boning up on my aggression."

"That would be heaven for me," Hunter told him, even though he knew they both had a long way to go before his ultimate sexual fantasy might be realized. Chase needed to get much rougher with him, needed to demonstrate more anger in their sexual expression if ever he was going to scare him silly.

Still, this one reservation about what was otherwise their extraordinary sex life was merely a minor quibble within the scheme of things. Hunter resolved not to turn and run, but to trust his gut instinct and remain patient, especially since he and Chase were off to so promising a start.

After so many years of just dreaming about it in his masturbatory fantasies, Hunter knew he had at last finally found the one man who, with some encouragement and guidance, could finally fulfill his darkest, most deeply repressed sexual longing: getting taken to the mat, held captive, and scared into a numbing fear while being forcibly raped.

No doubt about it. Hunter was in love.

*   *   *   *

Early Monday morning, after making passionate love one last time and then showering together, Chase drove Hunter the half hour it took them to speed through a fortunate lack of traffic, over to LAX.

They stood outside the security gate, forcefully hugging each other, their fantasy weekend suddenly at an all too abrupt end, each of them left with only this last, lingering farewell.

"Can't believe it's already over, Coach," Hunter whispered into Chase's ear. "Didn't I just get here? I had the best time ever."

"So did I," Chase whispered back, squeezing Hunter even tighter. "You may also find this odd, coming from me. I'm actually going to miss you."

Hunter smiled. "That means everything to me, Coach. I don't know what else to say. Just have to tell you again … you are my muscle fantasy dream man come true. So what are you doing the rest of the decade?"

"From the sound of things," Chase whispered back, "fielding compliments from you."

"I can think of worse ways to get through the future," Hunter said with a sly grin.

"Yeah, yeah," Chase sidestepped the compliment.

"You'll see," Hunter said seriously. "I'll never stop insisting you're still the man, my number one coach."

A dim, protective alarm sounded in Chase's head, warning him of an impending emotional overload. "Don't go getting all gooey on me again," he said firmly, and then suggested, "How 'bout we just take this transcontinental muscle romance one visit at a time?"

"Whatever you say, Coach. By now, you must know — you're the Boss!"

From somewhere high above, a garbled, semi-coherent message announced the final call for Hunter's New York flight. He and Chase hugged each other one last time, then with reluctance let go. Hunter lifted up the handle of his carry-on luggage, looked directly at Chase, and briefly studied his studly man up and down, capturing the emotional moment by snapping a mental picture he could summon at a later time.

Chase looked Hunter straight in the face and noticed a swell of tears piling up in the Kid's eyes. "You're not about to start crying, are you?" he asked, incredulously.

"I'm afraid so," Hunter confessed with a shrug. "Maybe I should have mentioned this sooner. I cry real easy."

"You mean like at hockey matches?" Chase asked, facetiously. "Inflated real estate prices?"

"I mean like when things get emotional," said Hunter. "As a kid, I was always sobbing. Don't tell me you never cry." Without waiting for a reply, Hunter swatted a tear from his cheek, solidly punched the side of Chase's arm, and then disappeared into the bowels of the security area.

Chase turned, strolled out of the terminal, and headed back toward the parking lot to retrieve his car. Along the way, he decided it was probably just as well Hunter lived three thousand miles away, seeing how he might easily turn into a genuine threat to Chase's calculated choice to remain a full-time, philandering roamosexual.

There was something oddly compelling about his surprisingly strong feelings toward Hunter that clearly set the Kid apart from his other muscle boys. To his credit, Hunter was making a highly favorable impression. Still, so far as Chase was concerned, fidelity represented little more than a Judeo-Christian notion instituted millennia ago by heterosexuals for the specific cultural purpose of keeping families together, disease from running rampant. Past that, monogamy for him was by then an antiquated conceit that made little sense in the day-to-day world of the modern active gay man, the roamosexual on the prowl.

Chase knew any affection he felt for Hunter could only get in the way of his long-held commitment toward never again getting entangled in another deep emotional involvement. He wanted nothing to come between him and the routine of his well-adjusted, carefully mapped-out existence. His life was a fine lawn in want of no further trimming, and last thing he needed in his perfectly manicured lifestyle was getting dragged into some impractical, long-term, long-distance romance.

In spite of his staunch commitment to never stop playing the dating game, to remaining forever single, he nevertheless decided to heed his own advice. It *would* be wisest for him to take their heated romance one cross-country call, one e-mail, one videocam session, one intercontinental visit at a time.

For the time being, Chase would not, as was more often his custom, readily disengage. At the same time he opted for a wait-and-see approach, he also reminded himself how imperative it was he not get emotionally entangled. Willingly, he would hang in there, even as he remained romantically resistant". He felt so on top of the situation, he decided to wait and let Hunter make the next move.

No doubt about it. He was in like.

*   *   *   *

High in the sky, flying almost without need of aerodynamics, Hunter couldn't get over the miracle in his life. His entire existence up until then had been little more than a walkup. He'd finally met the man who was the apotheosis of everything he ever fantasized about in his myriad mythical, muscular notions. However, he also knew full well that in no way was his irresistible object of desire any kind of easy takedown, any fast conquest. Chase, he knew, was more than resolutely set in his stubborn ways, clearly hesitant about diving in to anything deep or emotional.

Not a problem for Hunter. He spent the whole of his flight home from Los Angeles daydreaming about how he was going to get Chase to eventually move to New York, where they would live together in harmony as a loving couple. He envisioned the two of them enjoying a summer place together out on Long Island, maybe a cottage in the Hamptons — all the while building up a coterie of worthy friends, hosting vibrant dinner parties, going off on memorable vacations, raising bulldogs, becoming your basic A-gay power couple.

Long accustomed to enjoying success in his aggressive, business-related endeavors, Hunter slowly devised a clever strategy. Incorporating his business acumen, he mapped out a blueprint for an aggressive crusade, not unlike the marketing campaign he was setting up for his clients at the San Diego Bureau of Tourism. He never wanted anything so much in his life, because nothing had ever been this important.

Hunter committed himself to inconspicuously insinuating himself into as many aspects of Chase's life as he could manage until he won over his chosen partner. As he traversed the country, across all three time zones, he spent the entire flight ruminating over his course of action until his plan was set. His strategy seemed so foolproof, it made him smile.

He would simply make himself indispensable.

First thing Tuesday morning, after his early workout at the Executive Sports Club, as soon as Hunter got to his office, he made the few obligatory phone calls necessary to placate his most important clients. He checked in on his subordinates and made believe he was actually being attentive to the progress of their various campaigns. He then told Margo to hold his calls as he had little time for the vicissitudes of his burgeoning career, and had a far more pressing matter to pursue in the form of some very serious shopping to commemorate Chase's forty-ninth birthday the following week. Hunter thought of it as step one in his bid to win Chase's heart. Grinning with Cheshire satisfaction, he left his office building and marched quickly against a strong, autumnal wind, toward Fifth Avenue.

*   *   *   *

Birthdays never meant much to Chase. After turning forty-five, he figured it was all downhill from there and intended to treat his special day as nothing special. No fuss past a casual acknowledgment as to how speedily his lazy life was zipping by.

Late in the morning on the third of November, the day of his big four-nine, Chase donned his gym gear and downed his pre-workout protein drink. He was set to bicycle down to Gold's to meet up with Stack for their legs workout, when a delivery man arrived at his doorstep bearing a package that had traveled overnight, all the way from New York.

Chase signed for the delivery, closed the door, then opened the wrapping and lifted out two powder blue Tiffany boxes with white satin ribbons, each containing a three-by-five sterling silver picture frame housing a photo of the Coach snapped by Hunter.

- Chase in a serious pose, showing off his Guns of Navarone.

- Chase relaxing on a bench, his hands clasped jauntily behind his head, a broad smile across his face, the grandeur of the Santa Monica Mountains looming in the background.

Beneath the pair of framed photos lay another powder-blue gift box from Tiffany. Chase untied its white ribbon, lifted the cover and removed a five-inch long, two-pound, sterling silver paperweight in the shape of a dumbbell.

Chase didn't know what to make of so much consideration. Hunter wasn't the first kid to fixate on him. In the past, however, as soon as one of his muscle boys developed any kind of early infatuation and stepped over the line toward intimacy, that was always Chase's cue to cut them off, disengage, and move on. So why, he wondered, was he so accepting of how excessively Hunter was doting on him?

He was all set to call Hunter in New York, to thank him for the extravagance of his thoughtfulness, when the front bell rang once again.

Chase opened the door and was again greeted by the same delivery man that had just been there, only this time the fellow held out in his hands a nine week old, brindle and white male English bulldog puppy. The little male sported around its neck a huge, red-ribbon bow.

"Holy shit!" Coach muttered. "Who's that?"

"He's for you," the deliveryman answered, thrusting the little dog at Chase. "I was instructed to make two deliveries, one right after the other."

Chase cautiously took the puppy in his hands and held it up in the air. "Look at that crumpled face! I can't accept this beautiful baby!"

"Well, I'm sure not taking him back," said the deliveryman. "I was instructed only to pick up the package from Fed-Ex, the bulldog from the breeder in Tarzana, and deliver both of them here to you."

"Does he have a name?" Chase asked, as the little wrinkled pooch yawned in his face.

"I got no other information," the deliveryman smiled cavalierly, as he turned to head back to his truck. "Guess that's up to you."

Chase carried the little puppy into his kitchen, and by the time he finished placing a small bowl of water down on the tiled floor, he and the baby bully had bonded. While the bulldog furiously lapped up the water, splashing much of it on to the floor, Chase called Hunter at his office.

*　　　*　　　*　　　*

Margo knew she was wise to interrupt Hunter's meeting with an art director to let him know Chase was calling. Hunter quickly shooed both his secretary and his subordinate from his office and reached for the phone. "This is Hunter Rowe!" he announced, all business.

"Hunter — what in God's name have you done?" Chase asked from three thousand miles away.

"Well, if it isn't the birthday boy!"

"Have you gone bonkers?" Chase asked, gazing down at his new canine companion. "I know how much these babies cost, so you must know I can't accept anything this extravagant!"

"Don't be ridiculous," Hunter dismissed the notion. "We both agreed you need spoiling, and I decided I'm the best man to see that it gets done."

"So far, you're doing a fine job!" complimented Chase, before switching tones and asking defensively, "Hey — by any chance, are you trying to win over your old coach?"

"Nuts!" Hunter declared with unbridled enthusiasm. "I've been unmasked."

Chase ignored Hunter's verbally expressed ambition and contended, "You can't be pulling in so much income you can afford to throw it away on me."

"Hey, it's only money, Coach. And the Bulldog Association rated his breeders among the best in Southern California."

"I can see that," said Chase. "He's got perfect markings. Corkscrew tail, short, stubby legs ... hell, even rosebud ears. How can I thank you? What can I do to return these incredible favors?"

Hunter wrestled briefly with the question and knew he wanted to say, *Well, you could sell your house in Los Angeles and you and your puppy could move to New York and spend the rest of your life with me.* Instead, he allowed propriety and sensibility to prevail and instead told him, "I just wanted you to have the best damn birthday ever. Figured if I couldn't be there with you to celebrate in person, I'd splurge and send along enough reminders so you couldn't possibly forget me."

"Believe me," Chase told him honestly, "you're making an indelible impression."

"That's what I hoped to hear, Sir!" said Hunter, beaming ear to ear. "So would it be okay if I started calling my coach from work every morning, say around nine o'clock, your time, just to stir you awake with a short long distance hug, help you get your day off on the right foot?"

Oops! A tiny alarm went off in the back of Chase's head, signaling things might be getting a bit intrusive, even slightly uncomfortable. However, he was so knocked out by that magical bully pup, he relented and calmly told Hunter such an escalation in their daily contact sounded just fine with him.

"So, tell me ..." Hunter wanted to know. "Is the puppy cute?"

"Cute?" Chase laughed, even as the small bulldog strutted over and plopped down right in front of his new master. "He's probably the cutest little ugly bulldog I've ever seen."

"Great!" said Hunter. "Then you guys are getting along?"

Chase affectionately scratched the length of the playful baby bulldog's back and answered, "Let's put it this way: I've already fallen in love."

You and me both, Hunter thought to himself, and then asked aloud, "Any idea what you might want to name the little critter?"

"Who knows?" said Chase, thinking fast. "He's such a sturdy little tank and he's got such big shoulders. How 'bout we call him — Atlas?"

"Perfect!" said Hunter. "Atlas, it is. He can be the start of our bulldog dynasty. Now then, I have just one last question to ask the birthday boy ..."

"Shoot."

"Well, since it's your birthday," Hunter asked, timidly. "Would it be okay if I also just happen to casually mention ... you know — that I love you?"

Silence.

"Only if you promise not to make a habit of it," Chase finally allowed, light heartedly, but hoping to be taken at his word.

"Okay. I love you. There, I said it. Now go fuck yourself. And what about you, Chase?" Hunter asked, with feigned innocence. "Anything you care to tell me?"

Chase wanted to reciprocate, wanted to give in and tell Hunter just what he wanted to hear. But he also learned from experience how that volatile word had wrought him far more heartache than satisfaction. Rather than returning the sentiment, he instead managed to come up with a self-admittedly cheesy response, softly offering, at least with genuine sincerity and a smile, "Ditto, Kiddo."

"Hope you don't mind if I keep asking you this, at least every now and then, Coach, at least until you start asking the same question back to me."

"Be my guest," Chase answered flippantly, before settling into an actual vulnerable moment of candor, offering, "So far, I'd be lying if I didn't say you're doing an unexpectedly amazing job of keeping me captivated."

"Gosh, Coach," Hunter smiled. "I know it's *your* special day, but you just made *my* year!"

"Wish you were here to enjoy it with me," said Chase, surprising himself not so much because he said it, but also because he truly meant it.

"Don't you worry, Boss. I'm already busy at work, putting together plans for our next muscle reunion!"

"Thanks for everything," said Chase. "You've outdone yourself. Somehow, you've managed to become an important addition to my life."

Bingo! Hunter was elated because he knew he hit the bull's eye smack in the center of Chase's heart. "You and Atlas have a terrific birthday, Coach," Hunter concluded, smelling victory in the air as he hung up the phone and returned gleefully to work.

*   *   *   *

Chase and Hunter's daily phone conversations got chummier, more personal. Their e-mails grew progressively more affectionate, even intimate, as each of them in time shared parts of their innermost selves. Nightly, they visited one another, talking through computer speakers while viewing their bodies via web cams. Their long distance teleconferences inevitably ended up with them both naked and showing off for each other. And even though their virtual sex, their almost daily mutual masturbations over their cams, weren't nearly as satisfying as holding each other in the flesh, it sure crossed the finish line a close second.

Why, Chase wondered, had he not by then erected his usual walls of defense? Before Hunter came along, the first time any of Coach Chase's muscle boys used the word *love* in a complete sentence, they were quickly dropped from the squad. This time, however, Chase felt somehow relaxed about it all and took the bulk of Hunter's considerable attention in stride. He even came to accept his boy's seemingly limitless affection as the real thing. He could not yet bring himself to tell Hunter he loved him in return, but in a spirit of compromise, he began signing his e-mails: *Ditto from me and Atlas.*

Chase and the baby bulldog were made for each other. Atlas proved to be highly intelligent and caught on quickly to the demands made of civilized canine citizens. The bully pup was housebroken in less than a week. Chase trained his puppy to sit, to high-five with his left front paw, and to retrieve sticks and balls. Every time he looked at Atlas, he couldn't help but be reminded just how thankful he was to Hunter for bringing the little fireplug into his life, and how very happy, how uncharacteristically unthreatened he felt about the formidable deepening of their ongoing long-distance romance.

For Hunter, it was all going too well, and he kept expecting Chase to drop him, kept anticipating his boyfriend would call one evening to flat out tell him their journey had gone as far as it would and so he was calling it quits.

But such was not the case. That call never came. In fact, quite the opposite. As Hunter set up his next trip west in early January, Chase went out on a limb and invited him to forgo staying in a hotel and instead be his and Atlas' houseguest.

By increments, Hunter inched his way forward, slowly softening the sturdy layers surrounding Chase's once impenetrable armor.

*   *   *   *

It wasn't until several weeks later, while Chase was driving to the airport to pick up Hunter for his new boyfriend's second visit to Los Angeles, that he was unaccountably flooded by an inundating wave of anxiety and trepidation.

Hey ... Chase heard himself alert the back of his mind. *What if things don't click so well between us this time? What if spending a whole week together, day in, day out, around the whole fucking clock becomes too much, even unbearable? How'll I get through it? How'll I get rid of him? What if the honeymoon ends before it starts and we start bickering like so many other couples?*

What if ...?

Stop! Coach slammed the brakes on his escalating self-doubts and told himself to cease his negative ruminations, because he was still taking this long-distance romance slowly, cautiously, just one major muscle group at a time. *Calm down,* he warned himself. Nothing was set in stone — not yet, anyway. There was still plenty of wiggle room to back off the moment things turned the slightest bit sour. He reminded himself of his rule to never expose his vulnerability. Not to anyone. Surely, that was his ticket to remaining free of pain and in control.

Filled with lowered expectations and heightened anticipation, Chase drove into LAX and, after parking, paced back and forth inside the arrivals area. Overhead video monitors displayed gloomy news. Owing to a back-up in overcrowded skies, Hunter's delayed American Airlines Flight #211 would not be pulling into the gate for another thirty minutes.

*   *   *   *

Aloft at forty thousand feet, Hunter spent the whole flight from New York battling the worrisome butterflies of anxiety assaulting his insides. As his plane approached LAX, he grew fidgety, as if he were doing an ad for a hemorrhoid cream. When the pilot announced they'd be encircling the airport for who knew how long, waiting for clearance to land, Hunter wondered if the sweet torture would ever end. Checking out the distance between his seat and the front exit door, he vowed that come what may, he'd be the first passenger to exit the aircraft.

When at last the jumbo jet finally touched down thirty-seven minutes later, and the huge metal door near the front of the aircraft swung open, Hunter yanked his roller suitcase from the overhead bin and barreled from the plane. He spotted Chase standing there, waiting for him, and immediately felt a jolt of shivering excitement galloping down his spine. Hunter gleamed with pride because his new boyfriend looked so darn coach-like and appealing, so fucking super-daddy beautiful. Hunter's pulse quickened, his heart pumped rapidly and, between his legs, inside his Calvin briefs, his cock announced its own late arrival.

Finally face-to-face again after so many weeks, at first they both just stood still, sizing one another up and down, saying nothing, grinning wildly. Finally, Chase opened his arms wide for a big muscle hug.

Hunter released his suitcase handle, folded himself into his coach's emphatic embrace, and whispered into Chase's ear, "Great to be back in your champion arms, Boss."

"Great to have you here," Chase whispered back, hugging his boy still tighter.

When Chase took a step back, he spotted a layer of tears welling up in Hunter's eyes.

"Whoa!" Chase groaned, as he reached forward and captured on the tip of his finger a small tear about to tumble down Hunter's cheek. "Not this again?!"

"Can't help it," Hunter sniffled. "Just so damn happy to see you."

"Get a grip!" Chase demanded as he made a fist and solidly clipped Hunter beneath his chin. "Don't you know real men don't cry? Shoot back down here to reality, Boy, and show your coach some backbone!"

Hunter took a step back, snapped to attention like a good soldier, and smiled broadly with a stiff upper lip, a sharp salute and a quiet, grateful response, as gruffly, he barked, "Sir, yes Sir!"

After smooching like rabid teenagers from the moment they settled into Chase's car, parked at the far end of the parking structure, Chase finally eased himself away from Hunter long enough to drive out of the airport, toward the 405, headed for Laurel Canyon.

On their way home, as Chase's earlier pangs of anxiety melted, he realized his heightened uneasiness had been for naught. He felt calm, at ease. He and Hunter were connecting as solidly as their first time. With all systems good to go, Chase floored the gas pedal and raced ahead, twenty miles over the limit.

*   *   *   *

They barely stepped inside the front door when a frisky Atlas bounded from the bedroom, practically tripping over his bulky puppyhood in his fervent zeal to greet his master and his houseguest.

After Chase and the puppy had one of their raucous hellos, culminating in an obligatory puppy pin, Atlas then wiggled over to welcome Hunter to Hyde Park.

Hunter took to the three-month-old pup at once and knelt down to tickle the stout little fellow's teeny corkscrew tail. At the same time, Chase jumped forward and forcefully threw Hunter smack down onto the floor. He grabbed each of the his open hands, stretched his boy's arms out wide and nailed Hunter's knuckles flush up against the carpeting. Without another word, he planted his thick lips smack atop Hunter's open mouth.

Moments later, they were both in the bedroom, out of their clothes, and once again all over each other, rolling around naked on Chase's king-sized bed. Kissing ardently, they furiously rubbed hands across taut bodies, all over their flexed muscles.

Coach knew what Hunter liked, and so he jabbed away erotically at his boy's resilient six-pack. Hunter pretended the gut punching hurt more than it did, which heightened his excitement, and he responded by moaning dreamily.

As Chase again took Hunter down, the two of them in turn giddily re-enacted their well assigned roles as Coach and Star Varsity Wrestler, Father and Son, Marine Sergeant and Grunt Recruit, Man and Boy, Lover and Lover. Hunter silently favored their father/son role-playing. He felt a thrilling jolt of affection anytime Chase referred to him as Kiddo or the Kid or called him Boy.

Hours passed as Chase paved their erotic path, orchestrating every sensuous movement of their glorious muscle sex, their passionate lovemaking. Manipulating himself, Hunter shot three prodigious loads, while Chase popped twice, shooting his explosive payload on both occasions all the way down the length of his willing boy's open throat.

Finally exhausted, they lay in bed next to one another on their backs. Chase's arm rested securely around Hunter, whose head nestled cozily against Chase's shoulder.

"When we're living together in Hawaii," Hunter interrupted their reverie to daydream aloud, "we can do this *every* day."

Chase kept his eyes closed as he quietly played along with Hunter's ridiculous wishful thinking. "Why not twice a day?" he murmured sleepily and again drifted off.

*   *   *   *

The way their week together flew by, you might have thought they'd been cast under some benign sorcerer's spell. Days and hours slipped speedily away without their noticing. Each morning, as the bright hues of an emergent predawn slowly illuminated their bedroom, Hunter awoke leisurely and was content to lie still and simply take in the gratifying sight of the handsome, strapping fellow lying next to him in all his manly, muscular nakedness. From the vantage point of his infatuation, even Chase's intermittent snoring seemed quirkily sexy.

In time, Hunter might reach over to gently rub an affectionate hand across the length of his boyfriend's torso, slowly stirring his partner awake. After running one hand across Chase's butt, he positioned the other beneath his buddy's balls and then soothingly massaged both areas until he was greeted by the thickening emergence of Chase's fat cock. Talk about an idyllic awakening.

Every morning, they satisfied their mutual hunger with an audibly raucous eruption, after which Chase went into the kitchen to brew some Kona coffee and feed Atlas. At the same time, Hunter quenched his penchant for obsessive neatness by dutifully and fastidiously making Chase's king-size bed, perfectly tucked-in hospital corners and all.

After breakfast, Coach lounged on the couch reading the *Los Angeles Times*. Atlas remained curled up against him, blissfully snoozing and snoring. Hunter served his cleanliness muse as he turned into a whirlwind, fortifying his indispensability by buzzing about the house, dusting, mopping, sweeping, and polishing. He rendered spotless everything in sight, including the kitchen sink.

Once Hyde Park was literally gleaming, Hunter balanced a broomstick on his shoulder like a rifle and, after looking around at his compulsive handiwork, announced to the pristine room with unabashed pride, "I came! I saw! I cleansed!"

Chase raised a thumbs-up approval. "Good job. You proved anal retention has its rewards. So now that the house is in tiptop shape, can *we* go workout?"

*   *   *   *

Training together at Gold's was, for Hunter, a once distant muscle fantasy finally come to life. Ever since puberty, he daydreamed about pumping iron in tandem with a hunky bodybuilder. He always dreamt it would be an older, take-charge kind of man, one he loved deeply.

With Chase as knowing coach and Hunter his willing apprentice, they worked out well together. "Come on, Hunter," Chase coaxed encouragingly as Hunter fought to push up the bar on the bench press. "Big and strong, Kiddo. Come on. Just a bit more. I'm right here when you need me ... but it's all you!"

As a real-life coach, Chase was as accomplished as the character created for his alter ego. Knowledgeable and articulate about weight training, his choreographed workouts were intense and inventive. As they exercised their powerful bodies, he taught Hunter how they could best spot one another, sometimes rather sexily, teasingly, provocatively, but whether in front or behind, always following good form. Chase showed Hunter how to train like a pro as they performed drop sets, forced reps, and both static and negative contractions.

"Most importantly," Chase told his willing pupil, "whenever you're finishing a set and have nothing left to give, when you finally get down to muscle failure — that's when you gotta push out one, two, maybe three more reps. If not for yourself, then do it for me."

Hunter was impressed the way his coach varied their exercises and kept their training sessions fresh and stimulating. Workout to workout, whether pumping their pecs, bombing their biceps or trashing their triceps, with every exercise, their sturdy muscles constricted beneath the stress of heavy weights. As blood flowed swiftly throughout their systems, the vascularity in their arms and legs popped out ever more prominently. To their mutual exhilaration, the sexual tension between them escalated unabated. And every time they pumped iron together, they each got so fired up they felt compelled, just as soon as they returned home, right after downing their obligatory recovery drinks, to jump on each other's bones and make audacious and jubilant love all over again.

*   *   *   *

The only minor intrusion that interrupted their time together was a doctor's appointment Chase couldn't switch: a visit his primary physician set up weeks earlier for a urologist to re-examine what might be a possible hernia developing around his groin.

Chase's physician completed his examination and informed him his hernia had progressed to the point that it required surgery. A rudimentary, arthroscopic procedure, he was assured, but surgery, nonetheless. "And let's do this soon," his doctor cautioned. "Before it gets out of hand."

Hunter spent the afternoon tidying up Hyde Park before he tidied up Atlas, bathing, brushing, and then dabbing the bulldog's brindle and white pelt in several splashes of after-shave.

Chase walked through the front door several hours later, disheartened by his impending hernia surgery. His spirits were immediately lifted when Atlas lumbered over for a back scratch, and offered his signature high-five greeting. Chase greeted Hunter with a solid kiss and then told him the bad news about the hernia operation he needed from the strain of pumping so many heavy weights for so many years.

He had no problem with the uncomplicated procedure. But his doctor also told the Coach that after a short stay in the hospital, he'd have to rest, and that meant missing two, maybe three weeks of working out.

"Oh, that's not so long," Hunter tried to lift Chase's spirits. "Besides, your body can probably use the muscle rest. What's it matter, anyway? I'd still love you if you were another twenty years older and fifty pounds heavier."

Caught off guard in a rare moment of defenselessness, Chase allowed, "I sure hope you mean that."

"Of course I mean it, Coach. With all my heart. Sure, my muscle man's body is the greatest. Anyone who's ever seen you knows that. But what good is it if *you're* not in there to fill it out? It's *you* I want, Chase. Your body's just the beautiful gift-wrap. I love what's inside, and you can take that to the bank."

*   *   *   *

Chase wanted his workout partner, Stack, and their mutual friend, Craig, whom they hadn't seen in far too long, to meet his new boyfriend. So he invited them as well as Craig's lover, Adam, to a dinner party at Hyde Park Friday night.

Several days before Hunter's arrival, when Chase told Stack he and Hunter would be working out together while the Kid was in town, Stack took umbrage and predicted Hunter would forge a wedge between them. Chase assured Stack he'd never let that happen, and hoped all of them having dinner together might ease any such concerns.

As co-hosts for the evening, Chase and Hunter compiled a grocery list and then shopped together for the meal.

This is so much like being an old, married couple, Hunter thought contentedly as he and Chase wheeled their shopping cart down the aisles of Whole Foods, picking up essentials.

This is so frighteningly suburban and provincial, thought Chase, wondering in sharp contrast why the usually spacious aisles of the store seemed so much more narrow than usual.

Back at Hyde Park, Chase labored in the kitchen, organizing and preparing his northern Italian menu of mozzarella, basil and tomato *insalata caprese*, grilled Tuscan chicken and marinated, grilled vegetables.

Hunter stepped resolutely in for an encore of his anal retentive prowess and buzzed about, sprucing up Chase's home, even though it was already so spotless, you could perform a quadruple bypass on the kitchen countertop. He vacuumed the carpets, mopped the bathroom floors, changed the bed sheets, hosed down the patio, and set a dinner table for five.

It was fortuitous that Hunter was able to get so absorbed in his cleaning mania, since he was a nervous wreck the whole day, worried Chase's three friends might not approve of their dear buddy's choice of a new, younger muscle mate.

Stack was the first to arrive, hungry, thirsty, eager to meet Hunter and to brag about his erotic exploits with the twenty year old he met not twenty minutes earlier, down at the gas station.

Craig and Adam walked in a few minutes later, bearing gifts of wine and muscle hugs.

Way back when, long before Chase trained with his super-sized workout partner, Stack used to pump iron with Craig, a just-under five-foot-three — and that was on his tippy-toes — two-hundred-pound bodybuilder. The forty-one-year-old mini-mountain of a man had competed back in the gay games in Chicago where, proudly, he placed second in their Masters category. By any tape measurement, Craig was short. But by no means was he either little or small, as he made up in width what he lacked in height. His compressed muscular development, no longer capable of further vertical thrust, long ago overcompensated by expanding horizontally. The explosion of his physique, the mass-accumulated success story that made him look like he'd been put through a trash compacter, came about thanks to a series of steroidal cycles supplied to him by his then workout partner, Stack.

Craig was one bodybuilder who actually took it as a compliment when told he looked like a cross between a bowling ball and an Amana freezer. After years of a consummate devotion to pumping iron, the short, thick man built up voluminous quads that ballooned out from within his tight jeans, and his bulbous arms stretched tight the sleeves of his T-shirt.

Years earlier, not long after Chase started working out regularly at Gold's, Stack and Craig and he all became fast friends. A trio of best buds, they grew so tight as a cohesive, well-connected team, they eventually forged their own muscle fraternity, affectionately referring to themselves as the Three Dumbbells.

For a time, the Three Dumbbells were inseparable, the best of muscle buddies. They went to movies together, discovered exotic third-world restaurants together, and cooked for and entertained one another in their homes. They caroused through West Hollywood's bar scene on a regular basis, scoring like true champion roamosexuals. They each enjoyed one another's company, and cruising was always more fun with two other buddies. Carefree, they ran around town, each of them ready for his next sexual conquest. That is, until Craig met Adam.

Adam taught mathematics and served as the ice hockey coach to teenage kids whose parents had enough affluence to send their pampered offspring to Westlake Village, the pricey, ivy-covered prep school just over the hill, off Coldwater Canyon.

Attracted only to musclemen shorter than himself, Adam, who in his stocking feet stood all of five-foot-four, was the first to acknowledge how limited his options were. So when he first met Craig, he became immediately infatuated, not only because Craig was smart, well-muscled, ruggedly handsome and athletic, but also because he was an inch shorter. Theirs was a magical love match made in muscle Munchkinland.

Craig and Adam enjoyed a whirlwind courtship and, after only two months of spending all their free time together, working out and making love around the clock, they moved in together.

Neither of them saw it coming, but happiness turned out to be a tall order for the short musclemen. Adam soon turned into a possessive lover, one who felt the need to keep Craig all to himself. He insisted Craig stop working out with Stack, so that the two of them, he and Craig, could become workout partners. And seeing how he taught logarithms during the day, that meant they could only pump iron together at night.

So Craig and Stack stopped training together, while Craig teamed up with his new boyfriend, Adam, with whom he trained in the evening. Chase stepped into Craig's vacancy, and he and Stack started working out together.

After several years of living together in what might best be described as disharmony, Craig and Adam morphed into one of those couples who thought nothing of constantly confronting one another openly and without restraint. They conducted their petty marital squabbles with such frequency in front of their friends, as well as whomever else might be within earshot, that they became known, at least behind their backs, as the battling Bickersons.

As Craig and Adam grew codependent in the creation of their own turbulent inner sanctum, they slowly drifted apart from Chase and Stack, and it wasn't long before Chase, Stack, and Craig were no longer a trio.

Chase was delighted to see Craig. It felt great having the Three Dumbbells together again.

During dinner, Hunter practically worked his nuts off as he shifted his accelerated social skills into overdrive so he might win over each of the guests. He was intentionally so damn charming as to be positively disarming. Conversation during the reunion dinner was lively, centered mostly on typical gay LA topics: movies, muscles, and men.

Throughout the meal, Atlas waited patiently under the table, noisily vacuuming up any morsel of fallen food.

To Hunter's great relief, at least two of Chase's three friends seemed to genuinely take to him. Stack, still cold as ice, was another matter. Hunter had yet to crack the Goliath's façade of aloof disdain. Stack all but dismissed Hunter's few overtures of comradeship.

The mere fact that they were all dining together again after such a long spell apart prompted Stack to wax nostalgic. He recalled how strongly the Three Dumbbells bonded three years earlier when they last spent the weekend together at the bacchanal in the desert that was the annual White Party in Palm Springs. "Was that not the time of our lives back then?" Stack asked.

"Sure," Chase agreed. "Once you got past the brain damage we inflicted upon ourselves from all the drugs we consumed."

"Those were the days," Craig chimed in, reverently. "A weekend of unlimited sex with a series of beautiful strangers, all the while bonding on a major scale with your real life buds."

"Talk about your roamosexual paradise," sighed Chase.

"I propose a toast!" Stack raised his glass of red wine high in the air. "I say we all pledge right now to go out there again this April. All of us — together."

"Great idea!" Craig agreed. "Let's all do it. Me and Adam and Stack — another great reunion. And you, too, Hunter. You'll come with Chase."

"Yeah!" Stack agreed. "It'll be just like old times. Are we all in?"

Hunter was delighted to be invited into their exclusive club, and so when the former Three Dumbbells and Adam clicked their wine glasses, sealing their White Party pact, he joined in, hoping to be accepted as one of the boys.

After a dessert of sliced honeydew melon with fresh raspberries, Hunter left the table and walked out onto the patio for a hit of fresh air. Along with a few deep breaths of anxiety relief, he took in the view overlooking a twinkling West Hollywood off in the distance. He was soon joined by Stack, who also looked down upon the city as he confided, "Tell you the truth, Hunter, I couldn't be more astonished by all that's going on between you and Chase."

"How do you mean?" Hunter was eager to know.

"Well," Stack explained, "maybe it's because long ago, Chase and I established our very own Muscle Daddy Academy. The idea was to go through one cadet after another. I never thought Chase would ever actually take such a long break from playing our game of musical mattresses. It feels just like when Craig met Adam, him sticking this long with one guy."

"It's only been a few months and two in-person meetings," said Hunter, feeling oddly on his guard.

"Me and Chase, we've been best buds for a long time," said Stack. "I think I know him pretty well, so believe me when I say he's a long way from settling down."

"And believe me when I say I already know that," Hunter responded pointedly.

"Be honest," Stack asked, just as pointedly. "Don't you think he's too old for you?"

"Not when you look as good as Chase," Hunter was candid. "And this may be hard for you to appreciate, Stack, but some of us actually prefer older men."

Stack shook his head in wonderment. "Boy, you must have something truly special. Care to share your secret?"

"It's no secret," Hunter offered calmly with a playful wink, as he turned to walk back into the house. "As it happens, I brew a great cup of Hawaiian coffee."

*   *   *   *

The following morning, Hunter got up early to tackle dirty dishes still piled high in the kitchen sink from their dinner party the night before. After brewing a pot of coffee, he carried a steamy cup into the bedroom where he deftly awakened Chase with a round of soft kisses. Slowly, Hunter then maneuvered himself down between Chase's legs so he could play with the pretty piccolo that was his muscle buddy's thick cock.

They both knew this was the last day of Hunter's visit, and it infused them with a collective sense of melancholy. Even their workout together at the gym later that morning found them each exerting less energy than during their previous training sessions. It was as if they were instinctively weaning off one another by being less intense and not as focused on their workout as before.

After returning home from Gold's, they stripped out of their workout gear. Naked, they rubbed roaming hands over one another while Chase concocted their protein recovery drinks. They never made it to the shower, because by the time Hunter bounced his hairy pecs and Chase flashed his Guns of Navarone, they were once again all over each other, making love.

Afterward, while showering together, they discovered how far apart were their respective reactions to that visit's final sexual encounter. Chase said he thought their lovemaking had never seemed more meaningful, while Hunter grumbled because Chase had been far too gentle with him, not nearly threatening or menacing enough. "I was hoping to get scared stiff!" he half-joked, while soaping up Chase's back. "I never once felt imminent danger, not so much as a figment of harrowing jeopardy."

"Hey, Kiddo," Chase shrugged. "If it's danger you want, maybe you should join the Foreign Legion."

"I don't speak French."

"Then just rob a bank and get caught, okay? That way you can go to jail and finally have some real fun in the shower."

"Stop!" Hunter protested as he raised soapy hands of surrender. "You're getting me hard again!"

*   *   *   *

After being together for an entire week and never once running out of conversation, it was odd how subdued they both were as Chase drove Hunter out to LAX later that afternoon. Though low key, Hunter felt perfectly at ease with their calm composure as he sat next to Chase, his hand affectionately massaging the muscles of his Coach's strong quads.

"Haven't we been through this scene before?" Hunter asked, as they headed toward the security area after Hunter checked in at the ticket counter.

"You mean another airport farewell?" asked Chase.

"Sadly so," Hunter frowned like a little kid.

"I'd be lying if I didn't tell you I'm actually sorry to see you leave," Chase told him.

Hunter looked down at the floor and quietly suggested, "We've got to do something about melting these three thousand miles between us, Coach."

"What do you think we should do — blow up the Rockies?"

"Well, for our next muscle reunion, why don't you come to New York, stay with me? Fly in for a week or two around my birthday in the middle of February. I've got more than enough mileage to get you there and back."

"Sounds tempting," said Chase.

"I promise to make it real special, Coach. Come visit me and I'll spoil you like never before. And I want you to let me fly you to New York, First Class. Make sure you're good and rested by the time you get to me. Can't think of anything I'd rather do."

"You drive a hard bargain," Chase said with a smile. He was surprised when he next sensed a swelling of sadness rising up inside him. So he hit the brakes on this uninvited invasion of genuine emotion. "Know what I think might be best?" he asked as he handed Hunter his carry-on bag. "Why don't you just go the rest of the way yourself? I'm much better at hellos than good-byes."

"Don't tell me Mr. Ice Cube is starting to defrost!" Hunter made believe the idea horrified him.

"Of course not," Chase lied. "But I never liked airports. And these days, in this post Nine-Eleven world, they're downright totalitarian. Besides, I parked in that twenty-minute max zone. You saw how long it took us just to get your luggage checked. I better not risk getting a ticket. They're really strict around here."

"I understand," Hunter said with a sad smile. "It's just as well. I should get away from you before I start blubbering again. I was the one who suggested it'd be fine if you just dropped me off by kicking me to the curb."

"But I can't let you leave without a farewell muscle hug." Chase said as he took Hunter squarely in his strong arms. Hunter hugged Chase in return with all his might and then whispered into his ear, "Just give me one good chance to love you, Coach. That's all I ask. I've waited my whole life for you, for this, and I want to make it work as best I can … to give it all I've got … for both of us."

Chase returned Hunter's hug as tightly as he could, kissed his boyfriend's cheek, and whispered back, "So far you're doing a damn good job. Have a safe flight home."

"Will do, Coach," Hunter smiled and took a step back.

For several moments, they just stared at each other, saying nothing.

A few unbidden tears, not unforeseen, but nonetheless most unwelcome, abruptly welled up in Hunter's eyes.

"Uh-oh. You're going to start bawling on me again, aren't you?"

"If only I knew how to turn off the faucet," said Hunter as he swiped at a tear about to roll down his cheek.

"Didn't your Daddy teach you if you don't stop crying, you'll grow up to become a sissy?"

"My father never said anything quite that supportive, Coach," Hunter answered with a sad smile. He then tossed his carry-on bag over his shoulder, lifted the handle on his roller suitcase, leaned in toward Chase, and finally got up the guts to ask softly, from the bottom of his heart, "Hey, Boss — Have I told you lately that I love you?"

Chase couldn't help but smile. Reaching forward, he softly slapped the side of Hunter's face and wiped a tear tumbling down the side of the Kid's left cheek. Then he quietly whispered back, "Ditto, Kiddo!"

After taking a deep breath, Hunter snapped to attention, issued his bold soldier's salute, wiped away another nerdy tear running sloppily down his cheek, and then, smiling boldly, spun around and stepped onto the horizontal people-mover leading to the security area and the departure gate beyond.

Turning back, Hunter watched as Chase disappeared from view. He wiped away another tear and pocketed his handkerchief. Just what was it about him, he wondered, that always set him off so easily? Was he, beneath his solid frame and within his convincingly masculine projection, at heart still that skinny, little sissy boy from back when he was growing up?

As the people-mover streamed forward, Hunter thought back to long ago. Maybe in truth he'd always been a wimp. Maybe his deep need to be so successful in his work, his drive to rise to the top of his field, to be prosperous and strong and loved by a man as worthwhile as Chase, germinated from a seed of insecurity planted long ago.

As Hunter floated down the extended passageway, his finger flicked from his cheek a final droplet of hyper-sensitivity and he began thinking back. In a heartbeat, long-repressed images from his childhood flashed before his vacant eyes, and he painfully recalled several disturbing incidents as though they were yesterday.

$$*\qquad*\qquad*\qquad*$$

LIONEL ROWE — THE LION'S ROAR

Hunter's father, Lionel Rowe, was a lean, ruff-and-tumble, no-nonsense sportsman who overcompensated for his slight stature, and the congenital heart murmur with which he was born, by offering the world a defiant swagger that telegraphed his unflinching bravado. A bold soul, he didn't just go out of his way to seek adventure; he actually courted it as a way of life.

Back in the sixties, while growing up in Corpus Christi, Texas, young Lionel tagged along with his father on manly treks into the wilderness. And it was out there in God's country where young Lionel quickly learned life's most essential disciplines: how to shoot deer in sun-dappled dells; how to fly fish in swollen streams; how to lie in wait for hours in bone-chilling, murky marshes and then shoot down a flock of wild geese traversing a dawning sky in graceful V formation. How, in short, to grow up and become a *real* man.

Young Lionel strove to emulate the paternal role model that was his macho mentor. Over the years, he never once disappointed his dad as he literally followed in his father's footsteps until he, too, had evolved into a big game hunter, big sports fisherman, and that most vibrant and telling of manly attributes: big-time boozer.

A self-proclaimed king of the jungle, the Lion owned and operated Safety First, a private security agency that supplied such protective services as security guards at banks, bouncers who checked IDs at night clubs, and bodyguards trained to take a bullet if necessary for the captains of industry whom they were hired to protect.

Hunter's mother, Roberta, was a formerly shapely blonde and one-time party gal whose compulsive eating saw her good looks melt away into a blowsy appearance not long after she and the Lion were married.

Before exchanging vows, and well before Hunter was born, Lionel and Roberta's courtship was an uninhibited submergence into primitive sexuality. But things changed quickly not long after their shared pronouncements of everlasting commitment. Overnight, *I Do* became *I Don't* as each grew both complacent and contemptuous of each other.

Throughout his early years, Hunter grew up hopelessly short, painfully thin. His father was rarely around because he spent most of his time at the office. As violent crime in the Corpus Christi area soared, Safety First flourished. As demand for salaried protection eventually outpaced supply, Lionel was soon able to add another half dozen security officers to the payroll.

On the propitious occasion of Hunter's fifth birthday, his father decided the time had come for them to get better acquainted. He proudly proclaimed to Roberta that his son was ready to acquire his sea legs. True to his word, Lionel took his little boy down to the marina early the following morning, before dawn, where they boarded a huge fishing boat filled with a dozen other fishermen heading deep into the Gulf of Mexico.

It was an overcast, blustery day on the high seas, and after only an hour into their nautical journey, the tumultuous rocking of the enormous vessel churned young Hunter's stomach into so many knots, the little guy was rendered seasick. When everything around him started spinning in circles, his eyes rolled to the back of his head, and as the boat churned against a turbulent sea, he puked up his breakfast all over the railing of the poop deck.

Mortified, Lionel rushed down to the rest room, retrieved some paper towels, and quickly wiped up the last of Hunter's breakfast. Then, with most of the other fishermen watching, he smacked Hunter back and forth across the back of his head, scolding in rage, "Stupid boy! Couldn't wait for a bathroom? Couldn't hold it in until we got off the boat?"

Little Hunter felt too nauseated to answer, too embarrassed to look up and face his father. Instead, he sobbed tears of discomfort and, at the same time, forcefully heaved the last helping of that morning's cheese omelet and home fries over the boat's railing. Such was Lionel's initial effort at father-son bonding.

*   *   *   *

In the autumn of Hunter's seventh year, Lionel was still unwavering in his mission to make a man out of his frail, wimpy little boy. After practically dragging his recalcitrant son out of bed on another grey and chilly, pre-dawn Sunday, he suited the little guy up in rain pants, poncho, and wading boots. He exercised great caution as he handed over the BB gun he'd given Hunter the previous Christmas. Father and son then headed out to the muddy marshes in pursuit of some man-to-man duck hunting.

Hunter detested every single freezing moment of their misadventure and found the entire outing too cold, too wet, too dull, too muddy, and certainly too early in the morning. The seven-year-old boy hated all their downtime spent wading through shoulder-high weeds or crouching in silence, waiting for some dumb flock of ducks to take flight.

Father and son waited and waded and waded and waited, and Hunter did his best to stop shivering while remaining perfectly still. As the skies transposed from slate gray into an ever-darkening charcoal, a light, chilling drizzle descended, further dampening Hunter's already washed-out spirits. If winning his father's approval wasn't so imperative, he would have started whining long ago. Instead, he raised the hood on his poncho and gritted his teeth, thinking that, at least things couldn't get much worse.

But he was wrong. Things did get much worse. And fast. When a huge water spider unexpectedly crawled slowly up the side of his left leg, Hunter screeched a high-pitched alarm and leapt up in fright. He splashed the water wildly and screamed, pleading for his father to get the startling bug off him.

Lionel rushed over to help, and their frenetic sloshing about in the muddied waters flushed a flutter of birds from their shelter. A dozen distraught creatures flapped their wings in wild animation and fled in fright, squawking across the bleak sky as they got the flock out of there.

Enraged, Lionel knew they'd just blown their one best shot. "Shit! Shit! Shit!" he exploded, and again smacked the sides of Hunter's head back and forth with his open hand — hard. "Idiot boy!" the Lion roared. "Jumping around and carrying on like some pathetic little pansy! I can't fucking believe it. You've ruined the whole Goddamn shoot!"

*   *   *   *

They barely spoke as they drove home from the duck pond in Lionel's Ford pickup. Still reeling from his confusion over his father's violent overreaction to his own overreaction to the spider, Hunter tried as hard as he could to stop crying. Between sniffles, he still couldn't understand why something as stupid and obnoxious as a dumb old duck hunt could possibly be so important in his father's life.

"Stop crying like some silly little girl!" the Lion commanded.

"I can't help it," Hunter maintained, between sobs. "I don't mean to cry. I know it's bad."

"Then stop it, Hunter. God damn it. Just stop it right now!"

Lionel's harsh tone upset Hunter that much more, prompting him to cry that much harder. Nothing he ever did was good enough to win his father's approval. And the more his father ordered Hunter to stop crying, the louder and more strident grew his small son's protest. Hunter's insistent profusion of tears turned into a test of wills that escalated until the Lion snapped all over again.

Fuming with an explosive rage, Lionel pulled off to the side of the road, killed the engine and then let loose. He smacked his open hand against the back of his son's head and then slapped him left to right, before double back-handing him again and again, over and over, until Hunter was beaten into submission. Taken to the mat, the little boy went down for the count, and finally stopped bawling.

"You better learn this once and for all," Lionel scolded. "Real men don't cry."

They rode the rest of the way home in silence. Rendered timid, and unable to express either his distress or frustration, Hunter simply stared blankly out the passenger window. Every now and again, the pain from his humiliation forced him to emit a few pathetic whimpers. But the moment the Lion glared at him again as a warning, Hunter shut up.

As Lionel sped down the highway, he tried to fathom how his only son could possibly be such a wimpy little sissy, such a mama's boy. How could his own flesh and blood be so averse to the things he loved so dearly and treasured so highly? Rather than serving as the memorable father-son bonding experience Lionel envisioned, their would-be manly excursions onto the water and into the marshland had instead forged a major wedge between them.

At the time Hunter had little way of knowing how much his father's traumatizing abuses would one day become so commanding a source for his erotic urges.

*   *   *   *

For decades to come, Hunter would cherish his earliest memory involving sexual arousal. It occurred one Thanksgiving not long after he turned eleven, during his first exposure to professional wrestling.

Lionel and Roberta had invited Neil Henderson, the Lion's chief supervisor at Safety First, and several other guards from the agency, along with their wives or girlfriends, over for a turkey dinner.

After feasting and complaining about eating far too much, the women retreated to the kitchen, to clean up and delve into some serious girl talk. Lionel and his male buddies waddled into the living room to partake in the smoking of cigars while engaging in manly conversation.

One of the Lion's security men checked out the latest scores of ongoing football games, and then stopped switching TV channels long enough to focus on a pro wrestling match.

"Will you just look at the size of those guys?" the guard observed aloud, to no one in particular.

Hunter glanced over at the television screen and was instantly mesmerized. For someone as hopelessly short and pathetically skinny as he, it was quite an eye opener. The pair of wrestlers in the ring sported enormous muscles and, even though one of them was covered in so much body hair he looked more simian than sapien, and even though the hairy man's opponent bore a patch over one eye and displayed a barrel-chested torso blanketed in garish tattoos, to Hunter they appeared like Spartan warriors.

The two bulky musclemen glistened with sweat as they orbited in circles, stalking one another as, with great theatrics, they tossed each other around the ring.

"It's all fake, you know!" Neil Henderson complained, with knowing authority. "They just pretend to beat each other up. The outcome's all mapped out in advance."

"So if pro wrestling's so fake," asked another guest, "how come it's so damn popular?"

Hunter didn't know the answer to that question, and didn't really care, because the stiff boner suddenly bulging within his pants gave rise to the fact his libido had just body-slammed into his destiny.

That night in his room, alone in bed while drifting off to sleep, the magical image of those two burly men who earlier waged battle on TV popped into his mind once again and, gifted by the miracle of early pubescence, Hunter found himself sexually aroused. Sporting a boner felt so good, he flipped over onto his stomach and pushed his enlarging member back and forth against the bottom sheet of his bed.

Previously, he'd experienced brief episodes of getting nearly hard, but never given it much thought nor done anything to advance its purpose. However, there in the dark of his room that night, Hunter played around with his little boy boner, massaging his thickening flesh and then manipulating its pliant firmness until, while envisioning those two TV wrestlers pounding away at each other, he actually popped for the very first time. His unexpected orgasm shot up from somewhere deep inside him, emanating from a place far down in his young manhood. It rose up in a swelling gush, all the way up until a thick glop of goo burst out from the cleft in the head of his dick, and spewed forth in several fascinating and frightening squirts. His jackpot residue was an alien cream too thick to be pee, too cloudy white to be blood, too exotic to be dismissed, and far too exciting to be ignored.

From that mystical night forward, whenever he was home alone and fortunate enough to find two hot professional wrestlers on television pretending to beat each other up, he got instantly hard and quickly whipped out the baby oil he kept secreted in the back drawer of the night stand next to his bed. He then beat his little boy boner into a submissive state, manipulating his joystick so that his orgasm erupted the very moment one wrestler pinned the other.

Hunter's prepubescent passion progressed, and life finally found real meaning for him one rainy afternoon, while he was channel surfing on the small TV in his room. His sexual fixation catapulted up to a whole new level when he came upon a sixties gladiator movie starring Steve Reeves.

Holy shit! thought Hunter. *That's the most incredibly handsome, most perfect, muscular man I've ever seen.* By the time *Hercules Unchained* went off the air, Reeves the Magnificent had become Hunter's number-one new idol — the best built, most handsome muscle man of his dreams, whose fantasy image he summoned from then on, whenever he again whipped out his budding erection and beat off.

Every Sunday for the next few years, Hunter made it his business to carefully comb through the entertainment section of his father's newspaper, surreptitiously scouring the coming week's television listings, checking to see if any Steve Reeves or other gladiator movie might air on Adventure Theatre. On those outstanding occasions when they broadcast a Reeves film, Hunter sequestered himself in his room, baby oil and Kleenex at hand, and joyously whacked away, rhythmically stroking himself into a near stupor of euphoria over his revered muscle icon. He could only imagine the joy from being overpowered by such a Hercules. More often than not, Hunter popped a plentiful youthful load just about the same time Reeves defeated a villainous opponent during each film's requisite gladiator-wrestling contest.

*   *   *   *

The Lion always hoped Hunter would grow up to be as successful and formidable a wolf on the prowl as he had been in his bachelor years. Now that the teenager was practically a young adult, he knew the surest way to guide his boy into true manhood was to orchestrate his son's next rite of passage, and that meant duplicating the same ritual to which his own father had exposed him back when he was Hunter's age.

The week before Hunter turned fifteen, Lionel told him not to make any plans for Saturday night. He told his wife, Roberta, to enjoy a night out with the girls, as he was taking their boy out for some serious "men-only business."

On Saturday evening, Lionel and Hunter left the house around six and drove south for several hours until they ended up in Brownsville, a rundown industrial town just north of the Rio Grande. By turns nervous and excited, Hunter had no idea what his father was up to, but as always hoped to somehow finally earn some measure of favor in his eyes.

After driving through a shuttered, former business district, Lionel zigzagged his way through a series of dark back roads, until he turned a corner and pulled into a parking lot next to the Dixie Bar & Grill. It was a huge, ramshackle saloon smack in the middle of nowhere, and the Lion parked his pick-up amid a cluster of motorcycles and a fleet of enormous semi-trucks.

Bright, blinking, red neon letters glowing in the dark night above the bar's entrance sizzled and buzzed noisily with no lack of subtlety: *GIRLS! GIRLS! GIRLS!*

"Ready to down a couple of steaks and celebrate?" Lionel asked the birthday boy.

"Sure thing, Dad!" Hunter assured him, enthusiastically.

Lionel placed an awkward, fatherly arm of affection around Hunter's shoulder as they walked beneath the buzzing neon sign and headed into the cavernous, smoke-filled restaurant.

The joint was jumping. Over in one corner of the bar, rowdy college boys boisterously belted out raunchy fraternity drinking songs as they got progressively snockered, downing successive shots of salt-rimmed tequila. Off in another part of the room, plaid-shirted, foul-mouthed truckers surrounded a pair of billiards tables. Fat men puffed away on fat cigars as they got behind their eight balls and raucously shot round after round of pool. In the middle of all this manly revelry, a pair of buxom, topless go-go girls, clad only in tassels and thongs, pranced brazenly back and forth beneath dim red lights, along a narrow, elevated runway. A troop of aggressive bikers, clad mostly in black, hooted and whistled, encouraging one and all to stuff dollar bills into the dancer's G-strings.

A bleached-blond, buxom hostess, vehemently chewing on a tired wad of gum, escorted father and son through the dining area, over to a vinyl booth. After plopping a pair of menus down on their table, she headed back to the front of the restaurant.

As father and son sat down across from one another, Lionel looked around the crowded room and raised his voice to be heard over the rock and roll music blaring from speakers all around them. "How's this for titty heaven?" he asked, pointing toward a big-busted, talentless young woman atop the runway, holding onto a pole while a-rhythmically twirling purple tassels in provocative circles.

"Boy — titty heaven is right!" Hunter shouted back, instinctively doing his butch-best to sound stimulated.

When an elderly waitress with unruly hair arrived at their table, Lionel snapped the menu out from Hunter's hands and, without consultation, ordered them each a sixteen-ounce porterhouse steak dinner, cowboy rare, thank you, plus a pitcher of draft beer for himself and a tall ginger ale for the birthday boy.

They dined like proper cavemen, slobbering over thick slabs of crimson beef. Lionel filled Hunter's empty glass with some of the beer from his nearly empty pitcher. "Tonight's a special occasion. So drink up, Birthday Boy!" he ordered as they clicked glasses.

Hunter did as he was told, even though the brew tasted flat and bitter. "I thought alcohol interfered with your heart medication," he observed.

"Who gives a shit?" The Lion roared with typical bluster while draining his stein. "Are we celebrating tonight or not?"

An hour later, after finishing off their twin apple pies a la mode, Lionel excused himself and headed back over to the front of the restaurant, where he conducted a short chat with the buxom hostess who'd seated them.

"Okay, Hunter," Lionel announced the moment he returned to their booth and clapped his hands loudly. "You ready to follow me?"

"Lead the way, Dad," Hunter answered as he spooned down the last of his vanilla ice cream, and followed his father over to a darkened staircase down near the rear of the crowded room.

"You just go right up there!" Lionel instructed, pointing to a hallway at the top of the landing. "This is your moment to shine, Son. So just hightail it upstairs right now. Room five."

Standing directly behind Hunter, the Lion slapped his son's butt and propelled the scrawny lad forward. "And happy birthday!"

Filled with both curiosity and a discomfiting apprehension, Hunter ascended the long staircase, one step at a time. As he reached the landing and walked down the dimly lit red hallway, he was struck with an ominous tinge of anxiety. When he arrived at door five, he gulped audibly, and then gently knocked on the dark wood.

A tall, big-breasted woman in her late thirties, with flaming orange hair, attired only in an unfastened satin bathrobe, answered his call. "Don't tell me! Let me guess," she gushed in a raspy voice. "*You* must be the birthday boy!"

"Yep, that's me!" Hunter answered nervously, at least an octave too high.

"Well, come on in," the woman said invitingly, as she took a step back and opened wide the door. "I'm Dolores and we've been expecting you."

We? Thought Hunter. *Who's We?*

As Hunter took several hesitant steps into the room, another big blonde with beautiful legs, a decade or so younger than Dolores, came out from the bathroom, wearing only a pair of frilly panties and too many drops of some powerfully sweet cologne. "I'm Amber," she said warmly. "And you must be our little birthday boy!"

"Guess the word is out, huh?" Hunter answered awkwardly with a forced laugh, hoping to sound unruffled and worldly.

"I swear, they look younger every year," observed Amber. She sized Hunter up and down. "Okay, I just finished douching, so I'm fresh as a daisy. What say we get this dog-and-pony show on the road?"

Dolores was in full accord. "Ready for your birthday surprise, little man?" she asked, turning to face Hunter. "You wanna wash up first, or just dive right in ... so to speak?"

"Well ..." Hunter answered apprehensively. "I'm a little new at this. What's the usual procedure?"

"Procedure?" Amber bellowed, mockingly. "There ain't no set procedure, Birthday Boy. It's all up to you. We're just here to show you a good time."

"Great!" Hunter smiled awkwardly. "I love a good time."

"Wonderful!" said Dolores with a snap of her fingers. "So why don't you just go into the bathroom, take off all those silly clothes, then thoroughly wash your little man hands and scrub down your little dicky-dicky real quickie-quickie."

*   *   *   *

Hunter quickly undressed in the grimy bathroom and then, repeating Dolores' explicit instructions in his head, thoroughly washed his little man hands and scrubbed down his little dicky-dicky real quickie-quickie. After finishing his ablution, he stared into the mirror and tried figuring out whether he was nervous, excited, rattled, apprehensive, grateful, jittery, furious, confused, humiliated, empowered, or simply all of the above, plus downright terrified.

His very own father, hunter of game and catcher of fish, had not only brought him to a house of ill repute, he'd also actually paid for not one, but two, count 'em, two hookers for his son's pubescent passage into manhood. How lucky could a kid get?

Hunter's qualms raced through his head. Things were happening so fast, and since he had so little time to prepare, how would he know what to do, or even where to begin? What if it took him too long to finish his business? What if they made fun of his immaturity, his lack of experience, his dismally short and slender body? Most worrisome of all, would they report the quality of his performance back to his father once it was over?

Hunter interrupted his potential panic attack because the time had arrived for him to conduct himself like a real man, or at least like what his father considered a real man. He hoped, then begged, then prayed, then pleaded to be granted both strength and virility. He wrapped a towel around his narrow waist, stuck out his immature chest, took a deep breath, gave a less-than-confident wink to the kid in the mirror, turned the handle on the door, and stepped out of the bathroom and into the launching of his sex life.

*   *   *   *

Dolores and Amber lay sprawled out atop an unmade bed, both of them stark naked.

"Okay, Honey," Dolores waved Hunter over as he walked out from the bathroom. "Hop aboard!"

Hunter took a few hesitant steps toward the bed and allowed Dolores to hold his hand as she led him down to their crumpled bed sheets.

They all three lay on their backs, a curious ménage a trios, with Hunter sandwiched sensually between two ladies of the night, casual as you please. As six eyes stared up at the ceiling, at first no one said a word.

Amber finally broke the silence, asking, "So? Got a favored position, Birthday Boy?"

"I'm not really sure," Hunter answered with a smile. "How many are there?"

"More than you can shake a dick at!" Amber chuckled.

"Why don't we just get rid of this?" Dolores suggested, as she yanked Hunter's towel off him and tossed it to the floor.

Amber eyes opened wide in approval. "Hey, take a look at the kid!" She shrieked. "So young, so hung."

Dolores agreed. "Even soft, you can tell he's big, thick, just like his old man."

Oh, great! thought Hunter. *Just what I needed to hear.*

Hooker to the left of him, hooker to the right, the three of them lay naked in bed, and for a few more brief moments, none of them said another word.

Silence.

Amber wondered how long their john's pecker would stay soft. By no small coincidence, Hunter was wondering the same thing.

It soon became clear to Dolores that their inexperienced, underage client was not about to get things moving on his own, so she rose up on her knees and situated herself between Hunter's legs. After wrapping a soft hand around the little guy's flaccid member, she observed, sardonically, "Okay — time to find out if this one's a boy or a girl!"

Thanks, thought Hunter. *That's a real confidence booster!*

Dolores then opened wide as if readying for a dental probe and summarily popped Hunter's limp manhood into her big, lipstick-smeared mouth.

Amber also sat up, moved closer to their young client, took his left hand and placed it firmly atop her supple, fully formed right breast. "How's this big ole titty feel, Birthday Boy?"

Hunter gently massaged Amber's ample, well-shaped breast, and was greatly relieved when he actually felt vaguely aroused by its erotic resiliency. He then pressed the back of his head deeper against the pillow and closed his eyes.

"Now that's more like it!" Dolores announced, between slurps. "Our boy's in the air."

"Nothing to it," Hunter shrugged cavalierly, hoping to sound confident. Then, with his eyes still shut tight, his hand kneaded Amber's ample breast as she enticingly stroked his torso. Dolores spent the next few minutes expressing her exceptional oral talents. Hunter soon felt a fresh excitement rising up from somewhere deep within him.

Amber sensed their client's escalating exhilaration, and cheered him on. "Come on, Birthday Boy," she whispered encouragingly. "Shoot it now. Shoot all of it straight into Dolores' mouth."

Hunter moaned with pleasure and kept his eyes shut real tight, even as he allowed the tantalizing erotic images of the movie playing in his mind to help carry him over the top. As the birthday boy climaxed and shot his load, he cried out in a release of primal excitement. Dutifully, like the true pro she was, Dolores gulped down the thrust of his young sperm.

And the fantasy that made Hunter shoot, the image that transported him over the edge into delirious sexual success, was a vision of his personal muscle icon Steve Reeves, so big and strong, triumphantly wrestling his villainous opponent into submission.

*   *   *   *

Lionel was already tanked and a bit woozy from the two, three, or was it four more steins he'd guzzled while hanging out downstairs at the Dixie, nervously waiting around while his son lost his innocence. As he and Hunter drove home, he did his best to stay alert by volubly singing along with the medley of static-laced, hokey tunes blaring from a local country-western station.

Sitting across from his father, lost in thought while feeling potent and downright manly, Hunter just stared out the window, watching the dark night whiz by.

Lionel ruffled Hunter's thick, blond hair with his open hand. "So …?" he called out to his son, almost hollering so he could be heard over the music filling the cabin. "You haven't said much. How'd it go? Those girls show you a good time?"

"I'll say!" Hunter boasted, immodestly. "Talk about Titty Heaven!"

"Dolores said you were quite the little stud back there!"

"Guess she knows a real man when she sees one, huh, Dad!" Hunter suggested with a roguish chortle, relieved because things upstairs at the Dixie had gone so well; and also because he'd gotten not just merely a passing grade, but a good review.

"No need to thank your old man," Lionel grinned and gently slapped his open hand against the back of his son's head, a love tap. "It was the Lion's job to help you score your first taste of pussy!"

Satisfied they had finally shared a successful bonding experience, Lionel flipped the volume up on the radio as loud as it would climb, and boisterously sang along with the rousing twang of the country tune.

As Hunter went back to staring out the window, he was relieved his father deemed the evening a triumph. The chip off the old block couldn't help but grin. Not only had he somehow pulled off the formidable sexual challenge posed by his time spent with Dolores and Amber, he'd also managed to keep his father from discovering the truth about his taboo muscle fantasy.

*   *   *   *

Aside from the erotic wrestling scenarios that dependably accompanied his masturbatory fantasies, Hunter never dared allow himself to act on the lure of muscle. Instead, he sublimated his attraction to well-built men by vowing to do something about his own sorry scrawniness. And from his exploration of the muscle magazines he kept secreted beneath his bedding, he already knew that pumping iron, particularly for a growing teenager, was the surest ticket to his much sought-after muscle growth. He knew he wasn't about to develop a hot body just by wishing it. So the day before he turned sixteen, while in the middle of his junior year at Corpus Christi's Jefferson High, when Lionel asked his son what he wanted for his birthday, Hunter told his father he wanted to join Power Up, the recently opened, well-equipped gym not far from their home.

The Lion was mightily impressed his lanky son actually wanted to explore an endeavor as ostensibly manly as bodybuilding, so he not only gave Hunter his blessing, he even paid for a year's membership.

Hunter loved working out at the Power Up gym. He trained three afternoons a week, right after school, lifting weights with zeal and enthusiasm. After only several months, he began feeling a pronounced difference in the small mounds that began developing into his burgeoning biceps. He still looked about the same in his bathroom's full-length mirror, and that was somewhat deflating. However, just a few weeks later, he actually felt his pecs budding a tad more mass. He loved doing sit-ups because, with such low body fat on his slight frame, it took little time for an emergent six-pack to pop up across the breadth of his abdominal wall. Hunter gradually put on a few pounds, packing some discernable bulk onto his slender five-foot-seven, one-hundred-and-thirty-three pound frame.

Intramural wrestling was wildly popular throughout Texas, often attracting the most powerful jocks to its active calling. When Hunter's high school wrestling squad posted a notice announcing tryouts for new team players, he decided the time had come to finally do something about his clandestine, erotic attraction to the sport.

On the day of the tryouts, Hunter showed up in the school gymnasium half an hour early, determined to give it his all. What better way to exhibit his budding butchness, his blossoming jock-like sensibility, his no-nonsense masculinity?

Matched up, however, against a wily kid four inches taller and twelve pounds heavier proved to be his speedy undoing. Unable to mount any level of tangible defense, as well as only vaguely familiar with the most basic wrestling maneuvers, Hunter was swiftly pretzled, pinned, and then cut from the roster after only the first round of tryouts.

The rejection merely boosted his determination to make the squad. He revised his schedule, took aim at getting bigger and growing stronger by hitting the gym five times a week.

He talked his mother into whipping up huge omelets and thick hamburger patties for him at breakfast, and extra chicken breasts at dinner. He started forcing down enough banana-laced, high-caloric, protein drinks to supply his fast-growing body with a mighty three thousand muscle-building calories a day.

In his senior year, with an impressive fourteen pounds of new, well-proportioned muscle packed onto his once scrawny frame, eighteen-year-old Hunter felt fit enough to have another shot at trying out for the school's wrestling squad. His patience and perseverance paid off when, after his second tryout, he was accepted.

The young, would-be jock focused on his practice sessions, even as he worked extra hard at advancing his grappling style. After hours spent sweating on the mat, his skills improved and Hunter was eventually recognized as the team player who put up the biggest battle — at least until he was taken down and pinned. He continued working out with weights, pumping up after class. Bit by bit, he put on weight and grew stronger, even as he poured his heart, his entire body, his very soul into the sport. He relished with a feverish persistence the opportunity to feed his closeted fetish.

Unlike so many of his fellow teammates who often starved themselves as they slimmed down days before a contest, leaning out so they could qualify to wrestle at the top of a lower weight class, Hunter refused to diet so radically. Victory was important to him, but not at the expense of his prized muscle growth.

To his bewilderment and embarrassment, more often than not, he remained fully erect throughout a match. With his late teen testosterone surging, there were even several occasions where, while intensely entwined on the mat, and getting trounced and then pinned by his opponent, he also shot out a major load — a micro-atomic, orgasmic detonation drenching the confines of the protective, plastic cup within his jock strap.

He wondered if maybe he wasn't a little weird, since he got far more aroused whenever he was pinned and lost the match than on those rare occasions when he was victorious. A light bulb went off in his head the day he realized the only reason he worked hard at winning the odd match was because he didn't want either his coach or his team buddies to suspect that his true preference was to be taken down and overwhelmed, held in place until he was forced to submit and tap out.

What was it about the lure of defeat that appealed to him so much more than what for him was the letdown of victory? Since Hunter was by then so much stronger and in such good shape for his size and age, he could easily win most of his matches. More than savoring some supposedly sweet victory, however, he preferred to roll over and lose. He actually derived a quirky pleasure in letting his opponent get the better of him. While home in bed masturbating before going to sleep, he often fantasized about getting wrestled to the mat, roughed up a bit and, after getting pinned, forcibly raped in the shower by the best-built, most commanding wrestlers on his squad.

Wrestling also provided him with all the homoerotic stimulation he could handle, so he rarely felt any further need to carry his forbidden fruit, his offbeat fetish, to any next level. No need to wander over into those sinful dangers posed by the inevitable disease, degeneracy, and degradation he'd always been taught accompanied both anal and oral man-to-man sex. Even so, the psychosexual dynamics and mixed messages manifested by his teammates often left Hunter not just frustrated and confused, but also highly aroused. Take, for instance, any of those tantalizing homoerotic episodes that transpired post-practice, down in the locker room. After stepping out of their singlets and then soaping up in the showers, guys on the squad sometimes sported major erections.

Rather than concealing from their fellow teammates the surprising arrival of their big boy boners, the jocks instead just joked about them. None of them felt threatened or embarrassed about getting stiff in front of the other guys. Openly, they flaunted their hard dicks and brazenly showed off, comparing sizes or salaciously ribbing one another as they vied to see who among them boasted the biggest member or had the hairiest balls.

All this same-sex clowning around was always activated in the name of heterosexuality, all in the name of getting aroused *only* over women. Each wrestler in his turn invariably bragged about how gaga he was for girls.

The team's coach, Greg Howgart, a big, beefy bear of a goodhearted fellow, was one of those rare faculty types who actually cared about his young athletes.

Down in the locker room one late afternoon, team players were engaged in their customary moronic-sophomoric horseplay of having water fights in the showers, or snapping towels at one another while drying off.

When Coach Howgart walked in, he bellowed for his boys to stop the rowdiness and finish getting dressed. One of Hunter's teammates called out, asking Coach Howgart how come so many team players sported wood while wrestling or while showering, and what, if anything, it all meant.

The locker room turned suddenly silent as all ears pricked up to hear what their coach had to say.

Coach Howgart was nonchalant, even dismissive, as he remained calm, supportive. "Nothing to worry about, Guys," he told them with hardy assurance. "Happens to players on every team I've coached. Doesn't mean a darn thing. Soldiers get hard all the time in battle. It's all that adrenaline pumping through your system, releasing primitive energies."

Coach's words made sense and helped soothe whatever homoerotic concerns any of them may have been harboring.

"You see, Guys," one of the bigger wrestlers announced, even as he indiscriminately snapped the stinging tip of his towel smack against the naked flesh of the butt nearest him. "We're simply behaving naturally, like barbaric warriors! AAARRRRGGGGHHH!!!!"

*   *   *   *

By the end of his senior year in high school, Hunter received a letter announcing his acceptance into the School of Commerce at New York University. By then, the future Marketing major had also sprung up to nearly five-feet eleven in height, and, thanks to his muscle progress, tipped the scales at a much-improved hundred-and-sixty-five pounds.

Lionel acknowledged his son's acceptance into college in his usual passive-aggressive fashion, threatening his boy, "You screw up after all I'm shelling out for this higher education bullshit and I promise, I'll have you enlisting in the Navy so fast, you'll be scrubbing submarine toilets before you know what hit you."

"Thanks," Hunter responded, glibly. "Nothing like a bit of fatherly support to send me out into the world."

Lionel shrugged. "As you may have learned by now, diplomacy and tact have never been my strong suits."

For once, there was something upon which father and son could agree.

Before heading off to college in New York in the fall, Hunter took a part-time summer job, five afternoons a week, bagging groceries down at Kroger's, the local supermarket. It was mindless, boring work for not much money, and he could hardly wait for each tedious day to end, so he could bicycle over to the gym, and then get lost in the intensity of his workouts.

One afternoon, just before Labor Day, Hunter's mother heard from a relative back home in Houston, who called with the distressing news her elderly aunt had taken seriously ill and was fading fast. Roberta packed a few necessities and then Lionel drove her to the airport for her hastily arranged flight.

Lionel was driving to San Antonio that coming weekend to attend a three-day security conference. With his wife away, he didn't feel completely comfortable leaving Hunter all by himself without adult supervision. So he gave Neil Henderson, his right-hand man at his agency, a spare key and asked him to drop by once or twice over the course of the next few days. "Boys will be boys," Lionel grinned knowingly. "So just check to see he's not using the place for a beer bust with thirty of his buddies, okay?"

*   *   *   *

"I'll be back late Sunday night," Lionel cautioned his eighteen-year-old son as he headed out for his two-hour drive to San Antonio. "Just don't burn down the fucking house while I'm gone."

Hunter worked tiresome, robotic afternoons over the weekend at the supermarket, bagging groceries. When his work week finally ended late Saturday afternoon, he biked over to the gym, changed into his gear and then spent the next few hours using their Universal and Nautilus machines to push out a vigorous workout.

Bored to distraction, Lionel found his security conference deadly dull. He soon grew weary of exchanging business cards with so many half-ass jerks from so many other rubber stamp security firms. Making his stay there that much more tedious, the weather in the home of the Alamo was miserable, pouring with rain and laden with a stifling humidity. Even his clandestine chasing of women was a bust with nary a shapely enough set of gams or pair of stacked boobies cruising the bar or lobby areas to warrant his initiating a flirtation, let alone an anonymous pick-up.

When the final seminar in which he was enrolled, "Personnel Martial Arts Training," was canceled due to a lack of registration, he decided to check out of his hotel and drive home a day early.

Pumped and invigorated, Hunter left the gym and biked back over to his house where he unexpectedly found Neil Henderson cozily couch-potatoed in shorts and a sweatshirt, making himself very much at home. His father's good buddy had just finished downing his fourth bottle of beer while cheering the Texas Longhorns on to victory.

"Yo, Hunter!" the big, beefy man called out from the sofa. "Come watch this. Longhorns are twelve yards and two downs away from pulling ahead, seven seconds left to play!"

"My father's not here," Hunter told him as he squirmed out of his backpack. "He's in San Antonio."

"No shit, Sherlock," Neil was sarcastic. "That's how come I'm here. Your old man asked me to stop by, make sure you're doing okay. So — I'm stopping by!"

"Never mentioned it to me," said Hunter.

"Well, your father doesn't talk much."

"That's not exactly big news," Hunter observed.

"You fucking idiot!" Neil blew his stack at the television, "Fumble?! Can you believe he fucking fumbled the fucking ball? What a fucking asshole!"

"I'm going to shower," Hunter said, and turned to leave.

Neil was dumbfounded. "But you'll miss the end of the game."

"Sounds to me like it's already over," Hunter said and headed for his room.

*   *   *   *

Steaming hot water pelted Hunter's torso as he stood directly beneath the shower-head. It felt so satisfying after his workout, he luxuriated longer than usual in the cascade as it soothed his freshly stimulated muscles.

While shampooing with his eyes closed, Hunter couldn't help but visualize how appealing Neil just looked, spread out so lazily across the couch in his oversized sweatshirt and those thick, hairy thighs popping out from his gym shorts. And so what if he was saddled with a fairly prominent beer belly — the beefy guy still exuded a definite air of sexy manliness.

Hunter dried himself off, wrapped a towel around his waist and, feeling a subversive need to show off how well his young body was developing, sauntered back into the living room, making believe he was trying to find a postage stamp.

Sure enough, as Hunter made his way over to the desk drawer, the huge man looked away from the basketball game he was by then watching long enough to note, "Your dad tells me you've been working out, that you even made the wrestling team."

Hunter fingered his way through a mess of paper clips and rubber bands.

Neil sized Hunter up and down. "Looks like you've also put on some good muscle weight since I last saw you. Good job."

"Thanks, Neil," Hunter acknowledged nonchalantly, carefully masking how thrilled he felt about making a favorable impression. "I've been lifting over at Power Up."

"Sure shows!" Neil told him with genuine enthusiasm. "By the time you get to college, them coeds are gonna be all over your sweet little ass. Better prepare yourself, Buster."

"I can hardly wait," Hunter responded in his lowest register.

Neil sat up on the couch, placed his bottle of beer on the coffee table before him. "You know, I used to wrestle, too," he told Hunter. "High school *and* college. They always said it was near impossible to break out of my full nelson."

"Impressive," Hunter acknowledged, feeling downright exhilarated as he took a cautious step forward. "Is there some trick to it?"

"You betcha," Neil assured him. "The key's in the positioning of your feet: maintaining leverage. Go put on some shorts, I'll show you."

Filled with both an exhilarating and apprehensive sense of danger — the single emotion to which he was most drawn — Hunter dashed back to his room, tossed his towel onto the bed, stepped hastily into a pair of workout shorts, and then raced back into the living room.

Neil had by then pushed the couch and coffee table a few feet toward the wall and stood in the middle of the room, stretching his arms high over his head. With a firm clap of his hands, he pointed an index finger at Hunter and instructed, "Come here and get down on all fours. I'll show you my secret, starting from takedown."

Hunter quickly did as he was told, dropped to the floor, settled in on his hands and knees.

Neil pulled off his sweatshirt and tossed it onto the sofa, casually noting, "No sense getting this all sweaty, huh?"

Hunter looked fleetingly over his shoulder at Neil's huge, athletic pecs, his full, broad shoulders, the imposing size of his powerful arms, and tried curbing his mounting enthusiasm by looking down and fastening his eyes on a spot directly in the middle of the carpet.

Neil positioned himself down on one knee astride Hunter, and couldn't help but notice his young opponent's emerging stiffness. He placed his right arm around the teenager's back, and wrapped his left hand down around the kid's wrist, locking the two of them into the standard starting position. He wondered if he should give into one of the other demons with which he'd been wrestling for the past few decades by rubbing his shorts and his own emergent erection up against Hunter's young thigh. "Ready to wrestle?" he whispered into Hunter's ear,

Hunter gritted his teeth and seethed, "Let's rumble!"

Several minutes later, Hunter lay sprawled out on the living room carpet, flat on his stomach, bearing the full brunt of Neil's big body, which by then was piggy-backed directly on top of his. The strong security guard had Hunter completely incapacitated, held at bay in his signature full nelson.

"Can't break my powerful grip, can you now, huh?" Neil asked, tauntingly, as he slowly pushed Hunter's face down further toward the floor.

"Break your grip?" Hunter mumbled, rhapsodically. "I can barely breathe!"

Neil tightened his immobilizing grasp as he next rolled himself as well as his young opponent over on to their backs. Lying vertically atop one another, still piggy-backed, they both faced the ceiling.

As Hunter struggled in vain to free himself, he also experienced a quiet delight in how erotically satisfying Neil's thick hard boner felt pressed against the back of his shorts. He instinctively sensed it would be far too awkward to acknowledge both his and his opponent's stirring stiffness, so instead, he said to the ceiling, "Thought you were going to show me how to break out of this hold."

"You're right!" Neil answered, and slowly released Hunter from his resolute grip.

Hunter rolled himself away from Neil's torso, onto the carpet. Momentarily freed from his intoxicating incarceration, he rubbed the back of his sore neck.

Neil sat up in place and, while unexpectedly sliding out of his gym shorts, cavalierly suggested, "What say we get rid of these, as well, huh?"

"How come?" Hunter asked, trying hard not to sound too naïve or overly excited.

"Dunno," Neil shrugged. "It's just a real cool way for guys to wrestle together. That's how they used to do it ancient Greece, back when the Olympics first started, you know. Naked and all oiled up. The way real men used to wrestle. Besides ..." he coyly added, "Aren't our shorts just getting in the way?"

"In the way of what?" Hunter asked with only partial innocence.

"Well," Neil reasoned, "how do you suggest we grab on to each other's balls and start squeezing 'em like lemons if we're still in our shorts?"

Hunter never heard of such an idiotic tactic, but giddily accepted this out-of-left-field erotic maneuver as a challenge to his budding machismo. "Oh, a dirty fighter, huh?" he blustered with a forced bravado, even as he stepped out of his own shorts and joined Neil in his nudity.

*   *   *   *

It was a little after nine in the evening when Lionel pulled into his driveway and parked directly behind Neil's beat up Plymouth. Hunter's dad was pleased to see that Neil had obviously stopped by to look in on his boy.

The Lion arrived at his front door and heard the familiar sound of a sporting event blaring from inside. After unlocking the door, he walked in and stopped dead in his tracks when he was welcomed home by the sight of his son and his trusted business associate wrapped together on the Persian rug in the living room with no clothes on, gleaming with sweat, the two of them sporting major erections while contorted together in some bizarre consensual confrontation.

Lionel took in the incomprehensible surreal sight before him and bellowed, "WHAT THE FUCK'S GOING ON HERE?"

"Holy shit!" Neil unwrapped himself from his erotic hold on Hunter and scrambled to his feet. "Lionel! What are you doing home?"

"I live here, Goddamnit!" Lionel seethed. "What the fuck ...?"

"We weren't doing anything wrong, Dad," Hunter offered timidly, from the floor. "Just fooling around!"

"Wadda ya mean, fooling around?!" Lionel barked. "Why the fuck you both naked?"

Mortified, Neil reached for his shorts. "It was a guy thing," he shrugged. "No big deal. I was showing Hunter some wrestling moves. You know — for fun!"

"FUN?!" Lionel screamed at the top of his lungs. "Get out of my house, Neil! Just get the fuck out of my house right now, before I call the cops, you perverted prick!"

"Come on, Lionel," Neil tried making light of their humiliating predicament. "Believe me, it's not how it looks."

"Oh, really?" Lionel eyes enlarged with rage as he fumed, "How the hell does it look?"

"We were just practicing some holds," Hunter chimed in as he also jumped to his feet. "Just clowning around."

Lionel walked directly up to his son and smacked him hard, first against one side of his head and then the other. "CLOWNING AROUND?!" He repeated voluminously. "Grown men do not clown around, rolling around naked!"

"That's not what we were doing, Lionel," Neil insisted. "I mean, we got out of our clothes. But it was nothing like what you're thinking! We were just being jocks."

"JOCKS?!" Lionel erupted and again furiously slapped the sides of Hunter's head. "You get out of my house, Neil. Just get the fuck out of here right now!"

"Stop it, Dad!" Hunter implored, cupping his hands to his ears in a desperate effort to protect his head. "Please! Don't go all crazy on me."

"CRAZY?!" Lionel fumed, and again smacked Hunter across the back of his head. "You wanna see crazy, you little pansy? I'll show you crazy!"

"Please don't, Dad — No! — Stop!" Hunter pleaded. "I'm begging you!"

"Wassa matter?" Lionel roared and smacked Hunter again. "Little sissy boy can't take it, huh? Little big man would rather be a no good, naked, little fairy, is that it?"

Lionel went nuts, spun out of control and smacked the left side of Hunter's head, then his right, forcing his son back, one step at a time, still pummeling away at his face even after he'd backed him up against the wall.

"Stop it, Lionel, damn it!" Neil shouted, as he came up from behind his boss and thrust his arms beneath Lionel's armpits. "You'll hurt your boy!" Neil raised his arms higher and quickly clasped his hands around the back of his boss' neck, locking the Lion in one of his renowned full nelsons.

"What the fuck?!" Lionel complained. Suddenly incapacitated, his arms were forcibly stretched high above him in the air until his hands dangled as if he were a marionette's puppet.

"Just calm down and then I'll release you," Neil negotiated.

"Calm down?!" Lionel complained, while vigorously trying to wiggle out from Neil's immobilizing grip. "How dare you tell me to call down, you fucking child molester! Let go of me, Goddamnit! I'm gonna call the cops and then I'm gonna beat the shit out of you both!"

Neil summoned all his strength and tightened his gripping embrace to hold the Lion at bay.

A jabbing, shooting pain suddenly stabbed Lionel deep within the linings of his chest cavity, and his head felt like it was being crushed in a visor. He cried out, helplessly, "Omigod! I can't breathe!"

Lionel's eyes bulged wide in astonishment, his face turned crimson, and then his whole body went limp. Sagging like a rag doll, he collapsed beneath the weight of Neil's immobilizing grasp.

"Holy shit!" Neil muttered in disbelief as he carefully lowered his boss' suddenly flaccid body to the floor. "We gotta call an ambulance!"

As Neil hurried to the phone, Hunter dropped to his knees and took hold of Lionel's hand. "Oh, God, no!" he hollered. "What is it, Dad? What's wrong?"

Unable to breath, Lionel's entire body was aquiver as he gulped inaudibly for oxygen. Thickening veins popped up prominently along the sides of his neck. "Oh, God!" he uttered in his excruciating pain. "… My chest … heart … can't breathe. Help me … please."

The Lion saw his future fading fast and the reality of his imminent demise so petrified him, he began to sob. And as tears of pain, anguish, anger, and regret streamed down his cheeks, he was amazed to find Hunter hovering over him, uncharacteristically stoic.

The Lion took the briefest of moments to look past his own misery, straight up into his son's somber eyes and, with his last gasp of breath, asked sadly, "No tears for me, Son?"

Hunter remained steadfast. "Real men don't cry — remember?"

"Good boy," Lionel mumbled in a feint gasp as his eyes lost focus and his heart stopped beating. His body turned rigid before it went limp, even as the Lion's authoritarian rule, and Hunter's painful recollections of it, came to an abrupt end.

*   *   *   *

MEN IN LOVE

A tiny clock inside Hunter's head ticked off the days, hours, and minutes before the man of his dreams would finally get there, and he was adamant his VIP houseguest would have the best time ever.

Over on the other side of the country, Chase began entertaining the once wild notion that his budding courtship with Hunter might mature into a real-life love affair. And, while he still wasn't sure if he was ready for so drastic a change in his lifestyle, he still wanted to make this a special birthday for his hot muscle boy. He couldn't compete with Hunter's expense account or his magnanimity, but after rummaging through his closet, Chase found an old Tiffany sterling key ring still embedded in its powder-blue box; a party favor picked up years ago at some fund-raiser. He brought it to a local jeweler and had the name *Hunter* engraved on one surface of the circular pendant, *Chase* inscribed on its flip side.

Chase wondered why he was going to the effort. He knew Hunter had scored some emotional inroads, but was the Kid also slowly cracking the outer shell of his stalwart alter ego? Was Hunter getting through to him despite his best efforts at a stubborn defense? Was it possible this far younger man could actually dissuade Chase away from the random, rampant wanderings of his roamosexuality?

Of course not! Chase chastised himself while he finished packing for his trip east. *I like my life just as it is. Nothing on earth's about to change any of that.*

*   *   *   *

Hunter braved a taxi ride through gridlocked city traffic, all the way out to JFK, so he could pick up Chase. He arrived at the crowded baggage claim area just as Atlas in his traveling kennel whizzed by on the carousel.

Chase and Hunter tried keeping their hands off each other during their long cab ride back to Manhattan, but it wasn't easy. Atlas sat up between them, their designated chaperone, panting heavily when he wasn't licking their faces.

Early every weekday morning of Chase's vacation, he and Hunter worked out together at the Executive Sporting Club. Hunter proudly introduced Chase to all his gym cronies. If some of them sensed his houseguest might also be his lover, that was fine with him.

Following each of their workouts, Hunter hurried off for work, while Chase headed back uptown to take Atlas out for his morning stroll around the block.

Chase and Hunter met for lunch every day, sometimes with a friend Hunter wanted Chase to meet. Hunter returned home from work each day by five-thirty and the two of them reliably ravaged one another, making long, furiously sublime love. After resting a while, Chase and Hunter usually showered together, then dressed and went out to an expensive restaurant for dinner.

Hunter relished draining his expense account, loved spoiling his man silly, and always picked up the tab. Chase kept offering to pay a bill here and there, to split a check, but Hunter was adamant.

"You're my guest, Coach," he told Chase, after dinner at a popular new Asian/Cajun restaurant in Chelsea called Howe's Bayou. As Hunter cavalierly handed his American Express card to the waiter, he added, "Don't you know by now your number-one boy's number-one priority is keeping his big man happy, showing you a good time?"

"Well, I just want you to know how grateful I am," Chase told him.

Hunter smiled knowingly. Bingo! That was *precisely* what he wanted to hear. "Please," he laughed dismissively, "don't mention it." His brain, however, held a small party in his head as he sensed his calculated indispensability clicking into place. "What else are expense accounts for?"

Hunter wanted Chase to fall in love with The Big Apple. If his coach felt at home and happy in the cosmopolitan atmosphere of the big city, he'd be that much more willing to spend more time in New York with his boy. In Hunter's logic, it followed that as Chase grew ever more acclimated, it wasn't too much of a stretch from there to imagine him soon having no problem actually moving, relocating to the magic that was Manhattan. From there, it was an easy jump to envision the two of them setting up house and starting to live their lives together as a prominent gay Gotham power couple.

For his part, Chase was confounded as to why their explosive sex had yet to dull or wax routine. Wasn't that what was to be expected between two men? Didn't long-time lovers become over the years more like brothers, or sometimes sad to say, more like sisters? Rather than waxing predictable and stale, Chase and Hunter's sex life kept expanding, remaining consistently exhilarating, imaginative, and athletic.

Chase had never felt so comfortable around another man. His boyfriend provided so much undivided attention and genuine affection, he could finally just relax and be himself. He didn't have to work anymore at charming Hunter. He didn't even have to keep playing his part as the Coach. He could just be Chase, without all the self-imposed trappings of his alter ego.

Saturday was Hunter's twenty-ninth birthday, and at last, it was Chase's turn to dote on his boy. They arrived right on time for their eight o'clock reservation at Watermelon, Manhattan's hot, new, Upper West Side foodie shrine, just off Central Park West. Chase didn't care that the expensive menu was way over his limited budget. He wanted to return at least a fragment of the extensive generosity Hunter had been shoveling his way ever since they first met.

"Tell me something," Chase asked, while looking over the menu. "For your birthday — what would you like more than anything else?"

"Nothing much," Hunter answered honestly, without even thinking. "Even if you had to lie, I'd want to hear you say you love me."

"How about something a bit more realistic?" Chase asked, and made light of Hunter's seriousness by reaching over and punching him on the shoulder. "Why not a trip to the moon or a new Porsche?"

"Believe it or not," Hunter countered, "sometimes even real men actually come right out with it and say the dreaded "L" word. It's not *always* wimpy when guys do that, you know, not the end of the world, not if it comes from a place of real affection."

"Hold on a minute," Chase kidded the Kid. "I'll get out my violin."

Hunter dropped the subject and, just before they ordered dessert, opened Chase's gift: the engraved Tiffany key chain. He untied its white ribbon and lifted the top off the pale blue box. Deeply moved by Chase's thoughtfulness and ever the crybaby, he fought to hold back tears of happiness.

"Uh-oh!" Chase saw Hunter's eyes filling with liquid and announced, "Here comes the rain again."

After dabbing his eyes, Hunter finally brought up the speech he'd rehearsed regarding the sensibleness of Chase's returning again to New York very soon. "How 'bout next time," he suggested, cheerfully, "you visit for an extended stay, say maybe four or five weeks."

"Five weeks?" Chase repeated disdainfully, like it was a jail sentence. "If I stayed that long, I'd have to start paying rent."

"I'm being serious," Hunter ignored Chase's semi-sarcasm and continued unfolding his scenario. "You come back here maybe as early as April. Stay with me to mid-July. That way, we could find out what living together might be like in real time."

Chase said nothing as he sat at their table, smiling stupidly.

"So what do you think of my plan, Coach?" Hunter was eager to learn.

At first, Chase still didn't know quite what to say or how he should respond. The notion *sounded* appealing in concept. But if Hunter's seemingly well-rehearsed invitation was such a good idea, why were alarms of distress going off again in the back of Chase's head?

Chase didn't want to put any damper on Hunter's big night, so he chose to ignore those disturbing signals of near-emotional panic whispering in his ear, telling him to jump up from the table, run from the restaurant and head straight for the airport.

Instead, he remained composed, even downright stoic as, calmly and coolly, he told Hunter, "I'm willing to explore so wild a hair-brained plan, okay? My initial reaction is that it sounds like a fine idea. So I suggest we each think about it, make it a genuine consideration."

"Is that a polite way of telling the birthday boy to go fuck himself?" Hunter asked defensively, point blank.

"It's a polite way of thanking you for coming up with what sounds like a truly fine proposal," Chase clicked his wineglass against Hunter's in a one-way toast, and then took a sip. "Glad you put it on the table. At this moment, however, I just can't show any more commitment past finishing my wine. Anything else you need to know?"

"Yes!" Hunter answered, emphatically, making believe he no longer felt disappointed. "I need to get a serious and solid commitment from you at least about *something*. So what do you think looks best for dessert: the floating island or the chocolate soufflé?"

*   *   *   *

Ancient tribesman might have taken it as some dark omen when, as if on cue, the moment Chase and Hunter left the restaurant, after an alarming thunderclap, it began pouring heavily with a near freezing rain. Typical of what so often happens whenever there's a downpour in Manhattan, suddenly there was not an available taxi in sight. So they huddled together, beneath the protective cover of Hunter's black umbrella, locked arm in arm, and began to walk home in the bone-chilling downpour.

All about them, countless city lights reflected untold droplets bouncing melodically against the pavement in a glistening sheen of surrealism. The pounding rain soon turned into a punishing hail. Pedestrians sporting cumbersome umbrellas scurried up and down both sides of Fifty-Ninth Street, heading for shelter.

Chase and Hunter stopped at the red light across from the fountain outside the Plaza Hotel just as the hail seamlessly segued into snow. As it tumbled down around them, the Kid turned to Chase and quietly told him, "I want to thank you for a great birthday, Coach. I don't think I ever had a better time."

Chase placed an affectionate hand atop Hunter's shoulder and smiled. "Anything for Coach's Star Varsity Wrestler!"

Hunter took hold of Chase's hand and squeezed it with great affection. "I know this is gonna sound all mushy and maybe not as butch as you'd like, Coach. But you gotta let me have just one short nellie break so I can tell you something really important, okay?"

"It's your birthday, Kiddo!" Chase told him. "Fire when ready."

As snowflakes mixed with rain and hail pelted their umbrella, Chase could tell Hunter was about to say something very emotional, very serious, and something deep inside him sensed this was not the moment for sarcasm or flippancy.

Hunter stared directly at his boyfriend, and as a familiar reservoir of tears welled up in his eyes, he bravely told him, "I know how for the last ten years you've shied away from relationships, Boss. Sooner or later, everyone's bound to have a broken heart. It's part of life. But it's important you understand I've given you all my love. We both know I've never done that before, not with anyone. I've waited so long for you, for this, for us, my whole life, really. And so, not only am I giving you my heart, I'm also counting on you to take really good care of it."

Hunter's sincere expression was just the sort of affectionate display that, in the past, would have alienated Chase and sent him packing. At first, he didn't know how to respond, and said nothing, even as a wave of anxiety invaded his stomach. He knew they both had plenty going for themselves as a team, but still quietly wondered if the Kid wasn't rushing ahead, sailing into their one-on-one as lovers much too deeply, and far too fast. The last thing he wanted to do was break this sweet young man's heart, but still, he also needed to protect himself.

The light turned green, but neither of them bothered stepping forward. Instead, they lingered beneath their umbrella, shivering against the wild weather.

While wary about his complicity in sharing Hunter's bold romantic vision, Chase wanted to respond to Hunter's valiant vulnerability, to say *something* favorable about their emotional connection. So he looked him straight in the eye and honestly told him, "You don't have to worry, Kiddo. I know hearts are fragile. That's why I promise I'll be careful with yours, okay? You have my word."

Hunter was so overcome with gratitude and joy, he could refrain no more, and let loose the floodgates of his emotions. As tears of cheer ran down his cheeks, he wrapped his free arm around Chase, and enthusiastically kissed him on the lips. They stood on Central Park South in the mad mixture of the pounding rain, the freezing hail, the tumbling snow, kissing arduously, the two of them exposed and curiously unconcerned, propriety and passing pedestrians be damned.

Once back in the apartment, after getting out of their drenched clothes and drying off, Hunter told Chase he was eager to jump into an especially nasty muscle rape scene. By then, however, Coach had lost interest in Hunter's notion of fantasy lovemaking. He knew they could of course dream up some elaborate scenario in which Chase might play some threateningly nasty bad guy to Hunter's hapless rape victim. But after some delicate discussion, Chase steered Hunter away from acting out any elaborate, erotically driven, role-playing scenario, and instead convinced him they didn't need the distraction of performing. In place of those theatrics, Chase calmly offered Hunter the less complicated and, at least from his perspective, more desirable option of the two of them hunkering down simply as themselves and making glorious love. Which is precisely what they did.

Early on the morning of Chase's departure, as he and Hunter awoke, they hugged and kissed and, again following Chase's direction for the last time that trip, made sweet and gentle love. Gentle, that is, until, at the peak of their lovemaking, Hunter felt an intense orgasm welling up inside him, about to surge forth. When he could no longer hold back its ascension, he grabbed on to each of Chase's strong biceps and, summoning elements of his personal submission fantasy, abandoned their "vanilla" sex long enough to cry out with abandon, "Oh, yes, Daddy, fuck me! Fuck me hard. Go ahead — rape my little boy ass!"

Their rhapsodic climaxes burst practically at the same moment, and once they calmed down and caught their breaths, Hunter became subdued, even slightly detached.

When Chase noticed something was bothering the Kid, he finally asked what was wrong.

"It's no big deal," Hunter suggested. "I mean, you know I'm grateful for all the affection I've been getting. But there's still that other side of me that hungers for a more dominating experience."

Chase wasn't about to apologize for his passion being neither rough nor vicious enough for his sex partner. Still, he assuaged Hunter's evident frustration, promising, "Tell you what, Tough Guy. Next time we meet, I'll try to be a far nastier lover, okay?"

Neither of them made much more than small talk as they rode the elevator down to the lobby along with Chase's luggage and Atlas and his traveling kennel. They walked quietly out of the Hemisphere Arms, and on to Seventy-Third Street, where Hunter's doorman blew a manic whistle to flag down a passing yellow taxi which screeched to a braking halt, curbside.

Chase opened the passenger door, instructed Atlas to hop in, and then tossed his luggage and the bulldog's traveling kennel into the cab. He then asked the driver to take him to Kennedy Airport. "Well, Kiddo," he said with a dopey grin, as he turned to face Hunter. "I guess this is it … until next time."

"I'm afraid so, Coach. And you don't have to worry about what happens next between us," Hunter told him with unabashed confidence. "Got a few plans bouncing around inside my noggin."

Coach smiled as he took hold of Hunter, wrapped him in his strong arms and hugged him. When he took a step back, he saw Hunter's eyes welling up with tears. "I guess by now, I'd be surprised if you didn't get all weepy on me."

"What can I say, Coach? I have trouble with good-byes."

"Evidently," Chase smiled and clipped the bottom of Hunter's chin with his fist. "For now, why don't you get the hell out of here and get your hot butt down to the office? Go be the Boy Wonder of Madison Avenue."

Hunter snapped to rigid attention. As a tear glided down his reddening cheek, he saluted sadly and offered up a quiet, "Sir, yes, Sir!"

Chase crawled into the cab of the taxi, sat back with Atlas and, as the yellow transport took off, watched Hunter waving good-bye. As the taxi accelerated down the block, the Kid receded further and further into the bustling cityscape.

For the very first time, Chase started believing their crazy, bi-coastal, cross-country, against-all-odds muscle courtship might just turn viable, after all. Maybe a long-term, loving relationship between two men *was* possible. Maybe the twenty-year difference in their ages was not so formidable an obstacle. Maybe there was a way to melt those thousands of miles between them. Blow up the Rockies, indeed!

Maybe Chase would have to be the one, seeing how he had no steady nine-to-fiver as did Hunter, to take a shot at moving to New York for that extended stay they'd talked about; find out what it might be like, setting up house with Hunter, just as his sweet boy suggested. Maybe they could both eventually even satisfy Chase's long-held fantasy and someday make the move together to Hawaii. And, of course, there was the biggest *maybe* of all — maybe Chase wasn't destined to remain a roamosexual for the rest of his days. Monogamy suddenly seemed less like a dumb gig and more like a plausible prospect. With so many extraordinary elements coming together all at once, Chase could barely believe his life had suddenly stumbled into so much blessed bliss.

Strange, warm and enlivening sensations elevated his spirit. He appreciated how lucky he was to suddenly be a part of the kind of heavenly relationship you usually only hear about in love songs. For the first time in years, there was meaning in his life. Finally, without even looking for it, an honest-to-goodness romance had shown up at his doorstep, unannounced, and was not just sticking around, but also ripening, maturing, blossoming into a reality. No longer a loner, Chase finally met someone with whom he could be vulnerable, flaws and all; someone with whom he might actually get to share his life.

The taxi crossed the Fifty-Ninth Street Bridge, and Chase turned to look back again, back over the outline of Manhattan's dazzling skyline. He reflected back on the bounty of the week he'd just spent, and realized it was perhaps the most fulfilling emotional experience of his life. And, although he knew not how nor where their bi-coastal liaison might head next, or where it might eventually wind up, something inside him guessed he might never again in his life come to enjoy so much contentment, so euphoric a moment. While pondering all this, he surprised no one more than himself when he next began to cry. *Cry.*

Him: the Coach. Coach Chase: confirmed roamosexual and co-founder of his and Stack's Muscle Daddy Academy. Chase yanked his handkerchief from his pants pocket and wondered whether this inexplicable, uninvited rush of tears was emanating from his supreme happiness, or from some deeper, bittersweet regret? There was no way he could know for sure.

He was gratified that he and Hunter had just shared such an exceptional time together, but he also felt a wave of despondency washing over him because his euphoric bonding with his new boyfriend had come so swiftly to an abrupt end.

How much longer, he wondered, could their extended honeymoon last? And how different would things become between them once that happened? Would the extreme heat of their sexcapades eventually grow as stale and as flat as Chase anticipated? And just how much longer could they both keep lit the fiery torch of their scalding sexual attraction? Just how much time would pass, before, following convention, they would grow weary of one another and then, like so many loving couples before, devolve into the day-to-day antagonisms, the running hostilities, the typical over-reactions, the taking one another for granted, the half-truths and the panoply of grievances that so often characterized "normal" coupled relationships?

As the taxi barreled its way through traffic, retreating from the enchanted isle of Manhattan, it headed directly into the bowels of Queens, straight out to the airport.

Instinctively, Atlas sensed Chase's melancholy, and so he sat up and slowly licked Chase's face, gently lapping up the last of his master's bittersweet tears.

No doubt about it. Chase Hyde was in love.

* * * *

BOOK TWO:

TRUE JOCK

"I have been in love once, many times"

— Marlene Dietrich

CHASE HYDE — COACH-IN-TRAINING

When Chase's father, Murray Hyde, opened Hyde Motors in the late fifties in car-happy Southern California, it was the first dealership to offer pricey Jaguars in the rapidly developing Newport Beach area of Orange County. His successful franchise was ideally situated on the Pacific Coast Highway.

Chase's mother, Elizabeth, perennially tanned and always fashionably attired, was an attractive blonde whose vanity drove the upkeep of her appearance. From the day she returned home from the hospital with Baby Chase, she felt devoid of maternal instincts. Elizabeth also had a *thing* about dirt and germs, and detested the very idea of cleaning her baby's butt or wiping his runny nose.

In total contrast, the young father remained steadfastly dedicated to his son's well-being. Conscientious, caring, consistently on call, he willingly bounced out of bed in the middle of the night to warm a baby bottle and administer Chase's feeding. He never once griped about changing his infant son's soiled diapers. He never tired of humming a soft lullaby to the little fellow while rocking him to sleep. Murray was so attentive, he quickly captured his little boy's unflagging devotion.

Elizabeth didn't care to compete with her husband for their son's affections. Her partner's commitment to Chase was so consummate, she simply caved in to his more assertive nature, and did what any indifferent parent might — she hired a nanny to tend to the baby, and a cleaning lady to take care of the house. Slowly, she gave up trying to become a better mother as she abandoned the battle for their son and retreated into the cloudy comforts provided by alcohol. Vodka martinis became her drug of choice, oblivion her chosen objective, extended lunches in stylish Fashion Square with her equally unhappy, married girlfriends her main avenue of escape.

*   *   *   *

Chase was raised in his parents' sprawling house in an upscale area of Newport Beach boasting manicured lawns and flowering jacaranda trees. Other little boys in the neighborhood, especially those from broken homes, could only envy the indestructible bond Chase enjoyed with his father. The connection they formed was so strong, it held little room for Elizabeth. By her own choice, she wanted no membership within their private circle of closeness, the special domain of intimacy that became their exclusive For-Men-Only club.

On any given evening, as soon as Murray returned from his dealership, little Chase dropped whatever he was doing and made a mad dash for the front door so he could greet his father with their big nightly hug hello. In time, the two of them refined a ritual greeting of roughhousing in which Murray pretended his little boy was beating him up.

"Stop! Stop! You're killing me!" Murray howled with glee as he made believe the small fists Chase was pounding against his rugged torso were really hurting him.

"Look at me, Daddy!" Chase bragged, while hovering over his father and flexing his thin, little boy biceps. "Look at my big muscles!"

"Man-oh-man!" Murray pretended to be awed. "You sure are one strong little boy!" Murray wrapped strong, protective arms around Chase and hugged him tightly. "Hey, Kiddo," he asked, rhetorically, looking his son straight in the eye. "Who do you love?"

"DADDY!" Chase hollered out boldly, on cue, and returned his father's hug with all his might. "I love my Daddy!"

*   *   *   *

Bulldogs were the school mascot back when Murray attended Newport High, and he always felt an inexplicable attraction to the wrinkled, tubby fireplugs. Maybe that's why it came as no surprise when, returning home from Hyde Motors one early evening, he held aloft in each hand an adorable nine-week-old English bulldog puppy — a baby boy and a baby girl he named Napoleon and Josephine.

Having a pair of pups around their house would be good for protection, he assured his apprehensive wife. He put off telling her he also planned to raise a dynasty of champion bulldogs.

Whenever he was home, Murray played with little Chase and the bulldogs. All their roughhousing and camaraderie soon left Elizabeth swaying in the matrimonial breeze, all but fending for herself.

Eight weeks after Josephine ended her second heat, she began panting even heavier than usual one early morning, while circling in place, and scratching at the floor, as if fashioning a nest. It was soon apparent the bitch was going into labor.

Over the course of the next twelve hours, with both Murray and Chase supportively serving as mid-husbands, the beefy bulldog panted away non-stop beneath the vanity in the master bedroom and eventually gave birth to a litter of four perfectly wrinkled pups.

Assisting Josephine with the delivery of her bully pups was a glorious bonding experience for father and son. When he returned to his dealership the next day, Murray celebrated the birth of the pups by handing out expensive cigars to all his employees.

Elizabeth had never been particularly fond of dogs, found them too smelly and too messy, and never stopped expressing her disapproval of them.

By the time the four new pups started pooping all over the property, Murray knew his wife wouldn't like it, but he still went ahead and sold only two of the pups. He decided to keep Attila, the litter's only male, as well as Scarlett, one of Josephine's female pups, for his budding brace of bulldogs. The messy situation quickly turned into one more issue over which Elizabeth and Murray incessantly squabbled.

*   *   *   *

Murray never stopped playing ball with his boy. He pitched to the little fellow inside the confines of batting cages when he was seven, tossed a football back and forth with him in their backyard as soon as he turned nine, and shot hoops with him on the courts by the beach whenever he could break away.

When litter mates Attila and Scarlett grew up, they mated, producing still another bountiful, incestuous litter of three bully pups.

Again, Murray grew so attached to the little wrinkled beasts, he insisted upon keeping one of the little females, whom he named Bathsheba. And again he and Elizabeth fought hard, loud, and often about the constant mess and never-ending musky *essence de bulldog* perpetually permeating their home.

The bulldogs became a major part of their lives. One litter after the next, Murray and Chase grew so emotionally attached to their precious pups, they insisted upon holding on to at least one pooch from each set of offspring. At any given time, there were between five and seven bulldogs moping about the Hyde household.

Working as a team, Murray and Chase trained and then entered the best bred of their wheezing, drooling brood at AKC-sponsored dog shows all across Southern California.

With the passing of seasons, Jezebel begat Salome and Rasputin, who in turn produced Cleopatra. When it became Cleopatra's turn to mate, she had so many complications with her pregnancy, Murray's veterinarian performed an emergency Cesarean section which bestowed upon the Hyde dynasty a very wrinkled Godzilla, and a very youthful Methuselah.

In time, the walls of the Hyde den sported the framed blue-and-white Win, Place, and Show ribbons won by the bully champs, even as Murray's desk became cluttered with kitschy trophies.

Elizabeth gave up trying to maintain a reasonable home and eventually acquiesced, accepting the fleas hiding out in the carpeting and the dog hairs in plain sight everywhere as pieces of the sordid baggage her husband brought along, back when she so stupidly agreed to marry him in the first place.

*   *   *   *

A week before Chase's twelfth birthday, Murray surprised his family when he flew the three of them to Honolulu, first class, where they spent a week at the Royal Hawaiian Hotel on Waikiki Beach.

By the early 1970's, sun blocks and protective tanning creams with SPFs had only recently been introduced to a still disinterested public. On the first day of their Hawaiian vacation, Elizabeth stayed true to her Southern California beachside upbringing and, rather than safeguarding her hide, Mrs. Hyde instead slathered herself in the more popular, mythical mixture of baby oil laced with several drops of iodine. She planned to expose her skin for about thirty minutes, poolside. Her skin glistened as she stretched out on a chaise lounge. While basking in the semi-tropical sun, she polished off a trio of Mai Tais and soon drifted to sleep for several hours.

By day's end, Elizabeth was scorched, burnt, and soon so blistery, she had no choice but to spend the rest of the week inside their hotel room, hidden from the sun, coated from head to toe in aloe vera gel, while Murray and Chase both spent their vacation in the blue Pacific, learning how to surf.

The well-formed waves at Waikiki often roll in so slowly, it makes the world famous beach an ideal spot for beginners to pick up the basics of the age-old sport of Hawaiian kings.

Every morning of their vacation, Murray and Chase awoke early, downed a fast breakfast on the hotel's lanai, and then smeared a dab of zinc oxide across their noses before they picked up their rented surfboards and dashed into the ocean.

They spent the whole day surfing together, paddling out, bobbing up and down in the water, waiting and watching and doing their best to catch any elusive wave at just the right point, before jumping up on their boards for a wild ride. They were both natural athletes and so, after several days first spent mostly in frustration, both of them wiping out almost as soon as they got up, they each soon began getting the hang of it.

By week's end, father and son both managed to stay up on their boards, often maintaining their precarious balances while riding the three-to-four foot greenies to shore.

Chase loved surfing with his father in Hawaii. The warm ocean water that close to the Equator was an inviting, enthralling hue of azure blue. The temperate trade winds that casually breezed through the towering palms carried with them the intoxicating perfume of plumeria. Toss in the most dramatic of dazzling, Technicolor sunsets, and a just-turned twelve-year-old Chase was hands down the happiest he'd ever been in his young life.

By the end of their vacation, neither Murray nor Chase wanted to leave, while a still blistery Elizabeth could hardly wait to get the hell out of there. She'd grown weary of the cloying sweetness of island rum punches, and looked forward to reclaiming the purity of her precious Russian vodka.

Chase was still too young to know much about what he really wanted out of life. However, he was certain Hawaii was his paradise found, and he promised himself some time in his future he'd find some way to return.

*   *   *   *

Not unlike so many other pre-pubescent boys his age, Chase was your basic ninety-eight-pound weakling, just another scrawny Southern California kid.

However, not long after the skinny little boy turned twelve, he had his first exposure to major muscle that wasn't simply a cartoon superhero. It came about as a seemingly innocuous passing moment, one that, nonetheless, instantly turned into a life-altering milestone he would never forget.

It occurred one late afternoon after school, while his mother was still at the Newport Plaza mall with her girlfriends. Chase was in the den, lazily wrestling around with bullies Rembrandt and Methuselah, while half-watching some dumb afternoon game show. Before launching into their game of wits, the TV host congenially interviewed a contestant and learned that the big man was a bodybuilder recently named Mr. America. The host then asked if the champ wouldn't mind giving the audience a look at his prize-winning physique.

The country's current reigning muscle champion hardly minded, and happily exhibited his trophy-winning body. He pulled off his over-sized sweat shirt and revealed a mountainous mass of amazing torso muscles the likes of which Chase had never before witnessed.

While Mr. America flexed his big biceps and bounced his massive pecs up and down to the appreciation and bemusement of the studio audience, Chase stared at the screen in awe, even as he experienced his first full-blown, pre-teen erection.

He had no idea why the sight of such a well-built man flexing and showing off such spectacular muscles got him suddenly so curiously aroused, but the splendid tingling sensation running through his fast-developing gonads made him realize, even while still so young, that the future course of his sporting life was suddenly made clear. Inspired, he knew he would have to build up his own muscles so that someday he too might look even remotely like the incredible man on TV.

That night, when Murray returned home late from Hyde Motors, Chase greeted him with their usual roughhouse hello, and afterwards begged his father to buy him some exercise weights so that he, too, might grow up to look like the powerful muscleman he'd seen earlier that day on TV. Murray liked the idea, thought it seemed a fine way for his boy to start strengthening and building up his peewee body.

Several months later, on Christmas morning, when Chase ripped open a gift-wrapped box from beneath the twinkling, ornament-laden Douglas fir, he found a junior set of purple plastic dumbbells, each weighing in at thirteen pounds, one for every year of his young life.

Elated, Chase threw his arms around his father, hugging him with great affection and genuine gratitude.

"Glad you like them so much, little buddy," his father told him.

"Dad, these are great — just great — you have no idea!"

"Now just use them to help you grow up big and strong."

"You bet I will, Dad! That's the plan." Chase bellowed excitedly, and then turned to hug his mother and thank her as well for the great Christmas gift.

"Just be careful with those silly things," Elizabeth admonished her son while reservedly returning his hug. "They were your father's idea, not mine. Just don't be breaking things, swinging them all over the place."

"Don't worry, Mom," Chase assured her. "I promise I'll be extra-special careful."

Chase carried his prized new lightweight dumbbells into his room and immediately incorporated them by improvising the execution of several basic exercises. By the time he laid to rest the baby weights, a few minutes later, he already felt stronger.

*   *   *   *

From that day on, young Chase Hyde trained religiously, working out with his insubstantial weights every afternoon after school. Steadfast in his mission, he conscientiously curled the plastic dumbbells up and down until his thin biceps ached. He pressed his light weights over his head repeatedly, hoping to bring a hint of definition to his shoulders. Lying flat on his back, he extended his arms out wide, then forcefully squeezed them back together in an arch, all keyed up to build up his puny pecs.

One late afternoon, while exercising in his room, Chase lay on his back atop his bed, slowly and diligently pressing his thirteen-pounders up and down toward the ceiling. As his concerted set of ten reps neared their end, and as fresh blood coursed wildly throughout his chest cavity, he experienced what he quickly surmised was his first orgasm. The amazing sensation churned from somewhere deep within his groin before it rose up and then ejected from his urethra in a pulsating wave of spurts that spewed forth a thick gush of gism that blanketed his jock strap. The sensation of so much unexpected saturation felt so alien, he dropped his weights to the floor.

After the thrill of that first incredible orgasm, the confusing sensation over what his body had just discharged, Chase quickly connected the dots regarding his feelings for muscle. At the same time, he inadvertently unveiled the immutable blueprint for his forthcoming sexual identity.

He promised himself he would always, but always remain in training. He could never stop working out and would stay in the best shape possible. He would remain forever faithful to the fortress that was his body. He would focus on his new fixation: getting bigger and stronger, and building up more and more muscle by pumping iron. He would devote himself to bodybuilding, his newly self-anointed lifestyle.

*   *   *   *

One Sunday in May, Chase, along with Evita and Caligula, the latest puppy additions to the long line of Hyde bulldogs, spent another satisfying day with his dad at Hyde Motors. The late spring afternoon was sunny and pleasant, the showroom crowded with potential buyers.

Caligula, barely nine months old and still a scamp, spent the day wagging his butt and getting fawned over by visitors in the showroom. Evita, by then a more mature year-and-a-half, preferred spending her visit curled up in the back seat of one of the Jags, blissfully snoring away, her apnea in carefree abandon.

By early evening, almost time to close, Murray walked into the office and promised Chase that just as soon as he accompanied one final, highly motivated car buyer on the shortest of road tests once around the neighborhood, father and son would quickly head over to the local driving range. Their plan was to work on their golf swings by slamming through several buckets of balls.

As Chase watched his father walking behind the expensive luxury sedan quietly idling at the open garage door entrance, he also noticed the zealous would-be customer already in place behind the wheel of the Jaguar, clearly raring to go.

Before Murray had the chance to get there, however, the prospective auto buyer made a foolhardy effort to show off for his girlfriend who was waving at him giddily from across the showroom. When he depressed the gas pedal, he shifted out of neutral and inadvertently mistook reverse for drive. Instead of heading forward, out toward the street, the car lurched backward and slammed into Murray, knocking him down, pinning his pelvis beneath one of the rear wheels, and crushing the lower part of his body, right there in the crowded showroom, right in front of Chase.

"OH, NO — DADDY!" Chase screamed out as he bolted from the office into the showroom.

At the same time, the disoriented test driver realized the error of his idiotic move and switched gears. The gesture compounded the disaster when the Jag heaved forward and drove back over Murray's body, before it finally rolled out of the showroom, onto Newport Beach Boulevard. There, the muddled and by then terrified driver finally finished his road test when he slammed on the brakes and brought the sleek, new Jaguar to a screeching halt.

In the chaos and hysteria that ensued, with salesmen and customers running everywhere, screaming incoherently, Chase dropped to his knees at his father's side, cradled Murray's head in his lap, and sobbed, "My God, Daddy! Oh, no! Oh, no!"

Murray Hyde knew he was in serious trouble because he couldn't feel a damn thing. Dazed, he looked up in his state of extreme shock and, as streams of blood flowed out from the sides of his mouth and oozed from his nostrils, and his battered body quivered and shook, he quietly moaned, "Don't worry, Son — doesn't hurt. I'll be fine."

"Don't die, Daddy!" Chase pleaded in a pure panic. "Please don't die!"

Struggling to summon a last breath, Chase's father instead coughed up a final thought along with some blood as, with a soft mutter, he asked, "Hey, Kiddo — who do you love?"

"Daddy, Daddy!" Chase cried out in horror. "I love my Daddy!"

Fading fast, Murray Hyde managed a smile, even as his eyes froze in place, his head flopped to the side, and he was gone.

*   *   *   *

Murray Hyde's funeral, three days later, was a somber and relatively dignified affair, once you got past the melodrama of Chase's mother, heavily intoxicated, theatrically draping herself across her husband's coffin in the heightened hysteria of her inconsolable grief.

When a fourteen-year-old boy witnesses something as horrific as his own father's violent death, it takes a toll. Chase dealt with the tragedy the easiest way he knew how: by suppressing it. The youngster remained surprisingly composed throughout the secular service, almost as if he might be attending the funeral of someone else's dad. Even afterwards, at the cemetery, while his mother ranted, practically jumping into the open plot as they slowly lowered Murray's coffin into the ground, Chase remained non-reactive, present in body, but certainly not there in either mind or spirit. Instead, he concealed his inner desolation, and focused only on comforting his overwrought mother.

Elizabeth was in deep despair over her husband's untimely demise, not only because she was so unprepared for its random cruelty, but also because it saddled her with so much guilt. She'd been having a yearlong, extra-marital affair with one of the car salesmen in Murray's showroom. To alleviate her remorse, she drank. But the more she drank, the more remorseful she became. And the more remorseful she became, the more she drank.

* * * *

Jerry Petrillo was a six-foot-two, two-hundred-thirty-two-pound, beefy bear of an electrical engineer who worked at the Lockheed plant in Long Beach, where he designed interlocking wiring for fighter jets.

For a straight man in his late twenties, Petrillo was still in relatively good shape, once you overlooked the pronounced protrusion of his imposing beer belly. He lived in Newport Beach with his wife and their infant daughter, near the end of Chase's street.

Petrillo enjoyed spending time with his family and relaxing around his property. When he moved into the neighborhood a few years earlier, he designed and assembled on one side of his two-car garage a makeshift, eight-foot-square workout area.

The engineer constructed a sturdy bench press for his at-home gym, and installed a small weight rack filled with sets of dumbbells, ten pounds to sixty. He worked out on a regular basis, pumping iron, reaping the feel-good benefits of staying big and strong.

One afternoon, after school, Chase strolled down the block, Cleopatra and Zeus ambling along on either side of him. They had no need for leashes as they always kept apace. When Chase passed the Petrillo driveway, Zeus stopped in his tracks and suddenly sat down on the pavement and stared up the driveway. The garage door was raised, and that was when Chase first spotted Petrillo inside his workout area, astride his ersatz bench press, struggling to thrust his forty-five-pound barbell, loaded with two forty-five-pound plates on either side.

Drawn to the scene as if by some seductive siren, Chase sauntered up the driveway and, as soon as Petrillo finished pumping out the last rep of his weighty set, he sat up and extended an amicable, neighborly hello. "I like your dogs," he told Chase, as he caught his breath and scratched Zeus's backside. "Looks like they're strong and in real good shape."

"Looks can be deceptive," said Chase, bending down to pat his panting canine companions. "Cleopatra's going off to be mated next week and Zeus is an epileptic. He's on more medication than Elvis Presley."

"Impressive," observed Petrillo.

"Yeah," Chase agreed. "Before my father died, I promised him I'd keep the Hyde dynasty of bulldogs going."

Chase then told his brawny neighbor how he had started lifting very light weights in his room a couple of years ago, but that when it came to bodybuilding, he was still pretty much a novice. He then asked if Petrillo wouldn't mind demonstrating a primary exercise or two, as he was keen to get more deeply involved in the manly pursuit of building muscle.

The good neighbor patiently performed a pair of basic pecs exercises on his bench press, and then supervised as Chase pumped out a much lighter version. As Chase then headed home, Petrillo called out and invited his young muscle buddy to come back and work out with him any time.

Chase jumped at his neighbor's sociable offer, and early the next evening, walked back over to Petrillo's house. He arrived at the driveway just as the beefy man was starting his workout.

"Hey, Chase, good timing!" The big man called out. "How about if we pump some iron together?"

Petrillo was a born muscle coach, Chase a conscientious learner and eager team player. Despite their wide age difference and disparity in sizes, they worked out for the next hour together, pumping up their biceps and triceps.

The following morning, Chase felt empowered when he awoke and felt a welcome soreness in his upper arms. The pleasant ache signaled he had successfully broken down the muscles in play, setting them up for growth.

As if on automatic pilot, the eager, would-be bodybuilder returned to Petrillo's garage again early that evening, all stoked to work another pair of major body groups.

Petrillo was actually glad to see the teenager, even liked the idea of maybe taking him under his muscular wing. The friendly, supportive tone he then projected as he unveiled to Chase some of the intricacies of pumping iron convinced Chase he could not have found a more accomplished muscle mentor to excite him about the virtues of training hard.

After proficiently pumping iron together through several more workouts, the big man and the growing boy agreed to lift weights together on a regular basis. Chase and his older muscle guru pumped iron in the early evening, four times a week, as soon as the electrical engineer got home from work and right after Chase finished his homework.

Petrillo showed him how to properly use the long barbell, as well as the compact dumbbells and how to always — but always — incorporate perfect form. Petrillo insisted that every single rep be executed with precision. He made certain they used an appropriate weight with every exercise — never too heavy, never too light.

Petrillo was impressed with Chase's enthusiasm and dedication, grateful he'd finally found someone who so quickly caught on as to the best way to spot him when he went to failure pressing his heaviest weights. Although neither of them felt the need to acknowledge it aloud, Petrillo took on the role of deputy dad as easily as Chase eased his way into serving as surrogate son.

*　　　*　　　*　　　*

Chase's mirror soon began reflecting subtle, positive changes in his body. Along with his gradual progress, working out with Petrillo had another bonus: it allowed him to escape his unhappy home life, at least for a couple of hours.

It was a relief to get away from the invariably inebriated state in which his mother seemed to thrive. A closet tippler, Elizabeth Hyde stole furtive sips from her Stoli in the freezer, nipping away from early afternoon into late evening, until she blithely climbed into bed and passed out.

Chase trained with Petrillo in his garage with a consistent regularity for over a year, until his muscle mentor got bumped up to Chief Engineer at his aerospace company, and was transferred across the country, to their sister plant, in Lansing, Michigan.

When Petrillo moved his family two thousand miles away, he took all his belongings with him, and that included his improvised bench press and extensive set of free weights. Before he left, however, he worked out with Chase one last time, and encouraged his protégé to keep up with his pumping iron, especially since the youngster was making such impressive strides.

Chase took Petrillo's words to heart, and signed up for a membership at the nearby YMCA. There, he continued bodybuilding three, sometimes four days a week. While others swam laps in the indoor pool, played volleyball, or shot hoops in the gymnasium, Chase headed straight for the weight room.

Throughout his first year of high school, Chase often felt distracted in the school locker room when the best-built of his classmates stepped in and out of their gym gear. What invariably caught his eye was the young, finely tuned athlete: the freshman gymnast, the sophomore track star, the junior wrestler, the senior quarterback. At fourteen, the future hunk stood five-foot-five and, while actually starting to develop an athletic-looking physique, weighed in after gym class at a still lanky one-hundred-thirty-two pounds.

Finally a sophomore at fifteen, and bigger and stronger than the year before, Chase, along with so many teenagers in his beachside community, began trekking down to the ocean, where once again, he took up surfing.

Riding the waves of the oceans atop projectiles that looked like sleek ironing boards, surfing had by then transformed from a national craze into big business. Pastime for some, preoccupation to others, it made its way up and down the oceanic coastlines of the country, and carved its niche across the Gulf Coast and throughout the Caribbean. Chase treasured being a part of its ongoing cultural explosion, and looked forward to towing his big board behind him on rollers as he biked the few blocks over to the beach every weekend. He spent almost every Saturday and Sunday, from early morning until just after dusk, splashing about, riding the shore breakers. A major part of his excitement about improving as a surfer was that it kept kindled the precious memory of that glorious week he'd spent with his dad in Honolulu years earlier.

Chase conquered the waves on a ten-foot board long after they fell from favor and were summarily replaced by the shorter, more lightweight boards that were so much easier to maneuver when hot-dogging. The teenager had never been much interested in executing fancy tricks on the waves, so he felt no calling to ride a smaller board. What he enjoyed most was the way the heavier paddling required by the longer board broadened his delts, built up his pecs, added mass and shape to his biceps, his traps, and the width of his back. He also kept up with his bodybuilding, and continued lifting weights midweek down at the Y. With his pubescent hormones flowing, he developed rapidly, growing inch after welcome inch.

In his senior year at Newport High, Chase took a class in creative writing, and first began composing short stories. Creating imaginative plot lines came easily to him, and his writing instructor singled out Chase's compositions as the most skillful storytelling in the class.

By the time Chase graduated from Newport High, the persistence of his weight training had paid off. Nearly six feet tall, the eighteen-year-old tipped the scales at one-hundred-sixty-five pounds. He concentrated on crunching out so many sit-ups that he built up the kind of perfectly chiseled, adolescent eight-pack usually seen on champion gymnasts or Greek statues. And even if he was still youthfully lean and lanky, his emergent muscles were already well-defined, auspiciously carrying the gifted proportions he'd inherited from his dad.

Being smart only added to his appeal, and after he scored well on his college boards, he was accepted into UCLA.

As a high school graduation gift, Elizabeth acknowledged Chase's achievement by surprising him with his first car — a snappy, if used, dark blue Ford Fairlane convertible.

Before heading off to his higher education as a freshman the following September, Chase took the whole summer off. Every week, with Cleopatra and Zeus panting in unison alongside him in the passenger seat, with the top down and his surfboard projecting out from the rear seat like a missile, Chase headed south to Dana Point. When he arrived beachside at Doheny State Park, he pitched a tent and spent the next few days camping out and riding the greenies at what was then still the best kept secret surfing spot in all of Southern California.

By summer's end, Chase was an accomplished surfer. All his strenuous exercise, and so much paddling through the water, complemented by his time and effort in the gym, propelled him into a late-adolescent peak of great shape. All his overexposure to the Southern California sun had by then also bronzed the eighteen-year-old to a golden copper-brown.

Over the long Labor Day weekend at the end of his untroubled summer's sabbatical, the state beach in Dana Point was even more crowded with surfers and other visitors than at any time all season long. Chase pulled into Doheny early Friday afternoon and had the good fortune to grab one of the last available campsites facing the ocean. He quickly erected his small, two-man pup tent in the shade of a huge pine, and then placed Cleopatra and Zeus safely inside, where the old dogs could snore into the sea breeze while getting their much-needed beauty rest. He then toted his board down to the shore and spent the rest of his pressure-free afternoon gracefully catching sets of consistently rolling, four-foot waves.

Chase bobbed up and down in the water until long after the sun dipped below the horizon and the surrounding visibility grew so dim that he was forced to call it a day. After collecting driftwood along the beach, he built a small fire in the grilling pit at his site. Cleopatra and Zeus lay sprawled out on the sand next to the campfire, and the white noise of their synchronized snoring kept him company.

Chase wrapped a couple of potatoes in foil and buried them within the grill's fiery coals, slowly baking them. Once the roasted spuds were almost cooked, he took four sirloin burgers out from his small Igloo cooler and placed the defrosted meat evenly across the top of the grill. He also popped open one of the cans of Bud from the twin six-packs he'd brought along. The burgers cooked quickly. Chase flipped two of them onto a paper plate and hand-fed one to Cleopatra, the other to Zeus. The bullies slavered down their dinner with enough chomping, snorting and saliva-driven gusto to make any non-bulldog fancier quickly lose his appetite.

A well-built, athletic-looking fellow, scruffily appealing in a counter-culture sort of way, crawled out from the adjoining tent, and watched with amusement as Chase fed his ravenous beasts.

"Smells good, Dude," he called out. "Whatcha cookin'?" Clad only in a pair of torn, cut-off jeans, the surfer sported a full head of long and unruly, curly blond hair.

"Just some burgers, a couple of burnt baked potatoes, a few cans of not-so-cold brew" Chase told him.

"Dude!" The surfer cheered, good-naturedly. "Sounds like a major feast!"

"Well, these last two burgers are nearly ready," Chase told him. "You're welcome to join me."

The blond hippie hurried over to Chase's campsite. "I'm Tyler," he said amiably, extending an open hand in friendship. "Guess I must've crashed. Wanted to wake up while the snack bar was still open, so I could pick up some chow."

"Oh, you mean the ptomaine tavern? They shut down a few hours ago." Chase extended his hand in greeting. "I'm Chase."

"Glad to meet you, man," Tyler smiled as he shook Chase's hand. "Last night, I drove all the way from San Jose, just to get down here for the early morning waves. Man, they were smokin', totally bitchin'. Rode 'em 'til I crashed. But I ain't had a bite since breakfast."

"Then break your fast, Pilgrim," Chase said as he scooped the third burger onto a paper plate and handed it to his impromptu dinner guest. "Hope you like it rare."

"Hey, thanks, man," Tyler said, as he crouched down next to Chase and pulled a small tin box out from a pocket in his cut-offs. "Seeing as how you're supplying the nourishment, how 'bout if I contribute some merriment?"

Tyler popped open his small tin box, pulled out a sloppily rolled joint and held it up in the air, chuckling, "A little something from Mother Nature with no chemicals, no preservatives, just plenty of zip!" Tyler reached into his other pocket, extricated a cigarette lighter, fired up the joint, inhaled a whale of a toke, and then held it deep inside his lungs as he passed the contraband weed over to his host.

Chase didn't want to appear too innocent or uncool, so he cavalierly inhaled a deep drag off the joint and immediately launched into a hacking coughing fit.

"Go easy, man!" Tyler advised, patting Chase on the back. "This stuff is Northern California Sensimilla. Total dynamite, Dude. Acclimate slowly. Go on, man — take another hit!"

Chase inhaled a second puff, this time with less urgency, and then relaxed as the smoke filtered down his esophagus and into his expanding lungs. "Thanks, buddy!" he said, throatily, handing the joint back to Tyler.

Several hours later, full from hamburgers and baked potatoes, inebriated after downing six cans of Chase's Buds between them, and stoned from still more of Tyler's potent marijuana, they became fast surfing buddies.

Tyler was a twenty-year-old college dropout and major stoner who spent his nights driving up and down the California coast with his surfboard stored in the back of his dilapidated Ford woody station wagon. He was in the habit of crashing in one surfing spot after another, and was content to spend this phase of his life in pursuit of little more than the perfect beach, the perfect wave, the perfect joint. He supported his alternate lifestyle by selling grass to other surfers he met along his travels.

In time, the campfire's coals smoldered to ash. Chase and Tyler agreed they were each exhausted from their hours spent riding the waves earlier that day. They exchanged gentlemanly good nights before each then retired to his respective tent. Surrounded by his snoring bulldogs, Chase fell into a deep sleep in a matter of minutes.

Early Saturday morning, just after daybreak, Tyler opened the flap of Chase's tent and stuck his curly blond head inside. He held out a Styrofoam cup of coffee in each hand and surprised Chase and the snoring bulldogs when he announced, "Rise and shine, all you sleeping beauties. Snack bar just opened, and more importantly … surf's up!"

From within the questionable comfort of his sleeping bag, Chase stretched, yawned, and groggily asked, "What time is it?"

"Who cares?" Tyler shrugged as he handed Chase a steaming cup of coffee. "Time to hit the waves. They're coming in nice 'n steady. So far, not so much as a hint of wind. Great height, ideal shape, couldn't be more perfect. Up and at 'em, Chase. We ain't got all morning!"

*   *   *   *

They rode the waves together the entire day. While out on the water, Chase and his new surfing pal exchanged helpful board-to-board tips on how they might each improve their personal styles while navigating their precarious liquid paths to shore.

That night, as the sun went down behind him, Chase used the outdoor shower to rinse the salt water off his body. Back inside his tent, he stepped out of his jock strap and surfing trunks, and donned a fresh pair of gym shorts. After he gathered more wood and got another campfire going, he went to the tent next door and invited Tyler to again join him and Cleopatra and Zeus at his campsite, to grill up some wieners, scorch another pair of baked potatoes, and chug the last of his brews. Tyler accepted the invite and again offered to contribute to their extended cookout the reserve of his stash of marijuana.

Several hours later, once they were again blithely stoned as well as intoxicated and serene, the surfing buddies complimented one another on having such well-developed bodies, and talked about how dedicated they each were to staying in shape.

When a late summer rolling fog swept in from the sea and quickly blanketed the beach in a chilly covering of thick cloud, Chase and Tyler moved their party inside, within the covering of Chase's tent, where they shared the last of Tyler's stash. On their backs, next to one another, their only source of light was the smoldering of the joint passing back and forth between them.

"I got kind of a small confession to make," Tyler announced with a nervous chuckle, as he deeply inhaled and passed the end of the roach. "No big deal either way, man."

"Shoot!" said Chase.

"I really dig girls," Tyler confessed, his eyes peeled to the top of the tent. "Love the way they smell and feel. So don't get me wrong. It's not like I'm queer, or anything like that. But I'd be lying if I didn't tell you I also sometimes like to see another guy get off, but only if he's really well built like, you know ... like *you*."

"How do you mean?" Chase asked, half in innocence, half in sudden unbridled excitement.

"How 'bout I just show you what I mean?" Tyler answered, as he sat up, moved over and knelt between Chase's legs. "Just lie there on your sleeping bag and relax, okay? Might even help if you close your eyes. I'll do all the work, okay, man?"

As a major boner sprang to life within his shorts, Chase clasped his hands behind his head and allowed, "Take your best shot ... man!"

Inside the darkened tent, with near-zero visibility, and both bulldogs banished to a nearby corner, rhythmically snoring into the dark night, Tyler eased himself forward and slowly pulled down his surfing buddy's gym shorts.

"Cowabunga!" Tyler exclaimed in surfer speak the moment his hand came to rest around the girth of his buddy's cock. "You sure did a good job of hiding this big dog inside your surfing trunks."

"One of the plusses of using a jock strap," Chase acknowledged with a sheepish grin.

"This really turns me on, man. I'm gonna take it real slow, okay?"

"I'm not going anywhere," said Chase. "Take all the time you need."

Without another word, Tyler then began administering Chase's first, full-fledged blow job. Several minutes later, the surfer-hippie's unexpectedly talented mouth brought his new friend to the point of an explosive orgasm. Chase didn't want to disturb any of the other surfing aficionados already asleep in surrounding tents, so he tried his best to muffle the measured joy of his glorious release. Tyler had difficulty accepting the full size of Chase's robust thickness, and choked and gagged, even as he did his best to gulp down all of his surfing buddy's copious load.

Once the vehement passion of the moment passed, Tyler flopped back down and collapsed alongside Chase, shoulder to shoulder. Feeling oddly awkward, neither of them knew quite what to say as, slowly, they caught their breath. After another few uncomfortable moments, Chase drifted dreamily off into an untroubled slumber, and was soon snoring almost as loudly as Cleopatra and Zeus.

In silent slow-motion, Tyler eased his way out from Chase's tent and crawled into his own nearby shelter, where he, too, plopped down atop his grubby sleeping bag and crashed.

Chase awoke early Sunday morning, raised the flap on his canvas domicile, and was surprised when he saw Tyler's tent no longer there. His new surfing companion, with whom he had bonded so strongly, had evidently risen just before dawn and split. Rather than confront his guilt, Chase's newfound surfing buddy abandoned the campsite and his guilt without so much as a "Later, Dude!"

*   *   *   *

The dorms at UCLA had a strict No Pets policy, and wouldn't allow Cleopatra and Zeus to room with Chase. Elizabeth wanted no part of looking after the smelly beasts. She was too preoccupied with the maintenance of her intoxication and her shopping sprees over at Newport Plaza. But Chase was unwilling to part with the latest in the long line of his father's bulldogs, so just before entering UCLA in mid-September, he rented a small bachelor apartment a few blocks off campus, in Westwood.

By the time he started college, Chase had already faced as well as embraced his sexuality as a fact of life. After the excitement of his initial man-to-man carnal experience with Tyler, he was eager for further exploration. He already knew he didn't care much for the notion of monogamy. To a budding roamosexual like Chase, marriage or even settling into a long-term relationship with another man was little more than a one-way ticket to mediocrity, a heterosexually inspired invitation to a humdrum normalcy. For the time being, all he wanted was to fool around with the sexy masses of muscles on as many other well-built men as he could attract.

Freshman Chase put aside his principal avocation of surfing and again redirected his primary physical energies back into pumping iron. He threw himself into his workouts, lifting heavily and exercising hard, striving to slowly pack on still more size, yet at the same time, staying toned, cut, well-defined. He lifted with such fervor because he wanted to be at his muscular best whenever the next young man's hot body caught his eye. So long as he maintained his peak condition, he was confident he'd always attract the kind of muscular bodybuilder he preferred.

Since writing came so easily to him, Chase chose English as his major.

When not in class, many other male students joined rowdy campus fraternities, boisterously bingeing on steins of beer, while bragging incessantly, boasting about their endless pursuits of buxom co-eds.

When not in class, Chase spent much of his free time in the weight room of the school's gymnasium, steadfastly committed to his training. He enjoyed the company of like-minded bodybuilders, and could spot a well-formed set of biceps from across the quad. The way the material on a young man's tight sleeve stretched full when draping a thick and winning pair of guns was always a giveaway. Chase's sharp eye could detail how well someone was built from the breadth of a young man's back, from the slimness of his waist, even from the way the front of a snug shirt foretold a set of sexy pectorals lying in wait, just beneath the cotton.

Well-built jocks never had trouble attracting friends, and Chase was no exception. Other young men impressed with his athletic countenance were similarly drawn to his manly demeanor. Co-eds on campus found him highly attractive, and often found themselves charmed by his winning manner. Many of them flirted unabashedly in an effort to get to know him better. The moment he left a room, they often wanted to know if he was single and available. He was always polite with pretty girls who stopped to say hello. He kept private the predilections of his true nature, and rarely shared with them anything more than superficial conversation. His evident emotional distance, coupled with his charming reticence, his apparent unavailability, and the sense of mystery it created, only made him that much more appealing to their schoolgirl crushes. As a breeder, he would have been quite the ladies' man. Instead, he aimed his sights at the most attractive males of the species and became quite the man's man.

Having his own apartment afforded Chase a privacy not found in the rowdy dorms, so whenever he connected with a new muscle buddy, he had the luxury of inviting the hot guy back to his place off campus, under the pretext that they could hang out together.

Once back in Chase's small bachelor digs, he and his fresh, always well-built, still-closeted recruit kicked back as they downed a few brews and wrestled around with Zeus and Cleopatra. Sometimes, Chase and his new chum might smoke some weed if the other guy was carrying. After a while, Chase casually brought up such homo-erotically related topics as their training routines in the gym, or the progress of their mutual muscular development.

On those occasions when fortune prevailed and Chase ascertained that his new friend shared his fascination with muscle, he usually suggested they remove their shirts and show off their physiques for each other, maybe flex together before the mirror. Just as a *guy* thing, of course.

If Chase's bodybuilding buddy was eager to whip off his shirt, and if the bulge within the young man's shorts then sprang to life, Chase's guest could be counted upon to justify his behavior by mentioning *something* about how his real sexual orientation and erotic interest was, of course, focused mostly … on girls.

Chase was fine with that. Just because he had resolved his attraction to other men, didn't mean the guys he brought back to his place had to share his lack of discomfort. Still, no matter how strenuously they protested, while testifying to what they swore was their true heterosexual nature, Chase's closeted muscular recruits reliably took it to the next level, wanting to play out some long-repressed muscle fantasy.

Chase enjoyed indulging in lengthy and erotic sessions spent caressing groups of flexed muscles with another hot jock. Throughout any carnal encounter, Chase and his momentary muscle buddy always kept a safe emotional distance by never kissing, never going further than mutual masturbation, and certainly never ever fooling around with each other a second time.

Post orgasm, Chase's athletic classmates were often confused and guilt-ridden about their clandestine lapse over the edge of acceptability into the forbidden territory of same-sex behavior. Maybe that was why, whenever one of his new muscle buddies spotted him on campus afterwards, they usually went out of their way not to say hello.

So much consistent disengagement didn't bother Chase. After a while, he even grew accustomed to it. He was as eager to move on as were they. He had neither the time nor the patience for the pangs and pains of guilt, reasoning that if there was any problem, it belonged to society, and not him. He firmly believed anything as exciting and gratifying as being all over another man's muscular physique couldn't possibly be a bad thing.

*   *   *   *

Years of alcohol abuse did not serve Elizabeth Hyde well. When her metabolism shifted, her weight ballooned, her boobs drooped, and her butt sagged. She grew despondent over the loss of her youth and the departure of her good looks, even as her face inflated, and her once shapely thighs grew lumpy with cellulite. She went on a crash diet of iceberg lettuce, canned tuna and laxatives, lost thirty pounds and then put it all back on. Her boozy appearance aggravated her already troubled spirits and, as she spiraled downward into a blousy melancholia, she remained reliant upon still more vodka.

On Thanksgiving weekend of his sophomore year at UCLA, Chase drove down to Newport Beach and sat his mother down for a chat. He remained unruffled as he told her about the reality of his sexual orientation. He thought being honest was better than sneaking behind her back, or worse yet, faking his sexual preference by dating or sleeping around with women, the way so many other repressed young men his age were still doing.

Warily, his mother listened attentively to all he had to say. When his confessional concluded, his mother said nothing as she sucked down the last of her second vodka martini. Elizabeth rose slowly and crossed to the bar, where she stirred up still another batch, and then turned to face Chase so she could dismiss his inconceivable assertion that her son might be gay. She told him she was certain his revelation signified little more than a rebellious phase from which he'd soon grow weary.

"No way could you possibly be one of them," she added knowingly. "There's absolutely nothing effeminate about you. You're a surfer, a jock, a bodybuilder."

"What has that got to do with anything?" Chase wanted to know.

With a shaky hand, Elizabeth replenished her martini glass. It certainly didn't endear his mother to him any further when she then added, "Maybe it's a good thing your father didn't live to see this, Chase. It would have broken his heart. You know how much he loved you."

"I know how much he loved me, Mother," Chase countered. "And I also know he'd want me to be happy."

"Everybody has to be happy these days," Elizabeth observed with disdain as she sipped her refill. "Whatever happened to surviving through hardship?" After another sip, she suggested, "Let's not tell anyone about this, okay? Last thing we need is our friends and neighbors sharing in this kind of disturbing information. We'll wait until you're absolutely certain this is the path you plan to take."

Chase strained to be patient. "Mother, this is the path I plan to take. I suggest you adjust to it."

"You're probably just acting out some post-traumatic reaction to your father's horrendous death," surmised Elizabeth.

Chase threw up his hands in frustration and changed the subject. Rather than drawing them closer, Chase's revelation pushed the two of them, already sadly estranged, that much further apart.

*　　*　　*　　*

Elizabeth Hyde decided to finally face her dependency on alcohol and attend AA meetings at about the same time she was diagnosed with cirrhosis of the liver.

Six months later, Chase drove from his mother's funeral in Newport Beach, back to his bachelor apartment in Westwood, an orphan at twenty-two. In Elizabeth's will, she passed ownership of Hyde Motors over to Chase. He wanted no part of the dealership and his gruesome memories of it, so when the family attorney suggested they sell it and pocket the profits, he agreed.

After graduating from college in June, Chase chose to move closer to the center of gay life rapidly emerging in nearby West Hollywood. He worked with a real estate broker for several months until he found his four-unit complex up in Laurel Canyon and used his share of funds from the sale of Hyde Motors to secure the charming compound. Hidden in the hills, the income-generating property was woodsy, cozy and suited him just fine. Not long after the close of escrow, he woke up Cleopatra and Zeus long enough to move the three of them into the main house within the enclave he soon dubbed Hyde Park.

Chase and the bulldogs lived happily in the Hollywood Hills for the next six years. When Cleopatra went into what would be her last heat, she and Zeus mated. At the end of her gestation, via a remarkably trouble-free birthing, the bitch delivered a single, prize-worthy, bully pup. Chase was convinced the brindle-and-white pooch was the cutest of all the Hyde bulldogs. By the time he and the pup bonded, Chase knew there was no way he could part with the little fellow he dubbed Romeo.

*　　*　　*　　*

In gay-friendly WeHo, you never had to look far to find another hot-looking young man, and Chase acclimated quickly to life as a practicing roamosexual.

In New York, when men met, the first thing they wanted to know about each other was where the other guy worked. In Los Angeles, as men first made acquaintance, the first thing they wanted to know about each other was where the other guy worked out.

With that in mind, Chase put his surfing on hold, mothballed his board to the rear of his garage, and then visited several gyms in the area, checking to see which of them featured the best equipment, and the most conducive atmosphere for his training. At one of these pump palaces, he ran into a fellow alumnus from UCLA, who told him about a nearby space that taught gymnastics and for a limited time, was offering a three-month bargain trial membership. His former classmate added that for optimal toning, shaping and building of muscle, he could do no better than jumping into gymnastics.

*   *   *   *

KUTCHIE WALKER — LORD OF THE RINGS

The owner of the establishment had his name twice emblazoned in brass letters across the front door with no intended irony: Jim's Gym. Chase bounded into the high-tech studio on trendy Robertson Boulevard and found Jim Banner himself at the reception desk. Jim was happy to give Chase a quick tour of his four spacious workout areas. Each was a mirror-lined environment where the dynamic disciplines of acrobatics on the mat, gymnastics on the horse, balance on the rings, and tricks on the parallel bars were all taught and practiced. As Jim guided his guest into the fourth workout area, the one sporting the rings, destiny also accompanied Chase inside.

Chase almost stopped in his tracks when he saw in the center of the mirrored space, hovering several feet in the air, executing a consummate, complex trick high up on the rings, one of the best-built, and certainly the most handsome young man he'd ever seen. Chase watched in near wonder as the lean, powerfully muscled, blond gymnast, clad only in gym shorts, practiced his highly polished routine. The agile twenty-one-year-old flipped over and over in dizzying circles until, for his finish, he froze in place, his hands fully extended, his body suspended upside down in a gravity-defying handstand.

The soaring gymnast spotted Chase and Jim staring up at him, and so he put into play his best trick, not just for Jim's approval or to top off an excellent practice session, but also to impress the handsome newcomer.

At first, Chase figured the hypnotic vision before him might be an apparition, because no one looked *that* perfect. Mesmerized, he couldn't take his eyes off the daring young man on the high-flying rings. On a scale of one to Hunk, the accomplished jock registered off the chart. He flipped himself over again, faced forward, and froze in place as he stretched his strong arms out as wide as possible, orchestrating a seemingly flawless iron cross.

Enthralled, Chase watched as the fourth dimension ceased clocking in at its usual speed of reality and instead, passed before him preternaturally, as if he were seeing the graceful slow-motion poetry on a taped replay while watching the Olympics.

When Jim glanced over and caught Chase practically gawking in wonder at the gifted athlete, he happily boasted, "Oh, that's Kutchie — one of our most accomplished clients. He's a bit tall for a gymnast, but he's also a hugely successful fitness model. Around here, however, he's just our Lord of the Rings."

With elegance and agility, Kutchie flipped himself off the equipment and landed with a near-perfect dismount. The glare from the overhead fluorescence made the freshly pumped muscles of his incredible body gleam with sexy pockets of perspiration. The sinewy vascularity in his arms and legs reflected his agility and strength. At five-foot-nine and a hundred-seventy pounds, he appeared to Chase a paradigm of the all-American jock.

"Beautiful work, Kutchie," Jim called out, raising a high thumbs-up.

Once he was back down on level ground, as Kutchie reached for a towel, he also took a closer look at Chase. Chase returned the flirtatious appraisal and felt an immediate visceral connection. And they had yet to exchange a word. No doubt about it. Chase was in love.

As Kutchie walked toward the showers, Chase knew he had to say *something*; that he simply couldn't let the moment pass. "Very impressive," he finally blurted out as the flawless gymnast sauntered directly past him. "How do you make it look so easy?"

"Two secrets!" Kutchie answered, cavalierly, not turning around, but offering a sly smile while on his way into the locker room. "Practice and practice."

Chase was so inspired by Kutchie's knockout workout on the rings, he became an instant convert to the benefits of gymnastics. Eagerly, he followed Jim over to a nearby cubicle where he signed up for their three-month plan. He then stuck around, scrutinizing the exercise areas while making a point of not leaving the building before he again got to check out the gifted and incredible-looking gymnast.

Twelve minutes later, Kutchie finally hurried out from the men's locker room and bolted out the front entrance. Even dressed in street clothes, the freshly scrubbed blond looked like he'd have no trouble stopping traffic. Chase followed directly behind, practically in the young man's footsteps.

As he caught up with Kutchie and walked alongside him toward the parking lot, he emulated his wide strides and finally broke the ice. With a broad smile, he said simply, "Hello there. I'm Chase!"

"Kutchie."

They both stopped walking for a moment and shook hands.

"Nice to meet you ... Kutchie. Unusual name. Who came up with that?"

"It's a long story."

"Well, after seeing you on the rings, I signed up for three months," Chase said in earnest. "So I've got nothing but time."

When Kutchie smiled, Chase seized the moment to ask, "Seriously, that last trick you executed with such precision ... what's the secret?"

"Oh, please," Kutchie demurred with a wave of his hand. "The iron cross is a snap. I could teach your grandmother to do it. Just leave your biceps out of it, let your delts do all the work."

Chase slapped his open hand against his forehead. "Duh. Biceps out, delts in. Why didn't I think of that?"

"Tell me," Kutchie asked with a poker face. "Are you always this aggressive with guys you've just met?"

"Always," Chase answered, without a flinch. "Although I prefer to think of it as assertive and pro-active, yet projecting a cool confidence accompanied by commanding authority. It's not my fault you're so damn good-looking."

"Gee, there's an original line," Kutchie rolled his eyes. "Hey — are you by any chance trying to pick me up?"

"I don't know," Chase played dumb. "Is that the same as inviting you back to my apartment to look at my stamp collection?"

"I don't care much for stamps," Kutchie told him and continued walking. "Besides, you don't even know my last name."

"In that case," Chase caught up with him. "Why don't you tell me what it is?"

Kutchie stopped walking again. "Walker. Kutchie Walker."

"Glad to meet you. Mine's Hyde. Chase Hyde."

"As in Dr. Jekyll and Mister …?

"Precisely!"

"Hi, Mr. Hyde."

"Hello, Mr. Walker. Okay, now that we've gotten introductions out of the way, how 'bout we go back to my place so I can show you my coin collection?"

"Thought you said they were stamps?"

"Stamps, coins, you name it," Chase told him. "I have wide-ranging interests."

Kutchie was taken with Chase's brazenness, but also long accustomed to having guy's hitting on him, trying to pick him up. "Come on, now," he asked. "You're not seriously asking me to over to your place just like that, out of the blue, right now, after we just said hello and introduced ourselves, are you?"

"Only if the answer is *yes*."

"And what happens then?" Kutchie wanted to know.

"For one thing," said Chase. "I give a great back massage. Bet those sturdy muscles could use a strong rubdown right about now."

"Hmmmm" Kutchie hummed, suggesting the idea actually appealed to him. "That sounds good. So maybe the answer could be *yes*."

"If what?" Chase was eager to know. "Just name it, Kutchie. At this moment I'm only living for your happiness."

"Well, how 'bout if we head back to my place instead? It's real close."

"How close is real close?" Asked Chase, hoping his sexual interest wasn't too obvious. He was so excited, he also hoped the giant erection by then awakening inside his briefs wasn't manifesting its thick protuberance too blatantly from his crotch. He didn't want to appear as if he was only interested in sex, even though at that moment, there was nothing else on his mind, in his shorts, or on his agenda.

"Not far is a few blocks from here," Kutchie told him. "Plus if you like, I've got some primo pacalolo we can smoke."

As far as Chase was concerned, anyone using the Hawaiian word for marijuana was clearly his kind of guy. "You got a deal, Kutchie!" He exclaimed with a smile.

"I'm over on West Knoll," said Kutchie. "So why don't you just follow me?"

Behind the wheel of his car, Chase was all keyed up about seducing the hot gymnast as he carefully tailed Kutchie's flashy Thunderbird over to the young beauty's small, furnished guesthouse, just a few blocks away. By the time they both stepped inside the gymnast's cozy quarters, they were randy and revved up, eager to initiate a deep physical exploration of each other's musculature.

As promised, Chase stood behind Kutchie, gingerly massaging the young man's sore traps, while Kutchie rolled and then proffered the Hawaiian joint for them to smoke. After only a few tokes each, they were both so raring to go, the doobie got placed in a nearby ashtray, and the massage was put to rest. They slammed into one another full throttle and hugged hard and kissed deeply as they nearly tore off each other's clothes in their heated race to get naked.

Twenty minutes later, Kutchie was flat out on his back on his bed, savoring the full-bodied, enveloping sensation of his new friend's forward thrust way up inside him. The thick density of Chase's girth thumped against the Lord of the Rings' prostate with such pleasure-building intensity, Kutchie couldn't stop himself from begging for more.

"Oh, yes, that's it!" he cried out. "Fucking amazing. Don't stop! Please … please. Omigod … I can't hold back … I'm gonna shoot!"

As one orgasm ignited the other, Chase howled an ecstatic if unintelligible release and shot a major load deep inside the dazzling gymnast. Kutchie also lost himself in the moment as he climaxed while stroking his own dick. His copious smattering of semen bathed the ridges of his six-pack.

Chase was careful about gently pulling out from deep inside Kutchie's bubble butt as his erection slowly deflated and came down to earth with a perfect soft landing. Once they were no longer connected, while still fighting for breath, Chase collapsed on top of the Lord of the Rings. Kutchie welcomed Chase's full weight on him as he closed his eyes and allowed his mind to wander off into a blissfully stoned, semi-dreamland.

Moments later, by the time their pounding heartbeats and their collective deep breathing returned to normal, Chase slowly eased himself off of Kutchie. While lying shoulder to shoulder, Chase was certain their big bang had been nothing short of a transcendental experience. He told Kutchie how incredible he thought their sex was, and how he could hardly wait to see him again, to make love to him all over again and to do it next time with an even more abandoned passion.

Kutchie smiled sweetly at Chase and then the young beauty, as was his custom, swiftly disengaged. "You know," he casually told Chase, "I have a big evening ahead, and am kind of exhausted. So I think what I really need right now is to catch a quick muscle nap." He then suggested that after his arduous workout on the rings, followed by so strenuous a workout on the mattress, it would probably be best if he and Chase just wrapped things up.

No problem. Chase said he understood perfectly and, after planting an affectionate kiss on Kutchie's lips, bounced up off the bed and took a quick shower. After their perfunctory exchange of phone numbers, Kutchie walked Chase to his front door. Chase promised he'd call the next day and Kutchie, who had a facility for tactility, and could win over most anyone with the warmth of one of his mighty muscle hugs, gave Chase an affectionate embrace in farewell.

Chase drove home in a dreamy state. Not unlike most everyone else who ever had the great windfall to bed Kutchie, he, too, was thoroughly smitten with the great looking model. However, it wasn't until he awoke the following morning in his own bed, pining again for Kutchie while sporting a major boner, that Chase also first realized how hastily he'd been hustled out of Kutchie's apartment. Still, despite this irksome detail, Chase was so infatuated that he was eager to see the gymnast again, and as soon as possible. So he searched his jeans pockets for the young man's number, then called and left a message on Kutchie's answering machine, inviting him out for dinner and a movie later in the week.

Two days later, Chase had still not heard back from Kutchie. So he called his new buddy again and left another message. Three days after that, he tried calling one last time, but hung up when all he heard was a repeat of Kutchie's recorded voice.

By the end of the week, Chase had yet to hear back from Kutchie. Unaccustomed as he was to such a blanket dismissal, he felt strange being so callously ignored. He had little history with not calling the shots, no real life experience with the kind of pain that often accompanied flat-out rejection.

Chase decided there was no way he could let it end just like that. Great bang, muscle buddy. Thanks — now get the fuck out. He was determined to pursue the young beauty, even more so after the next message he left on Kutchie's answering machine also went unreturned. No problem. Chase liked nothing more than a daunting challenge to bring him back into the fight with eyes cocked and fists clenched.

*   *   *   *

While working out on the mats in Jim's Gym several afternoons later, Chase locked his arms into position and extended himself up into a passable handstand. From his inverted perspective, he suddenly spotted an upside-down Kutchie on his way into the locker area. Chase immediately dismounted and followed him in there.

"Oh, hi!" Kutchie smiled, surprised when he found himself actually happy to see Chase.

Chase smiled, too, and as pleasantly as possible, asked, "By any chance, did you happen to notice you haven't returned any of my last seventeen hundred phone messages?"

"Oh … you know how that goes," Kutchie answered with a hapless shrug. "I'm so busy, I haven't had time to burp."

"Hey, I'm not trying to take over your life, okay?" Chase told him, frankly. "But wasn't that you in bed with me last week? I thought we had a great time and connected so powerfully, hell, I just wanted to play with you again."

Kutchie shrugged again. "What can I say?"

"Well, for openers," Chase remained pleasantly calm, "you can tell me what's going on. Do you have a lover?"

"Hardly," Kutchie smiled.

"Then why the distance?" Chase asked.

Kutchie sighed heavily, long weary from always having to explain himself. "I thought by now you'd have gotten the message," he said simply. "I just don't like investing all the emotion it takes to go to bed with someone a second time."

Confounded, Chase quietly asked, "Come again?"

"Seeing someone a second time makes me feel penned in," Kutchie confessed. "Trapped."

"Trapped?" Chase asked. "You mean by affection?"

"No, not affection," Kutchie smiled. "As you can imagine, I have a charmed life and never had trouble attracting men. I can never get enough affection. It's probably my favorite thing."

"Then what is it?"

"Who knows?" Kutchie shrugged innocently. "Something inside me just shuts down whenever I feel threatened, and I'm threatened the moment someone wants to take advantage of my giving nature a second time."

"You only have sex with the same man once, is that what you're telling me?"

"You know, you catch on fast!" Kutchie jabbed Chase's shoulder with his fist. "I'm used to having guys come after me because, as we both know, not only do I look good, but I also throw a great fuck. I am everyone's all-American dream boy. That is the commodity I sell. So it bothers me when guys want to see me again because I'm sure all they want me for is sex, for the lure of my body."

"Do I have this straight?" asked Chase. "There are people out there fighting for the right to marry so they can spend their lives together, but you won't go out on a second date?"

"Not even once."

"Was there something missing in the way I made love to you?"

"Come on, Chase!" Kutchie confessed. "What do I know about making love? What we had was pure, unadulterated, hot, animal sex. And a hell of a lot of fun. But no matter how you analyze it, a fuck is still a fuck. And by now, I've already chalked it up as another notch on my anti-chastity belt and moved on. No offense."

"*No offense!?*"

"I mean — nothing personal."

"*Nothing personal!?*"

"You know, you don't have to repeat everything I say. I only have sex with a guy once, okay? A curtain comes down, the show is over, and I bolt. Besides, the more I get to know someone, the less I want to get fucked by him. Sometimes I wish I were capable of giving more."

Chase pretended to be offended. "You're saying all I represent is another conquest in your sexual marathon."

"A lion never settles down!" Kutchie postulated. "The king of beasts roams merrily from pride to pride, plowing all the lionesses he can get his paws on. Why should I be any different? But here's the funny part, Chase. I also like you. Hell of a lot more than most. You're the first guy I've met in ages I might want to see again on *any* level."

"I'm flattered," Chase said, sincerely. "So, how about if we switch agendas and try just being friends? Unless that's also too threatening for you."

"Not at all," Kutchie acknowledged. "Most guys disappear soon as I tell them there'll be no more hanky-panky between us."

"I'd say that's their loss."

"So you really wouldn't mind just hanging out together?" Kutchie asked with a smile. "Even though it means never, ever jumping on my bones again, despite the fact you want to be all over me because you know the shape of my muscles, combined with my dynamic personality, drive you so wild with desire, you're going to have to learn to control yourself?"

"Listen, Kutchie," Chase told him frankly. "I do like you a lot. Who wouldn't? You've got charisma to spare. And you bet I wouldn't mind jumping on that choice chassis again. But believe it or not, to me you're also more than just another sexually invigorating icon. So yes, I think I could handle being nothing more than buddies."

"But even if we won't be fucking again," Kutchie added with one of his dazzling smiles, "I've still got plenty of room for affection."

"*Affection?*" Chase asked, quizzically, like he'd never before heard the word.

"In case you don't remember," said Kutchie, "we had some during those brief moments just before we got undressed. But then sex got in the way and reliably messed things up. Now that we got the fucking out of the way, we can relax around one another, feel free to hug, kiss, eat out of the same bag of popcorn in the movies, cruise other men together, that sort of thing. Besides, we're too close in age. You're only twenty-eight. I'm attracted to older men — daddies."

"Fine with me, little boy" Chase volunteered. "I'll be your daddy."

"Please!" Kutchie protested. "I have enough daddies. Just be my friend. From what I've seen of the world, friendship outlasts romance any day."

Chase acquiesced. "I'm too smitten to let a mere lack of sex between us get in the way of what's bound to be our big romance, I mean friendship. So we've eliminated sex from the equation. Fine. I have more than my share, anyway. Maybe a frustrating, I mean fruitful friendship is just what I need."

The champion gymnast acknowledged Chase's willingness to stick around even after his sexual rejection by opening a small window of vulnerability, noting, "To answer your earlier question, my real name is Cameron. But when I was an infant, I was so cute and cuddly, so hand's down Gerber's-baby beautiful, my mother couldn't resist pinching my pudgy little cheeks and murmuring, "Kutchie-Kutchie-Koo … Kutchie-Kutchie-Koo. When "Kutchie!" turned out to be my first fully articulated word as I crawled across the living room floor, the nickname stuck."

✳   ✳   ✳   ✳

Chase and Kutchie ran around together for a few months, and as their mutual affection escalated into a brotherly camaraderie, they became the best of friends. Chase trained alongside Kutchie in their gymnastics classes at Jim Banner's. Kutchie gave Chase invaluable pointers on the parallel bars, showed him the ropes on the ropes, and coached the future Coach on stabilizing his dizzying dismounts off the rings.

Sex between them was no longer an issue, so their lack of lovemaking actually made it easier for them to be less guarded and more relaxed around each other. And while Chase felt a growing devotion for Kutchie, he couldn't help but retain a fragment of a willful lust that every so often popped to the surface. It was an uninvited craving that found him fantasizing again about pouncing on Kutchie's beguiling bones. However, with a bit of self-restraint, he kept his sexual yearning to himself.

The power of Kutchie's seemingly universal appeal was such that wherever he went, his charismatic presence produced a pronounced sexual tension. Whether shopping in the supermarket, working out in his gymnastics classes, or simply plying his craft while modeling on a shoot, he exuded a palpable erotic energy, a smoldering aura of sensuality.

The young model was pursued by men of all stripes. The lot of them were drawn to his dreamy beach-boy good looks and affable manner. Once they made his acquaintance, it was his trusting nature and his keenness to please that made his vulnerability all the more appealing.

Kutchie's attentive admirers were eager to get his hot little butt into the sack. In return, all Kutchie ever really wanted from his transitory daddies, most of them in their thirties, forties, sometimes even older, was an embracing armful of manly affection. His own father had walked out on him and his mother back when he was an infant, and growing up with no prominent fatherly figure left him aching to feel the warming envelopment of an older man.

As a pair of roamosexuals on-the-prowl, Chase and Kutchie ran around town night after night, hitting West Hollywood gay bars in the active pursuit of hot men. For them, every trick became an "ex" even before they undressed.

Kutchie's winning looks combined with his gift for captivation won over most everyone who came under his spell. On any given evening spent carousing, any number of men might become instantly infatuated with him. Kutchie merely needed to glance around the bar and, after assessing suitable candidates, zero in on that night's most desirous dad. Chase watched in awe as Kutchie sent forth his exclusive, sweet scent of seduction, and reeled in one incredibly hot daddy after the next.

Once Kutchie singled out his incipient sexual partner, he instinctively released a subtle spray of the cologne that was his magnet — a pheromone-laden vibration that signaled his willingness to be picked up. He sometimes acknowledged his interest with the introduction of one of his captivating smiles, and soon thereafter went home with his handsome, new gentleman friend, where he invariably found the sensuous satisfaction he so actively sought. After being pampered with adoration and tenderness, Kutchie's well-muscled legs were soon spread wide, high in the air, as his delicious bubble butt got feverishly fucked. The privilege of getting to plow Kutchie's heavenly body could be counted upon to lock in his trick's emotional attachment, guaranteeing the mature man would still be lusting after Kutchie long after they parted company.

*   *   *   *

From Chase's vantage point, Kutchie was absolutely right when he said he led a charmed life. Beautiful people often did. They attracted better mates, landed better tables in restaurants, often got better jobs with higher salaries. Their beauty was not just their gift to the world, but also their calling card. Along with the most striking of men and women, Kutchie was doted over, waited upon, catered to, and adored — often without his having to exert much effort or offer much in return.

A revolving door filled with good-looking, older men kept him in a perpetual, sensual spin. And Kutchie's pursuits found him obliging one beguiled gentleman after the next. And even though he granted many of his overjoyed pickups permission to passionately plow their peckers deep inside him, he also made certain none of them ever came within shooting distance of the fortress that was his heart.

Kutchie was the first to acknowledge how everything came easy to him, even as he counted his many blessings. He truly believed he'd been born under a lucky star. How else to explain the fact that he never got sick? A sore muscle ache after a strenuous workout on the rings was the closest he ever came to feeling bad. Whenever he hooked up with a hot, older man who wanted to make love, he felt no need to object when his sex partner defied convention and begged to breed him, to ride his beautiful bubble butt bareback.

Kutchie's rampant promiscuity was especially peculiar, because when push came to shove, he didn't really care all that much for sex. Far too often, the men who picked him up and penetrated him caused him no small amount of discomfort. Many were insensitive or insufficiently lubricated when they forged their cocks deep inside him. Sometimes his butt was sore, irritated and raw for days following an invasive get together.

His pickups made him feel valued and prized and vibrantly alive, which was why he didn't care when they were also near-strangers. He savored the attention, the affection they lavished on him during their brief time together. What Kutchie enjoyed most about the whole fucking experience was being held tightly, securely, and lovingly by another man. At least until his trick unloaded.

As soon as a session ended, his passing loving partner predictably expressed a sincere eagerness to see the young beauty again. That was when Kutchie switched off his seduction button. In the blink of an eye, the young hunk's sweeping need to feel snug in his surrogate daddy's strong arms vanished. He switched gears, broke free, tactfully maneuvered his confused pseudo-parent out the door, and moved on.

*   *   *   *

Chase and Kutchie became family for each other and with time felt less like former tricks and more like devoted brothers who shared a genuine love, one that transcended sexuality and carved a welcome caring deep within both their spirits.

One evening while they were cruising the bars along Santa Monica Boulevard, Chase told Kutchie, "I'm sure you already know that if you ever need me for anything, anything at all — I mean, if a day filled with trouble ever comes your way, I'll be there."

Of course when he offered his unconditional support, Chase had no idea that day filled with trouble for Kutchie was about to dawn.

On an overcast, fog-enshrouded Los Angeles morning, after Chase and Kutchie had gone out the night before for margaritas and carousing, Kutchie awoke, not just with a troubling, pounding hangover, but also with a furious case of the galloping trots. *Damn Mexican food!* He thought to himself while dashing to the john.

Kutchie spent a good part of his fashion shoot that day in the can. Every fifteen minutes or so, clad only in the Jantzen navy blue bathing suit he was modeling, he raced to the rest room for yet another runny evacuation. His painful peristalsis soon settled down and returned to normal, but his diarrhea remained more or less consistent for the next few weeks. Then, at Jim Banner's Gym one afternoon, after he and Chase went through the paces of a sweaty workout, climbing up and down the ropes and balancing on and off the parallel bars, Kutchie stepped on the scale in the locker area and was dismayed to see he'd dropped eleven pounds.

The following Wednesday, Kutchie woke up at three-thirty in the morning, soaked in perspiration, fighting for breath, coughing up blood, and shivering with chills from a fever of one-hundred three. He reached for his phone and called Chase.

Chase was at Kutchie's apartment in twelve minutes flat. After helping his fevered, ailing buddy into his car, he drove speedily over to the Emergency Room at nearby Cedars-Sinai. Along the way, Kutchie turned to Chase and, after coughing up a mouthful of blood-drenched phlegm, said softly, "I don't think I'm going to make it."

"Nonsense," Chase dismissed Kutchie's gloomy assessment, and kept his eye on the road, even as he affectionately rubbed the back of Kutchie's neck. "You can't take the easy way out and leave me just like this. Don't you know how many more men we have to conquer together first? Don't you know our great adventure has barely begun?"

Kutchie looked over and, even in his pain and discomfort, managed a small smile.

"Besides," Chase confessed. "I love you too much to lose you now."

"That means a lot to me," Kutchie muttered through his pain. "And I love you, too."

Kutchie was quickly admitted into the ER, where a team of specialists labored to clear the young man's lungs, before submerging him inside a transparent oxygen tent. While Chase paced nervously in the waiting room, Kutchie slipped into a deep coma.

A week and a half later, on a gloomy morning in January, three days before his twenty-second birthday, Kutchie Walker's generous heart stopped beating, and he became the first of so many of Chase's friends to succumb to the plague of AIDS that before long would go on to devastate the rest of the world.

A charmed life, indeed.

*   *   *   *

Kutchie's untimely death hit Chase hard, rendering him grief-stricken for weeks. His sense of loss was so profound, his stomach cramped in genuine pain. He also wished to hell he'd been more strident, shown more of a big-brother concern in warning Kutchie of the inherent dangers lurking within his unsafe promiscuity. He knew he should have been more take-charge when it came to Kutchie's health. He blamed himself for not getting his buddy to a doctor sooner, and kept coming up with lots of other red flags he should have pursued to head off the calamity.

The trauma over losing Kutchie also forced Chase to finally take a hard look at himself, at his own life: in point of fact, his sex life.

He needed to change his habits. He had to better protect himself against the onslaught he suddenly felt all around him. Gym buddies showed up out of the blue looking frail and gaunt, twenty, maybe thirty pounds lighter than just a few months earlier. Men on the street pulled low their baseball caps in a fruitless effort to hide unsightly, purplish discolorations on their faces from the ravages of Kaposi's sarcoma. Friends, acquaintances, pals all around him tested positive, dropped weight, got sick with pneumosistis, pained by neuropathy, numbed by brain seizures and paralyzing strokes — an entire community of men disintegrating in droves as they fell victim to the epidemic.

Along with most every one of his gay friends, Chase rushed to get tested for HIV. He wanted no part of any death sentence, but needed to know the truth. When the verdict on his blood work came back negative, he made a pact, resolving to thereafter engage only in safe sex. He vowed to stop diving into the deep, intimate pit of anal penetration with another guy; to wait at least until after they enjoyed a minimum of several dates, until he knew with certainty they were not only physically engaged, but sharing an emotional connection, as well.

He would not participate again in anal sex until he and his partner bonded; or, okay, whenever a bubble butt just too damn tempting to resist came along. Either way, from then on, whenever he partook in any sexual encounter, Chase promised himself he'd don a condom. He further promised himself that from then on, he'd no longer allow his dick to guide his existence. The big head had to step in to take control over the little head. Given his newfound sexual conviction, and since he rarely saw any muscle buddy more than once, the invasive intimacy of butt sex was soon little more than a distant memory.

Still, he had no complaints, especially since muscle sex was so satisfying. Flexing passionately, sexily, rubbing and massaging and kissing another bodybuilder was always fun and erotic, excitingly tactile and, as an added perk, disease-free. The man-to-man flexing of freshly oiled-up biceps never felt anything less than fantastic to the tender touch.

Chase also knew he needed to get lost in something. Motivated by his need to lift his cloud of despondency over Kutchie's death, he allowed his bereavement to carry him into a virtual escape. He slowly emerged from his doldrums by sitting himself down and starting to write.

He awoke early every morning, whipped up his egg white frittata breakfast of champions and his pot of Hawaiian coffee, and spent the next four to six hours hammering away at his computer. In writing, he found the solace and consolation he needed for his profound grief.

What he wrote about was Kutchie.

It just flowed out of him. He recounted the powerful connection of their fraternal bond, Kutchie's charismatic presence, his successful career as a top male model, his compulsive obsession with men, and his need to be loved by so many.

All the while he wrote, Chase never let up on the intensity of his training, never strayed from his own riveted fascination, his nearly life-long preoccupation with muscle.

Hyde Park's three rental units were all occupied. The income they generated covered the bills and kept him relatively comfortable. He was financially secure for at least a few more years. He led no extravagant lifestyle, and for the time being, needed no salaried employment. He spent the next year and a half incorporating his God-given gift for orchestrating words. By his own insistence, he pounded out his self-imposed daily minimum quota of four pages, before he gave himself license to wrap it up and head out to the gym.

The problem for Chase was that Jim Banner's gymnastics venue no longer held any fascination for him. The sight of the rings, the parallel bars, even the mats, were all painful reminders of his loss, so he gave up his membership there, purchased one at the Gold's in Hollywood, and once again took up pumping iron.

Morning after morning, word by word, one afternoon after another, page after page, night to night, chapter by chapter, Chase wrote and then wrote some more. He carefully crafted and composed a beginning, middle, and end — all of it focused on a main character modeled after Kutchie.

He attacked his writing program the same way he approached his bodybuilding: with consistency and patience. His creative undertaking developed and expanded until it blossomed on his hard drive into two-hundred-fifty satisfying pages. Once fully assembled, Chase then took the time to reshape, restructure, and re-edit the entire manuscript until it evolved into *True Jock*, his first novel. It told the homo-erotic tale of a show-stopping champion gymnast who, while up in the air, had no trouble mastering the rings which won him one medal after another. However, once back down on the ground, the gifted jock had far more difficulty forming bonds that lasted.

Once his first draft was complete, all Chase had to do was find a way to get his manuscript published.

*   *   *   *

Howard Kaufman was an up-and-coming agent at Writer's Ink, the prospering Hollywood literary agency. In his mid-thirties, he was also a dumpy tub of a man, seriously overweight, and way out of shape. Sexually speaking, the cherubic workaholic was one of those deeply repressed, practically asexual types who remained forever fearful of stepping forward to act on his hidden erotic impulses. He lived mostly for his work and felt content to keep the true nature of his sexuality tucked away, locked deep inside the walk-in closet of his own construction. He long ago convinced himself that he only cared to celebrate celibacy, and that his avid attraction to muscle, along with his extensive, forbidden fantasies involving bodybuilders, was nothing more than a harmless, innocent pursuit, a basic aesthetic appreciation of muscular male anatomy.

The primary reason the portly agent hung out around bodybuilders in the first place was because he harbored a dreamy fantasy that he and they might, by some cosmic miracle of illogic, get the chance to bond and become good friends. Kaufman was an avid muscle sycophant. Although he hadn't developed any significant tone himself, he lived for the excitement of observing it in others. He subscribed to a bunch of beefcake magazines, attended many of the bodybuilding contests around Southern California, and spent what little free time he had online, huddled over his laptop, combing sites featuring men with muscles.

Even though he secretly lusted and fantasized over photos of well-built men, Kaufman had also long ago convinced himself that he certainly had no *real* interest in doing anything *sexual* with any of them. His self-imposed self-restraint didn't stop him from imagining just what a pair of powerful, fully flexed biceps might actually feel like to the touch of his open, caressing hand. Actually, his decades-long secret yearning to squeeze, lick, and kiss the hard, contracting muscle of a strong bodybuilder was pretty much the only masturbatory image he ever envisioned any time he oiled up his johnson in some Johnson & Johnson and beat the little bugger into submission.

His consummate appreciation of muscle was the primary reason Kaufman so looked forward to getting away from the office mid-afternoon and heading directly over to Gold's in Hollywood. He appeased his guilt about being in such ghastly shape by spinning his wheels at a leisurely pace upon a stationary recumbent bike for half an hour or so, three times a week. Surrounded by the company of muscular men, he felt empowered, as if he were one of them. Riding the bike also gave the agent the opportunity — in between the tortoise-paced churning of his chunky thighs and his speed-reading of a screenplay or manuscript — to surreptitiously ogle the hot and hunky muscle men exercising all around him.

Kaufman and Chase had long ago established one of those polite-in-passing, *Hey, Wassup?* kind of familiar nods most gym members exchanged with scores of others. Chase spotted the curmudgeonly butterball scanning a different manuscript or screenplay every time he churned away lackadaisically on his bicycle. After a couple of gym buddies mentioned what a big success the pudgy guy was at representing writers, Chase brought his manuscript to the gym and kept it in his locker.

Several days later, as he walked into the locker room after a workout, he spotted Kaufman down at the end of a long, low bench, unbuttoning his shirt. Coach's chest and triceps were freshly pumped, his body glistened sexily with sweat, and he knew it was time to finally put his muscles to productive use. He stretched out of his tank top, tossed it over his shoulder and then, shirtless and shameless, walked over and introduced himself.

Chase didn't want to encourage any awkward advances, but he also needed to make a good impression. He was friendly, congenial, and just the slightest bit playful, all on a professional level, all in an effort to capture the agent's attention. It worked.

Once Chase sensed Kaufman was captivated, he reached inside his locker and casually pulled out a copy of his manuscript. His work firmly in hand, he asked Kaufman if he'd help him out by taking a look at his just-completed work of fiction. "I heard you're really good at what you do," Chase told him, frankly. "Maybe you could give me some input. Tell me how much editing my manuscript needs, where I might submit it, what I should do next. Fact is, I need a professional opinion."

Kaufman savored having his professional ego stroked by one of the top hunks in the gym. "Leave it with me," he told the budding author in a lethargic monotone, and begrudgingly accepted Chase's manuscript. He already knew any generosity of spirit on his part was a waste of his valuable time, so he qualified his acceptance with a caveat, adding "I'm swamped with material right now, but I'll try to get to it, eventually."

"Much appreciated!" Chase enthusiastically shook Howard's limp hand, as if they'd just sealed a deal, and was on his way.

Kaufman finished dressing and haphazardly tucked Chase's manuscript under his saggy upper arm. He left the gym, drove home and, while checking his phone messages, dumped Chase's creative effort atop the mountain of manuscripts that was his slush pile, a veritable tower of babble.

* * * *

As he did each weekend, Howard Kaufman spent Saturday afternoon speed-reading through his client's projects. The hard working writer's rep settled in on a thickly cushioned luxury chaise, poolside, beneath an open beach umbrella on his sprawling Brentwood property. He stretched out lazily, right alongside his SPF15 Estee Lauder bronzer, his pitcher of mango margaritas, and his bong of hydroponically cultivated marijuana, before reluctantly diving into his pile of typically dull and mostly unreadable reading material.

After flipping halfway through his top client's latest special effects-driven, sci-fi screenplay, he decided it was non-involving and mostly incomprehensible, even if commercially viable. He put the script aside and, reaching for the next item in his pile, inadvertently picked up Chase's manuscript.

Damnit, wasn't life already dreary enough for the chubby little man, what with his having to plow his way through the dribblings of the better-credited, higher-paid writer clients he represented? Kaufman felt justifiably less than enthusiastic as he opened up Chase's work. Not unlike most everyone else, the agent harbored the same built-in prejudgment concerning any creative capacities of bodybuilders. He sub-scribed to the prevailing cultural bigotry which dictated that men with muscles, by the very nature of their time-consuming dedication to their bodies rather than their minds, were not very likely to also be either talented or intelligent. Major muscles may have been what most every man once secretly longed for, but stereotypically, people often associated bodybuilders with sheer stupidity. Kaufman, too, believed *smart bodybuilder*, by its very definition, had to be oxymoronic.

Leaning back down against his plush chaise, Kaufman was all set to afford Chase's work his obligatory four to eight pages before he would then have read enough to turn its writer down in a fairly polite and sufficiently professional manner.

To his amazement, Kaufman found Chase's tome not only highly readable, but more importantly, downright marketable. Confounding expectations, he read *True Jock* in just several sittings and found it engrossing, insightful, and well written. It didn't hurt that it was also homoerotic as hell.

Kaufman called the author at home. After congratulating Chase on his effort, he said he wanted to sign him up and represent him as his agent so he could sell his book to a publisher.

Good for his word, Kaufman moved directly to his game plan, and straightaway after signing Chase to their standard, four-page, two-year contract, had his assistant Fed-Ex a copy of *True Jock* over to their New York office.

As soon as Chase's manuscript arrived on the other side of the country, one of the interns at Writer's Ink East made twelve reproductions and then, in an initial multi-ple submission, an associate agent then shipped copies to the various publishers pre-selected by Kaufman, accompanied by a glowing cover letter.

Three months later, after being rejected by most of the publishing houses, Howard Kaufman got a phone call from a senior editor at Gotham Books, who announced he not only thought Chase's work was quite promising, he also wanted to publish it.

Kaufman's next call was to Chase, to relay the good news.

*   *   *   *

While riding high, Chase also felt somewhat guilty about connecting so well, so fast. This nonsense about having to suffer for your art obviously didn't apply to him, as he had so easily scored at what was pretty much his first effort at bat.

Chase and his agent quickly developed a warm working relationship. Chase was relieved he no longer had to win Kaufman over through any mischievous flirtation. The agency would soon be making money off his mind, not his body, and he was pleased he could forego further posturing. From that point on, he and Kaufman were platonic and polite, working in tandem, strictly on a business basis.

Similarly, Kaufman had no trouble giving up the fantasy scenarios he had secretly embraced involving himself and Chase. He resolved that even though he'd never get to massage Chase's sore back or squeeze his flexed biceps, he felt sufficiently satisfied by the intoxicating interaction that was their social intercourse. He experienced a comforting exhilaration whenever he was around his new client, whether in a meeting in his office or working out at the same hour in the gym.

Kaufman looked forward to spending time with Chase as the two of them mapped out marketing strategies for his forthcoming first novel. Whenever they met, the agent savored the experience and imagined that if they went on to become inseparable business associates, might not a drop or two of his client's magical, muscular charisma also rub off on him? Surely, being seen with Chase would elevate the round little man's sex appeal, if only a notch. Hunkdom by association.

*   *   *   *

The budding author spent the next four months feverishly rewriting, reshaping his publisher's suggested edits. With each reworking, Chase proofread his manuscript until finally, with the last of his I's dotted, and with his T's and fingers crossed, he submitted his completed composition.

As *True Jock* went to press, the aspiring novelist was excited, but jittery and filled with anxiety and angst, all in anticipation of the reception his initial literary effort might receive. He forced himself into a state of restrained impatience, even as he also listened for the sounds of fame and fortune to show up on his doorstep, bathing him in rewarding waves of adulation and tribute.

Unfortunately for Chase, his new best buddies, fame and fortune, had other ideas as to the direction in which they were about to take his life.

Six months later, when *True Jock* was published, Chase's first novel was greeted with a minimum of fanfare. The few trade publications that reviewed it — Publisher's Weekly, The Kirkus Review of Books — suggested it was a fine stab at yet another lightweight first novel. None of them urged their readers to run out and buy a copy as it was nothing exceptional. One of the trades did at least acknowledge Chase Hyde as a writer of undeniable promise.

When *True Jock* failed to take off in the way Chase fantasized, he was deeply disheartened. So much for his dream house in the Hawaiian hills above Lahaina, overlooking the blue Pacific. So much for his engraved invitation to The Good Life. So much for lunches at Spago, ski trips to Aspen, Armani suits in the closet, the Beamer convertible in the garage, the brace of bulldogs drooling around the house, the live-in help, and of course that most prized link to his success fantasy: the parade of smart, hunky bodybuilders in a constant flow through his fruitful life.

*   *   *   *

After the disappointing reception for *True Jock*, the young author did what any disenchanted artist might do following his initial literary effort into oblivion. At home in Laurel Canyon, he rested on his laurel, and displayed little interest in any pro-active furthering of his literary livelihood.

His first book hadn't launched the flourishing career he envisioned, never earned him much money. With no publishers out there clamoring for his next bookish endeavor, he felt no pressing need to sit down and tackle another long-term project.

Committed to nothing so much as his training, Chase strove hard, not for the creation of more words, but for the betterment of his body. Year after year, as one decade dissolved into another, he worked out hard, slowly packing on ever more muscle, pumping iron with a reliable consistency.

Over time, the Gold's Gym in Hollywood developed into a magnet for many of the more serious gay bodybuilders in the area. Steroid abuse within its raucous halls ran rampant. If you wanted to join the daily parade of muscle hunks who showed up to work out, you did well to join the fray, furtively score a cycle of the unlawful juice, and then watch with impatient excitement as the muscles of your body rapidly expanded.

By the time Chase turned thirty-seven, he was long-settled into his chosen life-style. Oddly enough, he was not especially bothered that his life continued to lack significant purpose. Somewhere in the back of his mind, he knew his compulsive commitment to his training was ultimately a superficial pursuit. Still, as a slave to his libido, he stayed focused on building an ever-improving physique.

And it was while he was pumping his impeccable pecs at Gold's one sunny after-noon that providence threw Chase an unexpected curve ball when he had his first serendipitous encounter with Christian Falconer. However, to best tell the Byzantine tale of that major muscle mystery, we must first turn the page and start at its begin-ning.

*   *   *   *

BOOK THREE:

PUMPING IRONY

*"If we could be twice young and twice old,
we could correct all our mistakes"*

— Euripides

CHRISTIAN FALCONER — CHRONICLE OF A PROPHESY FORETOLD

After eight-and-a-half months of a challenging pregnancy, Ruth Hortense Falconer was bloated as a whale. Over the course of the first trimester of her gestation, the twenty-seven-year-old expectant mother suffered morning sickness and regurgitated daily. Once that unpleasant phase subsided, she put up with debilitating stomach cramps almost every afternoon, and needed to elevate her swollen ankles nightly. Owing to a voracious appetite, she also rapidly packed on an astonishing weight gain of nearly eighty-three pounds.

On a very wet and bleak, wintry Sunday morning, the once-petite woman was accompanied into the Evangelical Covenant church in Greenwich, Connecticut by her husband, the well-respected physician and pillar of the community, Dr. Andrew Falconer. Dr. Falconer assisted his wife as she waddled her misshapen five-foot-three frame down to the front pew. He took great care as he guided her onto a seat at the end of the aisle, just as the service was about to commence.

Ruth Hortense spent the next hour or so trying to ignore the immense pressure her uterus placed upon her bladder by getting lost in the comforting power of prayer. Far more spiritual than her husband, much of Ruth Falconer's daily energy was pre-occupied with her devotion to the Lord and service to her church.

Dr. Falconer and his wife attended services religiously every Sunday. He went along with her, not because he felt led by any divine calling, but because showing up for services every Sunday morning was expected of prominent, God-fearing people who comported themselves with a proper display of Christian values. From the way Dr. Falconer often spoke about those values, about how they were the best way to conduct one's life, you'd think he was also a firm believer in the word of the Lord. In truth, he did not believe in the resurrection nor did he feel any need to work toward his own salvation. Perhaps that was why, while paying his weekly spiritual debt to civilized society, he usually passed the time by getting lost within his erotic day-dreams.

While the choir sang, and their committed harmony lifted the communal spirits of the assemblage, the good doctor closed his eyes to envision bare-breasted, Rubenesque women filling his mouth with luscious grapes plucked straight from the vine. On this particular Sunday, Dr. Falconer's lascivious review of the best breasts he could summon was interrupted the moment the pastor opened his sermon with a fire and brimstone bang.

"The signs are all around us," the pastor warned, with an emphatic slap to the podium. "Even now, here in the mid-nineteen-seventies, as the millennium, with its promise of the Rapture and eventual redemption fast approach, we must prepare!"

Twelve long minutes later, as the pastor ended his weekly rant, the organist launched into a rousing rendition of *Onward, Christian Soldiers*. At the same time, Dr. Falconer hurried up the aisle, past all the pews, straight outside into the torrential deluge, to pull his car around front, where, as prearranged, he would pick up his wife.

Churchgoers wearing infectious smiles and offering neighborly nods greeted one another as they milled about inside the narthex of their house of worship, sipping from Styrofoam cups of coffee, munching on sugarcoated donuts. Mostly, they killed time while waiting for the torrential downpour of biblical proportions to subside so they could all head home.

Ruth Hortense stood patiently at the front entry, politely nodding to familiar parishioners as she waited for her husband to drive up to the curb in his shiny, black Cadillac.

The faithful who flocked to Ruth Hortense's charismatic church believed in the Bible as their revealed word, and remained ever-alert for any of the signs and wonders heralding what they were convinced was a certain and fast-approaching end of time.

Because of their ever-vigilant expectation of miracles, when one of the church elders, a tall, frail, rail of a man in his late seventies, walked straight up to Ruth Hortense and, with no invitation, gently placed his open hands upon her expanded stomach, most everyone milling about inside the church stopped whatever they were doing and took quiet notice.

It was obvious from the sight of the frail man's eyelids suddenly fluttering wildly in place, and his eyeballs bizarrely aswirl in dizzying circles inside their sockets, that he was intercepting a message from the Other Side.

Conversation in the vestibule quickly died down and all eyes watched as the aged man, widely known for his intuitive gifts, asked in a raspy voice, "Do you happen to know what gender your child is going to be?"

"No," Ruth Hortense sweetly told him. The expectant mother suddenly felt awkward, as if under the glare of a spotlight. Everyone within earshot remained silent as they waited to hear the pronouncement the revered elder was about to articulate. With a nervous smile, Ruth Hortense explained to the thin, old man, "Dr. Falconer felt there was no real need for any amniocentesis. We've decided to welcome whatever blessing the good Lord has in store for us."

"Well, my dear sister in Christ," the slender elder soothingly told her, "While observing you from across the room, I was struck with a vision, so I came directly over to share with you the joyous news the Lord just placed on my heart."

"Oh, yes, please, do tell!" said Ruth Hortense in the genteel, thick accent of her Atlanta upbringing. "I just can't hardly wait to find out what it might be."

The church elder rubbed his open hands slowly back and forth across the protruding basketball mound that was Ruth Hortense Falconer's swollen mid-section. At the same time, churchgoers looked to see if the old man's fingers might not be picking up some esoteric message from the contents nestled deep within the expectant mother.

As the elder shut his eyes tightly, he quietly proclaimed, "Here's what lies ahead. Exactly two hundred and seventy days following his conception, you shall be giving birth to a son."

"A son?" Ruth Hortense repeated, practically giddy with enthusiasm. "That is so exciting!"

"Yes," the elder agreed with the gestating woman as his eyelids flickered like wings on a hummingbird. "Expect a son who will be welcomed into this world at a weight of … hold on … I see numbers clearly now … ten pounds, six ounces."

"Ten pounds …?" a bedazzled Ruth Hortense repeated. "Six ounces?"

The bone-thin man wrapped up his vision, saying softly, "The Lord is gifting you with a boy so big, so strong, he is destined to grow up … a Samson."

"A Samson?" Ruth Hortense repeated in soft wonder, still clinging to her awe.

"That-Is-What-I-See!" The old man proclaimed loudly as he lowered his hands to his sides, popped open his eyes and snapped out of his preternatural reverie. "A Samson," he said again, quietly. "I doubt I've ever seen a vision so unambiguous."

As if the elder's extraordinary prophecy of so unexpected a foreseeable future wasn't revelation enough to elate Ruth Hortense's already elevated spirits, just then, up in the heavens, an alarming clap of thunder, followed immediately by an electrifying burst of white lightning, reinforced her exhilaration when, without warning, it jolted the room. Every little light inside the church flickered on and off in unison for a few moments before they all came back on, restored to full power.

"God's will be done." Ruth Hortense uttered in a faint whisper, even as she slipped into a blessed state of bliss. In a moment of revelation, she fully appreciated how Joan of Arc must have felt when the Maiden of Orleans bore witness to her own miraculous visit from the Holy Spirit.

After thanking the man for sharing his splendid gift of prophecy, and blessing him for the clarity of his intuition, Ruth Hortense turned and waddled back into the belly of the church, directly up to the altar. Alone in the majesty of so great a hall, she felt a true succor within the calming safety of her sanctuary. For physical support, she held on to a pew as she dropped clumsily to one knee and shed a few tears of deep gratitude. For spiritual support, she again gave her life over to the Lord and thanked Him for the blessing of His forthcoming bounty.

It came as no surprise to Ruth Hortense that on a day so filled with inspiration, the moment Dr. Falconer drove up to the curb, the heavy rain that had been pounding the pavement all morning came to an abrupt end, as if someone in charge upstairs assiduously turned off the shower faucets.

As Dr. Falconer jumped out of his Cadillac and trotted up the steps of the church to escort his wife back down to their car, Ruth Hortense gazed up into the sky and smiled with glee when she noticed directly above her a grouping of gray clouds breaking up. The dark clouds unveiled themselves theatrically, a wispy curtain parting until they exposed in the far distance a precious patch of blue sky.

Dr. Falconer carefully positioned his inflated wife securely into the passenger seat of his Eldorado and half-listened to her blabbering on about the incredible news of the elder's prophecy. The good doctor then cut her off mid-sentence as he firmly slammed shut the passenger door and yelled at her through the side window, instructing her to lock her door and buckle up. He then dashed around to the driver's side.

Ruth Hortense sat back uncomfortably in her seat, looked up at the sky, and her heart immediately started racing again the moment she spotted, deep within the parting of clouds, a near-perfect rainbow arcing its way across the open, blue portion of the sky.

"Look up at the clouds!" Ruth Hortense pointed her finger toward the heavens. "Oh, my God, Dr. Falconer … Do you see that? Oh, dear Lord!"

Dr. Falconer, by then in the driver's seat, rested his hands upon the steering wheel and looked up toward where his wife was pointing. "What are you going on about now, woman?"

"There!" exclaimed Ruth Hortense. "Look quickly! It's fading right now!"

Dr. Falconer looked up and saw nothing more than the passing storm.

"Talk about a divine blessing," Ruth Hortense gushed. "Lord, what a glorious day!"

"You call this foul weather a glorious day?"

"We just witnessed a rainbow up in the sky. A rainbow in all its glory. What can it mean if not a smile from God?"

"It can mean it's simply a rainbow!" Dr. Falconer countered, testily.

"Nonsense!" Ruth Hortense dismissed her husband's clinical pessimism. "Not after the prophecy we just received."

"Oh, please …" Dr. Falconer protested by exhaling in heightened exasperation. "Won't you for once try exhibiting some common sense? We always see rainbows this time of year."

"And what about the prophecy?"

"What idiotic prophecy?" Dr. Falconer asked impatiently, in his thick, Georgian-raised drawl.

"I knew you weren't paying attention!" Ruth Hortense remained patient as she again recounted all that just happened, from the laying-on of the clairvoyant elder's hands, to the celestial timing of the thunder and lightning, the lights going off and then back on inside the church, the sudden halting of the rain, and then the appearance of that heavenly rainbow.

Dr. Falconer responded by rolling his eyes to the roof of his Cadillac, the way he often did whenever the mystical side of his wife's spiritual nature got the better of her intermittent level-headedness.

Ruth Hortense was barely bothered by her husband's facile dismissal of her divination. She knew his logical, scientific mind stood between himself and the imagination it would take to join her in trusting how very special was bound to be their forthcoming, hallowed bundle of joy.

*   *   *   *

The expectant father, Dr. Falconer, was a prominent internist stuck in the collective Let's-All-Worry-About-What-The-Neighbors-Think sensibility that governed much of Greenwich, their well-to-do, Connecticut suburb. He was the son of German immigrants who had worked themselves to death, sacrificing to raise five children in rural Georgia. A self-proclaimed self-made man, the good doctor constantly begrudged the sacrifices and struggles he'd endured. He'd paid out every dime of his own tuition, and made ends meet by working his way through Yale Medical School, often holding down two, sometimes three jobs at once.

Dr. Falconer and his future bride met back when he was completing his internship at St. Mary's Hospital in Atlanta. Ruth Hortense, whose family had resided in the South since before the Civil War, was finishing up her nursing degree. At the time, she was as slender as she was slight, with a radiant smile and big, southern-belle blonde hair.

The intern found nurse Ruth Hortense both pleasing and charming. In addition to her wholesome good looks and lilting Southern charm, he liked the conservative, always-appropriate manner in which she dressed, the comely way she fashioned her big, blonde hair, and the inviting way she smelled whenever they went out. Since she couldn't have been more his ideal image of a doctor's wife, it wasn't long into their courtship before he asked her to marry him.

In her heart, Ruth Hortense knew the future doctor was an elitist and a condescending snob. Even so, she admired his analytical mind, his evident sophistication, his old-fashioned observance of etiquette, and especially the mature way he respected her privacy and always treated her like a lady. Thus, with no other suitors or prospects in sight, she accepted his passionless, practical proposal.

After a respectful courtship, and after Dr. Falconer completed his residency, he and Ruth Hortense hosted a proper Christian church wedding, followed by a relaxing, if indifferent and uneventful honeymoon in Bermuda.

Ruth Hortense didn't care much that when it came to making love, her husband lacked luster. Surely stability and common decency, in partnership with a shared respect, counted for more in a functioning marriage than did the surprise of sexual fireworks.

Dr. Falconer set up his medical practice in Greenwich, and invited Ruth Hortense to work alongside him, to serve as his receptionist, his nurse, his office manager. She agreed, and kept track of his appointments, balanced his books, collected fees, took blood samples, and injected patients with vaccinations and flu shots. Even after she became pregnant, Ruth Hortense continued running Dr. Falconer's office several days a week.

*   *   *   *

On her last scheduled visit to her obstetrician's office before her due date, Ruth Hortense's doctor examined her and heard two healthy hearts, mother-and-fetus, beating nearly in unison. He then told the large little woman that, given her enormous size and outlandish gain in weight, the best way for her to avoid traumatic wear and tear once in labor would be to let him perform a Caesarian section.

Ruth Hortense would have none of it. She refused to be under sedation when she delivered her miracle baby. She needed to be wide-awake and alert when she embraced her special child's momentous arrival into this world.

"May I be perfectly frank with you?" Ruth Hortense's obstetrician asked, as he leaned against his desk. "You're a nurse, so you know that even under the best of circumstances, giving birth to a baby is a lot like shitting a pumpkin."

Unaccustomed to such vulgar imagery, Ruth Hortense brought nervous fingers to her mouth and twittered in feigned mortification. "Ooh ... Doctor, please!"

"I'm sorry to be so blunt. But you need to know all indications suggest you're carrying an unusually huge package. I only heard one other heart beating inside you, but your uterus is full enough to be bearing twins, maybe even triplets. Why not make it easier on yourself?"

Ruth Hortense waved a dismissive hand in the air. She knew religion and modern medicine were often at odds with each other, so she chose not to tell him about the gift of prophecy she'd been given in church, and instead asked pointedly, "Be honest with me, Doctor. Do you really think, given the choice, the Virgin Mary would have slept through Jesus' birth?"

$$*\qquad *\qquad *\qquad *$$

Several days later, on the very bull's eye of her due date, while in the kitchen, scrubbing the detritus from their breakfast dishes, Ruth Hortense's water broke.

Dependably organized and well-prepared, Dr. Falconer took immediate charge of the situation. He took hold of his wife's pre-packed suitcase, already resting against the front door, lifted his car keys off their hook, led Ruth Hortense by the hand, and rushed her from their home. The good doctor drove his laboring wife through a pouring rain, as fast as the speed limit allowed, straight over to the emergency entrance of Greenwich General.

While en route to the hospital, Ruth Hortense lovingly massaged the circumference of her incredible growth and tried not to think about her escalating discomfort as she asked, "We're agreed he's going to be named Christian, isn't that right, Dr. Falconer?"

"Yes, yes," Dr. Falconer answered with impatience, as he carefully sped down the highway, his eyes riveted to the road ahead. "Christian's a fine, up-standing name. And what if it's a girl?"

When Ruth Hortense felt a sudden, sharp, stabbing pain shooting through her midsection, she gritted her teeth, panted heavily to relieve her burden, and answered with unwavering certainty, "He's not going to be a girl."

$$*\qquad *\qquad *\qquad *$$

For the next seventeen hours, as she remained in a near-constant painful state of labor, Ruth Hortense fought off her extreme suffering by visiting with the Lord. However, this was one time in her life when even the potency of prayer could not bring her any measured solace. The pain was so severe, it soon overwhelmed her.

Another few hours passed before the medical staff encircling their patient in the delivery room saw the top of a baby's head finally protruding from its mother's valiant cavity. Two more hours later, the obstetrician cradled a full head, a neck, and most of its left shoulder.

In her blinding agony, conjoined with what by then was her thorough exhaustion, Ruth Hortense screamed aloud in a torrent of incoherency. She was certain something had gone terribly wrong because it sure felt like she was ripping wide open. As her swollen eyes sent forth another slew of tears, and rivulets of mucous dribbled from the sides of her nose, she panted heavily, rapidly, and screamed out at the top of her lungs. She hollered with undignified, undiluted agony until finally, *finally*, she accepted the will of her doctor and gave him license to administer an epidural.

The injection numbed only her lower half and allowed her to actuate the remainder of her problematic delivery while she was still at least half awake. By the time the rest of her baby finally slid out from its dark, slippery vessel, straight into the awaiting physician's plastic-gloved hands, everyone in the delivery room breathed a collective sigh of relief.

"It's a boy!" announced the pediatric surgeon, triumphantly, as he clamped the newborn's umbilical chord, summarily severing the last physical vestige of prenatal bonding between mother and child.

Ruth Hortense closed her swollen, reddened eyes and offered up a silent prayer of gratitude.

"And what a big boy!" the obstetrician marveled, as he guardedly handed the wailing, squiggling infant over to a team of awaiting nurses. "Wait until you see him. I've never seen such a full head of hair on a newborn."

Ruth Hortense fought against the weariness of her drained body, fought valiantly against the drugs numbing her system, fought to remain awake just a while longer.

Once the big baby boy was cleaned and examined and wrapped in soft linen, he was weighed and then handed over to the new mother. "Here he is," the nurse said as she lowered the baby into his mother's outstretched arms. "He's sure a big little fellow. Weighed in at ..."

"I know," Ruth Hortense smiled down lovingly on her child and said, "Ten pounds, six ounces."

"Wow!" The nurse was surprised and impressed. "Right on the money. How'd you know?"

Ruth Hortense cradled her mystical, miracle infant against her full breast, and heralded his arrival into civilization by drawing his tiny face flush up against her left nipple.

As the suckling slowly accepted the nourishment of his mother's milk, they both drifted unhurriedly into a collective, finally trouble-free slumber. And not long after, the hearts of Madonna and child once again beat in near unison.

The gifted elder had been positively prescient about her baby being a boy, about the timing of his due date, about precisely how much he would weigh at birth. Everything was in place. Even in the semi-stupor of her thorough exhaustion, Ruth Hortense needed no further sign from above.

No doubt about it. Providence had deigned her Christian would grow up to become a Samson.

*   *   *   *

There never was a time when the newborn didn't attend church. Ruth Hortense insisted Christian be filled with the Holy Spirit as early as possible, and didn't plan to simply drop him off in the parish nursery with all the other infants while she and Dr. Falconer attended services. She made a point, just before they left for church every Sunday morning, to cradle her little big baby in her arms and breastfeed her chosen one, making certain he was fully mollified. Once his little belly was crammed with the calming influence of her fresh milk, a well-nourished Christian drifted into a contended slumber and then snoozed soundly through the duration of the service.

Dr. Falconer allowed his wife the freedom to foster Christian's spirituality, but insisted every other building block become his responsibility as he had ambitious plans for his son. He looked forward to seeing his boy follow in his footsteps by growing up to become a doctor. He expected his son would learn to appreciate life's more refined and agreeable pursuits.

"Our boy's going to speak French or maybe Italian," he informed Ruth Hortense at his pedagogical best. "We'll introduce him to the works of Rembrandt and Picasso, expose him to the world of opera and ballet, take him to the best Broadway shows and finest restaurants. Children are born without restraint, and must be tamed and tempered, taught civilized behavior. I'll see to it that he becomes the perfect little gentleman, and insist he put away his toys, clean up his room, be mindful of his chores, and learn to play the violin."

Ruth Hortense knew better than to confront her husband on his didactic musings, but felt compelled to ask, "Don't you think you might be overloading his plate a bit?"

"Nonsense, woman," insisted Dr. Falconer. "If he can't play a musical instrument, or doesn't speak a second, maybe even a third language, how will he ever get into Pre-Med at Yale?"

*   *   *   *

Christian Falconer was the tallest little boy at his third birthday party. Standing amid scores of colorful balloons blown up by his mother, and surrounded by a plethora of presents, he loomed at least several inches over all the other kids his age helping him blow out the candles on his enormous ice cream cake.

Dr. Falconer proudly handed his son what he claimed was a very significant gift. Christian giddily tore open the gift-wrapped box and pulled out a top-of-the-line, kiddy doctor's kit, replete with pulsating stethoscope, licorice tongue depressors, and a bottle of candied aspirin.

Christian stood to hug his father. However, the boy's gratitude was short-lived when he was immediately distracted by the sight of his mother wheeling in a shiny red, pedal-driven fire truck.

Ruth Hortense knew the gift was a major overindulgence, but while off shopping in Manhattan, she'd spotted it in the window at F.A.O. Schwartz, and just couldn't resist scooping it up.

The honored birthday boy spent most of his celebration zooming around his home, pedaling room to room astride his shiny new fire engine. The doctor's kit from his father remained on the floor in a corner, untouched.

The day after his birthday celebration, Ruth Hortense helped her three-year-old carry some of his new toys out to the backyard, so he could play in the fresh air while she baked a dessert inside. The little guy assembled his legion of tiny toy soldiers and lined them up along the pavement, alongside his shiny new fire engine, and his two brand new plastic action figures, each with its own moveable arms and legs.

Ruth Hortense bent down and picked up one of the action figures and asked, "You see this toy?" she jiggled it in front of her son. "Do you know who this is?"

"BATMAN!" Christian hollered out with glee.

"That's right, Sweetheart!" Ruth Hortense smiled as she picked up another plastic action hero and asked sweetly, "And who's this one?"

"INDELIBLE HULK!" Christian barked.

"Yes, Dear One!" the young mother smiled with warmth as sweetly, she corrected him. "That's the *Incredible* Hulk. And can I tell you something? When you grow up, you're going to look just like him!"

"Really, Mommy?" Christian asked excitedly as he tore the toy from his mother's hands and studied the voluminous muscles sprouting all over his compact plastic action hero.

"It's true, Christian. You're going to look just like him, except you'll be a whole lot taller, and not so green."

"Oh-boy-oh-boy-oh-boy!" the little gentleman jumped up and down in place.

"Now play nicely, Dear One. I'll be inside the house if you need me."

Ruth Hortense watched Christian lining up his army of toy soldiers along the pavement, and then walked through the rear door. Once back inside the kitchen, she got quickly busy, whipping together one of her prized apple pies. At the same time, she also kept a watchful eye on her boy, observing him playing outside.

Christian orchestrated a short, fierce battle, pitting his plastic soldiers against his two action heroes. But it was no contest as his massively muscled miniature super-men mercilessly kicked butt and knocked over a score of undersized infantrymen.

In little time, the three-year-old's short attention span snapped. Bored with the tumult of combat, Christian marched over to his shiny new fire engine truck. He studied his big toy, then looked up to the top of the roof of his house, then back down again at the tiny transport at his feet, and wondered if his new truck could remain in one piece if he threw it all the way in the air. Well, there was only one way to find out, so Christian wound up and whirled the twenty-seven pound truck around in circles a few times before flinging it up as high and as far away as his little arms could manage.

Ever on the lookout from her bay window, Ruth Hortense watched in wonder as Christian tossed the huge, heavy toy high in the air. When the fire engine soared overhead and landed near the peak of the roof, before it rolled down and got wedged within a rain gutter, she first made sure her boy was all right, and then hurried for the phone to call Dr. Marvin Tanner, a colleague of her husband's who specialized in problematic pediatrics.

*   *   *   *

Ruth Hortense waited impatiently as Dr. Tanner pored over the x-rays of Christian's skeletal structure. When at last the specialist looked away from the evidence, he calmly surmised, "I see nothing here to suggest we need take any direct action or change anything you've been doing. Your son may be three years old, but he's the size of most seven-year-olds, and already has the bone density of most ten-year-olds. If we lined him up alongside a hundred other boys his age, his height right now would put him in the top one percent, making him bigger, taller than ninety-nine of all the other boys."

"But, Dr. Tanner," Ruth Hortense tried making sense of the confusing x-ray images illuminated before her. "Just what does it all mean?"

"It means you're going to be doing a lot of grocery shopping," the physician answered, wryly. "From what these tests suggest, Christian's going to be an early grower who probably won't stop before he reaches who knows, six-three, maybe six-four."

"So then what do you suggest I do?"

"Well, when I observed him playing, he seemed quite agile. So if he were my boy," the pediatrician confided glibly, hoping to justify his fee, "I'd involve him in sports as soon as possible."

Transfixed, Ruth Hortense stared into the x-ray. "He'll need all his strength — I best not cut his hair."

*   *   *   *

For the first six years of Christian's life, Ruth Hortense insisted upon not giving her son a haircut. His lengthy hair, she imagined, was a necessary accessory, one of the more obvious signs of his emergent extreme strength. Even though Dr. Falconer protested that a boy Christian's age shouldn't be walking around looking like Goldilocks, Ruth Hortense remained adamant that their child not renounce his thick and curly, by then nearly shoulder-length locks of perfectly golden hair.

One oppressive August afternoon, Dr. Falconer decided it was time the social dictates of common decency took precedence over his wife's hysterical mysticism. He drove his son downtown, to Shorty's barbershop, where he insisted Shorty himself give Christian a proper military buzz cut.

By the time Dr. Falconer brought his boy home an hour later, Christian's biblical locks were ancient history. As they walked through their front door, Ruth Hortense took one look at her suddenly shorn child and flew into a hysterical rage. She cried, she stomped her feet, she carried on. Her full-tilt hissy fit was accompanied by sobs of southern-belle sorrow in tandem with a torrent of tears. When at last her explosion subsided, and just before she fled to her room, slammed the door behind her, pounced atop her bed, and cried unhappily into her pillow, she whined bitterly at her husband, "Maybe if you picked up a Bible once in a while, you'd already know — Samson never wore a crew cut!"

Half an hour later, as Ruth Hortense dried her eyes and straightened the bedspread, she also came to terms with the reality of her circumstance. Clearly, she held the mandate to help deliver Christian to his God-given destiny. Her husband refused to see the light concerning the ordained road map to their boy's future, so she had to step in to facilitate the fulfillment of his prophecy.

From then on, Ruth Hortense never stopped telling her son how extra special he was, never stopped reminding her extraordinary child about God's message of love, redemption, and salvation. She convinced Christian that the Bible was the inerrant word of the Lord, and every night, before she tucked in the youngster, they knelt by the side of his bed and prayed. Down on their knees, they clasped their hands and begged their dear Savior for peace of mind, for spiritual guidance, and of course, especially in Christian's case, for the good health and supreme strength that was his prophetic due.

One night, while praying with his mother, and with her full encouragement, young Christian first felt the presence of the Holy Spirit, and was then emotionally overwhelmed when flooded with a sense of forgiveness for everything he'd ever done wrong as a little boy. So moved was he by God's atonement for his sins, he gladly made the leap of faith required for Him to come into his young life and, with his mother's wholehearted blessing, Christian willingly accepted Jesus Christ into his heart.

*   *   *   *

As her son grew older, Ruth Hortense inundated him with toys, video games, and clothes — whatever his little heart desired. Not wishing to be outdone, Dr. Falconer also fought for his son's easily distracted attention by contributing acquisitions that were far more conspicuous. People needed to know that Christian wanted for nothing. That meant his son wore the most expensive clothes and attended the region's most prestigious schools. Dr. Falconer's Yale legacy would aid in assuring Christian's eventual acceptance into his alma mater. The ivy-covered path Dr. Falconer envisioned saw Christian majoring in biology, before going on to medical school, and ending up a respected physician in an upscale community. Like father, like son.

As for Ruth Hortense, she never wavered far from her fervent religious convictions, her irrefutable belief in the veracity of the Word. She welcomed meeting her family's monthly evangelical obligation by consistently tithing ten percent of their earnings. Before every meal, she implored Christian and her husband to join her in a short blessing, a prayer of thanksgiving. Though well intentioned, she repeatedly misquoted the Bible, often giving credit to the wrong chapter or verse.

She insisted her husband and Christian go with her to church every Sunday. While waiting in their pew for the service to begin, Ruth Hortense might take the opportunity to talk to Christian about a delicate issue over which she felt particularly passionate. "Promise me you'll wait until you're married before you make love to a woman," she beseeched her seven year old. "Anything outside of chastity at marriage is a mortal sin that will automatically stop you from getting into heaven. You just have to trust that God will send you a Delilah when He's good and ready. Are you listening to me?"

"Of course I'm listening!" Christian insisted, having no idea what she was talking about.

Christian's attention span was too limited for him to pay attention during church services, the temptation for his mind to stray too great. And when he looked down the pew and saw his father already zoned out, his eyelids drooping, it always gave him license to similarly flee from the boredom of the service and begin conducting in his head private story conferences all his own. Like father, like son.

The big difference, however, was that while Dr. Falconer reliably fantasized about voluptuous women deliriously slapping their humongous breasts back and forth across his face, Christian usually daydreamed about testing the superhuman powers of his action figures.

$$* \qquad * \qquad * \qquad *$$

Dr. Falconer knew that nothing suggested good breeding more than a working knowledge of fine music, so he introduced his lucky little heir to the works of Mozart, Beethoven, and Bach.

Sadly for Dr. Falconer, however, the only response his rowdy, energetic son ever displayed while being forced to sit still and listen to sonata after concerto after symphony over the family stereo on any given evening was his total boredom and complete lack of interest. Christian found the collective output of the masters of music more punishment than amusement, and nothing approaching enlightenment.

Despite Christian's resistance to the beauty inherent in Vivaldi and Wagner, Dr. Falconer hired a music teacher from a local junior college to teach the ten-year-old how to play the violin. And it took little time for Christian to develop a severe loathing for the prissy stringed instrument. As he put up with one silly tutorial after the next, the language of musical notes made little sense, and he would have much preferred playing with his action figures, or better yet, roughhousing with his schoolmates. Instead, he suffered through his music lessons, struggling to understand the screechy musical expression.

Once it became more fully clear to Dr. Falconer that Christian was not likely to become the next Itzhak Perelman, the frustrated physician adjusted his aspirations, and instead, had his son transfer his musical aptitude to next study the piano.

Christian's violin tutor was formally relieved of his responsibilities. The replacement musical mentor for the recalcitrant musician, one Miss Winifred Winslow, was a tall and willowy, aggressively unattractive woman, the very essence of old maid. She had thick eyebrows, long, bony fingers, and absolutely no facility for relating to children. She taught music robotically, practically by rote. During their hourly sessions, whether Christian was paying attention or not, Miss Winslow mechanically recited the inflexibility of the musical rules she memorized long ago.

Christian soon loathed the keys of the piano as much as he feared the strings of the violin. All those silly little ivories and far too many confusing notes — and who could recall or even care whether they were major, minor, flat, or sharp?

The whole effort was far too achingly dull for so overactive a boy who much preferred running around outside, playing touch football with his buddies, or dashing around the bases on his Little League team. He hated being the only player on the squad who had to run home right after practice three times a week for yet another stupid piano lesson. No matter how bitterly he complained, however, Christian couldn't get his father to release him from those stupefying lessons.

Six months after taking up the piano, eleven-year-old Christian could bang out little more than a rather hopeless rendition of "Poor Little Buttercup" from the Mikado, the simplest of musical compositions. After listening in on his son's lesson one day, Dr. Falconer confronted Miss Winslow. He wanted to know just why Christian was adapting to the keyboard at such a snail's pace. The boy's tutor claimed she had been hired only to instruct, and had little control over the pace of her student's skills. "And in Christian's case," she added ruefully, "his disinterest and easy distraction suggests this endeavor may not be the wisest avocation for him, after all." As Miss Winslow next launched into a dissertation on the connection between comprehending musical theory and actually banging out a tune, Dr. Falconer made believe he was listening intently to her and at the same time daydreamed about what she might look like outside of her blouse and twenty years younger, twelve pounds heavier, and four bra cup sizes larger. Miss Winslow finished talking just as Dr. Falconer snapped out of his momentary mammary reverie.

"I'm sorry," he said, politely. "Could you repeat that last part? I wasn't listening."

"Certainly!" Ms. Winslow retorted, pointedly. "I said your son has trouble paying attention."

Dr. Falconer didn't much care for the way the flat-chested piano teacher blamed Christian for his slow progress, to say nothing of her evident inability to tap into his hidden talent, and immediately relieved her of any further musical tutorial obligations having to do with his boy.

After his son's failures at musical aptitude, Dr. Falconer chose to take a step back and let Christian chart his own course for a while. He was curious to see down which of life's winding paths his progeny might next choose to wander.

∗   ∗   ∗   ∗

At his mother's urging, Christian began exercising on a regular basis. Each evening in his room, the twelve-year-old worked out. He did a score of push-ups, at least a hundred hard-crunching sit-ups, and ended his brief training routine with more pull-ups performed on the thin metal chin-up bar his mother set up at his request inside his walk-in closet.

After school one afternoon, instead of hitting his math homework, the pre-adolescent locked himself in his room as was his custom, and pounded out his push-ups, satisfied his sit-ups, and then walked into his huge closet, wrapped his hands around his chin-up bar, and started doing his customary dozen pull-ups, slowly raising and lowering himself up and down, up and down. To his surprise, smack in the middle of his sixth pull-up, while literally on the rise, Christian experienced his first pseudo-orgasm.

The minor explosion inside his jockstrap stopped short of being a full-blown, adolescent, spermatozoid release. His young body had yet to produce the testosterone which lay ahead, along with his first sprouting of pubic hair. But even without the bonus of any major expulsion, the life-changing sensation of whatever it was that just finished zapping through his gonads electrified him. The commotion in his groin felt so singularly satisfying, in fact, the young jock decided to see if he could make it happen once more, and immediately wrapped his hands around the metal bar. After only another five slowly-executed pull-ups, a smaller version of the same electrifying sensation once again encircled his gonads. Nothing ever felt so incredible.

Christian had no idea what was going on inside him, but treasured its rewarding sensation. Whatever in God's name it was didn't really matter, because he rejoiced in the bewilderment it left in its wake. He wiped his sweaty torso with a towel, and looked forward to the next afternoon when he could pound out a whole new set of pull-ups.

*   *   *   *

In the week following those landmark explosive episodes, Christian abandoned his sit-ups and push-ups. By then, the only exercise that held his interest, owing to the triggering effect it had on his testicles, was his blessed pull-ups. Every weekday, he hurried home after school to workout, eager to get to the privacy of his room, back to his slowly executed pull-ups and the extraordinary ersatz ejaculations that most often accompanied his ride.

After seven consecutive afternoons filled with exhilarating pseudo-orgasms, Christian began doing pull-ups throughout the day. His seemingly unquenchable excitement about provoking his newfound joystick into temporary rapture found him summoning his immature and as yet fluidless orgasms sometimes up to three or four times a day.

In just a few months, all this energetic concentration on nothing but those relentless pull-ups began manifesting positive physical results on the growing boy. One look at Christian's budding frame was all you needed to see the emergence of his athletic-looking musculature.

Christian felt a definite satisfaction in being taller and stronger than other boys his age, and was eager to develop superhero muscles all his own. He was so motivated that, shortly after he turned thirteen, with his mother's blessing, he bicycled into town to the local YMCA.

During his tour of the facilities that followed, Christian visited the indoor basketball and racquetball courts, the spacious areas reserved for calisthenics and gymnastics, the over-chlorinated swimming pool and the under-deodorized locker room. But it wasn't until the teenager was led into the weight-training room and saw all the equipment crowded in there, the multitude of machines, the cable stations, stacks of free weights, bench presses and barbells, that his eyes lit up. Oddly enough, when Christian observed how many of the mostly older guys working out in there were his size or even larger, he felt the same sensation of being filled with the Holy Spirit he sometimes sensed in church. He knew at once this was where he belonged and that pumping iron was God's gift to him.

After peddling home swiftly, he exuberantly told his mother how badly he wanted to join the Y. Ruth Hortense adored the notion and promised she'd discuss it with his father later that evening.

*   *   *   *

"Lifting weights rather than doing something practical like learning another musical instrument?" Dr. Falconer asked, incredulously, after his wife and he were tucked into bed and she brought up the feasibility of Christian signing up at their local YMCA. "Good God, woman. Show some common sense. What possible benefit could ever come from such a waste of precious time?"

"It could help make him big and strong," Ruth Hortense answered.

"He's already big and strong," Dr. Falconer insisted. "And he already devotes far too much of his free time to sports. Besides, this bodybuilding thing is beneath him."

"This bodybuilding thing is what he wants to pursue," Ruth Hortense insisted right back.

"I thought he might next take up the bass guitar. They say it's easier than the piano. Or how about the cello? It's not like YoYo Ma's had a bad life."

"He doesn't want to study music," Ruth Hortense insisted. "He wants to lift weights."

Dr. Falconer dismissed the very idea in his most didactic delivery. "It's simply not for our son. Lifting weights is the bastion of the hoi polloi: stevedores and blue collar riffraff."

"Oh, don't be such a snob," his wife dismissed his objection. "Can you think of a better way for him to fulfill the prophecy?"

"Please don't start on that nonsense again."

"Just you dare me!" Ruth Hortense answered sharply, her eyes wide, unflinching, as they met his.

When it came to most everyday elements of their well-ordered lives, Dr. Falconer always decreed precisely how things would be run: which magazines they'd read, which charities they'd support, which PBS shows they'd watch. But when it boiled down to the one or two odd issues in their marriage over which Ruth Hortense felt the most adamant, he had long ago learned there was simply no arguing with her.

"Fine, then," Dr. Falconer relented with a weary wheeze and one of his farcical eyeball rolls toward the ceiling. "Against my better judgment, Christian has my permission, if not my approbation, to go ahead and start lifting those silly weights."

There were times in Ruth Hortense's life when she asked herself why she stayed not just married, but committed to Dr. Falconer. She smiled benignly as she realized it was because of almost-tender, albeit infrequent moments like this. "Bless you, Dr. Falconer," Ruth Hortense sighed softly. She kissed the top of her husband's forehead with cordial affection, snapped off the light on the bedside table, rolled over onto her side, and, as she did every night, prayed herself to sleep.

"But I won't have him embarrassing me," Dr. Falconer warned in a stern addenda as he, too, turned his back on his spouse and stipulated, "He can only lift weights if he also keeps up with his studies." Then, picturing his nightly parade of big-nippled, pendulous jugs smacking him back and forth across his face in slow-motion, the good doctor allowed the arousal of his ritual to carry him into a placid slumber.

*   *   *   *

Christian focused all his youthful energy on his YMCA workouts, and stayed fully engaged in the building of his hormonally maturing body. Adding further euphoria to his zeal about his new endeavor, the big boy quickly discovered that by lifting weights, he could replicate the same thrilling, tingly, explosive feelings generated within his groin by his faux-orgasmic pull-ups. He got just as boned and often experienced the same explosive release when he worked out hard on the bench press. He looked forward to hitting the weights in the gym the way other boys his age looked forward to hitting the sheets at bedtime to beat off before falling asleep.

After just a few months of intense workouts, Christian's efforts begat genuine reward as he saw minor hints of major muscle groups taking shape on his chest, across the width of his shoulders and back, along the sides of his legs, across the ridges of his abs. Bodybuilding was a constant physical challenge, a test not only of Christian's hard-to-hold focus, but of all his strength. What more could he ask from a pastime?

The dedicated way the inspired youngster took to pumping iron did wonders to reinforce Ruth Hortense's deep conviction that her son was destined to build up his body. As she bore witness to his zealous fervor and the evident muscular development he was soon manifesting, she knew it was not just a casual blessing, but a true Godsend. Her son had found in his new hobby the perfect vehicle, one which would carry him to the heights, indeed, the widths, he needed to reach.

By the time Christian attended the exclusive Norton private school, the ninth grader was fast on his feet and agile with his hands. For him, bodybuilding and sports went firmly hand in hand. And to Dr. Falconer's utter dismay and Ruth Hortense's total delight, Christian took to football as if to the pigskin born. Big for his age, deft and aggressive, he brought to the field an ardent fervor and a clear facility for sports. Getting stronger as a result of lifting ever-heavier weights allowed him to become more aggressive, and made him that much harder to knock down as their sturdy defensive middle linebacker.

*   *   *   *

Christian spent much of his time daydreaming. Easily distracted, he could drift off whether in class, in church, or at home. No matter how hard he tried banishing the occasional erotic images that intruded into his flights of fancy, however, he couldn't stop himself from envisioning what it might be like, fooling around in vigorous horseplay with his teammates. In his head, they were sometimes decked out in football regalia, sometimes in varying states of undress. Mostly, he pictured his buddies simply strutting around the locker, skimpy towels encircling lean, chiseled waists, their young, powerful muscles on immodest display.

What Christian loved most about being a football player was not so much the actual game, which provided satisfaction enough, but more the incomparable feeling of closeness, the heartfelt male camaraderie he experienced when practicing with his teammates. He sensed a keen level of excitement whenever they changed into or out of their gear in the locker room, or whenever they all communally showered together after a practice.

On those sad occasions when they lost a game, the mood of gloom in the locker room was palpable. Some of the team players, overwhelmed by disappointment, broke down and wept openly. Whenever the Norton Vikings were victorious, however, the team was ebullient. Christian's own infectious high spirits invigorated the celebratory mood, filling the locker room with those feelings of camaraderie and bonding he so cherished.

Teenage boys best expressed same-sex affection by roughhousing like tiger cubs at play. Wrestling around half-heartedly with other jocks was about the only platform which gave them license to be tactile. Showering together after a successful battle was the most fun because that was when players blew off the most steam. You could count on lots of nasty harassing as guys ribbed one another mercilessly over the more vulnerable aspects of their personal adolescences.

If you bore a big butt, it became the butt of jokes. Large ears, big noses, humongous dicks were also fair game for ridicule. Got an obvious birthmark, boy? Step right up for a verbal drubbing. Facial zits, too much body hair, not enough body hair, too much body odor, or evident bad breath? You wouldn't even think about rinsing off before your weaknesses got derided, exploited, viciously mocked. Nothing was off-limits, and most everyone on the team got picked on for *something*.

Unscathed by all this, Christian was singled out only for his respected size, his surfacing muscles, his precocious strength. He loved it when his buddies noticed changes in his developing physique. The whole team knew him by his nickname, Samson, and he felt empowered by the positive attention it generated.

*   *   *   *

The novice bodybuilder sent away for a subscription to *Strength & Health*, and pored over every issue the moment the muscle magazine arrived in the mail. When he opened his April copy and came upon a full-page photo of Arnold Schwarzenegger, taken when the massive Austrian was training for yet another Mr. Universe contest, he couldn't help but gawk and gaze with reverence.

Saturated in sweat, the future Governor of California was draped over a preacher bench in full muscle contraction, pumping his biceps with a heavy E-Z-Curl bar at the Gold's gym in Venice, California. As Christian marveled at Mr. Universe's awesome biceps, an initial seed of aspiration was planted, because he knew right then he had found his future.

He fantasized how one-day he might get to also have his shot, training at the mecca of bodybuilding. He was raring to join the legion of young men who journeyed west yearly, dumbbells dancing in their heads, just so they could pump iron at Gold's, alongside the competitive bodybuilders who had first inspired them in muscle magazines.

*   *   *   *

In his junior year, during a football game, the sixteen-year-old recovered a fumble, but then got clobbered by four bruisers from the rival team. No bones were broken, but the lower part of his leg remained swollen for weeks. The aching injury sidelined the middle linebacker for the rest of the season.

Christian hardly minded. He knew an aggressive approach was the swiftest path to his full recovery, so he returned to the Y and worked out daily. Restoring his legs to the power they possessed before his injury fueled his motivation to become a still bigger bodybuilder. Christian traded in the aches he endured on the football field for the far more rewarding sweet discomforts derived from the strain of lifting weights in the gym. He pumped up and bulked up and, after three months of intense training, was not just fully recovered, but actually bigger and more powerful than before his unfortunate tackle. The huge adolescent built himself into such tiptop shape that he was encouraged by Coach Freemont, who ran the Physical Education Department, to train to compete in a teenage bodybuilding contest.

*   *   *   *

When he turned seventeen, Christian entered his first competition. By then, he stood six-feet-three-and-three-quarters and weighed a sturdy two-hundred-ten pounds. Nervous and scared witless, but nonetheless undaunted and fully determined, he registered for the Teenage Mr. Fairfield bodybuilding tournament, signing up in both their Novice and Teenage categories.

Dr. Falconer was off in Detroit, attending a medical conference, and still didn't even know about the competition. Thrilled to be included, Ruth Hortense gladly drove her boy to the event. She even went backstage with him to help prepare. She assisted in gingerly applying a final pair of coatings of dark skin toner onto his large, well-muscled body. The devoted mother watched with bursting pride as, curling light dumbbells, he pumped up. She grasped her hands around one end of a towel while he held tightly on to the other and bobbed up and down, doing so-called sissy squats to stretch his quads.

When Christian looked around the pump-up room and realized he was the only competitor whose able assistant was his mother, he felt ill at ease. Part of his father's obsessive concern-with-appearances had rubbed off on him, and last thing he wanted was to give the impression that he was some kind of mama's boy.

Onstage that afternoon, three dozen overbuilt, over-tinted contestants were instructed by a disembodied voice emanating from a distant sound system to go through their mandatory poses, all collectively executed in muscular unison. Each time the announcer called out a particular pose, the contestants assumed that position. A chorus line of bodybuilding exhibitionists flexed their best front double biceps, showed off their side chests, their rear double biceps, their abs and thigh poses, their side triceps, their front lat spreads and finally, their rear lat spreads.

Each contestant's name was then called out and they stepped forward one by one for their moment in the spotlight. When Christian's name was announced, it was his cue to hit that stage and do a solo performance of his pre-rehearsed posing routine. Suddenly downright petrified, his knees began to buckle and in near panic, his intestines turned to Jell-O. What if he confused the chronological order of the poses required in his well-rehearsed, individual flexing routine? What if the crowd didn't respond to his carefully chosen, pre-taped posing music? What if, under glaring lights, face to face with a live audience, he freaked out and just stupidly stood there, motionless?

Christian called off his anxiety attack and left his ruminations behind as he prosecuted his preprogrammed poses with all the simplicity of a youth-driven power coupled with a precocious grace. By competition's end, however, he was disappointed when he came in fifth among the Novices, and placed sixth among the eight other competitors in the Teen division.

*   *   *   *

Driving home after the contest, Ruth Hortense gushed about how proud she was of her boy, seeing how outstandingly well he placed for a beginner.

"Hey, Ma!" Christian interrupted his mother's burst of ebullience. "I placed fifth and sixth in my divisions, okay? I fumbled badly. Sure, I'm big and bulky. Just not nearly cut up enough."

"Nonsense," declared Ruth Hortense. "You did just as the Lord intended. Praise Jesus!"

Ruth Hortense was so overjoyed, she was barely fazed when Christian then told her she could no longer accompany him backstage to any future contest.

"But Dear One," she rationalized. "You saw all those boys. Every contestant needed help in getting ready. If I'm not there to paint and discolor you, who's going to do it?" She then suggested, facetiously. "Your father?"

"Sure — why not?" Christian exclaimed, hoping by chance that Dr. Falconer might be so taken with his boy's first genuine interest in an extra-curricular activity, he'd welcome the opportunity to serve next time as first lieutenant.

However, when asked if he'd help out, Dr. Falconer demurred. Typically aloof and icily polite, he claimed the scheduling of his upcoming medical conventions rendered him unavailable to assist Christian with his future contests. The good doctor then pointedly added that he wanted no part in anything as vain and senseless as Christian's unsettling devotion to so garish a display of overdeveloped bodies.

Several weeks later, Ruth Hortense and Christian drove for several hours down to Chester, Pennsylvania, where he would compete in the Mr. Teenage Philadelphia contest.

Upon arrival at the arena, Ruth Hortense, as pre-arranged, headed straight for the auditorium to sit and wait, while Christian went directly backstage to the pump-up area — on his own. Having dismissed his first lieutenant, Christian simply asked one of his fellow contestants if he wouldn't mind assisting in smearing his final two coats of war paint needed to turn his skin into a ludicrous shade of dark brown.

Onstage at his second contest, while again performing his solo posing routine, Christian was more relaxed, exuding an easy-going self-confidence. From all appearances, it seemed as if he almost broke into a smile. By competition's end, however, he was discouraged when he came in fourth among the seven young men competing in his Teen division.

With his energies focused principally on training hard for his contests, Christian's schoolwork took a familiar back seat to his passion. His considerable attention deficit was by then an as yet undiagnosed disorder. Dr. Falconer did what he could to improve Christian's grades by lording over him and sending him to his room nightly to hit the books. He deeply resented having to lower his inflated expectations for his son's academic and professional endeavors. It further disappointed him that, despite the personal, father-to-son legacy for which he had worked so hard to hand down, and despite his hard-earned social connections with the university faculty, it was painfully clear that his heir would never get into Yale.

At term's end of his senior year, when Christian shamefacedly brought home an especially dismal report card, a mortified Dr. Falconer hit the roof. "Good Lord," he berated his wife. "If your son spent a tenth of his time picking up books instead of those stupid weights, he might have learned something by now."

*   *   *   *

By July, the budding bodybuilder, still training to compete, placed seventh in the Teen Division of the Mr. Darien contest. He came in ninth in the same category at the Mr. Interstate competition, and was demoralized when he didn't place at all in the highly competitive Mr. Collegiate competition.

Christian's poor showing in his initial bodybuilding contests disheartened him. The main impediment to his landing a coveted second or even first place trophy was evidently his oversize. It was plain to see he was big and beefy, with the added plus of genetically gifted proportions. However, anyone in the auditorium studying all the bodybuilders flexing alongside him onstage could also see his drawback. Christian needed to become less bulky, better defined.

No one was more aware of his shortcomings as a bodybuilder than he. His impressive massiveness showed up in the mirror plain as day whenever he played his prerecorded music and practiced his posing routine. And when he finally opened up and shared his mounting frustration with his mother, she assured him she would look into it.

Late in the afternoon several days later, Ruth Hortense stopped by the Norton School, went down to the Physical Education office and asked to meet with Christian's former football instructor. Coach Freemont greeted Ruth Hortense, said he had a few minutes before his next gym class, and invited her to follow him into his nearby cubicle.

Coach Freemont was all business as he listened intently to Ruth Hortense's concerns over Christian's less than prize-winning streak.

"Mrs. Falconer," the Coach decreed with a loud clap of his hands. "Your boy's a big, natural athlete. He was sure fast on his feet, and always took a lot of punishment on the football field, at least until he got injured. But as I recall, he was also ... well, you know, a bit lazy, easily distracted during practice. That's why I was glad to see him doing so well with his bodybuilding."

"Both Dr. Falconer and I were thrilled when he found something he's so good at," Ruth Hortense lied sweetly. "So I was hoping you might be able to tell me why you think he's not placing better."

"May I be frank with you, Mrs. Falconer," Coach Freemont asked as he leaned against his desk and got directly to the point. "It's as simple as this: If you want Christian to be able to compete more successfully in this arena, you might consider modifying his training tactics somewhat." With a dispassionate shrug, Coach Freemont added, "There is, after all, a potentially viable option ..."

Ruth Hortense was all ears. "And just what might that be?"

Coach Freemont looked over his shoulder as if to ascertain they were still the only ones in his small cubbyhole of an office. "You must understand what I'm about to tell you now is strictly confidential and private, just between you and me ... completely off the record."

"Yes, yes, no problem," Ruth Hortense quietly agreed, and scooted her chair closer to the coach's desk in avid anticipation. "I only want to do what's best for Christian."

"Okay," Coach Freemont clapped his hands together once again. "You didn't hear it from me, of course. But what it comes down to is this: if you want your son to build himself up so that he might go on to compete as a viable player ... well, you may already know medical science has been making major strides in muscle enhancement. So you might look into getting him started on a cycle of steroids."

"I have no problem with that," Ruth Hortense offered with a surprisingly light-hearted shrug. "Do you know where we can get some?"

"That part's not so easy," Coach Freemont told her. "You can't get a cycle of ste-roids without a prescription."

"I know that," said Ruth Hortense. "I am a nurse."

"And your husband's a physician!" Christian's coach declared. "So why don't you just ask him?"

"Thank you, Coach Freemont," Ruth Hortense offered a big smile as she stood to leave the cubicle. "That is exactly what I plan to do."

*   *   *   *

That evening in their dining room, while Christian was still upstairs washing his hands, Ruth Hortense carried her roast beef platter to the table, and obsequiously placed it before Dr. Falconer for the deft wizardry of his anatomical dismemberment. As she handed over his carving utensils, she also calmly told him the upshot of her little chat that afternoon with their son's former coach.

Christian's father could not have been more adamant in his response. "Absolutely not!" He huffed vehemently. "Steroids are completely out of the question. We don't yet know anything about their long-term effects. Christian spends enough of his time in pursuit of that aimless hobby, as is. Good God, woman, don't you think he's already big enough? I simply refuse to imperil our boy's future well-being for some haphazard, untested, temporary pharmaceutical stimulus!"

As Christian bounded his way down the stairs and into the dining room, Ruth Hortense raised her hands into the air in her familiar gesture of surrender and quietly intoned, "Whatever you say, Dr. Falconer."

By the following afternoon, Ruth Hortense was on a mission, her own spiritual quest, if you will, as she sat down at her computer in her husband's office and spent several hours combing through science and medical publications, scouring research papers, and dissecting statistics, voraciously learning everything she could about this strange new subject of steroids: their use, their abuse, their good points and their bad.

After weighing the positive elements — rapid muscle growth, loss of fat — against the negatives — outbreaks of acne, an extended gut, mood swings, long-term effects to organs as yet undetermined — Ruth Hortense prayed to be blessed with some confirmation that Coach Freemont was right, and that steroids might be the path Christian needed to take. Since her son was still so young and healthy, she felt confi-dent that his hearty constitution, accompanied by the Lord's blessing, could easily assimilate such an untested supplement, and could well withstand or reject any lurk-ing side effect. Willingly, she placed the entire matter in God's capable hands.

God responded faster than Ruth Hortense ever expected. The following Wednesday, she was back at the desk in her husband's office, paying their monthly bills. Doctor Falconer was in an examination room behind closed doors, probing a tumor amassing on the neck of one of his patients. When Ruth Hortense opened the middle drawer in search of envelopes, her eyes came to rest upon her husband's blank prescription pad. Clearly the providential sign she had sought: there it was, just lying there in plain sight, all but calling out to her.

"Well, don't that just beat all?" Ruth Hortense muttered, not taking her eyes from the pad. Consistently vigilant, her husband reliably kept his prescription pad securely locked in the bottom drawer of his desk. An hour earlier, however, after he speedily scribbled off a Xanax prescription for an anxiety-addled patient, he uncharacteristically neglected to restore the pad to its permanent place in the bottom drawer and then lock it. In his haste, he instead tossed it haphazardly into the unsecured middle drawer.

Ruth Hortense removed the blank pad and laid it out flat on her desktop. Her husband always, but *always*, kept his prescription pad locked up. It was one of the countless idiosyncrasies from which he never varied. Yet, there before her sat the fast-track ticket by which her son might achieve the aspirations he had for himself, as well as the accomplishments she wished for him.

What else could this be? She asked herself, *if not yet another clear sign from the Lord?* The prescription pad was an unambiguous answer to a mother's prayer, and Ruth Hortense wasted no further time debating potential ramifications, complications or even dire consequences resulting from the forgery she was about to perpetrate. Instead, she simply took pen in steady hand and, casual as you please, studiously imitated the sloppy, gibberish style of her husband's infantile scrawl as, carefully, she wrote out a healthy prescription for the anabolic steroid, Deca-Durobolin. She then capped her deception by scribbling her husband's name at the bottom of the form.

Dutifully following God's dictate with her contribution to satisfying the prophecy, she returned the pad to its improper place in the middle drawer, where her husband was sure to find it. She then folded the prescription into her purse, clasped her hands together in prayer, looked high up past the ceiling, straight to the heavens above, and once again quietly intoned, "God's will be done."

*   *   *   *

Two days later, not long after Christian returned home from his workout at the gym, he got an urgent call from his mother. She told him to drop everything and immediately bike down to his father's office.

"Now pay close attention to me," Ruth Hortense instructed with uncharacteristic authority, half an hour later, as she shepherded Christian off into one of Dr. Falconer's examining rooms, and locked the door behind her. She purposely conveyed a serious air so he would pay careful attention to what she was about to tell him. "I need to take you into my complete confidence, Christian," she said intently. "You have to promise me, no, swear to me, right here on our family Bible, that what's about to transpire must never go past these walls — that it must remain a secret."

"No problem, Ma," said Christian. "Mum's da woid. I swear."

"I wanted us to have some privacy, so I waited until your father went to his hospital board meeting."

"Fine," Christian shrugged. "What the devil are you talking about?"

"First swear for me," Ruth Hortense insisted. *"Swear to God!"*

"All right, all right, I swear to God," Christian allowed with a lazy shrug of his shoulders. "What's so important?"

Ruth Hortense calmed down, came out with a bright smile, and snapped back to her more typically softer self, sweetly asking, "We both know Moses carried his staff to ease his path up and down Mount Sinai, right?"

"Of course, Mother. And that's why you called me down here?"

"Listen to me!" Ruth Hortense demanded. "And we certainly recall how God gave Samson all that beautiful hair to go hand-in-hand with his God-given gift of great strength, yes?"

"You only told me about a million times."

"Well, Darling, we also both know very well how God wants you to become a towering man among men."

"Yeah, Yeah … I've also heard that my entire life," Christian said as he rolled his eyes toward the ceiling in the same way his father often did when displaying impatience with Ruth Hortense.

"Okay, Son," Ruth reached for a syringe filled with a translucent liquid which rested innocently atop a nearby sterile towel. "The good Lord has put it on my heart to give you a blessed gift, a little something extra. Call them booster shots. You're going to bike down here every Wednesday for the next twelve weeks, while your father's at his board meetings, so I can administer them to you."

"What's in it?" Christian asked skeptically, staring at the scary-looking syringe in his mother's hand.

"Deca-Durabolin," his mother told him.

"Wow," her son muttered softly in total awe as his eyes lit up. "The steroid?"

"Yes, Christian," his mother registered surprise. "You know it?"

"Yeah," Christian answered. "I've heard guys talking at the gym."

Ruth Hortense placed her free hand softly against the side of her son's face with tender affection and looked him straight in the eye. "You can't tell anyone about this, ya hear? Not your former teammates, not any of your pals down at the Y, and most importantly, certainly not your father! Do you understand?"

"I sure do!"

"Good! Now turn around, zip down your pants, and drop your drawers."

"But, Ma," Christian protested and took a short step back. "You know I hate needles."

"Oh, don't be such a big baby," Ruth Hortense insisted. "It'll only sting for a moment. Surely, any pain you suffer will hurt me a lot more than it could ever harm you."

Christian couldn't argue with such irrefutable logic, and so he did as he was told. A brave soldier, he dropped his drawers, squeezed his eyes shut and, with visions of superhero muscles massaging his imagination, he relaxed his butt cheeks and accepted the needle's sting.

*   *   *   *

As the potent power of Christian's Deca cycle kicked in, the young bodybuilder's muscle growth accelerated its already impressive late-adolescent pace. Fired up by his mother's heavenly revelation, and inspired by his own drive to get the most benefit from the shots, he set his sights on upcoming contests, and soon began split training, working out twice daily.

In Christian's fevered quest to take in more than two hundred and twenty grams of muscle-building protein every single day, one gram for every pound of his body weight, he consumed massive amounts of food. Throughout the course of any given day, over five, six, sometimes seven meals, he gobbled up six cans of water-packed albacore tuna. In the same twenty-four hour period, he gulped down some forty-eight eggs, the lot of them spread out over four generous helpings of a dozen egg white omelets, each quickly whipped into shape and always lovingly prepared by his benefactress, Ruth Hortense.

Christian's impressive muscle progress paid off handsomely when, at his next contest, six weeks later, he placed second in the Mr. Teenage Collegiate competition. The month after that, he finally walked off with first prize in the Mr. Teenage New Haven contest.

The teenager grew, grew, and then grew more — so much so that by the time he was two-thirds of the way through his cycle, he had already packed on thirteen pounds of pure muscle mass. Not only did he get bigger and broader, but, as predicted, he got far more cut and better-defined then ever before.

When Dr. Falconer observed his son's hurried muscle growth — it would have been hard *not* to notice — a part of him was a bit suspicious, and found him wondering if his wife hadn't somehow cavalierly disobeyed his authority. On the other hand, there was a very small part of him that was actually impressed with Christian's apparent accomplishments, especially seeing how his boy, usually so easily distracted, was at last keeping his focus on a single endeavor. Still, there was no way Doctor Falconer could ever lend his support to so purposeless an enterprise as excessive muscular development. And since he would never deign to be seen at an event so *déclassé* as a bodybuilding competition, he never attended his son's contests.

He did, however, make a point of giving Ruth Hortense several scientific papers to read covering recent research enumerating possible harmful side effects arising from the abuse of steroid-based muscle enhancers. He also kept his prescription pad locked safely away where it belonged, in the bottom drawer of his desk. Once again, he was the only one with access to it.

*   *   *   *

Christian was elated by the gains his developing body achieved from his steroid cycle. He never tired of practicing his posing routine in front of the mirror, never stopped feeling downright awed by the sheer quality of change in both the shape and size of his impressive growth. His six-pack was shredded, his pecs and biceps bulged with mass, yet were well defined and vascular. Made stronger by his striking growth, his heightened motivation drove his intense split-routine workouts, and he never once stopped devouring the bounty of his mother's nourishing meals, never stopped fueling the machine he built into his prize-winning body.

Ruth Hortense took Christian shopping for his workout gear as well as all his supplements. She didn't protest when he picked out a particularly expensive protein powder, craved a costly pair of workout pants, or swore he couldn't live without another over-priced supply of L-Glutamine, the amino acid powder needed for muscle recovery that he added to his protein drinks. Devoted to her son's progress, she caved in to his every wish.

When Christian told her all he wanted for his eighteenth birthday was a car, she assured him she'd take care of it. However, when she mentioned the idea to Dr. Falconer as they dressed to drive into Manhattan to meet friends for dinner before the ballet, her husband initially bristled. "He's still too young and irresponsible," Dr. Falconer insisted, dismissively.

"But all his friends have their own cars," Ruth Hortense insisted right back. "Besides, if he has a car, he can start driving himself to his bodybuilding contests. I think he feels awkward, a bit pampered, having to be brought there by his mother."

"For good reason, woman!" Dr. Falconer huffed, sternly. "He *is* pampered. You've spoiled the boy rotten."

When it came to keeping up with the Joneses, Ruth Hortense knew how great was her husband's need for acknowledgement of his conspicuous consumption, so she shrewdly appealed to his soft spot, stating, "Dr. Falconer! How do you think it makes us look if he's the only eighteen-year-old in the neighborhood with no car?"

That hit home. His wife's rare moment of level-headedness made sense. "Fine," he told her. "But if we get him a car for his birthday, it can't be some dinky jalopy. He may look like an oversized ranch hand, but I want people to know he hails from affluence and sophistication."

As it turned out, Dr. Falconer was right. Once Christian got his driver's license, he certainly looked polished and sophisticated as he buzzed around Greenwich behind the wheel of his spiffy, new, Corvette convertible. His son's hot wheels may have been a hell of a lot more expensive than what the doctor originally wanted to spend, but he took a definite pride in knowing Christian garnered admiration and envy among his peers when zooming around his neighborhood. He knew his son's luxury sports car telegraphed the doctor's distinctive standing within their upscale community.

Several weeks later, on a perfect spring morning in mid-May, Christian was fully energized as he was about to drive over to Westport on his own for his next bodybuilding contest. Ruth Hortense accompanied her son to his new Corvette, which sat in their driveway, still freshly agleam, and reeking of all the prosperity Dr. Falconer could muster.

As Christian opened the car door, his mother took her beloved boy in her arms and kissed him in farewell. "Don't you worry now. I won't be late. I'll leave here in a while. But I won't go backstage, annoying you. I'll be out front, in the auditorium, cheering louder for you than anyone."

"I'm sure of that," Christian quietly lamented.

Ruth Hortense wished her son Godspeed and then casually slipped a brand new fifty-dollar bill into his hand. "Some pocket money for you, Dear One," she whispered. "Now go show them what a real Samson looks like!"

*   *   *   *

Zipping exuberantly along, a mere twenty miles an hour or so over the legal limit on the Connecticut Turnpike, Christian headed to the Interstate competition with the top down on his classy new convertible. On the road, he sang along vigorously to the music of a local Gospel station blaring from his stereo. He pulled into the Westport Park & Recreations Center and then, surrounded by a swarm of other competitive bodybuilders, hurried inside to the front of the auditorium to register and weigh in. He used the fifty-dollar bill his mother had given him to pay his contest entry fee, and then went backstage to the pump-up room to prepare.

By the time he was applying his fourth and final coat of Pro-Tan, Christian couldn't help but notice Tom Ketty, the handsome, older competitive bodybuilder alongside him who'd been stretching and pumping up with fifteen-pound dumbbells — and who also hadn't stopped looking his way.

Christian felt awkward and averted the older bodybuilder's eyes, even though he was eager to initiate some jock-to-jock conversation. He wanted to find out what this older guy was doing with his training that still kept him in such great shape.

It seemed as if the mature bodybuilder heard what Christian was thinking because he suddenly turned, introduced himself, and then suggested that he and Christian help each other finish getting tinted. "You know, if you're not fully darkened, those stage lights really wash out your muscles, make them look flat. I've been competing long enough to know it takes two people to get a whole body fully bronzed."

Christian smiled in agreement with the mature bodybuilder, adding, "And some places are harder to reach than others."

"I've learned that the hard way," Tom mused, as he sort of chuckled and placed his dumbbells on the floor. He was entered in the Master's Division, reserved for men over forty. "My best friend was supposed to help me out, like always. But he came down with the flu."

The Master's competitor applied a heavy coat of Pro-Tan across the breadth of Christian's back. The older muscleman's firm application of the tanning cream across Christian's lats and down the back of his hamstrings felt stimulating, even a bit unnervingly erotic. And it sure beat the pants off having his mother doing it for him.

Tom Ketty then turned around so Christian could do the same paint job on him. In short time, both men's skins, along with all the other competitors, projected a preposterously unnatural tone approaching varying shades of mahogany. Their collective darkened hues made many of them seem better-suited for a politically incorrect minstrel show than any beauty contest.

Once deeply tinted, Christian and the older bodybuilder slowly finished pumping up side by side. The windows in the huge facility were wide open, and a gentle,

warm wind bathed the crowded room in a welcome promise of the summer to come.
By the time Christian and the Master's competitor were ready to go onstage to perform their posing routines, they were pumped, painted, and jacked, the pair of them
ready to strut their stuff by showing off the fruits of their labors.

That afternoon in Westport, both Christian and his new muscle buddy fared
extremely well. Christian scored a solid victory when he won first place in the Teen
Division, while Tom, in a far more competitive category, placed third in the Master's
competition.

Backstage, after the presentation of cumbersome trophies, Tom congratulated
Christian with a strong, brotherly hug. They each then collected their change of
clothes and left the building.

"Well, Christian, if you ask me," Tom Ketty suggested as they headed toward the
parking area, "it is my firm belief that our mutual success today calls for some kind
of celebration."

"Sounds good to me," Christian told him. "What'd you have in mind?"

"Well, I've been diligent about my food intake for the last eleven weeks," Tom
decreed. "Haven't had so much as a potato chip. I think maybe it's time we broke
training!"

Christian smiled in cautious agreement, even though he had no idea what Tom
had in mind.

"Hey!" Tom stopped in front of his dilapidated Plymouth and hit the top of his
forehead like he'd been struck with inspiration. "My place is just a few minutes from
here. Right off the Turnpike. Why don't you just follow me? I chilled a six-pack of
Miller, figuring if I competed well, I'd celebrate. If not, I could drown my sorrow."

"Then what are we waiting for?" asked Christian. "Let's celebrate!"

*   *   *   *

An odd mix of musclemen, the forty-one-year-old and the eighteen-year-old settled into Tom's cramped bachelor apartment, and chatted innocuously about the
contest, about Tom's nine-to-five job as a loan officer at a local bank, about his last
few girlfriends, and about Christian's new car.

Christian was amazed how much chummier and chattier he and Tom became
after they each polished off a few bottles of Miller's. In training most of the time, the
young man was not yet accustomed to the effects of alcohol. Tom's unpretentious
hospitality, along with the intoxicating brews, helped Christian unwind, and they
both soon discovered they shared a ravenous excitement about bodybuilding, as well
as a common thirst for getting into ever-better shape. It took little time before they
both stood tall before Tom's full-length mirror, shirtless, performing for their mutual
reflections, encore highlights of their respective posing routines.

The Master's competitor offered Christian several helpful pointers regarding his
posing technique, and complimented him on every part of his beautifully developing
physique. He was also quick to point out with a forced chuckle, "And just so you

know — I'm not gay or anything. I love girls, I mean, especially women. Older, in-shape women drive me nuts. Hey, can we ever get enough pussy?"

"Never!" Christian agreed wholeheartedly as, in unison, they each struck their impressive Most Muscular poses for the mirror. By that point in their flexathon, Christian was more distracted by Tom's powerful presence than any conviction his host was espousing in justifying his sexual predilection.

"But on the other hand ..." Tom chuckled again, mid flex. "Maybe it's also impor-tant sometimes to — you know — expand our horizons. We both know you don't have to be a homo to appreciate how great another well-built guy looks. Besides, man does not live by breasts alone!"

"That's probably true," Christian half-heartedly concurred with a playful bounc-ing of his pecs.

The sight of this young, naive bodybuilder showing off with such a lack of inhibi-tion got Tom so whipped up, he quickly dropped the subject of his vaulted hetero-sexuality and instead just dropped to his knees. With no further rumination, Tom speedily untied Christian's workout pants, pulled out the big boy's stiff cock, and wrapped his mouth around it.

Flustered by this not-so-surprising turn of events, Christian was all set to protest, to forcefully push Tom off and back away, but the alien, ecstatic sensation coming from below his waist was so electrifying, he decided to postpone any protest.

In the middle of all his dizzying oral activity, Tom freed his mouth from the teen-ager's fully extended manhood long enough to mention that what they were doing, how they were fooling around, was strictly a manly diversion, in no way related to anything so perverse as same-sex attraction. "We're just letting off some steam after all that intense training," Tom assured him.

Their intimacy, such as it was, abruptly concluded anyway, when Christian, dis-oriented from his intake of beer, erupted prematurely and shot a copious load of late adolescent sperm directly into Tom's mouth. The third-place Master's winner gurgled euphorically while slurping down every last drop of the first-place Teen's bodily essence.

Oddly enough, as soon as Christian came, Tom's teeny apartment suddenly seemed so much seedier than before, and Christian felt both soiled and claustropho-bic. A wave of punishing guilt washed over him, and he excused himself. After quickly washing up in the bathroom sink, he slipped back into his tight T-shirt and workout pants, thanked Tom for a truly unusual experience, and then bolted from that den of iniquity in what between orgasm and departure, even for a beginner, may have been record time.

While driving home, Christian flashbacked over the day's seminal events — from taking off in hot wheels all his own, to flexing his way into first place, to then going off and flexing with Tom. However, he made a point to convince himself that the Master's competitor was right about the oddly erotic way things ended up. What transpired between them was simply a buddy-buddy bonding experience.

Masculine men with powerful, athletic bodies could roughhouse or fool around with each other now and again and still not be labeled homos, couldn't they? Besides,

Tom was the one who'd taken their connection further, committing that act of sexual defiance. Christian didn't want to be rude, which is why he hadn't bothered protesting his host's sexually stimulating beneficence.

Christian had never given much thought to his sexual orientation, and had always done a fine job of pushing away any stray, promiscuous notions his subconscious dared elevate to the surface. His level of denial found him convinced that when it came to other men, any interest lay purely in an appreciation of muscle, rather than any interest in their genitalia. By his very nature, he knew he was heterosexual and couldn't possibly be gay. He preferred pecs to pricks, liked delts more than dicks, appreciated abs above ass, and guessed he was merely passing through an awkward adolescent phase.

The choices in Christian's life required the certainty of his heterosexuality. He knew his fascination with muscular men was purely platonic and, God willing, temporary. He thought it no big deal that, aside from a few shy kisses exchanged in dimly lit corners at make-out parties, he hadn't yet really fooled around with girls. He always knew the proper Christian values by which he was raised would someday translate into his getting married and raising a family. At his mother's urging, hadn't he long ago given God that commitment? Freely, he'd embraced his mother's wishes, vowing his obedience *not* to engage in sexual relations until *after* he wed. He reminded himself how, given the rambunctious, amoral character of modern-day life, he needed to aspire toward a higher ethical conduct. He could only marry someone who also believed it was imperative they both remain virgins until their nuptials.

As if to confirm how daunting it was to wear his pledge of celibacy as a badge of honor, Christian gripped the steering wheel, cranked up the volume on his Gospel station, fully depressed the accelerator and, singing along at the top of his lungs, sped down the turnpike, a young, still straight, future breeder, barreling forward, directly toward the setting sun.

* * * *

To Christian's deep regret, the twelve weeks of his Deca cycle sped by far too quickly and, after his mother administered his final *booster* shot, he woke up one morning in the middle of the summer to discover the wind knocked out of his sail.

He saw it right there in the bathroom mirror before him, plain as the pecs on his chest. So much of his impressive muscle gain, the bulk of his added mass which had inflated principally through the process of water retention, was rapidly disappearing, evaporating like snow beneath a midday sun, sadly taking along with it too much of his glorious muscle progress.

It was all fading so fast, and Christian wasn't prepared to let it go. Not just yet. *Please Dear Lord,* he prayed. *Help me find a way to hold on to the bulk of my new muscle growth — if not for the rest of my life, then please, God, I beg you, for at least a little bit longer — maybe just long enough to carry me through the upcoming Mr. Central Connecticut contest.*

When Christian pleaded with his mother to secure for him another prescription of Deca and administer another secretive cycle, she told him she could no longer get to his father's prescription pad. "And even if I could," she added. "I'm no longer so sure they're such a good idea. Your father gave me some more material about steroid usage, and I realize now I may have erred in giving them to you. It could be harmful to your liver and I'm worried now about long-term damage."

"But, Ma!" Christian pouted in protest. "The Mr. Central Connecticut contest's just six weeks away. Don't you want me to compete at my best?"

"Of course, Dear One." Ruth Hortense forced a meek smile. "But what can I do? My hands are tied. Let's just be grateful for the nice results we got from that gift from the Lord. For now, I think it would be best for everyone if we simply drop the whole subject. For good."

But Christian refused to drop the whole subject. He asked around the Y and, after speaking to a few of the bigger bodybuilders, was surreptitiously handed the phone number of a guy who sold black-market supplements on the side.

Lance Petrie was that guy, and he was an enormous bodybuilder; a two-hundred-and-sixty-three pound muscle monster who weighed in with far more fat than muscle mass. He had spotted Christian working out in the weight room at the Y, and appreciated the eighteen-year-old's evident zeal for constructing his body. So when Christian approached Lance and asked if he knew anyone who could help round up another cycle of steroids, the mountain of a man assured the teenager he had come to the right source. "Meet me here tomorrow at four with three hundred-fifty bucks in cash. I'll have an eight-week cycle of Deca for you."

"Excellent!"

"This stuff is from Mexico," Lance told Christian with a wide grin. "Liquid dynamite. If you need syringes, that's another fifty."

"No problem," Christian told the behemoth. "My parents are in the medical field. I can supply my own needles."

As Christian sped home in his Corvette, he held a short wrestling match with his conscience as to the moral implications of what he was about to do, but had little trouble quickly pinning his self-doubts to the mat. Did he not, after all, have a clear obligation to do whatever was necessary to help him realize his Samson prophecy? Had it not been drummed into his head ever since his first push-up?

While his mother was in the kitchen, unloading freshly purchased groceries, Christian ducked into his parents' bedroom and into his father's walk-in closet where he grabbed one of the packets of cellophane-wrapped syringes stored in a box atop the highest shelf. Then he crossed over to his mother's walk-in closet and looked inside several of her purses until he found her checkbook.

Carefully, quietly, he tore off the bottom check. If anything, he reasoned, might it not be going against God's plan *not* to follow through with another cycle? Christian pictured himself onstage at his most recent contest in Westport, looking so accomplished and feeling so fit, sensing the audience's admiration, their positive reaction to him at the top of his form and at his muscular best; and the satisfying image was all he needed to make up his mind.

He cautiously wrote out a check made out to Cash and, at the bottom, meticulously forged Ruth Hortense's polished signature. Then he replaced the checkbook, snapped her purse shut and left his parents' bedroom.

After thanking God in advance for the blessing of the additional booster he was about to receive, he drove quickly over to Greenwich Savings and Loan and cashed the fraudulent bank draft.

*   *   *   *

Six weeks later, Christian once again placed first in the Teenage Division at the Mr. Central Connecticut contest, and surprised everyone, especially himself, when he came in third in the Men's Overall. Ruth Hortense was beyond thrilled. Even Dr. Falconer finally took a quiet, if unacknowledged, pride in his son's emerging success in his chosen preoccupation.

Christian's mother proudly displayed her son's trophies on the Falconer mantle. However, the doctor didn't care for the eyesores, and insisted the only purpose they served was to clutter the living room. "If you feel compelled to be so self-aggrandizing as to insist upon displaying them," he told Christian in his typically patronizing tone, "can you kindly do so in the privacy of your room? You don't see me hanging my medical diploma above our fireplace, do you?"

Christian took it all in stride and transferred his trophies to his room. By that point, he had long ago concluded the only thing he and his father had in common, anyway, was that they were both inhabitants of the same household.

*   *   *   *

Christian never cared much for school, had never been a good student, and certainly had no interest in attending college. Still, he figured it had to be better than, God forbid, getting a job and having to work for a living. So he attended New Haven Community College, where he was forced to feign interest in his mandatory freshman classes in English Lit and Fundamentals of Science. As he sat through ponderous lectures, boring instructors laid out age-old syllabuses. Christian lent but half an ear, and passed the class daydreaming and watching the clock.

The only thing Christian liked about community college was the gym where he trained on a regular basis for his next contest. By the time he completed his second steroid cycle, he was so impressed with his gains, he dreaded the thought of again watching all his hard work and blissful results dissipating into thin air. He hadn't seen his steroids contact down at the Y for at least several weeks, and when he asked around the pump room, was told that Lance had gotten busted when federal drug agents nabbed him in a sting operation which also rounded up half a dozen other Connecticut distributors of illegal substances.

Christian's only connection to his next cycle had dried up. Backed up against the wall and frustrated, the budding muscle champion had no choice but to aggressively take the matter once again into his own hands. He needed to steal his father's prescription pad as well as forge another of his mother's checks — without getting caught. The Mr. Tri-State contest was coming up in less than two months, and there was simply no other way he could compete at his absolute best against all those other steroid-enhanced muscle monsters.

*   *   *   *

When Christian returned home from the gym the following Saturday afternoon and found he was the only one in the house, he headed straight for the ceramic bowl on the table in the foyer and pocketed the set of office keys his father kept there. Then he hurried upstairs, found his mother's checkbook and ripped out a check. He left his house, jumped into his Corvette, and drove even faster than usual, straight to his father's office. He felt nervous, jittery, as slowly, he let himself in. After carefully unlocking the drawers of the office desk, he pulled out his father's prescription pad and flipped through all the receipts until he came upon the carbon copy of the prescription his mother had written for his initial cycle of Deca.

In his whole life, he was never more focused as he opened the pad to a fresh page and then diligently copied the prescription's exact formula — from the curves of his mother's handwriting to the imitation of his father's Latin scribble and down to the contours of his mother's own initial forging of Dr. Falconer's signature. And since he was already going through so much troublesome deception, Christian further figured, what the hell, he may as well write out the prescription for twice the dosage his mother first forged. Sensing a goofy feeling of surreal accomplishment, Christian replaced the prescription pad, locked the drawer, closed up his father's darkened office again, and sped back home.

*   *   *   *

An urgent phone call was placed several days later.

"Hello, Dr. Falconer? It's Jonesey, down here at the pharmacy."

".... Jonesey," the doctor acknowledged.

"I'm re-filling your prescription for that Deca-Durobolin," the pharmacist informed the physician. "But I'm a bit confused by the size of your order."

"There must be some mistake," Dr. Falconer insisted.

"That's what I thought. I mean, did you really want to double the dosage you prescribed last time."

"I beg your pardon?" protested Dr. Falconer. "What last time? I wrote no such prescriptions!"

"You mean you didn't authorize them?" The pharmacist asked, puzzled.

"Certainly not!" An indignant doctor protested.

"Well, then ... Good thing I called, huh?"

"Very good thing!" Dr. Falconer concurred. "And you can just rip up that forgery," he instructed the pharmacist.

"Well, you know, I'm also required to report such counterfeiting to the police. But I wanted to check first to see if maybe you'd rather take care of this, yourself, personally, and leave him out of it."

"Leave who out of it?" Dr. Falconer wanted to know. "For whom was the prescription written?"

"Dr. Falconer, it's made out to your son," the pharmacist said as he glanced at the prescription in his hand. "It's for Christian."

Fuming inside, Dr. Falconer icily insisted, "That being the case, Jonesy, I see no need to inform the police. I'll take care of this issue, myself. And thank you for calling."

*   *   *   *

"I WANT HIM OUT OF MY HOUSE!" Dr. Falconer bellowed into the receiver the moment Ruth Hortense picked up the phone. "If he's not gone by the time I get home, I swear to God, I'll call the police and have him thrown in jail. Is that perfectly clear?"

"What in the world?" asked Ruth Hortense, mystified.

"Imagine!" The good doctor huffed. "My own son, compromising his father's integrity and moral character — the very goodwill it took so many years to build up."

"Dr. Falconer, please …" Ruth Hortense interjected. "You're not making sense."

"Good Lord, woman, I am a respected member of this community. Why the very notion of so flagrant a disregard of my authority sickens my stomach. He's no son of mine, and I want him out!"

"Now, really, Dr. Falconer …" Ruth Hortense tried subduing her husband's outrage. "Whatever it is, it may not be his fault!"

"Not his fault?" Dr. Falconer raised his voice. "Can you imagine if Jonesey hadn't called to check with me, but had first gone to the police?"

"Jonesy at the pharmacy?" asked Ruth Hortense, catching on. "Why'd he call *you*?"

"Just imagine if the police had shown up at our door!"

"Oh, come now, Dr. Falconer," Ruth Hortense tried easing her irate husband with an infusion of southern charm, and asked in her sweetest, most coy, little girl tone, "Can it really be that big a deal?"

"HAVE YOU HEARD ANY OF WHAT I"VE JUST SAID?" Dr. Falconer erupted into the receiver.

"All I've heard so far is screaming." Ruth Hortense insisted bravely.

"Damn! I knew something was up when he grew so much bigger so damn quickly. But hold on. He didn't just break the law and forge my name once. Seems he also broke the law months ago, as well."

Horrified, Ruth Hortense brought an open hand to her mouth as she realized there was no way out. It was time to own up to her deception, to confess that the first forgery was hers. Ever-fearful of her husband's explosive wrath, however, she also knew this was no time to further enflame his ire by disclosing the truth. He first needed to calm down.

"He's such a big shot, let's see how well he does on his own," Dr. Falconer continued. "I'm cutting him off as of now, Ruth Hortense, do you hear me? RIGHT NOW! And that's final!"

"But, Dr. Falconer …"

"I'm sorry, but he has no respect for me, for us — for all that I've done for him, all we've done, everything I've tried to give him, and I want him out of the house and gone!"

"But, Dearest — there's something you should know …"

"I know all I need to know, DAMNIT!" the doctor hollered into the receiver. "So he better be out of there before I get home! He's cut off. Finished! And if you don't like it, you can just pack up and go right along with him. DO YOU HEAR ME NOW?"

Still shouting, Dr. Falconer slammed down the phone.

*   *   *   *

Ruth Hortense was often intimidated by her husband's forceful nature. But by the time she hung up the phone, she was also so upset, she came surprisingly close to taking him up on his threat. For the briefest of moments, she actually considered dropping everything — just turning her back on their regimented life in Greenwich and leaving, walking out alongside Christian, wherever he might be headed, precisely as her husband had dared.

On the other hand, wasn't it her duty, her destiny, to stick by her mate through thick and thin? Wasn't she still that righteous Christian woman who long ago swore to God that she would love, honor, and obey Dr. Falconer for the rest of their days, for better and for worse? But why, she wondered, was it so often so much worse and so rarely any better? She wondered if maybe Dr. Falconer wasn't right at least about one thing. Maybe what Christian really did need was to be on his own. With a deep sadness, she realized she could hold him back no more. Her son needed to get on with his life.

When Christian returned from the gym, freshly showered and fully pumped, he found his mother in his room, bedside, amid several opened suitcases. His folded underwear, his socks, assorted shirts, and several pairs of pants surrounded her.

"What's all this?" he wanted to know.

"Your father's kicking you out of the house," She quietly told him.

"Oh, shit!" Christian muttered as he quickly surmised, "He found out about the steroids?"

"He found out about the steroids," she repeated softly and placed several pairs of perfectly folded Jockey shorts into one of the open suitcases.

Christian's shoulders slumped forward as he looked down at the floor. "Was he furious?"

"Like you can't imagine."

"Damn. I'm so sorry," Christian said quietly.

"We would have been okay if you hadn't gone ahead with that second forged prescription. What in the world were you thinking?"

"I had to do it, Ma." Christian offered with a stupid shrug of apology. "The Tri-State show is just a few weeks away. How else could I compete?"

"Why didn't you come to me?"

"I did, remember? You said your hands were tied."

"Well, now we're in a fine mess," Ruth Hortense offered as she stood and walked over to Christian's bureau. She opened the bottom drawer and pulled out several sweaters. "We need to be fast. Get you packed and out of here, on your way. I'm thinking six pairs of underpants to get you started."

A little over an hour later, Christian piled his packed bags and his set of dumbbells into the back of his Corvette. Ruth Hortense handed him a sack filled with fresh apples, pears, raisins, almonds, several grilled, skinless chicken breasts wrapped in foil, plus a few bananas. "Here," she offered sadly, "something for you to snack on."

"Thanks, Ma," he told her, still somewhat bewildered by all that had so rapidly transpired. He lobbed the grocery bag onto the passenger seat.

Ruth Hortense looked down at the ground in shame. "I'm heartbroken about this," she said forlornly. "Lord forgive me. It's all my fault."

"Mine, too, Ma," Christian managed a sad smile of farewell.

Ruth Hortense reached into her pocket, pulled out a small wad of greenbacks along with a Visa credit card and shoved them both into Christian's shirt pocket. "Here," she said, forcing a hesitant smile. "A couple of hundred dollars and one of your father's credit cards. He rarely uses it and the bill always comes to me. So if you stay below the limit, he'll be none the wiser."

Ruth Hortense took her son in her arms, squeezed hard as she could and fought back tears while giving him a heartfelt hug. "Promise me you'll take good care of yourself," she implored. "Who knows? This may work out for the best. You talked about finding a place of your own, anyway."

"Don't worry about me, Ma," Christian told her as he returned her squeeze with just as much affection, and dabbed at the tear running down the side of her face. "I'm big and strong. I'll be fine."

"Call if you need me. And let me know soon as you're settled. Let me know where I can send more money. I know I won't sleep a wink before then."

"Will do, Ma," Christian said as he patted his padded pocket and then got in behind the wheel. Looking up at her, he rolled down the car window, took her hand and quietly asked, "How will I ever survive without you?"

Ruth Hortense smiled sadly and softly said, "I'll never stop praying for you, Son. Godspeed!"

*   *   *   *

While zooming down the access road, several minutes later, heading toward the Connecticut Turnpike and nowhere in particular, Christian weighed his options.

His first thought was to head directly over to Fairfield, maybe check into some cheap motel until he found an apartment. That way he could find a local gym and keep up with his training while he got ready to compete in the upcoming Mr. Tri-State bodybuilding show.

When he braked to a halt at a red light just across the entrance to the Turnpike, he thought fast. Should he turn left and head east, toward the familiarity of Fairfield, some thirty miles away, or should he turn right and drive out toward uncharted territory?

Sitting behind the wheel of his Corvette, both literally and figuratively at the crossroads of his life, Christian decided to put his trust in the Lord and begged the Holy Spirit to guide his next move. He watched the light turn green and at the same time made a snap decision, one prompted by little more than sheer impulse. As he accelerated forward, he also figured what the hell, this was as good a time as any to pursue the long-lived daydream that was his ultimate bodybuilding fantasy. As he floored the gas pedal, full throttle, and headed for the Turnpike's tollbooth heading west, a spontaneous, inexplicable erection sprouted within his shorts.

Next thing Christian knew, he was zipping along the highway of life, not headed the thirty miles over to nearby Fairfield to prepare for its upcoming contest, but off in the opposite direction, en route clear across the country, toward the mecca of serious bodybuilding that awaited him three thousand miles away in Southern California.

*   *   *   *

For the next five days, Christian drove way over the speed limit, across highways and interstates, racing pell-mell, stopping only to eat, sleep, or refuel, until he eventually wound his way to Venice, California. Finally in the muscle capital of the world, the champion bodybuilder checked into a dingy, thoroughly depressing room at the local YMCA.

When Christian phoned his mother, she was relieved he was safe, but also deeply concerned he ended up so far away from her. "I'll wire some money out to you right away," she told him. "And if you need me, I can fly out, help you get organized and settled."

The last thing Christian wanted was his mother there with him. So he told her he relished his newfound independence and planned to find some way to support himself, to become self-reliant.

"I'm so proud of you, Dear One," his mother acknowledged. "You're being so brave."

"Hey, Ma, we both gotta be brave."

Neither of them alluded to the reality that his breakaway independence was thus far contingent upon her continuing generosity.

As soon as she hung up, Ruth Hortense drove to her local post office, where she immediately cabled a cashier's check to Christian for nine hundred dollars. After that, she continued supplying him with a steady flow of cash through a stream of cashier checks, another fresh five, six, or seven hundred dollars arriving every week.

* * * *

Although uncertain about his precarious future, Christian cheerfully coughed up the cash for a six-month's membership at Gold's gym in Venice, and then began working out in earnest.

Daily, the young bodybuilder thanked God for setting in motion the events that brought him there. After checking out several dilapidated rooms in the neighborhood, he paid a first-and-last month's rent for a bachelor apartment situated at the rear of a graffiti-stained, multi-unit complex. His undersized habitat came partially furnished with a lumpy bed, a dysfunctional fridge, and an ineffective microwave. On the bright side, the dump was within walking distance of his gym.

Christian adapted quickly to his uniquely Southern California bodybuilding lifestyle. He thrived on pumping up alongside so many contest-winning superstars within the pantheon of muscledom, the biggest champions of the sport. Several were the very bodybuilders of massive proportions who first inspired him back when he studied their profiles in his muscle magazines.

Christian felt right at home at Gold's. When you're a massive bodybuilder his size, you couldn't help but appear to more normal perspectives as some sort of aberrance, an oddity of nature. Back home in Greenwich, wherever Christian went, his mega size stuck out like an oddity. He was never at ease over the constant scrutiny, whether negative — "*Yo, who's the muscle freak?*" — or positive — "*Oh my, who is that Greek God?*" sent his way. A great advantage once he started working out at the Venice landmark was that his eccentric size no longer seemed so ludicrous.

Whenever he pumped iron in any of Gold's cavernous rooms, Christian was surrounded by other muscle monsters, many of them men of similarly outlandish proportions who also subscribed to his doctrine that a bodybuilder can never get too huge. The biggest men huffing, puffing, and sweating through their workouts derived a sense of security in the commonality of their abnormal oversize. Many of them suffered from dysmorphia, a lack of visual objectivity. Hence their drive to get bigger, more muscular and bigger still. Erase the past. Lose that once-bullied slender little kid, that long ago chubby porker; leave your yearning to be someone else in the trail of your protein powder as, pound after muscular pound, you reinvent your image and expand into a physical entity large enough for two men.

And while Christian wasn't dysmorphic, per se, you could tell from the way he confidently pounded the heavy weights that he was an obvious member of the club, one of Gold's Big Boys: their unofficial, exclusive fraternity of larger-than-life muscle monsters.

Deeply focused on his training, the only drawback to Christian's bodybuilding bliss was his damn expensive cost of living. He hated shelling out the eight-twenty-five every month for his tiny digs. Then there was all the food intake and multitude of supplements he downed daily, all needed for stoking the furnace of his muscular upkeep. Despite his mounting expenses, he strove to stay in step with the monsters of mecca, and wished he weren't so damn poor, wished he could afford just one more cycle of steroids.

*   *   *   *

Back home in Greenwich, Ruth Hortense harbored a deep resentment over Dr. Falconer's merciless banishment of Christian. Dispirited over her family's schism, she struggled long and hard with her conscience as to what she might do about it.

No matter how hard she tried to release her sadness, let go her antagonism, no matter how often or ardently she prayed about it, for the life of her, she couldn't in her heart find a way to forgive him. While at home, she and Dr. Falconer barely interacted with one another. Their intermittent verbal communication was frosty and perfunctory, pseudo-polite at best.

After much fretting, she elected to maintain the status quo of the charade that was their marriage, and went mechanically through the motions of her obligations, serving as the doctor's dutiful wife, his reliable nurse. And although she went along with the sham, she also moved her things out of their master bedroom and took up Christian's vacated room as her own.

She was cautious and discreet while keeping alive her trans-continental connection with Christian, constantly providing his monetary needs. She juggled her husband's books with enough convolutions until she found a successful way to manipulate the Falconer budget so she could fire off additional cashier's checks to her son for another five or six-hundred dollars.

How would he ever survive without her, indeed.

Dr. Falconer hardly minded when his wife abandoned their conjugal bed. The only reason he'd elected to sustain their marital masquerade in the first place was for the sake of propriety. He could never admit failure, never suffer the black mark placed on a failed marriage. Not the good doctor.

Although the Falconers barely spoke at home, their social intercourse when out together in public was a whole other matter. He projected a facade that gave the impression his life with Ruth Hortense was hunky-dory. He rationalized that so long as their image as a couple appeared rosy, what did it matter that, in truth, such was hardly the case?

One night after the symphony, Ruth Hortense and Dr. Falconer were having a late supper in a chic Manhattan restaurant, making believe they were tolerating one another. As Ruth Hortense took a sip of her wine, she offhandedly dropped her baby bombshell. "By the way, I heard from Christian. He's living in Southern California."

The doctor bit into his Chilean sea bass, gritted his teeth, then nearly choked on his words as he spat out, "Seems he moved as far away from us as he could. Well, I say good riddance. He's your son now. The only way he might ever redeem his deceptive behavior would be to apologize, beg his father's forgiveness." Dr. Falconer poked the flaky flesh of his fish with his fork and added, "So unless there's something I truly need to know, let's not bring up the subject of Christian again. We'll see how well he does out there on his own. And you are *not* to send him any money, is that clear?"

"Would *I* do that?" Ruth Hortense asked, with the innocence of a saint.

*   *   *   *

Although it troubled her greatly to see their boy so estranged from his father, Ruth Hortense thereafter kept all interactions between Christian and herself to herself. She phoned him several times a week, usually while the doctor was examining patients. Bravely, she disobeyed Dr. Falconer's specific orders when she didn't stop wiring their son his weekly money orders. She secretly shipped him care-packages filled with much-needed basics: linen, washing detergents, tee shirts, whatever he requested.

Toward the end of February, after Christian had been in California six months, Dr. Falconer went shopping at an upscale electronics shop in downtown Greenwich. After looking around, he wrote a check for seven thousand four hundred fifty dollars to have a top-of-the-line stereo system installed in his office. The doctor knew how much income he turned over to Ruth Hortense to deposit each month, and trusted their bank account could cover so hefty a withdrawal.

He was surprised several days later when he received a note from his bank saying their dual checking account was overdrawn and that his check had bounced. Humiliated by such a financial disgrace, the doctor quickly set about clearing up this probable clerical error, and waited for Ruth Hortense to go shopping before he rummaged through her desk in his office. Soon enough, he found the reason their account suffered insufficient funds: a listing of several dozen checks made out to cash for five, six, or seven-hundred dollars.

As he continued rifling through his wife's papers, Dr. Falconer came across recent statements from one of his reserve credit cards, and became furious when he found a score of postings for hundreds of dollars charged to gas stations, restaurants, supplements from health stores — all in the Los Angeles area. Lastly, when he pored over their most recent phone bills, he found a cluster of collect calls placed from Venice, California.

Furious, feeling betrayed, Dr. Falconer called his MasterCard's 800 number and summarily cancelled his credit card account, effective immediately. Then he closed his office early and drove straight over to the bank, where he moved all funds from his and Ruth Hortense's joint balance into his individual account.

When she returned from her shopping, Dr. Falconer confronted his wife's maddening deception the moment she walked through the front door. "I'm cutting you both off," he announced sharply. "Both you and your son."

Ruth Hortense knew she'd been unmasked. She figured sooner or later her boorish husband was bound to find out about Christian's financial support. The doctor had only to open his eyes. She'd just hoped to postpone for as long as possible the ugly scene about to unfold. "Please, Dr. Falconer," she acquiesced, obsequiously. "I can explain everything,"

"I put myself through college, didn't I?" He insisted, rhetorically. "You think that was easy? Nothing builds character like hard work. You've made it too easy for him, and it's got to stop. If he wants to live the life of a sybaritic pagan in Southern California, he's going to have to support himself. Let him get a job, like everyone else. And no more collect calls from him."

"I'm so sorry," Ruth Hortense began to sob.

"Believe me," Dr. Falconer sternly insisted, "you're far too many years late for sorry. If he wants to talk to you, let him be a man and pay for it with his own money. I won't have our bank account drained just so he can build up his body while his mind evaporates in that vacuous culture out there. When I say he's cut off, I mean just that. He's on his own!" With an indignant snap of his fingers, Dr. Falconer twirled around and, still on his high horse, bolted from the room.

The next day, the good doctor relieved his wife of her trusted obligation to pay their monthly bills, and systematically turned all their finances over to their family accountant. He placed his wife on a strict allowance, one so prudent, she needed permission just to go out and get a manicure or join her girlfriends for lunch. He made certain she no longer had the funds, the financial means by which to again assist their wayward son.

When Christian's next three collect calls to Greenwich went unaccepted, and after he endured the embarrassment of having his credit card rejected at a gas station, he paid in coins to call his mother and, although it broke her heart, she told him his father had taken control of their finances.

"He wants you to be on your own — for good," Ruth Hortense told him, sadly. "He thinks it'll make a man out of you."

"I'm already a man!" Christian protested defensively.

"Maybe you should come back home, Dear One. All your father needs is one sincere apology and then everything can go back to normal."

"Thanks, Ma," Christian responded in all honesty. "I think I'd rather starve!"

*   *   *   *

As the last of Christian's cash rapidly vanished, he drove up the Pacific Coast Highway in his Corvette and visited several used-car dealerships. After negotiating and comparing a host of absurdly low offers, he signed over the ownership of his powder- blue status symbol. In exchange for his spiffy hot wheels, he received both a check for four thousand dollars as well as the keys to a beat-up Volkswagen Rabbit.

The big fellow looked somewhat foolish as, uneasily, he wedged himself behind the steering wheel and then drove off the lot in the little bug. Some tit for tat. Mile for mile, the smog-belching eyesore got great gas mileage, but in car-happy Southern California, where perception was reality, the chugging heap also telegraphed his financial hardship.

Christian went quickly through the money he received from the sorry sale of his Corvette, and was soon again down to the last of his cash reserve. He needed to find some way to keep going. While stepping into his jock strap in the locker room at

Gold's before a legs workout one afternoon, he overheard a couple of bodybuilders who were drying off after showering. One of them mentioned Chez Joey, a nearby, would-be ritzy steakhouse just about to open across from the beach. Christian's ears pricked up when he next overheard that their management was seeking strong men to carry big trays. After his workout and then a fast shower, he drove over to the restaurant.

The fidgety manager of Chez Joey who interviewed Christian was impressed with the young man's size and apparent strength. He was also under so much pressure to complete the hiring of his wait staff before the restaurant's scheduled opening that coming weekend, that he went against his better judgment and, despite the applicant's having no prior work experience in the field of food services, offered Christian a job as a waiter.

Two nights later, outfitted by management in a stiff, white shirt, black slacks, and one of their butcher's aprons, the muscle monster worked the busy opening of Chez Joey, delivering martinis, taking down orders, returning overcooked prime rib and underdone sirloin.

After the restaurant's successful start, Christian worked Chez Joey's lunch and dinner shifts, six days and nights a week. Working so many hours drained his energy. Between shifts, when he could summon the energy, he drove over to Gold's in his dumpy VW, and did his half-hearted best to keep up with his training.

He hated his new job, hated having to put up with snooty, demanding customers. He dreaded being bossed around by Chez Joey's well-to-do clientele — pencil-necked geezers and their over-coiffed wives. *"Hey, Boy — let's have some more water over here!"*— *"I said I wanted my steak well done!"* The stress of it all took its toll, and Christian's workouts began to suffer. His lack of proper muscle rest exacerbated his prevailing sense of exhaustion. As was so often the case when he lifted heavy, he couldn't be bothered with good form. And when he bent over in the gym one afternoon to dead lift a barbell loaded with two hundred pounds of plates, something in his spinal column shifted. A lightning streak of unspeakable pain shot across his lower vertebrae and he literally had to limp out of the gym.

The next day, still in excruciating pain, he visited a chiropractor who adjusted him and then concluded he'd need at least a dozen more treatments before his agility might even have a shot at snapping back to prime pumping-iron condition.

The chiropractic adjustments Christian undertook ate up most of the money he picked up from tips, and afforded him only temporary relief. Every time he returned to the awkward juggling of a table's worth of porterhouse steaks, his suffering returned anew, and his persistent back pain made him despise his job that much more.

*   *   *   *

One Saturday night at Chez Joey, as Christian waited on a table of uncharacteristically agreeable customers, he overheard them chatting about their welcome sanctuary, an evangelical church that was but a short drive up the Coast Highway, in the heart of Malibu.

For Christian, the timing was providential. He didn't need to report to work again until the dinner shift the following evening, and decided to use his infrequent off-time to attend the Sunday service. Given the potent power of prayer, he hoped the Lord might help him find some way to alleviate his pecuniary woes.

The Evangelical Church of Malibu, with its fresh coat of white paint and towering steeple set against a cloudless sky, sat perched atop a wind-strewn bluff, overlooking the ocean. As Christian pulled into its parking lot the following morning, it seemed the perfect picture of a Hallmark card.

For those who believe God's hand is in *everything*, it could be argued that nothing less than an inspired intercession was in play that holy day because, also in attendance, already seated in her customary pew, was Pipsi Sterling, a petite, twenty-year-old socialite/celebutante. Both tastefully and expensively attired, she projected not only an air of unaffected sophistication, but also a vivacious demeanor. One glance at her chic Prada pants-suit or her perfectly coiffed hair or her freshly manicured nails was all it took to see she was as well-groomed and pampered as the prize-winning horses she raised at her nearby mini-ranch on the other side of the Malibu Hills. At five-feet-two and one hundred six nicely-proportioned pounds, she appeared so stylish and displayed such infectious merriment, it was easy to overlook the reality that she was, beneath her perfect hair and meticulously applied make-up, rather plain-looking.

Pipsi smiled brightly as she waved at other church members. Then, from that first heavenly moment she laid eyes on Christian as he walked into her sun-drenched house of worship, she was struck with an immediate, almost mystical, attraction to him. Pipsi couldn't help but smile in appreciation at the huge newcomer's imposing presence as he lumbered his way down the aisle.

Preoccupied with looking for a place to sit, Christian failed to notice the young woman smiling so gleefully at him as he plopped down in the pew directly behind her. The sun shining through the stained-glass window at the back of the church bounced off Christian's colossal frame and cast a giant shadow across Pipsi, spreading itself as a penumbra across the scope of her forward vision. At the same time, an unfamiliar sensation within her system began pounding heavily with runaway adrenaline. When she turned around to sneak in a better glimpse of him, their eyes locked momentarily. He caught her bedazzled stare, smiled politely, and lowered his head.

Pipsi quickly diverted her eyes over to the stained glass window. Still, their brief gaze was all she needed. One look at Christian and she was a goner. It was the oldest cliché in the book: love at first sight.

Embarrassed at being caught gazing so blatantly at the huge young man, Pipsi zipped around again to face front. Her palpitating heart confirmed her preposterous conviction that the larger-than-life bodybuilder who just smiled so sweetly back at her was the man for whom she had always waited.

Whereas many women felt intimidated by the sheer oversize of muscle monsters like Christian, and had little interest in watching them flex or pose, Pipsi was an exception. She felt totally enthralled by the sight of a well-built muscleman. To her mind's eye, the way Christian was built was nothing less than an answer to her prayers.

And speaking of prayers, for the duration of the service, Christian prayed. He prayed as hard as he could, humbly placing it all in His hands: his uprooted instability, the pounding pain in his lower back, and, of course, the major mess of his monetary predicament.

Sitting directly in front of Christian, Pipsi spent the entire service staring down at the umbrella of the shadow the big fellow spread before her. All the while, she shifted her attention from him to hymn to Him. She prayed that after the service ended, she might get to introduce herself to the hulking object of her sudden thrall and infatuation.

Alas, prayers are not always answered, and Pipsi's well-thought-out ploy to welcome the strapping young man to the Evangelical Church of Malibu was short-lived. The moment the service concluded, even before the organist launched into a rousing rendition of *Amazing Grace,* Christian zipped up the aisle, barreled out from the church, and drove his dilapidated Rabbit down to Gold's for a light chest and triceps workout before he headed to work.

$$* \qquad * \qquad * \qquad *$$

As the pain in Christian's spine intensified, he grew ever more desperate to find some way to give up his backbreaking job at the restaurant. Problem was, he hadn't worked long enough yet to qualify for unemployment insurance, and he still needed a steady flow of cash to pay his chiropractor who adjusted his injured lower back three times a week. No matter how destitute, however, he remained intent upon putting aside enough money to finally score steroids for his next cycle. He hated being so far from even near-contest shape, and resented the fact that he could no longer turn to his mother to help him get out of the fleabag that was his pocket-sized bachelor apartment.

At Chez Joey, still suffering from his ongoing back pain, Christian still carried full loads of steaming dinner platters out to his tables. However, stabbed by a knife-like spasm in his lower back while carrying one especially weighty load one dinner hour, he lost control of his tray and sent seven sizzling steaks crashing to the floor with a thunderous clamor. Once the mess was cleaned up, the manager warned Christian that if he screwed up again, he'd be out of a job.

The next day, between shifts at the steakhouse, Christian milled about the Starbucks located around the corner from Gold's, nursing a double espresso. He hoped its caffeine jolt might blast him with sufficient energy to prosecute a halfway-decent biceps and delts workout.

When he finished reading one of the new postings on the bulletin board in the back of the coffee shop, he figured it had to be a hoax. However, given his dire financial predicament, he wanted to be certain, so once again, he carefully read the curious message …

FINANCIAL FREEDOM FOR FUTURE CHAMPION

Extremely generous, older gentleman interested in mentoring and providing full financial support to aspiring bodybuilder. Your only job will be to train full-time, get in top shape for a contest.

I want to reward your hard work in the gym by taking care of all your needs, and that will include not only use of your own room in my impressive living quarters, but also luxury travel to contests, plus all the food you need to consume, all the muscle-building supplements you need to get big (hint, hint, tee-hee!). For a bodybuilder with the right attitude, I'll even toss into this golden opportunity an ample spending allowance.

Significant additional cash can also be earned for competing successfully. Ideal protégé is driven, focused, goal-oriented, and eager to show off the fruits of his labors.

No sexual favors required or expected in return.

A slave to muscle, all I want is to bask in your glory.

Robin — (310)659-8069

Even as Christian hastily jotted down the number, he still suspected there had to be a catch. Why would anyone ever be so philanthropic without expecting something in return? Another piercing pain arched its way across his lower back, and he envisioned the nightmare of discomfort that lay ahead for him in a few hours, toiling at Chez Joey. When another spasm abruptly seized his lower back, he decided, what the hell, he had nothing left to lose; so he turned and headed for the pay phone.

*   *   *   *

ROBIN KINCAID — MIGHTY MOUSE MUSCLES

Hopelessly short, banister-thin and outlandishly wealthy, Robin Kincaid was a sixty-two-year-old trust fund baby who fashioned a career in the carefree management of his diverse investments. Even without the aid of his financial advisors, the entrepreneur had an uncanny knack for trusting his instincts and making ever more money. His financial independence allowed him to devote the bulk of his free time to serving as a major muscle sycophant.

In his official capacity as mentor to muscle, Robin sponsored aspiring bodybuilders, often traveling with them around the country, indeed the world, attending bodybuilding contests in grand style. Most often, the "protégé" under his current tutelage also competed in the show. A devout worshipper, Robin lived to admire muscle and was never so proud, never more vocal than when he attended a contest. Standing as high on his tippy-toes as his diminutive, five-foot-three-and-three-quarters-inch frame would allow, he zealously cheered the posing routines of his current muscle boy.

As for his own sorry physique, Robin was soft and scrawny, a veritable wisp of a man. Tipping the scales at barely one hundred twenty-three pounds, his inferior physical appearance was rendered that much less imposing once he opened his mouth and out popped his pipsqueak, Truman Capote voice.

Robin's mother died while giving birth to him about the same time his widowed, industrialist father scored a lucrative contract to supply the plumbing for a fleet of submarines built for the US Navy during World War II. He got rich, literally worked himself to death, and then left a chunk of his considerable fortune, several million dollars, to his eleven-year-old heir.

Ten years later, once Robin assumed his legal inheritance, the astute twenty-one-year-old invested his freshly acquired funds in blue chips and gold reserves. As the market soared and his earnings doubled and then tripled in relatively rapid time, his financial advisors began referring to him as their investor with the Midas touch.

Robin fashioned for himself an extravagant, decades-long lifestyle, most of which revolved around the opulent splendor of Kincaidia, his ten-thousand-square foot villa spread over an acre and a half of immaculately manicured grounds, tucked away in Trousdale Estates, in the middle of the "Platinum Triangle," between Beverly Hills and Bel Air.

*   *   *   *

"Robin Kincaid's residence!" announced Lester, the buttoned-up, British houseman.

"Yeah ... Hello ..." Christian stammered into the phone. "Uh ... is ... a ... uhm ... Robin there?"

"Whom shall I tell Mr. Kincaid is calling?" Lester asked with a stiff-upper lip.

"My name is Christian. I saw his posting in the coffee shop. But if this is a bad time ..."

"No, not at all," insisted the houseman. "I'm sure Mr. Kincaid will be delighted to speak with you. Hold on while I see if he's available."

Robin Kincaid was lounging in his library, but quickly put down the latest issue of Flex magazine when Lester buzzed the intercom to announce a lad named Christian was calling about his ad.

The little man quickly clicked a button and squeaked breathlessly into his cell phone, "Hello, this is Robin! So, Christian, tell me, are you by any chance a serious bodybuilder?"

"Well, yes," said Christian, wondering what business he had making this call in the first place, wondering why the high-pitched fellow on the other end sounded so unbearably eager. "I'm calling about the ... notice you put up."

"Excellent!" Robin bolted straight up in his lounger. "Please ... please do tell me a bit about yourself."

They shared a short, amiable chat, one which Robin enjoyed that much more once Christian mentioned a few of his trophies and titles won in bodybuilding contests. The potential protégé then agreed to meet his prospective sponsor the following late afternoon, up at Robin's place, right after the gym, just before he had to return to work his restaurant's dinner shift.

Robin suggested Christian not shower at the gym, but instead, simply bring a change of clothes with him so he could clean up there before heading back to the restaurant. "That way, we'll have plenty of time to visit," Robin added with a nervous giggle. He then assured Christian they'd be enjoying nothing more than a casual, friendly chat. "Simply think of it as a relaxed and informal, no-obligation, get-together. If nothing else, we can unwind on my terrace, see if we get along, find out if we're on the same page. How's that sound, Son?"

"I guess it sounds fine, Robin."

"Super-duper!" Robin peeped, unable to mask his giddy exhilaration. "See you here tomorrow afternoon at Kincaidia."

∗   ∗   ∗   ∗

Lester served cocktails on Robin's elegant terrace overlooking the Santa Monica Mountains, and it was all rather civilized, nothing at all what Christian had expected. Robin Kincaid, stylishly attired in Armani slacks, Polo pullover, and Ray-ban sunglasses, reclined on a lounger, sipped his iced Ketel One vodka, and held court with such gentility and worldly panache, he seemed to Christian nothing less than the perfect little gentleman.

Christian, straight from his workout at Gold's and still sexily geared up in gym shorts and sweaty blue tank top, gulped downed his banana-laced, whey protein recovery drink with such animal abandon, he seemed to Robin nothing less than the perfect caveman bodybuilder.

The late afternoon sun wove a hazy pattern of broken light as it popped in and out from behind a thin whisper of clouds in the smog-encrusted sky. "Sometimes, near the end of the day," Robin whimsically quipped as he sipped, "I enjoy a dry martini with a twist of fate."

Twenty minutes of idle chitchat flew by and Lester brought out an enormous platter of cold jumbo shrimp over crushed ice, and placed it atop the tiny table between their chaises. Christian dove right in. As he bathed one jumbo shrimp after another in the accompanying fiery cocktail sauce, he and Robin continued their tête-à-tête.

What they talked about mostly was Christian. Robin wanted to know *everything* about the big boy: his entire history as a muscleman, how he became a bodybuilder, the specifics of his training routine, his history of steroid use, when he last competed. Robin was animated, somehow endearing in his zeal and gracious while fawning all over his guest. Christian was surprised about how relaxed and unexpectedly at ease he felt, given how unsettling was the peculiar situation.

As Christian told his ostensible benefactor about his successes on the teenage competitive bodybuilding circuit, Robin fought to subdue his curiosity. When Christian then related the prenatal prophesy that his mother received about him growing up to become a Samson, Robin's dark-brown eyes widened in their sockets. Hearing all about Christian's prophetic destiny came as magical muscle music to Robin's pointy little ears. "Omigod, that is such a great, Godly omen," he giggled joyously. "As it happens, my very favorite muscle fetish is watching feats of strength."

"You like strong men, is that it?" Christian asked.

"Do I ever! Just take a look over there!" Robin pointed proudly into the house at a wall-to-wall mahogany bookcase whose over-filled shelves were cramped with his personal library of superhero movies. Robin's prized collection of video tapes and DVDs, more than a hundred and sixty films in all, sat lined up in rows like blank dominoes. If there were a movie made in the past fifty years featuring a muscleman, gladiator, or superhero, Robin owned a copy. Everything from *Tarzan of the Apes* to *Hercules Meets The Three Stooges*. Each strong-man movie was earmarked with its own special scenes featuring demonstrative displays of power, so Robin needn't waste time and could fast-forward directly to them whenever he longed for sexual stimulation: Hercules getting unchained, Tarzan cavalierly swinging from vine to vine with Jane in his strong arms, Goliath struggling, curling his biceps toward his ears while pulling together two teams of runaway horses.

"Even with all those muscle gods in my collection," Robin told Christian, "you can still be my number one Samson, any day!"

Christian didn't know quite how to respond. "Well," he shrugged awkwardly and dragged another jumbo shrimp through the cocktail sauce. "You seem like a real nice man."

In truth, Robin was a real nice man. But he was also a spoiled little rich boy whose cockeyed sense of power derived from knowing he could buy most anything or anyone. Owing to his profusion of funds, he was long accustomed to purchasing whatever his current whim might dictate, and felt perfectly at home paying his way in and out of everything, which explained why he so often got whatever he wanted. And if he didn't, the tiny titan could spin himself into a wicked tantrum of a hissy-snit as melodramatic as any mad queen twice his size.

Robin banged the side of his chaise with a little fist to emphasize his candor. "I want to put everything on the table, up front, so there can be no misunderstanding between us. That's the only way I might even begin to consider entering an accord like this, okay?"

"I agree," said Christian. "It's important we understand each other. So what is it you're looking for?"

Eager to please, and hoping with all his heart to win Christian over, Robin whipped out his vulnerability card and confided how badly he needed to share his life with someone. He discussed his strong desire, indeed the sheer joy he derived from promoting a budding bodybuilder. All of it, of course, executed without asking *much* in return.

"In point of fact," said Robin, temporarily removing his sunglasses and staring directly at Christian. "For only a smattering of attention and a modicum of male camaraderie, all I've ever asked of any protégé is for him to take advantage of this golden opportunity to focus on nothing but his training. I just want to sponsor a future champion."

"Nice!" said Christian, pleased with this turn in the conversation.

"You know," Robin next informed Christian with knowing authority, "great composers all had sponsors. Beethoven, Mozart, Tchaikovsky, all those musical geniuses.

Not a one of them would have had the time needed to compose the monumental music we now enjoy if someone hadn't been footing their bills."

"I never knew that," said Christian, gulping down the last of the chilled shrimp.

"So why shouldn't I take advantage of my net worth and use it to help promote a future champion bodybuilder? All I want is the chance to give a dedicated muscleman the opportunity to focus on nothing but his training." Robin offered an ebullient smile, an affectionate wink, and took another sip of his dry martini. "Christian, my boy," He declared. "I have this hunch that with you as my muscle boy, and me as your sugar daddy, we could get along famously."

Christian didn't know what to say. "I'm flattered," he finally responded.

"So how does all this sound, Son?" Robin was eager to know.

Son? Thought Christian, as he studied Robin's gleeful face. *Nothing about this odd little man reminds me of my pompous old man. Hell, maybe that's a good thing.*

When Christian didn't answer the question, Robin again sought to recapture his guest's wandering attention. "Christian?" he asked, pointedly. "How does all this sound?"

Christian forced a smile and confessed, "Well, quite frankly, it all sounds too good to be true. Why would you do all that for me?"

"Easy," exclaimed Robin. "I'm rich enough to do as I please."

"Do you mind if I ask how you got rich?" Christian asked with the candor of true curiosity.

"Not at all," Robin boasted, hoping to sound sincere. "I made my fortune the old fashioned way. I inherited it."

"Nice work," Christian acknowledged, with a smile.

"And I can assure you, Son," Robin added. "Everything I'm offering is on the level. I'm just this big ole fan of men with muscles who also has an altruistic need to help someone like you realize his dreams. Anything wrong with that?"

"No, of course not," said Christian. "That's good to hear. I'd love to be able to train and do nothing else. That's what I liked about the note you posted. Nothing would make me happier."

The moment he spoke, Christian realized he probably sounded too needy, so he quickly added, "Well, nothing would make me happier that is, so long as things stay within my comfort zone."

"Keeping you comfortable is exactly what I'd have in mind," gushed Robin, trying to sound not the least bit salacious. "How 'bout for starters, why don't you shower, then let me take you out for a big steak dinner, put some meat on those big, beautiful muscles?"

"I wish I could," said Christian, downing the last of his protein drink. "But as I said yesterday, I gotta be back at the restaurant before five. We open again at six, so maybe I should shower now."

"Wonderful idea!" Robin lit up. "I'll have Lester escort you over to the Temple I just finished renovating."

"The Temple?" asked Christian, puzzled.

"Yes," Robin answered, with a silly snicker. "Since I worship at the altar of muscle, I like to think of my pool house as my temple of pleasure. That's where you'll live should you decide to become my protégé and allow me to become your sponsor. You'd be so comfortable all alone out there … all the privacy you could ever want."

"That's good to know," said Christian. "Because I really appreciate privacy."

"So do I," Robin cheerfully agreed, masking his eyes with his hand, peek-a-boo, pretending not to see. "And any bodybuilder that becomes my high priest of muscle must also live in a temple, no? And I'd never take so much as a step inside the pool house unless I was invited."

Lester guided Christian out to the pool house and Robin, once alone, wondered if he should feel any remorse over never being fully upfront with any of his potential protégés. He lied to Christian about what would eventually be expected of him because he needed first to hook the lad in, and then slowly coax him, via the entice-ment of his extravagant generosity, into what he anticipated would become their gradually escalating sexual adventures.

*   *   *   *

Robin's sleek, nearly all-glass pool house was contemporary in its design. Christian wandered through the Temple's tastefully furnished living area and into its marble bathroom. Pewter faucets, indirect lighting, and the open shower with its eighteen thundering showerheads were all more opulent than anything he'd ever seen.

Any wall space in the enormous bathroom that wasn't covered by mirror or glass was blanketed with custom-framed photos of competitive bodybuilders with their trophies, all of them Robin's previous protégés. Just across from the shower, a pair of cedar doors led to an in-house sauna, right alongside a small, cozy steam room.

After unwinding in the shower for twenty minutes and then drying off with an Egyptian cotton bath towel plucked fresh from its heating rack, Christian relaxed in the sauna and then the steam room. Both conveniences worked wonders to soothe the sore muscles of his overtaxed torso. He shaved with one of the sterile sterling razors provided, and as the Polo shaving foam tickled his skin, he realized that luxu-riating in so much comfort had actually relieved some of his stress.

Scrubbed, shaved, and dressed for work in his stiff, white, long-sleeved shirt and black slacks, Christian tossed his soiled gym gear into his backpack and lumbered back outside, onto Robin's patio, to thank his diminutive host for his hospitality and be on his way. The sun had just dipped below the far-off mountain peaks and its lingering, late afternoon residual glow bathed the entire extravagant property in a smattering of flattering amber.

"I'm outta here, Robin," said Christian, extending his hand. "Thanks for the use of the pool house. You built quite the temple."

"If you don't mind, young man," Robin forced a congenial chuckle. "Don't leave just yet. I'm sorry, but I just don't like the idea of you lifting all those heavy trays, given the state of your troubled lower back and all. You might hurt yourself, do some serious damage. Who knows how long you'd be away from the gym then?"

"Yeah, I worry 'bout that all the time," Christian said in agreement. "But I feel a little better now. Your dry sauna and steam room helped an awful lot."

"I had a hunch they might," Robin smiled cheerily. "And as you see, they'd both be here for you around the clock, whenever you needed them."

Another sudden, stinging ache surprised Christian as it jolted his lower back again, then quickly dissipated. "But it's not as if my back doesn't still hurt," he said, rubbing the spot. "While the pain's not nearly as severe as before, some of the spasm's still there. I can feel it when I walk."

"Then don't walk," Robin suggested. "Know what I think? I think the smartest thing you could do right now is call Chez Joey, tell them you're in far too much discomfort to work tonight."

"Wish I could, Robin," said Christian, truthfully. "But Friday's one of our busier nights. I can't afford to lose that much and I'm already in deep shit with my boss."

"No problemo," Robin giggled. "Tell you what. How 'bout if I give you however much money you might have earned, wages, tips, and all? That way, instead of waiting on other people at the restaurant tonight, you'll come along with me, we'll get you off your feet, and we'll let others wait on us. You're used to serving steaks, right? Well, what say tonight we get one for you? One big, juicy slab of beef. You'll still get the money you would have made, plus I'll toss in another thirty per cent tip of the whole amount from me."

"Wow," said Christian. "You'd really do that?"

"It's like I told you," Robin answered. "All I want is to make it comfortable for you. Now how does all that sound?"

"Well, Robin," Christian answered in all honesty. "Kind of like everything else since I walked in here: all just too incredible to believe."

*   *   *   *

Christian called Chez Joey and told them he was too immobile to work the dinner shift, and then Robin and he drove in the little man's splashy Mercedes 550 SL convertible down to the Palm in West Hollywood. Along the way, Robin called ahead to secure a reservation.

Half an hour later, while Christian plowed voraciously through his sixteen ounces of prime-aged, Kobe beef, Robin picked away at his steamed four-pound Maine lobster. By then, the odd little man had sized up Christian to his total satisfaction. He sensed a true comradeship and compatibility between himself and this shy, evidently dedicated bodybuilder. He concluded the young man passed his eligibility test with flying colors. Although they just met, Robin felt no qualms about inviting the twenty-year-old to move in and become his next protégé.

"I am so eager to sponsor another champion bodybuilder," he gushed. "But, instead of you creating a symphony, like Mozart or Beethoven, all you have to do is build the best muscle body possible. Does this sound like something you could embrace? Might you be my Mozart of muscle?"

"I'm still not sure," Christian answered honestly. An electrifying ribbon of fresh pain stabbed a short-lived return visit into his lower spine, then vanished, but not before it served as painful reminder of his chronic back problem.

Robin spotted the passing look of discomfort on Christian's face and asked, with genuine concern, "What's ... wrong?"

"It's nothing," Christian answered quietly and stretched his sides, hoping to find a moment's relief.

"How does a hot Jacuzzi sound, back at my place, right after dinner?"

"Sounds perfect," said Christian. "But I don't know if I should. I didn't bring a bathing suit."

Robin sensed Christian's uneasy apprehension and quickly assured him, "Oh, you don't have to worry. It'll be purely therapeutic. You'll be in there all by yourself. I don't even like spas. Too darn hot for me. And don't you worry about being naked. I've got plenty of swimwear."

Robin stopped picking away at his half-eaten lobster and, after Christian devoured the last of his red meat, they drove back up to Kincaidia. As they walked through the front door, Robin was atwitter. "I'll just run and get you some trunks for the Jacuzzi," he said as he excitedly clapped his hands and scurried off to his bedroom. Back in a flash, the little man handed Christian a skimpy pair of red posing trunks and pointed toward the pool house. "Why don't you go change in the Temple?"

Christian smiled politely, quickly crossed the living room, stepped out onto the lushly landscaped rear patio, and then walked back once again into the pool house. There, he removed his clothes and stepped into the borrowed posing suit.

A heating rack in the bathroom warmed several thick, white bath towels. Christian wrapped one around his waist, tossed another over his shoulder, and then sauntered out into the cool night air, back over to the pool area.

Robin was reclining on a chaise alongside his Jacuzzi, watching with great interest and practically salivating as Christian dropped his towel onto the tiles and stepped down into the hundred-and-four-degree swirling, soothing water. A true muscle queen, Robin always felt bodybuilders looked sexiest in their posers, briefs, or boxers, even more so than when they were butt-naked. He watched with lecherous glee as Christian slowly submerged himself down to the top of his shoulders, and felt compelled to tell him, "Those posers look rather magnificent on you, young man."

Christian smiled modestly and looked down into the churning water at his basket. "Thanks. They sure seem to fit quite well."

"Then why don't you just keep them?" Robin offered, waving his hand as if it were a magic wand.

"Hey," Christian said softly. "Gee — thanks."

As Christian relaxed in the healing water, Robin sat quietly across from him, gazing stupidly at his guest's massive physique. The whirlpooling jets eased some of the stress in Christian's back, relieved some of his pain.

Twenty minutes later, after rinsing off again within the elegant shower inside the pool house, Christian dried himself, stepped back into his clothes, and then again joined Robin back inside the main house, in the comfort of his host's elegant, wood-

paneled library. Warming things up, Lester had ignited a cozy fireplace, and for further ambience, lit a dozen Rigaud candles all about the room.

The little squeaky man and the huge baritone bodybuilder sat across from each
other in over-sized leather Barcelona chairs. While Robin sipped an aged Cognac
from an immense brandy snifter and Christian enjoyed a glass of Evian, they discussed the feasibility of Robin's offer, negotiating unresolved details involving
Christian's immediate future.

"Don't take this the wrong way ... I don't mean to pry," Robin told his guest.
"But I think this could be important. You never once mentioned anything about
your sexuality."

"Well, Robin," Christian said rather frankly, "Although I'm just a little uncomfortable right now discussing something as personal as sexual relations, the truth is, I
just haven't had much experience."

"Oh, really?" Robin sat up in his chair.

"Truly," Christian answered quietly, and quickly added, "But I can tell you, one
thing I know for sure — I'm straight."

"How can you be so certain?" Robin asked, feigning innocence.

"There are some things you just know," said Christian, firmly, and then came
right out with it, admitting yes, okay, he was still a virgin, still hadn't gone all the way
with a woman; and no, of course he certainly never did anything like that with a
man. He was mindful not to mention anything about his long-ago, unfulfilling sexcapade with his older muscle buddy after that bodybuilding contest. However, he
also wanted Robin to be aware of his devotion to God, so he told him all about it,
concluding with the news of his strong lifelong conviction to remain chaste until he
wed. When Christian saw a look of curious puzzlement cross Robin's face, he immediately asked, "Is that a problem ... a deal-breaker?"

"Not necessarily," Robin told him. "Just so long as you don't insist on rubbing my
nose in it. So you're religious, is that it?"

"Yes, Sir. God is the author of my reality. I pray to Him and to His Son, and so
even if I wanted to, I couldn't have sex with another man. I don't want to lose God's
blessing."

"Fine with me, Christian — whatever gets your adrenaline flowing."

"I'm grateful I have such a close relationship with the Lord," Christian candidly
admitted. "We have an amazing communication."

"Excellent!" Robin gushed. "Can you put in a good word for me?"

"Sure thing," Christian smiled, good-naturedly. "But it's not like that. It's more
... internal."

That suited Robin just fine. He loved being driven into the uncharted waters of
infatuation by so-called *straight* bodybuilders who professed they were unavailable,
while at the same time affecting a confusion over the reality of their true sensual,
sexual sensibilities.

Robin planted his nose inside his goldfish-bowl-sized brandy snifter, inhaled the
fumes therein, and confided how, even though he had always greatly admired beautiful physiques on well-built bodybuilders, he'd also never even once taken the time to

pick up a weight to build up any muscles of his own. The last thing he ever wanted, or insisted upon, he confided, was any *mutual* muscle appreciation. "I dream about just little ole me being the one doing all the doting, all the worshiping and admiring. That's why you'll have to be the one doing all the lifting, all the hard physical work."

"Not a problem," said Christian. "I love working out."

"And I love hearing that," said Robin. "But you're gonna have to agree to work your butt off, do whatever it takes to propel yourself into the best shape of your young life. And while you focus on your training," Robin offered as he twirled the fragrant intoxicant inside his snifter, "I can help by doing all the rest: taking care of your protein intake, your six, seven, eight meals a day, plus the entire medicine cabinet full of those hard-to-find supplements you'll need. I have the best contacts for the fastest-reacting muscle-enhancers on the market. You want steroids from Thailand? One call away. From Mexico? Here overnight."

Robin was happy to see Christian perk up at the mention of steroids and quickly added, "All I want is for you to let me help you become a true champion. Together, as a team, as sponsor and protégé, with all the caring affection of a doting father and loyal son, we can get you there."

"Wouldn't that be something?" Christian quietly asked, while sorting out his anxiety. "But isn't there something else you'd expect in return? Be honest."

"I'm *always* honest," Robin lied. "Ask Lester if you don't believe me. And yes, there is a little something I'd want that will keep me in good humor."

Uh-oh, Thought Christian. *Here comes the hard part.* "And what might that be?"

"Well," Robin announced sheepishly, "I'd want you to pick me up in your arms every evening, carry me to bed, and tuck me in."

That's it? Christian asked himself. "And what else?" He asked, suspiciously, as he wondered where else this was heading.

"And nothing else," Robin beamed. "That's the beauty of sponsorship. So wadda ya say?"

"I don't know," Christian shrugged and forced a smile. "I suppose it sounds ... good."

"Good?" Robin asked, incredulously. "It could be downright glorious. Now — how soon can we begin? Please tell me tomorrow morning, first thing's not too soon."

"I think I'd be more comfortable knowing that if I did agree to give something like this a shot, we'd be doing it, you know, on a trial basis."

"Fine with me," Robin squeaked excitedly. "You move in here and enjoy what I have to offer. Should you find it's not for you, just let me know and we go our separate ways, no hard feelings."

"You certainly make it sound appealing," Christian said with a forced smile. "I'm a bit overwhelmed by all this. So if it's okay with you, I'd like some time, maybe a day or so, to think about it."

"I was about to suggest that!" Robin exclaimed. "No sense rushing in unless you're really ready to commit yourself to an all-out, going-for-the-gold training program.

It's a big decision. You take your time, give it some thought, and then say yes. It's as simple as that."

Christian downed the last of his Evian and stood up. "Guess I better be on my way, huh?" he said politely, reaching out to shake Robin's hand. "Thank you for dinner."

Robin shook Christian's hand, and then wrapped his thin arms around the big boy's small waist. "How 'bout a big ole muscle hug goodnight?" he asked. "When you're living here, I doubt I'll ever want much more from you than that."

Christian was happy to oblige with so sweet a gesture, and hugged Robin back with what he hoped was ample affection. Robin found their short embrace wonderfully homoerotic, and it rendered him positively euphoric. He felt as if his feet no longer touched the floor as he floated across the living room and saw his guest through his rotunda entrance and out the front door.

*   *   *   *

Back in his tiny, cramped apartment several hours later, Christian lay in bed, staring blankly up at the dark ceiling, unable to sleep. He weighed the pros and cons of his actually doing something so off the wall as moving in with Robin and letting the odd, old, diminutive gentleman become his muscle mentor, his … patron.

Could he or couldn't he? How badly would he be disturbing his already troubled spirit? Should he or shouldn't he? How deeply would he be damning his eternal soul? Would he or wouldn't he? How much would he be selling out? More specifically, how much would he have to be putting out?

Christian flipped himself over onto his stomach to consider the other side of the coin, contemplating how much better his life would be if he didn't have to show up twice a day at Chez Joey, how great he would feel packing on some solid muscle, propped up and propelled by another potent cycle.

Frustrated, he flopped around all night, wrestling his demons as well as his angels, back and forth, weighing the ups, the downs, the plush plusses, the moral minuses. By the time the first rays of dawn burst through the slits in his blinds and started brightening his ceiling, Christian had yet to make up his meandering mind.

Starbucks was abuzz with caffeine-fixated customers when Christian, still undecided about Robin's proposal, walked in to order his ritual, pre-workout double espresso. As he sipped his steamy energy bumper-upper, his contemplation was rudely interrupted when, with no warning, another wrenching, spasmodic pain sliced across his lower back with an impact so commanding, he reached for a tabletop to steady himself. He rubbed his hard-to-reach, impaired area and wondered if he was even *capable* of getting through his workout, let alone his upcoming shift at Chez Joey. Then he thought about how less agonizing his aches would feel if only they were being soothed by Robin's therapeutic Jacuzzi; and that idyllic image, snap, just like that, put Christian over the top. He stood up straight as he could manage and carried his container of coffee over to the bulletin board at the side of the store. After glancing around to make certain no one was watching, he removed Robin's

Bodybuilder Wanted notice and then hurried to the pay phone to call his once and future benefactor.

*   *   *   *

The intermittent piercing pain in Christian's lower back began subsiding as soon as he called Chez Joey to tell the manager he was quitting his job. It was the first time since his arrival in Southern California that he actually felt something approaching ebullience. After packing everything he owned into his two suitcases, he hastily composed a thirty-day notice-to-vacate his cubbyhole of a living space and stuffed it inside his apartment manager's mailbox. Then he drove up to Kincaidia.

An elated Robin swung open the front door to welcome Christian, and excitedly clapped his open little hands repeatedly, like a kid in a candy store just given permission to gobble up all the M&Ms. "Oh, come in, come in, oh, please do come in!" He gushed, even squeakier than usual. "My, oh my, don't you look extra large and wonderful today?"

"Thanks," said Christian. "But I can't bring my things inside just yet. At least not until you tell me once more you fully understand we're trying out this sponsorship stuff strictly on a trial basis."

"Why, of course, Mr. Samson!" snapped Robin. "A trial basis, it is. That was my idea in the first place, remember? Let the games begin!" Robin then gleefully instructed Lester to help the muscle monster unload his boxes from the dilapidated VW.

While Lester carried Christian's suitcases out to the Temple, Robin suggested Christian store his beat up, plebian Rabbit in the rear of Kincaidia's four-car garage, and then handed him the keys to one of his own stable of autos — this one his bright yellow Porsche convertible. "It's yours, Christian," Robin said excitedly. "For your unlimited use."

"Wow," was all a subdued Christian could think of to say.

As Christian unpacked his belongings and put away his clothes on the shelves and in the drawers of the Temple's walk-in closet, Robin made several phone calls. "First thing we gotta do is straighten out that bum back," he told his new protégé as he then set up a fresh series of appointments with Christian's chiropractor.

In a grand gesture, one actuated to ensure that Christian felt that much more welcome, Robin next presented Christian with another endearing surprise. "What wouldn't your sugar daddy do for his hard-working muscle boy?" he rhetorically asked with a wicked grin as casually, he handed over to his protégé a satin Gucci shaving kit.

Christian unzipped it and pulled out numerous boxes filled with vials of Deca, Sustanon, Winstrol, Primobolan, even the exorbitantly expensive Human Growth Hormone. There was enough contraband chemistry for several full and potent cycles of steroids, accessorized with packets of rubbing alcohol and a slew of sterile hypodermic needles.

Christian was so elated by the sight of such an abundance of quality juice, he was all set to jump up and express his genuine gratitude by giving Robin a big old muscle hug. But he controlled himself and was instead civil and courteous, offering with quiet reserve, "This is great, Robin. Thank you so much."

"Happy to help out!" Robin exclaimed. "My gut instinct tells me things can go very smoothly for you and me. I have confidence in your devotion to your training. And while it's true you must suffer for your art, your sugar daddy's here to alleviate any pain, to make your life more comfortable than you ever imagined."

*   *   *   *

Robin's newest protégé moved into Kincaidia, and for a while, things went unexpectedly well. And even though so many aspects of Christian's unorthodox relationship with Robin felt awkward, there was also much to appreciate about his new living arrangement. The Temple was a handsomely appointed pool house, audaciously elegant and luxurious, yet still comfortable. Meticulously manicured lawns and lushly landscaped gardens provided serenity and privacy to Robin's prime property. His enormous salt-water pool featured cascading waterfalls, and the bubbling jets in its adjoining Jacuzzi worked wonders, soothing Christian's lower back. Beneath a canopy, poolside, sat a shaded, open-air workout area. The mini-gym featured an incline bench plus a pair of racks bulging with gleaming silver dumbbells for any on-property pumping of pecs.

Thanks to Robin's sky's-the-limit magnanimity, Christian's sponsor hired, in quick succession, a nutritionist to maximize his diet, a music coordinator to edit tunes for his posing routine, and a highly qualified, two-hundred-fifty-dollar-an-hour personal trainer skilled at sculpting competitive bodybuilders into peak condition. Christian's big weakness onstage was a subtle suggestion of clumsiness evident in his transitions between poses. He needed to appear less forced, more graceful. So Robin hired him a posing coach.

Robin also insisted upon paying his protégé's considerable chiropractic bills, and as Christian's once-chronic pain subsided, the split routines in his almost daily workouts slowly returned to their former full-throttle intensity.

Christian assuaged the challenge to his moral authority, along with his intermittent pangs of guilt over his hustler-like setup, simply by burying them in the recesses of his consciousness. He made a special point to stay clear of church, at least for the time being. As he eased into his luscious new surroundings, rather than dwelling on remorse, he instead accepted his unforeseen predicament as divine providence. He also took time every day to thank God for the drastic change in his quality of life, for the sudden bounty of his many blessings.

Robin never undressed in front of his protégé, not while getting ready for bed, not anytime. He wouldn't so much as sunbathe shirtless at the pool. Christian never once saw his sponsor's exposed torso, and that was just fine with him. The small man claimed he was simply too mortified by his sorrowfully scrawny frame, and that it would be an affront to nature if he ever disrobed before someone of Christian's physical stature. "The only thing I ever exercise," Robin light-heartedly told Christian, "is my option to be lazy."

As for what was expected of him in return for Robin's bigheartedness — at first, there was but one muscle fantasy Christian was called upon to enact and, although a bizarre request, he found it neither troublesome nor threatening.

Night after night, their major role reversal ritual never varied. Just before going to bed, clad in his monogrammed, satin pajamas, what Robin wanted more than anything in the whole world was to be lifted up and tucked into bed. So Christian honored the fantasy and picked the little man way up, lifting him as if he were a little boy in Daddy's big, strong arms, and then carried him over to his Chippendale bed, where Christian tucked him in. Lost within his satin sheets, the diminutive man stared up at Christian, and in his most infantile voice invariably whimpered, "Was your sugar daddy a good little boy today?"

There was a part of Christian that almost enjoyed Robin's infantile scenario. He found it quite doable and small price to pay since he was no longer scrounging for rent money, no longer destroying his back, waiting on tables. "Oh, yes," he cheerfully placated the little man. "Sugar daddy was a very good little boy."

"But just how good?" Robin always pouted, a peevish five-year old. "Tell me, please-please-please-please. How good?"

"I'll tell you how good," Christian always answered. "Sugar daddy was such a good little boy, I'm gonna let him feel the power of one of my big biceps." The muscle monster then raised his arms, lowered his guard and popped one of his pythons before Robin's widening eyes, telling the poor little rich boy, "Hold on tight and squeeze as hard as you can."

With glee, Robin wrapped both his hands around Christian's proffered magic muscle and squeezed as hard as he could. The sensation of fondling such perfectly shaped, trophy-winning strength sent him sailing into an inner tantrum of delirium. The psychological make-up of the little man was almost the antithesis of a basic Napoleonic complex. Whereas most short men yearned to be bigger, taller, and stronger, Robin was perfectly content to remain undersized. He relished being the little man worshipping an enormous muscle monster because his mini-stature granted him license to baby-talk perpetually, to pout at will, and unendingly play a capricious Peter Pan who never grew up.

Christian signaled he was finished flexing, insisting, "Now, you be a good little boy, and get your rest." After flipping off the light switch, while closing the door behind him, the dutiful houseguest quietly intoned, "Night, Sugar Daddy. Sweet muscle dreams."

"Night, Son," Robin always whispered back, and then rolled over into a fetal position, and closed his eyes.

*   *   *   *

To commemorate his and Christian's productive first month of cohabitation, Robin flew them both to Las Vegas, first class, where they attended the Muscle Mania bodybuilding contest. He wanted his protégé to see the level of competition he'd be facing at his upcoming Mr. Muscle Beach show three months hence. They stayed at Caesar's Palace, in an extravagant penthouse suite overlooking the Strip.

At the contest, Christian felt embarrassed to be seen alongside Robin, and prayed they wouldn't bump into anyone he knew. The last thing he wanted was for anyone to think he and the little man were an item, or God forbid, that he might be Robin's *boy*.

By marked contrast, Robin was positively swollen with pride having Christian in stride. He shepherded his protégé around the Strip in a chauffer-driven limo, treated him to expensive steak dinners, and was so happy about how well things were going, he treated himself and his new bodybuilder to a manic shopping spree.

Robin bought a solid-gold letter opener for himself and gifted Christian with brand-name shirts, designer slacks, top-of-the-line gym gear, custom-fitted posing shorts, Versace sunglasses. "Whatever you want," he told his muscle boy. "If it tickles your fancy, Son, we'll tickle my bank account."

Reclining in the back of the limo, Christian surveyed the shopping bags they'd accumulated over the past few hours, patted his benefactor's hand and told him, "I want you to know how grateful I am for all you've done for me."

"What do I live for but your happiness?" chirped Robin. "And I have just one teensy-weensy favor to ask in return."

"And what might that be?" Christian asked, warily.

"Well," Robin twittered in his seat, a jittery schoolboy. "I know it's over three months away, but when the time comes, could I be the one who helps rub that tanning gook over your body when you compete in the Venice show?"

Christian was relieved the request was so easy to satisfy, and assured his benefactor without hesitation, "You bet, little man!"

Robin got so fired up over the prospect of serving as Christian's First Lieutenant, he rifled through his billfold, whipped out his black American Express card, and merrily handed it over to Christian straightaway, declaring, "This is for you, dear muscle boy. Be prudent and use it wisely, lest my accountant have a coronary!"

"I don't need that," said Christian, handing the card back. "You've already given me so much."

"Nonsense!" Robin declared and pushed the card back in Christian's face. "Keeping you happy, well-fed, well juiced, and surrounded by runaway luxury — that's my highest priority."

*　　*　　*　　*

Christian trained harder than ever and injected more than ever, and his magical muscularity accelerated as if inspired by some genie who'd granted him his wish. His bulking-up diet found him devouring daily ten thousand calories which distributed four-hundred grams of muscle-building protein throughout his system, paced over seven small meals and three protein drinks. Finally feeling pain-free, coupled with his conscientious training and the benefits of being back on cycle, soon manifested itself as rapid muscle growth. In little time, he packed on another twelve pounds of mass. Christian practiced his posing routine with regularity, and when he flexed before the Temple's wall-to-wall mirror, he was so encouraged by what he saw, he could only ask of his reflection, *Who wouldn't want to live in this lap of luxury?*

As Christian's body amassed ever more muscle, Robin remained patiently in wait before he would start insisting on getting more bang for his buck. Whenever a new protégé moved in, the tiny titan insinuated himself incrementally, one demand at a time. He didn't want to scare away any of his muscle boys, at least not at first. So he was cautious about escalating the physical liberties he'd eventually insist upon taking. He sometimes took a sadistic glee in seeing how swiftly a new protégé acclimated to the luxurious good life he presented so cheerfully and with such largesse. He'd weave the net that was his philanthropic extravagance and then sit back and watch with calculation as his prey settled into the glorious excesses offered at Kincaidia.

The little man loved pouring his resources into each of his protégés. At least until he tired of their presence. As soon as his escalating demands exceeded his current boy's comfort zone, Robin abruptly cut short his philanthropy, sent the bodybuilder packing, and routinely began the recruitment process, scouting the city's gyms all over again. For his disgruntled protégés, returning to the dim reality of their previously impecunious lives was often a daunting challenge.

Living large, Christian had no inkling of Robin's agenda and soon grew comfortable around his patron. One night, during their ritual of tucking Robin into bed, he even invited his benefactor to squeeze not just one, but *both* his flexed guns.

Robin loved getting lost in the euphoric touch of Christian's flexed biceps as they always sent him into an ecstatic, blissful state. The big problem with ecstatic, blissful states, though, is that they often have a short shelf life. And so, even as Robin enticed Christian ever more deeply into his opulent extravagance, he also knew their eccentric affiliation was already doomed to failure.

*   *   *   *

TROUBLE IN TROUSDALE

After two months in Kincaidia, Robin was ready to start getting from Christian a bit more putting-out for all he was shelling out. At first, his escalating expectations seemed almost sweetly innocent.

For openers, he soon wanted to exchange his and Christian's brief muscle hugging encounters not only when Christian was on his way out the front door, but also the moment his protégé returned from his workouts. "If that makes you the least bit uncomfortable," Robin suggested, arms open wide along with a winning smile. "Just let me know now, okay?"

Not a problem, thought Christian. *I can manage that. Robin hasn't crossed over the line.* The massive muscle monster was happy to hug the merry moneyed munchkin. By his very nature, Christian had always been tactile and affectionate. He felt perfectly at ease warmly embracing another man, especially when it was someone like a fellow teammate for whom he held some affection. And Robin seemed such a sweet, gentle and quirky little squirt, it was hard *not* to like him.

So Christian gave himself license to be hands-on, touchy-feely with Robin, volunteering as much pseudo-affection as he could muster without having to re-introduce any further level of guilt into his already troubled spirit.

Tests of strength were Robin's number-one favorite muscle fantasy. And Christian still had no problem when the little man's next erotic request was to let him bear witness while Christian exercised his muscles, or even better, performed some Herculean task. "If you have any problem with that," Robin suggested, arms flung wide with another big grin. "Just let me know now, and I'll back down, I swear."

Christian had no problem showing off for Robin. Willingly, he dropped to the floor whenever Robin issued one of his giddy requests for him to pound out forty formal push-ups, or give him a hundred hard crunches. He also never once minded having to swim those thirty, forty, sometimes even fifty requested laps in Robin's glorious pool while the little man sat by and stared dreamily at him. He even enjoyed showing off whenever Robin begged him to rip a phone book to shreds, relished watching as the diminutive man-child jumped up and down and clapped his little hands, squealing girlishly, with idiotic delight.

"Jeepers-creepers, Christian, could I trouble you for just one more teensy-weensy muscle favor?" Robin asked in sing-song one night while they were out, enjoying yet another expensive steak dinner.

"What'd you have in mind this time, little man?" Christian wanted to know.

"Well," Robin's eyes went wide with excitement as he asked animatedly, "along with getting tucked into bed and granted permission to squeeze my big boy's flexed biceps, how 'bout if you also throw in a little nightly back massage? Huh? If that might be any kind of problem, just let me know now."

"Won't be a problem," Christian told him, good-naturedly. "I can manage that."

After fourteen consecutive bedtime back massages, Robin was the happiest grown-up little boy in the world. Then, on the fifteenth night, as soon as Christian finished massaging Robin's undeveloped rhomboid muscles, the frail little man flipped over onto his back and baby-talked, "Would you mind sitting here with me, by my side? I'd like you to stay with your little boy sugar daddy until he falls asleep."

Christian felt a bit uncomfortable with that request. But Robin still hadn't crossed over the line. Thus, the additional elements of their nightly ritual were set in place. Christian tucked Robin into bed, flexed his biceps and then massaged his benefactor's back. He caressed the back of his small head, and then stayed with him, bedside, until his sponsor drifted off to sleep. All in all, still a small price to pay, Christian reasoned, for the many blessings he was enjoying in return.

*   *   *   *

Robin's established pattern soon found him growing bored with his spiraling requests. As each of his muscle fantasy expectations were realized, they soon grew monotonous and were no longer enough to fully satisfy the sugar daddy. In search of a new titillation, Robin next insisted Christian involve them both in a nightly feat of strength.

Not a problem. The ritualistic fantasy enacted from then on began as Robin lay flat out on his back atop his bed and went rigid. It then became Christian's challenge to lift the little man high up into the air, way above his shoulders, as far as Christian's long arms could stretch. He then pressed Robin's stiffened little body up and down, up and down, with several reps of shoulder presses, as he turned his host into a hundred and twenty-three pound barbell of flesh and bone.

Frozen in place, Robin's little boy pecker shot dependably straight into the air as it popped out from his pajama bottoms. Robin maintained his undersized boner throughout every weight-lifting movement of Christian's clean lift-jerk-and-press. The little boy who lived deep inside the multi-millionaire felt an invigorating thrill from feeling safe and secure while getting lifted up and down by the exhilarating power in Christian's Samsonian arms.

Christian was humiliated by the lifting process. He felt embarrassed by the appearance of Robin's puny pecker improperly protruding out from inside his pajamas, and resented having to cater to Robin's infantile fantasies. However, so long as he wasn't being asked to perform any nasty gay sexual favors, Christian knew he could still tolerate the surreal situation.

$$* \qquad * \qquad * \qquad *$$

Five weeks out from the Venice Beach contest, Christian's training took over his life. He pumped harder than he ever thought possible, and miraculously managed to hold on to most of his awesome size even as he trimmed down and cut up. One flex in the mirror and he knew he looked more freakizoid-muscular-amazing than at any time in his bodybuilding career.

Christian's cocktail had him juicing with the exorbitantly expensive human growth hormone, which alone set Robin back several thousand a month. The contest-bound bodybuilder then further supplemented his voltage HGH with varying doses of Primobolan, Sustanon, and Cypionate for the growing of muscle, as well as insulin for the burning of fat. He downed six Dianobol tablets daily to help cut him up. As prophylactic, he also took little pills called Novadex, anti-estrogens sent into his system to make certain his testosterone didn't escalate to the point it converted. God forbid that should happen and Christian sprout a pair of dreaded bitch tits. Pendulous breasts on a woman were one thing. On a man they were a catastrophe, a slap in the face from Mother Nature that could only be corrected by costly cosmetic reconstructive surgery.

Magnanimously, Robin didn't so much as flinch when he shelled out a jaw-dropping five thousand dollars for Christian's potent fourteen-week cycle. He giddily watched as Christian pyramided his dosage up and then up still further, until the water retention from his commanding cocktail sculpted his inflated muscled mass with Herculean size, splendid cuts, and remarkable shape.

Christian had it all worked out in his head. He planned to arrive onstage at the Venice show at the very peak of condition, a picture-perfect two hundred fifty-two pounds. Shooting for that goal, he carefully calibrated the dosages he'd need for the remainder of his extensive cycle. Two weeks later, he was giving himself shots in the upper butt every other day, then every single day. Finally, ten days away from the contest, he refused to face the reality that he could well be compromising his future good health, and began stabbing himself with his profusion of highest quality juice twice a day.

The more Christian's muscles developed and grew, the more of them Robin wanted to explore. He soon insisted that Christian always be shirtless whenever they were at home together. Christian didn't much like that idea, but felt so beholden for all he was getting, he went along with Robin's request.

Pretty soon, life with Robin was no longer so hunky-dory. Christian often felt cheap and uncomfortable about always being ogled, and hated whenever Robin glared lustily at his shirtless torso. At night, as he tucked Robin into bed, he started telling himself, *maybe this wasn't such a good idea*. By morning, when he awoke pain-free, surrounded by luxury, and ready to focus only on his upcoming contest, he reminded himself, *maybe this wasn't such a bad idea*.

By the time Christian introduced severe carbo-depletion into his pre-contest regimen, he was ingesting significant amounts of quality protein every two or three hours. His multitude of meals came from a boring diet that found him consuming one plain turkey breast after another, one drained and unadorned can of dry albacore tuna, one vapid egg-white omelet following the next. Three of his daily meals consisted of a pound of rare hamburger coupled with half a grapefruit, a peculiar combo said to work wonders in cutting him up by removing what little fat remained on his oversized frame.

As the quirky demands of Robin's muscle fantasy fetishes escalated, the daily interactions between provider and protégé soon grew progressively more strained than sexy, more prickly than pleasant, more combative than compatible. When Christian began distancing himself emotionally, Robin didn't seem at all phased by the change in his muscle boy's attitude. The more Robin kept adding to his list of muscle-motivated demands and expectations, the further Christian retreated. The more Christian retreated, the further apart they grew. Christian went mechanically through the motions of doing what was expected of him, but it soon became clear to Robin that his protégé's faux affections were more the reactions of a compliant servant than any devoted son.

The escalating friction between them soon turned so unpleasant that Christian promised himself he'd restore his sense of self by packing up and leaving his oddball, luxurious confinement in two weeks time, right after the Mr. Muscle Beach show. He'd find a new place to live, even go out and get another job if necessary. Anything had to be better than this loss of dignity.

No longer at ease with the rules governing their roles as sugar daddy and muscle son, Christian needed to renew his troubled spirit. He delayed going to the gym the following Sunday morning, and instead sought a familiar spiritual solace when he drove up the Coast Highway and returned once again to the Evangelical church in Malibu. He arrived just in time for their eleven o'clock morning service.

Also in attendance at the service that morning was socialite Pipsi Sterling. The moment she spotted Christian lumbering his way down the aisle, thank heaven, her eyes brightened and her spirits soared. Even from several pews away, Pipsi was already so thoroughly smitten, so completely infatuated, she could only pray Christian might take notice of her. She wished she didn't feel so intimidated by him, and tried as hard as she could during the long service not to be too obvious every time she slyly turned around to steal another unobtrusive glance his way. She knew this was no time to be coy and vowed to find a way to meet him sometime before he left church services that day. Besides, she was hosting one of her elegant brunches right after church, and had faith he'd make the perfect last-minute guest.

The inspiring church service did wonders to soothe Christian's crisis of conscious-ness; at the same time it revitalized his unflappable commitment to the Lord. He was grateful that he was again inside a house of worship, thankful he could once more put his trust in God's capable hands. Given the depth of his guilt over how far he'd fallen in his walk with the Almighty, he hoped the penance he offered in prayer dur-ing the ceremony might somehow alleviate at least a slice of his shame.

As soon as the service ended, churchgoers started filing politely out of the vesti-bule. Pipsi looked all around the faithful flock for Christian. When at last she spot-ted him leaving the men's room, on his way out of the lobby, she knew she had to make her move. Filled with an unexpectedly bold determination, she held her chin high and headed directly toward him. As they passed by one another, she *accidentally* brushed up against him and finally got his attention.

"Welcome to our little heavenly haven," she practically sang out. "I'm Pipsi Sterling and am just so glad to see you back here, praying with us again."

Christian was flattered. "Why, thank you," he returned her handshake. "I'm Christian. Christian Falconer. I enjoyed today's service. Gave me a welcome moment of peace."

"When I didn't see you again after your last visit, I thought maybe you weren't coming back."

"I've been real busy, getting ready for a contest," he told her. "I'm a body-builder."

"Yes, I noticed," Pipsi smiled with ironic understatement. "I also wanted to intro-duce myself to you today mainly because, well, you see, I've invited some friends over to my place, which is nearby, for an after-church brunch." Without pausing for a breath, Pipsi insisted, "And don't tell me you have other plans because I know a big, strapping fellow like you has just *got* to eat sometime, and I simply won't take no for an answer." Pipsi opened her purse, whipped out a business card and, along with her most effervescent smile, slipped it into Christian's hand. "Truly, I would love it if you would join us. Here's my address."

"Brunch sounds great," said Christian, accepting the gracious offer and pocketing the card. "I'm so hungry, I could eat a horse."

"Well, I hope you'll settle for steak and eggs." Pipsi said, with a forced chuckle. "As it happens, I raise six glorious stallions, for riding and for showing. None, however, are for consumption."

"Poor choice of words on my part, huh?" Christian shrugged and amended his hyperbole. "How's this: I'm so hungry, I could eat a house?"

"Now that's more like it!" Pipsi beamed cheerfully. "I'll salt the French doors in advance of your arrival."

✳   ✳   ✳   ✳

Way over on the other side of the Malibu mountains, Robin was feeling glum and blue as he always did whenever he had to face the sad fact that yet another of his sponsorships was drawing to a bitter close. The silver lining, however, was that it also signaled he could again initiate a renewed search for his next star protégé. Why, just the notion of going through yet another glowing honeymoon period with still another hard-working bodybuilder tickled him silly. Ever tactful, he'd waited until Christian drove away from Kincaidia earlier that morning before instructing his houseman to once again tack his *Bodybuilder Wanted* notice onto bulletin boards around town.

So when a young man with a deep, sexy voice called several hours later to say he was a huge bodybuilder who had just read one of Robin's notices, the small man wasted no time in quickly setting up an interview for later that afternoon.

Owing to a timely coincidence, the twenty-two-year-old bodybuilder was not only new to town and flat broke, he was also desperately seeking immediate lodging. He added he was most receptive to receiving both comfort and support. Robin perked up and asked the prospective protégé, "How 'bout we meet over cocktails later today? I'm rather fond of the patio outside the Polo Lounge of the Beverly Hills Hotel? Do you know where that is?"

"I'm sure I can find it!"

"Cocky!" Robin chuckled with a grin. "I like that in a young man. Let's see how well we interface with one another, okay? And don't you worry. Should we click, I'll be most eager to make sure you'll be very, very comfortable."

✳   ✳   ✳   ✳

The brunch at Pipsi Sterling's English country "cottage-in-the-woods" was elegant without being pretentious. The heiress's expensively furnished mini-mansion sat way up in the Malibu hills, perched out on a breezy bluff, overlooking the ocean. Her six prized, chestnut-brown horses lived in their own pampered comfort in an air-conditioned stable abutting the main house. Next to the stable was a rustic corral. A free-form swimming pool sat on the other side of the sumptuous mini-estate, and the entire bucolic property was encircled by a grove of flowering Brazilian pepper trees.

Three of Pipsi's closest female pals were the last to arrive at her Sunday brunch. Their hostess quickly pulled them aside and took them into her confidence as she discreetly pointed toward Christian, by then walking around, outside in her garden.

She implored her girlfriends to go over to him and sing her praises. "Be sure you tell him nothing but wonderful things about me," she practically pleaded. "It's really important. Do this for me, puh-leaze!"

Christian ambled about the meticulously landscaped, two-acre property. As he slowly sipped freshly squeezed orange juice from a tall Stueben flute, he was greeted most cordially by Pipsi's three emissaries of goodwill. Accompanied by a few silly giggles, they introduced themselves and immediately went on about how much they all loved their darling hostess.

"She *always* has a smile on her face," gushed the first of Pipsi's girlfriends. "Even when she's in a sour mood. I don't know how she does it."

"Don't be silly," countered the second. "When is our little Miss Pipsqueak *ever* in a sour mood? She always sparkles!"

"Pipsi's father, as I'm sure you know," the third girl confided to Christian, beneath her breath, "is the prominent landscape architect, Hubert Sterling."

"I didn't know that," said Christian with one of his characteristic shrugs of ambivalence. "Who's Hewlitt Sterling?"

"Hubert!" The first young lady stepped forward and corrected him with a sweet smile. "He's a *big* wheel in the community. Very successful, extremely wealthy. Interests in all kinds of financial pies."

It was true. Pipsi's father was not just a successful landscape architect, but also a venture capitalist and a real estate tycoon. Depending upon whom you asked regarding his business dealings, Hubert Sterling was either a pillar of the community or a snake in the grass. While not much was widely known about the rest of his financial empire, his one high-profile, most visible enterprise was the wildly successful Beverly Hills landscaping enterprise, From the Ground Up.

In celebrity-conscious Southern California, From the Ground Up was justifiably regarded, at least in florally conscious social circles, as *Gardeners to the Stars*. Their reputation was well-earned as they created rolling lawns, extravagant flower beds and over-the-top topiaries for the lavish estates of Steven Spielberg, Hugh Hefner, and Barbra Streisand, among other famous household names.

Christian smiled politely at Pipsi's lady friends, excused himself and went back into the house to get another glass of orange juice. When he passed the living room, he saw that the mantle over Pipsi's fireplace was laden with almost as many trophies awarded her horses as Christian had earned back when the Falconer mantle was still cluttered with those awkward-looking accolades won for his efforts in bodybuilding. Christian wondered why so many dust-collecting trophies, whether for bodybuilding, golf, or Best in Show, often looked so cumbersome and ungainly. Evidently, Pipsi was as passionate about her horses as was he about his training.

Luncheon was served. Christian downed several protein-packed plates filled with steaks and eggs and chicken breasts, and stopped eating long enough to thank his hostess for the high quality of her bountiful buffet.

"Oh, I always eat healthy," Pipsi told him. "Have for years."

When Christian smiled politely, Pipsi felt pressured to say *something*, anything to hold her large guest's attention. "My parents sent me to school in Switzerland," she boasted, apropos of nothing. "I speak French, Spanish, German and even a little Italian."

"Nice," Christian commented. "I speak no foreign languages, and that includes English."

Pipsi smiled, Christian shrugged again, and she sensed he was getting ready to say good-bye. So she cut him off at the pass, and asked vivaciously, "Why don't you stick around a while longer? We've barely had a chance to visit. Besides, the other guests will be gone in another couple of cups of coffee. If you like, you and I could go for a horseback ride up in the hills."

Christian lit up. "Sure, why not?" he smiled and shrugged his eager acceptance.

*   *   *   *

Their lazy horseback ride through the scenic woodsy trails of Malibu Canyon, atop Pipsi's champion stallions, Star and Rapture, was both pastoral and calming. As their horses moseyed alongside each other, clip-clopping for several hours over the dirt path, the metaphor was not lost on Pipsi that she and Christian were riding off together into the Malibu sunset.

She told him all about the buying and selling of champion show horses. He told her all about his training for the Muscle Beach contest coming up in two weeks. Off in the distance, as the last of the sun slid behind a thin snippet of clouds and slowly slipped from sight, she mentioned she'd always thought it would be fun to go to a bodybuilding contest, but had never before met anyone so closely involved. However, now that she had, she added emphatically how she would absolutely love to see one.

Christian wanted to invite her right there on the spot, but couldn't because he didn't know how'd he'd ever explain why Robin was also there, no doubt doting all over him as he so often did, subtly signaling his ownership by pawing him with his soft, creepy, little hands.

*   *   *   *

Back in town, Robin was driving toward his appointed rendezvous with his potential next protégé. As always, when auditioning a new boy, he was a-twitter with anticipation.

Despite his trepidation and the fear of rejection he carried since childhood, the introductory meeting between Robin and his new bodybuilder buddy went far better than either of them expected. Cody, who hailed from a cookie-cutter town just outside Fresno, arrived at the Polo Lounge sporting a winning smile and a tight muscle shirt. Fresh off the freeway, the strapping lad was another none-too-bright monster bodybuilder who'd fled the boredom of suburbia and now needed a place to stay. Still, from what Robin saw, Christian's potential replacement was a diamond-in-the-rough, star-in-the-making. Just like Christian, this big boy was also a super heavyweight competitive bodybuilder. Unlike Christian, Cody had already accepted the reality of his homosexuality. And given the high level of the young man's bodybuilding aspirations, Robin felt certain they would have no trouble setting up some practical living arrangement.

When Cody rested his folded arms on the table and squeezed his already alluring eighteen and a half inch, vascular guns in a near-flex, it was all Robin could do to contain his sensual excitement. He felt a little stiff one sprouting up inside his underpants as, giddily, he laid out the usual litany of luxuries Cody could expect should he agree to move into Kincaidia.

"Hey, man," Cody announced with a big smile, "I'm more than ready to jump in right away. Damn. Let's do this. I'll be honest with you, Robin. I get real turned on by a man with a big wad. Damnit, I don't really care what you look like or even how old you are. Just so long as you're in there with the bucks."

"That'll be me, Cody!" Robin boasted. "Just let this sugar daddy spoil his muscle boy while you get ready for your next contest."

"I love spending money," Cody offered candidly. "Especially when it's someone else's. And I ain't no cheap hustler. In return for all you're offering, I'll do whatever makes you happy."

That did it! Robin's rising little pecker shot up from half-mast to full sail and throbbed with a lustful merriment. When an over-eager Cody next promised he'd also welcome showering Robin with an abundance of affection as reward for his proposed outpouring of generosity, Robin knew fortune had smiled on them both, because once again, he'd found his next protégé.

*   *   *   *

Roughly two hundred forty thousand clippity-clops and some two hours later, Christian and Pipsi trotted off the bridle path and steered their horses back into her corral. After dismounting their steeds, Christian thanked Pipsi and told her he needed to get going. He was already hours late for that afternoon's scheduled steroid injection.

"Can I ask you a personal question?" Pipsi asked as she walked with him to his car.

"Shoot!"

"I was just wondering ... how many times have you been in love?"

"Who, me? None, so far," Christian answered honestly. "I spent so much of my life till now focused on my bodybuilding, there's never been room for anything else. How 'bout you? Any lovers?"

"Who, me?" Pipsi answered playfully. "Well, I promised my two fathers, both Hubert and Jesus, I wouldn't fall in love until I was certain I could stay committed forever. Heck, I even promised them both I'd be truly conventional and remain chaste until I wed."

"Hey, no kidding!" Christian was pleasantly surprised. "Same with me!"

"Nice to know someone else feels the same way," Pipsi offered.

"Yeah!" Christian agreed, wholeheartedly. "What's so wrong with that kind of old- fashioned thinking, anyway?"

"Not a darn thing!" Pipsi answered approvingly, as she leaned forward and gave him a warm hug good-bye. Christian leaned over and returned her affection.

"Nice car," She observed, running a perfectly manicured finger along the side of the yellow Porsche.

"Thanks," said Christian, quietly. "Belongs to a friend."

"What would we do without rich friends?" Pipsi asked, rhetorically.

"My car's a beat-up, old VW," he told her with one of his lopsided shrugs.

"What's it matter, anyway?" she asked, philosophically. "All cars can do is take you where you want to go. The rest is simply window dressing."

As Christian popped opened the door to Robin's Porsche, Pipsi raised her finger into the air as if struck by inspiration. "Hey — would you like to escort me this Saturday night to a black-tie supper gala my parents are hosting at the Beverly Hilton? It's for diabetes, their favorite charity."

"I'd love to go," Christian told her, honestly. "But I'm afraid I don't own a tuxedo."

"Oh, puh-leaze!" Pipsi giggled. "That's the least of our worries."

Christian was eager to accept, but he knew he was expected to spend that night with Robin. Their interaction had gotten so frosty of late, so borderline bellicose, he didn't want to further stir the pot. Reluctantly, he declined her gracious invitation, saying with a sad shrug, "I already have plans for Saturday."

"Ah, too bad," Pipsi tried masking her disappointment by smiling politely as she stretched to softly kiss his cheek. At the same time, she tucked another business card into his shirt pocket. "Here's my private cell number," she said softly and patted his huge pecs several times, making sure it was safely lodged. "Will you call me?"

"Of course I will," said Christian.

"I mean it," Pipsi was adamant. "When a woman says she'll call you, she means when she gets home. When a man says he'll call you, he usually means sometime before he dies. So please call. I'd love to chat more, maybe workout with you sometime. Have you show me what I'm doing wrong."

"I'd love to train with you," Christian told her. "But you might run into some trouble spotting me while I'm benching five plates on each side."

"Naw!" Pipsi facetiously flexed her lean, surprisingly well-shaped biceps. "I can handle it. I'm quite strong. Or we can just go out for another horseback ride."

"I think I'd like that a lot!" Christian told her with a genuine smile, before he squeezed himself behind the wheel of Robin's flashy sports car and took off.

*   *   *   *

Christian returned to Kincaidia, refreshed by his idyllic afternoon roaming on horseback through the Malibu hills. When Lester informed him Mr. Kincaid was not yet home, but still at his "business" meeting, the bodybuilder headed straight for the privacy of his pool house. As he stepped out of his clothes, and into a pair of Polo sweatpants, he removed Pipsi's business card from his shirt pocket, and carefully placed it down next to his bedside phone.

One cocktail hour, two martinis and three sheets to the wind later, Robin returned after dark to Kincaidia, all wound up and fully animated, having all but sealed the deal to become the power behind Cody's forthcoming ascension into the ranks of championship bodybuilding. The young muscle dynamo told Robin he'd seriously consider his proposal and get back to him very soon.

Over in the pool house, Christian stood before the wall-to-wall mirror, practicing the troublesome transitions in his posing routine for the approaching contest, when Robin barreled in.

"Robin!" Surprised, Christian dropped his towering double biceps stance and turned away from the mirror. "What are you doing out here in my part of the house?"

"*Your* part of the house?" Robin was aghast. "I bet you sure like the sound of that, huh?" With an ironic chuckle, he then added, "I guess I must have gotten lost!"

"Something wrong?"

"Something sure is!" Robin brayed like a tipsy five-year-old as he garbled inaudibly, "*Your* part of the house: that's what's wrong! That's the only thing, in fact, that *is* wrong. Everything else is once again damn near perfect. So I want my welcome home muscle hug and I want it right here and damn it, I want it right now! You got any problems with that?"

Not a problem, thought Christian, gritting his teeth. *I can manage this. The Venice contest — two weeks away. Stay calm. Robin still hasn't crossed over the line.*

Christian hoped he might get back to nailing down his posing routine if he administered one fast hug and sent his recalcitrant benefactor on his way. So he took a short step forward and reluctantly opened wide his arms, ready to embrace Robin.

By then, however, the half-pint had other ideas, insisting, "And I don't just mean your everyday hello-good-bye muscle hug. I mean a major squeezeroony. And one more thing," he sneered, with a snitty snap of little fingers. "I also want to see you in one of your posing trunks while we hug. Any problem with that, let me know right now."

Not a problem, thought Christian, getting more annoyed and very quickly losing patience with this bothersome distraction. *I can manage this. Calm down.* He disappeared into his walk-in closet to choose among the pairs of posers Robin had bestowed upon him during their Vegas shopping spree. As always, Christian hated being so blatantly objectified and, as always, he felt he had no choice but to put up with it.

While Christian changed in the Temple's closet, Robin wondered whether Cody, his new likely protégé, had called yet to accept his offer, and so he ambled over to Christian's bedside telephone to retrieve his messages. At the same time, he looked down at the business card lying against the phone.

Christian strolled nervously out of the closet clad in a pair of yellow posers. He didn't like it when Robin was in this kind of nasty mood, so he was eager to get this over with as soon as possible.

"Who in God's name is Pipsi Sterling?" Robin wanted to know as he looked up. The sight of his muscle boy looking his glorious best instantly captured his attention.

Christian sauntered over in all his muscledom and hovered over Robin. "Just a girl I met at church."

"Good! Then you won't be needing this," Robin sneered, dismissively, and quickly ripped Pipsi's business card to shreds. "Now then," he stifled a hiccup. "Where's your sugar daddy's great big muscle hug?"

Inwardly fuming, Christian closed his eyes, bit his lower lip, followed form and gave Robin a strong squeeze. Robin wrapped his slender arms around Christian's waist and squeezed back with all his might. "Oh, yes!" He proclaimed. "That feels real good. Well, at least for a start."

Christian released himself from the disparity of their Mutt-and-Jeff hug and took a short step back. "For a start and for a finish, Robin, remember?" he remained resolute. "We agreed on our rules!"

"Did we?" Robin asked, twisting his body to and fro, an intoxicated, cantankerous child. "Well, maybe it's time for us to start making up some new rules! Wadda ya say?"

"I think I've had it up to here with all our rituals and rules."

Robin felt bolstered knowing Christian's understudy protégé replacement was practically hovering in the metaphorical wings, waiting to come on. So the small man screwed up some big man courage and semi-slurred his squeaky words, announcing bluntly, "Okay, Samson. Now that your trial period is over, it's time to own up."

"I have owned up, Robin. More than I ever expected or wanted. Done whatever you asked. Everything we agreed upon, and more."

"Big deal!" Robin snapped his fingers. "The truth is your sugar daddy's been nothing but patient, coddling you long enough, and now the piper must be paid."

"You wanna give me that again?" Christian asked cautiously and guardedly took a step away from Robin.

"Time now to give back a little bit of all your sugar daddy's been giving you."

"You're drunk, Robin," Christian said calmly, pulling his pair of sweat pants back on, over his scanty posers. "Maybe you should go to bed."

"Not yet, damnit!" Robin cried out, far too loudly. After stifling a cumbersome belch and then another hic-cup, he took a couple of deep breaths and pouted, "How long did you think this was going to remain a free ride? Don't you know muscle charity only goes so far? Seems to me you have no sense of gratitude, and now your patron saint, your very own fucking angel of muscle is tired of jacking off every night after you leave my bedroom."

"That's not my problem," Christian insisted. "I've kept up my part of the bargain. And this has been anything but a free ride. I've been paying heavily with my soul and with all the companionship I could muster. And you're wrong. I am grateful, very grateful for all you've given me."

"Then prove it to me!" Robin huffed.

"How?" Christian asked cautiously.

"I know something you can do!" Robin exclaimed with sinister calculation. "Something that just might help improve matters around here a whole lot. Wanna guess what it is, Son?"

Christian bent forward and looked straight into Robin's face. "Why don't you just tell me?"

Robin's eyes darted down to the carpet and remained fixed there as quietly, he worked up the courage to baby talk, "I want my big muscle boy to drop his big sweat pants to the floor along with his tiny posers, so his little sugar daddy can finally administer an all-out, muscle worshipping blowjob!"

Now, *that* was a problem — one Christian couldn't possibly manage. Robin had crossed over the line. Without thinking, Christian brushed past his benefactor, returned to his walk-in closet and started packing. He reached for whatever was nearby, and tossed some basics into one of his threadbare suitcases: several T-shirts, underwear, workout gear, sneakers, a couple of jockstraps.

He packed none of Robin's gifts — not his chic Armani slacks, nor any of his Polo shirts, not his Jocko briefs, nor even his custom fit posers. Lastly, he extracted from his wallet Robin's black American Express card and left it on one of the shelves. Suitcase in tow, Christian burst back out from the closet and bolted from the pool house.

Suddenly filled with remorse, Robin ran up to his ward from behind, shouting after him, "Please! Please! Don't go!"

They hurried through the main house side by side, and Christian remained unbowed as he headed with a fevered determination for the front entrance. Robin stepped in front of the door and wailed like a five-year-old having a meltdown in the middle of a supermarket. "No-No-No! You can't leave! Please, please forgive me? I'm so sorry, so sorry!"

Christian looked straight down into Robin's face and told him sincerely, "That makes two of us!"

"I know I've been a bad little boy," Robin confessed. "But you can forgive me, can't you? Please, please, please?"

"I need some time alone," Christian told him. "Time to think."

"If you leave me now," Robin wagged a naughty-naughty finger at his protégé. "You may not be able to come back."

"I'll take my chances!" Christian told him. Then, holding his mounting anger at bay, he stormed out of Kincaidia.

Christian jumped into the Porsche and sped straight down to Venice. As he zoomed along the Santa Monica Freeway, pressing the pedal twenty miles over the speed limit, he was alarmed when it hit him that in his blinding rage and sheer haste, he'd forgotten to pack his Gucci shaving kit which housed the last of the steroids needed to finish his cycle before the contest.

An hour later, Christian was back at the YMCA — same dump, different room. He forked over all but the last of his cash from Robin's most recent "allowance" allotment for a full week's rent. He used the pay phone in the lobby to call Kincaidia. He told Lester to let Robin know he'd be dropping by the next day to pick up the rest of his things, particularly the last of his steroids, and also to exchange the keys to Robin's sporty Porsche for his own tarnished VW.

"Very good, Sir," said Lester, typically reserved. "I'll relay the message to Mr. Kincaid."

∗   ∗   ∗   ∗

Christian was already in a foul mood when he drove Robin's Porsche into Kincaidia the following afternoon, pissed off because he was by then already half a day late for his next shot of precious juice. He also felt anxious about having to again confront Robin, and worried how complicated the little man might make it for him to pick up his essential stash.

The bodybuilder's VW had been moved out from the rear of the garage and now sat at the front of the property. Christian attributed his seething, bubbling anger to 'roid-rage and, as he rang the front doorbell, ordered himself to calm down.

Lester opened the front door. "Good afternoon, Christian."

"Where's Robin?"

"Conducting a business call to London, I believe," Lester answered in his composed monotone. "I was instructed to show you to your things." Lester handed Christian the keys to his VW and then calmly escorted him through the house, outside to the pool area.

Cody, Robin's new, super heavyweight bodybuilder protégé, was already poolside, stretched out atop a chaise, soaking up the afternoon sun in a pair of powder-blue posing trunks. His entire body bounced in sync with the dance music blaring privately from his earphones. Neither he nor Christian took notice of each other as Christian stepped into the pool house.

Lester had evidently already packed the rest of Christian's things inside the boxes he brought with him back when he first moved in. The cartons sat stacked in a corner of the room.

Christian headed directly for the night table. When he found its drawer empty, he turned to Lester and demanded to know, "Where's my shaving kit, Lester? You know what I mean: the little Gucci kit with the zipper. Robin gave it to me!"

"You'll have to discuss that with Mr. Kincaid," Lester responded blandly. "I'll let him know you're here."

Christian made several trips back and forth, toting his boxes outside. After cramming his meager worldly possessions into his undersized Rabbit, he returned to the pool area to retrieve his steroids and be on his way.

Robin was by then also poolside, shaded beneath a wide-brimmed summer hat, stretched out on a chaise, alongside Cody.

"I came to say good-bye," Christian told him. "Here are the keys to your Porsche. Thanks for everything."

"You're very welcome, I'm sure," said Robin, icy and aloof.

"Just one last thing," Christian responded, all business. "I need the rest of my cycle."

"Cycle?" asked Robin, like he never before heard the word. "I don't know anything about *your* cycle. The only cycle of which I have any acquaintance is the one Cody just started."

"Who?" Christian asked, confused.

"Oh!" said Robin, feigning surprise. "How rude of me. Guess you two haven't met. Christian, this is Cody."

Robin patted Cody's enormous, freshly shaved, muscular thigh, and raised his squeaky voice loud enough to be heard over the earphones blasting into Cody's ears. "Yo, Cody, say hello to Christian!"

Christian's replacement protégé opened his eyes, raised his head, and pulled off one of his earphones long enough to acknowledge, "Wassup, man?" Then he dropped his head back against the pillow, to focus again on his music and his tan.

Christian ignored Cody as he told Robin, "I need the rest of my cycle. You know that. For the competition. I don't want anything else. Just give me the rest of my juice and I'll get out of here."

"How's this for a small world?" Robin boasted. "Just like you, Cody, lying here next to me at a bountiful two hundred thirty-two perfectly proportioned pounds, is also entered in the Mr. Muscle Beach contest. And, like you, he's also here on a trial basis. Unlike you, however, he's going to have a clear advantage two weeks from Sunday since he's also now on a major cycle."

Christian glared at Robin with mounting anger.

Robin reached behind the pillow on Cody's chaise, and pulled out the Gucci shaving kit in question. "Is this by any chance what you're looking for?" he asked, disingenuously.

"You know it is!" insisted Christian.

"I swear, this world gets smaller every minute!" Robin mused.

"Give it to me, Robin," Christian grumbled, swiftly losing the last of his patience. "They're mine. They were a gift from you, so they belong to me. You know I need them for the contest!"

"Tough titty!" Robin squeaked, and punched a tiny fist into his chaise. "Just before you got here, I told Cody he could have the rest of your steroids, and that means all of them!"

Christian knew he was about to lose it, so he clamped his open hand against his abs in an involuntary effort to hold his mounting fury at bay. Instead of jumping forward and grabbing hold of Robin, which is what he felt like doing, he instead squeezed the keys to the Porsche on the Tiffany key ring in his hand, and raised his arm out before him. With a jiggle of his keys, he negotiated, "You can have the keys to your house and your car back as soon as I get my shaving kit."

"Keep the stupid keys for all I care," Robin shrugged, ambivalently dismissive.

"Why are you doing this?" Christian wanted to know.

"Because someone has to show you boys that brains eventually win out over muscle every time. And you can keep the damn car. You think I care? I'll just report it stolen."

"But what happened to our agreement?"

"Our agreement was for a trial period," Robin said as he got up off his chaise and, hugging the shaving kit to his chest like it was a football, stood tall as his weenie frame would allow. "Well, we had our little trial period, didn't we? Didn't quite work out. Pity. You let your sugar daddy down and now it's over. To paraphrase Oscar Wilde: 'There is no good or evil — there's only charming and tedious.' And you, my boy, have become tedious. So why don't you hand over the keys and just get the fuck out?"

Frozen in place, Christian clenched his teeth and seethed, "For the last time, Robin, give me my shaving kit!"

"Make me!" Robin giggled, as he abruptly darted straight into his pool house. A mischievous little boy at play, he quickly slid closed the enormous sliding glass panel and secured its dead bolt, locking himself inside. The little man then shouted loud enough to be heard through the thick glass. "Ha! Ha! Guess what? I was the one who acquired all those wondrous drugs for you, paid for them with my own money. Nothing here belongs to you anymore, you stupid jock. So why don't you just turn around and go back to your loser life?"

Christian snapped.

Enraged, he hauled off, tossed the Tiffany key ring into the deep end of the water, and then stomped straight over to the small, al fresco gym area at the side of the pool. Once under its awning, he wrapped both his huge hands firmly around the long, forty-five pound barbell. Even though the heavy piece of equipment was locked and loaded with a forty-five pound plate on each side, Christian yanked the hundred thirty-five pounds from its perch atop the bench press like it was a paperweight.

In a mighty display of power lifting, he resolutely pressed the hefty burden up into the air, and kept it balanced high over his head as precariously, he walked the barbell over to the front of the pool house. The muscle monster then fulfilled his prenatal prophesy as, with Samsonian force, he thrust forward the weighty metal projectile and slammed the loaded barbell flush against the floor-to-ceiling panels of the bolted glass double doors, the pillars of Robin's sacred Temple. The brutal force of its paralyzing impact immediately smashed to smithereens the entire sliding glass entrance.

The sight of his just-recently installed, thirty-foot, polarized-glass wall suddenly being reduced to shards of rubble before his eyes, shocked Robin. Its accompanying thunderous crash, which echoed throughout the surrounding Bel Air canyon with a booming reverberation, further scared the living daylights out of him.

As the all-glass entryway crumbled, the architectural integrity of the pool house was so compromised, the roof cracked and the front half of the structure toppled over. It came crashing down and collapsed onto the patio, creating in its wake a dark cloud of dust.

Cody was so startled by the sight of Christian tearing down Robin's house of worship, he popped out of his earphones, jumped up from his chaise and darted straight for the safety of the living room inside the main house. No way was he about to get into any hostile confrontation with some psycho muscle monster erupting with that much incendiary 'roid rage.

With menace in his eyes and nostrils flared like a bull loose in the streets of Pamplona, Christian stormed threateningly past all the shattered glass and headed into the pool house, hell-bent for Robin. He ignored the crashing, crushing crescendo of steel and glass collapsing all around him as he confronted his former patron. Furious, verging on flipping out of control, he no longer thought sensibly as he grabbed the little man by the side of his shoulders and effortlessly lifted him high up off the floor, high over his head, way up into the air.

Robin remained frozen in terror as Christian shook him back and forth harshly, like a rag doll. "Gimme back my damned 'roids!" he bellowed threateningly.

Too terrified to talk his way out, Robin quickly let go of the Gucci bag. "Take 'em!" he cried out as the bag hit the floor. "Just take 'em and get out!"

Christian released his hostage, discarding Robin as if he were a used towel. As Robin plopped to the floor with a thud, Christian knelt down and scooped up his shaving kit.

Robin remained spread-eagled across the carpeting, trembling in place because he was scared so senseless and at the same time, never in his life so exhilarated.

Christian speedily zipped open the shaving kit, checked to make certain all his remaining vials and hypodermics were accounted for and still in one piece. One or two of the tiny vials were cracked open from their fall, but all else was intact. Satisfied, he tucked the Gucci bag securely under his arm, stepped over a mound of shards, and stomped his way back into the main house. He tried calming himself down from his raging outburst, and was slowly returning to his more familiar senses, when he passed Cody in the foyer.

Robin's new protégé expressed his neutrality by raising huge, well-chiseled arms of surrender high in the air as he told Christian, "Hey, man, I got no beef with you."

"Good," Christian told the new kid on the block. "Tell Robin I'm sorry about the damage. Tell him, maybe, if he hadn't been such a little jerk about it ..."

"No problem — I'll do that!" Cody said assuredly as he rushed ahead to open the front door for his predecessor. "Hey — got any advice for me, like you know, maybe the best way to handle Robin?"

"Yeah," said Christian as once again, he walked out of Kincaidia, this time with his integrity. "Practice your baby talk!"

*   *   *   *

PIPSI STERLING — SET FOR LIFE

Not long after he brought down the pillars of his pagan captivity, Christian found himself once again ensconced in his lamentable room at the dilapidated Y. He didn't calm down until he emptied his Gucci bag and prepared to administer the overdue shots for the end of his cycle.

In his haste to release the highly regarded elixir into his bloodstream, he haphazardly stabbed the needle into his left upper butt cheek and broke a vessel. A burst of blood spurted onto his bed. Christian hurriedly smacked a Band-Aid over the eruption, stemming the flow. *Not a big deal,* he told himself, as he lay down on the lumpy, by then bloodstained sheets, and again repeated his mantra to himself, over and over, before he fell into a fitful sleep: *You must suffer for your art.*

Early the next morning, an ache throbbing through his glutes awoke Christian. When he looked down and found an unsightly, swollen, purplish bruise over the puncture wound, he decided since things couldn't get much worse, he may as well try to get in touch with Pipsi. However, since Robin had torn her business card to shreds the day before, he had no idea how he might reach her.

When he went down to the lobby and called Information, the operator told him yes, there was a "P. Sterling" registered in Malibu, but the phone number was unlisted. *Just as well,* Christian figured. *God must have other plans for us. Besides, what would she ever want with a fallen, penniless sinner like me?*

Resigned to failure, he headed back to his room to unpack the last of his cardboard cartons. When he unfolded the khakis he'd worn the day before at Pipsi's brunch, the other business card, the one she first handed him in church, fell out from a pocket and flipped about, seemingly airborne as it glided gracefully to the floor.

Christian had forgotten all about Pipsi's other business card. He quickly pocketed a handful of change from the top of his dresser, and then high-tailed it down to the pay phone in the lobby.

When her message center answered, Christian was nervously chatty. "Yo, Pips, it's Christian calling," he tried sounding cheery. "You know, from Sunday's horseback ride? And, uhm, well, if that invitation is still open, you know, for that black-tie event this Saturday, I'd sure like to go with you. I don't have any formal clothes, but I have a blazer and a dark tie if that's okay. I'm here in Venice, in a room at the YMCA with no phone. It's a long story. Anyway, how 'bout if I call you again, tomorrow morning at nine, just before my workout, okay? I hope you'll be there so we can talk. Later, Miss Pips!"

When Pipsi picked up Christian's message, she was overjoyed. She immediately called and postponed her early breakfast meeting the following morning with her financial advisor, and then phoned to postpone her nine-thirty a.m. manicure. Her top priority was to be home Tuesday morning when Christian called back.

By ten past nine the next day, Pipsi paced the floor while staring at her still-silent phone. By nine-twenty, as she thought about contacting him at the Y, the phone finally rang. Praise God — it was Christian calling.

"Hey, Pipsi. It's me."

"I was so happy to hear from you last night," Pipsi exuded enthusiasm. "And yes, the invitation for this Saturday is most assuredly still open."

"Great," said Christian. "So — okay if I show up in my blazer?"

"I don't see why something as trivial as formal attire should be any kind of stumbling block for us, do you?" Pipsi asked, still bubbling over with her signature liveliness. "How 'bout we talk about what you'll wear when we speak on Saturday? What are you, anyway, about a fifty-six-large?"

"Why, yes, I am," Christian was impressed. "How did you know?"

"Lucky guess," Pipsi confessed with a girlish giggle.

*   *   *   *

On Friday, the day before Pipsi's parents' charity fundraiser at the Beverly Hilton, Christian returned to the Y after his workout and, as he passed the front desk, the manager called out to him, "Oh, hello there, Mr. Falconer. This came for you by messenger." The manager pointed to a black garment bag hanging from a hook on the back of a nearby door. Bright red letters on its plastic covering announced: *Another Rental from Ted's Tuxedos.*

Christian carried the hanging bag up to his small room, unzipped it and pulled out a classy Brioni tuxedo, accompanied by all the accoutrement needed for formal attire: eighteen-inch neck, thirty-six-inch sleeve dress shirt, snappy black bow tie, ebony studs and cuff links, even footwear: black formal socks, size thirteen Gucci black patent leather shoes.

After a quick, hot shower, Christian tried on the tuxedo. Practically a perfect fit.

"How'd you know my measurements?" he asked Pipsi, a short while later, when he called from the pay phone in the lobby to thank her for her thoughtfulness.

"I have an eye for detail," Pipsi cooed. "But I did have to guess about your shoe size."

"You know, I'll have to pay you for the rental," Christian told her, knowing he couldn't possibly afford any such thing.

"Don't be silly," Pipsi dismissed the notion. "It was my invitation. Besides, you'll feel more comfortable looking like all the other penguins. Please just have your formal wear packed when the messenger picks it up first thing Monday morning. I wasn't certain about your inseam, so I also put the tailor at Ted's on standby in case you need any last minute alterations."

"Won't be necessary, Miss Pips," Christian gloated. "You did a great job. I'm good to go."

"Wonderful," Pipsi purred. "Then I'll see you tomorrow night, you big bruiser, up here at my place, all spiffy and polished, right at seven."

*   *   *   *

Christian stood tall in front of his bathroom mirror, brimming with renewed confidence as he sized himself up. He may have felt somewhat confined, even inflexible in the stiffness of his rented tuxedo, but he sure looked sharp and handsome. And of course huge. It amazed him how much Pipsi's bubbly effervescence, her surplus of sweetness, had become not nearly so off-putting, so cloyingly annoying as when they'd first met.

He stuffed himself into his clankity Rabbit and drove up to Malibu.

A vision in organdy ruffles, Pipsi opened her front door and was so taken by her escort's sartorial splendor, she threw her arms around him and gushed, "My-my-my, don't we look elegant!"

"Thanks," Christian deflected the compliment. "I'm afraid my car's real low on gas. I didn't want to stop at a station, you know, all dressed up like this. Could we take your car?"

"Sure thing," Pipsi answered happily. "But only if you drive."

"You sure you don't mind?" Christian asked.

Pipsi giggled good-naturedly and tossed him the keys to her Jaguar convertible. "Once I peeked outside and saw the wreck you drove up in, heck, that's exactly what I was about to suggest!"

*   *   *   *

Their black-tie fete at the Beverly Hilton was as rigid and reserved as Christian anticipated. Decked out in formal finery, several hundred guests milled about, stopping here and there to exchange air kisses, or perhaps conduct brief networking bursts of polite conversation.

Serving in their roles as gracious host and hostess, Pipsi's father, Hubert Sterling, and her mother, Lucille, stood at the ornate entrance leading into the Grand Ballroom, animatedly greeting arriving guests.

By the time Pipsi finished introducing her date to several couples, Christian got the impression that many of the guests at the fundraiser had bought their seats and tables less out of enthusiasm and more out of some sense of obligation to the Sterlings. Whether it was the Sterling's high social standing within the Beverly Hills community, or Hubert's varied, some might say sordid, business dealings, Mr. Sterling was evidently a dynamic force within the community.

Toward the end of the twentieth century, back in those irrationally exuberant gold-rush days on Wall Street, Hubert invested his capital with enough dumb luck to catapult him into the Super Millionaire's Club, that legion of *nouvelle riche* for whom money became no object and ostentation no impediment.

Pipsi led Christian over to the receiving line so she could introduce him to her parents. One look at her folks and Christian thanked God Pipsi had inherited her mother's physical structure and not her dad's.

Hubert Sterling was a big-bellied bear of a man. By sharp contrast, his wife, Lucille, was petite and delicate, just like Pipsi. With a strong handshake and a manly slap to Christian's back, Hubert then mortified his daughter when he bellowed raucously, in his gravelly James Earl Jones projection, "So this is our little girl's new fella, huh?"

"So nice to meet you, Christian," Sterling's elegant wife said softly, with a sweet smile. As Lucille leaned forward to welcome her daughter's date to their fundraiser with a polite peck on his cheek, she also whispered a confidence into his ear. "Just want you to know, Pipsi never tells us diddley squat. Still, she's said nothing but wonderful things about you."

Christian was flustered but flattered. "Thanks," he answered, awkwardly. "Pipsi and me, I mean Pipsi and *I* just met. But I can tell your daughter's a wonderful girl. I mean woman."

"You were right the first time," Hubert chimed in with ebullience. "To me, she'll always be a little girl. *My* little girl"

Embarrassed by her father's exuberance, Pipsi rolled her eyes to the chandelier, latched on to Christian's hand, and quickly led him away from her parents' receiving line. With a broad smile, she proclaimed theatrically, "Come, Christian — let us move on in search of liberating libation."

*   *   *   *

Throughout the evening, Pipsi slowly sipped never-ending refills from a flute of champagne. Christian felt a bit out of place among so many unfamiliar people, especially with so many of them taking notice of his prominent oversize. Still, he was not about to calm his jitters by breaking training, not with the Venice Beach show less than ten days away. Instead, he stuck to carbonated water on the rocks.

Hours later, by the time they returned home to her country cottage, Pipsi was tipsy.

"Maybe you shouldn't drive all the way back down to Venice," she suggested, kicking off her high heels. "Not after all I've had to drink. Why not spend the night?"

"You mean here with you?" asked Christian, rendered defenseless by her brazen, unexpected invitation.

Pipsi picked up on her date's reticence and was fast to assure him with a nervous giggle, "Oh, it wouldn't be sexual or anything," Pipsi said. "I just like being with you. And friendship is far more important than sex, any day, don't you think? You can sleep upstairs with me, or you can have your own room down here. Your choice."

"Well, how 'bout if I just hold on to you for a while?" he asked, knowing how well that had worked with Robin. "At least until you fall asleep?"

"Can't think of anything I'd rather have you do," Pipsi said as she took the muscle monster by the hand and led him straight up the stairs to her bedroom.

Christian spent the night in Pipsi's frilly bedroom, lying in his boxer shorts alongside his little princess in her baby doll pajamas in her queen-sized bed. They cuddled cozily together, like spoons. In their respective slumbers, she purred while he snored.

Awash in the plush comfort of Pipsi's pastel-pink Frette satin sheets, the big guy stretched awake around nine and watched as an already-showered and smartly dressed Pipsi carried a bountiful breakfast tray into the room.

"Like the phoenix from the ashes, the slumbering giant arises!" she bubbled animatedly with one of her silly giggles as she placed the overloaded tray atop his lap. "Isn't this the most beautiful morning imaginable?"

"I suppose it is," Christian agreed amicably.

"Well, don't worry 'bout me," Pipsi gushed. "I've already eaten! Heck. I've been stirring your darn oatmeal for the past half an hour, waiting for the brontosaurus to budge. Hope it's not overcooked."

"It couldn't be better," Christian told her eagerly, as he dove into the spinach and feta cheese omelet abutting the huge bowl of oatmeal on his plate. "Thanks. This is just great!"

"Enjoy!" sang Pipsi. "And if you like, once you're finished, we could go to church."

"Great!" Christian answered. "I've got a pair of khakis and a denim shirt in the back of my car."

"Perfect," gushed Pipsi. "And I've been thinking. You looked so darn dashing in your formal clothes last night, why don't you just hold on to them? I'm committed to several other upcoming black-tie events this season, and would be honored if you'd again be my escort."

"Abtho-lutley!" garbled Christian, his mouth filled with spinach and feta.

"Now you stay here and eat. God knows, a growing boy needs physical nourishment before spiritual enlightenment. I'll go feed the horses."

Pipsi clicked on the television, tossed her remote to Christian, and then hurried out to the stable.

*   *   *   *

As they sat through the Sunday church service, Pipsi and Christian felt the eyes of the congregation upon them. They each relished being seen together. The wave of positive support flowing their way from parishioners made her feel proud to be with him. Not just a towering hunk, but thank heavens, in this day and age, of all things, a believer, as well!

Similarly, from his perspective, Christian knew that having Pipsi by his side instantly inflated his standing in their house of worship. Parishioners craned necks as they checked to see if there might be a new church couple in their midst. The vibes of the congregation's consensual approval made the big fellow feel respected, admired, and once again certifiably heterosexual.

During the seventy-minute service, the Evangelical Church of Malibu's fresh, new twosome sat pressed together in their wooden pew and prayed. Pipsi prayed to God, asking that Christian might grow to care for her as much as she was nuts for him, while Christian prayed that Pipsi would keep up her rescue of him, keep showering him with her seemingly boundless attention.

After the service, with the top down on her blue Jaguar, as they drove back to her place, Pipsi knew God's will was at work when Christian told her he needed to head straight back to the Y. His week's stay there was up and he had to checkout by three, go apartment hunting and find some new place to live.

Calmly, Pipsi felt no hesitation when she next invited her new friend to become her houseguest. "Why don't you just move in and stay with me a while?" she asked as they pulled in to the hidden driveway leading to her property. "You can keep all your things in my guesthouse. Heck, it's just sitting there."

Christian jumped at her generosity. "You mean it?" he asked incredulously, as he turned off the engine and handed Pipsi her car keys.

"Well, of course I mean it," she answered happily. "I'd love that. You can just stay here until you find a place of your own."

Christian leaned over and kissed Pipsi once, sweetly on the lips. Then he pulled out his own VW car keys, opened the Jag's door, and cheerily told her, "See you back here in a couple of hours!"

After gathering his meager worldly possessions and checking out of the Y, Christian stuffed everything into his Rabbit, got behind the wheel and stopped for a moment to pray. He thanked God for taking such good care of him, for helping him land so squarely on his feet. Then the muscle monster drove back up the Coast Highway in his travesty of a jalopy, all the way to little Miss Pipsi's country cottage in the woods.

*   *   *   *

That night at Pipsi's, Christian again slept with his new benefactress, his big arms engulfing her as they snuggled together, positioned like pretzels in the middle of her bed.

Early the following morning, right after his next scheduled heavy injection of steroids, as he devoured Pipsi's hearty breakfast of steak and eggs, Christian explained he needed to go into his full-steam-ahead, pre-contest mode.

Pipsi claimed she found the notion of helping her houseguest prepare for his contest simply the most exciting adventure imaginable. She then offered to do whatever was needed to help get him ready for the show.

"Well," Christian told her, frankly, "I've got my workouts and the rest of my cycle injections lined up. So if you can help out with my food, you'll be saving the day — again. You see, all I really need now, in addition to working out, is to eat. That's all. Just feed the machine. And of course ..." he then added, almost under his breath, "finish my cycle."

"Aren't you worried about that?" Pipsi asked. "Aren't steroids dangerous?"

"They sure are!" Christian agreed, wholeheartedly. "Especially if you abuse them. That's why, soon as I finish this last batch, that's it. No more for me. I'm giving my body a rest."

"In that case," Pipsi sang out, "I'd be thrilled to enlist."

*   *   *   *

The surest way to forge a path to Christian's heart, Pipsi prayed, was through his stomach. So she went directly to work and hired a cook to prepare his meals.

At that point in his pre-contest training, the muscle monster was cutting up, downing mostly protein, so the chef stayed busy, roasting whole chickens and racks of lamb, grilling sirloin steaks, searing ahi tuna, and baking fresh Chinook salmon.

Pipsi purchased a food scale to make certain Christian got the exact amounts of protein he required for any particular meal: a pound of sliced turkey breast here; three-quarters of a pound of filet mignon there. "Heck," she told her mother over the phone with a girlish giggle, while supervising as the cook grilled three pounds of fresh jumbo shrimp. "We're down to the wire here, Mom. Gotta dash. Christian's Mr. Muscle Beach contest is this weekend. I have no time to chat … we're too busy feeding the machine."

Pipsi's effervescent bursts of mirth might have put off many a man, but in her own peculiar way, she captivated Christian. So many things about her reminded him of his mother. He loved how classy she was, how she took such good care of him, the doting way she fussed over him, how supportive she was about his training.

As the last of his cycle further shaped his muscles, Christian focused intensely on his upcoming show. The illusion of near-perfection the steroids helped create on the outside, however, was not necessarily matched by the progress within. Christian fought to be valiant as he put up with the unpleasant side effects from his massive doses of juice. The 'roids toyed with his liver, threw off his blood chemistry, and created in his nervous system an electrolyte imbalance that delivered debilitating cramps into his thighs and calves. The last of his cycle also gave him insomnia. His trouble sleeping, along with recurrent headaches, plus the annoying outbreak of unsightly and itchy rashes popping out over the back of his arms and across his glutes, only added to the irascibility that was his 'roid rage.

When he responded to some petty issue by snapping at Pipsi, he realized he hated all his misplaced anger and, after apologizing painstakingly for his unacceptable outburst, again promised that as soon as the contest was over, he would get off those damn steroids for good.

*   *   *   *

As the contest approached, Christian was injecting himself two, sometimes three times a day. He had no illusions that his contraband cocktail might not one-day come back to bite him in the butt, but for the time being, all that mattered was showing up onstage that weekend in the best damn shape of his young life.

The steroids rampaging through Christian's system dissolved his residual fat even as they packed still more mass onto his already astonishing frame. One day out from the contest, when the muscle monster boldly flexed his imposing double biceps pose in Pipsi's full-length mirror, he was thrilled when he saw how the illegal fluids, along with his strict diet, in conjunction with his heavy lifting, had all coalesced to work their magic. Finally in top contest shape, massive yet cut, he tipped Pipsi's scale at two hundred fifty-three perfect pounds. His abs were so shredded, Pipsi said she wanted to grate some of her imported Reggiano Parmesan on them.

The night before the contest, Christian was far too pent-up to sleep. Wide-awake, he lay on his back in bed, next to a peacefully slumbering Pipsi, repeatedly replaying his upcoming posing routine in his head. As the numerals on the bedside digital clock shifted from 2:00 to 3:00 to 4:00, he became more frustrated over his insomnia. It wasn't until the first early glimpses of a black and purple predawn began seeping through slits in the bedroom curtains that Christian finally drifted in and out of a sporadic rest. By the time the alarm clock sounded at seven-thirty, he awoke exhausted. He struggled to get out of bed and knew he'd be relying on sheer adrenalin to carry him through the day.

Pipsi prepared a pre-contest breakfast high in complex carbs, meant to make more pronounced in prominence his vascularity and heighten the cuts in his musculature. The idea was that after so many days of severe carbo-depletion, a serious, sudden infusion of fat into his system on the day of a contest would give his body a much sought-after ripple effect. After downing his stack of pancakes, his oatmeal, his protein-packed egg white omelet, the young competitor showered and then shaved his entire body. Pipsi assisted with those hard-to-reach spots like the back of his legs.

Once he was freshly painted in his first couple of layers of tanning cream, he gave himself that cycle's final injection of Deca mixed with Primobolan and Trenbolone. After quickly assembling his gear, he and Pipsi then headed straight down to Venice.

*   *   *   *

Backstage in the crowded, cavernous pump-up room of the Santa Monica Civic Auditorium, a bevy of bodybuilders were preoccupied, stretching and exercising with light weights, while rubbing layers of thick, darkening grease over every inch of their exposed skins. Contestants far more accustomed to lumbering around their homes in loose-fitting sweat suits were now preparing to step out in front of a muscle-happy audience, exposing their powerful physiques for appraisal and approval, clad in nothing but the teensiest of posers.

This time out, Pipsi was Christian's trusted First Lieutenant, and she dutifully darkened the breadth of her boyfriend's back and rubbed on and painted the back of his legs. As she adoringly applied the dark goop, his enormous body morphed several shades of brown deeper. Christian realized how comfortable he felt having Pipsi at his side, meticulously massaging the darkening cream into his skin. It sure beat the hell out of getting darkened by Ruth Hortense or, God forbid, Robin.

And, speaking of Robin, God forbid, when Christian looked over, he spotted the diminutive fellow off in a corner of the room. Robin was smiling giddily as he bounced up and down on his tippy-toes, while diligently oiling up Cody. Christian caught the little man casting now and again furtive glances his way, but chose to ignore him.

Instead, he scanned the room and sized up his competition. He couldn't help but observe how so many lady friends assisting competitors were, for the most part, well, homely. Traffic-stopping hunks teamed with lackluster women. Go figure. It made Christian feel more comfortable about having Pipsi helping him get ready. *Say what you will about my gal, Miss Pips,* he thought while concentrating on his posing routine for the mirror. *With all the dogs in this room, at least she's the pick of the litter.*

A harried stage manager, all-business, rushed straight to the center of the warm-up room to bellow his authoritative two-minute warning: "Attention! I wanna see all bodybuilding contestants lined up, ready to go out onstage, and that means right now!"

As the bodybuilders lined up to file out the double doors, the stage manager looked over the contestants, counting heads while calling out his pertinent last-minute advice: "And remember, you're trying to impress the judges, so don't forget the four Do Nots: Do *not* dance; Do *not* do Karaoke; Do *not* repeat your poses; and most importantly, Do *not* shake your butt in the judges' faces."

As Christian and Pipsi joined the other contestants headed toward the wings of the stage, whom should they run into but Robin and Cody.

"Why, Christian, hello!" Robin was ebullient, acting as though he'd run into a dear old friend. "Imagine running into you here?"

"Hello, Robin," Christian quietly acknowledged.

"You look so cut up," the little man offered. "So contest-ready. I'm impressed. You remember Cody, don't you?"

"How could I forget?" Christian forced a smile.

Robin placed an affectionate arm around Cody's waist. "My boy's also cut up and contest-ready, no?" he asked, before adding pointedly, "He's been staying with me in the main house while my pool house gets rebuilt. And this morning, when he showed his daddy his peak perfection, I promised that when he walks off with the top trophy today, I'm going to buy him a large Dodge pickup."

Pipsi had no idea who this oddball little jerk might be, but she was not about to let anyone intimidate Christian. "Why don't we just wait and see what the judges decide?" she suggested ardently.

For a moment or so, no one said anything. "Well, Christian," Robin broke the awkward vacuum. "Aren't you going to introduce us to your ... *friend?*"

"Robin and, umm, Cody," Christian muttered, practically beneath his breath. "This is Pipsi."

Robin shook Pipsi's hand enthusiastically. "Any friend of Christian's ..."

Christian tried sounding as gentlemanly as possible as he cut off the conversation with a brusque, "Okay — Best of luck!" Then he grasped hold of Pipsi's hand and led her away. As they walked toward the stage, Pipsi turned to Christian to ask, "How in then world did such an awful, little man like Robin ever raise such a huge son?"

"Robin's not his biological father," Christian told her, dryly. "Cody was adopted."

*   *   *   *

The lights in the cavernous auditorium dimmed down, and when they came back up, their harsh scrutiny illuminated forty-three over-inflated, over-darkened bodybuilders, overcrowding several platforms on the stage. In another era, so many well-oiled musclemen on display would have meant you were attending a slave auction in ancient Rome.

The so-called pre-judging segment of the contest next unfolded, and the competitors were directed by a disembodied voice to simultaneously pose and collectively flex their way through the seven mandatory poses. Five finalists in each weight division then got singled out to go on to compete in the second part of the program, where they'd perform their individual posing routines for the audience. Both Christian and Cody made it to the Super Heavyweight run-off.

Bodybuilders often enacted a variety of strange rituals just before going onstage to perform their personal posing routines. Some smoked pot, while one or two others snorted a hit of cocaine. Other guys swore a shot or two of vodka calmed their nerves and even heightened their vascularity. Some muscular lunatics even injected a hazardous substance called Synthol directly into their biceps, instantly inflating their mass, however disproportionately.

Christian was scheduled to go on right after Robin's new protégé. While waiting in the wings, he tried not to feel discouraged by Cody's audience-pleasing routine. He refused to compromise all the confidence he'd built up, and instead filled himself with the same excess assurance he exuded in the past when posing onstage before a cheering audience. He needed none of those last-minute tricks or myths used by others, as his secret weapon was the power of prayer.

A few moments later, when they announced his name, he puffed his pecs out as far as they could expand and walked nervously out to the center of the stage. Swimming in an abundance of testosterone and brimming with vitality, he begged God to accompany his every move. As his upbeat posing music began blaring over the sound system, Christian launched into his well-practiced routine.

As was long his custom, he hit all his marks, all his buttons, and managed to eventually win over the audience's collective approval. His chemical cocktails were so well timed, his muscularity peaked on the very day of the competition. When his posing music reached an earsplitting crescendo, he froze in place, made an angry warrior's face, firmly flexed his splendid double biceps peaks high above his head, and wowed the crowd.

The contest's last event was a manic collective posedown meant to finalize the pecking order of winning muscle. Christian stood alongside Cody, as well as the three other super heavyweight finalists, and the moment the posedown bell sounded, each contestant did his best to out-flex and outshine the rest of the competition.

Aiming to intimidate, Cody interrupted his posing long enough to move downstage and stand directly in front of Christian. When he dramatically flared his lats before the crowd, the audience roared its enthusiasm.

Unwilling to let Cody steal his thunder, Christian wasted no time and also stepped forward, directly before Cody. Instinctively incorporating the last of his reserve, he squeezed himself into a vein-popping most muscular pose, one he held on to until the posedown came to an abrupt end. The crowd went wild, cheering with excitement.

At contest's end, Cody was awarded third place among the super heavies, while Christian came in second. Christian picked up another trophy when he also placed third in the men's overall. Cody didn't place in that category at all, and Christian quietly gloated and silently thanked God for allowing honor and decency to triumph over decadence and deceit.

*   *   *   *

That night at their private victory dinner at Valentino's in West L.A., Christian and Pipsi celebrated his fine showing in the contest. He finally broke training by joining her in sipping several glasses of Veuve Clicquot. After toasting his accomplishment, Pipsi announced she had a post-contest surprise all her own, and then invited him to unwind from the pressures of his training by joining her for a week of sybaritic pampering at the Golden Door Spa in Arizona. "I reserved one of their private casitas for the two of us," she gushed, animatedly. "All you have to do is pack your toothbrush and your jock strap. My platinum credit card will take care of everything else."

The abundance of amenities offered at the two-thousand-dollar-a-day luxury resort helped Christian swiftly adapt to being overly spoiled and thoroughly indulged. The bodybuilder and the heiress languished together through a blissful week of submitting their bodies twice and sometimes thrice daily to the rejuvenating pampering procedures presented at the world-class spa.

The resort had a well-equipped gym, but Christian felt no motivation to workout. For the time being, he just wanted to unwind. So he and Pipsi passed on the low-calorie "spa" cuisine, and Christian quickly developed a fast liking for the expensive bottles of vintage red wines and rich desserts they enjoyed with their elaborate dinners.

After getting pummeled by a score of stimulating mud, coffee, and clay massages, exotic seaweed wraps and ancient Asiatic muscle rubs which zeroed in on their pained pressure points, Pipsi and Christian felt fully relaxed, free of aches and stress. Lathered in sun-blocked protection against the strong Arizona sun, they lazed around together, poolside.

After seven days of living lavishly, as they headed back home to Malibu, Christian realized how much he relished the good life and concluded he was ready for a lot more.

Now that they were acknowledged as a couple, Pipsi gingerly arranged her crowded social calendar, making certain she and Christian would go everywhere together, hand in hand. She struggled to decide which among her myriad invitations she wanted to accept. She was eager to show off her new beau. Fancy dinners in elegant homes competed for their attention, along with all manner of cocktail parties and celebrity-laden, charity fundraisers. For a young woman just shy of turning twenty-one, it was amazing how many A-lists already sported the young socialite's name.

Christian felt a lot better once he was finally off cycle. The multiple side effects he experienced soon dissipated, his unsightly rashes cleared up, and his painful headaches ceased pounding. He no longer lost his temper at the slightest trigger, and was once again able to sleep through the night.

Pipsi was overjoyed at seeing how much sunnier Christian's disposition was, how much less burdened and more light-hearted he seemed, how much easier he was to simply be around. However, it took but a few short weeks of over-indulging in all that good food and great wine before their glamorous lifestyle began having a negative impact on Christian's prized physique.

He never would have guessed how satisfying a glass of aged port could taste at the end of a meal, served with some fine stilton on a slice of Anjou pear. Who could have imagined how hard it might be to decline a chocolate soufflé when ordered ahead in a fancy restaurant? And when it came to all those fine vintage red wines he and Pipsi were imbibing with almost every dinner, what the heck, where was the harm in enjoying just one more glass … or three?

Both off-cycle and off-season, most of the water-retention that had previously inflated the muscle monster's powerful body quickly subsided. The fat burners in his contraband Deca no longer kept his sculpted six-pack from getting covered over by a sorry protrusion of gut. He was still big and strong, still a gigantic jock. But after another two months filled with so much more breaking of training, Christian soon sported more the sturdy physique of a powerlifter than any contest-ready bodybuilder.

Even though he felt burned out by the training process, Christian still managed to get over to Gold's once, maybe twice a week. Even so, his workouts were flat and uninspired. With no contest target to shoot for, Christian's workouts were little more than a walk-through. He used only light weights and exerted but a minimum of effort simply for the sake of basic bodily maintenance.

*   *   *   *

One early April evening, while Christian and Pipsi dressed for still another fashionable dinner party, this one over in Brentwood, they watched a report on the local news about a series of Southern California wild fires. Stoked by warm Santa Ana winds, fiery pockets of destruction were ravaging several communities in the parched, drought-stricken area, and that included their Malibu neighborhood.

"Nothing to worry about, Darling," Pipsi assured her boyfriend. "This is Southern California. Wildfires, mudslides, earthquakes, celebrity sex tapes, celebrity homicides, race riots, freeway snipers, plastic surgery disasters, melanoma run amuck — all part of everyday life."

Somewhere around two in the morning, a strong rush of wind fanned the furious flames of a nearby forest fire even as it sent snippets of sparks aloft, over into the nearby valley, and then directly down into the Malibu canyon. Christian and Pipsi awoke abruptly when they heard the alarming, wailing screech of approaching sirens, along with the gravelly humming of a trio of helicopters suddenly hovering in the sky overhead. The pungent odor of fire was redolent in the air.

Christian jumped out of bed in his boxer shorts. Pipsi threw on her bathrobe and followed right behind him as they trotted downstairs and rushed outside to her stable just as it burst into flames.

Alarmed and distressed, Pipsi panicked. "Oh, my Lord!" she screamed. "The horses! Oh, no! Star and Rapture! Please, God, no!"

"Stay here!" Christian shouted and, without thinking, ignored both the spreading flames and the mounting toxic, charcoal clouds of fuming smoke speedily engulfing the structure as he flung wide open the stable's huge front door and ran straight inside.

Too petrified to follow him, Pipsi did as she was told and stood in place, motionless. She watched in abject horror as Christian disappeared into a darkness of billowing smoke. As the flames leapt up before her, the fire quickly spread the contagion of its voracious appetite wildly across the full breadth of the stable.

Christian remained inside the burning structure for what seemed an eternity, and Pipsi was terrified. Feeling helpless, she watched as the devouring flames leapt from the top of the stable and hop-scotched over to her house. As her roof ignited, she looked back into the smoky chasm of the stable and cried out, "Help! Help! Please! Oh, God, no! Christian, where are you? Please! Please — get out of there! Never mind the horses. ALL I WANT IS YOU!"

Pipsi next heard the clanging bells and screaming sirens of an approaching fire engine thundering up her driveway, and ran down to rally them. By the time she returned to the burning stable moments later, a team of conscientious fire fighters in hot pursuit dragged a pair of hefty, cumbersome hoses behind them.

When a major section of the stable's structure suddenly collapsed, its booming crashing sound horrified Pipsi. "Oh, God, no!" she hollered out. "Christian, where are you? Please! Please get out of there!"

As the far section of the stable's roof cracked and then buckled, Pipsi saw the heavy side door suddenly sliding open. Five of her horses, one more startled and skittish than the next, then escaped from their fiery confinement as they raced wildly away from the flames, out into the safety of the corral, as fast as each of their four long legs could carry them.

Peering into the thick smoke, Pipsi tried containing her fright by praying. "Please, God, please!" she intoned in a near hysteria. "Take the stable, Take the house. I don't care. Just bring Christian back to me, Lord. Please! Bring him back safely and I promise I'll never let him go, not ever again!"

Pipsi buried her face in her hands and stood there frozen, not budging, not thinking clearly as she ignored the clatter of firemen rushing straightaway into the blazing inferno rapidly enveloping her property. She remained lost in prayer until she looked up again and spotted the glorious sight of Christian emerging from a thicket of dark smoke. Riding bareback atop Star, he coaxed Pipsi's favorite equine companion out of the burning stable's front door as he led her prized show horse away from the enveloping flames and out of harm's way.

∗   ∗   ∗   ∗

The flames that overwhelmed Pipsi's property were eventually extinguished, and the exhausted firefighters packed away their hoses beneath an overcast, gray dawn. With their sirens once again wailing, they then moved on to catch up with their brethren combating a blaze by then devouring homes on an adjoining hillside.

Christian and Pipsi drove down to the Malibu Inn. After checking in to a room, they spent the next several hours dozing on and off, locked in each other's arms.

Later that morning, still shell-shocked from the trauma they'd suffered together, Christian and Pipsi drove back over to investigate what remained of her once charming country cottage in the woods.

Water damage left by the team of determined firefighters was more destructive and far more extensive than any destruction the fire had brought to the property. In their determination to contain the inferno, the crew hosed down everything in sight. Pipsi's handsome furniture, her closets brimming with designer clothing, her dishware, her books, her fine art, her worldly goods, all lay in ruins, sopping wet.

Hand in hand, Christian and Pipsi wandered through the still smoldering remnants of her home, searching for anything salvageable. As Pipsi reached down to pull out a contorted, melted snippet of one of her horse show trophies, Christian came upon the waterlogged fragments of what had been his recently acquired Brioni tuxedo pants.

Strangely enough, Pipsi seemed barely phased by so much devastation. In truth, she had little cause for complaint. God, after all, answered her prayer when he delivered Christian, who in turn delivered all her beloved horses to blessed safety. Her boyfriend's selfless chivalry clarified her love for him, and now that her valiant hero was safe, her prized horses rescued, she wanted to show how boundless was her gratitude. As for replacing her possessions, that merely required a little of her time and a lot of her money, and Lord knows, she had plenty of both.

*   *   *   *

MONEY TO BURN

Hubert Sterling was set to seal the deal on the sale of several investment properties he owned in an upscale section of Hancock Park. One of them was a classic, California-Spanish, three-bedroom house, replete with gardens, tiled patios and a swimming pool. As soon as he heard the news about the calamitous fire that destroyed his little girl's Malibu home, the successful businessman immediately took the Hancock Park house off the market and handed it over to her as a temporary residence in which she and Christian could cohabitate.

Pipsi welcomed the huge project of replacing her material goods and tackled the assignment as might any sensible, self-respecting heiress. She went shopping. She and Christian spent several days traipsing the money-lined, quality stores along Rodeo Drive in Beverly Hills. They picked up Wedgewood china, Baccarat glassware, and Christofle silverware, among other necessities of life. Bloomingdale's and Williams-Sonoma supplied their kitchen appliances and bathing and dining needs. Saks Fifth Avenue and Lord & Taylor provided dresses, suits and shirts. They scooped up casual wear at Abercrombie & Fitch. Gucci was a must for shoes, Prada for accessories.

Whenever Christian saw a garment or furnishing he admired, he had only to point it out, and it was added to their shopping cart. For Pipsi, nothing was too good, too expensive for her beloved. They had a blast replacing their wardrobes, her furniture and all her houseware items. It was like starting over together fresh, as a committed couple. Her fire insurance would eventually reimburse a hefty chunk of her loss, so she gave herself full license to go out and spend, spend, spend. The daughter of the Gardener to the Stars hired one of the acknowledged Interior Designers to the Stars to quickly furnish their new Hancock Park dwelling. She next interviewed several architects about drawing up blueprints and preparing bids for the designing and rapid reconstruction of her Malibu property.

For the time being, Pipsi boarded her horses at a stable over in Burbank, not far from the riding trails that wound their way through Griffith Park. She drove over to groom Star and Rapture, and take them out for rides, several times a week.

A week before Pipsi's twenty-first birthday, Hubert Sterling took his daughter to lunch at the Ivy. As she picked at her lobster salad and he devoured a huge bowl of pasta primavera, he asked his pride and joy just how he might best honor her fast-approaching poignant milestone.

"There's only one thing I really want," Pipsi replied quietly. "And that's Christian. I love him so much, Daddy."

"What is it about him?" Hubert wanted to know.

"Who knows?" Pipsi giggled frivolously. "I love his transparency, his lack of guile. I love that even with his massive size and imposing power, he's always so gentle with me. I love that he's also a believer, and that he hasn't forced me into anything, hasn't minded remaining chaste until we decide what's ahead for us. I love the way he treats my horses. Gee, Daddy, I guess I love everything about him."

Hubert said he understood and took on her request as nothing less than his fatherly duty. As he cupped her chin lovingly in his hand, he solemnly promised her, "I'll get right on it."

The moment he returned to his office, Hubert Sterling instructed his executive assistant to call Christian at Pipsi's to set up a meeting between them as soon as possible.

*   *   *   *

The plush offices of Hubert Sterling Enterprises took up the entire fifteenth floor of a Century City high-rise. Hubert's executive assistant led Christian through the bustling complex, toward the plush corner suite, and asked if he wanted anything. "Coffee, juice, Perrier?"

"Nothing for me, thanks," Christian responded, politely.

"There's the big fellow now!" Hubert called out with enthusiasm as he greeted his guest at the door to his office. "Thank you for coming. Now we can have ourselves a man-to-man, heart-to-heart."

"I appreciate that, Mr. Sterling," said Christian, taking a seat in a handsome leather chair.

"Not *Mister* Sterling!" Pipsi's father roared with a hearty slap to Christian's back. "Please, call me Hubert. Nothing formal here. Just two big men having a little chat."

"Okay … Hubert," Christian smiled. "By all means, let's chat."

When Hubert's intercom buzzed, he whirled in place, flicked a nearby switch on his gargantuan desk and bellowed, "Hold all calls!"

"Yes, Mr. Sterling," an obsequious voice peeped over the speaker.

Hubert turned to again address Christian. "Now then," he plopped down on the tan ultra suede couch next to Christian's chair. "Where were we?"

"About to have a little chat," said Christian.

"Of course!" Hubert exclaimed, inspired to be back on track. "Right. Now let me be totally frank about this, okay?"

Christian forced himself not to appear too much in awe of the corporate opulence by which he was surrounded as he shrugged and answered, "Sure. Why not?"

"Okay. As you know, you and my daughter have not been seeing one another very long."

"No, not very long," Christian agreed. "Just a few months."

"Still, Pipsi tells me it's been enough time for her to make up her mind about you," Hubert boasted. "She believes that God brought the two of you together for a purpose."

"Oh, I believe that, as well, Sir," said Christian, in all honesty.

"And I'm sure you already know how important my little girl is to me."

"Of course I do," Christian answered emphatically. "She's lucky to have such loving parents."

"Truth is, I've worked my ass off to give her everything she ever wanted or even thought she might need. All the doll houses and perfumes, all the clothes. The best boarding schools. Family vacations in the Seychelles and the Caribbean. Shopping trips with her mother to Paris and Milan. Theater trips to New York and London."

"She's mentioned all that," Christian acknowledged.

"I've indulged her every whim, pampered her every passion, never denied my little girl anything," Hubert bragged, without apology. "When my little princess told me she wanted to grow up to become a cowgirl, I bought her a pony for her eighth birthday. Doesn't every father? When Pipsi turned thirteen, she wanted to learn to ski, so I purchased our three-bedroom bungalow in Lake Tahoe. Lucky for me, it also turned out to be a great investment. Do you ski?"

"No," said Christian. "But I've always wanted to learn."

"Perfect!" Hubert blurted out with pride. "Pipsi's a great instructor. She'll have you zipping down the slopes in nothing flat. Let me see, what else? Oh, yes. When my little girl announced she wanted to spend her sophomore year, not back at Wellesley, but in India, of all places, what'd I do? I sublet a furnished apartment for her in an elegant, gated community in downtown Mumbai."

"I know," said Christian. "I saw the pictures she took there and all the art she brought back."

"So why am I telling you all this?" Hubert asked as if he didn't know, and then answered his own question. "Because I want you to understand how nothing has ever been too good for my little girl, nothing out of reach. Not expensive cars, not designer clothes, not fancy jewelry, not show horses, not luxury travel, not real estate. Am I making myself clear?"

"Not exactly, Sir."

"Okay," Hubert exhaled with a slight sigh of impatience. "I guess what I'm getting at is that age-old question fathers have never stopped asking: just what exactly are your intentions with my daughter?"

"Intentions?"

"Just where are you planning to take this ... *courtship*? What kind of a future, if any, do you envision for yourself and Pipsi?"

"Well, Pipsi and I are having a great time together," Christian allowed.

"Yes, that's what she's told me," Said Hubert. "And that being the case, maybe you should think about taking this to the next level, Christian. You might think about showing me how serious you are."

"Oh, I can assure you I'm serious, Sir!" Christian maintained, with conviction.

"In that case," asked Hubert. "Have you given any consideration to the notion of ... matrimony?"

Caught off-guard, Christian smiled innocently and asked, "Don't you think we're a little young to get married?"

"Nonsense," Hubert dismissed the notion. "Lucille and I were not even twenty-one when we walked down the aisle."

"But I haven't even got a job yet. How would I support her?"

"I've got it all figured out!" Hubert asserted with authority as he banged his fist on the desk. "Answer me this, young man: Have you ever thought about a career in landscaping?"

"You mean as in lawns and trees ... flowers?"

"Precisely!"

"I'm afraid I don't know much about gardening," Christian admitted.

"Hell, neither do I," Hubert said, frankly. "My staff at From The Ground Up figures out all that crap for me. I only bought the business after I received their bill for some work they did around my place. I figured, if they can legally get away with that kind of highway robbery, I want in."

"But what could I do there?"

"Let me tell you something, Christian. A business, just like skiing, is something you can learn. Truth is, I don't like what I've been seeing in my landscaping firm's last few financial statements. Something's screwy, and I still can't figure what it might be. I need someone inside, someone I can trust who will accurately report back just exactly what's going on down there."

"And you think that could be me?" Christian asked, incredulously.

"Yes, Christian. I do think that could be you. And I'm prepared to pay a handsome wage for that kind of loyalty. So what do you think?"

"Well ... I'm flattered," was all Christian could think of to say.

"Let's cut to the chase, Son," said Hubert, as good-naturedly as he could muster. "I'm sure we can fix whatever in the world is stopping you from taking my daughter's hand in marriage. As you know, I am a man of some influence. Together, we can overcome any obstacle in our path."

"Sure," Christian agreed. "Maybe some day down the road."

"But the two of you living together like this," Hubert maintained. "Both of you attending the same church. It's unseemly."

"But we have yet to do anything in the way of ..."

"Please! I don't want to hear. I know Pipsi's a good girl. Years ago, she promised me and her mother she planned to wait."

"And I've been mindful about honoring her wishes," Christian said softly.

"Well, if you were truly honoring her wishes," Hubert postulated theoretically, "you might give some thought to embracing the conjugal blessings bestowed by the sanctity of marriage."

"Some day, sure," Christian said guardedly. "But marriage is a very big step."

When Hubert realized he wasn't making the smooth progress he'd anticipated, he switched tactics. Leaning forward, he drew himself closer to Christian and lowered his voice, asking, "Can I take you into my confidence?"

"Of course you can, Sir."

"What I'm about to tell you must not go further than this room. You cannot discuss it with Pipsi, can't mention it to anyone, not another living soul. Is that clear?"

"Perfectly clear, Sir," Christian nodded in agreement. "You have my word."

"That's good!" said Hubert. "Because, well, you see, Pipsi's mother isn't well."

"I had no idea."

"No one knows about this. We've been keeping it under wraps," Hubert lamented. "Some damn blood disorder, her white blood cell count gone crazy."

"I'm so sorry."

"I appreciate that," Hubert said with humility as he reached forward and placed a trusting hand on Christian's knee. "Normally, I would wholeheartedly agree with you about taking something like this a bit slower. But I'm afraid we may not have the luxury of time. What I'm trying to tell you is that Lucille may not be around much longer."

"That's terrible."

"That's right."

"How long is not much longer?" Christian asked, concerned.

"Who knows?" Hubert shrugged. "She's seen several specialists. With all my affluence, none of them has yet come up with a satisfying solution. Every doctor's given me a different time frame."

"So what can I do?"

"Glad you asked," Hubert sat up straight again, pleased with the direction their little chat was now headed. "Remember: Pipsi knows nothing about this. What my wife needs now is to see her daughter wed. Maybe, with God's grace, she might even stick around long enough to welcome our first grandchild into this world."

"I see."

"How crazy is our society?" Hubert asked, pointedly. "If you want to use a car, you gotta first pass a driving test. But to become a parent, all you need is an orgasm."

"… I … uhm … don't … think.…"

"You and Pipsi are both practicing Christians," Hubert interrupted. "That means your kids can be raised as little eager believers, as well. And Pipsi's mother and I can hardly wait to become grandparents."

"Well, that's all fine and …"

"Okay, let's move on!" Hubert clapped his hands and changed the subject. "Name some place you always wanted to go, say like on a vacation, or if you went off on your dream honeymoon? Go ahead. Any place at all. Name it."

Christian considered several destinations and then suggested, "How 'bout Tahiti?"

"Perfect!" Hubert sang out with glee. "How 'bout two weeks at the Bora Bora Lagoon Resort as a honeymoon present?"

"Sounds like it could be … fun," Christian uttered softly.

"And I've got a few other perks in mind," said Hubert, starting to sound more like an infomercial announcer than a prospective father-in-law. "I'm prepared to pay, not only for a huge wedding *plus* your honeymoon in Tahiti, or any other highfalutin' place on God's green Earth you care to go. Once you're home, I'll start you out with a substantial salary and name you Head Supervisor at From The Ground Up. To show you how serious I am about all this, I'll also toss in matrimonial gifts of a size-able bank account for your living expenses. And how 'bout a brand new, top-of-the-line Jaguar XKE convertible, as well? That way, you and Pipsi can have matching Jags. Don't all newlyweds? So how's all that sound?"

"It's a lot to absorb," said Christian. "But I can't even afford to buy Pipsi an engagement ring."

"I'm one step ahead of you," Hubert responded. "In addition to everything else coming your way, I also want to toss into the mix the three-and-a-half carat Cartier diamond ring Pipsi's mother has been waiting to pass down for just such an occasion. What do you think of that?"

Somewhat overwhelmed, Christian told Hubert, "I really don't know what to say."

"Well, you might think about saying *Yes*. You're going to need a more permanent place in town while Pipsi's Malibu cottage gets rebuilt, no? Well, instead of putting the house you and she are now sharing back on the market, why don't I just hand the title over to the two of you? All part of your honeymoon package. At Sterling Enterprises, we aim to please!"

"Well, so far, you're sure doing a fine job."

"Let me tell you something, Son," Hubert postulated. "The first hundred mil-lion's the toughest. After that, it's all gravy."

"No doubt," Christian agreed affably before adding, "And you make it sound so easy."

"It *is* easy. Easy as you hopping on board. That's not so hard to understand, now is it?"

"No, Sir," Christian said, softly. "Not hard at all."

"Lucille told me you and my little girl are heading up to our place in Tahoe later this afternoon."

"Yes, Mr. Sterling, we sure are."

"HUBERT!" Hubert bellowed.

"Hubert," Christian quietly corrected himself.

"Spending a week there, celebrating Pipsi's birthday?"

"Yes, Sir, that's the plan."

"Well, that should give you some time to sort things out. Take a good look at your life, Son. See what a difference a few smart decisions can make. As you may have surmised by now, in the interest of keeping my little girl happy, I'm prepared to offer the moon."

"Not a problem, Hubert. I promise to keep Pipsi happy."

Hubert stood up, walked over to his desk, opened its center drawer, reached in, and pulled out a small dark blue velvet box, which he handed over to Christian. "Here's that ring I mentioned. Perfectly cut, every facet in place. A gem of a gem."

As Christian opened the small Cartier box and looked at the impressive jewel gleaming in his face, Hubert walked up to him and asked, "You know what I had to pay for this kind of craftsmanship? Don't ask. In fact, take it with you," he suggested. "That way, you'll have it on hand should you decide to pop the question." Then, still hovering over the muscle monster, he admonished sternly, "Let me sum it up for you, Son. You get married; I'll see that you prosper."

Christian wasn't sure how he should respond, so he just sat there and shrugged idiotically.

The captain of industry didn't have the slightest qualm over lying about his wife's diminishing condition. The truth was Lucille was never in better health. However, in the world of high finance in which Hubert Sterling dealt daily, little white lies meant little more than Machiavellian means to ends.

Pleased with the presentation of his extravagant offer, Hubert issued himself a resounding seal of approval, walked directly over to his floor-to-ceiling window and looked out at his sweeping panoramic view. Looming far off before him to the north sat the parched Santa Monica Mountains. Over in the distant south, a shining cluster of towering silver spires revealed downtown Los Angeles. Looking west, the tycoon squinted as he stared at a shimmering Pacific Ocean stretching into a limitless horizon.

Hubert's eyes widened as he surveyed the breadth of his domain and then, summoning his life's philosophy, he extended his hands out wide and, sealing Christian's fate, asked rhetorically, "Now, then ... who says money can't buy happiness?"

*   *   *   *

The North Shore of Lake Tahoe was the most captivating place Christian had ever seen. Encircled by lush forests of firs and snow-capped mountains, the handsomely furnished, Sterling family three-bedroom "bungalow" sat at water's edge, a stone's throw from the California-Nevada border. Its wraparound deck overlooking the lake boasted a breath-taking view. Christian and Pipsi so enjoyed their time together while celebrating her birthday week, the days just slipped away.

For two people interacting with no one else around, they got along exceptionally well. As the relaxing week flew by, neither of them ever once lost patience or felt confined or found cause to offer so much as a critical comment.

Every night, after a candlelit dinner at one of the local restaurants, topped off with yet another bottle of great red wine, they returned to Pipsi's family retreat. As a roaring blaze from the fireplace pulled the evening's chill from the air, they snuggled together on the couch.

Pipsi cherished the time she spent alone with Christian, and hardly minded that the one thing missing from their romance was any measurable level of eroticism that ever moved beyond hugging and kissing. Somewhere deep within the recesses of her mind, she sensed something was a bit askew, even somewhat atypical about Christian's seemingly repressed sexual expression. Other devoted, born-again believers she dated in the past were for the most part all perfect gentlemen. Still, there were times when, like most single women out there in the dating pool, she had to stick up for her virtue and fend off the occasional aggressive, unwelcome sexual advance.

By sharp contrast, Christian was the first man she ever met who seemed to possess no sexual agenda whatsoever, no pro-active plan to get past first base, to win her over through seduction. Even sleeping together in the same bed, the muscle monster never once offered anything more than a heartfelt hug or an affectionate kiss on her lips, just before saying good night and switching off the lights.

Oddly enough, the admirable self-control that was Christian's passive and stand-offish sexual unavailability only made her lust after him that much more. She felt so joyful just being with him, she simply chose not to ponder any demons of sexuality with which he may have been wrestling.

One late night in Tahoe, as they sat nestled together on the couch before the fireplace, shoulder to shoulder, taking little sips from the cognac in their shared brandy snifter, they occasionally interrupted their sharing of confidences with gentle kisses.

She privately wished he would be more aggressive, that he might take greater advantage of their romantic setting. At the same time, she didn't want to push him past whatever kept him comfortable. She needed to respect his wishes, his timetable. She knew his Christian virtue was commendable, and while she was grateful for his evident respect for their declared shared commitment to chastity, it also left her feeling more than a little frustrated.

Still later that evening, by the time the blazing logs in the fireplace were reduced to embers, Christian sensed her longing and, while wishing he felt the same way, also wanted to honor the promise he made to her father to make her happy. So he took her in his big arms, held her tightly, insinuated his tongue into her mouth, and initiated a soft French kiss.

Momentarily lost in the ethereal excitement of their first genuine, semi-passionate moment, Pipsi took hold of Christian's hand, brought it up to the front of her sweater, and placed it over her small yet well-formed left breast. When he squeezed it softly, he was amazed at how pleasantly resilient it felt to his touch. At the same time, while their lips remained locked and their tongues intertwined, she casually stroked the outline of his powerful chest. Brazenly, she then allowed her hand to trespass slowly down his torso until the tips of her fingers casually brushed up against the outline of his fly. When she discerned the evident stiffness lying in wait within his pants, she gently stroked the thick bulge. Nice to know that even after all the alcohol they'd consumed, he was still aroused.

When their lips parted, he smiled because she looked so happy; and she smiled, relieved because the rigidity of his member was solid proof at last of his interest, if not his action.

A short while later, as they crawled into bed and Christian drifted quickly off to sleep, Pipsi reminded herself that, from her own limited experience, she already knew sex was highly overrated. With that in mind, she turned over on her side so they could sleep tush to tush, and decided she was in no rush. She would remain patient and attentive while awaiting however long it might take before her boyfriend was finally ready to initiate any further sexual advances between them.

* * * *

They celebrated Pipsi's twenty-first birthday on Sunday, the day before they were set to head home to Los Angeles. By late afternoon, the birthday girl chilled a bottle of vintage champagne alongside several pounds of jumbo shrimp. Christian told her he wanted to take advantage of the glorious spring weather, and went hiking by himself through the woods.

After aggressively climbing to the top of a nearby hill, he leaned against a smooth boulder, caught his breath, and looked across the dazzling panoramic vista stretched out before him, as far as the eye could see. Down below, several luxury yachts anchored in a nearby marina were getting scrubbed down, while way out on the water, half a dozen polished sailboats glided smoothly over the glistening lake. Christian took in the striking vista, and then sat down atop a rock to take stock of his life, weighing the pros and cons of Hubert's tantalizing offer.

He knew darn well that when it came to finding a mate, he was never likely to get it all in one package — not a good body *and* a pretty face *and* solid social connections *and* an impressive financial portfolio *and* a pleasing personality. So, in exchange for the comfort of Pipsi's surfeit of security, as well as the great gift that was evidently her unconditional love, could he not learn to overlook the little woman's flaws, most specifically her abundance of exuberance, her annoying giggles, and alas, her lackluster looks? *"Judge not, lest ye be judged,"* he quoted to himself in silent reprimand.

Christian picked up a nearby pebble, tossed his frustration down into the lake, and then lay flat back atop the rock, staring up at the sky to contemplate the upside. He certainly got along well with little Miss Pips. And there was something truly appealing about her sweet if sometimes too kinetic spirit. She was always pleasant, always easy to be around. Besides, he reasoned, over the centuries, hadn't most men married for money? Isn't that what dowries were all about? Christian knew his motivation was stronger than that. He'd be marrying in large part for money, true. But for him, the best wedding present of all might just be the cloak of decency that would accompany all the other trappings.

Could he move past the fact that although there were elements about her he loved, he just wasn't *in* love with her? Christian trusted and believed he could easily learn to love Pipsi more profoundly and reminded himself, *With faith, all things are possible.*

While on the subject of faith, another significant element he liked about their friendship was that Pipsi was also a believer. Together, they shared a collective bonding in their commitment to Christ. Surely, that was a huge plus.

Christian counted his blessings. He had never known such comfortable contentment, and had never felt more respected. He thanked God for his bounty, and begged the Holy Spirit to continue guiding him in his walk. He told himself Hubert was wrong. Only a fool would believe money bought happiness. Just below that, however, money could at least deliver no end of comfort. And comfort, God knows, was surely a close second.

Thinking about all he'd been through since arriving in Southern California, the muscle monster realized how downright fortunate he was to have found, especially after that sordid debacle with Robin, such a wholesome companion, so fine a potential life partner as Pipsi.

And so what if his *romance* with Pipsi lacked passion? His own parents never expressed a sense of sensual fulfillment, and from what he'd seen among even the most intensely involved couples, their depth of passion over time seemed destined to dissipate and cool off.

As in the past, he still secretly yearned now and again for the physical contact of another muscular man's body. His fascination with muscle, he knew, was never more than a temporary temptation, a distraction he long ago trained himself to hold at bay. He also felt, even given his rather limited exposure, that a successful relationship with another bodybuilder was little more than a juvenile fantasy all but impossible to fulfill.

After further furious rumination, and after another hour or so spent in quiet prayer, Christian decided it would be a mistake not to acknowledge that God had sent Samson his Delilah. So what the heck, he figured, he may as well snatch the gold ring and settle for the valued qualities of security and respectability, social standing and solid commitment. He was bound to be blessed from above by a God who could only smile upon so wholesome a union. He also knew he would be showered down here on earth with an unconditional love from a good woman. How could he not be happy with all that?

Christian removed from his pants pocket the small velvet jewel box Hubert had given him. He popped it open, lifted Lucille's sparkling diamond ring into the air, and was impressed by how its flawless facets reflected the late afternoon sunlight. His mind made up, he resolved to return to the Sterling cabin on the sparkling lake and, right after dinner, while lowering their noses into their shared snifter of Cognac before the blazing fireplace, he would heed Hubert's advice, get down on one knee, and with God's blessing, ask Pipsi to marry him.

A gust of wind down on the lake fueled the sailboats with a burst of speed. The late afternoon sun painted the entire vista in a golden blush of springtime rebirth. Christian raised his face to the heavens and silently acknowledged with deep sincerity, *Thank you, Dear Lord. I sure don't know what I ever did to deserve all this, but I can promise, at our wedding, you'll be the guest of honor.*

*   *   *   *

HOLY MATRIMONY!

As an unseasonable torrential downpour drenched the expansive back lawn of Hubert and Lucille Sterling's palatial Holmby Hills property, Pipsi and Christian stood holding hands before three hundred twenty-two invited guests or three hundred twenty-three, if you include God. Family and friends sat clustered together in flowered rows of white folding chairs, beneath the shelter of an enormous transparent, vinyl tent. They watched in quiet reflection as the young bride and groom committed themselves to the holy sacrament of marriage.

Hours earlier, when Pipsi first awoke on the day of her wedding, she parted her drapes, saw the threatening skies of a rapidly gathering storm, and immediately turned to the Lord. She begged Him to smile on her forthcoming union by scattering the dark, thickening clouds. His approval of their blessed union would be most evident if He just took a short break from His ubiquitous schedule to favor them with some beautiful Los Angeles weather sometime before her wedding's end.

On the other side of the bed, Christian awoke on the day of his wedding, and also looked outside at the approaching menacing clouds. *So much for sunny Southern California,* he thought.

With every passing hour, the skies grew ever darker. By mid-afternoon, as the three hundred twenty-two or twenty-three wedding guests of Hubert and Lucille Sterling drove up the driveway of their regal mansion, their dark day was brightened by a cornucopia of roses, orchids, tulips and calla lilies, all of them white, all exquisitely arranged in extravagant over-abundance.

Hubert Sterling had no trouble spending the three quarters of a million dollars which covered the wedding expenses, and never once complained about a single opulent or ostentatious over-charge. He lodged not so much as a quibble over the extravagance regarding the pounds of beluga caviar brought in from the Caspian Sea. He didn't grumble about the exorbitant rental of the see-through, vinyl tent erected days before on the grand lawn behind his house; or even about the sturdy dance floor constructed over the Olympic-sized swimming pool. Without once wincing, he signed checks for Pipsi's thirty-five-thousand dollar Vera Wang bridal gown, as well as the celebrated fourteen-piece dance band that would keep guests bopping up and down for hours.

Despite his boundless budget, the one thing the real estate baron couldn't purchase at any price was good weather. By mid-afternoon, as a chamber string quarter solemnly plucked out their selection of Mozart's greatest hits, and as Hubert escorted the blushing bride, his own petite, precious princess, down the white, flower-petal-laden aisle, that was the moment the heavens opened up with a torrential downpour.

As Pipsi and Hubert inched their way down the floral-draped aisle, step after tiny step, toward the ersatz altar, it was a good thing the bride was holding on to her father's arm for support, because she was trembling from a combination of fear, anticipation, excitement, and from the unfamiliar spotlight of so many eyes suddenly riveted to her. When she heard the forceful pelting of the heavy rainfall bouncing off the transparent roof high overhead, she looked up at the thundering deluge, and wondered for the briefest of moments if God wasn't frowning on her union with Christian.

She immediately dismissed her silly superstitious concerns the moment she looked ahead and saw her fiancé standing tall and brawny, smiling nervously at her from his place way down at the flower-filled, makeshift altar. Even though Christian hadn't trained much since his contest, months earlier, and even though much of his muscularity had gone smooth, even a bit soft since he went off cycle, he still looked so big and rugged, so darn huggable-loveable, she immediately quickened her pace and headed alongside her father down the aisle. Full steam ahead, she stopped trembling and proceeded directly to the fulfillment of her lifelong matrimonial fantasy.

*   *   *   *

At the lavish reception immediately following the nuptials, wedding guests refused to let the unseasonably foul weather dampen their hearty party spirits. Joyously, they consumed untold amounts of lobster from Maine, oysters from Chesapeake Bay, stone crabs from Florida, and *pate' de fois gras* airlifted the day before from Strasbourg. Eagerly, they emptied myriad magnums of Moet and Mumms.

Among the many jubilant guests in attendance at the lavish wedding were Christian's parents, Dr. Falconer and Ruth Hortense. They had flown out to Los Angeles to have a trial rapprochement with their wayward son, and of course to meet their future daughter-in-law.

It had been Pipsi's idea. She felt it was important that Christian re-connect with his parents and try to make amends with his father. She insisted he invite his parents to their wedding. She prayed such a blessed reunion might put to rest any lingering resentment and end his father's estrangement.

When Christian and Pipsi drove to the airport to pick up Ruth Hortense and Dr. Falconer a few days before their nuptials, his father claimed he was delighted to meet Pipsi, even as he remained cordial yet aloof, greeting his son with a firm handshake.

By pointed contrast, Ruth Hortense was overcome with emotion as she threw her arms around Christian exuberantly, and then dissolved into a puddle of tears.

Merry celebrants at the reception soon forgot about the storm raging without as, within, they grew progressively more stuffed, ever more drunk, and lost more of their inhibitions as they boogied away the late afternoon on the dance floor.

Weeks earlier, while finalizing honeymoon details, Pipsi decided one sure way to avoid any wedding night jitters would be to simply not have any self-imposed "wedding night." Instead, she arranged for them to head directly from their reception, straight to the airport, where they'd hop on their late flight to Tahiti.

After keeping her cherished chastity at bay until they wed, she purposely postponed their connubial bliss, extending their abstinence by waiting at least one more night until they were ensconced in paradise. After all their patience, they would then feel relaxed enough to finally initiate any lovemaking. She relished the fantasy of the two of them being joined together as one, right there in their own Garden of Eden.

Hour after hour, the raindrops pelting the plastic sheeting of the transparent party tent grew ever louder as the raging storm intensified. The volume on the dance band's speakers was raised decibels higher and then higher still to compete against the rainfall's imposing clamor.

Toward early evening, all the celebrating began winding down. Guests lined up outdoors, along both sides of the circular driveway, preparing to send Pipsi and Christian off on their honeymoon. And then, just like that, it abruptly stopped raining.

Pipsi stepped out of her lavish, beaded wedding gown and changed into a chic skirt and blouse more appropriate for a full night's air travel. Christian pulled off his formal matrimonial attire and donned dark slacks, a pale blue Oxford shirt, and a Polo blazer. The bride and groom then headed together out of the house and into their brave new world.

Family and friends flung rose petals and tossed confetti and blew soap bubbles at Christian and Pipsi, showering them in an enchantingly colorful blizzard of fluff, as the newlyweds hurried arm in arm toward an awaiting limousine.

Standing beneath the arched entrance to their home, hosts Hubert and Lucille Sterling shared a bittersweet moment as the reality of their sudden empty nest hit home. Feeling joyful and sad at the same time, they snapped on a pair of happy faces and waved good-bye to their little girl, his little princess.

Down at the limo, Dr. Falconer and Ruth Hortense opened the passenger door for the newlyweds. Pipsi ducked her head as Christian assisted his bride into the limo. Dr. Falconer then stepped forward and placed a stoic hand on each of Christian's shoulders. Swallowing his pride, he softly told him, "I'm so proud of your positive turnaround, Son, and want you to know I never lost faith. Always knew my boy would one day wind up on his feet, a fine gentleman. Have a wonderful honeymoon!"

Christian was so moved by his father's unexpected affirmation, he threw wide his big arms and embraced him. Finally ready to re-knot their family ties, Dr. Falconer conveniently relegated their schism to the back of his mind, gave in to his well-guarded instincts, and actually returned the hug, warmly embracing his long-lost son as if he were … a long-lost son.

Wedding guests surrounding the limo oooh-ed and ahhh-ed their collective approval of so loving and genuine an outpouring of father-son warmth. Caught up in the emotion of the moment, Ruth Hortense expressed her extreme euphoria by breaking down and sobbing effusively.

Christian broke away from his father's embrace, kissed his whimpering, overjoyed mother and then, as he ducked into the limo and nuzzled next to his bride, a most unusual phenomenon occurred.

Off in the far distance, just above the horizon, enough of the prevailing cloud cover had by then parted to reveal a portion of the lower sky spewing forth the last of a dazzling summer's sunset. At the same time, high up in the atmosphere, a preter-natural fusion of shadow and brightness, clouds and descending sunlight came together to form the full color spectrum of a magnificent rainbow. It arched its way overhead into a flawless semi-circle, spreading from one end of the horizon to the next, even as its colorful arc painted a path clear across the heavens. It was the first full rainbow Ruth Hortense witnessed since that day outside church almost twenty-two years earlier, when she was first given the prophesy about Christian.

Pipsi and Christian gazed out the limo's window in awe at the inspirational vision. Under normal circumstances, a rainbow in Southern California was a rare enough occurrence. But for it to appear so magically, so out of nowhere, just at that moment, on their very wedding day, along with the clearing of the clouds, made Pipsi realize her prayers had been answered.

As the limo drove off in the direction of the sunset, headed toward the airport and their late departure, the bride placed a loving hand flush against her bridegroom's cheek, and whispered sweetly into his ear, "You see, Darling. God's given us His stamp of approval, after all. We are truly blessed."

Truly blessed, indeed.

*   *   *   *

Christian and Pipsi killed time in Air France's comfortable First Class Lounge for several hours. By the time the newlyweds finally boarded the plane for their flight to Tahiti, they were both pretty much wiped out. It wasn't merely the stress leading up to their big day, but also their hangovers from all the champagne they imbibed at their celebration. They each looked forward to catching some much-needed sleep. Even in the plush spaciousness of their reclining leather seats, however, the nine-hour flight from Los Angeles to Papeete was anything but restful.

Mother Nature, perhaps still in her playful mood, gifted their 747 with stop-and-go pockets of severe turbulence. As a result, neither Pipsi nor Christian managed to get any discernible rest. By the time they finally stepped off the plane in their Garden of Eden at five the following morning, they were not simply fatigued, but jet-lagged as well.

Their connecting flight, the Air Tahiti-Nui puddle-hopper to the neighboring isle, was delayed several hours, and so Christian and Pipsi didn't check into their luxurious, thatched-roof, private *bure*, built over the translucent, turquoise waters of the Bora Bora Lagoon Resort, until early afternoon. By then, Mr. and Mrs. Christian Falconer were each so thoroughly spent, they didn't even bother to unpack as they quickly crawled into bed.

Lying side by side, Pipsi softly combed her fingers through her new husband's thick hair and kissed him amiably on his lips. "I can't believe I'm finally here with you. And it's important you know that even after all this time, I'm in no hurry. Honest. All that matters to me is that we love each other."

Christian returned Pipsi's sweet kiss on the lips and quietly asked, "God only knows what I ever did to deserve you."

Pipsi laid her head upon her groom's immense chest. "Let's try to get some rest," she said, closing her eyes. "We have all the time in the world. Heck, Darling, we have the rest of our lives."

*   *   *   *

On the third night of their lavish honeymoon, liberated by the effects of several rum drinks, Christian finally made love to his bride. After waiting so long, after the build-up and all the hoopla, after so much anxiety and trepidation, in the end, it turned out to be no big deal.

After dinner, as they lay in bed together in their candlelit hut, Pipsi had only to place an affectionate hand on his manhood before he responded by springing to life. Once aroused, he kissed his wife gingerly and then moved his hands up and down, fondling her slight, tight body. He made a point of clearing his mind of any uninvited erotic images doing their best to confuse his uneasy libido, and focused, instead, on how agreeable was the supple warmth of her pleasant lips, how satisfying was the sheer resiliency of her sweet little B-cup breasts.

His stiffness made him feel indomitable. He was, after all, young and robust, with a surfeit of testosterone, and had no trouble remaining stiff as, slowly, he entered his wife. He then maintained his rigidity throughout the exhilaration of his score of deep thrusts. He summoned none of the masturbatory images of his muscle superheroes, and focused, instead, only on the satisfying sensation of his huge dick finding so much unexpected sensation from its vaginal massage. The entire she-bang ended with his strong and potent orgasm.

Although neither of them needed to express it as they drifted into their collective post-coital slumbers, Pipsi and Christian each felt as though they'd finally gotten over a major hurdle. Now they could both relax and simply enjoy the rest of their honeymoon, swimming, sunning, sightseeing, minus the pressure of all that performance anxiety. Christian had successfully made love to a woman and, in so doing, proved to his bride, to the world, to God and, most notably, to himself, that he was, as he always trusted, soundly heterosexual.

Pipsi was never more euphoric, Christian never more relieved.

*   *   *   *

The newlyweds spent two glorious weeks honeymooning in Tahiti before they returned to Los Angeles and set up house. Christian was enthralled with the pot of gold he'd found waiting at the end of his and Pipsi's connubial rainbow. And by the time he and his bride ironed out the few inconsequential kinks that accompanied the period of adjustment that predictably followed their heavenly honeymoon, their living arrangement suited him just fine.

They each made a point of catering to the other's quirky pet peeves. She tried hard as she could to stop interrupting him when he spoke, while he made a point to no longer drive quite so fast when she was in the car with him. She did her best not to giggle as an automatic response to most anything he said, while he worked at being less easily distracted whenever she delved into minutiae over the renovation of their Malibu country cottage.

Christian was at peace having the quiet comfort that came from knowing there was someone in his life who truly cherished and adored him. He especially appreciated the lengths to which Pipsi went toward keeping her big man happy.

And keep her big man happy, she certainly did. The bride's chef continued cooking for them, stoking Christian's extra-large frame as if he was still bulking up for a contest. However, since he was no longer on steroids, his metabolism wasn't so easily assimilating his intake of fat. Along with the huge portions of food placed before him each evening, he and Pipsi also decanted another expensive bottle of red wine. And no matter how full he got, Christian always managed to find room for at least one of the cook's dependably special desserts. Dark chocolate fudge layer cake, anyone?

Soon enough, Christian's water weight evaporated, his inflated muscles lost much of their chemically-induced mass and, like a tire troubled with a slow but steady leak, his champion body went flat and smooth, then soft and burly, then big and beefy, and next actually began slouching toward schlubby/chubby. How far the mighty had fallen.

Living large came effortlessly to Christian, and he grew progressively less concerned with the importance of his staying in training, ever lazier about getting over to the gym. He soon lost patience with the heavy, often gridlocked traffic he encountered on the Santa Monica Freeway when he drove from Hancock Park out to Gold's in Venice. Rather than hitting the gym five or six times a week as in his pre-contest mode, he grew lethargic and found it a major accomplishment just to get over there once or twice a week. When the troublesome bulges in his lower spinal region again started causing him discomfort, there were entire weeks when he didn't work out at all.

As for his so-called career in landscape architecture, Christian's high-paying position at From The Ground Up required little work and less thought. The sign on his office door may have read Supervisor, but the only supervising in which he ever engaged was the overseeing of his expense account. When he spoke to his father-in-law about his lack of weighty responsibilities, Hubert Sterling assured him that all he was expected to do was keep an eye on the comings and goings of the staff, and to report back to him at Sterling Enterprises any activities, especially any expenditure by his employees, that might seem excessive or suspicious.

And as for the newlywed's intermittent sex life during the first year of their union, Christian never had difficulty servicing his bride the few times they made love. By never varying from their missionary position, Christian maintained his firmness and kept Pipsi mollified, satisfied, fulfilled.

The morning after they went out for an expensive dinner with her parents to celebrate their first anniversary, Christian awoke early, got out of bed and showered. While drying off, he glanced over at the mirror. When he barely recognized the overweight, out-of-shape, twenty-four-year-old young man frowning back at him, the once shredded fellow who not so long ago was a competitive contest winner realized he'd been off-season far too long.

He flexed tentatively, timidly, for the mirror and resolved to reverse the damage, get back into training, back into shape. He also acknowledged how he'd gotten far too spoiled to have any patience with gaining back all that muscle slowly, the natural way. His back to the wall, he asked around at the gym, was given a few contacts, and soon scored another cycle of steroids.

Christian returned to his training with vigor, not simply for his own self worth, but also because he suspected that, although Pipsi said she didn't mind how he looked, claiming she would love him no matter how far from contest shape he strayed, he still preferred it when she swooned over him, and not when she was playing big sister to his Pillsbury dough boy.

After twenty-four months of again training hard, being more careful about his diet, injecting the steroids without a break from one cycle to the next, he lost his excess fat and slowly built himself back up until he was nearly at the peak of his form; not quite the contest-ready condition of his teen years, perhaps, but at least most of his prominent gut was gone. Big and defined, he was once again a major muscle hunk.

Toward the end of every one of his muscle-enhancing cycles, Pipsi reminded him of his promise to get off the juice. And each time Christian segued into another cycle, he promised his wife it was the last time he'd be turning to the 'roids. And each time when he changed his mind and started shooting up again, Pipsi was disappointed, but let it pass.

Soon enough, Christian got fed up with the long drive out to Venice for his workouts. Their Malibu property was almost all rebuilt, and he and Pipsi would soon be going out there on weekends. So for the time being, he transferred his membership over to the nearby Gold's in Hollywood.

The muscle monster had to pump his way through several workouts before he adjusted to his new gym's prevailing openly gay atmosphere. The bulk of their membership seemed so much more homosexual than anything to which he'd been previously exposed. The entire feeling of the health club, in fact, was so much gayer than the more uptight and — at least on the surface — hetero sensibility he encountered when pumping iron over in Venice. Guys in the Hollywood gym were not only friendlier, but also far more affectionate with one another. Members thought nothing of embracing another muscle buddy in greeting, sometimes even exchanging a short, affectionate kiss, smack on the lips of all places.

Men hugging and kissing one another so freely, so openly in public, was alien to Christian, and the sight of it made him both nervous and somewhat envious. The facility, to its credit, had the best equipment, plus the most motivating, driving energy of any of the other workout spaces in the area. Christian soon relaxed and simply took in stride all that high profile, same-sex affection, all those flirtatious cruises telegraphed his way, the constant homoerotic innuendoes so often floating around the locker area. He was training in Hollyweird, so what the hell, he figured, boys will be boys.

In truth, there was also an unexamined, inconspicuous part of him that actually felt titillated about being in the midst of so many well-built men expressing themselves so openly, whether on the gym floor or in the locker areas. He also experienced a slight, perverse level of satisfaction, a twinge of affirmation, whenever he found a hot guy checking him out.

The wedding ring on his finger not only signaled his lack of availability, it also made him that much more appealing to other gym members, who could only lust after him from across the gym floor. Still, when he left for the gym one perfectly sunny afternoon in early spring, right after shooting himself up with his latest cocktail of Deca, Cypionate, and Trenbolone, he had no way of knowing how dramatically and drastically his life was about to change.

*   *   *   *

DIVINE INTERVENTION

As Chase Hyde strode into Gold's, he was psychologically pumping himself up to physically pump himself up. After stretching and then walking uphill for twenty minutes on the treadmill, and then knocking out a hundred crunches on the slant board, he trotted downstairs to the main floor for a chest and triceps workout. The buff thirty-eight-year-old initiated that day's weightlifting routine at the pec deck, planning to pyramid up with ever-heavier weights over the course of several sets.

By a random stroke of life-altering serendipity, Christian Falconer also walked into the gym that early afternoon. He was also there to pound out his own extra heavy chest workout. After changing into his workout gear in the upstairs men's locker area, Christian headed downstairs and lumbered his hulking frame over to the pec deck. He watched as one of the gym members meticulously pumped out a warm-up set, and was impressed with the guy's imposing physicality.

"Hey, Buddy," the muscle monster grumbled in a no-nonsense, deep register that sounded more like he was gargling marbles than articulating in English. "How many more sets you got?"

Chase released a lengthy exhale, looked up at Christian, and held up three fingers.

"Okay if I work in with you?" Christian asked bluntly.

"Be my guest," Chase answered, good-naturedly, as he stood up and relinquished the equipment.

They switched places and Chase watched as Christian impatiently adjusted the weight. The big man removed the long, metal pin on the weight stack and shoved it into one of the lower apertures, rendering the machine an eye-popping eighty pounds heavier. The muscle monster then plopped himself atop the padded seat, inhaled deeply and seemed to stop breathing as he fought to push out ten remarkably sloppy reps.

For Chase, it was so uncomfortable to witness, he felt obliged to say *something*. "I'm exhausted, and all I did was watch," he acknowledged, as they again traded places and Chase lowered the weight back into a more normal range, and then effortlessly stepped into his alter ego persona as the Coach. "If I can make a small suggestion, Big Guy," he put it out there, as pleasantly as possible. "You're in great shape and clearly can handle a lot of weight. So it's not like you're doing anything wrong, per se. Still, I bet you'd get a lot more bang for your muscle buck if you dropped down to a lighter weight and did fewer reps with better form."

Having offered his insight, Chase took his own deep breath, and then carefully launched into his next set, slowly pushing the pair of metal handles forward in an arc while concentrating on feeling the force of the weights hitting his pecs.

Christian was one of the bigger muscle monsters in the gym, one among a smattering of heterosexuals who worked out there. So he certainly wasn't used to getting slapped down with any weighted criticism faulting his training style, even if it had been offered in the interest of constructive input. Taken aback by Chase's presumptuousness, the big guy quickly put a clamp on his 'roid rage and, instead of lashing out, just stood there impatiently, his huge arms at his sides, his fists clenched, more or less fuming. He said nothing as he carefully studied Chase up and down while the Coach prudently prosecuted his every rep with faultless form.

After releasing the handles, and before they again traded places, Chase lifted his hands into the air, palms up, and motioned with a gesture that seemed to ask, *There! Was that so hard to do correctly?*

Agitated, Christian again plopped down on the pad, wrapped his hands menacingly around both sides of the steel machine and, unable to camouflage his bellicose tone, dared Chase to make this an issue, asking, "You think my form sucks, is that it?"

"That's it," Chase brazenly told him. "But don't get me wrong. You've got a trophy body, even off-season. That's the good news. But the bad news is you also have a tendency to sacrifice your form to protect what is probably a bum lower back, prone to injury. Struggling is fine. Hey, life's a struggle. But never at the expense of good form. That's why I say your best bet is lower the weight, increase your reps, slow it to a crawl, nail your lower back against the pad, tense your core, don't forget to breathe, and oh, yes, stay in contraction the whole time. Your back hurts less, your muscles grow bigger, everybody wins. How hard could that be? Any questions?"

Christian absorbed all that, and answered the challenge. "Well, the good news is that what you say about improving my form may be sound advice. But the bad news is I've been lifting most of my life and never paid much attention to either better form or sound advice. And I especially don't appreciate hearing opinions from people I don't know."

Chase was not intimidated. He dismissed Christian's blustery bravado with a genial smile and thrust out his hand. "In that case, I'll introduce myself before you tear off my face. I'm Chase Hyde."

If this older guy wasn't so appealing, an easily-riled Christian might have quickly exploded and simply decked Chase right there at the pec deck, or at least told him to go mind his own fucking business. But the smart ass was also evidently so successful at the construction of his own amazing musculature, Christian figured maybe Chase knew what he was talking about — that there just might be something to his unsolicited advice.

On his next set, the muscle monster actually made an effort to better control the handles on the machine. He held his breath and rhythmically pressed the heavy weight forward and then back, forward and back again, pumping out his reps at a much slower, more evenly controlled tempo. He thrust his lower back flush up against the pad, and kept his midsection tightened.

"Now you've got it!" Chase cheered Christian through his first few reps and then audaciously placed his unsolicited hands at the back of Christian's triceps and carefully assisted, spontaneously spotting the muscle monster as he strained to pump out his last few reps.

"Hate to admit it," Christian released the weight and muttered reluctantly, "that felt a lot better."

"Figured it might," Chase told him with confidence as, trading places once again, he sat back down at the machine. After lowering the weight on the stack back down into his range, he again synchronized the precision of his heavy breathing with his flawless form, as ever so slowly, he pounded out his next set.

This time, it was Christian who stepped forward to spot as Chase struggled through his last few reps. "Thanks, buddy!" said Chase, after going to muscle failure on his last rep. "Nothing like a good spot."

"You read my mind!" Christian said good-naturedly as they again switched places.

Before Christian started slamming out his next set, Chase again felt obliged to hand out still another pointer. "And one last thing, Cowboy," he said bravely. "If you'll stop holding your breath during the exercise, and start breathing out heavily while you're pushing, and inhaling deeply as you come back, you'll bring so much oxygen into your lungs, so much blood into your pecs, you'll float out of here like the Goodyear blimp."

Once again, Christian didn't know quite how to respond, couldn't decide whether to bristle or to listen. He never liked instructions, but also figured maybe, just maybe, Chase once again knew what he was talking about.

The muscle monster said nothing as he executed his next set. This time, he exerted not just slower movements, but also sucked in deep breaths followed by heavy exhales, just as Chase suggested.

It took Christian six exuberant reps before his pecs popped up and pooped out as he went to muscle failure. Chase assisted with a perfect spot as Christian struggled to complete the exercise. As the big man then fought to catch his breath, he relinquished the machine back over to Chase and felt obliged to confess, "What a difference. That felt great. Thanks."

"Glad to help," Chase said calmly, before sitting back down again on the pad. "I've been at this a while, so by now I can spot a guy's flaws from across the room. I've got a whole trunk full of short cuts. Little ins-and-outs can make a major difference in getting the most from any workout."

For his final set, Chase again dropped the weight back down to his more sensible level, and Christian again spotted him. Instinctively, the Coach repeated his fine form along with his systematic deep breathing. "How come I haven't seen you in here before?" Chase asked the muscle monster after he finished his set.

"Just joined a few weeks ago," said Christian, as he sat down and again wrapped his huge hands around the handles of the machine. "I was training at the Gold's over in Venice. But my wife and I moved here a while ago, to this part of town, into Hancock Park, so this gym's much closer, more convenient."

After Christian properly pumped out his final set, he stood up and shook Chase's hand. "That was helpful, Coach!" he conceded, unintentionally calling Chase by his nickname. "Got any more insights?"

Enjoying the affirmation, Chase smiled modestly and invited the muscle monster to join him for the rest of his chest workout. Christian jumped at the chance, and as the two of them shuffled over to the other side of the gym, he signaled his hearty enthusiasm by pounding his pecs like a mighty gorilla.

At the incline bench, Chase demonstrated for the big fellow a whole new way to exercise his upper pecs: lowering the barbell down slowly, then holding it in place, actually bringing it to a full rest atop his chest for a beat before thrusting it back up with an explosive, fully controlled burst of energy.

"What a great pump!" Christian roared, as soon as he finished banging out his fourth set. "My hard-to-hit upper region is thrashed."

The sturdy bodybuilders finished their chest routine on a cross-cable exercise, and then Chase invited Christian to stick with him for the rest of his workout. Like a grateful puppy, Christian followed Chase from the cables over to a flat bench, where they used a heavy E-Z curl bar to bang out escalating sets of skull-crusher extensions for their triceps. After their final set, Chase shook Christian's hand. "Good job, Buddy," he complimented the muscle monster.

Christian spun in place, whipped off his tank top and appraised himself in the wall-length mirror directly behind the machine. With so much fresh blood rapidly engorging his pectorals from the pump, he was gratified to see the thick vein that ran across the length of his left pectoralis growing ever more prominent, practically popping out from beneath his skin. Bouncing his massive pecs for his reflection, he smiled with great satisfaction and exclaimed, "Man, you really know your stuff."

"That's why they call me the Coach," said Chase.

"Really enjoyed working out with you," Christian told him frankly, before next surprising both himself and Chase when he next added, "You're the first person I've been able to talk to in here since I joined this gym. Everyone acts so afraid — like if they look at me too long, I'll give them a black eye."

"Believe me, I know just how they feel."

Christian smiled and genially brushed his fist across the side of Chase's left shoulder. "You're a real smart ass. So how 'bout if you and I head out for a cup of coffee or something?"

The notion sure sounded fine to Chase. "Make that a high-protein recovery drink, Buster, and you're on," he answered, even as he returned the gesture of male bonding by landing his own hard-fisted thump smack against the solid mass of Christian's freshly pumped pecs.

*   *   *   *

The two big musclemen sat huddled over a tiny table in a corner of the Hearty Healthy Cafe on nearby Melrose Avenue, fortifying themselves with recovery drinks. While slowly sipping their banana-laced, milky mush, they talked animatedly about bodybuilding, clearly their shared passion.

Since none of Christian and Pipsi's friends from the church lifted weights or even belonged to a gym, the muscle monster found it refreshing to finally connect with someone clearly as dedicated, well-versed and as seemingly heterosexual as himself. Christian and his newfound buddy judiciously dissected such weighty topics as dropsets, forced reps, interval training, Creatine-loading, carbo-depletion, cycles of steroids, and training for a contest. Christian told Chase how, as a teenager growing up in Connecticut, he enjoyed some measure of success as a competitive bodybuilder.

Chase was impressed. "Doesn't that take a lot of work, training for a contest?"

"Only to the exclusion of everything else," Christian acknowledged.

"Well, you worked hard and it paid off."

"Thanks," Christian appreciated Chase's affirmation and added, "But you know, there's a lot more to it than just the building and sculpting of the body. Just like anything else that's made to look easy, flexing takes lots of practice before you get good at it."

"Really?" Chase took a slug of his protein drink. "It always comes so easy to me. I figure what's the big deal about posing on stage?"

"Believe you me," Christian turned a bit defensive. "There's a world of difference between flexing for fun in front of your mirror at home after a shower, and successfully hitting all the major poses in a choreographed routine — all before a cheering audience under blinding lights, while sporting the world's smallest bathing suit."

"Sounds scary," Chase agreed. "That's why I'd rather flex for a private, appreciative audience of *one*. I mean, besides myself."

As they downed the last of their recovery drinks, Christian suddenly felt there were a few other heavyweight issues he wanted to get off his heavyweight chest, so he asked his new muscle buddy, "Hey, would you mind hanging out some more? How 'bout if I go grab us a couple of coffees?

"It's late," said Chase. "I should get going."

"But I really enjoy talking to you!" Christian conceded and then stood up, lumbered back over to the counter, and bought them each an oversized coffee. Chase realized he wasn't going anywhere for a while, so he graciously accepted the cardboard container and started sipping.

It didn't take long for the stimulation of the buzz to kick in, because Christian spent most of the next hour opening up to Chase, unraveling aspects of his private life. It was as if he'd been waiting to meet just the right understanding person who might commiserate with his situation.

With surprising candor, Christian's caffeine-induced reverie next found him sharing how, even though he dearly loved his wife, with whom he'd been eternally joined for over three years, he also missed bonding with men who shared his bodybuilding sensibility. Christian claimed he enjoyed hanging out with other muscular men, solely as the strongest of companions. The muscle monster then fondly recalled how empowering, even intoxicating, was the presence of male camaraderie permeating the sweat-drenched atmosphere backstage, while he pumped up alongside other bodybuilders against whom he would later compete. Christian claimed he missed all those virile elements of fraternal fellowship. "When I moved to Southern California," Christian told him, "I wanted to workout at a gym alongside other guys with some size, you know, closer to my physical stature, my devotion to training. That's why I first started lifting over at the Gold's in Venice."

"Makes sense," Chase observed. "You wanted to pump with the big boys."

"The first few months I trained there, I felt a bit intimidated."

"Intimidated?" Chase was confused. "How come?"

"Who knows?" Christian shrugged. "I suppose all those huger-than-life contest winners working out all around me made me feel small, undeveloped."

"Undeveloped?" Chase asked, incredulously. "You're the size of the Hollywood Bowl!"

"I wish!" Christian chuckled. "Still, seeing all those gargantuan guys made me want to be as big as them, as cut and massive, wanted to be a part of their world. That's why I've never really stopped doing the 'roids."

"Well, all that juice has sure done its job," Chase said, encouragingly.

"I know," Christian agreed, hoping he wasn't sounding too immodest. "I've always loved bodybuilding. All I've ever wanted to do is train, eat, and get big — train, eat, and get bigger still. Growing up, I knew I had no choice. Pumping iron just called to me. That's why I'm so lucky I met Pipsi."

"That your wife?"

"Yes. I'm real fortunate," Christian explained. "I married for both love and money."

"Always a good combo," Chase agreed.

"Yeah. My wife's father runs a bunch of businesses, including a very successful landscaping enterprise in Beverly Hills. Gave me a real cushy job there, along with a huge salary. I've been promised a promotion to Vice-President plus a full partnership in Sterling Enterprises just as soon as we bless them with a grandkid."

"Sounds ideal," said Chase.

"It is," Christian agreed. "I'm paid a lot just to work a few hours every day and do very little. But I feel out of place there."

"Why's that?"

Christian shrugged his huge shoulders. "What the hell do I know about the flowering cycle of any fucking petunias?"

"Let's face it," Chase hit the table with his fist. "Petunias are for pansies."

"Exactly!" Christian smiled. "But I really do like my cushiony job, such as it is, mostly because it gives me all the time I need for my bodybuilding, plus all the money I need for what seems like my never-ending supps."

"That's good," Chase agreed. "Because those puppies can get real expensive."

Christian acknowledged he had little patience with the time it took to build natural muscle, and was now nearing the end of yet another cycle. Chase was anything but surprised. One look at Christian was all anyone even vaguely familiar with bodybuilding needed to see he was amass with superhuman muscles, and that his inflated look could only have been built into such buffed, puffed poetry with the boost from prodigious amounts of steroids.

"I can appreciate the allure of steroid cycles," Chase told the muscle monster. "I just don't like all those yucky side effects."

"Yeah, like what?" Christian asked, slightly defensive, as if he didn't already know.

"Oh, little things," answered Chase. "Headaches, baldness, bipolar mood swings, aching joints, strokes and blood clots, nausea, impotence, high blood pressure, heart disease, enlarged prostate, urinary and bowel problems, bloated bellies, shrunken testicles, reduced sperm count, and have I left anything out? Oh yes, kidney and liver damage."

"Thanks!" Christian said, facetiously. "Now I feel a whole lot better. Always figured I'd die young, anyway."

Christian confided that giving up so much of the gains made during a cycle was often such a letdown, it compelled him to jump right back in and start shooting up another vicious cycle soon as the last one ended.

All this talk of muscle camaraderie excited Chase. He was well-aware of the sexual sparks, however subdued, that were sailing back and forth between him and the muscle monster with a not so subtle intensity. So Chase confronted the situation head on, put it on the table, and cleared up any misconceptions by getting his side of things out in the open right away. "Unlike you, Christian," he said openly. "I'm a happily *un*-married, single gay man — one who doesn't plan to settle down, mainly because I'm ever on the prowl for the next hot bodybuilder and the sharing of some hot muscle sex."

Christian reacted rather calmly, yet with definite surprise as he lamented, "And here I was sure you were straight. You seem so … heterosexual."

"Right," Chase answered. "And maybe you need to have your gaydar upgraded."

"Maybe I do," Christian acknowledged. "Hey, you know, I'm a big fan of muscle, same as the next guy. But fooling around with it's just too risky."

"And just what would a straight, married man know about muscle sex, anyway?" Chase asked, flat out.

"Don't get me started," said Christian, raising hands of surrender into the air. "I'm not so totally innocent, you know. I tried it once, right after a bodybuilding contest. Turned out to be a disaster. But at least I got it out of my system."

"Oh, really?" Chase wanted to know. "Who'd you fool around with?"

Christian candidly aired the dirty laundry of his brief homoerotic sexcapade, confessing how, years earlier, he experimented in a sexual episode of mutual muscle appreciation with one of his fellow competitors, after a bodybuilding contest. He also hastened to add their brief encounter had been anything but gratifying, because he felt dirty and was wracked with major guilt the moment he finished squirting his thick seed into the guy's mouth. "So after that," Christian admitted to Chase. "I fought hard to suppress any same-sex urges which came up, and just walked away from exploring other muscular men on that level. Turned out to be a smart choice, since it's also the safest way to stay clear of disease ... and even more importantly, stay in step with the Lord."

"The Lord?"

"Yeah, the Lord. Ever hear of Him?"

"You mean the Big Kahuna?"

"Yes," Christian frowned. "That's who I mean. But that's another reason I don't allow myself to get aroused anymore by muscle. It goes against my religion. I'm a Christian."

"Ah, Christian the Christian," noted Chase.

"Doesn't get more Christian than that, huh?" Christian observed with a wry grin. "When I injured my back, I had trouble bending over. So I started going back to church, getting myself straight with the Lord, thinking He might help me heal faster. And that's where I met Pipsi."

"God sure works in mysterious ways," observed Chase.

Christian edged his chair closer to Chase and lowered his voice, like he was about to reveal some dark family secret. "When my wife was born, her mother named her Pearl. But her father hated the name, so he started calling her Pipsi, and it stuck. Pipsi was never much of a Pearl, anyway." Casting big blue eyes to the floor, Christian then quietly reflected, "She gives me so much of my strength."

"And here I figured it had to be all that spinach!" Chase suggested.

Christian smiled, took a giant swig of his coffee, landed another friendly punch to the side of Chase's arm, and then candidly confessed, "Anyone can see you're a great looking guy. Still, you should know the main reason we can't share any sexual intimacy together, I mean besides my being a married, heterosexual man, is my commitment to God. Men and women were created for one reason: procreation."

Chase knew he'd sound too sarcastic if he offered any flippant contradiction, so he just listened as Christian then added, "My resolve to restrain myself from sin made me stronger, better prepared emotionally to stay focused, not simply on my walk with the Lord, but also on my training; and I guess you could say also to my being open to one day meeting a woman like Pipsi. You know what I mean?"

"I don't think so," answered Chase, who was by then mostly confused by Christian's circuitous logic. "You're saying something like women are more respectable, spiritually healthier."

"And here I thought you weren't paying attention." Christian smiled, grateful for Chase's clarity over his own convoluted conclusions. "With women, there's less chance of rejection once the sex is over. They'd rather build nests, so they don't disengage."

Chase nodded in empathetic agreement. "Jesus Christ, everyone knows men are snakes!"

Christian lowered his head to the floor and softly implored, "Would you mind not taking the Lord's name in vain?"

"I beg your pardon?" Chase asked, confused. "What did I say?"

"You said *Jesus Christ* ..."

"I did?"

"Just now."

"It was accidental," Chase explained. "Christ, I certainly didn't mean to offend."

"There — you did it again."

Chase played back his inadvertent insensitivity and turned serious. "It won't happen again. I promise."

"Don't worry," Christian conceded. "It's more my problem than yours. I just get uncomfortable when I hear His name thrown around like that."

"I understand completely," Chase said with a smile. "And admire anyone on a spiritual journey. Having a complex Messiah complex just makes you more interesting to me. Actually, I'm relieved. When you said there was something you needed to get off your chest, I thought you were going to confide something awful, like you're a serial killer or a Republican."

"Nope," said Christian. "Just a devout believer who is often so wracked with guilt about my here-and-there oddball attraction to other muscular men, I've spent most of my adult life running as far away from it as I could get. And yes, that probably includes getting as big as possible and, to some extent, maybe even my hurrying down the aisle to marry my bride."

Chase looked directly into Christian's blue eyes, trying to decipher what kind of mixed message the muscle monster was sending, what kind of emotional connection he might be trying to make. Sure, the big fellow claimed he was happily married, even predominantly straight. So why, then, was he so effortlessly bringing up his attraction to muscle, as well as his experimental, if limited, homoerotic past?

Wrapping up, Christian told Chase how he needed to fully embrace his commitment to married life, how much he loved their spacious home, how hard he was trying to become more dedicated to his beyond-boring job, how committed he was to forever finding favor with the Lord and, in the process, how determined he was to keeping tucked away those seductive sirens summoning so many of his muscle fantasies, his sinful same-sex urges. "Let's face it, friend," Christian acknowledged.

"Everyone knows a sustained, successful, sexual relationship between two men isn't feasible, practical, or even morally justifiable. And if you don't believe me, just ask anyone at my church!"

"I can tell you've given this a lot of thought," said Chase.

"So, if it's all right with you," Christian concluded. "Since we worked out so well together today, how 'bout if we have another go at it again next time you train, find out if we're compatible enough to maybe become full-time workout partners and who knows ... maybe even friends?"

"Fine with me," Chase acknowledged. "I know I'd sure enjoy being flirty, I mean friendly, with you."

"Walk me to my car, okay, Smart-Ass?" Christian suppressed a smile as he stood to leave the coffee shop. "We can exchange phone numbers."

When Chase looked at Christian quixotically, the muscle monster quickly added with justification, "So we can set up our next workout. You don't build muscle through dumb luck, you know. It takes good genes and hard work."

"And sometimes steroids," Chase interjected.

"Yes," Christian smiled in agreement. "Sometimes those, too."

Chase enjoyed toying disarmingly with straight men, especially those experiencing some confusion over the direction of their own sexuality. And Christian, he could tell, was prime teasing material.

As they walked toward the parking area, Christian turned to Chase and said, "Thanks for the extended coffee break. I'm not usually such a blabbermouth, but I don't know, I guess after not giving you a fat lip earlier today, I actually grew to like you, even though you are a misguided, bone-smoking, Philistine pagan."

"You're too kind!" Chase smiled and retorted, "And I like you, too. Even if you are an intolerant breeder and a major closet case."

"I am not a closet case, okay?" Christian insisted. "Haven't you been listening to me? I admire muscle, but refuse to be turned on by it."

"Suit yourself. Besides, what do I know? I've harbored this probably ignorant lifelong presumption that when it comes to building muscle, most men are either gay or confused."

"Is that supposed to be a compliment?" Christian asked, feigning naiveté.

"Hey, Pretty Boy, if the jock strap fits ..."

Christian and Chase walked up to an emerald-colored Jaguar XKE convertible and from thirty paces away, Christian unlocked its doors with a push of a button on his key chain.

Chase stood there and just stared at the car. "You have a Jag," he murmured in quiet wonder.

"Doesn't everyone?" Christian laughed, purposely obnoxious, as he settled in behind the wheel and stretched his arm over to the glove compartment. "I know I have a business card in here," he said as he rifled through a clump of papers cluttering his glove compartment.

"Amazing," Chase uttered, in near wonder. "Could it be an omen?"

"More like one of the wedding gifts from my father-in-law," Christian answered.

"We used to have them."

"Wedding gifts?"

"Jags," said Chase. "My dad had a dealership in Newport Beach. Hyde Motors."

"Good!" said Christian as he handed his business card to Chase. "Then it was meant to be!"

"I like this challenge," Chase admitted freely. "Can we plan on meeting back at the gym tomorrow? Let's say one o'clock for back and delts?"

"I'll be there."

"But I gotta warn you, Christian." Chase made a stern face. "When it comes to working out, I'm a bit of a task master. You're going to have to get up off your lazy butt and work hard for your Coach."

"I know," said Christian. "I was there today, remember? That's why I want to train with you. And you don't mind being friends with a straight man?'

"Not at all," Chase smiled. "Hell, I'm no heterophobe. Some of my best friends are breeders. Maybe we can have one of those meaningful, straight man-gay man, thick-as-thieves, warriors-in-flexed-arms, look-but-don't-touch kind of platonic-moronic relationships."

"You know, I like Los Angeles more and more all the time," Christian said as he started his engine, floored the pedal, and then with a wave goodbye, zoomed out from the parking lot. Looking hot in his hot wheels, the muscle monster zipped down the street with the top down, his radio blaring a gospel station, the wind at his back, buff and beautiful, not a care in the world.

Chase watched the Jag head toward Melrose Avenue traffic and, all outward appearances to the contrary, was convinced the huge fellow was still battling too many personal inner demons to render him sexually viable. Didn't matter to Chase. The prospect of getting past Christian's unavailability may have made the muscle monster that much more appealing. But Chase sensed he was also so preoccupied with the parade of men passing through his life, that maybe what he sorely needed was a true friend. Having sex with other men was easy, but finding and keeping best buds was a whole other matter. Besides, the muscle monster said he was happily married, totally committed to his bride. Chase had no interest in either being a home wrecker or investing all the time and energy it would require to win over and seduce someone as seriously conflicted as Christian seemed to be.

*   *   *   *

Not only did Chase and Christian work out together the following day, their teaming up proved such a muscle-pumping-thumping success, they spent the next two months at the gym as workout partners. They exercised well together and shared a common synergy, as they each sensed how to smoothly spot one another to best advantage. Their collective hard work paid off handsomely and they both achieved significant muscle progress, despite the wide weight variance they used during any given exercise. Chase, for example, bench-pressed two big forty-five-pound plates on each side of the barbell, a two-hundred-thirty-five pound weight, respectable by any normal bodybuilding standards. By contrast, Christian's driven sets pyramided up until, at the peak of his exertion, his racked bench press was packed with five big plates on each side of the barbell, a whopping four hundred ninety-five pounds — more than impressive even by the mightiest of muscle monster parameters.

Each of them was vigilant, extra cautious when spotting. They both made certain the one doing the lifting reached maximum contraction over the course of any set. Each of their slowly executed exercises found them straining hard for a beat or two at the peak of every contraction. Chase never let up on his unflagging insistence they both execute every rep of every single set incorporating nothing less than Coach's unwavering precision, his steadfast insistence on perfect form.

With Chase as his muscle mentor, to say nothing of the major boost the big man was getting from all the contraband juice in perpetual percolation throughout his system, Christian quickly packed on yet another twelve pounds of solid muscle mass.

When the guy at the gym in Venice who sold Christian his last few cycles of illegal enhancers retired from his illicit sideline and moved to Key West, Christian took the loss of his contact as an omen he should give his body a rest and not do another cycle right away. By the end of eight weeks, when his latest 'roids cycle came to an abrupt end, however, the muscle monster fretted over how quickly his latest progress would rapidly diminish and dissipate. Deflated over such a prospect, and ever-fearful he might, heaven forbid, start looking less like the Michelin tire man, he elected not to give his body's precious organs the chemical respite for which they cried out.

Instead, he discreetly asked around at the gym until one of the locker-room regulars referred Christian to another muscle monster in the gym — a bodybuilder named Stack Robinson. Christian found Stack at the cables station and waited for the big guy to finish his set before he introduced himself and brought up the subject of unlawful enhancers. Stack was all business as he warned Christian how hard it was to come by quality steroids in such lean times, which was why his prices had soared. "Anything picked up on the black market these days is gonna cost you," he informed Christian, who shrugged and mentioned that price posed no problem for him. Stack sealed the deal, telling Christian to meet him in the main parking lot the following afternoon.

* * * *

Chase and Christian trained together with an easy-going camaraderie that also allowed room for the occasional playful tease. While in the gym, they might punch each other good-naturedly on the arm between sets, or maybe snap a towel tauntingly at the other's butt when drying off after they showered.

One afternoon, while getting into their gym gear before exercising, for example, Chase took an appraising look at Christian stepping into his dark blue SafeGard jock strap. "You know," he taunted his workout partner. "For a straight guy, you sure got a cute butt."

Christian accepted the compliment and returned the tease. "Dream on, Coach!" he said, patting Chase on the back. "We both know you'd like nothing more than to plow your nasty way up into these unavailable, virgin cheeks."

"Sure, maybe if you were more my type," quipped Chase. "But I'm somewhat fussy. I prefer men with muscle!"

"Ha. Ha." Christian made believe he wasn't amused as he flexed one of his trophy-winning, nineteen-inch biceps smack in Chase's face. "What's this baby look like to you?"

"You mean besides a lot of water retention?" Chase asked with feigned innocence.

"Let's get out on the gym floor!" said Christian. "You're such a smart ass, today I'm gonna work you so hard, you'll limp out of the gym."

"I love it when you talk dirty!" Chase growled as he followed the muscle monster out of the locker room.

*   *   *   *

When Christian finally told Pipsi he had found a workout partner, she wanted to know everything about Chase. The moment she learned her husband's new friend was also still single at thirty-eight, she insisted they not only invite Chase to their next dinner party, but that they also include one of her unmarried, born-again gal pals from their church group, in the hopes sparks might just fly between them. Christian played along, told her he thought it was a fine idea. At the time, of course, Pipsi had no way of knowing the only real sexual sparks that might fly back and forth across the table at any dinner party she might host would be between Chase and her husband.

Christian fought hard to repress those erotic distractions that now and again sprang up in the midst of his workouts with Chase. The sight of Coach's body in contraction while he lifted a loaded barbell, his sexy muscles flexing to capacity, his impressive veins popping, was a particularly alluring image, one the muscle monster couldn't shake from his head.

There were even times when, while lying in bed next to a sleeping Pipsi, Christian closed his eyes and pictured himself wrapping his hands around Chase's flexed biceps. The mere visualization of the erotic image was sufficient stimulus to get him solidly boned. He always switched channels at that point, and quickly changed the broadcast in his mind, as he focused instead on his salvation by turning to prayer. *"Please, Jesus,"* Christian silently prayed. *"Let the satisfaction I get from being a successful bodybuilder quench my hunger for muscle."*

He asked God to please allow the empowerment he felt from having men and women alike stare at him with admiration be sufficient in making him more comfortable with himself and not less. He prayed to God to let the ecstatic feeling he often got when lifting weights be sufficient in satiating his sometime sorrowfully sinful appetite for fooling around with another man. Well, okay, not just any other man. By then, Christian knew what he most needed to hold at bay were those far too constant sexual fantasies circulating behind his eyes and interrupting his focus, those erotic pictures challenging his prosperous lifestyle, those irrepressible, constant muscle fantasies involving — Chase.

＊　　　＊　　　＊　　　＊

Week after week, the sexual tension infusing Chase and Christian's workouts continued to escalate unabated, this despite Chase's conscientious effort to respect Christian's religious convictions as well as his marital status by curbing his flirtatious impulses when they were at the gym. But it wasn't easy for either of them to put a cap on all their playful teasing, their fooling around, mainly because they were both so good at it. As they grew closer, Christian felt he might just soon explode if he didn't get to put his arms securely around Chase's sexy waist. Just once, that was all he needed, just one major squeeze and his curiosity would be satisfied. He yearned to hug Chase, even if only briefly, to finally feel a piece of the power within his buddy's beautifully developed body.

With every workout, Christian slowly came to accept the realization his repressed attraction to muscle was not about to dissipate, no matter how hard he prayed, no matter how conscientiously he struggled to banish those alluring visions of a shirtless Chase that kept popping up in his head. He made a point *not* to think about his workout partner, especially on those increasingly rare occasions when he made love to Pipsi. Still, no matter how hard he tried to drive from his overactive imagination those uninvited, erotic images, they would simply not be slaked.

His mounting sexual confusion ultimately came to a head one late afternoon after they both left the gym following a strenuous and exhaustive legs workout. Christian got behind the wheel of his XKE and reacted more like a zombie on auto pilot as he soon found himself absent-mindedly following Chase home, showing up without notice at Hyde Park's front door, just like that, unannounced, and ringing the doorbell.

＊　　　＊　　　＊　　　＊

Chase had just pulled off his tank top and was on his way into the kitchen when the bell rang. Shirtless, he opened his front door and was surprised to find his workout partner at his doorstep. "Didn't we just say good-bye?" he asked.

"Yes, of course we did," Christian stammered. "But I thought maybe we could have a recovery drink together. Can I come in?"

Chase opened wide his door, and with a sweep of his hand suggested Christian follow him.

"Thanks, Coach."

As Christian followed Chase through his living room and into his kitchen, a slow moving Romeo, by then twelve years old, got down from his perch of privilege upon the couch and shuffled his way into the kitchen to join the party.

"Who's this?" Christian asked as he bent down and scratched the aged bulldog's coat.

"That's Romeo," said Chase. "Poor old geezer's the last of the Hyde bulldogs."

Christian lowered his hand and Romeo offered up a paw for a high five greeting. Christian gently slapped his hand against Romeo's extended appendage and wondered aloud, "How could something so downright ugly also be so darn cute?"

"That's what I ask him every time his snoring wakes me." Chase answered as he pulled his huge tub of Cell-Tech protein powder from the shelf. "Okay — what's up?" Chase then asked innocuously, casually tossing a pair of freshly peeled bananas into his blender, all the while doing his best to conceal his excitement over the real reason Christian might be there.

The sexual tension between the two of them had bubbled up for weeks and was by then frothing over. Chase had long sensed this moment might be coming. To some degree, he'd been anticipating it, even though he still had little idea how he might respond should their measurable mutual attraction be finally laid bare. Chase also knew he had to be the one to remain strong and vigilant, resistant for them both. He knew he mustn't give in to any primal animal lust, didn't dare dive into the dangerous dynamics of fooling around with an unavailable, guilt-saddled, married man who was also a born-again Christian. More importantly, he didn't need to encourage any sordid sexual relationship with his own workout partner, a circumstance that could only compromise or jeopardize their productive training program. Chase recalled that longstanding golden rule of bodybuilding: You don't pop with whom you pump!

Still, Christian *was* standing right there before him in his kitchen, so sexily inflated, his thick, freshly pumped quadriceps popping out so enticingly from within his tight, black bicycle shorts. Drenched in post-pump perspiration, the muscle monster's tank top clung to his enormous torso and made prominent his nipples. Chase found the whole visual so stimulating and bone provoking, he wasn't sure how much longer he could pretend not to be aroused.

Christian also sensed it was finally time to bring their shared yearnings out from behind their carefully drawn curtains of studied denial. He knew Chase was far too much of a gentleman to ever make a first move, so it was up to him to initiate the jump to any next level. Anyone observing the two of them interacting together at the gym could have told you their sexual tension was building so intensely for so long, something was bound to snap.

And snap it finally did. Christian took a short step forward and initiated a surreal bouncing of his massive pecs. He then placed a hesitant hand atop Chase's shoulder, stared down at the floor and nervously said, "There's something I think we should try, just this once and then never again, so we can be done with it and then that's it, we can go back to the way things were, I swear. That okay with you?"

"Well, of course it's okay with me," Chase assured him. "What the hell are you talking about?"

"But," Christian kept his eyes peeled to the floor and took a deep breath. "We both have to understand that no matter what might happen between us right now, that we never ever talk about this, not ever; because it'll be the one and only time we're ever gonna try something weird like this, ever, ever again. Are we both completely clear about this, Coach?"

"Clear as cement," Chase answered, hoping not to sound too flip.

"Problem is," Christian offered an apologetic shrug, "I'm just not quite sure how to get it going — don't know how, where to start ..."

"Let me see if I can make this a little easier," Chase suggested, even as he raised his arms in the air and flexed hard his celebrated biceps. "Why don't you just grab on to these big boys?"

As Christian raised his head, his eyes popped wide open. "Oh, man, I've been dreaming about doing just that for so long. I'd love to." Reaching out, he wrapped both his giant hands around the left Gun of Navarone, the big one. "Incredible," he moaned, practically melting, as he carefully squeezed Chase's supple left biceps muscle. "I swear, feels even better than I ever, ever dared dream!"

Complimented and excited, Chase smiled his gratitude and flexed his left gun still harder.

Christian pressed his body smack up against Chase's as he held onto his workout partner's big, left baseball biceps, as tightly as he could, squeezing it for dear life itself, almost as if he was trying to crush the mighty orb until suddenly, his whole being began to shake, and he cried out, "Oh, no! No! Oh, my God — I'm gonna shoot!"

Astonishing them both, Christian went from zero to sixty in nothing flat until he was practically overwhelmed by a near-paralyzing wave of inexpressible euphoria. A glorious, pulsating sensation wracked his entire body as a thick gusher of sperm exploded out from his cock, saturating the crotch area of his bicycle shorts.

Chase kept his arm tightly flexed throughout the duration of his workout partner's extensive orgasmic outburst. Christian's extended release kept shooting, one robust spurt after the next, a gushing geyser gone berserk. Throughout it all, he never once let up on his unyielding grasp of Chase's solid muscle. Fully drained at last, Christian released his vice-like grip and simply let his body slump into Chase's strong arms. For a few moments, neither of them said anything.

"Very impressive," Chase finally observed quietly, as he held on to Christian while the muscle monster's breathing returned to normal. "You just shot a major load without once touching yourself."

Flustered, mortified, uncomfortable, and by any measure confused, Christian then said coyly, "What a mess, huh? Guess I better go clean up."

While Christian scurried off to the bathroom to take a speedy shower, Chase finished concocting their recovery drinks.

A few minutes later, clothed again in his freshly stained workout gear, Christian walked out of the bathroom and could not tear out of there fast enough.

Chase handed Christian his protein shake, but he waved it aside, suggesting, "You drink mine, okay? I'm late. Don't you see it's late? I should have been back at the nursery by now. I gotta bolt!"

And bolt he most assuredly did, leaving Chase standing there in the middle of his kitchen, a freshly blended, whey-protein recovery drink in each hand.

*   *   *   *

The next day when they met at the gym, things between Chase and Christian seemed strained and ill at ease mostly because, aside from Christian's behaving a bit more understated than usual, they both acted so downright … normal. As they pumped their backs and then their biceps, neither Chase nor Christian said a word about either Christian's unexpected drop-by visit the day before or his remarkable premature orgasm.

By the end of their sexually frustrating workout, Christian knew he could no longer resist his compelling need to again take hold and envelop his training partner. So he turned to Chase and asked if he could once again invite himself back to Chase's for yet another fortifying recovery drink adding, for assurance, "And I promise this time, I'll drink it."

Chase didn't think it was such a good idea, and reminded Christian how awkward was his withdrawal immediately following their previous day's rendezvous. "Didn't you notice how tense we both were during our workout today?" Before Christian could respond, Chase added, "Let's close this chapter, put it behind us and go back to being great workout partners. I'd rather not toy with anything that might threaten that."

"No, no, no," Christian assured him. "I'm well aware of all that. You don't have to convince me. That's why I promise this'll most certainly be our very last … uhm, private time together — one final pop for the road, that's all. I just need to feel those monster guns one more time. I swear to God."

Well … Chase figured. *If the big guy's up for it, if he can deal with his psychological demons, hell, so can I.* "Okay, then," he told Christian. "Why don't you follow me home?"

*   *   *   *

Their reunion in Hyde Park's kitchen found them both less forthcoming, more hesitant than the day before. Without words, Chase threw together ingredients for the blending of their recovery drinks. Christian studied Chase lost to the focus of his purpose, and decided to send his guilt packing long enough to drop his pretense at restrained civility. He walked up from behind and wrapped his arms securely around Chase's wide shoulders. He then bear-hugged his workout partner tightly as he could. "Damn, why do you have to feel so good?" he asked softly.

Chase turned to face Christian and returned the affectionate hug. He then eased himself away, took a short step back. "Okay, Big Boy!" he looked Christian up and down. "Show me what you got! And this time, try to refrain from erupting while you flex those freshly-pumped, massive guns for your Coach!"

Christian happily obliged and assumed his commanding double biceps pose. Chase kneaded his fingers gingerly into their erotic pliancy and then raised his own big arms and flexed them for Christian. The muscle monster reached out for them like they were winning lottery tickets, and Chase sensed his training partner was once again steaming hell-bent toward another premature eruption.

"Whoa!" Chase called out, and lowered his flexed guns as he took a step back. "Don't want you popping your balloon before we bring out the birthday cake. We just got started."

"You're right," Christian agreed, as he also took a step back, stared up at the ceiling and inhaled deeply, hoping to calm his mounting excitement. "I'm sorry, Coach. I just so love the feel of your biceps. Never felt anything like them."

"No need to apologize," Chase told him. "I'm flattered."

Christian looked directly into Chase's eyes. The muscle monster then quietly asked, "As long as we're here, could I try something I've thought about pretty much since we first met?"

Chase ignored the mammoth erection awakening within his gym shorts. "Sure, go ahead."

Christian eased a hesitant hand directly behind Chase's neck and then stepped forward and brought his lips smack against Chase's, kissing his workout partner flush on the mouth.

What the hell's going on? Chase wondered, even as Christian's tongue parted Chase's lips, and eased its way beyond his workout partner's teeth, deep into the hollow of his mouth.

Chase's extravagant erection sprang to its full rigidity, solidifying the reality that he was by then far too excited to stop. So he tabled his concerns over what kind of disturbing emotional consequences might later befall this not so unexpected erotic turn of events.

When at last their lips parted, Christian looked nervously at Chase. "Never kissed a man before," he said softly. "Five o'clock shadow sure makes an impact. Tickles. Where'd you ever learn to kiss like that?"

"Haven't I told you?" Chase answered with a smirk. "I *majored* in kissing." Reaching forward, Chase locked his own hand around a small tuft of hair at the back of Christian's head, squeezed it tightly, and brought their faces back together for another deep kiss.

"You must have graduated with honors," Christian mumbled, between kisses.

"Slurpa cum louder than everyone else!" Chase mumbled back.

"Do all men kiss like this?" Christian wanted to know, between kisses.

"Only those with lips," Chase answered, maneuvering Christian into another feverish embrace. When they once again came up for air, Chase asked with concern, "Are you okay with this?"

"Who knows, anymore?" Christian peered down at his sneakers and answered with a confused shrug. "I know it's not right. But I couldn't hold back any longer, just had to try kissing you. Just this once, okay?"

"Glad you finally did," Chase said as he affectionately cuffed Christian's chin with his fist. "Saved me the trouble." Chase leaned over and kissed Christian up and down the side of his thick neck, just below his ear. When Christian moaned a sweet, pleasurable exhale, Chase knew he'd struck an erogenous zone on the big fellow, and so he slowly swathed his tongue all across the sensual area.

Minutes later, they were both in the bedroom, standing tall and naked before Chase's full-length mirror, flexing their huge guns for the benefit of their dual reflections. They hugged each other tightly and shared wet and sloppy kisses as their hands played around with each other's impressive erections.

Chase popped open the drawer in the night stand next to his bed, pulled out a plastic container of grape seed oil, snapped it open and slathered some of it all over Christian's torso. He oiled up the muscle monster's solid pecs, his flexed biceps, his dense delts, his chiseled abs.

Christian stopped flexing long enough to take the posing oil out of Chase's hand. He lifted the plastic container overhead, aimed the bottle down at Chase's chest, squeezed hard and showered Chase's upper pecs with a steady stream of the translucent liquid. As the line of thin, clear liquid saturated the expanse of Chase's pecs and dribbled down his torso, Christian used both his hands to rub the glistening fluid into his workout partner's mighty chest. Using his enormous fingers, Christian dug in still further, deeply massaging Chase's pronounced traps.

"Ah!" Chase sighed with satisfaction. "The glory that was grease!"

Chase bounced his smooth, impeccable pecs with evident pride, and the sight of their glistening animation got Christian so stirred up, his own love muscle expanded still further, even as it spat forth several drops of pre-cum.

Chase retrieved the grape seed oil from Christian and casually emptied the last of it all across the Cinerama sweep of the big man's colossal lats.

After several more minutes of erotically rubbing each other, while sharing a hot and slippery mutual masturbation mixed in with extended flexes and deep, passion-filled kisses, Chase pulled back the covers on his king-sized bed and then aggressively pushed Christian down on top of it. He sprang into the air and with his full weight, landed directly on top of the muscle monster.

"You feel real good on top of me, Coach!" Christian said, still catching his breath from the crushing impact of Chase's powerful body. When he looked down at the bedding, he observed, "Hey — we're getting this oil all over your sheets!"

"Who cares?" asked Chase, rolling over to his side. "I'll wash 'em."

After another heavy kiss, it was apparent their shared passion was rising to a crescendo. Christian never felt more excited, more engaged. As Chase's grape-seed-oily hand wrapped itself around Christian's thickened cock and started wanking on it, Christian looked straight into Chase's eyes, and followed the Coach's lead. The moment he took hold of Chase's enormous fat cock, he was amazed. "Holy shit!" Christian gazed in wonder at Chase's stiffness. "How come it was never this big in the locker room?"

"I confess," said Chase. "There is a gun in my jock strap. And yes, it's happy to see you."

As they kissed and masturbated each other, their excitement escalated until Christian felt a climax welling up from deep within his groin, and he knew his rocket's bursting was both imminent and unstoppable. Since this was the last time they'd be fooling around together like this, the heat of the moment gave him license to make the most of it by fully lowering his inhibitions. So he sat up and straddled himself across Chase's waist. "I'm so close," he implored. "I'm gonna shoot if you'll just do something I've pictured in my mind, all too often."

"Name it, Cowboy," Chase answered with a smile. "I aim to please."

"Okay," Christian summoned one of his favored, long-suppressed flights of fancy. "Could I shoot my load — just this once — all over your big left gun, while you're flexing 'em both for me?"

Excited by the imagery, Chase raised his arms and proudly flexed the Guns of Navarone as hard as he could. "Do it, Christian," he told him as he flexed still harder. "Pop some snow on that peak!"

That did it. Launched, Christian's libido soared into lift-off and he shot like a cannon. His milky pockets of gism hit the bull's eye smack on the prominent, thick vein that ran along the peak of Chase's fully flexed left gun, exactly as envisioned for so long in Christian's imaginings.

The sight of Christian's explosion incited Chase to erupt with his own full release. As an ecstatic tingle pulsated throughout his body, he eased his head against the headboard, tilted his pelvis, and saturated his own hard abs with copious spurts of his ample load.

*   *   *   *

The feverish sexual tension that paved its irrepressible path to their first fully realized carnal encounter was finally behind them, and thereafter, Chase and Christian invariably found themselves heading straight back to Chase's house following their workouts. Once there, before anything happened, Christian was dependably emphatic as he made it clear this was the last time they'd be flexing together.

Then they'd grab hold of each other and plunge right in, catering to their mutual muscle fixations.

Whenever they fooled around, their muscle reunions never lasted long. Ten minutes was about the extent of any of their erotic encounters. Christian got so speedily excited, his genital thermometer shot up until he could no longer hold back. His premature orgasms allowed him to take a quick bite out of the forbidden fruit that was his attraction to muscle, before returning him directly to the contemplation of his guilt.

Chase grew accustomed to Christian's pattern of unparalleled excitement followed by premature ejaculation followed by deep remorse followed all over again the next day by unparalleled excitement.

"Odd," Christian observed after one particularly swift, near record session. "With Pipsi, it takes me forever to cum, but with you, I can pop almost as soon as you touch me." After sighing, he then confessed his guilty pleasure. "Here's my dilemma: I want to worship the Lord, but I also want to worship your biceps. Problem is, I feel fine about the one, but filled with guilt over the other, especially since muscle sex with you is so much fun. I love getting lost in both of you, but since I can't serve two masters at once, I'll be damned if I know what to do about it."

*   *   *   *

By the time Chase's twelve-year-old bulldog's crippling arthritis made it difficult for the aged canine to get around the house, Chase acquiesced to his vet's advice and finally had his chronically-pained pup put down. As with the demise of all the bullies that preceded him, Romeo's death took another emotional chunk out of Chase.

The redeeming feature to his grief over the last of the Hyde bulldogs was the way in which Christian stepped forward to console Chase's sorrow. He reinforced their deepening bond by providing compassion, commiseration, and a strong shoulder to lean on.

After several more weeks of all-out, muscle-pounding workouts predictably capped by powerful and always final sessions of furious muscle sex up at Hyde Park, Christian surprised them both one afternoon when he claimed he was finally ready for further exploration and experimentation.

"Fine with me," Chase told him. "What'd you have in mind?"

"Well," Christian said nervously, "I'm curious to find out how a blow job might feel from you. Pipsi's not too interested and not very good at it. And I hear guys give better head than women."

"It's true," Chase agreed. "Men are better cock suckers, lesbians better muff divers,"

"Then maybe we should try that sometime," Christian suggested, bravely.

"Muff diving?"

"Cocksucking!" Christian corrected him. "And maybe if I get excited enough, I'll even be able to try going down on you. Just don't count on it. That club you're carrying looks like it could choke a guy to death. And just so you know, don't start getting any bold ideas about any rear entry, okay? No way you'll be plowing your way up this boy's ole Hershey Highway," Christian told him. "No anal sex for yours truly, thank you very much. No one's taking down this hot virgin butt!"

"Never?" asked Chase.

"Maybe when hell freezes over," Christian mused. "But everything that leads up to that might be fair game, if that's okay with you."

"I'm more than happy to lead you down that jaded path," said Chase. "If by chance I never mentioned it — virgins are my specialty!"

*   *   *   *

At first, Christian was ill at ease acclimating to the sheer volume of the Fifty-First State. As Chase's hardened flesh navigated its way into his mouth, the muscle monster learned to gradually fasten his gums around its substantial girth. Chase then patiently instructed him on how to slowly relax his throat muscles so he could best accept the whole of his Coach's manhood and, with practice and patience, learn to eventually administer the best blow job possible.

It was a first for Christian, and he took to it like a pro. In fact, he adjusted to the rigors of the cocksucking challenge with a far more gleeful sense of abandon than he ever demonstrated on those infrequent occasions when he contemplated going down on his wife. Pipsi hardly minded because, sensing his reluctance in that erotic zone, she never encouraged it. Sharing mutual, narrow marital sexual appetites suited both her and Christian just fine.

Christian's fooling around with Chase was a whole other matter, and he was able to finally let loose a sexual exuberance the likes of which he never before experienced. The muscle monster felt as if he'd waited his whole life to finally emancipate most of his deeply repressed muscle fantasies.

Chase's concern that any escalation of their intimacy might have a negative impact on their training proved to be ungrounded. If anything, their workouts were never more focused. Day after day, workout to workout, three days on, one day off, like clockwork, the training partners could simply not get enough of each other. They could not polish off a day's training without also feeling an urgent calling to hightail it straight back to Chase's place for what Christian consistently swore would be one last final round of pure, unadulterated muscle sex.

After another few weeks of post-pump eroticism, Chase was eager to ease his new sex partner into the next level of man-to-man interaction, and suggested he finally induct Christian, despite his previous protestations, into the mysterious world of man-to-man anal intercourse.

But Christian remained adamant he still wanted none of it. Fooling around in the uncharted territory surrounding the foreboding, forbidden zone of rear entry was, he claimed, just too perverse, too Old Testament sinful, and certainly way too gay for anything he might tolerate. So long as they stayed away from sex involving their butts, Christian could rationalize his fall from grace wasn't quite so steep, and he could still repent, could still seek mercy when begging God to forgive his wayward escapades.

All the big bodybuilder ever really wanted when they were alone together, in fact, was to play with Chase's muscles, maybe dive into a bit of fellatio. But when it came to anal sex, he rationalized that remaining unsullied in that area meant everything else in which they partook was merely experimentation, little more than playful fooling around with another muscle buddy — still just a guy-to-guy thing. Besides, no anal sex also meant since they weren't actually fucking, he wasn't *really* cheating on his wife. Most prominently, Christian was convinced that so long as he remained butt-chaste, he still wasn't truly gay.

One afternoon, the workout partners were in the gym, winding up twenty minutes of walking rapidly uphill on adjoining treadmills, warming up before pumping up. Christian further chiseled his abs by forcefully crunching them like an accordion with his every pounding step. "My wife insists I invite you to a dinner party we're having," he told Chase, between crunches. "She's heard so much about you, she doesn't understand why I haven't brought you around. Besides, she's eager to fix you up with one of her single girlfriends. It's next Friday. Can you make it? I already told her you could."

"Don't you think that might be a little … uncomfortable?" Chase asked.

"Well, sure," Christian agreed. "But she'll think it's strange if you don't show up. Besides, it could give you a chance to see where I live, see what my life is like when I'm away from you. And now that we're friends, you'll have to meet Pipsi *sometime.*"

Chase felt flattered Christian was finally opening the door to the other side of his double life. As their twenty minutes on the treadmill ended, he accepted the invitation and asked, "What's for dinner?"

"I have no idea. But my wife entertains with great style. You two will probably hit it off, fall in love, run away together, and leave me to die old and alone. Let's hit the weights."

∗   ∗   ∗   ∗

The following Friday evening, Christian and Pipsi hosted their dinner party for eight guests. After champagne and hors d'oeuvres in the living room, Pipsi led everyone into their flower-filled, candlelit dining room.

Four of the invitees were two young married couples whom she knew from their church in Malibu. Rounding out the attractively appointed dining table were Chase and, right next to him, by no accident, the fix-up of Pipsi's dreams, Ms. Lisa Fleming, a sweet and soft-spoken, surprisingly attractive, twenty-something blonde who worked in Beverly Hills as a dental technician.

Neither the irony nor the symbolism was lost on Chase when Pipsi inadvertently plunked herself down between him and Christian, the wedge keeping them apart. The young Mrs. Falconer looked around her candlelit table and, after parting with one of her girlish giggles, requested rhetorically, "Shall we ask a little blessing?"

Everyone at the table held hands and lowered their heads as Pipsi quietly prayed aloud, "Lord, we thank you for this bounty and for the blessing of dining with dear friends, both old and new. In Jesus' name, Amen."

As everyone seated around the table muttered a soft "Amen," Chase figured it couldn't hurt to score a few brownie points with The Big Kahuna. So he, too, raised eyes to the ceiling, joined their chorus, and mouthed a silent, "Amen."

Pipsi and Christian's dinner guests supped on medallions of veal, steamed haricot verte, roasted Yukon potatoes, several bottles of a vintage California pinot noir, and a serious breaking-of-training dessert of white chocolate mousse topped with crème fraiche. Over the course of several courses, Chase was on his best behavior, trying to make a good impression. Lisa was intrigued by her dashing dinner companion and seemed eager to learn everything about the handsome bachelor with whom she'd been paired.

While not fully enjoying the charade, a part of Chase also quietly reveled in it. Rather than play into how awkward he felt in the prickly situation, he remained polite and articulate, and continued to charm, even after Lisa, his "date," began unabashedly flirting with him.

Chase was no stranger to having women come on to him. He even welcomed their affirmation. Lisa was no exception. She and he played coyly with each other throughout the meal and just before dessert, while the rest of the table was engaged in a heated dispute over the rigors of divorce and joint custody, she leaned into her dinner companion to ask, "So tell me, Chase ... have *you* ever been married?"

"I have never been married," Chase told her. "How about you?"

"Twice, I'm afraid," Lisa answered, with a guilty shrug. "My therapist says I'm only drawn to men who are unavailable."

"And why's that?"

"Who knows?" she batted pussycat eyelashes. "Maybe I've been misguided while waiting to be swept off my feet by Mr. Right."

In Pipsi's role as Cupid, she had arranged for Christian to drive over earlier to pick up Lisa and bring her to the dinner party. Mrs. Falconer was then at her playful best when, right after dinner, she pulled Chase aside and casually asked if he wouldn't mind driving Lisa home. Ever gallant, Chase assured his hostess it would be his pleasure.

While everyone else gathered in the living room for decaffeinated coffee, brandies, and polite conversation, Christian brought Chase into his den so he could show his workout partner the many framed photos hanging on the walls, photos taken at some of the former champion's bodybuilding contests back when he lived in Connecticut. Chase couldn't help but be impressed.

Unable to keep his hands to himself any longer, Christian reached out, wrapped his huge arms around Chase's waist, and forcefully hugged him. Chase initially accepted the vigorous assault of affection, but then remembered where they were, and whispered into Christian's ear, "Are you nuts, you big galoot? This is no time to be naughty! There are six born-again lunatics in the other room. They catch us like this, they'll stone us to death."

Christian released his firm grip. "Sorry," he muttered as he turned to leave the room. "I needed to hold on to you — just once."

An hour or so later, the dinner party slowly broke up. Chase obliged Pipsi's request and gave Lisa a lift over to her immense, Orwellian condominium complex, just on the other side of the hill, in Studio City. Along the way, he politely half-listened to her lively dissertation on the underappreciated value of the semi-annual dental check-up. Lisa hoped she wasn't rambling, but knew she was being uncharacteristically frothy and loquacious. She felt inexplicably nervous around Chase, and had no idea why she was behaving like an infatuated teenybopper. She also wondered if maybe he liked her at least as resolutely as she was excited by him.

Chase pulled his Jeep up into the driveway of Lisa's multi-unit building complex, and then escorted his date to her lobby entrance.

"It was such a pleasure meeting you," Lisa told him while clumsily fumbling through her cluttered handbag for her front door key.

"Thanks, Lisa. You, too!"

"Ah, here it is!" Lisa exclaimed as she lifted up her key and, after twisting it in the lock, asked guilefully, "So — would you like to come in for a nightcap?"

"Maybe if it weren't so late," Chase answered, hoping to sound agreeable. "Big day tomorrow!"

"I understand," Lisa tried masking her disappointment by placing her arms around Chase's waist. "Then how 'bout a hug goodnight?"

"Sure thing!" Chase placed his arms around the dental technician's shoulders and affectionately returned the hug.

"Wow!" Lisa held on to Chase as she hugged him tighter. "Most guys I date have nothing but fat around their middle. You're solid as a rock."

"I work out with Christian, remember?"

"Two big muscular men, huh?" Lisa asked, almost mischievously.

"That's us!" Chase boasted as he released his date and took a step back. "You like muscles on guys?"

"What girl doesn't?" quipped Lisa. "They're the first thing we look for in a man — right after personality, intelligence, sense of humor, compassion, humility, and oh, yes, net worth and character."

"In that case, I'll start working on my character," Chase said with a grin.

A playful Lisa again lowered her hand into the jumble of her handbag and fingered around until she pulled out her business card, which she then slipped into Chase's hand. "Why don't you give me a call? Maybe the two of us can get together — have a bite or something?"

Chase knew Lisa would be reporting back to Pipsi first thing the following morning every detail of their ride home, so he pocketed the card and played along with the hetero hoax by offering his dinner companion a perfectly agreeable smile along with what he hoped might pass for a semi-responsive, semi-flirtatious wink. "You never know," he told her with an amicable wave of his hand. "Maybe you can x-ray my teeth sometime."

*   *   *   *

At the same time, back in the heart of fashionable Hancock Park, Christian and Pipsi had already cleared the dinner dishes, blown out their multitude of candles, turned off the lights, and were by then upstairs in the master bedroom, getting ready for bed.

Christian stood in pajama bottoms before the bathroom sink, brushing his teeth, while Pipsi sat straight up in their king-sized canopy bed, toying with their remote, absent-mindedly flipping channels.

"So …?" She called out, loudly. "You think by any chance Chase liked Lisa?"

"How would I know?" Christian yelled back to her from the bathroom, while rinsing his mouth. "Didn't everyone like Lisa?"

"You know what I mean, Silly! As a potential girlfriend. That's why I asked him to drive her home, give them some time alone. They sure seemed to be clicking nicely when they left here."

"How could you tell?" Christian wanted to know. He was puzzled by the sudden pang of jealousy he felt at the notion of Chase and Lisa hitting it off. He switched off the bathroom light, walked to the foot of the bed, and stared at his wife staring at the TV.

Christian couldn't tell if it was the vintage wine they'd had at dinner, the skyrocketing level of his 'roids-induced testosterone count, or more likely, the release he needed from all the sexual tension created by the look-but-don't-touch presence of his workout-partner-cum-secret-lover at their dinner party. Whatever it was, the muscle monster was suddenly rendered randy.

It had been some time since he'd last made love to his wife, and a tiny voice inside his head advised him the time had arrived to again service the little woman. He felt a need to reinforce and assure not just her, but especially himself that he still had an undiluted interest in their lovemaking — that he could still hit his mark and perform like the hetero muscle champ he was. He also wanted to avoid raising any red flags, didn't want Pipsi getting suspicious about him and Chase.

Christian crawled calculatedly into bed, snuggled cozily right up next to Pipsi, authoritatively took the remote from her hands, and snapped off the TV.

"Oh, Hun-ee," Pipsi protested mildly. "I wanted to see what's on HBO."

"I've got other plans for us," Christian told her as he stretched to dim the lamp next to their bed.

Pipsi was exhausted from the dinner party and looked forward only to blessed rest. But since it had been quite some time since she and Christian had last been intimate, she answered the scriptural dictum of her conjugal commitment and submitted to his will.

Minutes later, Pipsi was not just surprised, but also made breathless by the vehemence manifested in her husband's lovemaking. She had never known him to be quite so aggressive, never before found him so carried away in his seeming euphoria. Most surprising was that some previously unknown quirk deep within her actually found excitement in this new uninhibited, nearly overwhelming Colossus who was suddenly so heatedly expressing himself as he vigorously insinuated himself into her dainty body.

Once deep inside her, Christian thrust away with uncharacteristic intensity. He felt gratified that the carnal sensation of being back within the mysterious membrane walls of his wife's sacred treasure still imparted so much damn exhilaration. He was thankful to know he was, given his recent sexual drift to the other side, functioning again like a *real* man.

This is what I want, Lord, he told himself as he made love to his wife. *This is all I need.* He locked eyes with Pipsi's and forcefully pinned her shoulders to the sheet with his strong hands. He then held her at bay incorporating the same dominating vehemence Chase usually showered on him.

Liberated by the wine that had inebriated him, as well as fueled by the uninvited, yet tantalizing images of a naked Chase suddenly racing across his mind, his escalating passion soon carried him to the brink of orgasm. His intoxication further allowed him to vehemently verbalize his enthusiasm in the same manner he often did as he approached one of his premature orgasms when he was with Chase. As he began to ejaculate, he exaggerated the dramatic effect of his climax when boisterously, he shouted out an unexpected and certainly un-Christian-like volley of "Fuck! Fuck! Fuck!"

While next emptying his spasms of seemingly limitless euphoria inside his wife, he also unexpectedly brought Pipsi to the first and what would turn out to be only vaginal orgasm she ever experienced throughout the duration of their wedded bliss.

As for Christian, the mental picture he summoned as he shot his seed deep inside his wife was the erotic image of Chase vehemently fucking him.

*   *   *   *

Overnight impressions of Pipsi's dinner party varied.

The following morning when she placed her call of thanks, Lisa told Pipsi she'd had a simply superb time, and hoped she wouldn't have to stare too long at the phone waiting for Chase's forthcoming call.

Pipsi was delighted she finally got to meet her husband's new workout partner. Chase seemed like such a fine man and, with so few eligible bachelors out there, if for some silly reason he and Lisa didn't click, she had in mind three or four other single lady friends from their church group all lined up, ready to step in to take her place. Might not one of her sisters in Christ turn out to be just the right match for Chase?

As for Chase, he felt ill at ease taking advantage of Pipsi's hospitality. Now that they'd met and he'd looked her in the eye, the situation seemed so much more *real*, which only made him feel that much more uncomfortable about dating a married man.

And Christian was not just delighted to have spent so perfect a dinner party with the two most important people in his life; he could also hardly wait to again get the three of them reunited. After their initial evening together, Christian went out of his way to set up the kind of social outings that included both Pipsi and Chase. The three of them went out together several times, once to a fancy restaurant, once to a Sunday church service, once to a movie.

Christian derived some perverse pleasure in simultaneously spending time with both his wife and his boyfriend; this, despite the fact that Chase felt justifiably awkward around Pipsi. Rather than bringing them all closer into some harmonic trio, as Christian altruistically envisioned, Chase believed their threesome merely compounded his and Christian's deception, and added unnecessary weight to the muscle monster's already considerable baggage.

For the first time since coming out so many years earlier, Chase felt oddly comfortable about the notion of monogamy. And even though he and Christian had yet to delve into anal sex, the muscle monster so satisfied his sexual appetite, Chase no longer felt what had been his driven need to seek out other men.

Christian appreciated Chase's newfound fidelity, and decided the time had come to stop having it both ways. After the night of their dinner party, he stopped having sex with Pipsi altogether.

Pipsi barely took notice. Sex for her was more an obligation to quench her husband's sporadic carnal appetite than any kind of measurable, pleasurable diversion. There was also a small segment within her complexity that observed how Chase and her husband seemed inordinately close for two straight men. However, she conveniently relegated so dark and suspicious a cloud of doubt into an area of her mind that simply refused to contemplate such folly. Instead, she stayed busy with the ongoing reconstruction of their stately manor in Malibu, and got lost in the pleasure derived from spending so much time with her horses.

Month after month, Christian and Chase's muscular romance thrived. Chase was crazy about Christian. Christian was nuts for Chase, even as he remained devoted to Pipsi. Her presence in his life provided him not just with the security, stability and respectability he craved, but also with a deep sense of spirituality he found comforting and fulfilling. For a short while, all three of their lives appeared relatively rosy and surprisingly stable, despite the circuitous convolution of their unusual situation.

Throughout their brief halcyon period, they each in their turn basked in the comforting notion that their odd arrangement was somehow playing out just fine. The three of them all felt blessed, even if in a collective denial about the stormy weather which lay in wait, just around the corner.

*   *   *   *

Christian injected the last hypodermic needle of his latest cycle into his upper butt, and suffered a separation anxiety so severe, he decided on the spot he had to score just one more round of 'roids. Stack, his source at the gym, was away for a month. Christian was not ready to part with the muscle gains he'd built back up, and needed to search elsewhere to satisfy his dependency on supplemental support.

Hubert Sterling, Christian's father-in-law, hailed from a large, close-knit family that rendezvoused for a week every year at Lake Tahoe, usually around Thanksgiving. When Pipsi informed her husband of the dates for that year's family reunion, he begged her to let him off the hook. He didn't much care for her aunts and uncles, had less in common with the spoiled brats that were her cousins. Besides, he further explained, if she went by herself to the family gathering, he could take a few days off and fly down to Mexico and pick up the drugs he so badly needed for his next cycle.

Of course he'd promised Pipsi he wasn't going to do steroids anymore. "And I won't," Christian assured her, supplanting his promise with yet another promise. "Right after just one last, final cycle."

Unlike in the United States, south of the border you needed no prescription to buy steroids or any other prescriptive drugs. They're all sold over the counter in every *farmacia*, as easy to procure as baby aspirin. When you consider how much mark-up you had to shell out for a cycle of 'roids on the black market, it cost about the same to fly down to Mexico, stay in a nice hotel, cover your meals and also pick up your steroids.

When Christian asked his workout partner to join him in Puerto Vallarta over the holiday weekend, working out and relaxing in the sun, Chase jumped at so rare an opportunity to have Christian all to himself.

*   *   *   *

Chase and Christian's visit to Mexico was their mutual muscle fantasy come true. Christian booked a cozy *casita* at *Descanso Del Sol*, a charming inn tucked into the hills above the seaside town of Puerto Vallarta. The glorious view from their court- yard overlooked an azure Pacific Ocean. He and Chase rose early each morning and began their day hugging, kissing, and flexing erotically for each other. After shooting intense orgasms, they tossed on tank tops and shorts and walked into town where, ravenous from their morning debauchery, they consumed huge Mexican omelets. Fortified with protein, they then strolled over to the local gay beach, where they worked out together at Tito's Gym, a surprisingly well-equipped, al fresco facility, set up on the sand, under the sun, not a hundred feet from the waves breaking at the shoreline.

They trained together, pumping iron for an hour and a half, sweating and panting under the warm, late-morning sun. When they completed the last set of their final exercise, the bodybuilders raced into the ocean in their Speedos for a rejuvenating swim.

Hours later, back in their room, tanned, pumped up and once again horny, Chase and Christian celebrated their passionate muscle sex all over again. After napping and then showering and dressing for dinner, they strolled back into town, to find an open-air restaurant and dine by the light of the moon.

Along the way, they popped into the local *farmacia*, where Christian purchased the steroids required for his next few fourteen-week cycles.

Escaping the realities of his life in Los Angeles freed Christian in ways he never anticipated. Getting away from his doldrums at the nursery, away from the plush comforts of his home, away from the ministrations of his devoted wife, all conspired to let him explore previously uncharted sexual territory. When he and Chase fever- ishly kissed, he finally stopped fretting over any moral implications of so previously forbidden an endeavor and, instead, simply accepted its rewarding sensation.

For a few untroubled days, while they were together in this idyllic setting, their muscle sex grew so passionate, it became more like fervent lovemaking. Surprisingly enough, there was none of the requisite discussion beforehand by Christian, offering his usual insistence their encounter be the very last time that they'd be indulging in such illicit practice.

An even bigger surprise came when the muscle monster felt none of his usual pangs of post-orgasmic guilt, no sense of deep remorse for his sinful fall. Getting away from home somehow allowed the former champion bodybuilder to break free from his chains of convention, and he finally gave himself no restrictions on return- ing Chase's genuine affection. Most tellingly, while vacationing with Chase, Christian experienced not a single premature orgasm.

Throughout the months of their illicit romance, Christian had been very clear and rather vocal about having no interest in butt fucking. To neither of their sur- prise, he held on to that conviction throughout their vacation. At least until their last night in Puerto Vallarta.

Over dinner at a candlelit restaurant up in the hills, overlooking a churning ocean, overlooking reality, Christian unexpectedly claimed he no longer felt blinded by his dogma. Never more relaxed, never so at peace, having never felt so connected to another man, the muscle monster confessed he felt far removed from his pervasive peer pressure back home. "Spending this time with you has been incredible," Christian told Chase. "And since I may never again have an opportunity like this — well, you may find this hard to believe, but … well, tonight, I want … I can't believe I'm saying this, but tonight, when we get back to our room, that is if you're up for it, I want you to fuck me."

Caught off guard, Chase hadn't anticipated this sudden turnaround. "Are you sure?" he asked.

"Quite sure," Christian responded. "Maybe it's time I found out what all the fuss is about."

Elated by the notion, Chase stepped up to the plate. "I couldn't agree more. But I'd have thought you'd want to take me down, not the other way around."

"Naw," Christian was candid. "I have enough on my hands whenever I'm intimate with Pipsi. I'd rather have you inside me. I figure that's the one place my wife can never be. So, will you let me bottom for you, Coach?"

The question struck a nerve in Chase, who took the occasion to share his top/bottom philosophy. "I don't like those terms," Chase told him, candidly. "I've never liked the labels placed on gay men. They're modeled after the heterosexual paradigm and are inappropriate."

"You've lost me."

"It's like this," Chase explained. "Gay men are the only people who can literally both fuck and get fucked. Give as well as receive. This is not a minus, but a plus. Even the terms top and bottom are pejoratively loaded and misleading. Top suggests winning and masculine. Bottom telegraphs losing and feminine."

"They're false assumptions?"

"Correct!" Chase mounted his soapbox. "Especially since neither's necessarily the case. There are plenty of butch bottoms out there and plenty of big sissy tops. And guys who only top to keep their machismo intact are missing out on a big piece of the gay puzzle."

"Okay, Coach, you've convinced me," Christian held up an open hand of surrender. "I'm ready for my piece of the puzzle. Let the games begin!"

*   *   *   *

Chase couldn't get back to their quaint casita fast enough. He needed to hit the sheets before Christian changed his mind. He lit a few votive candles and tuned in a local radio station airing sentimental Mexican love songs. He grabbed Christian and kissed him deeply while they helped each other out of their tees and shorts.

Naked, Chase held onto Christian's shoulders as he slowly eased the big fellow down onto the bed until he was flat on his stomach. He stretched the muscle monster's solidly defined arms out wide on either side of him, and reached for a supportive feather pillow which he shoved beneath Christian's hips, slightly elevating the perfectly formed mounds of his thickly muscled bubble butt. Chase then placed his own hands beneath Christian's underarms and interlocked the fingers of both his hands, ensnaring his boyfriend's thick neck as he clamped Christian into a sensual full nelson.

Christian was fully erect as he welcomed his voluntary incarceration. After burying his face deep into the pillow, he shut his eyes tightly and moaned softly.

Chase carefully eased his stiff cock up against the space that divided Christian's rounded cheeks, then cautiously eased its fat head flush up against the outer membranes of the muscle monster's smooth anal orifice.

"How's that feel?" Chase asked softly.

"*Hmmmmm*," Christian whimpered, faintly. "So far, so good. Don't hurt me. But don't stop."

Chase was not about to stop. As he rubbed the fat, mushroom head of his thick cock up and down between Christian's beefy cheeks, he ripped open the foil wrapping on a jumbo-sized Trojan, slipped it on over his dick, and then slathered the length of his hardon with the oil from a fresh bottle of lubricant. He then took great care as, gently as possible, he eased the tip of his huge erection up against Christian's fleshy opening. After taking a deep breath, he pushed his cock gently but emphatically forward. Carefully, yet firmly, he forged his fat flesh further in until he almost gained access through the fleshy cleft.

"You're very tight!" Chase whispered into Christian's ear. "Just be calm. And breathe. I'm right here, Big Guy. It's just you and me. Now let me in."

Christian closed his eyes tighter, buried his face deeper into the pillow, gritted his teeth and tried to relax. No easy feat. "Please don't hurt me!" he whined into the pillow.

"I'm not going to hurt you, you big baby," Chase said softly as he kissed the back of Christian's neck. "I'm going to make love to you. But first you have to let me in. You just need to relax."

"Listen, Buddy!" Christian spoke directly into the pillow. "I'm lying flat out on my stomach and there's a big, naked man on top of me, straddling my bones, about to poke me with what I can only describe as a weapon of mass destruction. How am I supposed to relax?"

"Leave it to me," Chase whispered into Christian's ear. "Take a deep breath. Let it out. Open up. Let me in. It'll be a perfect fit, and I promise. I'll go very slowly, every loving inch of the way."

Christian exhaled deeply and as Chase spread the big man's cheeks, its aperture magically unraveled, a camera lens made of flesh, ready for its close-up.

Little by little, Chase's big dick slowly penetrated the muscle monster's soft, previously impregnable anal cavity; and as he slowly entered this uncharted territory, he also closed the book on Christian's hallowed virginity. Once he was all the way in, Christian moaned again, at first a sort of purr that grew into a gurgling-growl, all fuelled by a wild, new sensation of pleasure.

Deep inside his partner, Chase next introduced a series of deliberate yet gentle thrusts which soon escalated as, with each jab inside Christian's butt, Chase grew ever more assertive until he was soon hammering his partner with a solid rhythm both exciting and intense.

As Christian grew more acclimated to the strange, surreal sensation, he forced himself to drop his macho defenses, at least for the time being, and at last submitted, finally allowing Chase to become the first man to cut through his homophobic fears and penetrate him.

Chase stayed locked deep inside Christian as commandingly, he flipped the muscle monster over, onto his back. After lifting the big man's powerful legs into the air and wrapping a huge arm around each of Christian's enormous thighs, he draped a leg over each of his own shoulders. Again, he pressed all the way in and remained buried deep inside Christian's tight muscle butt as he kissed him fervently on the lips.

Christian quickly acclimated to the unfamiliar, primal sensation of Chase's pounding rhythm, and was soon following Chase's lead, lifting his butt up off the bed in sync every time Chase hammered hard against his anal membranes. Working in tandem, they propelled themselves up and then back down again as they followed Chase's slow, controlled pace, his deliberate lunges in and his tantalizing pelvic thrusts out. Their sensuous movements worked in blissful synchronization as they pumped back and forth, up and down.

The intensity of their lovemaking, the fact they were so literally united, filled each of them with a profound closeness. They made love, and their magical bonding escalated so fiercely that they were both soon ready to explode.

"I'm gonna shoot!" Christian announced excitedly while panting heavily. Even as he raised his big arms and flexed his sexy double biceps to show Chase all his might. "Can't hold back anymore!"

"Do it, Christian!" Chase grunted. "Do it for me. Shoot all over your fucking hot abs!"

Christian cried out his ecstatic astonishment and erupted with a vociferous, extended ejaculation. Without ever once touching his own genitals, thick gobs of the muscle monster's orgasm erupted from his hard cock, splattering pockets of thick gism across the length of his torso, saturating the ridges of his sculptured six-pack.

The sight of Christian getting so lost in his euphoric explosion got Chase so whipped up, he felt a jolt of exhilaration rising up from the base of his balls and into his rigid shaft, until at last it shot an opaque reserve of creamy gism out from within. Chase howled as his orgasm detonated way up into the linings of Christian's no longer quite so chaste cavity.

Spent, Chase carefully withdrew from deep inside Christian's anal canal, snapped off his rubber, tossed it to the bedside waste basket, and rolled over onto his back.

For the next few minutes, as they lay shoulder to shoulder, neither of them said a word, neither of them so much as stirred. They just stared up at the ceiling and dozed cozily in and out of a semi-somnambulistic consciousness. Slowly, they caught their breaths and drifted back down from their rapturous high. Without having to voice it, they both knew they had just experienced some kind of wondrous cosmic fuck, one of those once-in-a-lifetime events too few people ever find the good fortune to experience: a moment captured for posterity as the depth of their emotional connection actually surpassed their physical attraction.

No doubt about it. Hell had frozen over.

*   *   *   *

In one of those unexpected dramatic developments that no one saw coming, once exposed to it, Christian relished getting butt-fucked more than he ever could have imagined. And for the next few hours, he just couldn't get enough.

Seemingly insatiable, he insisted Chase make love to him over and over again, practically begging his muscle mentor to take him down with all the full athletic intensity, both physical and emotional, that his training partner could muster. They made love four or five times. Chase soon lost count of his and Christian's spectacular orgasms.

As Christian grew ever more oriented to the thrill of having his prostate erotically massaged, his bubble butt adapted to the alien sensation created by Chase's inner thrusts, and he soon felt transported. The full intensity of Chase's thick, solid flesh pounding away so deeply within him was like nothing he had ever experienced. He couldn't believe it took him so long to finally get past his resistance to the ultimate in carnal taboos. Their incredible consummation bonded him to Chase more strongly than anything he ever fantasized might be possible between teammates.

The following morning, Chase was slowly awakened by the sensual sensation of Christian's fingers sensually massaging into awareness the nipples on his pecs.

"Imagine how exhausted we'd be by now," Christian whispered into Chase's ear. "If we'd started fucking at the beginning of our trip and not the end."

Even in his fuzzy lack of focus, Chase sensed Christian wanted to be made love to yet again. "Somehow I think we could have managed it," Chase whispered back as he and Christian then shared a long, sweet good-morning kiss.

They made sublime love all over again, building toward the heated intensity of another rapturous orgasm. As he shot, the muscle monster spewed forth an uninhibited volley of vulgarities, paradoxically and inadvertently conjoining his guilt-ridden, sybaritic lust with his faithful observance, hollering out, "OH, GOD, CHASE, I LOVE YOU! OH, GOD, I LOVE YOU SO FUCKING MUCH!"

By the time they finally finished fooling around, they were already running late and hastily hurried to check out of their hotel. Christian surreptitiously packed into his suitcase all his freshly acquired steroids. As the juice was contraband in the U.S., he needed to smuggle it in. He hid his tiny vials of clear contraband liquid deep in the middle of a pair of rolled up sweat socks. He stuck the dirty socks in with the rest of his soiled underwear inside a plastic bag, which he packed inside his valise. Along with his contraband drugs, Christian also made a point to pack into his luggage a pile of fresh guilt.

He and Chase both donned loud Hawaiian shirts and huge sombreros they purchased at the outdoor market. They hoped to look more like tasteless tourists than vile, vial-carrying drug runners.

They flew early that evening back home to Los Angeles. However, it wasn't until he and Chase were aloft that the realization first hit Christian. *How did this happen?* He asked himself. *After years of denial, doing everything to avoid it, turns out I really am gay, after all — just like any other flaming bone smoker — and not only gay, but in love with another man. Holy shit!*

Pipsi wasn't due back from Lake Tahoe for another day. As the pilot announced the plane's descent into Los Angeles, Chase studied Christian's saddened face and tried elevating his spirits by inviting the muscle monster to sleep with him that night in his bed up in Hyde Park.

Christian smiled. That was just the invitation he hoped to receive, the perfect cap to their fantasy vacation. He even insisted upon taking Chase to dinner that evening at a fancy restaurant.

*   *   *   *

Their dinner that evening at Neptune's Net, on the beach in Malibu, was the ideal romantic ending to what seemed more like a magical getaway than just some routine excursion across the border to pick up contraband commodities. Chase told Christian how grateful he was to him for finally giving so much of himself. The only reason he didn't allude to their dream vacation as a honeymoon was that one of the grooms was already married.

Once back at Hyde Park, Chase and Christian embraced each other and began kissing even before they got past the front door. They each sensed something bittersweet about the joyous lovemaking that ensued. Even in their heightened excitement, something within each of them couldn't shake the fact that Pipsi was returning home the following day, and that meant they'd both have to swiftly adjust to Christian's no longer being quite so independent a muscle spirit. Without having to verbalize it, they both knew their fantasy of putting Christian's double life on hold was nearing its end, and there was nothing either of them could do to change that.

While sleeping together throughout the cool hours of the night, they clung to each other with even more subconscious tenderness than usual, each of them quietly aware they wouldn't be sleeping together again in so comforting a manner, so secure a feeling of belonging, for who knew how long?

When they awakened early the next morning, they made rapturous love all over again. After collectively detonating still another powerful mutual orgasm, they remained entwined while their heartbeats returned to less frenetic levels of pulsation. Then, out of the blue, Christian quietly mentioned he had something to confess.

"And just what might that be, Big Guy?" Chase wanted to know.

"Simply this, Chase," said Christian. "I'm not so sure I can keep this to myself any longer. Sure, it's crazy, and I know I never anticipated this, but the fact is, I think I've fallen in love with you."

There, he said it. For the first time in his life, he actually told another man he loved him and, oddly enough, and to both his surprise and relief, a bolt of lightning didn't rocket down through the ceiling to take him out in a ball of fire.

Caught unawares by Christian's surprise confession, Chase was at first uncertain as to how he might best respond. Rather than risk what might later be regarded as a regrettable reaction, he instead grabbed a chunk of hair at the back of Christian's head and planted a big wet, deeply sensual kiss of gratitude on his boyfriend's thick, sensuous lips.

*   *   *   *

Half an hour later, Chase and Christian sat across from each other at the breakfast table, sipping steaming Kona coffee and downing protein from Coach's muscle-building, six-egg-white frittata.

The caffeine in Christian's coffee had its usual jump-start effect and, after his second mug, he went on about how surprised he was by his own true feelings. After gulping down the last of Chase's expensive Hawaiian Jo, he looked his workout partner straight in the eye, wrapped Chase's hand in his own, and further confessed, "I'm finally prepared to give it all to you, Chase. My whole heart. I want you to take it and I'll be right here for you if, in return, you'll also give me yours. That is, if by some miracle, you're up to accepting all the love I have to share."

Gulp!

There it was, fallen onto the breakfast table with a thud, a five-hundred-pound barbell, suddenly scattered amid the empty frittata dishes. Christian had again uttered the dreaded L word, and not just at the height of an ecstatic sexual release. L-O-V-E. Amazing, how immediate and dramatic an effect those four little letters can have on the dynamics of a relationship.

Chase did his best to appear unflustered as he squeezed Christian's hand in return, and leaned forward to again kiss the big man on his full lips. "Thank you," he acknowledged softly, not knowing what else to say. "That means a lot to me."

"In love with another man …" Christian softly reflected, as he peered down into his coffee mug. "Who would have ever guessed, huh? Me, Christian Falconer, your basic macho-jock muscle monster, in love with another man."

"Life," Chase suggested in understatement, "doesn't always work out the way you expect."

"Back when I was a kid," Christian recalled, "we used to pick on all those fruity guys in school. Fuck, man — now I've become one of 'em. Can you imagine what the guys on my football team would say if they knew I was in love with a guy?"

Chase didn't have the answer to Christian's question, and wasn't even sure if he was also in love. At his core, he had little idea what true love should even feel like. Since he never delved past minor infatuations, other than his platonic love for Kutchie, this was uncharted, alien territory. Christian's unsolicited pronouncement touched him deeply, and he wanted to believe and accept as genuine the sincerity of the muscle monster's affections.

Was it time to finally break away from his familiar pattern of turning his back on any romance the moment it got too hot, too intense? Maybe Christian truly was different from most other men. Maybe he wouldn't disengage if Chase dared to return his love.

Chase took Christian's hand, held on to it tightly, and figured what the hell, he might as well take the big man at his word, may as well take this *love* business out for a test drive. He opted to stop making sense and quietly responded, "Well, guess what? As fate would have it, I'm in love with you."

*   *   *   *

Hesitantly, reluctantly, Chase and Christian simultaneously let down their mutual, heavily fortified defenses as, avidly, they accepted each other's devotion, and luxuriated in a joyful extension of their honeymoon period. Even after Pipsi returned from her family reunion in Tahoe, Chase noticed how little her renewed presence fazed his workout partner. Was it Chase's imagination, or was Christian spending less and less quality time with his wife, and more and more with him?

For the next few glorious weeks, Christian felt no measurable guilt about sneaking away from his father-in-law's nursery to spend time with Chase. With every passing day, he grew ever more comfortable about their same-sex relationship. Christian's premature ejaculations were no longer an issue, and they made love for hours.

In his few fleeting moments of lucidity, Chase suspected that nothing but an unfulfilled dead-end lay ahead for both of them in their uneasy match-up. However, he also realized he had little choice but to see their affair through to its conclusion, especially since he was so infatuated.

Both bodybuilders began acknowledging aloud their devotion and commitment. The thin veneer of denial which previously protected Christian's facade finally cracked open, and he and Chase found themselves offering each other wholeheartedly corny expressions of affection on the order of, "You mean the world to me," or "I care so much, I'd take a bullet for you," every time they got together, whenever they parted company and, of course, every time they made love.

Chase had never before offered anyone all his love. He had never once, in all his years of taking down so many well-muscled lads, told even one of them that he loved them, not even casually or in passing. Kutchie was the first and last man for whom he felt any sense of true commitment, and outside of their slam-bang one time together, they hadn't even remained sexual partners.

Christian was the first man since Kutchie to carve his way so deeply into Chase's spirit, so much further than any one before, and he soon started feeling fine about articulating those theretofore dreaded, dangerous, and forbidden words: *I love you.*

It wasn't long before they were repeating those sentiments to each other — exchanging declarations of total affection in every way, from soft whispers to loud proclamations. Christian never tired of hearing Chase express his feelings, never stopped offering back those three life-affirming, dreamy words to his lover man.

For these two big men, it turned into a captivating interval of unmitigated emotional outpouring. As ravenous sybarites, they luxuriated in their deeply intense and highly fulfilling sexual activity. Lost in the ecstatic embrace of their heated romance, they each began to see the slightest chance that, with a bit of luck and a lot of obstacles to overcome, they might somehow actually find some way to get past their significant impediments.

The fundamental shift in their emotional connection was soon evident even in their body language during workouts. An impartial observer watching them interacting in the gym might have thought they were intoxicated from the spirited manner in which they traversed from barbell to dumbbell, from bench press to Nautilus machine.

Christian sometimes rested a warm, encouraging hand atop of one of Chase's sturdy quads and pressed down hard, sensually, into the thick muscle as his workout partner fought hard to hammer out an extra rep or two while finishing off a set of heavy leg extensions.

Similarly, when Chase stood behind Christian as he sat at the Smith machine and spotted the muscle monster, he softly counted out every rep and offered encouragement as the big man executed super-heavy shoulder presses. "One, two ... That's it, Christian ... three ... all you ... that's four ... big and strong ... excellent ... five ... push it up, Buddy, pump hard ... six ... gimme three more ... push harder ... that's it ... yeah ... just two more ... big delts, Babe ... biggest in the gym ... come on, Christian ... just one more ... for me ... last one ... push hard, do it for your Coach ... you got it, Big Guy. Good set!"

$$*\qquad*\qquad*\qquad*$$

Christian's carefree days of guilt-free abandonment didn't last long. All too soon, the demons that tore at him long before he professed his undying love for Chase began slowly creeping back into his restless spirit. One early morning, he just couldn't sleep. Lying flat on his back in bed, wide awake in the soft gray first light of an early dawn, next to a still-slumbering, softly snoring Pipsi, he stared up at the shadows dancing on the ceiling, and ruminated over his forbidden romance. Plagued by a troubling insomnia for several nights running, he wondered in that wee hour just how much longer he might be able to juggle so many mortally sinful balls in the air.

It bothered him that in a perfect world, he'd be lying next to Chase rather than Pipsi. Still, he knew he had to remain committed to his heaven-blessed union. During his infrequent moments of objective clarity, a part of Christian knew his affair with Chase, by the very drawbacks of its deception, was destined for disappointment. But he also knew he was in love with Chase. He loved the way he and his workout partner connected, loved exploring and worshipping every single inch of Chase's nonpareil musculature. He loved it when Chase flexed the Guns of Navarone for him while he beat his thick meat until he shot. Although he couldn't know it at the time, that tantalizing vision and its erotic imagery would turn into a favored masturbatory fantasy, one that would stay with Christian the rest of his life.

As for the present, Christian knew he had strayed far from the fold. There could be no successful future in his sinful male pairing. Even so, no matter how often he tried to walk away from Chase and return to his walk with the Lord, he just couldn't bring himself to do it. Not yet.

Christian's turbulent daybreak rumination was interrupted by the peeps of a small bird chirping somewhere out in the yard. The muscle monster tried composing the words he might summon should he decide to come clean and tell Pipsi about his affair with Chase. But no matter how he phrased them, he knew she would only feel betrayed should he ever confess so twisted a revelation. When Christian again heard the songbird's cheerful tweets greeting the sun's first rays, he rolled on to his side and tried as hard as he could to ignore its sweet tone so that he might fall back to sleep.

*   *   *   *

On any given day, while driving over to the gym, Christian resolutely promised, no *swore* to himself he would definitely *not* be going back to Chase's house in Laurel Canyon once they finished pumping up. He begged God for the strength it would require to help him from being led astray and yielding to temptation … yet again.

His resolve was unfailingly short-lived. By the time he walked into the gym, he had only to take one look at Chase, waiting for him at the barbell rack, looking so hot and sexy in his tank top and gym shorts, and the muscle monster's resistance melted. In the time it took to turn off a lamp, Christian miraculously managed to table the sum of his righteous intentions, and from that moment on, looked forward to again following Chase home as soon as they finished their workout.

After all this depraved sex, thought Christian, in a burst of rationalization. *After so much damned sinning, hell, what's one more lapse?*

The deal he made to himself as he smiled back at Chase was that he'd postpone his chafing remorse and not let it resurface again … at least not until after he shot his load.

But then — as if by magic, and no longer to either of their surprise — the moment Christian's spiritual conviction elbowed its way back into the forefront of his troubled psyche, his curtain of guilt descended between them. That was when he took an emotional step away from Chase and temporarily withdrew.

Adding to their stress, the latest stacked cycle of steroids Christian insisted upon injecting, often rendered him so wired, they made his sudden, one-hundred-eighty-degree mood swings that much more unpredictable. The 'roid rage generated by his overload of testosterone could find him calm and easygoing one moment, then suddenly expressing his frustrations in explosive outbursts the next.

No matter how much eruptive anger Christian displayed, however, he always calmed down, always came back, and consistently apologized to Chase for his behavior. He begged forgiveness from his boyfriend, asked him to please understand it wasn't him. It was the consummate shame he was feeling, amplified by the outlawed drugs he was injecting, that were causing his explosive overreactions.

After weeks of watching Christian running the gamut of emotions from friendly and warm to distant and aloof, from pleasant to moody to downright 'roid-raging hostile, Chase finally sat the big guy down to let him know it was crazy for them not to make some much-needed changes. Chase spelled it out and bluntly told Christian he could no longer have it both ways — could no longer hold on to both his blistering guilt and their torrid affair. In the final analysis, Christian had no choice but to choose between them.

"Time to make up your mind, Big Guy," Chase told him candidly, one late afternoon while they were lying cozily together in bed after still another blazing session of lovemaking. "All this back and forth between your home life and our love life is driving you crazy and making me far too uncomfortable. So, here's the deal: you either stay with me and walk away from Pipsi and your extravagant lifestyle, or you break up with me and stay with her. It's obvious by now you can't have it both ways. I never thought I'd end up playing The Other Woman, and I just can't do it anymore, okay? Pipsi or me, Pal — one or the other, but not both."

"Don't force me to choose," Christian warned. "You know I don't take well to threats."

"This is no threat," Chase assured him and planted an affectionate kiss on the big guy's lips. "It's simply the way things are. You know how I feel. Now the choice is yours."

"But you know how much I love you," Christian said, burying his face deep into Chase's pecs.

"And I love you, too," Chase said softly. "But you have to decide."

"You make it sound so easy," said Christian. "First, my mother took care of me. Then Robin took care of me. Now Pipsi takes care of me. Obviously, *someone* needs to take care of me. And I don't think you're prepared to do that."

Chase nodded in agreement. "I can barely take care of myself. That's why I've been trying to help you find some way to set all this straight with God."

Without warning, Christian erupted, banged his fist hard on the night table and bolted up in bed. "What the hell would you know about me and God?" He barked angrily. "This isn't something I can set straight, damn it! It's not negotiable. It's God's word, period. What we're doing is a sin! Can't you see that? Maybe if you took this whole Christianity thing a little more seriously, you might better appreciate the hell I've been going through."

Christian huffed his way into the bathroom, slammed the door shut and tried wrestling with his demons by calming down with a hot shower. While soaping his chest, he wondered how long his life with Chase could remain tucked cozily away in the back of his chaotic, cluttered closet. He knew he dreaded the thought of losing his lover, and that was when he first considered finally facing head on his incipient homosexuality. Maybe what he needed to do was reveal to his wife the sordid reality of his true inner self. On the other hand, maybe not.

Christian twirled off the shower faucets, reached for a towel, and wondered how much longer he could continue reaping the considerable comforts bestowed upon the son-in-law of his wife's prosperous father. Was it time to strike out on his own and try building from scratch some entirely new alternative career somewhere else?

By a remarkable coincidence, the muscle monster's major dilemma over which road to take was decided for him one night in early May. Chase and Christian finished yet another heated, intensely sexual and very loving encounter, and then followed up their lovemaking with an equally heated and intense shouting match over whether or not Christian should finally drop the charade and confront Pipsi with the truth.

While driving back home to Hancock Park, Christian examined his life and weighed his options. As he mulled over the pros and cons of which way he should turn, he came to a halt at a red light two blocks from his house, and made up his mind.

The time to stand up and take responsibility for his actions, he decided, had long passed. *"A real man faces his destiny!"* He said half aloud, mindfully slapping the top of his steering column. *"An honest man tells the truth."*

At last, as his clouds of confusion parted, he knew what he had to do. His mind made up, he would sit Pipsi down and confront his hidden inner demons by pouring out all that was on his heart. He would start with a few cups of coffee, start rambling, and then just let it all out, simply tell her the awful truth.

As Christian pulled into the circular driveway leading to his front entrance, he sensed a momentary peace, along with a calming sense of closure.

At long last prepared to confess everything, he would just get it all off his massive chest, let his dear wife know in no uncertain terms that he couldn't hold back any longer because, truth be told, her sinning husband was not merely unfaithful, but also in love with another man.

*   *   *   *

"We have to talk." Christian apprehensively summoned the courage to say to his wife, halfway through dinner, while gobbling down Pipsi's perfectly seared Albacore tuna. "There's something I have to tell you."

Before he got the chance to blurt it out and lift the heavy burden of his deep deception, Pipsi was characteristically coquettish as she also confessed, "Small world, Darling. Because I have oh, a little something or other to tell you."

"And what might that be?" A patient Christian feigned interest even as he temporarily tabled spilling the beans.

"Do you remember the night of our last dinner party a couple of months ago?" Pipsi asked animatedly.

"Vaguely ..." Christian answered, warily.

"Well, Darling, after Norm and Sally and Lisa and Chase all went home, do you remember how you and I enjoyed some ... private time and ... well, I went to see Dr. Sandler today."

"And what'd he say?" asked Christian.

"Oh ... simply that I'm twelve weeks pregnant."

Pregnant ... The word reverberated in Christian's head and bounced around his cerebral cortex until it waned into a diminishing echo. Yes, his mind assured him. That was the word she just used: Pregnant. As in: *With child.*

That was all Christian needed to hear. He sprang out from his chair, knocking it over as he dropped to his knees directly before his wife, and then wrapped his huge arms around her tiny waist. Overcome with emotion and elation, he buried his face deep into her lap and began to sob.

While wailing into Pipsi's stomach, Christian quickly prayed God would see his hyper-emotional outburst as nothing less than his sincere act of repentance, a contrition that might somehow, over time, miraculously start wiping away some of his extreme blameworthiness.

"Don't you see?" Christian mumbled, between sobs. "My prayers have been answered. I'm so damned, I mean I'm so darned overjoyed ... You have no idea!"

Pipsi gently stroked the back of her husband's neck. She was pleased to see how elated he was with this blessed news. "Yes, yes, Darling, I know," she said softly, and kissed the top of his head. "So now that we have my good news out of the way, you said there was something you had to tell me?"

Christian raised his head and looked straight into his wife's eyes. "Tell you?" He asked, mystified, and then lied, "Oh, that — it was nothing, believe me. Nothing of any consequence."

Pipsi wiped away a tear running down her husband's face. "I waited until you got home before calling Mommy and Daddy. I can hardly wait to hear Daddy congratulate you on becoming his new Vice President and senior partner!"

"What'd I ever do to deserve you?" Christian wanted to know. "I'm just a dumb jock."

"Who cares, Darling?" Pipsi planted another sweet kiss on her husband's forehead. "Just so long as you're *my* dumb jock."

Christian tightened his strong nineteen-inch arms around Pipsi's teeny waist, drew her closer, and again broke down and wept uncontrollably into her lap.

✳   ✳   ✳   ✳

Christian cut Chase off faster than you could say, "It's a boy!" — dropped him without benefit of any detailed explanation. He did, however, take the trouble to leave a short, blunt, phone message on Chase's answering machine, saying he would no longer be drawn into any of Chase's prohibitive, sinful games, and that they could no longer train together as workout partners because he was not only switching gyms, but also praying to God, begging the Lord to grant them both forgiveness for having drifted so far from the revealed Word. He hoped Chase might have a good life and never mentioned a word about Pipsi's pregnancy.

Christian returned to his expectant wife full time, got back into step with his walk with the Lord and, as promised, accepted the huge raise that went along with his promotion to a full partnership at Sterling Enterprises.

By sharp contrast, Chase took a devastating emotional punch, straight to his gut. Losing not just a wonderful lover and hot boyfriend, but also an invaluable workout partner all at the same time, left him confounded. The defeat hit Chase hardest in his ego, and forced him to retreat behind the barricade of his carefully constructed persona.

Chase had always been the first to walk away from any deepening relationship, and was not used to losing, not when it came to romance. He would not allow Christian's sudden disengagement to distress him. He needed to display no outward emotion that might manifest the stinging rejection he felt so deeply. He needed to remain stoic and strong, needed to get past the rejection, needed to put Christian's crushing dismissal behind him. To those ends, he resolved to be vigilant before ever again letting down his guard, before he might ever again offer his love so openly to another person. Hard as nails was the stance Chase elected to project. Why bother going after heart and soul, he figured, when all you really needed to get by was muscle?

From that day forward, Chase pursued nothing but hard, fast and erotic muscle sex, period. Slam, bam, thank you, man — now get dressed and get the fuck out. No more senseless hanging around, getting to know his trick after a sensational orgasm. No more warm and fuzzy online sentimental blather on the order of: *I like long walks on the beach at sunset, or snuggling up in front of a cozy fire with a hot toddy and a hotter body.* No more sleepovers or second dates. On those infrequent occasions when he might see a guy again, it was only if their muscle reunion was spaced weeks apart.

Emerging from all this pain and disappointment was Coach's cardinal commandment: *Love is for losers.* No sooner was his latest trick out the door than Chase couldn't help but wonder, *Who's next?*

Chase assumed there were some couples out there, guys who'd been together twelve years or so who still had sex once, maybe twice a week. God bless 'em. Most partners, however, Chase was convinced, let their physical intimacy lapse once an outside flirtation muddied the waters, or after their first quarrel or financial crisis, or maybe at the first sign of a wrinkle on their lover's brow.

Beyond his fresh, self-imposed declaration of emotional independence, Chase worked hard at getting himself over Christian in the same way he had gotten past the trauma of Kutchie's death: by diving straight back, not only into his training, but also into his writing.

He knew the time had long since come and gone when he should have returned to his craft, anyway. So he resolved to get back on track with his ho-hum career and simply sat down one morning and began the protracted process of pounding out another long form project.

Once again, Chase returned to his former solid working habits. Up early, and staying glued to his computer, writing until he strung together those four pages he insisted become his minimal daily output. He wouldn't even permit himself license to leave for the gym until he was totally satisfied with that day's assembly of words. The subject of his work was an obvious choice.

What he wrote about was Christian. He concocted a picaresque tale about the great difficulty a deeply religious, contest-winning bodybuilder has in confronting his homosexuality.

After six months of intensive writing, the purge that paved his productivity paid off when he completed a first draft of his second novel, a tome he titled *Pumping Irony*.

Prior to his affair with Christian, Chase always played along with the fantasy he created in his alter ego as the Coach. After his heart was broken, however, he simply took on its mantle as nothing less than the genuine article. Simile waxed into metaphor as his nickname became cold reality. In a seamless segue, he morphed his alter ego into his libido and overnight went from acting out the part of the Coach, to in essence *becoming* the Coach.

Casting Christian out from his troubled psyche helped Chase relieve much of his pain. Once he again felt free, he locked up his heart and tossed away its proverbial key. After that, he never again strayed from his pledge, his commitment to remain above the emotional fray. That is, until the time ten years later when he met Hunter Rowe.

But that of course, is our other story.

*   *   *   *

BOOK FOUR:

MUSCLE BOUND

"A true friend stabs you in the front."

— Oscar Wilde

HAPPILY NEVER AFTER

Chase returned home from his transcendent stay with Hunter in New York City and quickly settled back into the familiar grind of his daily routine: the gym, the gym, and the gym. The major impact on his life by then, ten years after getting over his affair with Christian, was how he felt about his new boyfriend. Not only did Chase actually miss Hunter more than he ever expected, he could also hardly wait for them to be reunited. Without ever really looking for it, he had uncovered the art of loving, of being loved in return. Erotic images of the Kid constantly played on his mind, not unlike a recurring tune you can't shake from your head. He treasured the secure feeling deep in his gut that once again there was someone in his life about whom he cared so damn deeply. Waking up exhilarated each morning gave him newfound purpose. Hunter's very essence seemed to accompany him throughout his day, wherever he went. It was as if the very spirit of his hot muscle boy had moved in and taken up a welcome residence within the confines of his psyche. Soon, their daily phone chats and numerous e-mails were no longer enough to quench his desire. He needed to be lying in bed next to Hunter, the two of them kissing exuberantly, holding on to each other, and, of course, indulging in their personalized grand and glorious love-making.

*   *   *   *

On a late Friday afternoon in April, Hunter's week-old request for a meeting with Dan Esterhausen, one of his agency's seven vice-presidents, was finally granted. Industry chatter about the Boy Wonder's crackerjack promotional campaigns was so flattering, that three of the town's top agencies were competing with offers to woo him away from Broad & Harris.

Through the protocols of expensive lunches at The Four Seasons and extended cocktails at 21, senior management at these rival agencies were luring Hunter over to their side of Madison Avenue. Each in their turn dangled the carrot sticks of significantly higher salaries, plus tantalizing incentives, bonuses, and perks.

Inflated with confidence, Hunter bounded into his four o'clock appointment five minutes early, still rehearsing his list of demands for more money and greater responsibility. He was fully prepared to walk away, in search of greener pastures, should his terms not be met. Once ushered into the executive's office, however, he was gratified when Vice-President Esterhausen told him how the top management at Broad & Harris was so satisfied with his productivity, they were officially raising his salary another $1000 a month.

Hunter smiled and sank deeper into the soft cushion of the ultra suede chair. Esterhausen went on to further assure Hunter that since he was delivering such exceptional results, much to the satisfaction of their clientele, he was also fast-tracking the young man toward an early vice-presidency, a promotion that could conceivably come through before year's end. Hunter made an effort to appear humbled by so laudatory an affirmation of his standing within the firm.

"However," Esterhausen went on, waxing philosophic, "as we know by now, here on Madison Avenue as in life, there's no such thing as give without take. So, in return for your salary hike, you're going to need to give even more of yourself, Hunter, to become even more of a team player. We all know Broad & Harris' most preferred personnel are those loyal and fully focused staff members who are even more married to the firm than to their own spouses."

"Fine with me, Mr. Esterhausen," Hunter said candidly. "Hell, in many ways, I already feel married to the agency."

"That's the kind of can-do spirit we like around here," Esterhausen exclaimed, punctuating his enthusiasm by punching his fist into his hand.

Hunter made a point to *not* project the excitement he felt, even as a joyous flutter of butterflies giddily tickled the pockets of his intestines. Rather than jumping up in uninhibited joy, he stood, stepped forward and projected an all-business demeanor as he firmly shook the vice-president's hand. "Sir, I truly enjoy my work here at Broad and Harris," he calmly told him, "and I plan to give it everything I've got!"

Going back out there as a fully committed team player, Hunter lifted his shoulders high as he left the Vice-President's office. The moment he returned to his desk, he called Chase in Los Angeles to report his major career news, and to assure him that even though he'd be working harder than ever, devoting ever more time and energies to his chosen vocation, he also emphasized that Chase was still foremost in his thoughts, still the most vital emotional element in his life.

*   *   *   *

The surgeon who performed the hernia operation on Chase was pleased with the success of the procedure, but also insisted that Chase put his training on hold and stay away from the gym for at least a month while his groin area healed.

A few mornings after that, Hunter called with exciting news. "Hey, Coach" he sang in greeting. "Didn't I promise I'd figure out some way to bring us together for another major round of muscle fantasy fulfillment?"

"What have you got up your long-distance sleeve?" Chase was eager to learn.

"Oh, just this," said Hunter, hoping to sound nonchalant. "The powers that be are sending me out west again, this time for a two-day marketing conference in San Diego, ten days from now."

"So far, so good! Go on."

"Here's my plan. From there, I'll just hop up to L.A. to pick you up, and then I'm finally taking some of my hard-earned vacation time, plus a ton of my long-accumulated mileage, because the two of us are heading out for a week in mid-April, you guessed it, Coach: all the way to Hawaii."

"You gotta be shitting me!"

"Hey, what kind of a marketing wizard would I be if I couldn't make my dream man's dream fantasy vacation come true? It was a no-brainer. I've even upgraded us so we'll be flying there First Class."

"Is this for real?" Coach asked, elated, but also wary, wondering if Hunter wasn't playing some kind of mischievous prank.

"What can I say?" Hunter laughed. "Your boy felt the crowded Coach class just wasn't good enough for his classy Coach."

"This is nuts!"

"Wait. It gets better. I just finished sealing the deal on a one-week's ocean view condo, one with its own lanai, up in the hills above Kona. Just as you always dreamed. You can teach me how to surf. I'll teach you how to drink rum. It'll be you and me, Coach. The two of us, fucking our brains out while having great muscle sex under waterfalls for a whole week, practically honeymooning in fucking paradise."

"Sounds beyond great," Chase quietly told him with evident disappointment in his voice. "Just one problem. Those dates won't work for me. The thirteenth's the day I head out to Palm Springs with Stack and Adam and Craig for the White Party. You were going to see if you could move things around so you could join us, remember? We've been planning it for months."

"We're talking Hawaii here," Hunter offered, in a facile dismissal of Chase's conflict of interest. "This is *your* fantasy, Big Guy. Not mine. And my dates for San Diego are locked in. It's business. Can't be changed. Don't you think your friends will understand?"

"No," Chase lamented. "I don't think they will."

"If they're true friends, they will," said Hunter. "They want what's best for you, no? And what's best for you would be to get back to Hawaii. Isn't that what you said you always wanted? Besides, Boss, maybe it's time you realized … it's all just you and me. Everyone else is just scenery."

"Cute," Chase acknowledged. "And there's another problem. Money. You know the couple living in my back unit the past few years? They moved out a month and a half ago and so far, not so much as a nibble from a new tenant. The market sucks right now. I keep lowering the rental price, but still no takers. So until I get back into some positive cash flow, I just can't afford that kind of extravagance and …"

"Excuse me, Coach," Hunter interrupted Chase's discourse. "Did you hear anyone on this end of the conversation mention anything about shared costs? Didn't I just tell you I'm in the business of making dreams come true? What kind of fantasy fulfillment would this be if you shelled out for it?"

"But I just can't accept that kind of generosity," Chase said, stubbornly. "You're not *that* well-off … well, not yet."

"Don't be silly. This fantasy's on me. Let's be grateful at least one of us is flush right now. Tell you what: how 'bout if once you've written your third novel and after it takes off, you can fly us both to Paris for dinner?"

"Kid, you got a deal!"

"Besides, it's me, Hunter — your number one muscle boy. And what's more, I plan to take care of *everything:* the condo, the rental car, all meals, our recreation — hell, the whole damn luau."

"But what can I do in return?" asked Chase, dizzied by such affirmation.

"Just show up in your sexiest shorts and keep those big Kahuna guns flexed in my face, Big Daddy!" Hunter answered, all smiles. "Besides, by now you must know, what's mine is yours."

"I can't go to Hawaii with you," Chase protested. "I haven't been to the gym in almost a month."

"Like I care!" Hunter responded, forcefully. "Hey, it's you I love. Your beautiful body's just frosting on the cock."

Chase lowered his defenses. "You sure drive a hard bargain."

"Does that mean we're on, Coach?"

"That means you better start waxing down your surfboard, Dude. You got yourself one totally stoked surfing buddy! Cowabunga!"

*   *   *   *

Invigorated and filled with heightened expectations, Chase and Hunter landed at the airport in Kona in collective high spirits. Chase left Atlas under the supervision of his tenant, Gloria Bishop, and Hunter left the pressure of his professional life back in New York. After picking up their rental car, they drove high into the hills, to the gatehouse of an upscale gated community, where they picked up the keys to their spacious ground-level condo. The one-bedroom unit, a handsomely furnished, top-of-the-line property, came replete with full kitchen and a private, lushly landscaped lanai with its own knockout panoramic view, overlooking the blue Pacific. Paradise, indeed!

By the time they unpacked and showered, it was time to unwind and watch the sunset astride the handsome loungers out on their lanai.

Naked of both clothes and inhibitions, they quietly watched as the celebrated Hawaiian sunset didn't disappoint. A dazzling panoply of color tinted the sky as the sun lingered lazily over a far-off ocean horizon. Spectacular and dramatic, the fiery star dissolved into an endless sea at the end of the world. Its bucolic majesty reminded Chase of the great Hawaiian vacation with his parents decades earlier.

Chase and Hunter experienced the entire metamorphosis into twilight with no need for words. Silently, they lay side by side on cushiony chaises, collectively observing the calming pastel-blue sky. They watched in reverence as it muted leisurely into an unabashed blush of bright crimson, and then toned itself back down, gradually deepening into vibrant shades of orange and yellow. In its final moments, the day climaxed when the sky slowly segued into a gradation of gray that slowly blended into the blue-black mystery of evening.

Once night fell, Chase and Hunter drove down into Kona and exchanged flirtatious gropes beneath the tablecloth during their candlelit dinner of grilled mahi-mahi, served on the lanai of one of the local seafood restaurants. Chase was finishing up his regimen of post-op antibiotics and still couldn't drink alcohol. Hunter, however, announced he was so happy to be away from the stress of work and so deep into vacation mode, he granted himself license to break training. Proving his point, he had one mai-tai and then ordered another, and then went ahead and slurped down a third.

After dinner, the muscle buddies pulled into a nearby supermarket to pick up a few staples. Hunter was still so becalmed from all the rum he drank, he stayed in the car and catnapped while Chase went shopping.

While standing in line, waiting to check out, Chase's cart was filled with their week's worth of groceries. One of the locals behind him, a woman in her fifties, far too tan, with lined, leathery skin from decades of worshiping her sun goddess, struck up a friendly conversation. She let Chase in on what she insisted was privileged information about a local hidden trail that led up to Kanikinichi Falls, a little known, secluded waterfall high in the hills. She whispered this information to him as though she was passing along top secret data regarding the natural wonder best-visited, she claimed, right after a heavy rain. That was when the cascade would be at its most thunderous.

By the time they returned to their condo, Chase was drowsy from jet lag, Hunter wobbly from mai-tai overload. So they quickly undressed, fell into bed and, by the soothing, soporific lull of the ocean's distant roar, quickly dozed off, locked in each other's strong arms.

*   *   *   *

Given the prevailing weather patterns in that area of the world, Chase wasn't surprised by the intensity of the pounding jungle rain that greeted them the following morning. The tropical storm soaked their "dry" side of the island for more than three hours.

By early afternoon, as the stormy clouds receded and the sun put in a welcome late morning appearance, Chase searched his map of the island until he found the hidden trail he'd been told about down at the market. He and Hunter then drove inland, over to the foothills of a nearby mountain range. After removing their tee shirts and donning backpacks, they hiked for two hours, foraging up an unmarked trail, way up off the beaten path, and soon found themselves traipsing through an enchanted tropical forest as they headed up, up toward the secluded waterfall.

When they stopped to take a break, Chase pulled out from his backpack a pair of bananas as well as a few handfuls of the macadamia nuts he'd packed for their hike.

Hunter was feeling ebullient about being in so idyllic a setting, and felt so completely devoted to Chase, he decided to commemorate the moment with a sincere, if sappy, gesture of affection. So he pulled out his small backpacking knife, walked up to a giant Norfolk pine in the middle of the thickly wooded area, and preceded to carve into its bark the shape of a small heart. Inside the heart, he then carefully etched their initials: **H.R. & C.H.**

Chase was genuinely moved by Hunter's sweet thoughtfulness.

"I know this is gonna sound all mushy and maybe not so butch," Hunter announced in warning. "But you gotta let me have just a short nellie break so I can tell you something that means a lot to me, okay?"

"Fire when ready!" Chase told him.

"Okay," said Hunter, as he placed a hand on Chase's shoulder. "Call me a sentimental old fool, but with everything going so well for us, and since it's so damn beautiful up here, I felt this urge to create some permanent record, some gesture demonstrating the strength of our love."

"You're right, Kiddo," Chase chided Hunter. "You're a sentimental old fool."

"That we know," said Hunter. "So now I'll pop the question: will you marry me?"

"Of course not," Chase snickered and punched Hunter smack in the shoulder. Hard.

"Ouch!" Hunter rubbed his shoulder with his open hand. "Too middle class conventional?"

"Too mundane heterosexual!" Chase responded.

"Okay, then, instead of getting married, how about if we instead make some kind of pledge of commitment to one another?"

"What'd you have in mind?" Chase asked, guardedly.

"Who knows?" Hunter smiled with a roguish shrug. "Some kind of vow, a sort of ... *covenant* between us, a solemn pledge to remain together for as long as we both shall love."

"You know that kind of talk makes me want to puke," Chase said causally.

"Normally, I'd say yes," Hunter agreed. "But right now, right here, with me, I'm not so sure. I think maybe you might like the idea of such a bond."

Chase wrapped his arms around Hunter with a warm embrace. "You mean, right here in front of God and Mother Nature and Father Time and anyone else who might be listening?" he asked.

"Yes," Hunter shot back. "Right here in front of the whole damn universe!"

Chase was so moved by Hunter's daringly sentimental, clearly loving gesture, he kissed his boyfriend solidly on the lips. "Fine with me!" he consented.

"I love you so much more than I ever expected," Hunter said with assurance as he took the plunge. "And so happily, I enter this loving covenant between us."

Hunter opened his heart with such a lack of reserve, Chase felt he had no recourse but to return the sentiment. Strange thing was he actually felt comfortable about joining in. On the spot, he decided it was time to start giving back some of the unending love the Kid had been spewing forth for so long. So, while standing alongside that Lord Norfolk pine, Chase took Hunter's unconditional commitment to heart and elected to let down his own guard, to finally reciprocate. He not only honored Hunter's long-sought request, but also topped his boyfriend's daring outpouring of saccharine sentimentality by actually dropping to one knee and taking hold of Hunter's right hand.

Caught up in the sheer euphoria of their captivating moment, with the dappled sun sprightly flickering all about, and the branches of surrounding pines seductively swaying in the warm breeze, he looked up at Hunter's beautifully sculpted torso, and softly asked, "Okay, Hunter ... since you asked for it, I've got exactly three words for you ..."

"Go fuck myself?"

"Close," Chase answered. "Simply this: I love you."

At long last, there they were, right out in the open: the most important three words Hunter waited half his lifetime to hear. However, even as he was moved to tears of elation, there was also something else about hearing that sentiment for which he had pined, something about hearing Chase finally returning so sincere an emotional response, something about it finally being expressed so freely, that just didn't sit right with him. Inexplicably, it didn't elate his spirit in the way he always dreamt it would. Rather than feeling the ecstatic reaction he'd so long anticipated, something unfamiliar within Hunter's temperament churned uneasily. He couldn't decipher whether the school of piranha suddenly circling his core was an acidic reaction from too much pineapple juice at breakfast, or some uninvited survival mechanism of apprehension and mistrust. He decided so much sudden unease was most likely a natural reaction to finally winning over his soul mate, to finally finding his true life partner.

So he elected to ignore whatever minor disturbance might be lurking about, unsettling his insides, in favor of accentuating what he knew unequivocally to be his true feelings. Looking down into Chase's blue eyes, he told him, sincerely, "Now don't throw up, but since you've already won my heart, I'm now giving it to you for safekeeping."

Chase rose up off bended knee and again kissed Hunter squarely on his sensual lips. When they broke from their tender embrace, the Coach noticed a reserve of tears welling up in Hunter's eyes.

"You're not going to start bawling on me again, are you, Baby?"

"Hey," Hunter wiped away a tiny tear. "I never claimed I wasn't the emotional type."

Their impromptu covenant established, their rest break concluded, Chase rose up and, after another deeply felt lip-lock, they again slipped into their backpacks and continued their journey uphill. Their plan, once alone up in their tropical Eden, was to undress and then romp around Mother Nature's bucolic wonder naked until they'd eventually make grand and impassioned love while frolicking beneath the surging flow of the falls which lay in wait.

Unfortunately, by the time they climbed to the top of the mountain and reached the falls, Hunter came down with one of his infrequent but nonetheless devastating migraines. He couldn't believe he was so far away from his Imitrex, left behind back at the condo. Almost as bad as the piercing pain by then lightning-flashing its punishing path across his vision, he and Chase further discovered when they finally reached the top of the hill that more than twenty other guests of the island, the lot of them obnoxious, had also been struck by the very same inspiration.

These camera-toting tourists, having in common only a desire for seclusion amid scenic grandeur, had evidently also heard the secret falls were a must-see after a heavy rain. In place of the calming solitude each of these visitors so vigorously pursued as they hiked to the top of Kanikinichi Falls, what these serenity seekers came upon instead was just another flock of squawking fellow travelers.

Hunter took one look around at all the rowdy people splashing about the natural spectacle and became instantly furious. Annoyed, he overreacted and took out the pain in his head and the disappointment of their trek on Chase, erupting, "Damn it! We came all the way for *this*? What a stupid, moronic waste of time!"

"I was told no one knew about this place," Chase countered.

"And you believed them! Let's just get the fuck out of here, okay?" Hunter insisted with unexpected vehemence. His outburst seemed especially surprising, coming so soon after the profound moment of loving and bonding he and Chase shared only half an hour earlier on their way up to the falls.

Without waiting for a reply, or even to see if Chase was following him, Hunter whirled around and headed straight back down the so-called secret trail.

By the time they reached the bottom of the footpath, Hunter was by then again becalmed, and he apologized for losing his temper. He blamed his mini-snit up at the falls on the untimely onset of his pounding migraine. Compounding matters, once he saw how futile had been their long hike, the pain in his head simply got worse.

As soon as they got back to their condo, Hunter downed a couple of his prescription migraine tablets. Unfortunately, his medicine delivered no measurable relief. He knew he was in far too much discomfort to either eat or drink, and was certainly in no condition to make love. Instead, he chose, right after showering, to forgo dinner. He knew from experience he had no choice but to retreat to their bedroom. He turned the air conditioning up high, shut the blinds and drew closed the curtains, blocking out all invasive light. Then he took a couple of Ambien and crawled into bed. He hoped a long night's rest might help get him past his throbbing pain.

*　　*　　*　　*

Early the next morning, Chase opened his eyes and smiled with satisfaction when he found his handsome lover lying in bed next to him, flat on his stomach, half awake, starting to stir. He still felt exhilarated from having finally expressed his love so openly the day before, and he gently stroked Hunter's butt cheek with his open hand and whispered softly into his ear, "Morning, lover boy."

Still half asleep, Hunter opened bleary eyes, but quickly buried his head deeper into his pillow and grumbled something unintelligible.

"Okay if I open the curtains?" Chase asked as he popped out of bed.

"No! Don't do that!" Hunter called out harshly from beneath his pillow. "Hate the light!"

"Sorry, Pal," said Chase, stepping back from the window. "Still got that awful migraine?"

"Damn it, yes!" Hunter complained bitterly into his mattress. "And on our vacation, too. Talk about bad timing, huh? I'm so sorry, Chase."

"No need to apologize," Chase assured him. "What can I do to help?"

"Can you find me a new brain?" Hunter asked, half in earnest.

"How 'bout some breakfast in bed?"

"How 'bout if you just leave me alone?" asked Hunter. When he looked up and saw Chase taken aback by his sharp invective, he quickly added, "Trust me, it's nothing personal. Honest. But whenever I get one of these fuckers, it drives me into a stinking, rotten mood, and it's best if I'm just left alone."

"Damn, I was going to take you surfing today."

"I know," said Hunter. "But I can't. Go by yourself, okay? That's what you can do to help."

Chase raised hands of surrender. "If that's what you want."

"It is," Hunter assured him. "I'm feeling kind of paralyzed. I should be better in a few hours."

After reaching for his surfing trunks, Chase blew Hunter a kiss, and then left him alone in the darkened bedroom to sleep through his significant pain.

*   *   *   *

Chase jumped into their rental car and drove over to a nearby black sand beach known to be ideal for surfing. After slathering his body in waterproof sunblock, he rented an old-fashioned long board, which he took under wing and then charged forward, into the shimmering water. After hopping up on his knees, he paddled out several hundred yards, toward the general direction of Japan.

Bobbing up and down in the water, he then spent the next several hours carefully picking out the cream of the crop among the six or seven waves in any given set rolling lyrically toward shore. As he singled out a wave he wanted to catch, he paddled vigorously ahead of it and fought to stay abreast until just the right moment when he propelled his board forward with sufficient momentum for him to hop up off his knees and land on his feet.

Chase was left-handed, so he goofy-footed, planting his left foot in front of himself, his right directly behind, and securing them both to the waxy surface of the board as he caught the wave. Maintaining his precarious balance, he then rode the roaring, graceful, sensuous force of nature until his ride ended in a thunderous burst of energy. The wave rolled to the end of its run and folded over, splattering into oblivion as it disappeared into the shoreline.

The moment his exhilarating ride ran out of the steam, Chase hopped off his board and, as if on autopilot, promptly flipped about and once again paddled fiercely back out toward the horizon.

*   *   *   *

High up in the hills, Hunter passed the hours inside his darkened room, restlessly flopping about beneath the sheets, catching intermittent catnaps, doing his best to sleep off the excruciating daggers still slicing their way into his cranial cavity.

By late afternoon, when Chase returned to their condo, looking vibrantly suntinted and feeling stoked from his great day in the water, Hunter was still fighting off his demonic migraine.

Chase brought a tray filled with a pot of herbal peppermint tea and a few pieces of whole-wheat toast to Hunter's bedside, but his boyfriend had no appetite for nourishment. He wanted only to further knock himself out again, to escape his paralyzing pain, so he swallowed another couple of Ambien and was sound asleep by seven that evening.

Hunter slept straight through the night, which turned out to be a good thing, because when he opened his eyes early the following morning, the stabbing pain in his head had all but subsided. When he gently nudged Chase awake, his boyfriend stretched his arms out to Hunter.

"How's that miserable headache?" Chase asked softly.

"Much better, thank God," Hunter told him. "I'm a new man."

Chase leaned over and gave Hunter a short wake-up kiss on his lips. "I was worried about you."

"You and me both, Boss."

"Hey, Kiddo …" Chase asked as if out of the blue. "Have I told you lately that I love you?"

Hunter smiled back at Chase.

"It feels so strange," Chase observed as he made a loose fist and gently clipped Hunter under his chin. "I mean in a good way, to actually say those words out loud! I feel positively liberated," he further confessed. "Had I known it'd be this easy, I would've said it long ago, back when we first met."

Hunter quickly stepped over Chase's syrupy bout of sentimentality by confiding, "You can't imagine how much better I feel, now that my headache's all but gone."

"In that case, let's get moving!" Chase threw back their top sheet and excitedly jumped out of bed. "You won't believe how great it is out there on the water. We're on a mission, Kid. Coach is going to teach his boy to surf!"

*   *   *   *

They drove back to the black-sand surfing beach Chase had discovered the day before. After renting and then waxing down a pair of long boards, Chase again conscientiously smeared his body in sunscreen, even as Hunter cavalierly opted to forgo such mundane protection. He claimed he needed to catch up with Chase's head start, and was determined to return to New York the envy of his office, as deeply tanned as possible.

Chase and Hunter stopped at the shoreline where the Coach offered a few basic pointers regarding the sport of Hawaiian kings. Then they each hopped atop their boards and paddled far out into the water, where they bobbed up and down and watched as successive sets of two, three, and four-foot waves rolled by.

Chase's Surfing 101 tutorial didn't seem to assist Hunter's adaptation to the sport. While he displayed an immediate and rather fierce sense of competition, he also endured one humiliating wipeout after the next. Hunter grew frustrated when he couldn't effectively navigate his board right off the bat. After a series of further futile efforts, he simply gave up his self-imposed rivalry, and then, glum and defeated, paddled his board back to the beach.

Ashore, atop his huge beach towel, Hunter watched with restrained resentment as Chase got up repeatedly and with apparent ease before he then gracefully rode his board all the way into shore. Hunter spent the rest of the day splayed out on his back, basking under the soothing, semi-tropical sun. Chase remained far out in the water, thoroughly inspired by how well he was catching the waves. His surfing skills were especially impressive when you consider he was by then almost fifty years old and had been away from the sport for so many years.

With nothing around to stimulate his own waning interest, Hunter soon grew bored lying atop all that beautiful black sand. While dozing on and off, it dawned on him he really didn't much care for beaches. Nothing but itchy, abrasive sand everywhere, and not even the most basic of amenities. He realized he much preferred just lazing about, poolside, sunbathing atop the comfort of a plush chaise, feeling elegant and pampered, while casually sipping a rum punch.

By the time they returned to their condo late in the afternoon, Chase sported a healthy-looking patina of light tan, while Hunter's face, torso and thighs had by then transmuted into a bright fire engine red, a most unwelcome dividend of his unprotected overexposure beneath a sun far more searing than he thought possible.

Even after he stood beneath a steaming hot shower for fifteen minutes, his burgundy skin was still inflamed, disturbing to the eye, painful to the touch. Adding to his woes, his head by then throbbed with a bothersome, low-grade fever.

Hunter could barely move without feeling pained. He tried alleviating his burning soreness by smothering the seared areas of his face and body in the sticky salve extracted from a branch of the aloe vera plant sprouting on their private lanai.

By the time they both crawled into bed later that evening, Hunter was once again far too impaired to even consider making love. When Chase switched off the light on the bedside night table, he kissed Hunter on the top of his head and asked quietly, "Hey, Mr. Lobster Face — would it help if I told you that I love you?"

"A lot of good that'll do me," Hunter answered, sarcastically. "My skin's on fire. I ache all over. Everything's burning, I wish I was dead, and I love you, too. Good night."

＊   ＊   ＊   ＊

When Hunter awoke the following morning, he felt frustrated after one quick glance in the mirror told him he had no choice but to stay out of the sun, at least for another day or so. His severe sunburn had barely abated, and his troubled torso by then sprouted several billowy pockets of blisters. He was adamant, however, that Chase not disrupt his own intended agenda, and insisted his head Coach head out solo for another day of riding the waves.

Chase had little trouble giving in to Hunter's wishes and, right after breakfast, hurried back down to the sunny, sparsely populated black sand beach, where he rented another surfboard and again eagerly hit the waves.

As he bobbed up and down, straddling his long board between sets in the briny water, Chase once again became the big Kahuna of yesteryear. Thoroughly ecstatic, he savored so golden an opportunity to rekindle the euphoric feeling of jock empowerment set off by so many of his magic aquatic carpet rides. The very outdoorsy nature of the adventure brought back cherished memories of the outstanding experience he and his father shared back when they learned to surf together the last time he visited the Aloha State. He felt as if, miraculously, he had escaped modern civilization, left both reality and twenty-first century civilization behind in the dust, and was off on his own idyllic, surfing safari.

At the same time, back at their condo overlooking the ocean, Hunter improvised his own form of escape atop one of the cushiony chaises, beneath the shade of an enormous sun umbrella on their lanai. His frustration over still being unable to cultivate his tan, offset by his relief that his migraine had passed, afforded him full license to get lost in the anesthetic infusion delivered by a steady stream of rum punches.

Back down at the ocean, Chase caught one wave after the next. While bobbing up and down out on the water, between sets, he was befriended by a scraggly looking fellow surfer who paddled up alongside him and asked — somewhat disingenuously — if it would be okay if Chase and he shared the next incoming wave. This island-born Hawaiian had darkly bronzed, weathered skin and sported shoulder-length, ebony hair.

After a few communal rides into shore and several exchanges of amicable pleasantries, the native Hawaiian candidly announced that Chase seemed like a cool enough dude, which was a good thing because he just happened to be carrying some dynamite pacalolo for sale. The native Hawaiian claimed his locally grown Kona Gold was not merely the best marijuana in the world, he even offered to back up his claim by letting Chase indulge in a sample hit or two to see if he liked it.

Sure sounded fine to Chase, so he and his surfer buddy paddled in tandem to shore and then traipsed up to the parking lot. Inside the dope dealer's clutter-strewn Toyota, they shared a bowlful of his demon weed. Several puffs later, Chase was so sky-high, he decided he'd be a fool not to score such potent proffered grass, especially since he was still restricted from drinking alcohol. After retrieving his wallet from the glove compartment of his rented car, he handed over a hundred dollars and surreptitiously accepted a sixth of an ounce of the illegal substance, more than enough to last him and Hunter through the rest of their holiday.

Chase then returned to the water and, after a few more hours spent soaking up another perfect surfing day, he drove back up to their condo. Once inside, he found Hunter sloppily splayed across his chaise, flat out on his back, half asleep, and also by then three sheets to the trade winds.

Chase sat down on a nearby chaise and, using one of several rolling papers his surfing companion cum dope dealer threw into the slapdash purchase, rolled a slapdash joint.

Hunter raised a somnolent head long enough to slur he wanted no part of any such contraband. "I don't like breaking the law," he pontificated. "Besides, the few times I tried that stuff, it made me cloudy, drowsy."

"You mean as opposed to the rum drinks which make you bright and perky?"

"Something like that," Hunter stumbled over his words.

"Suit yourself," Chase shrugged, and lay back against the cushion as he lit up.

They each stuck to the devils they knew and, soon enough, Chase was stoned, Hunter was drunk, and even though they reclined adjacent to each other on the same lanai, they may as well have been miles apart.

Stretched out side by side on their chaises, Chase reflected in stoned silence on the sheer poetry of the extravagant light show Mother Nature was producing way down at the horizon. As brilliant shades of yellow, red, and orange burnished the sky, Hunter glanced over and stole a look at his boyfriend. In his rum-infused reverie, he was puzzled as to why he never before noticed how large were the pores at the top of Chase's nose. Didn't the Coach ever scrub his face? And while he was at it, how come he'd never before spotted that ugly pair of irritating hairs sticking out from Chase's left ear? It wasn't likely such simian whiskers simply popped up overnight, was it? *Yucch*, thought Hunter, as he wondered how Chase could have overlooked those off-putting omissions of good grooming. Rather than mention anything about these disturbing transgressions, Hunter instead elected to get up and go inside to mix himself another rum punch.

By bedtime, Hunter was far too drunk and still too disabled from his sunburn for them to even think about fooling around. Despite anticipated plans to spend their week in the blissful setting making endless love, for the moment, at least, they simply exchanged a short kiss on the lips, followed by a verbal exchange of Chase saying "I love you," and Hunter slurring a responsive "Jy wove juu, too".

They then turned their backs on one another and, tush to tush, fell quickly to sleep.

*   *   *   *

From the moment he looked at himself in the mirror the following morning, Hunter saw how blistery and still blotchy red was his face. It would take another few days before he could again expose his damaged skin to the sun.

Chase, still post-op following his recent hernia procedure, was told by his doctor that while he could go surfing, he needed to refrain from lifting heavy weights for at least another couple of weeks. Hunter, however, was eager to hit the gym. When they drove into town after breakfast, Chase dropped Hunter off at the local Gold's, and then hurried back to his nearby black-sand surfing beach.

Hunter always felt initially disoriented when working out in a new gym, at least until he grew familiar with the lay of the land. He didn't appreciate the trouble it took to figure out how to properly approach unfamiliar machines alien to his routine.

One look around the crowded gym floor and he quickly observed how this particular Gold's was filled mostly with motley, overweight tourists, many with unrealistic expectations of speedily working off some of their rum drinks, some of their roast suckling pigs. He was one of the few hot bodybuilders working out in the cavernous space, and that included the small percentage of clientele who registered positively on his gaydar.

Meanwhile, down at the beach, far out in the water, Chase was filled with a boundless energy as he paddled back and forth on his rented board, riding to shore a successful succession of four-foot waves. Exhilarated by such ideal surfing conditions, and still ebullient about Hunter and their covenant, he felt confident he could grow a little less supple, less defined, even wax a tad tubby, and it would have little impact on their commitment to each other. Only days earlier, Hunter had promised that in his loving eyes, Chase would remain forever his studly Coach.

Maybe that was why, after being told so often how much he was adored, not just for his sexy body or his handsome face, but also for his facile mind, Chase realized he could finally ease away from his obsessive need to remain in perennially perfect shape.

It's a well-known, if disturbing law of science that while it takes forever to get into great shape, the only thing needed for muscles to initiate their descent into atrophy and deterioration was a short interval of inactivity. Chase's body had not only lost some of its elasticity, but some of its appealing muscle tone as well. The hours he spent surfing and splashing about in the water were a good enough aerobics exercise. But they couldn't make up for the weeks he'd been banned from the gym. Not surprisingly, his powerfully muscular body, forced into a physician-directed time off from the weights, began to look flat, on its way to going soft.

Hunter finished his workout in just under ninety minutes and then, his biceps and delts freshly pumped, hurried from the gym and, as pre-arranged, jogged down to the nearby black-sand beach, to meet up with Chase. His annoying sunburn still stung, so this time out he applied a strong sun block, wore a baseball cap, and kept his tee shirt on as he trotted down the wooden steps leading to the shoreline.

The moment Hunter landed on the beach, he sought the shaded protection of a nearby palm tree. He plopped down on his towel, locked his arms around his knees, and watched until he spotted Chase far out in the glistening ocean, disappearing in and out of view along with the rise and fall of waves in his path.

While squinting against the sun's harsh glare, Chase caught a glimpse of Hunter, sitting on the beach, and so he paddled in toward shore to greet him. Even covered up against the sun and with his cap on, even blotchy and beet red, his boy still looked so damn hot and handsome.

Too bad Hunter wasn't feeling the same degree of appreciation for Chase. Previously unobserved flaws in his boyfriend suddenly became magnified, and Hunter willingly tuned in to uncovering them even as he watched Chase step out from the ocean, plant his board upright into the sand, and then jog toward him, all smiles. As Chase approached, Hunter couldn't help but wonder if his imagination wasn't playing tricks on him.

Take a close, hard, look. Hunter heard a dim voice tapping against the back of his head as he watched Chase looming ever larger as he approached. *Go ahead. Don't his pecs seem a little less full, his famed guns not so imposing? How'd his six-pack lose so much muscle tone? And what's with those love handles starting to pop out, alongside his midsection? Big deal if he had that minor surgery.*

Chase jogged over to Hunter and his wet body glistened against the sun as he hovered over him. When Hunter looked up, he was saddened to see his Coach in a whole new light. While a part of him was busy uncovering Chase's imperfections, another inner voice insisted he needed to suppress such worrisome, negative observations. Rather than registering any of his flourishing disillusionment, Hunter instead smiled up at Chase, and conveniently tabled the notion that everything was not quite so ideal with his once-perfect partner there in that all but flawless setting.

Even after Hunter tried ignoring the obvious, however, his disturbing concerns would simply not quiet down. They had, in fact, only begun to surface.

A perfect example came the following morning when they were both out on their lanai, finishing their breakfasts. Hunter took another probing look over at his Coach in his shorts, sipping his guava juice, and couldn't help but again notice his bodily imperfections. And there was nothing funny about those laugh lines around his eyes, so much more evident there under the harsh scrutiny of morning light.

For the life of him, Hunter couldn't understand why he hadn't before spotted these evident flaws on his one-time hero. He felt curiously betrayed when those shortcomings he noticed the day before on the beach rose up again, confirming his ongoing disappointment.

Cultural reality dictates there are three mortal sins of gay sexual attraction: Ugly, Fat, and Old. Chase was certainly not ugly. And even though he wasn't in the best of shape, he was by no means fat. However, was it Hunter's imagination or was Chase starting to appear, not just mature, the way Hunter had always liked his muscle men, but slowly slouching toward the irreversible mortal third sin of looking … *old?*

*   *   *   *

It only took those first few days of settling into the breezy, laid-back rhythm of the Hawaiian lifestyle before Chase felt fully free of stress. Surrounded by so much natural beauty, as well as enlivened by the warm trade winds blowing the sweet, intoxicating aroma of plumeria everywhere, he was filled with a welcome sense of calm. The more time he spent surfing, the further behind he left the pressures of urban living, and the more relaxed and sublime was his disposition.

By sharp contrast, Hunter felt disenchanted with Chase's Hawaiian fantasy. Maybe that's what was partly at play when he began finding still further fault with Chase, soon nitpicking or arguing with him over most any little thing — from what his boyfriend should wear to the beach, to how disgusting it was he chose, before turning in, to floss his teeth in bed rather than in the bathroom. Hunter complained whenever it rained. He carped over the smallest detail, like insisting the air conditioning stay at full blast while they slept, rather than leaving open wide the double French doors leading to the lanai and letting in the pleasant trade winds.

Overnight, in the blink of an eye, one short revolution of the planet, Hunter inexplicably began acting less than polite. Finally familiar with each other's quirks and imperfections, he no longer needed to hold back cruel or insensitive thoughts, no longer needed to bother being quite as considerate of Chase's feelings as he might have a week earlier.

Their vacation turned into a test of wills. If Chase wanted to go for a swim, Hunter wanted to grab a bite. When Chase wanted to go snorkeling, Hunter said he'd rather rent motor scooters.

Chase was soon wise to the pattern of Hunter's quarrelsome demeanor, and made a point to remain patient. He guessed their sudden bickering was what naturally followed once two people, confident in their love, began spending all their time together, with few other human interactions. Hunter, after all, was thrown that sucker punch when he got hit hard by the one-two combo of his incapacitating migraine, compounded by his severe sunburn.

Chase also couldn't help but observe that Hunter was drinking a lot more, and surmised it was his excessive alcohol consumption that no doubt brought out this previously undetected aspect of his personality. He concluded, upon reflection, that there was no major trouble brewing between them. They were simply going through a normal period of adjusting to one another while learning how to get along. The Kid, after all, had given him his heart, hadn't he, and lest he forget, the Coach had only a few days earlier turned over his in return, back when Hunter carved their initials into that Norfolk pine. A covenant as strong and powerful as theirs was not so easily broken, not so cavalierly revoked, now was it? Of course not. Case closed.

*   *   *   *

By the following morning, the blistering, burning pain inflicted upon Hunter's hide had begun to subside. He claimed his skin was healing to the point he was ready to get back to the business of cultivating his tan. He also told Chase that he didn't really care to return to the beach. Instead, they both amicably agreed to spend the day following their personal pursuits.

Chase headed back to the ocean for another round of riding the waves, while Hunter again passed the hours out on their lanai, alternating between lounging in the shade, and then, with his body finally wisely sheltered in sunscreen, basking for brief periods in the sun. Whether lying either in the pleasant safety of the shade or beneath the searing sun, however, he drifted in and out of a lazy half-consciousness, again escaping reality by stealthily sipping one rum punch after the next.

As Hunter moved deeper into his inebriation, the more disturbing became the mounting negative notions that kept seeping out from some dormant corner of his mind. They gnawed at him and slowly drained his passion, his loyalty, while whispering nasty, petty, internal observations about his Coach. *Why in the world didn't Chase cut his hair before our trip?* Hunter heard himself wondering. *Doesn't he know how much more I like it when his head has a military buzz? And how come his snoring never bothered me so much before? He snores louder than Atlas — and that's going some.*

Chase returned in late afternoon from another splendid day of surfing. By then, an already inebriated Hunter announced he had come down with cabin fever and was itching to get out. He suggested they clean up and head down to Kona, find a restaurant for dinner, maybe hit a few bars.

Chase said he'd rather just hang out, take in another sunset, grill up a couple of steaks, maybe watch some dumb horror movie on TV. "You can get more hammered on your rum drinks, I'll have a few tokes, and we can both chill."

"Hey, Shithead!" Hunter burst with a vehemence that came out of nowhere. "I'm on vacation, remember? It's not my fault you still can't drink alcohol."

The foolish petty squabble that ensued, their first explosive row, escalated until it soon exposed surprising and unattractive sides to sub-personalities neither of them had previously witnessed in the other. Chase was confused by Hunter's inexplicably harsh invective, but was convinced his boyfriend's negativity was exacerbated by his inebriation. The Coach realized there was no winning so unwarranted an argument, so when he sensed himself verging on his own explosive outburst, he instinctively knew he'd be far wiser to just get out of there, and fast. That's why, after glibly suggesting Hunter get lost in another rum punch or two or three or four, he left their condo and hiked down to the bottom of the hill. He spent the better part of the next hour working off steam, trying to calm down by taking an extended, vigorous walk along the water's edge. Far off in the distance, way out over the ocean, a shimmering golden sun leisurely melted into the horizon before it slowly disappeared, floating toward the other side of the world, on its way toward gifting China with their forthcoming sunrise.

While sitting alone and watching the dreamy day's end, Chase got lost in the confusion of his thoughts. As his mind wandered, he couldn't help but appreciate the irony that he was enjoying one of the most gloriously romantic sunsets he'd ever seen … all by himself.

Surely, he should have been expecting this, shouldn't he, the abrupt conclusion of his and Hunter's honeymoon period? Sooner or later, it had to happen. Wasn't that a given when two loving people tried getting closer with each other? Wasn't it something all couples eventually experienced?

Chase convinced himself this first full-blown, yet frivolous lover's quarrel about nothing of consequence was merely an opening salvo in the plethora of obstacles bound to cross their paths as they built their relationship. Now that the curtain had fallen on the overture of their honeymoon, Chase was ready to see it rise again on Act One of their real association. Relationships, like anything else, he reminded himself, were often hard work.

Chase felt confident his own commitment to Hunter was airtight, and that since he was the far older and thus arguably wiser of the two, he took it upon himself to clear up any unpleasantness that popped up from time to time in their romance. They'd only recently exchanged vows of solid commitment, so Chase felt reassured Hunter wasn't going anywhere.

Okay, so they each lost their temper — hardly the end of the world. Chase knew he needed to just calm down and adapt, learn to take such sporadic obstructions, such occasional petty spats, in stride. *Everyone says compromise is the essence of relationship,* he told himself. *So what can I do but forgive and accept his flaws, his foibles, and ask him to do the same with mine? All part of the game.* After talking himself into getting past this blow up, Chase picked up his pace and headed straight back up the hill, to heal the hurt by kissing and making up.

∗ ∗ ∗ ∗

Alone in their condo, Hunter stirred up yet another rum punch. *Hey, man,* he reminded himself. *I'm still on vacation.* He carried his fresh cocktail out onto the lanai and plopped down atop a chaise to further contemplate just what might be going on between himself and Chase. Hunter's worrisome ruminations were cut short when his boyfriend returned from his sunset walk along the ocean. Chase's hands were clutched together, held out before him, as if he was protectively carrying something delicate. He sauntered over, slowly opened his hands and brought forth a perfectly shaped seashell. He handed the empty husk to Hunter, saying, "I just watched a great sunset, and felt so bad you weren't there to enjoy it with me, I figured I'd bring back a small gift from the sea."

Hunter opened his arms wide, a clear invitation to a bear-hugging, and Chase jumped directly atop his boyfriend's body, squeezing tightly, forcefully kissing him smack on his lips. They made out for a long while, fiercely kissing while exchanging profound gestures of affection as they wiped clean the slate of their earlier discord.

"I'm sorry we fought," Chase mumbled, between deep kisses.

"Me, too, Coach," Hunter whispered back softly, forcefully hugging Chase to his chest.

"Hey, Kiddo," Chase whispered to Hunter. "Your big Kahuna's got a big kahardon for you. So how 'bout if we head into the bedroom, where Coach can take down his Star Varsity Wrestler in a more seductively conducive setting?"

Excited, Hunter jumped up off the chaise. "I'm more than up for it, Coach," he said excitedly. "And how 'bout if this time we finally do it my way and play out my rape fantasy?"

Chase suspected that Hunter's muscle rape fantasy was driven far more by a false bravado than any true desire. He was by then familiar with the erotic scenario playing out in Hunter's vivid imagination. He knew Hunter's long-dreamt fantasy found him getting gang-banged in the shower by the hottest players on the wrestling squad. Fair enough. But Chase also suspected it was more the attention from so many well-built men that appealed to Hunter more than any mistreatment he truly wished to endure.

Chase couldn't really be sure how serious was his lover when they started kissing again and Hunter insisted, "Do it to me, Coach. Be really rough with me this time, okay? Let's drum up this damn rape scene, make it happen for real, so I can get it out of my system."

"Don't you know by now? Chase offered wryly. "You can't rape the willing!"

*   *   *   *

They went at it for several hours.

Nothing like making up after a lover's quarrel, thought Chase, once his cock was securely harbored deep inside his hot muscle boy.

"Yes! Yes, Coach!" Hunter cried out as he approached an ecstatic orgasm while having his prized bubble butt slammed into a most willing submission. Lying on his back, his powerful legs elevated, one perched over each of Chase's huge, rounded delts, Hunter looked up at Chase in the dim candlelight, and marveled at the sheer sensual sensation that accompanied getting pounded into a state of near rapture.

While part of Hunter was relishing this sexual encounter, another side of him also knew the whole scene still just wasn't being played out quite rough or tumble enough. "Fuck me harder, Daddy!" Hunter insisted gruffly, before pleading, "Hurt me, Daddy. Please. Go on. Slap me around. Make me your prison bitch! Do it. Make me your goddamn pussy boy!"

Chase fucked Hunter as hard as he could. He hammered away with all the manufactured fury he could muster. But sustaining an ongoing anger didn't come easy to him. Not only that, he also didn't much care for Hunter's recently introduced role-playing between them as Father/Son, mostly because it made him feel, well ... *old.*

It was always great fun playing off his alter ego as the Coach. However, this suggestion of his moving up a whole generation to play Daddy felt alien, uncomfortable, and far too close to home. What Chase really wanted, no matter the difference in their ages, was a soul mate, and not someone over whom he could lord or control as an abusive parent.

At the same time, he wanted to keep his muscle boy happy, to cater to his lover's cockeyed fantasies and off-kilter fetishes. But the simple truth was Chase actually derived the greatest pleasure from just lying together with Hunter, slowly luxuriating in their passionate affections. He preferred smothering his lover in wet kisses rather than caving in to Hunter's perverse wish to be manhandled and roughed up. He was confused by Hunter's oxymoronic notion that making love was akin to the infliction of pain and torment.

"Oh, Daddy, fuck me!" Hunter again cried out ecstatically as his testicular juice, like mercury from the bottom of an erotic thermometer, ascended the narrow, fleshy hollow of his erection, until it spewed forth in half a dozen thick squirts. "Oh, Yes, Daddy! Fuck me hard!" he cried out in rapturous excitement as his wild geyser erupted in convulsive spasms. "Give it to me harder, Daddy. Oh, yes — Rape my little boy ass!"

*   *   *   *

WHO'S YOUR DADDY?

Hunter awakened to a dawning sky and a symphony of birds chirping on the lanai in concert with Chase's snoring alongside him. Unable to go back to sleep, he stared at the ceiling and relived their extended sex scene the night before. Clearly, some undefined element in their once cosmic connection was no longer there. Something in their balance of power had shifted and the glue of sexual yearning so prevalent between them was suddenly missing.

Hunter felt safe and secure whenever he was wrapped in Chase's strong arms, comforted whenever the two of them, enveloped in some post-orgasmic euphoria, drifted in and out of slumber. But lying in bed that early break of day, while observing golden rays painting the walls of the room in a coat of sunshine, he couldn't understand why their lovemaking was no longer as satisfying.

And with Chase's ineffectual pretense at being menacing the night before, well, it all came across just so damn … tame. Where, for instance, were all the mounting fears he needed instilled in him before being pushed over the edge? Missing. And what about those titillating threats, that omnipresent sense of danger he begged his Coach bring to their sexual encounters? Nowhere. And whatever happened to the heightened eroticism springing from their pseudo-aggressive gut punching, their simulated pec slapping, the homo-erotica unleashed those few times he and Chase half-heartedly engaged in their faux wrestling? Gone. Gone. Gone.

It's finally happened, Hunter concluded. *Our incredible lovemaking has become … routine!"* Confused and aggravated, he decided that if Chase was unwilling to take him down in the brutal, dominating fashion for which he pined, then damn it, he'd find someone else who would.

Hunter slipped silently out of bed, careful not to disturb Chase as he tiptoed into the walk-in closet to get into his gym gear. After pocketing a banana and a protein bar, he treaded softly out of their condo and drove down the hill, into Kona to work out at Gold's. He trained back and delts, and then, feeling strong and pumped, capped his exercise program with half an hour's fast-paced, uphill climb on the treadmill. Step after conscientious step atop the circulating belt, Hunter strode in place and, as he walked, he returned to his disturbing ruminations.

It became perfectly clear that he and Chase were heading down different paths. Hunter had been patient, waiting for their primal passion to progress, until it evolved into a far more primitive and manly violence, more of the tough, erotic wrestling that had always gotten him sexually aroused. But by then it was obvious that what Chase really wanted was to be loving and caring, expressing himself through the mundane comforts of basic vanilla sex.

It also dawned on Hunter as he marched forward on the treadmill, going nowhere fast, that past his and Chase's evident sexual incompatibilities, he was also suddenly feeling more than a little hemmed in, claustrophobic, which was really odd, given the wide-open spaces of their lush surroundings.

What surprised Hunter most of all, the element that left him the most saddened and dismayed, was how weary he'd grown of hearing Chase saying *I love you.* So much gushing sentiment got real old, real fast; and what at first was charming, appreciated, even welcome, grew swiftly trite and cloying, if not downright un-*masculine*.

Yes, he'd been the one who first asked for it, practically begged for it, even felt at times like he couldn't live without hearing Chase express his love openly. But once his wish was granted, he discovered that what was fine in fantasy sure seemed lame in reality.

In a burst of specious reasoning, Hunter concluded that if his Coach could walk out on him — if only for a while — simply because of their silly squabble the night before, while they were alone together on vacation no less, then who's to say Chase couldn't also just as cavalierly dump him? Who's to say his once and future life partner wouldn't throw in the towel and step back from their relationship right after their next petty disagreement, disengaging without once looking back? Hunter knew with dead certainty that kind of rejection could only shatter him, leaving him devastated.

Somewhere in the back of his mind, Hunter knew they'd hit a tipping point, and that his survival mechanism needed to kick in. And that was when he realized that the best way to protect himself from having so emotional a trauma inflicted upon him, either now or in the future, was to safeguard his soul.

How? By getting out before he got hurt. *Maybe it's better to be the first to retreat,* he convinced himself in a fast-constructed justification. *Do it now, before Coach loses interest, drops me without so much as a second thought. That's all I'd need now — with all my stress at work!!*

In a sad emergence of clarity, Hunter grasped how severely the tables had turned. And he also knew, even though he had yet to fully admit it to himself, that things between Coach Chase and his Star Varsity Wrestler would never again be the same.

*   *   *   *

That evening, the last night of what at least started out as their dream getaway, Chase grilled fresh mahi-mahi with some local vegetables and they ate outside, at the candlelit table on their lanai. While finishing the last of their supper, Chase suggested they again stay in that evening to prepare for their early-morning departure. "You know, pack our bags, clean up the place, maybe get in a bit of rolling around together."

Hunter had other ideas. He claimed he was feeling so much better, and finally looking so good now that his nasty sunburn had finally segued into the glowing suggestion of a healthy tan, he preferred they go out, explore Kona's nightlife.

"What nightlife?" Chase asked. "We're in the subtropical boonies, remember?"

"Well, I checked online before I left New York," said Hunter. "Discovered there's a gay bar called Coconuts that recently opened right down at the bottom of our hill. I say we head down there, check it out."

"Why in the world would we want a gay bar now?" Chase protested. "Everything we need is right here, particularly each other. And you know I still can't drink. Besides, the music is always so deafening in those places, we wouldn't be able to carry on any kind of conversation."

"Oh, don't be such an old stick in the mud," said Hunter. "Besides, don't you think it could be fun, flirting with some of the local boys? You gotta know we'd be popular there."

"Who cares if we'd be popular?" asked Chase.

"I do, for one!" Hunter admitted. "And since when are you no longer interested in validation?"

"I don't know," Chase shrugged. "Maybe since I met you."

"Well, that's fine for you, Coach," Hunter argued. "But I'm not about to spend the last night of our vacation penned in up here like some washed up, geriatric shut-in, moving about on a walker. You know, sometimes I get the feeling you'd rather hug than screw."

"You know, sometimes I would!" Chase confessed.

"You confuse me."

"And you confuse me," Chase shot right back. "At least we still have that in common."

Their inane disagreement over how they should spend their last evening quickly escalated into a foolhardy quarrel, an unpleasant confrontation that culminated when Hunter stormed into the bedroom and slammed the door shut.

Sometimes it's not so big a jump from adoring to abhorring, and Hunter made the leap with lightning speed. When he emerged a few minutes later, he had changed out of his splashy Hawaiian shirt and was clad in a tight fitting, navy blue muscle tee. He snatched up the rental car keys from the kitchen counter, headed for the front door, and pointedly told Chase, "You can stay here, counting the stars and smelling the plumeria if that's what makes you happy. I'll be down at Coconuts should you come to your senses and choose to join me."

*   *   *   *

For the next two hours, Chase lay on the lanai, flat-out atop a chaise, trying to recall a time in his life when he felt so unhappy, so lonely. When his cell phone rang, he hoped it was Hunter, calling to make amends. "Hello?" greeted Chase, clicking in.

"Yo, Coach!" A familiar voice called out from twenty-eight hundred miles away.

"That you, Stack?" asked Chase.

"Bet your sweet ass!" answered Stack. "We're here at the White Party in Palm Springs, in our room at the Wyndham — me and Adam and his husband, Rumplestilskin ... I mean Craig. You remember the Bickersons, don't you? I've been living with them all weekend. It's like watching Divorce Court."

"God, it's so great to hear from you guys!"

"I kid, I jest," Stack yelled out to Adam and Craig, and then went back to talking to Chase. "These guys are so touchy. Truth is, we're having a blast. We all dropped some X about forty minutes ago, shoved it up our butts for smooth assimilation, and soon as it took effect, we got all giddy and fuzzy and silly, and so before heading down to the tea dance, decided to call you."

"I'm beyond flattered," Chase said with a smile.

"Yeah, yeah," Stack chuckled. "Maybe it's because we're all now high as kites, stoned to the tits, but try as we might, none of us could remember why you're not here with us now. We were all going to come to this together, remember? So we interrupted our euphoric stupors to find out how our absent Benedict Arnold is doing."

"Doing fine," Chase lied. "But believe me when I say I'd be a lot happier right now if I was there with you guys."

"So …?" Stack wanted to know. "You hula-crazed muscle studs been fucking your brains out?"

"Oh, you know," Chase answered in a soft voice. "Here and there."

"I can just imagine!" Stack snickered.

"Coming home tomorrow," said Chase.

"And about fucking time," Stack responded before he got distracted and called out, "Okay, you two, just calm down a minute, will ya? Don't be such animals. Hey, Coach — they're both waving at me, itching to get moving. Mad queens desperately seeking dick. What can I tell you? Everyone says hello-goodbye, and sends their regrets and their love. Now go fuck yourself. We're outta here — gonna go check out the hot bods down at the tea dance."

"You guys are so great," said Chase, feeling a swell of emotion affecting his voice. "Thanks for calling. Means the world to me."

"Hey, Coach," Stack offered a surprising strength in his wisdom. "Men are like buses. Miss one and another comes along in ten minutes. Real friends are in it for the long haul. Have a safe flight."

∗   ∗   ∗   ∗

Hunter ambled into Coconuts, the dimly lit, sparsely-populated bar with eardrum-popping music, down at the bottom of the hill. The prevailing butch ambience in the air was so forced, the place was downright gloomy. Many of the seedy bar's clientele were geared up in varying degrees of leather. Coconuts, clearly, was no venue for any gathering around the piano for a medley of show tunes, not in this self-conscious den of self-imposed hyper-masculinity.

It was a saddened Hunter who perched himself atop a bar stool and then grew progressively disheartened while polishing off three rum punches and reflecting upon the dazzling speed by which his affections for Chase had waned. One minute all his love was there, the next gone, vanished, swept out with the evening tide.

Hunter sighed sadly, and when he looked across the pool table, he spotted an older, extremely well-built, muscle-daddy type, leaning against the wall, grinning at him while taking a swig from a bottle of beer. The big guy was sexily shirtless in black leather vest and tight jeans. A tight leather band hugged the peak of his huge left biceps.

Hunter wondered if he wasn't being cruised. *Do I detect sexual tension in the air?* He thought to himself. *Hey! Things just may be looking up.*

Doing his best to maintain a semblance of sobriety, no easy feat by then, Hunter semi-smiled back at the older, hunky guy, signaling that his return tease meant he was at least partially interested in taking their across-a-crowded-room flirtation to the next level.

*   *   *   *

Back up on their lanai, still recumbent upon a chaise, beneath a limitless, starry sky, Chase couldn't decide which made him feel worse — not being in Palm Springs, partying with his best buddies, or again feeling so oddly disconnected from Hunter after their latest disagreement. His mood shifted back and forth between feeling furious and wanting to be forgiving. After much contemplation, he concluded he had to be the one to again set things straight with his lover. So once again, he swallowed his pride, slipped into his flip-flops, bolted from the condo and took a long, fast-paced stroll down the long, winding hill.

A nearly full moon illuminated Chase's path as he walked through the starlit night. The seductive, warm trade winds blew forcefully against his back, propelling his forward motion. The sensuality of the air, redolent with the sweet perfume of night-blooming jasmine, accompanied his walk.

By the time he reached the bottom of the hill, Chase had worked up a slight sweat, so he removed his colorful Hawaiian silk shirt and crossed over, onto the main highway that encircled the outer perimeter of the island. He heard the thumping of distant music, looked ahead and spotted a red, blinking, neon sign, perhaps a thousand yards down the road, unabashedly flashing the word *Coconuts* against the darkness of the night.

In Chase's mind, he would surprise Hunter by showing up at the bar, and then forcefully taking his lover in his arms and kissing him grandly before all the patrons. That way everyone in the place would know Hunter was his boy, all his.

As he drew closer to the watering hole, however, his hastily constructed fantasy quickly soured as it dissolved into a nightmare. Chase squinted into the dark night to make sure he was seeing correctly. Sure enough, way across the street, he caught a glimpse of Hunter, strolling out of Coconuts. Walking right alongside his boyfriend was some big muscle man in jeans and a black leather vest.

Chase ducked speedily out of sight, darting behind a nearby palm tree. From his unobstructed view, he saw the big bruiser mount a Harley-Davidson chopper parked right in front of the bar. He watched in near disbelief as Hunter climbed on right behind and locked his arms around the cyclist's waist. With a voluminous rattle, the stranger gunned his side pedal. The motorcycle took off, zipped down the highway, and was soon gone from sight.

Chase wasn't sure if he was confused, confounded, conflicted, or merely miserable. He knew he felt betrayed. Turning in place, he shoved his hands into the pockets of his safari shorts, walked back along the highway, and then all the way up the hill, back to the condo, sulking and stewing, sweating and steaming, every sad step of the way.

By three-thirty in the morning, Chase was still tossing around in bed, too restless and upset to sleep. Half-awake, he sensed Hunter tiptoeing back into the room.

Sill wobbly from his inebriation, Hunter flipped the air conditioner up to high and closed the French doors leading to the lanai, effectively cutting off the night breeze. He stepped clumsily out of his clothes and crawled slyly under the sheet. Hoping not to disturb Chase's semi-slumber, he sidled cozily right up alongside him. With a giant exhale indicative of his thorough fatigue, Hunter then placed an affectionate arm around Chase's broad shoulders, and closed his eyes.

Chase eased himself away, toward the edge of the bed, and Hunter felt gripped by a pang of culpability. So he leaned over to provide a smattering of placation, a momentary penitence, whispering into Chase's ear, "Hey, Coach, sorry you didn't come — would've been a lot more fun."

Even in his semi-sleep, Chase wouldn't allow Hunter's message to resonate. Instead, he stirred, eased himself still further away, and muttered incoherently, "Trying to sleep." Then he again drifted into as deep a sleep and as far away from Hawaii as his troubled mind could carry him.

*   *   *   *

Not long after sunup, Chase awoke and slipped quietly out of bed. He whipped up a quick breakfast and then hastily crammed his vacation wardrobe into his suitcase. Hunter got up a short while later and half wobbled into the living room, holding his open hand against his forehead in a futile effort to stabilize his pounding headache. "Morning, Coach," he said coyly, subdued, as guiltless as he could muster in a classic *Boy, was I drunk last night* bearing.

Chase fastened the top of his suitcase and looked up. "Hunter ..." he acknowledged, just as disingenuously ambiguous. "So ... how'd it go last night?"

"Oh, you know," Hunter lied. "Once again you were right. Nothing down there but a bunch of out-of-shape losers hanging out, downing beers."

"Really?" asked Chase, pretending to be mystified. "No big muscle daddies on motorcycles?"

Oops. Bamboozled, Hunter realized he'd somehow been unmasked. He looked squarely over at Chase, and asked, "How'd you know?"

"I saw."

"Saw what?"

"You leaving the bar with him."

"Where were you?"

"Watching from across the highway."

"Then why didn't you stop me?"

"I'm not your father, remember?"

"Oh, shit!" Hunter muttered and, still pressing his hand to his forehead, plopped down on the couch. "I'm ... so sorry."

Chase waved a dismissive hand. "Forget sorry. How was it?"

"How the fuck should I know?" asked Hunter. "I was so damn drunk, I could barely see straight, let alone remember either going off with him or anything that happened after that."

"And that makes it okay?" asked Chase.

"I didn't say that," Hunter was defensive. "Hey — I've got a roaring hangover, okay? Can we talk about this later?"

"Fine with me, Kiddo," Chase shrugged as he toted his suitcase over to the front door. "Why talk about it at all? It's only our relationship."

"I got scared, okay?" Hunter blurted out, trying to justify his betrayal.

"Scared?" Chase asked. "Of what?"

"I suppose the whole thing." Hunter answered. "You. Me. The two of us together. Plus I was angry. Upset. Feeling a little, I don't know … hemmed in, I guess. Smothered by your attention.'

"Isn't that what you wanted from me?"

"Well, that's what I thought I wanted," said Hunter. "I mean, I did. I know I did. But then, once I got it, it suddenly wasn't as important as I first thought, not as fulfilling as I always expected. Last night, what I really needed was to simply get off on my own, at least for a while, okay? I thought it would be good for us. You probably wouldn't understand."

"No, probably not," Chase agreed.

Hunter felt too ill at ease, so he stood up and returned to the bedroom to pack his bags. At the same time, he called American Airlines and learned there was room on a flight leaving for San Diego twenty minutes before his and Chase's scheduled departure to Los Angeles. He knew spending the night in L.A. with Chase, before then heading out the next morning back down to San Diego, and then home to New York, would be far too awkward. So he quickly shuffled his itinerary and switched his reservation so that he'd be flying nonstop from Kona to San Diego International instead of LAX.

*   *   *   *

During their long, tense drive to the airport, Hunter kept his baseball cap pulled way down over his eyes as he tried to catnap, tried keeping at bay the sunlight aggravating his aching hangover. Resting as best he could, he kept his eyes shut tight, with his brain in low gear.

Chase dropped Hunter off with their suitcases, and then drove over to Budget to return their rental car. He then took the shuttle back to the American Airlines Terminal, and caught up with Hunter, still waiting on the extended line to check in. After receiving their respective boarding passes, they each passed through the security area, and then Chase accompanied Hunter over to his gate for his recently switched flight to San Diego.

"Well," said Hunter, forcing a smile. "I guess this is it, huh, Coach?"

"So it would seem, Kiddo," said Chase. "Hope your hangover clears up soon."

Hunter took a small step forward, put his arms around Chase, gave him an affectionate hug, and quietly said, "I hope you'll find a way to forgive me."

"So do I," a subdued Chase responded, honestly. "I know things got a little out of hand toward the end, but still, I want to thank you for the trip."

"Hey, if I can't spoil my Coach …" Hunter didn't finish the thought.

When they drew away from each other, Chase lifted his left, by then solidly tanned arm, its famed muscularity prominently protruding from his short-sleeved Polo shirt, and quickly flashed a private flexing of his huge biceps muscle. "Say so long to the Guns of Navarone," he suggested, at least half-seriously.

Hunter did as he was told and sized up Chase's great python. Something melancholy gurgling in his gut told him to take a real close look, because he suspected he might not get to see it again. "Still the sexiest around!" he told Chase, sounding more bittersweet than complimentary, before adding, "Hey, maybe we can work through this. What do you think?"

"I think the least we can do is try," said Chase.

Hunter forced a smile and felt a need to further appease Chase before concluding their awkward departure. So he lied and added, "I've got more upcoming business trips to San Diego. You know me. I'll find some way to get us together again real soon."

Chase forced a noncommittal smile of his own.

"I'll talk to you once I'm back in New York, okay?" After kissing Chase softly on the stubble of his two-day growth, Hunter turned and headed down the long corridor leading to his plane for San Diego. Along the way, he didn't bother turning back and waving for what, every time they'd previously parted, had been a final gesture of farewell.

*   *   *   *

Flying over the blue Pacific toward San Diego, Hunter downed the last of a rum punch given him by one of the First Class flight attendants as he pulled out and opened his laptop to finally focus on the huge backlog of paper work he'd brought along, but had neglected while on vacation.

Several pages into perusing a dull, detailed proposal for a new convention center in downtown San Diego, he reclined in his seat and exhaled a sizeable sigh of relief. Right off the bat, he realized how less pressured and more comfortable he felt once he liberated himself from Chase. Odd, he observed, how cloying and needy, how downright smothering his boyfriend became, especially toward the end of their trip.

For the first time, Hunter looked at the typical pattern of couples, and realized it wasn't until the honeymoon was over before you discovered those traits you liked least about your partner. That was when you started to bicker and squabble, before you kissed and made up, and then fought again, before you finally ended the familiar sequence by fucking and making up. By the time you began having mini-snits in public, you were officially a couple. After so many years spent pining for all that, Hunter realized that wasn't what he really wanted out of life, after all.

As he reclined further into his leather-bound seat, he indulged himself in a few moments of a much-needed escapist pleasure, and sent forth from the back of his head the handful of scattered, graphic images he could summon from the night before.

He closed his eyes and recalled how sexy it was to ride through the breezy, dark night air on the back of that huge Harley Davidson chopper. He relished how, as soon as he and that studly biker arrived at the big man's trashy apartment, he was forced to service the aggressive fellow for several exciting hours. He reveled over how nasty and demanding his caustic muscle daddy had first been, and then how tender and thoughtful he turned, post orgasm, when he ferried him back over to Coconuts on his chopper, where Hunter picked up his car and then drove back up to the condo.

And so what if their carnal time together had been cold and unattached, free of any warmth or affection? It was erotic and satisfyingly abusive, exactly what he needed. And even when his dominating muscle daddy surprised him with that explosive urinary orgasm into his mouth, it wasn't all that bad, given its surreal context.

"Lucky for you," Hunter once again heard his dominator warning him as he opened fire and emptied his bladder, "I downed so many fuckin' brewskis, it'll taste more like sea water."

Oh, that's a real comfort, Hunter recalled thinking as he succumbed to the strong man's total domination.

Rather than sitting there, however, reveling in his sexual reverie, or wasting further time ruminating over the way his personal feelings for Chase had taken a one-hundred-eighty-degree turnaround, he instead returned to poring over his tedious report on the future growth of San Diego.

Hunter felt highly gratified that his agonizing hangover had subsided, and was soon so engrossed in his work, he made no effort to even acknowledge the unpleasant reality that so far as any future with Chase was concerned, he had already disengaged and was by then long gone and far away.

*   *   *   *

Also flying over the Pacific, heading in the same general direction as Hunter's plane, albeit further north, toward Los Angeles, Chase found it ironic that the First Class seat next to him on the crowded aircraft was unoccupied. He was mystified because, even after all the crushing disappointment and rejection of the past week, his loving feelings for Hunter, rather than dwindling had, instead, somehow intensified.

Okay, so they fought and bickered over the silliest of details. And Hunter had certainly been an insensitive, uncivilized jerk, so haphazardly trashing their "sacred" covenant that had been the Kid's damn idea in the first place. For reasons he could neither understand nor articulate, Chase felt more committed to their union than ever. And once he acknowledged his confusion over that sad conclusion, he also appreciated how he had no alternative but to do whatever it might take to get the two of them back on track. He needed to find some way to get both himself and Hunter past this ridiculous setback, so they could again go forward in harmony as the loving, functioning couple he still trusted was their destiny.

When it came to fidelity, men were snakes. That was old news. And gay men, Chase learned the hard way, were often the biggest asps of all. Monogamy seemed to be mysteriously missing from their genetic make-up. He wondered if a small slice within the gene for homosexuality might not also contain a propensity toward roamosexuality.

Chase knew he needed to forgive Hunter for his temporary drift from reason, his foolhardy flight from the fidelity to which they'd at least superficially agreed. He reasoned that if the growing pangs of their affiliation never went through any challenges, never suffered any rough spots along the dusty road toward stabilization, then maybe there wasn't much worth fighting for in the first place. He knew he needed to fight to regain Hunter's commitment and vowed to restore Hunter's need for him.

His concern about any lingering ill feelings between himself and Hunter were quickly back-burnered early that evening, as soon as he returned to Hyde Park. When he opened the front door, he was surprised when Atlas didn't rush over to gaily greet him. Chase walked through the house, looking for his bully pup, but his canine companion was nowhere around.

At last, Chase came upon a post-it attached to his refrigerator door. The note had been pasted there by Gloria Bishop, his tenant who looked after the ten-month old bulldog while Chase was in Hawaii. In a scribbled-scrawl, Gloria asked Chase to call her as soon as he got in.

"Sorry to have to tell you this, Chase," Gloria said softly, timidly, after answering her phone. "But two days after you left, Atlas had a small seizure. I thought it might be an isolated incident, and didn't want to bother you in Hawaii, so I let it pass. Then, yesterday, while I was walking him, he had another convulsion, far worse, and then … well, he didn't come out of it."

"What do you mean, didn't come out if it?"

"I mean he remained unconscious," Gloria told him. "So I rushed him over to your vet in the Valley. They said he suffered a *grand mal*, whatever that is. He's there now, still in a coma, and apparently on life support."

"Oh … no …"

"I feel awful. I was going to call you on your cell, but since there wasn't much you could do, and since you were due back today, I figured, why ruin your dream vacation?"

"Thanks," Chase told her. "I'll drive over there right now."

*   *   *   *

Anxious and distraught, Chase drove like a madman up to the top of Laurel Canyon and then down into Studio City, straight over to the Pet Pals Clinic on Ventura Boulevard.

"Your bulldog doesn't seem to be in any pain," the veterinary assistant on duty assured Chase as she led him through the rear section of the clinic, past a dozen or so sickly dogs and cats housed in stacked wire cages. The pathetic whelps of saddened abandonment combined with the cacophony of pitiful purrs coming from four-legged patients in distress, intensified Chase's anxiety.

He looked down upon his sweet brindle-and-white pup spread flat out in his enclosure, lightly panting away in his puppy stupor. One of his little paws was connected to an IV, the other attached to a life-support tube monitoring the arrhythmic beating of his young heart.

"Hey, there, Atlas," Chase said softly as he opened the door of the cage. The sight of his beloved tubby little pup, comatose and so sadly incapacitated, so extremely vulnerable, was heartbreaking. "How you doing, little guy?" Chase asked quietly. "Hey, Buddy — it's Daddy."

Atlas's eyes half-opened for the briefest of moments, but they didn't register any cognition.

"I'm here now," Chase told him, getting chocked up. "And I'll make sure you get through this."

The assistant on duty told Chase the veterinarian mentioned something about the next couple of days being pivotal to the bulldog's recovery, and suggested he call the following morning to speak to the doctor, personally. Chase said he'd do just that, leaned over and planted a tender kiss on the top of Atlas' head, then closed the cage door and left the clinic.

When he returned to Hyde Park, he placed a call to Hunter. Transferred to Hunter's message center, he left word about how critically ill Atlas was. He then asked Hunter to please call as soon as he picked up the message upon returning home to New York from San Diego.

First thing the following morning, Chase called Pet Pals and spoke to Dr. Walters. His vet told him Atlas was responding to treatment, was already off life support, and again breathing on his own. *Thank God*, thought Chase, breathing his own sigh of relief. "If he continues improving like this," Dr. Walters prognosticated. "We'll move him out of Intensive Care, and he can probably go home a few days after that."

*   *   *   *

Chase realized the rocky road he'd mapped toward his reconciliation with Hunter might be bumpier than he first anticipated when, after several days, he still hadn't heard back from the once-attentive man he used to call his boyfriend.

When he returned to the vet's to pick up Atlas several days later, he wondered if he might not need his own life support when he picked up his bulldog's medical bill for $6580. Chase had no idea how he was going to cover so exorbitant a fee, but none of that really mattered once a wobbly Atlas wiggled over to him and began joyfully licking his master's face. Rather than worry about his dire financial situation, he turned to the all-American solution and told the receptionist to charge the invoice to his credit card.

Chase felt a whole lot better once Atlas was back home where he belonged. His bully pup had dropped a few pounds, was looking a bit frail and lacked energy. He even appeared somewhat depressed as he moped about the house at an even more sluggish pace than was his custom. He had little of his normally voracious appetite, and spent most of his day curled up on the couch, snoring away, lost within the protective cloud of his own muscle rest. Chase hoped his furry buddy was just going through the process of recovery.

After a week of being molly-coddled and fussed over, Atlas regained much of his considerable appetite, was once again energetic and playful, more like his former frisky self at the height of his puppydom. Chase decided Atlas needed a special treat, and drove his canine life partner to the doggy park just off the Mulholland Drive bicycle path. As always, the pooch had a joyous time there, romping about off his leash, perkily playing with the animated pack of other pure breeds and mixed mutts visiting the pet sanctuary in the hills.

Quite the social animal, Atlas played while sniffing out the private parts of other four-legged guests at the park. After half an hour of scampering about, fetching Frisbees, retrieving balls, and prancing zanily all over the lawn, Chase and his bulldog headed back over to his master's Jeep. Along the way, without warning, Atlas lapsed into another grand mal seizure. He shook in violent, horrifying convulsions and collapsed onto his side atop the parking lot pavement.

Helpless, Chase dropped to his knees and, not knowing what else to do, held onto his pup's trembling head as Atlas lay there shaking uncontrollably, his jaws snapping haphazardly at the air.

After a few moments, his violent contortions induced a massive stroke. Atlas slowly extended all four of his paws straight out, and then, just like that, he stopped shaking, stopped convulsing, went rigid, and then limp. Sprawled out on the cement pavement, his tongue hung out of the side of his mouth.

A small group of curious park visitors, mountain bikers off the path, and fellow dog owners, slowly gathered around Chase and Atlas to investigate the commotion. Chase stared down upon his motionless pup. It all happened so quickly, it took him a beat to grasp that Atlas, sprawled out on the pavement before him, was dead.

*   *   *   *

Chase brought Atlas's lifeless body back over to Pet Pals and, after being told they would take care of everything, left his beloved bulldog with them.

As he drove back over Laurel Canyon, he began to weep. And couldn't stop. He pulled off the road and sat in his car, bawling for several minutes until he was again fit to drive.

Back home at Hyde Park, the house seemed eerily empty, oddly silent without Atlas lazing about. The fact that Chase still hadn't heard from Hunter since returning from Hawaii the week before only compounded his heightened sense of gloom. He knew he needed to give his muscle buddy breathing room, but he also felt a deep need to cater to his own vulnerability and share his god-awful news. So he called Hunter's office. Big mistake.

Hunter's secretary, as if by rote, mechanically rattled off the fact Mr. Rowe was in a meeting and not available. Chase toughed it out and left a short message on Hunter's voice mail, telling him the sad news. Four days later, Chase still hadn't heard back from Hunter, either by phone or online, so he made one last effort to call him at his office.

Hunter had just finished conducting a five-way video conference and, when the phone rang, assumed it was one of his associates calling back to compliment him on the superlative job he'd just done. Hunter's secretary was off on a coffee break, so he picked up the phone himself, announcing, "This is Hunter Rowe!"

To his chagrin, it was Chase on the line. "I've been meaning to call you," Hunter lied after a volley of awkward hellos. "Been buried in work since I got back."

"That's okay," Chase said quietly, hoping to sound conciliatory. "I figured you've been busy."

"Really swamped here at work," Hunter was emphatic. "Just keeps piling up, like so much horse shit, more and more every day. This month alone, we picked up three new accounts. Major clients!"

"I understand," Chase acknowledged. "Just needed to commiserate with you about Atlas."

"Oh, right," said Hunter, matter-of-factly. "Poor puppy. I got your message, but you can't imagine what a madhouse it's been here. I haven't had a moment to myself since I got back. Can you believe I haven't even hit the gym yet?"

"No gym?" Chase was amazed. "Wow, I guess you *must* be under a lot of stress."

"Like you can't imagine!" Hunter assured him. "I'm real sorry about Atlas."

"Thanks," Chase answered gratefully. "Feels good to touch base with you again."

Hunter felt some perverse satisfaction having Chase now pursuing him, and no longer the other way around. Still, there wasn't much more he could contribute now that his interest in their future together had lost its momentum. Besides, his day was far too crowded with high-pressure commitments to facilitate any further time for this conversation. "Can I be frank with you?" he asked.

"Shoot!"

"Okay — back when we first met, my workload was a hell of a lot lighter, my responsibilities fewer, so I had plenty of time to concentrate just on you. Not any more. I'm under the gun here. Besides, let's be honest. You don't really need me. You have it easy. From what I can tell, your life is focused on the gym, and that's about it."

"So what's your point?" Chase asked.

"I don't know," Hunter told him, candidly. "Just doesn't seem especially productive."

"Okay, so I've been in a bit of slump," Chase came to his own defense as he wondered why he was the one made to feel guilty about trying to keep alive their friendship. "But I've been thinking about starting another project. Maybe another novel."

"Good idea!" said Hunter, encouragingly. Then, not wanting to appear *too* hopeful or supportive, quickly added, perhaps a bit too pointedly, "And about time!"

"You probably think I'm still mad at you for going off with that biker, don't you?" Chase asked, pleasantly as possible. "That's all in the past, like it never happened. I've gotten over it. Can't you?"

"Oh, please …" Hunter waved a dismissive hand. "That was just a stupid one-night stand. What's that got to do with anything?"

Chase fought to remain calm. "You know, getting over Atlas's unexpected death might be just a little easier if I knew you were still here in my corner."

"Don't you think I know that?" Hunter asked, purposely ambiguous.

"And I'd also feel a whole lot better if I knew you still loved me …"

"Hell, Coach …" Hunter sighed with exhaustion and rolled his eyes to the ceiling. *Patience*, he told himself. *Just placate him, and then get off the phone.* "You must know part of me will always love you." Hunter said flatly, like he was choosing a linoleum pattern. "But right now, by necessity, you're no longer the most important element in my life, okay? I need to concentrate on my career."

"I have no problem with that," said Chase.

"Tell you what," Hunter suggested, sternly. "It'll help a lot if you'd stop calling me so much. I've got enough on my plate. How 'bout if I get back to you as soon as I have some free time?"

When Hunter's chilly suggestion was greeted on the other end by three thousand miles of long- distance silence, he asked, "Did I lose you?"

No, thought Chase, with a deep breath of frustration. *Did I lose YOU?* "I'm right here," he finally answered.

"I've got to be midtown in twenty minutes to meet clients," Hunter told him. "I can't be late."

"I understand."

"Good!" Hunter quipped as he scanned the first page of a lengthy survey enumerating consumer reactions to a new Colgate whitening toothpaste being test-marketed around the Baltimore area. "Thanks for calling. We'll talk again as soon as I have time to breathe, okay?"

"Sure thing," said Chase, hoping to sound agreeable and understanding, rather than disappointed and annoyed by Hunter's disturbing ambivalence.

"I got a meeting to get to."

"No problem," Chase said, sadly.

"Thanks for calling, Coach. We'll talk soon, okay?"

"I hope so, Hunter. I've really been missing you."

"Holy shit!" Hunter exclaimed as he looked at his watch. "Will you look at the damn time?"

"Why don't you just tell me the truth?" Chase finally came out with it and asked, frankly, "Why don't you just admit you don't give a shit?"

"Fine!" Hunter was defiant, his patience worn thin. "I pushed you away, okay? That what you want to hear? I disengaged. Happy now?"

"Happy?" Chase was flabbergasted. "How could that make me happy?"

"I gotta go," Hunter announced with an unapologetic shrug. "Good-bye."

"Wait a minute …"

"I can't be late for this meeting," Hunter insisted. Trying to justify his actions, he concluded, "And I'm sorry, but no one likes needy. You never once catered to my darkest needs, never once scared the shit out of me like I wanted. So here's the bottom line: you need to find yourself another star varsity wrestler because I'm out of the match."

"But what about …"

"That's it, Chase. I have nothing more to say!" Proving his point, Hunter hung up the phone and darted from his office.

On the other side of the country, Chase stared into his receiver as it buzzed its irritating disconnect.

*   *   *   *

Overnight, Chase spiraled downward into an emotional tailspin and for the next several days roamed about the house in a state of bewildered disenchantment. Sadly, it was not until he faced the cold reality of Hunter's rejection, combined with the fact that Atlas was not coming back, before he fully realized how desperate he felt without them, how he missed his pup, how he still needed Hunter.

Compounding his dismay, the Coach was slapped with yet another rude awakening when he next discovered how prominent was the gap suddenly placed in the middle of his everyday existence with Hunter and Atlas suddenly no longer a part of it. The Kid had done such a thorough job of making himself so completely essential, and now that his laser-guided attention was no longer beamed directly at Chase, it was dearly missed. Chase had been so comfortable, luxuriating in the barrage of devotion Hunter showered on him, that the moment it was so abruptly withdrawn, the vacuum created in its wake hit Chase with a wallop. Hunter's paralyzing dismissal of their covenant clawed away at his insides, even as it broke apart the foundation of his common sense.

Lifeless, he propped himself up against the pillows of his bed and half-watched an endless parade of mindless teen comedies movies on HBO. A dense haze of defeat encircled his troubled spirit as it seeped through his system. He felt himself drowning in a tidal wave of anxiety.

Out of nowhere, without provocation, and for no apparent reason, he wept. Seeing a flock of graceful doves traversing the sky outside his window could trigger a torrent of tears. Watching the devastation from an earthquake in Chile on CNN made him sob in empathy. Viewing a litter of puppies in an Alpo commercial made him bawl as he wallowed in self-pity while poring over cherished photos of Atlas.

Lying in bed, morose and lifeless, Chase wondered just why the world looked so damn peachy all the while he was in love, and then turned so dismal and gloomy the moment his heart was broken.

Nothing made sense anymore. Even after sobbing his way through a score of emotional outbursts, he still felt no sense of release. His stomach churned in constant agitation. With no discernible appetite, he ate but rarely, and when he did, picked at his food. His insides ached as though he was being pounded in the gut. His head throbbed as if he'd been slammed with a two-by-four. He had trouble sleeping. His muscles felt sore and achy. His phone messages went unreturned. He stopped showering and shaving, didn't even bother going to the gym. His mood grew dark, then darker still, even as his energy deserted him, and his outlook on life waxed ever more grim.

The most painful aspect of his suddenly dysfunctional behavior was that, for the life of him, he could not get Hunter off his mind. You'd have thought the very essence of his one-time, would-be, lifelong partner had moved in, set up some spiritual residence deep within his psyche, like an uninvited tenant who not only didn't pay his rent, but also refused to vacate.

Chase hadn't experienced a hurt this badly or felt this devastated since Kutchie got so deathly ill, since his affair with Christian ended so badly, so irretrievably, more than ten years earlier. Since that time, he had purposely chosen to remain aloof, carefully kept up his guard, and never allowed his emotions to influence any relationship. Until he met Hunter.

Maybe if the Kid hadn't been so damn persistent, so thoroughly resolute in having Chase loving him so fully in return, and if only Chase hadn't been so stupid as to relent, all his emotional distress could have been avoided.

As his sense of gloom and despair deepened, he knew he could not afford to lose them both. He had to let Atlas go. That was a given. But he was not willing to also give up his partner. During any minute of the day, any hour of the night, as he ached with a yearning worthy of an addiction, he also knew he had no choice but to find some way to see them reunited.

*   *   *   *

Chase was toying with his remote, still mindlessly flipping channel to channel several days later when the front bell rang incessantly. He dragged himself out of bed and lumbered to the door.

Stack stood there in a tank top and workout shorts.

"Oh … it's you," Chase muttered. "Come in." He turned and headed back to his bedroom.

"Coach, you look like shit," Stack told him frankly as he followed right behind. "And did you notice you haven't returned my last three thousand messages?"

"Haven't checked my machine," said Chase. "Haven't done much of anything."

"Is that why your place is such a mess?" Stack wanted to know as he looked around at the atypical disarray. "What the hell happened? How was Hawaii?"

"Dandy," Chase said, subdued. "Hunter and I broke up."

"Damn!" Stack reacted with surprise. "Hey, I'm real sorry, pal."

"I know," Chase said, wearily. "I am so fucking crushed. I feel paralyzed. Oh, yeah, one other thing. Atlas had another seizure and died."

"Holy shit," Stack said, almost inaudibly. "Well, no wonder you're such a wreck."

"No wonder," Chase agreed.

"So what happened with you and Hunter?"

"How the fuck should I know?" asked Chase. "Turns out the one thing I couldn't give him was abuse. Plus I broke the eleventh commandment, our cardinal rule: Love is for losers. Now I have to figure a way to get back on track."

"Good thing I stopped by to make sure you're okay. Now that I'm here, why don't you pull your shit together and come with me to the gym? Let's work out together."

"I can't, Stack," Chase semi-moaned as he crawled back into bed, under the covers. "Right now, I'm too fucked up. I'm not up to working out ... not up for anything."

"Hey!" Stack tapped into his alpha-male. "Show me some backbone here, will ya? Hell, man, you're the goddamn Coach, remember? Not some lovesick teenager. Snap out of it, get over him, and move on. Just like the old days. Let's go!"

"I want to, Stack. You think I enjoy feeling like this?"

"I sure as shit hope not!" Stack grunted and pulled back the covers. "Come on — get your lazy butt out of bed. We'll hit the gym. You'll feel a whole lot better once you're pumped."

"Thanks, Stack," Chase forced a smile as he leaned against his pillows. "Soon as I come out of this fucking fog. I promise. Right now, I just need some more time to myself."

"Something good's gonna come from all this," Stack assured Chase. "You'll see. Remember back long ago after you and Christian broke up? If he hadn't switched gyms, you and I might never have hooked up as workout partners."

"Don't try to cheer me up, okay?"

"Fine, Coach," Stack said with assurance. "You wanna have this meltdown, go ahead. But he's sure not worth it. And now that it's come to this, I can tell you the truth: I never liked the little jerk."

"Never?"

"Not for a minute!" Stack insisted. "We all thought he was trying to pull you away from us — keep you to himself. Personally, I thought he was a selfish little prick."

"Why didn't you tell me?"

"Because you didn't want to hear it," Stack stated bluntly as he headed for the door. "Okay, I'm taking off. These powerful pecs need to be pumped. Plus, I gotta start worrying about securing my afternoon blowjob. You coming with me, or not?"

"Not today," said Chase, sinking deeper into his bed. "All I want, besides having Hunter and Atlas back, is to be left alone."

"Hey," Stack said, on his way out of the room. "I'm real sorry about the bulldog."

"Thanks for coming by," Chase said quietly.

"Cheer up, okay?"

"Yeah, Stack," Chase answered, mordantly. "That's just what I'm about to do."

*   *   *   *

Another few days dragged by and still Chase felt no better. By turns deflated, demoralized, and depressed, he was also, after charging Atlas's exorbitant medical bills to his credit card, deeply in debt. His mortgage payment was already three weeks late. He was slouching into economic distress, and needed to get out of debt immediately. His biggest source of income, Hyde Park's two-bedroom rental unit behind his house, was still vacant. There was only one way Chase could meet his mortgage payments over the next six months and also gratify Atlas's vet tab. With no other funds available, he swallowed a hefty early withdrawal penalty and cashed in most of his IRA.

Even after mailing in his mortgage payment, along with its excessive late fee, and paying off his credit card, Chase's bleak financial situation seemed the least of his worries. He could do little more than obsess over how damned fast things soured between himself and the man with whom he'd made a covenant, a man with whom he pledged undying, enduring loyalty.

Chase moped about the house for another week. He still hadn't returned to the gym and, with little appetite, dropped seven pounds. Walking around in a cloud of misery became his leitmotif, mordant self-pity his primary expression.

After a few more days of lying around, emotionally immobilized by his anguish, he realized that if this intense period of grieving went on much longer, it was bound to extract a costly toll on his body, his mind, indeed, on what remained of his depleted spirit. He felt himself starting to lose it. By the time he hit bottom, in the depths of his unhappiness, he also knew it was time to either give it all up and quit, or somehow find a way to climb up from his desolation.

In the end, Chase refused to let his grief over Hunter drag him down any further into his void of despondency. If he was to retain a shred of dignity, a shard of his carefully manufactured persona as Coach Chase, he had to beat Hunter at his own game.

He knew he'd been taken down for the count, emotionally, physically, financially and, after much consternation, he decided the time had come to get past his mourning, end his grieving, and heal the damage. In the end, it was up to him and him alone to come to his rescue. He resolved to get out of his deep funk, lick his wounds, and get back to what had been his real life. Defeat was no longer an option and Chase knew he was on the road to recovery the moment his anguish morphed into resentment. Resentment swiftly segued into a seething anger, and from there, it was but a stone's throw into mounting rage. Chase took a hard look at his dour image in the mirror. He then promised his reflection he'd move past his pain and get even. No matter the sacrifice, no matter the cost, if it was the last thing he did, Chase Hyde swore he'd reap his revenge.

How dare that little prick drop me, thought Chase. For the first time, he understood the mentality behind crazed stalkers who grew so obsessed with their former lovers, they developed a perverse need to shadow their every move. He fully comprehended why some men felt compelled to call, waking their former partner in the middle of the night, just to hear their groggy voice before hanging up on them. It suddenly made perfect sense why Don Jose was driven to strangle Carmen after she ruined his life by running off with that big-time bullfighter. The two-timing harlot got what she deserved. He commiserated as never before with the betrayed husband who returns home from work one evening and snaps, goes to his closet, whips out his Winchester, strolls into the kitchen where his wife is peeling potatoes, and calmly empties a round of bullets into her two-timing torso.

If humans have an innate psychological mechanism for reciprocity, a natural willingness to repay kindness with kindness, Chase decided it followed that we must also carry within us an inherent need to repay betrayal with revenge. He'd fallen victim to the kind of insane, all-consuming love the French call *amour folle*. He refused to be the one ending up as the loser in their battle of the same sexes, and that meant this was fucking war. No way some half-assed, so-called Boy Wonder of Madison Avenue was about to just waltz in, step all over his life and, in the process, crush his ego and diminish everything he'd spent so many years constructing.

He had to climb out of his physical slump and emerge from his emotional trauma not just a better man for all the pain, but triumphant. He needed to slam the brakes on the breaking of his training. Chase was quickly closing in on fifty, and knew damn well that if he didn't work at it full time, his hunk status would swiftly vanish. Last thing he wanted was to end up as just another overweight, former jock with a sad pouch and a beefy muscularity gone soft.

He committed himself to getting back into top shape, to building his body back into even better condition than before his recent surgery, before his agonizing heartbreak. He would achieve this, not solely to force Hunter to realize the error of his misguided break-up, but also for his own pride and peace of mind.

Chase stopped feeling sorry for himself as soon as he began channeling his considerable fury into the scheming of his payback. He spent the next few days working on just how he might best accomplish his goal. He was a writer, after all, and the bulk of his fiction had always been spiced with dramatic contrivances. How hard could it be to fabricate a real life scenario of reprisal and retribution?

Formulating his revenge became Chase's main focus, his new obsession. He planned to give Hunter the most intense muscle fantasy of his life. And since by then Chase knew Hunter so well, he also knew how to deliver the goods. *He wants scared?* thought Chase. *I'll give him SCARED!*

After mulling over the formulation of his strategy, Chase slowly came up with a wild plan of attack, an outlandish ruse to get even. He knew Hunter had another upcoming business trip to San Diego scheduled for the beginning of August. As the blueprint of a well-plotted vengeance hatched in his head, he initiated his war plan.

For openers, he needed to use the time before Hunter's upcoming visit to San Diego to get back into top condition. Energized and motivated, he was determined to return to the gym in full force. He long ago learned from working out with both Christian and his workout partner, Stack, that to optimize his bouncing back as rapidly as possible, the most gainful means to attaining his goal was to change his mind about his long-standing prejudice against ever using steroids.

Backed up against the wall by extraordinary circumstance, Chase was out for blood. His mind made up, he didn't wait another moment before he called Stack, and told him he was finally ready to return to the gym, and back into heavy training. Chase also told his massive workout partner he was ready to start injecting into his butt the kind of illegal cocktail that would speedily help him lose his recently acquired, unwanted body fat, and at the same time pack on a hefty ten to fifteen pounds of major muscle.

Elated by this news, Stack promised to prepare for his muscle buddy the most aggressive cycle imaginable, and further guaranteed he'd be pushing his workout partner harder than ever before. He concocted for Chase a potent cocktail of anabolic steroids that would see his body peaking in all its miraculous muscledom by the time Hunter got to San Diego, in seven weeks.

Chase's evil plan to win back Hunter's love was so audacious, his strategy so seemingly foolproof, it made him smile.

He would simply make himself irresistible.

*   *   *   *

BRUTE FORCE

Chase put all his energy into his training, pumping iron at the gym with a determination the likes of which he hadn't exuded in decades. At the same time, he also initiated thrusting into the top of his butt the thrice-weekly hypodermic needles filled with the muscle-building elixir provided by Stack. It was a potent cocktail comprised of varying cc's of Deca, Equipoise, and Winstrol.

The hundred-eighty-degree turnaround in Chase's attitude regarding steroids meant that any of their heralded side effects, those unsightly rashes, the explosive 'roid-rages, the risk of blood clots, baldness, strokes, damage to his vital organs, a plague of locusts, and so on, were all put on hold, conveniently relegated to a back seat in his priorities. He didn't care that any improvements to his physique would for the most part be impermanent. And so what if his liver collapsed by the time he turned sixty? He was in pain at forty-nine, and for the time being unconcerned about the muscle cramps he endured, and the bouts of diarrhea he suffered. He wasn't even bothered that in the process, his heart might suffer damage. Hell, it was already broken.

Stack was so excited about Chase's change of tone, he not only sold the juice to his workout partner at cost, he even allowed Chase to slide in paying for it until he was once again flush.

Chase not only went into overdrive with his training, he also started writing again. It wasn't like he planned it. He simply felt compelled to move his thoughts into words, so he just sat down one morning, started banging away, and let it all pour out. Inspired by the depths of his receding despondency, the prose flowed out of him in a surging burst of creativity, practically nonstop. It was as if he'd never been away from his imagination.

First thing every morning, Chase pounded away at his computer. The plot came to him in fragments, like pieces of a giant jigsaw puzzle scattered across the floor, pieces he slowly strung together and eventually connected into a working outline. A full story soon spewed forth, and his writing turned into a cathartic river of self-expression, a needle slowly sewing the split tendons of his shaken spirit. Long branches of words spilled across his monitor screen like a stream of water pouring into a bottomless pool. Page after page, his once again fertile mind gave birth to a tall tale borne of joy and pain, a budding narrative that slowly evolved into a promising manuscript. As he typed away furiously, the story practically wrote itself as his ideas became a vibrant venue for venting his venomous rage, a near frenzied, yet somehow cleansing, perfect storm of words.

What he wrote about was Hunter. How they met. How he was shamelessly romanced and duped into their torrid affair. How they fell in love. How they broke up, and how he was shattered. Compelled to unveil their saga, he sensed the best way to retain his emotional stability was to get it all out, and so he dedicated himself to constructing an ever better manuscript, while at the same time, building an ever better body.

He wrote day and night, from the time he got up until late afternoon when he left to meet Stack at the gym. He simply wrote it as he remembered it, feeling oddly at ease, but nonetheless committed to airing his dirty laundry directly from his memory and onto his keyboard as he resurrected the entire saga of Hunter and Chase.

Being a novelist, he changed their names and stretched his dramatic license when it suited a plot point. But for the most part, he just typed away as his new writing project, along with the restoration of his former muscular prominence, became his life's assignment.

He wrote and trained, wrote and ate, wrote and slept, before he'd start all over again, repeating the fevered process the next day and then the next. Never before this driven, never so filled with purpose, Chase wrote late into the night. He screwed his courage to his dual missions, and damned if anything was going to distract him before he saw both projects through to fruition. He wrote for hours every morning, and then carefully injected his steroids before biking down to Gold's — getting it off his chest on the computer and then pumping up his chest at the gym.

Thanks to the contraband substances coursing throughout his system, along with Stack's ongoing encouragement, he was soon lifting weightier weights, pressing heavier barbells, curling bigger dumbbells. He rested no more than ninety seconds between sets, broke into a sweat while doing aerobics, and constantly varied his workouts, purposefully shocking his muscles as he hit every major group hard, all the way to muscle failure on every set. He trained hard, then harder still, before biking home to feed the machine with still more protein, and then sitting down again to return to his writing.

He assembled the rough outline of a beginning, middle and near conclusion, and as his story raced to its finish, Chase was amazed at how poignant it was to experience again upon his monitor screen the entire sad affair, and how much he also enjoyed setting up the elements of his vendetta, the planning of his forthcoming, bittersweet revenge.

*   *   *   *

Thirty-two stories above Madison Avenue, at seven-thirty in the evening, Hunter sat hunched over the desk in his office, poring over consumer reactions to his promotional campaign for San Diego tourism. A recently delivered white paper bag from Sal's Luncheonette filled with his dinner of double cheeseburger, greasy fries, and a vanilla Coke sat unopened before him.

Since returning from Hawaii, weeks earlier, he had become so preoccupied with his work, he was eating far more sloppily, mostly out of frustration, hoping it might relieve some of the escalating stress he felt at work from the executives hovering over him. Unfortunately for him, the huge workload he'd delegated to his subordinates before he flew off on vacation had been neither implemented nor followed through with the efficacy he had requested. Now, with his overbearing supervisor breathing down his neck, he had no choice but to finish the bulk of the damn paperwork himself.

Every work day, Hunter got to his office early, a little after seven, so he could polish off his ponderous paperwork before the phones began ringing, usually around eight-thirty. That meant he no longer made the time to get his training out of the way first thing in the morning. Owing to his increased work load, he also had no choice but to work late into the evening. Too often, he just called out for fast food which, twenty minutes later, was delivered to his desk.

It wasn't as if Hunter was avoiding the gym on purpose, or so he told himself. He kept meaning to get there. Staying in top shape, however, was simply no longer the high priority it had once been. Besides, every time he tried blocking out time for a workout, for the rebuilding of his softening body, he was invariably distracted by some ongoing drama at the office, something involving his main focus: the renewed obsession that was the forward march of his career. Besides, by the time he left work, he was too sapped of energy to hit the weights. Maybe that was just as well since by then, his devotion to muscle had pretty much dissipated.

After conducting a lengthy dialogue with his inner demons, Hunter concluded how ultimately superficial and shallow was the adolescent lure of muscle. While he was still disappointed over how swiftly his romance with Chase had soured, he also needed to face the naked truth: his vanity-driven pursuit of muscle was clearly *not* what he really wanted or needed in his life. And so he altered his priorities, shelving the quest for an ever better body in pursuit of his career ambitions.

Big deal if muscles were pretty to look at, even highly satisfying and titillating to touch, squeeze, or fondle. In bare truth, weren't they also mostly facade and pretense, more surface than substance, more armor than engine? Weren't muscles more a transient blessing than any kind of permanent fixture, more a cosmetic accoutrement than anything that might ever prove truly useful?

Hunter turned the page on his report, studied the myriad research data, and began jotting down pertinent stats he'd incorporate into his accounting to the corporate brass. As he marked up his marketing report, he also opened the white bag sitting before him, pulled out the cardboard container of now limp, tepid home fries, and began chomping away.

After several more weeks of eating poorly, sleeping fitfully, and never once getting back to the gym, Hunter's rigid six-pack began receding beneath the thin outer layer of fat that bit by bit began protruding around his midsection. Weakened, the striated cuts that once flourished across his thick delts and the well-carved cluster of his strong back muscles were swiftly fading.

He was still fairly hard and smooth, still genetically well-structured. But, as anyone who ever abruptly stopped working out can attest, inactive muscles begin to atrophy with a blinding speed that's most often in direct proportion to however long it took to build them up in the first place. With so much inactivity, his body, for the first time since he first emerged as a hunk, years earlier, began looking more like that of a beefy former jock's than the near contest-ready bodybuilder who had been jogging along that black-sand beach in Hawaii just a month and a half earlier.

*   *   *   *

Chase stayed busy writing, working out, and finishing his cycle. To neither his nor Stack's surprise, the steroids worked their anticipated wonders on his body. Day after day, he could both see and feel his powerful muscles on the increase, noticeably ever more massive, as they rounded out and expanded thanks to their chemically induced water retention.

The girth of his biceps bulged until his guns once again pressed tight against the sleeves of his tee shirts, seemingly poised to rip out from the material. By the time the Guns of Navarone swelled to eighteen inches, they never looked more full, cut or sensuous. When he pumped his pecs on the bench press, they became engorged with a fresh supply of blood and with every set, he forced his vascularity into greater prominence. His traps grew thicker in prominence, his cobra head lats flared out, and his teardrop quads thickened, never so huge, never more muscular, never so sexy. His twelve new pounds of inflated muscle shot his weight up to two hundred seventeen. His body fat dropped down to three and a half percent. His six-pack abs looked again like your grandmother's waffle iron. He was all muscle, all sinew, finally all ready for mayhem.

At the peak of his cycle, he studied his newfound mass in the mirror and for the first time understood why so many bodybuilders became addicted to the speed by which their steroid-induced muscles developed. The betterment of his body was proceeding right on schedule. And now that he'd nailed the physical element needed to entrap Hunter, he raised the curtain on the psychodrama he was about to unfold.

Chase went online and created an entirely new handle for himself, a novel name he came up with and then incorporated when he composed an introductory, "anonymous" e-mail he planned to send to Hunter.

In his misleading missive, he pretended to be someone else, a fictional character of his own creation. Chase edited his handiwork several times, until he was finally satisfied with his fabricated composition. Excited, he read it over one last time:

From: RuffMuscleGuy@aol.com

To: HunterRowe@Yahoo.com

Hunter —

This may be a real long shot, but after seeing your hot pictures posted on BigMuscle. com, and reading in your profile that you're planning to visit San Diego at the beginning of August, and more importantly, that you're looking to be dominated by a big, aggressive muscleman, I figured I had nothing to lose by writing to tell you what's on my mind.

I'm a 28-year-old bodybuilder who's been married for several years. My wife and I are no longer intimate. We stay together because by now we're good friends, and also because, in all candor, her father owns the bank where I work. So there's a bright future for me if I stay there.

Since I live a double life, I have no choice but to always be discreet. I work in a very old-fashioned environment and no one here knows about my attraction to other muscular men. While I know little about the gay scene here in San Diego, I do still like to break away when I can for an intense session of hot muscle sex with a well built fellow who looks — well, frankly, who looks a lot like YOU.

My wife knows nothing about this side of my personality, and would be devastated if she ever found out. For that reason, it is essential we maintain total secrecy.

Here's the catch: I'm also a former competitive bodybuilder who still trains harder than anyone you'll ever meet, and who perversely enjoys nothing so much as totally dominating my sex partner. I don't even care much for sex with another man if I can't be rough, threatening, maybe even hostile.

I feel a genuine sense of accomplishment on those infrequent occasions when I stray from my domestic situation and take the opportunity to discipline a willing boy, physically and verbally. And I know I'd get off on demonstrating my awesome power, showing you just who's in charge, before leaving you begging for more.

When I first saw your photo, I felt an instant connection when my big dick jumped up and got stiff, and I knew I wanted not just to fuck you really hard, but to also set up the kind of fantasy in which I might restrain you. That way, I could show you what I'm made of by raping your hot little muscle butt, hammering you as forcefully as you can take it, assaulting you until I drive you into a near stupor.

You also need to know that I'm a conservative and well-respected businessman, one who wears a suit and tie to work. So you can trust that I'll respect your sexual needs and willingly work within your limits.

I've attached a recent picture of myself, and must insist you delete it just as soon as you view it. I can send others once you've earned my trust. Once again, my need for discretion must remain paramount.

Ignore this note if none of this works for you. But if the scene I've laid out strikes a chord, and you want to be conquered, dominated, maybe even fucking raped by a massive and muscular, six-foot-three, 250-pound, Total TOP bodybuilder, and if you talk, eat, and sleep muscle, and want to be pounded by it, then get back to me on this right away, you little punk, because I'm clearly your man for the job.

For now, you don't need to know any more about me. My mystery must remain part of my power. Your only job will be to follow orders, to comply with my carnal whims, and obey my every command. For me, that's the only way a scene like this can work — with you as my willing prison bitch, my hapless pussy boy, and me signing off for now as,

Your Ruff Muscle Guy

Chase finished rereading his outlandish concoction and felt a curious sense of accomplishment. So far so good. Before sending it off, he carefully selected and then attached a photo from his files. The picture he sent was one of the many shots he had taken more than ten years earlier and still kept stored on his computer for purposes of nostalgia. And the winning photo he sent clear across the country through the magic of cyberspace was a shot taken in a Jacuzzi at sunset in Puerta Vallarta of his former lover, the muscle monster and latter day Samson … Christian Falconer.

*   *   *   *

Hunter arrived at work just after ten on Saturday morning, and walked quickly across the quiet, nearly deserted corridor leading to his office. Weekends were the best time to get the most work done as there were so few disruptions and he could concentrate on the backlog of his obligations. He was by then so preoccupied with Broad & Harris, he had not only stopped going to the gym, he also no longer found much free time to play online. He only logged on to the Internet now and again to check e-mail that might be business-related.

He also resolved to stay true to his pledge to put what had been his unending, unfulfilling search for muscle far behind him. He promised himself that any future romantic, man-to-man liaison would have to be based upon the depth of his potential partner's mind, rather than the width of his lats. Proving his point, he deleted Chase's name from his Buddy List, and no longer even cared to know when they were both online at the same time.

First thing he did as he sat down at his desk and turned on his computer that weekend morning was to log on to the Internet, to quickly check his e-mail. He waded through his pertinent business correspondence, and then deleted myriad unwanted Spam mail heralding programs to enlarge his penis or reduce his cellulite, offers to get in on the next hot stock market tip, or enticements to purchase lurid porno sites. At the bottom of his New Mail, Hunter was instantly aroused the moment he came upon a curious item with an attached pic sent from someone with the tantalizing handle, RuffMuscleGuy.

While apprehensive, he opened the missive at once, read it, and then got even more excited when he downloaded the attached pic and sat there, awed when he saw for himself how dazzling and sexy was this new, nameless muscle monster on his monitor. He ogled the photo of a chiseled, near contest-shape Christian, standing in a Jacuzzi, showing off his champion muscularity by flexing his incredibly huge biceps. The bodybuilder seemed the very paradigm of his ideal muscle fantasy. *Hey,* thought

Hunter. *Maybe I am still drawn to muscle, after all!* The letter and the accompanying photo got Hunter so wound up and instantly boned, he stared at the vision while re-reading the missive.

Somehow this huge bodybuilder had managed to press every one of Hunter's erotic buttons, even his most repressed fantasies, casually dropping his favorite buzz words: aggressive, dominant, rough, verbal, and of course, his most coveted of all fantasy fetish dream scenarios … *rape*.

Hunter's enthusiasm was further heightened by the notion that his potential dominator insisted he remain emotionally unavailable to him. If anything, their cross-country distance lent a heightened air of intrigue and excitement to what he hoped might turn into their upcoming rendezvous. *Let it just be physical,* Hunter reasoned, now that he'd decided Chase was right: Love *was* for losers. *That's all I'm looking for. Who needs to be romanced over a candlelit dinner? What I need right now is one fucking hot and super-heavy muscle rape fantasy played out in real time.*

Waiting not another moment, Hunter hit the Reply key and gleefully stirred up his muscle fantasies, opening his eager response in submissive salutation: *Sir! Yes, Sir!*

*   *   *   *

Chase biked home from the gym late Saturday afternoon, all the way up Laurel Canyon, kicking in with his last spurt of reserve energy to pedal pell-mell up the steepest part of his skyward driveway that led to Hyde Park. Pumped but winded, he quickly blended his recovery protein drink and as he slurped it down, carried it to his computer. He felt big and strong and back in business when he logged on to RuffMuscleGuy, the new online handle he'd only recently created, and was emboldened when he found waiting, under New Mail, a reply from Hunter to the missive he'd sent earlier.

From: HunterRowe@Yahoo.com
To: RuffMuscleGuy@AOL.com
Sir! Yes, Sir!
After receiving your note and seeing your hot pic, I'm sure glad I mentioned in my profile that I'll be visiting San Diego at the end of next week. I'm going there on business, staying at the Omni Hotel. And while I'm there, I can't think of anything hotter than having a big, hot muscleman like you taking charge of this willing boy, Sir, but only if I deserve to earn the full force of your astonishing power.

I'm flattered someone with your sense of command wants to manhandle me, and grateful you were so candid as to how you want to fuck me, and Yes, Sir, rape my hot muscleboy butt. I've had this decades-long fantasy to develop a temporary emotional attachment to a captor, and I'm thrilled I might at last have that particular role-playing fantasy realized.

I usually go for older men, but in your case, I'm eager to make an exception. Would it be possible, Sir, for us to talk on the phone before meeting? Or if you have a cam, how 'bout if we first check each other out in motion on our computers?

And if it's okay with you, I'd also like you to be verbally abusive with me should we meet.

I've attached three of my most up-to-date photos, taken on a recent visit to Hawaii, and beg you to send me any more pics of yourself. I am at your disposal, pure putty in your strong hands, Sir, and look forward with high hopes and great anticipation to being turned into your willing and obedient muscle boy.

Hunter

             *   *   *   *

Chase felt gratified by both the rapid reply and the rabid tone of Hunter's avid response. The Kid had succumbed to Coach's entrapment like some silly schoolgirl. His dizzying fickleness, his speedy rebound, further fueled Chase's considerable anger. *That cheap little tramp,* Chase thought, with a sardonic grin. *Took no time for him to latch on to a new object of adulation — even if it is me. So, if it's a goddamn rape scene my former lover boy wants, then that's what he's going to get, big time!*

Set in motion, the tangled pieces of Chase's puzzle were falling smoothly into place as planned. Bolstered by his resolve, he moved forward in setting up the next stage of his forthcoming meeting of the muscles. In his response to Hunter's note, he slipped again into his newly invented tough guy persona. He also sent along with it, for reinforced enticement, a few more pictures of Christian flexing his champion muscles.

From: RuffMuscleGuy@aol.com

To: HunterRowe@Yahoo.com

Glad you're on board, Sailor. As you can well imagine, I'm very particular as to just which men I choose to intimidate and dominate. But those sexy photos of you in Hawaii made me want to fuck your hot muscle ass that much more.

Are you ready for the details of our "rape" scene as I insist they be enacted? If I spell them out, you'll have to agree to fulfill every facet of what will be expected of you, all of it done to the letter. And, if for any reason you are unable or unwilling to meet any of these requirements, we can just drop the whole fucking business right now. There are plenty of other muscular guys out there eager for my abusive attention. I trust we're clear on this? If any of my demands don't work for you, be honest and let me know. Otherwise, I'll expect your complete cooperation. Got it, Boy?

One other thing: What did you think of Hawaii?

Your Ruff Muscle Guy

Hunter had a major hardon the entire time he read RuffMuscleGuy's note. He wasn't yet sure just what erotic demands his potential muscle master had in mind, but whatever they were, he felt confident he could meet them. He hit Reply and responded immediately ...

From: HunterRowe@Yahoo.com

To: RuffMuscleGuy@aol.com

Rest assured, Sir, you've now got my full attention and complete cooperation. By all means, fire away and send the lurid details of our carnal scenario — I eagerly await, prepared to oblige.

I fly into San Diego Wednesday afternoon, July 30th, and leave Saturday morning, August 2. As I'll be buried in boring meetings until late Friday, would it be all right with you, Sir, if we set up our encounter for Friday evening?

Oh, and Hawaii was kind of a disappointment. Turned out my former boyfriend wasn't the hero I thought.

Thanks for your latest pics, Master. They're driving me nuts. You are my dream muscle fantasy cum true.

Your Muscle Boy,
Hunter

Two days later, Hunter logged back on the Internet and excitedly read Ruff Muscle Guy's response …

From: RuffMuscleGuy@aol.com
To: HunterRowe@Yahoo.com

Maybe it's a good thing your boyfriend disappointed you in Hawaii, or you might not have been available for our explosive encounter. You've got yourself a rape date, Muscle Boy — Friday night, the 1st of August, your room at the Omni.

Here's how my Rape Rules come together:

On the night we meet, I want you in your hotel room, lying on the bed, flat out on your stomach, butt-naked. Your orders are to turn off all the lights, except the one in the bathroom. You are to go to a sex shop beforehand and purchase a hooded mask, a small, plastic ball with head strap to stuff into your mouth and stretch around your head, as well as two sets of handcuffs. That clear, boy?

Your head needs to be completely covered so I don't have to look down on your miserable face, and you don't get permission to see mine until I'm good and ready. Your mouth needs to be blocked so that any enthusiastic cries of your aching discomfort remain muted. Past that, I don't want to hear from you. You still with me, Pussy Boy?

You are to lock one section of each set of open handcuffs around each of your wrists, and snap-shut the other part to the bed post. That way, your hands will be restrained as soon as I get there, and I can get straight to work.

You are to place a box of Extra-Large condoms, as well as a big container of lube on the nightstand next to the bed.

If you own a DVD camcorder, bring it. If you don't, buy one and start recording it at 9:30. I want you to document our encounter so that once back in New York, you can savor the drama we create whenever you want to relive the realization of your lifelong fantasy.

You are to leave the door to your room closed, but unlocked, understood? I'll get there soon as I can break away — somewhere between ten and midnight.

Now all that's left is for you to let me know if you're still up for this. Get back to me ASAP. I trust I've made myself perfectly clear.

Your Ruff Muscle Guy,
Christian

Hunter replied immediately.

From: HunterRowe@Yahoo.com
To: RuffMuscleGuy@AOL.com
*Thank you, Christian, Sir! I am perfectly clear about every detail of our pseudo rape
fantasy scenario, and even as I applaud your creativity, I can hardly believe how well our
muscle fetishes mesh.*

*Just one request, if you please, Sir. I'm not so sure I can hold onto my excitement until
we finally meet. So can't we please talk on the phone beforehand, even if it's just once,
maybe see each other on videocam, so we can lock in our connection? I guess I just need to
be reassured this is on the level and that we're on the same page. I wouldn't want to enter
any sexual scene I couldn't handle.*

Your Muscle Boy,
Hunter

When Chase received Hunter's acceptance, he also answered back at once.

From: RuffMuscleGuy@aol.com
To: HunterRowe@Yahoo.com
*Glad you're still on board, Punk, and you need not worry about me respecting your
limits. You just utter the word "Give!" and I'll back off.*

*Until your takedown, however, the less you know about me, the better. It's possible we
can become friends after I've brutalized you. But until then, since the success of our erotic
mission depends upon our near anonymity, I must insist the less I know about you the better. It's what excites me most about this escapade — that I'll know so little when we meet,
we can let the intangible lure of our physical attraction guide us. That way, I won't get the
time to uncover any blemishes. Attached are another half dozen of my most recent pics.
Now get to work, boy. You've got a heavy load to carry.*

Your Ruff Muscle Guy,
Christian

Hunter read the letter and, while he couldn't have been more aroused over his
new muscleman's sexy response, he was also struck by a pronounced sense of hesitation. The disturbing apprehension washed over him and he wondered if he might
not be signing up for a sex scene so extreme, he might not be able to handle it. What
if it turned out more painful than he could tolerate?

The idea of being gagged with a plastic ball or restrained with handcuffs had
never fueled any aspect of his long-lived rape fantasy. Furthermore, the notion of
having to cover his head in a hooded mask made him that much more wary. It was
one thing to quietly harbor his enticing daydream of being roughed up by a big
muscle stud. Playing it out in actual sado-masochistic nastiness was suddenly a whole
other matter.

His bluster was easy to project whenever he was online. The anonymity of cyberspace allowed Hunter to unleash his dark side from within his colorful imagination.
Enabled by the safe enclave of his computer, it took no pains to project an air of
erotic bravado. But acting out such a tough-love fantasy with any sense of physical
verisimilitude might be something else entirely.

Hunter wondered if maybe he shouldn't just back off and flake out on the whole
project. But then, the moment he gazed upon the additional set of captivating pho-

tos his incipient dominator had attached to his e-mail, he felt his cock thickening as if trying to break free from his briefs. After ogling the invigorating photos of Christian sent by Chase, Hunter dismissed his trepidation and tabled his hesitation.

His dream nemesis looked so all-American wholesome, so clean cut, beyond well-built and downright likeable, Hunter sensed the big bodybuilder was simply setting up this extreme a scene in part because it was what he suspected Hunter sought. In his heart, he trusted that once they were actually together, it would play out more as the rough-and-tumble psycho-drama, the role-playing muscle fantasy he'd always sought, rather than any harrowing scene he might not be able to manage.

As that old locker room dictum suggested: when the little head gets big, the big head gets small. Maybe that was why, the entire time he typed his response to Christian, Hunter remained erect. He was excited about this forthcoming misadventure, even though he knew he and his hunky tormentor might not be in sync as to how their fantasy rape scene might play out. But its very uncertainty was also what made it so downright thrilling, which was why Hunter was so eager to initiate this new chapter into his sexual canon.

Trusting his gut instinct, he confirmed all systems were go, that his muscle master's willing boy would be following his instructions to the letter, exactly as directed.

He didn't want the new object of his attention to think he was either well practiced or blasé about all this, so he made a point to finish up his e-mail by noting:

And I think you should also know, Sir, I've never actually participated in any scene quite as elaborate or extreme as the enticing, sado-masochistic encounter you've laid out. In truth, I'm not really looking to get pained or hurt. That's not my fantasy. I just want to be taken to the outer limits of erotica. I guess with me, it's more a psychological thing.

Still, I'm truly excited by the erotic prospects of our hookup and hope you'll be patient with me as willingly, I follow every detail of your extensive demands.

Your Muscle Boy,

Hunter

To further stimulate his "new" muscle buddy's interest, Hunter attached a few more pictures of himself. They were three of the most flattering body shots of his torso, his legs, his butt, all snapped while he was flexing his muscles, back when he was in far better shape, all taken at the beach in Santa Monica months earlier by Chase, no small irony, since Hunter had no idea that was to whom they were being returned.

With Hunter so driven by his work at the agency, he still made no time to work out. The definition in his muscles lost shape as, slowly, they flattened out. With his lack of activity since returning from Hawaii, combined with all his sloppy eating, he quickly padded on ten pounds of unwanted flab, evident mostly around his midsection's love handles. However, by embracing his affinity for denial, Hunter trusted that once they finally met in that dimly lit hotel room, his studly Ruff Muscle Guy wouldn't even notice the inconsequential nuisance that was his recently attained gain in weight.

*   *   *   *

Chase's muscle growth from his cycle, along with his intense training and his strict dieting, all came together to whip him back into top shape. Stack was mightily impressed with his workout partner's speedy progress, insisting Chase was never more muscular, never more the total hunk.

Toward the end of his cycle, as adjunct to his cardio program, the Coach began bicycling in calculated spurts along the winding bike path on Mulholland Drive. It was a mostly flat, but still demanding trail, and with every forced ride through the late July heat, Chase pedaled his way into a fine sweat, even as he oxygenated his lungs, beefed up his heart rate, cut fat, and strengthened his legs.

One early afternoon, just a couple of days before his planned trip down to San Diego and his destined rendezvous with Hunter, Chase was biking the entire six-mile path and stopped at a nearly deserted scenic overlook to catch his breath and cool down. The San Fernando Valley lay stretched out before him, but owing to a toxic haze of gray-green smog blanketing the region, the distant San Gabriel Mountains were barely visible.

Glistening with sweat, Chase pulled off his tee shirt and used it to wipe his body dry. He leaned his bike against the side of a wooden bench and then sat down to catch his breath and take in the panoramic view.

Life's predictable unpredictability sat down alongside him that afternoon, and at first Chase didn't take notice as distant voices approached from the adjacent parking area. A few moments passed before he next heard a bustling noise passing through the tall grass directly to his right. When he turned, he saw an ugly-beautiful English bulldog prancing toward him, seemingly in a big hurry to greet anyone in his path.

As the bulldog wiggled his merry way over, Chase dropped to one knee. "Hey, there, Mr. Pretty Bulldog," he said in greeting as he rubbed the pure breed's fawn-and-white coat. "What are you doing out in this heat, besides panting a lot?"

"That's Samson!" Chase heard a little boy call out behind him.

Chase turned to find a cute little kid standing there. "Samson, huh?" he asked.

"That's right," the little boy answered. "It's because he's so strong. He's named after someone in the Bible."

"Yes, I know," Chase told the kid. "He sure seems sturdy."

As Chase patted the frisky bulldog, he heard a disembodied voice from behind a nearby row of fir trees call out, "Jericho, where'd you go?"

"I'm over here, Dad!" the kid hollered back. "Here by the lookout."

"Ah — I see you guys already made a friend," said the little boy's father as he came up from behind Chase.

Chase turned away from the kid's canine Samson to discover a real-life Samson. After so many years, walking directly toward him, was his former lover — Christian Falconer.

"It can't be …" Chase muttered in disbelief, as he stood tall. "Christian?"

"Chase …?"

"I don't believe it."

"What are you doing up …?"

"I was training on the bike path. Stopped for a breather."

"It's so great to see you. Come 'ere and give me a big old hug." Christian stepped forward, wrapped his huge arms around Chase, and affectionately squeezed him in greeting. When he let go, Christian knelt down alongside the little boy. "Jericho, I'd like you to meet Chase. He's an old friend. Chase: this is my son, Jericho."

"Hello, Jericho," Chase shook the little boy's hand. "Nice to meet you."

"Jericho's not a name in the Bible," Christian's son informed Chase. "It's a place with very strong walls."

"That's good to know," said Chase. "I love strong walls."

Jericho turned to Christian. "Okay, we've seen the view. Now can we go down to the Universal Citywalk, Dad, huh, can we?"

"In a bit, Son," Christian told his boy. "Why don't you first take Samson over to that field of grass, see if he wants to poop?"

"Okay, Dad. You gonna come with us?"

"I'm gonna stay here, talk to Chase a bit. But we'll keep our eyes on you."

"Let's go, Samson!" Jericho sang out with juvenile excitement as he ran off, the bulldog galloping behind him, playfully snapping at his heels.

Alone together at the top of a hill, looking over an endless stretch of suburban landscape, Chase and Christian stood and stared at one another, and at first neither of them said anything.

"Your son is adorable," said Chase, breaking the awkward silence and sitting back down on the bench. "Looks just like you, too, except of course he's much smaller."

"What must it be by now, over ten years?" Christian asked as he sat down next to Chase. "And you look better than ever. How's that possible?"

"Let me think," Chase answered, inflated by Christian's assessment. "Well, I still train like a madman. I still eat mostly healthy. And one other thing. I'm just finishing my first cycle of steroids."

"Unbelievable!" muttered Christian. "Wish I could say the same. I can't do them anymore. Came down with heart problems a few years back. Then, last summer, I had an embolism, you know, a blood clot. Almost killed me. Doctors said it was an offshoot from all my juice abuse."

"Holy shit!"

"Guess it was long overdue, huh?" Christian acknowledged. "But I also don't have time for the gym the way I used to. Fatherhood'll do that to you. It rearranged my priorities."

Despite Christian's news of recent health problems, the years had been good to him. Far less the colossus of yesteryear and not nearly so massive, he was still good-looking, if beefier, still strapping, if appearing more powerlifter than bodybuilder.

Chase and Christian spent several minutes reminiscing, catching up.

"I live in Palm Springs now," Christian told him. "Moved there several years ago to start a gay church."

"Come again?"

"It's a long story," Christian responded with a smile. "By the way, I read Pumping Irony, the book you wrote about us."

"Hope it wasn't too painful," Chase said, honestly.

"Actually, I thought you were too kind to me," Christian responded. "You must know how bad I felt about cutting you off back then. I never wanted to hurt you. But I was in turmoil, and confused. I had no one to talk to, didn't know how else to break it off."

"No big deal," Chase told him. "It only broke my heart."

"You think it was easy on me?" asked Christian. "Wasn't like I had a choice. When Pipsi got pregnant, my sense of guilt and obligation took over my thinking, and I bailed. Simple as that."

"Well, it was your decision. Hope it worked out for you."

"Yes and no," Christian answered. "When I started having trouble with my ticker about five years ago, I also sat down with myself and took stock. And that was when I had an epiphany."

"A Moses moment?" Chase asked.

"Something like that," Christian answered, good-naturedly. "I've always known my behavior in this lifetime influences what happens in the next. And while the Bible is still the word of God, we need to adapt to the times. Hey, we stopped stoning people who cut their hair or dared to work on the Sabbath. We no longer own slaves. So once I realized I could be gay and still follow Christian doctrine, I owned up to my true nature. That's when I sat Pipsi down and told her about my same-sex attraction."

"How'd she take the news?" Chase wanted to know.

"Better than I expected," said Christian. "I knew she couldn't handle me fooling around with another woman. But somehow, a man posed less of a threat. She claimed there was no way she could compete against such basic differences in anatomy. So we had an amicable separation and that's when I moved to Palm Springs. We've been separated now for a few years, but Pipsi and I are still great friends. She was gracious enough to assist in getting me up and running with my ministry — even helped me furnish my condo out there. So now Pipsi lives in our house in Malibu, and I use our Hancock Park home on weekends. I come to LA every other weekend to pick up my son and drive him out to be with me in Palm Springs. We share joint custody of Jericho, and of course, little Samson."

"I can't believe it," Chase patted Christian on the back. "You got a bulldog!"

"How could I not?" Christian asked with a shrug. "I've wanted one of those fireplugs ever since I first wrestled around with Romeo. So now, for the first time in my life, I'm on my own, actually supporting myself, while spreading the Word and letting gay men in my ministry know Jesus still loves them."

"Imagine," was all Chase could think of to say.

"Yeah," Christian said with another of his once-familiar shrugs. "I preach they can still be saved even if, like you, they're hopeless, philistine, bone-smoking pagans."

"Why didn't you contact me after you split with Pipsi?"

"You must know I wanted to reach you again," Christian answered, honestly. "And I know this is a cliché, but first I had to find me. Besides, after blowing you off the way I did, I figured you never wanted to hear from me again."

"Well," Chase agreed. "I was pretty miserable after you jumped ship. But I can't get over running into you after all this time. You've been in my thoughts a lot lately, mainly because I've been impersonating you online."

"Huh?"

"A guy I know in New York I was seeing — been sending him your pictures."

"But why would you need to impersonate me?" Christian wanted to know. "Just look at you! You do fine on your own."

"Well," said Chase, calmly. "I needed to entrap this guy because I'm thinking about slitting his throat."

"Who's the lucky fellow?"

"It's a long story."

"Nice," said Christian, indicating he hadn't been paying attention. "So, what'cha ya working on now?"

"Just finishing up a first draft of another novel," Chase told him.

"Is this one also semi-autobiographical?"

"You know what they say: write what you know!"

"I suppose," Christian agreed. "So how does this one end?"

"I won't know until after this weekend," answered Chase.

Jericho came dashing back through the tall grass, Samson right behind him, still nipping at his heels. "Hey, Dad!" he hollered out. "Now can we go down to Universal City?"

"Sure, Son," said Christian, squatting down to pick up the nine-year-old who, with hurricane force, ran into his father's strong arms. Christian lifted Jericho high up in the air and swung his little boy around in a dizzying circle before placing him down again, securely on the ground.

"Guess we better get going," Christian told Chase. "I promised Jericho we'd visit Spiderman before heading out to Palm Springs. Don't want to get stuck in rush hour traffic." The proud father looked down at his boy. "Okay, Son," he asked sweetly, "Can you say good-bye to Chase?"

"Bye, Chase!" Jericho waved with a big smile.

"Nice to meet you, Jericho. You and Samson, that is."

Christian took a firm hold of Jericho's hand, picked up Samson's leash, and turned to head back to the parking area. "Good luck with … everything," He told Chase. "Maybe I'll give you a call sometime. Still at the same number?"

Before Chase could answer, Christian's hand was pulled to distraction by Jericho, who was fired up to see his superhero at the amusement park. Christian smiled awkwardly, shrugged characteristically, and waved in farewell.

*   *   *   *

THE RAPES OF WRATH

When Hunter landed at the San Diego airport late Wednesday afternoon, a hot sun lorded over a cloudless blue sky, and the glare from its naked harshness withered everything beneath its infernal grasp. After snatching his suitcase from the carousel in the baggage area, Hunter picked up his rental car from Alamo, left the baking heat of the airport, and drove straight over to the Omni.

After checking in, he rode the elevator to the fourth floor, walked to the far end of a semi-circular corridor and entered his comfortably luxurious room. He could not have been more keyed up as he unpacked, could not have been more jittery or nervous, more filled with trepidation and anticipation about the potential extremes of his fantasy rape scene coming up Friday night. He was so wired, he had no idea how he might first get through the next two days, both of them filled with nothing but yawn-inducing business meetings.

If time goes fast when you're having fun, the opposite was most assuredly the case for Hunter, whose busy agenda found him catatonically pinballing from one sluggish sales meeting to the next. The moment his final scheduled conference concluded late Friday afternoon, Hunter bade farewell to his bureaucratic associates from the Department of Tourism and Chamber of Commerce, and hurried from their downtown offices. He drove out from the parking garage, directly into the gridlocked traffic by then blanketing the freeway. He did his best to contain his agitation as his rental car inched forward at a snail's pace, all the way back to his hotel.

By the time Hunter finally returned to his room, he hoped to relax with a long shower. Not so easy. Even with the room's air conditioner turned to high, he was still sweating as if he was about to overheat. He was far too keyed up to sit still and watch TV. He got the willies just thinking about the way things might unfold once his muscular tormentor finally arrived later that evening. He needed to calm himself, to subdue his mounting hesitation over this oddest of forthcoming fantasy fests. He also needed to ensure that he wasn't setting himself up for a rendezvous with some crazed lunatic.

For safety's sake and as a backup, Hunter rode the elevator down to the lobby, strolled over to the welcome desk, and there found the assistant concierge on duty.

"Hello. I'm Hunter Rowe. Room 421."

"Good evening, Mr. Rowe," the young man behind the desk responded, cordially and attentively. Fortunately, Hunter sensed, whether from his own gaydar, or from the fellow's deferential gesticulation, or perhaps simply from the hungry look in the employee's eager gaze, that the amiable assistant concierge was a member of the tribe. An emblazoned blue nametag prominently attached to his bright blue jacket lapel announced he was Max.

"Can I be frank with you, Max?"

"Certainly, Sir," the assistant concierge assured him with an infusion of disingenuous congeniality.

"This is a little awkward, but later this evening, I'm expecting a guest, actually a guy I met online."

"I see," Max acknowledged, suddenly very interested in their conversation.

"And I'm sure you know how we can't always trust these things."

"I'm sorry to say, Sir, I think we've all had our share of online disappointments and disasters."

"I'm so glad you understand. So please, Max, take this," Hunter pressed a crisp twenty-dollar bill into the assistant concierge's hand. "I'd like you to be my eyes for me?"

"Sir?"

"When my guest checks in with you, and you call to tell me he's in the lobby, I'll ask for your appraisal. Simple as that."

"Well, Sir, I doubt I'm qualified to judge what you might consider ..."

"Don't be silly," Hunter assured him. "We all know what a hot hunk looks like. He'll either have it or he won't. The guy I'm meeting is supposed to be big, tall and muscular, a competitive bodybuilder. So when you call my room, I'll ask if he's for real — and all you have to do is say yes or no. If the guy who shows up doesn't look like he belongs on the cover of a magazine, I want to know about it. Because if there's even the slightest doubt, I'll just hop in the elevator and meet him down here, myself. Okay?"

"I'll be working until midnight, Sir," said the assistant concierge, as he pocketed the hefty tip. "So no worries, Mr. Rowe. I'll be here when your guest arrives and will take care of it for you."

Satisfied with their arrangement, his safety net more or less anchored, Hunter gave his friendly assistant concierge a thumbs-up, and headed for the elevator.

Beset again by an anxiety attack as he returned to his room, Hunter's stomach churned in distracting knots. Even so, he retained a stiff erection the entire time he unpacked his bag of sex toys. Following orders as dictated, he placed a packet of extra large condoms and a tube of lube on the nightstand next to the bed. After opening the two sets of handcuffs purchased back in New York, he locked them in place on the posts at either side of the headboard. He positioned his dark hood atop a bed pillow, right alongside the plastic ball he'd later use to gag his mouth. From his shaving kit, he retrieved the tab of Ecstasy he'd brought from New York, and placed it by the phone on the night stand. He next loaded his camcorder with a six-hour DVD, placed the small device unobtrusively atop the room's plasma television set, and focused it on a wide shot of the bed, all set to shoot.

Hunter waited until nine-thirty before he lit half a dozen votives which he placed strategically around the room. *Nothing like a bit of ambience to set the right tone, get my muscleman into a nasty, aggressive mood,* he thought to himself with a mischievous grin.

His tasks completed, Hunter removed his shorts, pulled off his tee-shirt and socks, and then, buck-naked, crawled into bed ... and waited.

*   *   *   *

By the time Friday night's traffic finally started easing up, around nine-thirty, Chase was zooming past La Jolla, just north of San Diego. Jittery from too much caffeine, he took time away from obsessing over his revenge on Hunter, and thought back to his surprise chance encounter with Christian just a few days earlier. How providential to run into his former lover at that overlook. And talk about an unexpected turnaround in Christian's lifestyle! Chase wondered how different their lives might have turned out had Christian come to terms with his gayness a decade earlier.

Rather than ruminate as he sped along, he forced the memory of Christian to the back of his mind and channeled the irritability fueled by the last of his steroid cycle into the stoking of the anger he would soon need. As he exited the freeway, he wondered just how far he might take this proposed barbaric torture scene. The pieces of his deceptive puzzle had fallen into place and its outcome, he realized, was still anybody's guess.

One thing Chase knew for certain, as he drove into the self-parking garage of the Omni Hotel a little over an hour later, was that whatever else transpired, he planned to take Hunter down with all the fury he could muster. Chase would exact his revenge by intimidating, threatening, and humiliating Hunter. He was unequivocally intent upon violently penetrating his former lover boy, and then savagely slamming him so damn hard, the Kid would quickly regret ever fantasizing, and then so stupidly fomenting in the first place the initiation of this preposterous, over-the-top, fantasy rape scene. Chase wondered if his strong thirst for retribution might not send him spiraling out of control.

Fuck it, he decided. All systems were too good not to go, and by then it was too late to back out. Chase pulled into the parking area set aside for visitors. He killed the engine and reached over into the rear seat for his backpack. When he unzipped it, he peered inside and studied the menacing carving knife he'd brought along, trying to decide whether to actually bring it with him or leave it behind in the car.

He decided this was no time to alter any aspect of the blueprint outlined in his forceful retaliation, so he left the knife intact, got out of the car, flipped the backpack over his shoulder, and headed directly for the hotel lobby.

*   *   *   *

It was a little after eleven in the evening when Chase walked into the spacious Omni lobby and spotted its security-conscious "All Visitors Must Be Announced" sign posted at the entrance. So he walked up to the reception desk and asked the assistant concierge on duty to please call a guest named Hunter Rowe. "Tell him Christian is here."

Hunter jumped for the phone as soon as it rang.

"Good evening, Mr. Rowe. This is Max down in the concierge's office."

"Hello, Max. Boy, am I glad to hear from you."

"Christian is here in the lobby," the assistant concierge told him.

"Well?" Hunter asked keenly. "What's he look like? Is he a big guy? I mean big and muscular?"

"Yes, Sir," said the Concierge, trying to affect a noncommittal tone. "Most definitely."

"Tell me honestly — is he also good looking … handsome?"

"Oh, yes, Sir." The Concierge gushed. "Our room service is very — *Very* good. I can't imagine you'd be disappointed."

"Oh, great, that's excellent," Hunter beamed. "In that case, send him right up."

"Room 421," Hunter heard the concierge say to his rape date.

For a few moments, Hunter heard nothing, until the assistant concierge came back on the phone to add, "Okay, Mr. Rowe, he just stepped into the elevator. And you don't have to worry about a thing, Sir. I think anyone would agree your guest is a major hunk."

Giddy with excitement, Hunter popped out of bed and unfastened the lock on the door to his room. Then he flipped on his camcorder. As he crawled back into bed, he reached forward to pick up the little pink tab of X on the nightstand. Spurred on by Max' positive appraisal of the man en route to his room whom he had yet to meet, he trusted his instincts as he shoved the Ecstasy tablet up his butt.

Lying on his stomach, he fastened his left hand to one of his sets of handcuffs and snapped it shut. Semi-incapacitated, he fit his right hand into the other pair of cuffs and pressed the manacle against the headboard until it snapped closed. Lastly, he dropped his face to the pillow, slipped his head through the base of the dark hood he'd placed there, and then bit down on the small red plastic ball, partially gagging his mouth.

Lying there in the sensory depravation of his self-imposed, sudden darkness, he could barely contain his rampant excitement. Nervously, he closed his eyes and waited for his rough intruder to break into his room and then break into him.

*   *   *   *

The moment Hunter heard the door to his room slowly opening before it was then quietly shut and locked in place, he felt the muscles in his body tightening. As his would-be assailant stealthily approached the bed, Hunter's vivid imagination went straight to work, got the best of him, and made him instantly hard.

Chase quietly tiptoed into the candlelit room, placed his backpack on the floor, next to the bed, and pulled off his tee shirt. Looking down, he studied Hunter's naked body glistening against the soft flickering of the votive candles.

Hunter looked sadly vulnerable lying there, splayed out on his stomach. His face was buried deep into the pillow, precisely as instructed, his restrained arms and legs were spread out wide, and his butt was slightly elevated in the air, just prominent enough as he squirmed slowly to and fro to express an enticing body language boldly, bluntly signaling: come fuck me!

Chase glared down at his bound, gagged, hooded prey, and sized up his quarry. Sure, Hunter's legs still looked good, big and muscular, as always. But Coach was surprised when he also observed the Boy Wonder's wonderful torso had gone more than a little soft. He appraised Hunter's recently added weight, and couldn't help but be amazed by the unappetizingly prominent love handles the Kid had sprouted since they were last together in Hawaii.

Chase leaned one hand down into the small of Hunter's back and then used his other to slap the Kid harshly across the top of his butt. *Hey, Fat Boy!* He thought to himself. *Leave you alone for ten minutes and you slouch into a minor tubby!*

The sting of the hard slap caught Hunter by surprise, and he moaned a soft purr of contentment, letting his Ruff Muscle Guy know they had initiated their sexual psychodrama on just the right note. And even though he was never more petrified, there was, at the same time, a major section of his subconscious which also rejoiced in the intensity of his indefensible incarceration.

Hunter slowly wiggled his butt back and forth, begging for another slap, hoping it might just escalate into a genuine spanking. *But why,* he also wondered, *doesn't my Ruff Muscle Guy talk to me? He hasn't said a word since he got here. Doesn't he know how much I need to hear the threatening tone in his voice? Didn't I specifically request verbal abuse?*

Now that Chase finally had Hunter where he wanted him, he pondered what nasty deed, what hurtful item on his long list of vengeance he should first employ. When he looked about and noticed the half dozen votive candles Hunter had elected to place around the room, he decided it was imperative that Hunter understand right from the start that this was no idyllic romantic interlude, no sweet lover's tryst in some secluded hideaway. Hunter needed to know his charming touch of prissy ambience was never a part of the specific instructions he'd so carefully laid out, and so he decided to punish Hunter harshly for the inappropriateness of such gross insubordination. So he walked around the room and collected all the small, flaming glassware. After again slapping Hunter harshly across the top of his butt, he raised the first of the burning votives high above his head, tilted it over onto its side, and watched as the melted wax slowly drizzled out. Chase then incorporated the medium of the free flowing, scalding liquid to paint Hunter's back in a series of squiggly lines reminiscent of the work of a twisted Jackson Pollack.

"YEOW!" Hunter cried out in a shocked and pained signal of distress. Horrified by such unexpected, extreme abuse, the Kid yanked at his wrists as he struggled to free himself from his self-imposed incapacitation. *What the hell's going on?* he wondered as his body shook in pain and his erection went flaccid. *This is more than what I wanted, not what I signed up for at all. I better straighten this out and fast.*

"Hey, Buddy," Hunter moaned in a stifled garble through the obstruction of the plastic ball covering his mouth. "You've got me all wrong, Ruff Guy. I'm just not into *this* much pain, okay? Not really. Nothing this extreme, Christian, please-Sir-please! I just liked the idea of it, remember? Just the fantasy of the threat. Please, Sir! I'm tapping out, okay? There, I said it. I quit! I hate this fucking pain! I quit! I Quit! I QUIT!"

Chase leaned over and adjusted the ball covering Hunter's mouth until it was more firmly in place. From then on, as Chase returned to painting Hunter's back up and down in the dribbling of the melted wax pouring out from the remaining five votives, it no longer mattered how loudly Hunter complained, because his muffled protests were practically muted.

As Hunter writhed atop the bed, vigorously overreacting to the shock of so much unexpected burning discomfort, it suddenly dawned on him he might really be in true danger. What, after all, did he actually know about this stranger? Had he, in his irrational and lustful eagerness, rushed into his ideal fucking rape fantasy scenario with far too much fucking exuberance?

It all sounded so promising, so erotically stimulating, and relatively safe on his monitor screen in cyberspace. But once he was there, in the midst of so much more mayhem than he ever dared dream, so much more severe discomfort than he anticipated, a paralyzing, traumatizing fear the likes of which he'd never known took charge of his sensibilities. It corkscrewed out of control even as it overwhelmed his ability to reason. Unfortunately for Hunter, by the time he realized his date rapist might be truly dangerous, more Charles Manson than Charles Atlas, it was far too late in the match for him to either protest or break free.

Fuck, no! thought Hunter, his mind racing a mile a minute. *What if my Ruff Guy isn't who he said he was — not at all? Damnit, I can't even see what he looks like. What if he really means to hurt me, even kill me ... slice me up! Holy shit! This is all going way too far, much too quickly! And why the hell won't he talk to me?*

"I give!" Hunter screamed out another muffled cry for help, incorporating their pre-arranged plea of surrender. *"I give! I give! I give! Please, please, Sir! I give! Stop, please — I give."*

Chase watched warily as Hunter squirmed on the bed, and couldn't understand why he wasn't feeling more satisfied. Though puzzled by his sudden ambivalence, he skipped past all his other pre-programmed options and moved to the last, most threatening phase in his plan of attack. He climbed atop Hunter's back, straddled his waist and then reached forward, grabbed Hunter's forehead, and forcibly pulled the Kid's head all the way back until Hunter moaned in horrified, desperate anguish.

Hunter never felt more tormented, more threatened. Distraught, he realized that in truth he shared none of his Ruff Guy's notion of what was involved in his fantasy rape scenario. All he wanted was to have his wild vision finally acted out. He certainly never agreed or expected to be submitted to this degree of sado-masochistic cruelty.

By then, the Ecstasy was kicking in and his mind reeled as it spun wildly about in every direction. He couldn't tell, in his steadily advancing state of disorientation, if he was under the control and at the mercy of a true erotic dominator, an experienced and expert sadist, or some horrifying, serial killing sociopath. One thing of which he was damn certain, however, was that in his entire life, he'd never been so fucking terrified.

Chase held Hunter's retracted head firmly in place by pulling on a clump of hair at the back of his head. At the same time, he carefully reached down into his backpack and pulled out his huge carving knife. When he next ran the flat side of the steel blade up against the front of his captive's neck, Hunter got so instantaneously startled and alarmed, so petrified and excited, so threatened and inexplicably erect again, he screamed out a desperate, extended, yet still-muted cry for help. Abandoned by all his senses, including logic, his body tingled and trembled as he screamed out a final, unintelligible cry of both pain and joy because he couldn't tell if he was about to cum or to shit.

So he did both.

As Hunter lay in his spoils, Chase took one whiff, dropped his blade to the carpeting, hopped off the bed, and looked down upon his fouled, naked prisoner. Not a pretty picture.

Hunter, flat out on his stomach, his arms fully stretched out before him, was still imprisoned by his own metal clamps. He wriggled in place, yanking against his captive wrists in a futile effort to set himself free. Struggling like a trapped, wounded animal, he wallowed in his repellent waste.

And then, snap, just like that, before Chase could ponder what retaliatory act of vengeful cruelty he might next wish to employ, everything changed. Like a sink full of dirty water whose rubber stopper gets yanked away, all his considerable anger swirled down the drain. In the passing of a nano-second, Chase's impassioned need to get even, his driving desire to settle the score, suddenly no longer mattered. All the extraordinary passion he'd manufactured in justifying his license to hurt Hunter, to beat the hell out of him and forcibly take down his ass, vanished. Along with it, all the great affection he'd built up for his boy, the full reserve of his love, once so freely given, also disappeared. He might as well have been gazing down upon a total stranger.

Confused by this unexpected turnaround in his aggression, Chase stopped to examine his sudden loss of hostility, especially odd coming after so much preparation, so much advance entrapment. He finally had Hunter where he wanted him, but instead of feeling victorious, a sad disappointment washed over him, shaking him, and he felt an odd and sudden sense of closure about the two of them.

Gone was his need to get even. All his obsessive infatuation over Hunter since their breakup essentially dissolved. At the same time, the convoluted knots and butterflies that battered his stomach for so much of his waking life since returning from Hawaii somehow miraculously untied themselves and ceased their relentless fluttering.

As the rancid, invasive aroma from Hunter's regrettable accident filled the room, its revolting pungency quickly rendered Chase semi-nauseous. He realized he never really wanted to rape Hunter, and so he aborted his assault and tossed his knife into his backpack, turned and headed for the door. On his way out of the room, he felt an obligation to at least exit on a harsh note. Hunter needed to know he wasn't getting off scot-free. And so, to piss him off with a final touch of passive-aggressive antagonism, Chase turned off the comforting air conditioning in the room, flipped on the heat, and guided the thermostat as high as it would climb.

As the cool air stopped flowing, and a wave of discomforting warmth swooped into the room, Chase grabbed the full ice bucket from atop the nearby bar, dumped its contents all across Hunter's back, and tossed the empty ice bucket to the floor.

He left Hunter in his hotel room, lying in bed, incapacitated. Hunter's reddened wrists remained cuffed to the bedposts, the gagging ball stayed stuffed inside his mouth, the discomforting, sensory-depriving hood still covered his head.

Chase drove home at eighty miles an hour, speeding like a demon the entire hundred-thirty-five miles, all the way up the near-empty 405 San Diego Freeway, back home to Los Angeles. Along the way, he felt an unexpected lack of satisfaction and a deep sense of regret because he'd squandered so much energy in extracting the payback that was his hollow revenge.

*   *   *   *

BREAKFAST AT EPIPHANY'S

Abandoned, Hunter remained sprawled out atop the queen-size bed, still flat out on his stomach, still bound, gagged, masked, sensory deprived, and by then, aswim in the foul gook of his sickening wastes. Unable to mobilize himself past a pathetic fidget, and incapable of crying out for help with any credible audibility, he spent the unending hours of the night which followed tied up in knots, both real and emotional. As the pitch of night finally bled into dawn, he was not only still smeared in the unmanageable mess made during his emergency evacuation the night before, but also by then awash in his profuse sweat brought on by his hotel room's steamy temperature.

As he marinated in his own soured juices, excessive sweat dripped out from his overheated torso and eventually stained the sopping wet sheets in the sweltering room like a Rorschach test gone berserk. Unable to sleep, and finding it impossible to find any relief from his contorted torture, he was never more miserable or repulsed. Further dampening his bedding as well as his spirits were the small pools of ice cubes gone to melt. They blended into pockets of puddles along with the disturbing rivulets flowing from his bursts of sweat and his by then uncontrollable spurts of urine.

Bound, masked, and gagged, only his mind was free to wander. As he replayed the abandoned rape scene repeatedly in his head, he recalled highlights, bits and pieces of his agonizing fright. He vacillated between feeling a sense of total humiliation at having driven away his would-be perpetrator, mixed together with a most surprising near exhilaration over having experienced the opportunity to finally get nearly scared to death. Lying there in his misery, it dawned on Hunter that lurking just on the other side of revulsion lay attraction. As if by magic, his spirit reversed its descent into morbidity and instead mushroomed upward until his active imagination found him by turns hating and then embracing his sickening predicament.

Hours later, around ten that morning, the cleaning lady assigned to the fourth floor tapped her knuckles against his door. When the diminutive immigrant from San Salvador heard no reply, she used her passkey to unlock the door.

During the last year and a half while working at the hotel, the small, hefty woman had walked in on her share of bizarre and messy scenes. Still, as she entered room 421 that sunny San Diego morning, the cleaning lady stopped in her tracks when she came upon the unsettling sight of a hotel guest all tied up in bed, wallowing in his fetid wastes.

"Ay, caramba!" The hotel maid muttered in disbelief, beneath her breath.

She was all set to hurry from the room, straight over to the phone in her supply closet down at the end of the hallway, to call downstairs and notify Security; but then she heard Hunter whimpering incoherently while frantically bobbing his head up and down, seemingly summoning her over to him.

Hesitantly, the housekeeper walked over to the bed, fearfully removed the plastic ball from his mouth, and then lifted the hood from over his head.

Hunter expressed his eternal gratitude, and then implored her to open the drawer on the night table next to his bed and find the keys to the twin sets of handcuffs he'd placed there the night before.

"Please, Mister," the hotel maid insisted, quickly pulling open the drawer. "This is terrible, terrible. I must call Security for you, yes, okay?"

"No-no-no!" Hunter raised his voice. "Don't do that! No Security ... *Por favor*! Just find the keys ... right in there."

"You sure, Mister?" The maid asked as she lifted up the keys in question, and then used them to liberate her hotel guest.

"Yes, of course I'm sure," Hunter forced a fake merriment as he rubbed his raw, aching wrists. "This was all just a prank. A silly joke by friends who went a little too far."

"But what friends would do such a thing? So ... disgusting!"

"Believe me, it's quite all right. I'm fine. Really."

The housekeeper peered down at the bed. "This looks *muy, muy malo* — very, very bad."

"Yes, I'm sure it does," Hunter smiled. "But it's no problemo. Honest."

Finally freed of his incarceration, Hunter got up off the bed and limped over to the bureau. He rubbed his raw, swollen wrists and stretched the pained, cramping muscles of his back and legs as he found his wallet, reached in for some money, and slipped into the maid's hand a fresh hundred-dollar bill. "Here — take this ... please," he said, quietly. "Muchas gracias."

"*Dios mio ...*" said the maid, gawking at the crisp C-note in her hand.

"You go now, okay?" Hunter instructed. "I need some time alone," he added, as he walked over to the thermostat, turned off the roasting heat, and flipped the air conditioner back up to high. "Please — come back later to clean."

"You sure, Mister?" asked the housekeeping attendant.

"Quite sure," Hunter fought to remain amicable. "This was all just a silly joke. No need to worry. I'll be checking out soon. Really, I'm fine!"

Suddenly all smiles, the short, stocky cleaning woman pocketed the generous tip and bowed in humble gratitude. A conscientious worker, she swooped up the rumpled, soiled bedding, rolled the dirtied sheets into a huge ball of linen and then cheerfully carried the entire mess out of the room, closed the door behind her, and went about her business.

*   *   *   *

After thoroughly scrubbing every inch of his tormented body in the shower, Hunter called room service, ordered steak and eggs along with a pot of fresh coffee. Then he removed the DVD from his camcorder and slipped it into his laptop.

Hunter then sat back on the couch, hit Play, and watched in wonder, horror, and even a bit of awe as the eerily erotic scene played out in two-dimensions on his computer screen. At first he couldn't decide whether he was furious, complimented, or merely puzzled when he saw that his mystery Ruff Muscle Guy named Christian turned out to be, not some lunatic schizophrenic stranger, but his former lover, Chase.

Even in his bewilderment, he maintained a raging erection the whole while he viewed the action as captured in the dimly lit drama. He couldn't help but marvel at how downright satisfying, rather than appalling and repulsive, it felt to vicariously relive the entire carnal misadventure. However, even more surprising than the fact he'd been so thoroughly set up and hood-winked, was the shocking sight of his Coach looking so damn hot and muscular.

How could he have transformed so quickly? Hunter wondered. *What the hell's going on?*

For the life of him, Hunter couldn't get over how much of a change for the better Chase had managed in so short a time, how much more mass he'd added to his beautifully defined physique. He was flabbergasted because when last they were together in Hawaii, Chase, at the time still post-op, was not just showing a little bit extra, but also registering just this side of out of shape. *How could I have ever thought Chase was getting old?* he wondered.

Perplexed and unsettled, Hunter watched in amazement all over again the entire confrontation, start to finish. Ironically enough, he soon realized that, even with all the medieval discomfort he'd endured, so much degradation and disgrace, for some crazy reason, and he sure couldn't explain why, but he suddenly felt jubilant and alive. Most importantly, he also came to realize that while he had been completely misguided in taking that first hesitant step away from their commitment, he had never truly fallen out of love with Chase.

Hunter reasoned that if Chase had gone to all that trouble just to give him the wild sex scene he'd always sought, then it followed his Coach must still care deeply for him.

Hunter knew he was supposed to go back to New York City the next day, and that he had to be in his midtown office by nine come Monday for a videoconference. But he also knew that before then, he had to follow his gut and his heart and head to Los Angeles — and fast.

He called American Airlines to rearrange his itinerary. He planned to drive straight up to Chase's place and spend enough quality time with him to make amends. They could stay together, patching things up until Hunter would have to leave to catch Sunday evening's red-eye out of LAX to JFK. He would taxi back to his apartment at dawn, shower, change, and then head midtown, arriving just in time for his meeting at nine o'clock. Perfect.

After altering his travel plans, Hunter quickly packed his things, checked out of the hotel, and then drove his rental car straight up the 405, all the way to Chase's compound in Laurel Canyon.

En route, he rehearsed how he planned to confront Chase and admit the errors of his ways. He would apologize unequivocally for his senseless, premature disengagement. He would beg Chase's forgiveness, even as he embraced his former and future lover. He would open himself up in all his vulnerability, even if that meant throwing himself at Chase's mercy. He would insist they get back together, and he would not take no for an answer. Finally, he vowed not to leave Los Angeles before the vows of their covenant were reinstated.

$$* \qquad * \qquad * \qquad *$$

Chase finished that day's writing and read over the five new pages he created earlier that morning. Pleased with his new third act ending, he closed down his computer and changed into his safari shorts and tank top, prepping to bike down to the gym to meet Stack for that afternoon's heavy workout. While in the bathroom brushing his teeth, the phone rang. When his message machine picked up the call, Chase lent half an ear to hear who might be on the line.

"Hey, Chase. It's me, Christian ..."

The moment Chase heard Christian's voice, he hurried out into his living room to listen to the incoming message.

"You know, I've been thinking about you a lot since running into you the other day," Chase heard Christian say nervously into his machine. "What are the odds, huh? Great seeing you, though, and still looking like a champ. Jericho wanted to know if biking around the city was what made you so big and strong. I told him no, you were just a natural born superhero. And, Chase, I was wondering if you'd like to, you know, maybe get together with me, I mean with me and Jericho ... well, how 'bout me, Jericho, and Samson, the weekend of the Fifteenth? That's when I'll next be coming in to LA to pick them up. Talk about a lot of baggage, huh? Anyhow, I'm in Palm Springs now and would love to hear from you. So, if you'd like to maybe pick up where we left off, give me a call, okay? 760-837-8461. And hey, if I don't hear back from you — I'll understand. Take care, Coach. And God bless."

Christian's message ended and Chase stared at the answering machine. What to do? Should he return the call, jump back in, and tell Christian he was receptive to another wild ride? Or had he been too hurt from the damage he'd endured? Had he hardened so much over the last ten years that he was no longer either willing or capable of making so huge another leap of faith? Maybe Christian had evolved by then into someone Chase didn't know anymore. Was the former champion bodybuilder burdened, like he just said, with too much baggage? Could Chase adjust to sharing his life with a single parent? Did he really want to open himself up one more time to all the pitfalls and explosive land mines buried in the winding path that led to partnership? As Chase returned to the brushing of his teeth, he drew a mental picture of himself and Christian visiting Disneyland with little Jericho, and winced at the idea of waiting on an endless line for hours in a hundred-degree heat just to ride the spinning teacups.

Surely life's most dependable element was its never-ending capacity to surprise. Christian's unexpected resurfacing in his life, after bringing so much joy and then causing so much unhappiness, was simply too daunting for any immediate response. Chase studied himself in the mirror over the sink and couldn't decide if he was more frustrated or frightened by the notion, so he decided to just head out to the gym, where he could mull over his options while he and Stack pounded out their workout.

He left the bathroom and threw his backpack over his shoulder. On his way out the door, as he looked around for a pen, so he could replay the message and write down Christian's phone number, he heard a sudden, insistent buzzing of his doorbell.

Chase opened his front door and was actually surprised when he found Hunter standing there, smiling grandly, like he'd just won the lottery.

"Hi, Coach!" Hunter sang in a greeting so nonchalant, you might have thought he dropped by for a cup of sugar.

"Hunter," Chase said, subdued. "What the hell are you …?"

"I had to see you again, to thank you for setting up that incredible scene down in San Diego. It was brilliant and disgusting and fucking amazing."

"How'd you know it was me?" Chase asked, calmly.

"I recorded the whole thing, remember? Just as you insisted. Got it in my laptop in case you want to watch your handiwork."

"No, thanks," Chase answered. "Listen — you caught me at kind of a bad time. I'm just on my way to the gym. You know Stack — can't keep the big guy waiting."

"But I drove all the way up here to tell you I've changed my mind about us."

"And you think that matters to me?" asked Chase.

"Come on. I know you still care for me, Chase. Why else would you have put so much effort into setting up so complicated and crazy a charade in the first place?"

"Good question," answered Chase, matter-of-factly. "I thought I needed to get even. Thought it might be satisfying, maybe even therapeutic to win back some of my pride and return some of the humiliation you dished out so cavalierly. I thought it might make me feel better. But as you know, things don't always work out the way we expect. Turns out, I was mistaken. I derived no pleasure and found no fulfillment in any of it."

"Oh, come on," Hunter dismissed the notion. "For a while, it was the sexiest moment of my life. You must have felt some of that heat."

"Not really," answered Chase. "But I do need to thank you for getting me good and motivated, not only to get back to my writing, but also back into shape."

"I'll say!" Hunter chirped. "My God, Coach, you never looked better. How'd you do it? How'd you get your abs back so fast? Why do you look so great?"

"Just as you'd expect," Chase was candid. "With a lot of hard work and a little help from our friends at the pharmaceutical companies."

"But why now?" Hunter asked. "Why, after you said you'd never do steroids?"

"I changed my mind."

"How come?"

"Because I made a huge mistake," Chase told him. "I thought you were worth the sacrifice of my long-range health. I was not about to be dismissed, dropped by some punk kid who couldn't form a real emotional attachment if his gym membership depended upon it."

"Look who's talking!" Hunter protested. "How many lovers have you had in the last few decades? Hey, I know I was wrong, okay? After dreaming about it for so long, I finally had the shit scared out of me. Now I realize that's not what I was looking for, not really. All I want is you, Coach, and so here I stand, ready to work with you on building the foundation of that great relationship we both wanted."

"You only want me back because you know you can't have me," Chase asserted.

"Not true!" Hunter protested.

"Hey, Kiddo, men and women always love those best who love them least."

"What the fuck does that mean?"

"It means it's not going to happen," said Chase. "We are not getting back together. Besides, you must know me by now. I'm only attracted to other bodybuilders, to well-muscled boys. Granted, it's a shallow pursuit. But I can't help it. It's the way I'm wired. You know the rules: no muscle, no music."

"Oh, come on," Hunter pouted. "You're a writer. Can't we just start a whole new chapter?"

"And do what?" Chase asked pointedly. "Scare the shit out of you every night? That's not what I want to do with my lover."

"Fine!" Hunter declared. "We'll go back to vanilla."

"We're not going anywhere," Chase stated flatly. "You're going back to New York, and I'm going to the gym."

"But I can get into top shape again," Hunter reasoned. "I can do it in nothing flat, Coach. You'll see, I'll do it for you, just for you!"

"Don't bother," Chase said with a smirk. "I set up that fantastic scene in San Diego, not just to show you I could deliver what you thought you wanted, but also to teach you a lesson."

"It worked, Boss!" Hunter declared eagerly. "Your boy will never forget what you did to me down there. Sure, I wouldn't have minded it a little less brutal, certainly a lot less messy, not so painful, not quite so incapacitating, and maybe not leaving me isolated overnight. But hell, all in all, you finally delivered the fear I always dreamt about, and for that, I will always love you."

"Nice to know one of us found some sense of satisfaction," said Chase. "And it kind of worked for me, too. You got a taste of all you so easily gave up, and I've gotten you out of my system. So I guess now we're even."

"I suppose we are," Hunter agreed, sadly.

"So you see, everybody's happy," Chase said with a forced smile. "And you can relax. I never planned to do you any real harm. Never would have used that knife. I just wanted to scare the shit out of you."

"Well, you succeeded beyond my wildest expectation!" Hunter observed with evident embarrassment. "That was awfully messy, huh? So how 'bout if we blot it out and start over?"

"I don't have time for this. I gotta get to the gym."

"But I'm here for you now, Chase. That's why I shuffled my travel plans and drove all the way up to LA. It's me, Hunter: Coach's Star Varsity Wrestler. And I'm all yours!"

"Sorry, Hunter," Chase again shrugged his ambivalence. "One shot to a customer. I have no interest in getting back together. I'm not just over you, I'm also far too busy right now. I've got the first draft of a new book to finish, several prospective muscle boys to audition, a milestone birthday fast-approaching for which I must be in top shape and, to that end, a major chest workout in fifteen minutes with Stack. I can't be late. So if you'll excuse me ..."

Just before going out to his garage to retrieve his mountain bike, Chase realized he still had one last piece of business he needed to take care of before he could wipe the slate clean and start out spanking new. He left Hunter at the open door, walked over to his answering machine and looked down upon the blinking light indicating a message lay in wait. Without hesitation, he then pressed the Delete button, erasing Christian's message.

Pleased with his choice, he strolled past Hunter, closed the front door behind him, crossed to his open garage and retrieved his titanium twelve-speeder from its hooks on the wall. Hunter followed after him like a fixated puppy.

"Chase, wait!" He blurted out. "It took me some time to figure it out. But now I know I truly love you. Never really stopped loving you. Honest. Not completely. That's why I drove up here, Coach, to tell you I changed my mind. I was wrong, okay? I admit it. You must know we're too good together to throw it all away."

When Chase said nothing, Hunter added, "And I'll be in great shape. You'll see, even bigger, better than before. Hell, I'll even do a cycle just like you, if that's what you want. You won't be able to keep your hands off me!"

"You can do what you want," Chase told him. "It no longer matters to me."

"That's nuts," said Hunter. "How can it no longer matter?"

Chase looked straight at Hunter and said, calmly as possible, "As you so easily said to me not so long ago — I have nothing more to say."

His feelings expressed, Chase mounted his bicycle and steered it down the driveway leading out of his property. He flipped his transport into its highest gear, stomped down on the forward pedal and took off on his steep downhill ride, straight toward the gym for a balls-to-the-wall workout. Once again muscle bound, he carried his roamosexuality atop his shoulders with pride, even as he left Hunter standing there in the middle of Hyde Park's driveway, crushed and confused, his mouth agape.

"Wait, Coach, come back!" Hunter called after him in a booming voice of desperation. "I'll make it up to you, I promise! Just don't leave! Don't you see? All I want is you!"

The Boy Wonder of Madison Avenue watched in disbelief as his Coach pedaled down the steep hill, turned a corner in the road, and was soon gone from sight.

"Chase! Don't leave!" Hunter called after him, even as tears of regret began streaming down his cheeks. "I made a mistake, okay? Please don't go!"

Pedaling still faster, Chase pulled away from his bittersweet victory. All the way down the hill, he could still hear Hunter's fading, futile cries calling after him. His former lover's plaintive wails reverberated across the ravine until their echoes were absorbed into the canyon. Chase turned a deaf ear and aimed his sights only on the path ahead.

As he descended the hill and turned onto Laurel Canyon, the last of Hunter's distant pleas were interrupted by the sound of a high-pitched wolf whistle sailing through the summer air. Chase responded to the source of the flirtatious appraisal by glancing over his shoulder. For the briefest of moments within the periphery of his vision, he caught sight of a handsome, shirtless fellow with broad shoulders and big biceps smiling at him.

No doubt about it. His fans were everywhere.

*   *   *   *

ABOUT THE AUTHOR

David Marlow is the author of the novels I Loved You Wednesday (Putnam), Yearbook (Arbor House, a Literary Guild Selection of the Month), Winning is Everything (Putnam) and Surreal Estate (iUniverse).

On television, he wrote for "Knots Landing". His original comedy, "Daughters' Darling", was produced at the Laguna Playhouse in Laguna Beach, California. As a journalist, he contributed to New York and People Magazines, as well as the Chicago Tribune, corresponding from every continent except Antarctica.

He grew up in New York City and now lives with his partner in Palm Springs, California. He began bodybuilding at sixteen and has stayed in training as a lifestyle ever since.

His earlier novels have all been republished and are available at iUniverse.com.

For more information:
www.DavidMarlow.com
To contact the author:
DavidMarlowPS@aol.com

320

1995

9 780595 447398